"I know you walked
with a servan

She walked in these lands and released a nest. My own servants should not have allowed her to escape, but their actions serve me regardless. You will spy out a fitting sacrifice, one whose blood is rich and strong. Because if you don't, then on Hallows' Night the hunt will track the girl you call your cousin until we corner her."

Dismembered and her head thrown in a well.

I felt my courage flayed off my skin, an obsidian dagger slicing away filaments of hope.

Oh, Blessed Tanit. Gracious Melqart. Noble Ba'al. The threat of mage Houses, princes, and Romans hunting Bee through Adurnam seemed pathetic now. The mansa had been right, hadn't he? We should have gone with the cold mages, for then none of this would have happened.

None of this would have happened *now*. But the Wild Hunt would track her down eventually, if not this year, then the next. It was only a matter of time for Beatrice Hassi Barahal, who walked the dreams of dragons in the unwitting service of the courts' enemy. No one could stand against the Wild Hunt. No one.

Praise for *Cold Magic*:

"An exuberant narrative with great energy and inventive world building...I utterly loved it."
—Fantasy Book Critic

"Elliott pulls out all the stops in a wildly imaginative narrative that will ring happy bells for fans of Philip Pullman's His Dark Materials trilogy."
—Publishers Weekly

Books by Kate Elliott

The Spiritwalker Trilogy
Cold Magic
Cold Fire
Cold Steel

Crossroads
Spirit Gate
Shadow Gate
Traitors' Gate

Crown of Stars
King's Dragon
Prince of Dogs
The Burning Stone
Child of Flame
The Gathering Storm
In the Ruins
Crown of Stars

Jaran
Jaran
An Earthly Crown
His Conquering Sword
The Law of Becoming

Writing with Melanie Rawn & Jennifer Roberson
The Golden Key

Writing as Alis A. Rasmussen
The Labyrinth Gate

The Highroad Trilogy
A Passage of Stars
Revolution's Shore
The Price of Ransom

COLD FIRE

THE SPIRITWALKER TRILOGY: BOOK TWO

KATE ELLIOTT

www.orbitbooks.net

Copyright © 2011 by Katrina Elliott
Excerpt from *The Hundred Thousand Kingdoms* copyright © 2010 by N. K. Jemisin
Maps by Jeffrey L. Ward

Orbit
Hachette Book Group
237 Park Avenue
New York, NY 10017
www.orbitbooks.net

Orbit is an imprint of Hachette Book Group. The Orbit name and logo are trademarks of Little, Brown Book Group Limited.

The Hachette Speakers Bureau provides a wide range of authors for speaking events. To find out more, go to www.hachettespeakersbureau.com or call (866) 376-6591.

The publisher is not responsible for websites (or their content) that are not owned by the publisher.

Printed in the United States of America

First mass market edition: August 2012

10 9 8 7 6 5 4 3 2 1
OPM

Dedicated to the memory of Steve Larson, teacher, musician, theorist, lover of games, punster, oenophile, and all-around great, funny, brilliant guy. Gone way too soon.

Atlantic Ocean

IVERNIAN
CONFEDERATION

ICE

Tara

Deva

Ebora

BRIGANTIA

ORDOVICI
CONFEDERATION

Isca

Reiacum

Lindon

Sulis

Temes R.

TRINOBANTES

DUMNONIA

Londun

Camlun

Porto
Dumnos

Adurnam

CANTIACI

Area of detail

ATREBATES

Audui

CATULANIA

Reiacum

TRINOBANTES

Havery

Arras

Siccauna R.

Sulis

Temes R.

Camlun

VENETI DUKES

Lutetia

PARISI

Salru R.

Newfield

Londun

CANTIACI

Remi

TARRANT

Lemanis

Cantiacorum

Cena

Adurnam

Audui

Turo

Senones

ATREBATES

GALLIC PRINCES
AND DUKES

Alesia

Meens

ARVERNIA

Lemovis

Liyonum

Rodanus R.

ASTURIAS

Xixon

Burdigala

Porto Victoria

Garumna R.

Bracara

CANTABRIA

ZAZPIAK

Tolosa

Coimbra

Iruña

BAT

Carcaso

Numantia

OYO

Termes

Ibenu R.

Massilia

LUSITANA

Okilis

Segeda

New Oyo

Porto Lisso

Lisia R.

IBERIA

Tarraco

Ampurias

Ebora

Ituci

Oba R.

Saguntum

Tartessos

Carmona

Ebussos

Gadir

Malaca

Nova Carta

Mediterranean Sea

© 2010 Jeffrey L. Ward

EUROPA

★

1837 (AUGUSTAN YEAR)

Boreal Ice Sea

ICE.

BALT NOMADS

Baltic Ice Sea

• Carn

BELGAE

Boreal R.

NEURI

LUSATIA PRINCIPALITIES

Tretchtum•

Anvers•

Noviomagus

Sala

Kumbi

Colonia•

WAGADOU FEDERATION

Rhenus R.

New Jenne•

Zavist•

EMPIRE OF THE AVAR

Trevorum•

Maiacum•

New Gao•

TENE DUKEDOMS

Bruna•

PANNONIA

Argentum•

Ister R.

Vendunia•

Buda•

Raurica•

HELVITIA

ICE.

• Grad

Emona•

Mediolanum•

Tergeste•

Zena•

EMPIRE OF ROME

ILLYRIAN PRINCES

Nikaia•

Asa•

Salona•

Alalia•

Rome•

Tharros•

Neapolis•

Skodra•

Dyrres•

EMPIRE OF ROME

Qart Hadast•

Motya•

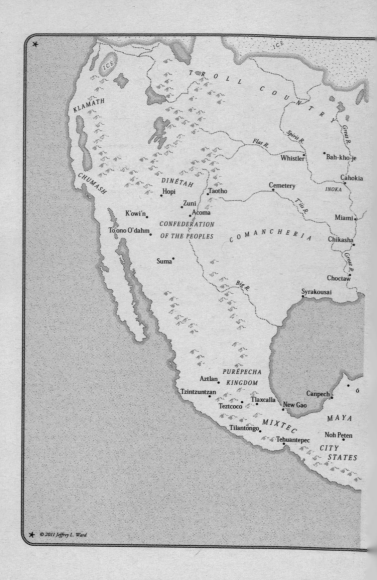

© 2011 Jeffrey L. Ward

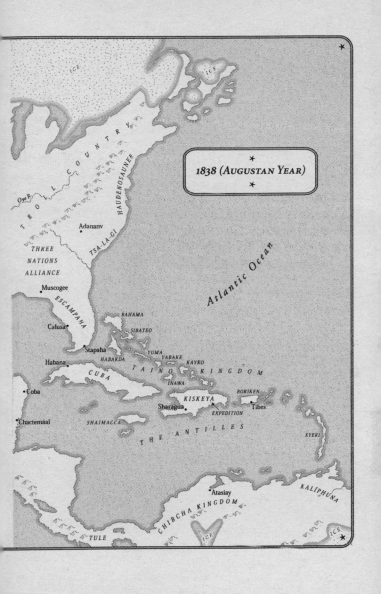

ICE

TROLL COUNTRY

Oyo R.

HAUDENOSAUNEE

Adananv

TSA-LA-GI

THREE
NATIONS
ALLIANCE

Muscogee

ESCAMPAHA

Calusa

BAHAMA

SIBATEO

Stapaha

HABAKDA

YUMA

YABAKE

KAYKO

Habana

CUBA

TAINO   KINGDOM

INAWA

Coba

KISKEYA

BORIKEN

Sharagua

Tibes

EXPEDITION

Chactemáal

SHAIMACCA

THE   ANTILLES

EYERI

Atasiay

KALIPHUNA

CHIBCHA KINGDOM

ICE

TULE

ICE

*

*
*

1838 (AUGUSTAN YEAR)

*

ICE

Atlantic Ocean

Acknowledgments

My thanks to the knowledgeable people who advised me on matters both large and small:

Fragano Ledgister (the Caribbean and theories of revolution), Gerald Rasmussen (politics), Marie Brennan (long hair), David B. Coe (tariffs and taxes), A'ndrea Messer (natural history aka science, as well as substantial assistance with the map), Jay Silverstein (empire and Mesoamerica), Alexander Rasmussen-Silverstein (there can never be enough Napoleon), Raina Storer (buttons & cookies), and Alyssa Louie (putting me in touch with the right people), like my sagacious physics advisor, Kurtis Nishimura.

My excellent and invaluable beta readers include Alexander Rasmussen-Silverstein, Katharine Kerr, Sherwood Smith, Jay Silverstein, Darcy Kramer, N. K. Jemisin, Edana McKenzie, Victoria McManus, Rebecca Houliston, Alberto Yáñez, Mark Timmony, A'ndrea Messer, Karen Williams, and Rhiannon and David Rasmussen-Silverstein. My apologies to any I've inadvertently left out. Special thanks to Christopher Kribs Zaleta for catching what everyone else missed.

I revised *Cold Fire* during the early part of 2011, a period when revolution became the headline and the hashtags I follow on Twitter began with #sidibouzid and #bouazizi and moved on from there. Many courageous people struggle for self-determination. I hope their voices can be heard.

Author's Note

The Spiritwalker books take place on a different Earth, with magic. Almost all the names and words are real, not made up. Although the world may seem like an attempt to write alternate history, it isn't true alternate history. It's more like a fantasia of an Earth that might have been had conditions included an extended Ice Age, the intelligent descendants of troodons, nested planes of interleaved worlds, and human access to magical forces that can redirect the normal flow of entropy.

Calendar Notes

The "Roman" days of the week commonly used in this world are Sunday, Moonday, Marsday, Mercuriday, Jovesday, Venerday, and Saturnday. The months are close enough to our own that they don't need translating. From the Celtic tradition, I've used the "cross-quarter days" of Samhain (November 1), Imbolc (February 2), Beltain (May 1), and Lughnasad (August 2), although it's unlikely Samhain was considered the turn of the year.

Creole

Part of this story takes place in the Antilles, the Caribbean, which has developed within a very different history from the one that shaped our own world. For that reason I decided to create my own creole rather than attempt (badly) to replicate any of the various historical or modern Caribbean dialects or patois.

With the heroic assistance of Dr. Fragano Ledgister and additional advice from Katharine Kerr, I instituted specific linguistic rules common to creoles and applied them with a few nods toward the languages that would have been part of Expedition's creole, most importantly Taino but secondarily Latin and Bambara. Obviously because I write and think in English I did also borrow heavily from elements of modern creoles as well. Insofar as the three levels of creole (as per Mervyn Alleyne's definition of a hierolect, mesolect, and basilect in Jamaican English) used in this book sound reasonable to the reader, it is due to the generous advice I received. Any faults and flaws are my own.

Our Caribbean, by the way, has an astonishing and marvelous literary and musical tradition so extensive there is not room here to even begin to discuss it, but I would urge you to explore it on your own.

COLD
FIRE

1

It was a cursed long and struggling walk hauling two
heavy carpetbags stuffed with books across the city of
Adurnam. That it was night helped only because the darkness hid us. The bitter cold turned our hands to ice even
through gloves. A dusting of new snow crunched beneath
our boots. My half brother Rory ranged ahead, on the
watch for militia patrols.

The prince's curfew had emptied the streets. In a normal year every intersection would have been lit with a fire
in honor of the winter solstice. Inns and taverns would
have remained open all night, awash with ale and free
oatcakes. But after the riots that had wracked the city,
people and businesses had locked their doors and shuttered their windows. It was so quiet I could hear my
cousin Beatrice's breathing as she trudged along beside
me with a bag across her shoulders.

"Cat, are we almost there?" she asked.

"I'll carry both bags," I offered, even though the one I
carried felt like a bag of bricks.

"It's not the weight. It's the dark."

The night was hardest on her. Clouds covered the sky,
and we avoided the few main thoroughfares that had
gaslight and kept to side streets where it was darkest.

With a curfew in force and people fearful they would run
out of oil and candles, few night-watch lanterns burned
on porches. Both Rory and I could see abnormally well
in the dark. That was one of the reasons my family called
me Cat instead of Catherine. We led the way, while Bee
had the more difficult task: She had to trust us.

Rory loped back. "Patrol coming."

We shrank into the shadow of an alcove. I set down
my bag and slipped my ghost-sword from its loop on my
outer skirt. It looked like a black cane, but at night I could
twist its hilt and draw a sword. I waited, poised to strike.
Rory tensed like a big cat about to spring. Bee sucked in
and held a breath. Ahead, a troop of mounted men clattered toward the nearest intersection.

Rory sniffed, then licked his lips. "I hear other people,
too. I smell iron and that nasty stuff you call black-
powder."

In the house nearest us, a shutter shifted as someone
inside peeked out. I closed my eyes, tasting the air and
listening with senses far sharper than Bee's. The wind
carried the clop of hooves but also a hiss of men whispering, the click of a boot heel on stone, the lick of flame and
the sting of burning.

"Stay here," I whispered, shoving the heavy bag into
Rory's arms. They obeyed.

In the interstices between our world and the spirit
world lie threads of magic that bind the worlds together. I
drew the threads as shadow around me to conceal myself
from ordinary sight. Staying close alongside the buildings, I skulked forward. In the intersection, no one
moved, but I heard the jingle of harness grow louder as
the soldiers approached. Movement stirred in an alley to
my right. A tiny flame flared, lighting the shape of a mus-

tachioed mouth and the gleaming barrel of a gun. After a hissed whisper, the flame was snuffed out.

I stepped back against the wall of the building at the corner just as the first rank of turbaned mage House soldiers rode into view. Sparks flowered. At least ten sharp gunfire reports echoed down the houses. Horses snorted and shied. Two soldiers crumpled forward. One tumbled from his horse. His boot caught in the stirrup, and the panicked horse dragged him sideways. A volley of crossbow bolts loosed by the mounted soldiers clattered against the buildings on either side of the alley. A glass window shattered, and bolts thunked into wood shutters.

"They're bad shots!" shouted a man from the alley. "We've got them, lads! Fire!"

But instead of loud reports, the only sound was a series of deadened clicks.

The mage troop swept forward as a seam of icy white light ripped across the air as if an unseen blade cut through the night to penetrate to daylight behind. A bright, cold fire bubbled out from the rift. The light moved as if pushed, spheres like lamps probing the alley and the stone faces of the buildings to reveal thirty or more men in hiding. The hiding men desperately tried to shoot, but their shiny new rifles simply failed to fire. The presence of an extremely powerful cold mage had killed their combustion.

With my back pressed against the stone, I willed myself to be nothing more than stone, nothing to see except what anyone would expect to see looking at an old, grubby, smoke-stained wall. Even so I dared not move, though I knew cold mages could not see through my concealing threads of shadow. A man dressed not in armor but in flowing robes rode forward from the back of the troop. His was an imposingly dignified figure with his graying black hair plaited into many tiny braids and his black face drawn down in an angry frown. I knew him: He was the mansa, the most powerful cold mage in Four Moons House and therefore its master.

In that knife's-edge moment before the men in the alley broke and ran, the mansa lifted a hand as he addressed a comment to his companion, a middle-aged blond Celt dressed in the uniform of the prince's militia. "They are smuggling in rifles despite the ban on new technology. Just as we suspected."

The temperature dropped so precipitously that my eyes stung and my ears popped as the pressure changed. With a whispering groan, metal strained. Men screamed as the iron stocks of their rifles twisted and, with a sound more terrifying than that of any musket or rifle shot, shattered as easily as if they were glass. Many writhed on the ground, torn and bloodied by the shrapnel. A few staggered away down the alley, trying to escape.

"Capture them all!" shouted the militia captain in a braying tenor.

"I want any who survive," said the mansa, studying the scene with a brow smoothed by his easy victory.

"You mean to execute them?"

"No. I mean to bind these rebellious plebeians into clientage. They, and their kinfolk, and their descendants will all be bound to serve Four Moons House. To execute them will merely inflame their kinfolk to further rebellion. But if these discontented men drag their households into servitude with them, that will breed resentment among their own kin for their folly in fighting against the natural order and losing what freedom they have. With your permission, of course. They're your subjects."

"A wise course of action. That will make the radical agitators think twice."

Blessed Tanit! His companion was the prince of Tarrant himself, the very man who ruled the principality centered around the city of Adurnam, on the Solent River, in northwestern Europa.

Really, I could think of no man I wanted to meet less than these two. As the soldiers mopped up the scene and the mansa and the prince sat in perfect amity at the center of the intersection, chatting about some man's thwarted marriage prospects, I edged backward until I felt it safe to remove myself from the wall and hurry back to the alcove where Bee and Rory waited. I shoved in between them, trembling.

"What happened?" Bee whispered. "I heard shots. And then screams."

"We have to backtrack. The mansa and the prince are with those soldiers."

"Are they hunting for us? Does the mansa know we escaped?"

"I don't think so. He said nothing of it. I still think his people won't discover we're gone until morning. Give me a moment." I shut my eyes, the better to envision the map of Adurnam I carried in my head, with its winding streets, secluded alleys, and dangerous warrens.

"You're shaking," said Bee, putting an arm around me.

"Men just died. And it was a shock to see the mansa again. By law Four Moons House owns me. He has a legal right to recapture me. And if he catches us, he will find a way to own you, too."

"I think we should go now while they're busy eating the wounded and dying," said Rory.

Bee stiffened. "You imbecile, we don't *eat* people—"

"Hush. Rory's right." I stroked his arm, because he liked that, and he gave a rumbling sigh. "We need to go while they're busy mopping up. I've got a better route. We'll creep back to Old Temple and go along the river. We'll be hard to follow if we cut through the goblin market."

I slipped my cane back into its loop and picked up the bag. We crept back down the street as quickly as we could, but no scouts rode our way. If anyone inside the shuttered houses noted our passing, they called no alarm. Eventually we relaxed a little.

"Do you think these lawyers and radicals will really take us in?" Bee asked.

"We have to hope they will, Bee. I don't know where else we can go otherwise."

"I'm very cold, Cat," said Rory. "I just want a warm fire and a nap."

"Are there fires that aren't warm?" muttered Bee as she strode along. Clearly, fear and anxiety had wound her tight. Even with our greater height and longer strides, Rory and I had trouble keeping up. "Winters that aren't cold?"

"Men who don't fall in love with your magnificent beauty at first sight?" I added, knowing she could not resist the bait.

I felt her grin by the way she struck a counterblow. "Why, dearest, I don't think I'm the one who got fallen in love with at first sight."

"I don't need reminding about that!"

"What? Didn't you like him a little in the end? Aesthetically, he is very handsome, despite the impressively arrogant personality. And *you* are the one who kissed *him*, after all."

Fortunately, the night covered my blush. "I really don't know what to think about him, Bee. And furthermore, I am not interested in having this conversation right now or possibly ever."

"Hush! You two are so loud."

Because Rory was right, we kept walking and stopped talking, but the exchange had restored Bee's usual bloody-minded cheerfulness. She even dawdled in the long promenade of the goblin market, examining the stalls of knives. By the time the cocks crowed, we had staggered onto Enterprise Road, where all kinds of foreigners, radicals, technologists, and solicitors lived. Unlike in the other districts of Adurnam, every street and even the humblest lanes in this neighborhood were lit by gas lamps. Their glow illuminated the predawn traffic of men and trolls coming out of and going into coffeehouses and unlocking offices. A few cowled goblins hurried away to burrow into their daylight dens. A woman opening up a shop paused to watch Rory saunter past, for he had the kind of self-satisfied grace that attracted the eye, and he knew it and liked it.

"Stop smiling at people! You'll draw attention to us!" I muttered.

"I see men looking at Bee, and *even at you*," he retorted. "Why shouldn't I get looks, too?"

Fortunately I spotted Fox Close, a lane tucked away between a tavern and a coffeehouse. By the time we turned down the lane and reached the law offices, dawn had come and the gaslights were being shuttered for the day. We halted on the stoop to look up at a newly painted sign. Pin-perfect orange letters shone against a feathery brown backdrop: GODWIK AND CLUTCH.

Who would ever have thought that two dutiful daughters raised in a quiet Kena'ani merchant household would throw themselves on the mercy of trolls and radicals?

"I hope this works," Bee muttered as we dropped the bags on the steps.

I plied the knocker. As we waited, I untangled my cane where it had gotten caught in a fold in my skirts.

The door opened. A troll stared at us. It was hard to know whether trolls looked more like birds or lizards. They stood tall and lanky on hind legs in a way that made me think of human-sized upright lizards, yet what looked like scales was a covering of tiny feathers. The way this one cocked his head first to one side and then to the other to get a good look at us with each eye also reminded me of a bird. He wore a jacket in the human style, and its drab brown cloth set off a truly spectacular scarlet-blue-and-black crest of feathers that ran from his upper spine to the crown of his head.

"May the day find you at peace," I said hastily. "My name is Catherine Hassi Barahal. This is my cousin Beatrice. And my brother Roderic. We're here to see Chartji. The solicitor."

"You're that one. Chartji warned me: 'Let her in quickly shall she come standing at the door.'" He hopped back, startling Rory and Bee. Seeing the two bags and their brass clasps, he bent forward to look more closely first at the clasps and then at my cane as if he could see the sword hidden beneath the magic that concealed it in daylight. "Oo! *Things!* Shiny things!"

A male voice came from inside.

"Who's at the door, Caith?" A strikingly attractive man stepped into view, wiping his hands on a grimy cloth. Seeing us, he grinned most enchantingly, as if his day had just become utterly delightful. "Catherine! And your charming cousin Beatrice. And another companion, I see."

"My brother, Roderic."

"Well met, indeed! Did you tell them to come in, Caith? Please, step inside at once and close the door." He nodded at Rory as we hustled in. "I'm Brennan."

As we walked down the main passage, he explained the young troll Caith's complicated kinship relationship to the solicitor Chartji. He showed us into what had once been the sitting room. There we found Maester Godwik seated at a desk with pen in hand.

The old troll looked up at once, his vivid black-and-green crest raising and spreading as he saw me. "The Hassi Barahal in her mantle! What an exceptionally pleasant surprise. Let me crow on the rocks at sunrise! And this...the cousin, I presume. And..." He studied Rory, who looked like an ordinary young man with golden, innocent eyes and thick black hair twisted into a single long braid. "Interesting. I've not seen one like you before. Well met. Please enter our nest."

There was one other person in the room, a bespectacled woman sorting among the pieces of a shattered printing press. She looked up, so surprised at Godwik's words that it was obvious she hadn't noticed us come in. Yet her smile seemed genuine. "Catherine!"

Brennan set our bags down in the room as the solicitor Chartji walked in behind him. Because Chartji was female, her scale-like feathers were as drab as Caith's jacket, and the feathers of her crest were only one color, a bright yellow. She was carrying a bowl of water cupped in one ink-stained three-fingered hand. "I thought you might come! Drink first. That's the proper way. Then we'll talk."

Their manner was so very encouraging that I began to allow myself to hope we had made the right decision to come here. As we passed around the bowl, each taking a sip of water in the traditional Mande custom of welcome, a knock rattled the door. Caith pattered away down the hall. I heard the door open.

After a pause, Caith called out, "Brennan! There's a rat here who says you're expecting a messenger. He says a rising light marks the dawn of a new world."

Brennan said sharply, "Get him in fast and shut the door!"

We all spilled into the hallway, me with my hand on my cane. If the others were armed, I could not see their weapons. I nodded to Rory, and he went partway up the stairs to get the advantage of height. Three armed men surged through the open door and into the entryway like soldiers clearing a path for their captain. I recognized them, for I had met them on the road not ten days earlier. All three were foreigners, and one was actually a woman dressed as a man. She stepped back outside, and a moment later a middle-aged man walked up the steps and came in.

He was tall and imposing, with brawny shoulders, black hair streaked with silver, and the features of a person born of mixed Iberian, West African Mande, and Roman ancestry. In other words, he had a prominent hook nose and a face long and broad and bold enough to carry it off. He wore a shabby wool greatcoat and a faded tricornered hat rather the worse for wear. Although he had the bearing of a man accustomed to wielding weapons, he wore none except the expectation that he was in command.

His gaze fastened immediately on the petite, bespectacled woman even though, of all of us standing in the entryway, she certainly looked the least physically imposing. "Professora Kehinde Nayo Kuti, I presume," he said.

They eyed each other like dogs trying to decide whether they'll have to fight over a bone.

"I expected you would send an ambassador to open talks between our organizations," she said.

"I am my own ambassador. As I must be, in these troubled times."

Blessed Tanit! I had first met this man on the road, where he had been traveling in the guise of a working man named Big Leon. I could not imagine how I had ever thought him merely a retired soldier no different from any other man who has survived an old war.

"You walked into Adurnam alone except for three soldiers?" Brennan was saying. "With all the mage Houses and every prince in northwestern Europa hunting for you? That seems rash!"

"And irrational," added Kehinde in a calmer voice. "We could turn you over to the prince of Tarrant for a significant reward."

In disguise as Big Leon the humble carter's cousin, he had hidden the crackling strength of his gaze and the coiled power of his presence. No longer. "But you won't. For you see, I am never alone. The hopes and ambitions of too many people are carried on my back."

"You're Camjiata," I said.

The man born Leonnorios Aemilius Keita had earned the name Camjiata, lion of war, by leading armies to victory. Everyone knew the Iberian Monster believed it was his destiny to unite the fractious principalities, dukedoms, city-states, and backward tribes of Europa into one glorious empire. He had tried once, and he had almost succeeded.

"Of course I am Camjiata. Who else would I be? At last, after the patient work of many years and many hands, I am free."

Chartji stepped forward, offering the bowl of water.

He doffed his hat and drank it all in one gulp. "And now we have business to do and no time to wait."

"Did you come looking for me?" asked Bee. I could not tell if she was terrified, or exhilarated, or making ready to punch him in the face, but she had her sketch-book open to a page where she had at some point in the last few months drawn a picture of him standing exactly where he was now, in front of the closed door in the entryway of these law offices. "Did she tell you how to find me? Your wife, I mean? The one who walked the dreams of dragons?"

"Yes. It was the final thing Helene said to me before they killed her. She told me that the eldest daughter of the Hassi Barahal clan would learn to walk the dreams of dragons. Find her, she said, because you will need her, as you have needed me." He lifted a hand in the classic orator's gesture used by the Romans in their ancient empire. It was simply impossible not to stare at him if he wanted you to do so, as he did now. "Helene said that the eldest Hassi Barahal daughter would lead me to Tara Bell's child."

"B-but I'm Tara Bell's child," I choked out, for I felt my heart had lodged in my throat.

"Of course you are. You could be no one else but who you are. So must we all be, even Helene, who knew that the gift of dreaming would be the curse that brought death to her."

I alone heard Bee whisper, "*Death?*" as she went pale.

He had gone on. "Even at the end, the gift compelled

her to speak. Those were the very last words I ever heard her say. She said, 'Where the hand of fortune branches, Tara Bell's child must choose, and the road of war will be washed by the tide.'"

I was not too stunned by these portentous words to miss the way Kehinde glanced at Brennan, or the way he gave a shrug in reply as his gaze flicked toward Bee.

"A fanciful turn of phrase," said Kehinde to the general, "but as I have a pragmatical turn of mind, can you tell me what you think it means?"

A longcase clock standing beside the coat rack ticked with each swing of its pendulum. A carriage rattled past outside. Camjiata watched until we were all looking at him and waiting for him to speak. He smiled softly, as if our compliance amused him.

"Why, the depths of the words are easily sounded. She meant that Tara Bell's child will choose a path that will change the course of the war."

The gazes of seven humans and three trolls left his face and fixed on me.

"Which means you, Catherine Bell Barahal. Because that child is you."

2

I am not a young woman who craves attention. Unlike my beloved cousin Beatrice, who is my dearest and most trusted friend in all the world, I make no effort to bring myself to the notice of all and sundry in the most forceful and spectacular way imaginable. I have the sort of character that prefers the shadows where it can bide quietly or, as Bee might say, sneak about without being caught.

So I did not at all like to find myself with every pair of eyes—except of course for my own since that would have been impossible—staring at me. Words usually come easily to me. But I had seen carnage on the streets. I had been awake all night. I really just wanted to close my eyes and sleep.

Instead, I stood for a moment as mute and seared as if I had been struck by lightning. Then I got angry.

"You may believe that because I am Tara Bell's child that I mean something to you and your schemes and plans. But I came with my cousin to these law offices to get help with our own private legal matters. Not to aid an escaped criminal!"

The door rattled softly at his back. He stepped away as it opened a crack. The woman dressed as a man squeezed in. As everyone relaxed, the general chuckled. His amusement made the air change quality as if holding its breath before the sun—or a storm—breaks through.

"Some call me a criminal, while others call me the Liberator," he said in the rich Iberian lilt he had not lost despite thirteen years confined on an island prison. "Like you, I came to these law offices on an entirely different matter. I truly did not expect to meet you here, Catherine." He nodded to acknowledge Bee. "Nor did I expect to meet your cousin, the young woman who walks the path of dreams. Not so soon, and not in Adurnam. And yet, why not here? Why not now? That we meet here and now merely reminds me that destiny directs our paths. We cannot escape what we are."

"That may be, but we can escape those who try to imprison us."

"Have I said anything that makes you think I am trying to make you my prisoner?"

"You must forgive me if I don't seem very trusting right now. For the last two months, I've been running from people who want to kill me. My cousin and I just escaped from house arrest. So I don't see how I can really trust you."

"If we are both being hunted, doesn't it make sense for us to become allies?"

"Allies in what?" I demanded. "Isn't your war over? Didn't you lose? Weren't your armies dispersed, and your allies punished? Didn't your enemies in the Second Alliance march home satisfied with their victory and your imprisonment?"

I wasn't sure how a man of his infamy would parry such a reckless attack, but he merely smiled drily. "A worthy salvo. It reminds me of the prickly unanswerable questions I would hear from your father Daniel when we were young. The struggle for liberation is never over as long as the old order crushes those who seek freedom. I intend to reform the laws of Europa and free the population from the oppressive rule of princes and cold mages. You could do worse than to join my army, as your mother did."

"We're not your soldiers," I said as I glanced at the woman who stood beside him.

A black-haired foreigner, she wore a man's jacket and trousers. A falcata, a short sword in the Iberian style, rode low on a belt loop at her left hip. Her eyes had the epicanthic fold of a person whose birth or ancestry rested in the mysterious lands of the Far East, but the most striking thing about her was the ragged two-tined white scar that forked across her right cheek. Was she one of his famous Amazon Corps, as my mother had been?

"Just because my mother was an officer in your army doesn't mean I am under any obligation to you," I added.

"You are mistaken if you believe nothing binds me to you."

Snow poured down my back could not have made me more cold. A horrible premonition seized me, together with a throat-clawing curiosity. *I had to know.* "What do you mean? You're not going to claim to be..."

"Oh, la!" Bee pressed the back of a hand to her forehead in a gesture worthy of the cheap sort of theater. "I am overcome by these confrontations and alarums! All these revelations and unexpected meetings are simply *too much*. If I do not sit down this instant, I shall *collapse*." She had perfected a throbbing quaver with which to soften the listening heart, but her voice retained an edge of determination that suggested her collapse would be accompanied by a tantrum no sane person wished to endure. When she grasped my elbow, her grip was like the clamp of a trap. From the cutting look she gave me, I could tell she wanted to *have words with me*.

The general touched a hand to his heart. "I am at your disposal, Professora Kuti. With you, I assume, is the legendary Brennan Touré Du. Tales of his daring exploits reached even my lonely prison cell. I have been assured your connections are legion, your intellect first-rate, and your commitment to the cause of justice and reason unparalleled."

Although Kehinde appeared to be nothing more than a petite woman with a quiet demeanor and an enthusiasm for technological puzzles, she met the general look for look. "You will understand that our chief concern is to assure ourselves of your dedication to the cause of justice and reason."

He nodded. "Alliances can only be formed where trust is assured."

"Let me then defer to our host, Maester Godwik."

Godwik raised his feathered crest of black and green. "It is our custom to offer a chance to wash, drink, and eat before any negotiation commences."

The general laughed. "As I well recall. The first of your kind I ever met were gunrunners. It took a cursed long time to get down to business though we were in the midst of a battle waged over a hill. I would be honored to wash, drink, and eat with you, Maester Godwik."

All three trolls showed teeth in an expression that mimicked a human smile. Given that they had fearsome teeth bristling in predatory snouts, the effect was more unsettling than reassuring.

"Caith," said the old troll, "please go join the watch at the corner."

Caith whistled an answer and went out the front door, accompanied by Brennan and the older foreign soldier. The younger soldier took up guard at the front door. By the way he kept glancing at Bee and then away, it was obvious he was taken with her voluptuous figure and magnificent beauty.

Maester Godwik gestured to Bee, Rory, and me. "We have not yet greeted you properly either, my young friends. Await us in the kitchen, if you will. General, this way."

Along the right wall were two staircases, one of which ascended to the first floor above us while the other, tucked beneath it, descended to a half basement. Godwik limped down the basement stairs while Chartji went upstairs past Rory. After a glance at Rory, the Amazon followed Godwik downstairs, the general and Kehinde at her heels.

"Look at those knives!" whispered Bee admiringly, still clutching my arm.

The young foreigner had unbuttoned his greatcoat. Beneath, he wore a harness of knives buckled over a quilted jacket of dull twilight blue. A belt strapped around his hips braced a pair of illegal pistols. He had straight black hair not unlike my own, and a brown complexion that resembled Rory's. The cast of his features, his wide cheekbones and high forehead, gave him the look of a man far from the house where he had been born and none too impressed by the place he found himself now. He met Bee's bold stare with a challenging one of his own.

"You're not of Mande or Celtic or even Roman ancestry," I said. "Where are you from?"

He measured me up and down and without replying looked back to Bee.

She lifted her chin in imperious dismissal of his rudeness. "Rory, bring the bags."

She tugged me toward the stairs, but when we were halfway down to the basement, alone on the dim stairwell, she yanked me to a halt. "Cat! You were about to ask Camjiata if he was the man who sired you! In front of everyone. Don't you remember anything we were taught at home?"

"I know! I don't know what came over me. I forgot myself in the heat of the moment. I just couldn't help but think that since he knew my parents, he might know who it was."

"Of course you want to know. But if Rory doesn't even know who your and his sire is, why would the general?"

"My mother might have told him."

"Your mother Tara Bell? Do you know the only words I remember her ever saying to us? *'Tell no one. Not ever.'* I doubt she told him anything, even if she was under his command. Also, you definitely shouldn't have mentioned we were under house arrest."

"I know!" I agreed grumpily. "But the radicals already know we're trying to escape the mages. And since Camjiata knows *what* you are, he's surely guessed the mage Houses want you."

"It doesn't matter what he would guess. *Tell no one.*"

"*Keep silence*," I echoed, a phrase that had been drilled into us by Bee's mother and father.

"That would be too much to ask from you, I agree!" she exclaimed, but then she hugged me. "I know you're tired, Cat. You've traveled so far and learned such shocking things, not to mention escaping certain death and saving me from what would have been an exceptionally unpleasant marriage. So babble nonsense, which you do so well, and leave me to negotiate."

"I can keep silent!"

She laughed, and we clattered down the rest of the steps and along a narrow passageway past an empty bedchamber, a pantry, and a scullery. At the end of the passageway, a half flight of steps led up to a back door. We turned into the kitchen. A cast-iron range was fixed under the stone arch of an old fireplace. Its burning coal soaked the kitchen in heat.

I set my black cane across the big kitchen table. A cutting board and knife sat atop the work-scarred surface next to a heap of parsnips, a bowl of dry oats, a pot of freshly churned butter, and an empty copper roasting pan. Bee set her sketchbook on the corner of the table, then dragged off her hat, gloves, and winter coat and threw them over the back of a chair. She crossed to the long paned window set high in the wall and got up on a stool to look out into the back. Being taller, I could see out the high window without using a stool; the view looked over the backyard, a long, narrow court enclosed by high walls and paved in flagstones. There was a cistern, a pump, a stone bench dusted with snow, and a carriage house abutting the high back wall next to a closed gate. Godwik was leading Camjiata, the Amazon, and Kehinde across the back court to a peculiar little building. It reminded me of a domed nest because it looked as if it had been constructed from feathers and sticks and wreathed with ribbons and wire from which hung mirrors, glass, and bright shiny things. A solitary crow perched on the jutting center post.

Bee sighed gustily, shoulders heaving, as she hopped down. "Oh, Cat! I thought by coming here we would have a chance to rest and decide what to do next at our leisure. Instead, it's as if we're caught by a tempest at sea. We're blown hither and yon without ceasing by the gods' anger."

"I don't think the gods have anything to do with this. I think it's all these cursed people who won't leave us alone who are the problem. Why did I think lawyers and radicals would be a safe harbor? Is there anyone we can trust?"

On the ground floor above, footfalls made the floorboards creak. The front door opened and closed, and someone descended the basement stairs. Bee grabbed the knife off the table. I picked up my cane.

"Here you are." Brennan entered the kitchen with that impossibly friendly smile, which I could not help but return even as I flushed, lowering my cane. An important and glamorous radical who traveled across Europa to foment revolution could not be interested in a callow young female like myself. Even if he was carrying our carpetbags. "What's in these?" he asked with a laugh.

"Gold bricks," said Bee, at the same time as I said, "Pig iron."

"I would have said books, but what do I know?" He set down the bags by the door and indicated the window with a lift of his chin. "No need for knives. Godwik could eat the general if he really wanted to. Even at his age."

Bee snickered. I clapped a hand over my mouth to stifle a laugh.

Rory sauntered into the kitchen. His slender build made his strength easy to underestimate until he leaped for the kill. "So nice and warm! At last! A nap by a proper fire."

"I wondered where you'd got to," I said. "Bee meant you to carry those bags."

He blinked innocently. "Did she?" He sank down onto the bench, picked up a parsnip, sniffed at it, and with a disdainful grimace set it back down. With a sigh, he stretched the length of the bench in a boneless sprawl whose languor I admired in large part because I knew that at the slightest sign of trouble he could spring up and attack.

The heat was making me sweat, so I shrugged off my coat and draped it over Bee's. In the backyard only the Amazon was visible, standing beside the closed gate. A clock stood atop the cupboard. Its ticking punctuated the silence as Brennan considered his work-hardened hands.

"I come from the north, as I think you recall, Catherine," he said, "from a mining village in Celtic Brigantia. A few days' walk from the village where I grew up, you come to the ice shelf. The ice rises from the land like a cliff. When the sun shines, you can see the ice face from miles away. It blinds because it is so sharp and bright. Professora Kuti and Maester Godwik can tell you all about the color, texture, weight, height, volume, and consistency of ice. But because I grew up so near the ice, among hunters as well as miners, I can tell you that the ice is alive. Not as you and I are alive. It's not a creature or a person. But it lives, although I couldn't tell you how or why."

"A fascinating tale, but what has it to do with us?" I said. Yet I could tell by Bee's frowning expression that he had caught her interest, although I could not be sure whether it was his story that intrigued her or his looks, his air of worldly experience, and the likelihood he had bested more than one man in more than one nasty fight.

"When I was a small boy, my grandmother told me about a girl who was one of her age-mates. In my grandmother's youth, the ice reached all the way to Embers Ridge, where we now light the bonfire on Hallows' Eve. One year at midsummer the girl walked out on the hunt with her older brothers. When they reached the ice, she stood all day as if dazzled. When the sun set, she woke. She told them she had seen visions—dreams—in the face of the ice. They went home to consult with the village *djeli* and the elders. But what happened was this: The things she saw in the face of the ice came true in the year that followed."

Bee inhaled sharply.

Brennan's gaze settled on her. "She married, but birthed no children. For five summers more, she walked north every solstice to the ice and walked home after and told the elders what she had seen. No one spoke a single word outside of the village of what she did. They knew better than to draw attention to a gift which is also a curse. Do you know what happened to her?"

The clock ticked ticked ticked.

"She died on Hallows' Night," said Bee in a voice as hard as an oracle's.

He had the look of a man who has seen things some might call the stuff of nightmares. "The authorities at the prince of Brigantia's court were told she had drowned. In fact she was torn to pieces on Hallows' Night in the forecourt of the temple of the hunters Diana Sanen and her son Antlered Kontron. Her severed head was found in the village well."

He paused. We said nothing. What was there to say?

"She had been pursued and killed by the Wild Hunt. As the Thrice-Praised poet Bran Cof sang, 'No creature can escape the Hunt, no man outrun its teeth.'"

The clock ticked over the new hour. Its chime so startled me that I flinched.

Brennan paced to the window. The Amazon had wrestled open the heavy bar that secured the back gate. A red-haired man in an old coat slipped inside the yard from the alley behind, and the Amazon went out. As Brennan turned to address us, the red-haired man barred the gate.

"It is well known," Brennan continued, "that before he took the name Camjiata, Captain Leonnorios Aemilius Keita married Helene Condé Vahalis. She was the daughter of a powerful mage House, although she was a cold mage of only negligible power. But it was rumored she walked the future in oracular dreams. People said the young general's victories were achieved because he knew how to interpret her dreams to his benefit. Camjiata just implied that you, Beatrice, are one of those young women—and they are always young—who has discovered she walks the path of dreams. It seems obvious the general wants you because he thinks your dreams can give him an advantage in war. Meanwhile, obviously the mansa of Four Moons House wants you to keep you away from the general, since it was the mages and the Romans who defeated Camjiata the first time. Yet it seems to me, if you are such a woman, then mage Houses, princes, Romans, and even escaped generals are not the worst threat you face."

3

Brennan looked out the window again, watching as the red-haired man traversed the length of the yard while kicking up the snow that dusted the paving stones.

"Excuse me." He flashed one of his spectacular smiles and went out. We heard him go up the back steps and open the back door. Gray light gleamed through the paned windows. The peculiar hut glittered as if polished gems lay hidden in its layers. A crow still perched atop the center pole. Brennan intercepted the stranger with a friendly gesture and a smile.

"At least," said Bee in a low voice, "the awful news was delivered by the handsomest man I've ever met."

"Bee!"

"How do you suppose he got the appellation *Du*? Brennan Touré Du. Du means 'black-haired.' Yet he's enchantingly fair-haired."

I clucked my tongue to show I was not so susceptible, even though I was. "He's positively *ancient*. Over thirty, anyway. That's even older than your handsome admirer Legate Amadou Barry. Or have you forgotten him?"

She fixed me with the smoldering gaze that caused young men to fall catastrophically in love with her, professors to quake, shopkeepers to hasten forward to serve her, and young women our age to wish they could be like her, so proud and queenly. Then she dabbed away a tear. "Please! Amadou Barry offered me an intolerable insult! As if I had asked for it!"

"You're not to blame for the proposal Amadou Barry made to you, Bee."

"I know." She blushed and looked away as if ashamed. "But before that I told him things I shouldn't have, because I thought he genuinely loved me. I thought I could trust him."

I frowned as I leaned on the table, pinning her gaze with my own. "Bee, you were alone and frightened and scared. You did nothing wrong. And I'm sure he was very persuasive. Until that unpleasant moment when he offered to make you his mistress."

"As if it were the best thing I could ever hope for!" She made stabbing motions with the knife. "This! For him!"

"Sadly, men are the least of our problems right now." I grabbed Rory's ankle. "What do you know about Hallows' Night? Murdered victims? The face of the ice? The Wild Hunt?"

His penetrating gold gaze was as opaque as a cat's. "I know I'm hungry."

"Do you not know, or are you not telling?"

"Hallows' Night? Murders? The face of the ice? I don't know what those things are."

Because he looked exactly like a young man, it was easy to forget what he truly was and that he didn't belong here. "Fair enough. I believe you. What do you know about the Wild Hunt?"

"I eat flesh. The Wild Hunt drinks blood. Even my mother trembles, for when the horn sounds, she would make us all hide. But everyone knows no one can truly hide, not if yours is the scent they pursue. I never saw them in all my life, but I have heard the hunt pass by while I cowered."

Bee weighed the knife in her left hand as she considered the parsnips. "We thought we need only escape the combined forces of the mage Houses and the local prince. Now I'm warned I was born all unknowingly with a terrible gift of dreaming that will result in my being dismembered."

"That knife is so sharp I can taste its edge." Rory rolled up to his feet as Bee glared at the hapless parsnips. "Upset people shouldn't wave knives around."

"I didn't ask *you*!"

He rubbed his eyes with the back of a wrist, the gesture very like that of a big cat, lazy and graceful and a trifle out of sorts. "They never do ask me, although they ought to," he said with a contemptuous sniff. He stepped out into the passage.

"It's just hard to imagine he really is a saber-toothed cat," whispered Bee.

"I heard that!"

"Then don't eavesdrop!" Bee called after him.

He padded up the main stairs toward the front entryway.

I went to the door, but the low passageway was empty, so I crossed back to the table. "That was certainly a disturbing story, but you must admit, Bee, we don't know if it is true. Maybe Brennan was trying to frighten us into cooperating with them."

She shook her head as she set a parsnip onto the cutting board. "Then he'd do better to ask why he and his comrades first met you while you were traveling in the company of a cold mage, when everyone knows cold mages are the enemies of Camjiata. Maybe he thinks we came here to spy on the radicals for the mage Houses."

"It would be just as easy to say that Camjiata and the Hassi Barahal house set me to spy on the mages."

"I wish that's what Papa and Mama had meant to do with you. Sent you to spy on Four Moons House, I mean. I could forgive them for that." She pulled a hand over her thick black curls and pulled them back as if to tie them in a tail, a gesture I knew meant she was troubled and nervous. "What I find so puzzling is why the general would walk into the city of Adurnam. He knows the ruling prince here is his sworn enemy. Doesn't he fear he'll be recaptured? How does he hope to get out of here without being caught?"

"All I know is the last place we want to be is in the same house as the most wanted man in Europa. Could you put that thing down before you stab me with it?"

She skewered me with a gaze that would have felled stout oxen, had they been unfortunate enough to cross her path. "I am a Hassi Barahal. I never put down the knife!"

I began to smile, but something in the tense way she began slicing the parsnip into even roundels killed my words.

She finally looked up with a crookedly trembling smile. "I don't want to die like that."

"Oh, Bee." I hugged her despite the knife.

In the silence, a lamp hanging from a hook on the wall by the door hissed patiently as it consumed oil. The back door opened. I released her and grabbed my cane. She raised the knife. The red-haired man appeared in the kitchen door, cheeks ruddy from the cold. Seen close, he was younger and better-looking than I had thought, especially when he grinned to greet us.

"Salvete," he said as he edged around the chamber, sticking close to the wide cupboard with pots, pans, and unchipped crockery set in neat display on its open shelves. One might almost think him leery of coming too close, although I could not fathom what might disturb him about two perfectly well-mannered young women, even if one was grasping a large kitchen knife and the other what must appear to be a polished black cane, the kind of ridiculous accessory carried by young men of wealth who were more concerned with fashion than utility.

"Peace to you," said Bee. "Are you with the general?"

He reached the stove and held his gloved hands over it with a grateful sigh. "Whew! I just can't get used to this cursed cold."

"You're not from the north?" Bee asked.

He looked pointedly at her knife. She set to work on another parsnip.

"I was born northwest of here, in fact. But I've been living as a *maku* in the city of Expedition for the last ten years. I'm Drake, by the way. James Drake."

"I am Beatrice Hassi Barahal," Bee said with her best queenly grandeur, "and this is my best beloved cousin"— she hesitated—"Catherine Bell Barahal."

He offered a formal bowing courtesy, gaze shifting from her to me and back again. His eyes were so blue they were like a sizzle of bright hot light. "I must always be at the service of such remarkably pretty young women."

Self-consciously, I smoothed my hands over the waist of my rumpled jacket and my well-worn and somewhat grimy riding skirt. I wasn't used to such brazen compliments.

Bee's stony demeanor cracked, and she responded with a smile that made his eyes widen. "But you must tell us more," she said. "Expedition is in the Amerikes. How exotic!"

"Between North and South Amerike in the Sea of Antilles, to be exact, where the Taino and their fire mages rule. The winters aren't cold there. Not like here, where cold mages rule beside princes and every soul lives under the shadow of the ice." His fine blue gaze skimmed the length of my cane. "I can't figure how a girl like you would be carrying cold steel. You're not a cold mage."

"Are you one?" I demanded.

He chuckled. "I don't bite, so no need to guard against me." His words were accented with the musicality of a western Celtic dialect overlaid with flat vowels that hinted at foreign lands.

Despite his pleasing grin, I burned with an acrid, suspicious question. "How do you know this is cold steel?"

"Maybe someone told me." His chuckle suggested he would say nothing more.

"You didn't answer my question," said Bee. "Are you with the general?"

Drake glanced out the window. "Ask him yourself, for here he comes."

Camjiata and Kehinde crossed the yard to the back door. I did not see Godwik or Brennan. Upstairs a door closed, and footsteps paced the length of the house. I heard the professora speaking to the general as they came down the passage.

"—But the airship was destroyed. It is certain a cold mage devised the sabotage."

"So I was informed yesterday when I entered the city," the general replied. "A shame. It would have made for a spectacular departure from Adurnam."

"To think of destroying such a remarkable and beautiful object, both in design and concept! A new means of crossing the ocean between Europa and the Amerikes! Such antipathy toward invention and technology lies beyond my understanding. Such people ought not to hold power over the lives of others. But without the airship, how will you cross the ocean?"

They came into the kitchen, Kehinde blowing on bare hands to warm them.

"I've already set a new plan in motion," Camjiata said as he walked to the table. He picked up Bee's sketchbook before she or I realized he meant to so brazenly invade her private things.

"Unexpected," he said as he flipped through the pages, many of which bore sketches of good-looking young men. "Yet as a way to record hopes and dreams, it's quite as useful as words."

Bee looked first as if all blood had drained from her face. Then she flushed in an exceedingly dangerous way that only ever presaged her rare but explosive blasts of volcanic temper. Just before she blew, Rory glided back into the room exactly as if he'd felt a warning rumble. He slipped up next to her and draped an arm over her shoulders in a way that made it look as though he were both soothing her and stopping her from stabbing the general.

Without looking up, Camjiata spoke in a coolly amused voice that made me think he knew exactly the effect his intrusion into her sketchbook was having on her. "Patience, and I'll explain. The women who walk the dreams of dragons walk the path of dreams each in a unique way. Helene heard words of tangled poetry. I learned to unravel her words to reveal meetings and crossing points yet to come. For you see, she who can read the book of the future can wield her knowledge of the future as a kind of sword, one with an edge sharper even than cold steel."

"Such a gift is a curse," I said hoarsely.

He studied the page that contained the sketch of him standing in the entryway. Bee had drawn it days, or weeks, or months ago. "Maybe it is. But the women who walk the path of dreams have no choice about what they are. Do you know how my beloved wife died?" He turned another page. His brows furrowed as he considered lines that seemed to depict nothing more than a bench set against a wall under a flowering vine.

"On Hallows' Night dismembered?" Bee choked out.

Rory tightened his arm around her.

The general glanced at her, and then at me, and last at James Drake, who had gone back to warming his hands over the stove. He lifted his chin. "Go on, James."

Drake's lips curled down. For an instant I thought he was going to refuse a direct order, but instead he left the kitchen and went upstairs.

Camjiata smiled at a charming sketch of fanciful clock-faced owl. He closed the book and straightened, his gaze like a spear piercing Bee. "Helene had gone to visit her family. She was a cold mage out of Crescent House, far in the north. I did not go with her. I had administrative duties that needed my attention, a legal code to shepherd into the world. We were both taken by surprise, I suppose, or perhaps we had begun to think we could not be taken by surprise because she walked the path of dreams. On that Hallows' Night, a storm demolished Crescent House's entire estate. All that was left in the morning were splinters, shattered stones, and faceless corpses. The main hall lay untouched but sheathed as in a glove of unmelting ice. As for Helene, her body was left on the steps of the main hall. Her limbs had been torn off. And she was decapitated. Her head was found at the bottom of a well that went dry that very night."

I shuddered. Outside, blown bits of icy snow pattered against the thick glass in a rising wind.

"What do you want?" whispered Bee.

"What matters," said Camjiata, "is what you want, Beatrice."

It wasn't just fear that was making me feel cold. It was actually getting colder. The cozy glamour of the fire wavered. The red glow began to shrink, and pieces of coal to settle. The fire flickered and all at once gave a weary gasp of defeat. Ash puffed and sank.

Rory sniffed. "That's magic," he said.

"Oh, no," whispered Bee.

Only the presence of a powerful cold mage could suck the life out of a fire from a distance. As on an inhaled breath, the house tensed to silence, as if waiting. The ghostly hilt of my sword stung like nettles against my skin as cold magic whispered down its hidden blade. A preemptory knock rapped so loudly on the front door that the walls vibrated.

Kehinde stepped to the kitchen door and looked into the passageway. "Come with me, General. We have a bolt-hole."

"Grab your coat and mine, and go out the back with Rory," I said to Bee, for she was the one the cold mages wanted. "We'll meet at that inn where we slept before."

Camjiata paused at the threshold, so unruffled by this emergency I admired his calm. "What do you mean to do against cold mages? For I recognize their touch."

I pushed past him and headed for the stairs. "I'm Tara Bell's child, aren't I? The Amazon's daughter. I have a sword, so I mean to fight them."

4

I found James Drake at the front door instead of the nameless young foreigner. Drake's lips were tilted up in a funny kind of smile, giving him the look of a man who is expecting a gift or a slap. He set a gloved hand on the latch but snatched it back.

"It's like ice!" he hissed.

My sword's hilt waxed cold against my palm. Had the cold mages found us missing and already tracked us down? Or had they discovered Camjiata was in Adurnam and come for him?

"Stand back." Gritting his teeth against the latch's cold burn, Drake opened the front door.

Seen past him, a man stood on the stoop, cane in hand.

"These are the offices of Godwik and Clutch, lawyers," said Drake, as though to a simpleton. "Callers are admitted only by appointment."

"Isn't it redundant to inform me that these are the offices of Godwik and Clutch, lawyers," said the man with the cane, "when the sign out front informs me both in word and in picture of that very fact? Naturally I do have an appointment with the solicitor named Chartji. Otherwise you can be sure I would not have ventured into a neighborhood like this one for legal aid."

Some men have the unfortunate propensity to look exceptionally well in the clothing they wear, and the effect must therefore be amplified when they dress with full attention to the most fashionable styles, the best tailors, and the most expensive fabric. In fact, he wore a greatcoat of an exceedingly fine cut, magnificently adorned by five layered shoulder capes rather than the practical one or the fashionable three. Its wool was dyed with patterned lines and sigils that reminded me of the clothing the hunters of his village wore when out in the bush. Altogether, the coat was one worn to be noticed and admired.

It was also unbuttoned, as if the ferocious cold did not bother him at all. Beneath he wore a dash jacket tailored to flatter a well-built, slender frame and falling in loose cutaway folds from hips to knees. The fabric's violently bright red-and-gold chain pattern made me blink. How any man could wear cloth that staggeringly vivid and not look ridiculous I could not fathom. Yet there he was, him and his annoyingly handsome face. I should have known.

"My very question," said Drake with a cutting smile. "What *is* a cold mage doing in this neighborhood? A mage of your ilk must despise the scalding technology of combustion. He must regard with contempt the clever contraptions and schemes made by trolls and goblins in their busy workshops. Which rise all around you, in all their industrious vigor."

I expected sparks to fly. The two men, as they say, stared daggers.

"So polite of you to inform me of what I must despise." The man on the stoop examined Drake as he might a man who has the bad taste to dress in provincial fashion when venturing into the city. "But unnecessary, since I've found I can make such judgments for myself."

Drake's free hand curled into a fist. A tremor kissed the air, expanding like the unseen pressure of a hand or an invisible dragon's sigh. I tasted smoke. A ripple swirled as shimmering heat across the threshold.

"Stop that!" The cold mage raised a hand as if brushing away a fluttering moth. The pressure and heat ceased so abruptly I coughed.

He looked past Drake and saw me. Wincing back as if he'd been struck, he lost his footing and staggered down a step before catching himself. His surprise gave me hope. Maybe Four Moons House and the mansa had not yet tracked us down.

He jumped back up to the door, his gaze fixed on me the way a hammer seeks a nail.

The cold magic pulsing from him coursed down my sword's hidden blade. If I twisted my draw just right, I could pull a blade into this world out of the spirit world where it currently resided. Not that cold steel would avail me much against Andevai Diarisso Haranwy, the very cold mage who had destroyed the famous airship. I was surprised the incognito guards Camjiata had posted on the lane had not raised the alarm, but then again, you could not identify a cold mage by looks. He might be any particularly well-dressed young man born to a family of high status and notable wealth. They could not have known he'd been born to neither but risen to both.

"You'll have to return another time, Magister." Drake started to close the door.

The man I was obliged to call my husband thrust out an arm and, with the tip of his cane, halted the door's swing. He pushed inside, closed the door, and on the entry mat paused to stamp snow off his polished boots and tap the dusting of snow off his hat.

"I have an appointment with the solicitor Chartji," he said as he set hat, cane, and gloves on a side table. "You cannot deny me entrance."

With his lips pressed together and his dark gaze mocking, he surveyed Drake with the disdain that came so easily to him. Drake's clothes were indeed undistinguished, although practical and sturdy, but in any other company a man with Drake's striking eyes and attractive face might expect his looks and smile to render his clothing invisible. In this company, he just looked drab.

As the gazes of the two men met, Drake's blue eyes seemed to blaze. My lips stung as with the bite of a kiln's heat. My lungs felt choked by unseen smoke and ash. My skin crawled as if licked by invisible tongues of fire. I gasped, sure the air was about to burst into flame.

A chill descended as decisively as a curtain falls at the end of an act. The burning taste of fire was utterly extinguished. Ice brushed my lips like a cold kiss, but it was only sensation, not actual frozen water.

Andevai uncurled a fisted hand as if he were carefully releasing a captured bird. "You're strong, but not nearly strong enough." He spoke in a bitingly arrogant tone whose sheer cool vainglory would have been sufficient to bestir a herd of calmly grazing elephants into a maddened, city-flattening stampede. "It's a bit dangerous, don't you think? Playing with fire?"

Drake's grin popped, but he looked furious, not amused. He took a step toward me. With narrowed eyes, Andevai placed himself between me and Drake. Then he met my wary gaze.

I had last seen him two days before. He had not changed. His hair was cut close against his black head, and his beard and mustache were trimmed very short and with absolute perfection, no doubt to encourage young women to look at him. The less said about his beautiful brown eyes, the better. Especially when I recalled the unkind and even cruel things he had said to me when we had first been thrown together, when he had dragged me against my will from the only home I had ever known.

His voice was soft now, emotion tightly controlled. "I suppose your presence here means you have managed yet another escape, Catherine."

"I can't tell you anything. Your allegiance lies with Four Moons House."

He regarded me coolly enough that I felt obliged to admire his composure, considering the things he had said at our last meeting.

"Considering the things that were said at our last meeting," he said, as if his thoughts aligned with mine, "it may surprise you to hear that my arrival here has nothing to do with you."

"Considering the things that were *said*!" I muttered, for it was hard to know what to say to a man when, the last time you saw him, you had shared a potent kiss. But I found words. "Every mage House has advocates trained in the law who can argue cases in the law courts. What use can you possibly have for Chartji's services?"

"A question I might ask you."

"You might, but my answer would be the same as yours."

He flashed a smile of such astounding sweetness and humor—as if he appreciated my wit!—that it would have been easier for me if my heart had simply stopped and I had dropped dead. I had not known the man could smile like that.

His smile vanished and he said in a serious tone, "Perhaps you'd best sit down, Catherine. Are you going to faint?"

"I never faint," I said hoarsely. "I'm just tired from all the *escaping* my cousin and I have had to do."

"You never answered her question, Magister." The spark in Drake's tone made my neck tingle as with a warning. "Why on Earth would a magister visit the offices of an ordinary solicitor who is also a troll? Have you lost something you want back?"

It was clearly a wild guess, but Andevai swung around as fast as if he'd been ridiculed. When his gaze met Drake's, such a flare of mutual dislike flashed between them that it felt as if all the air had been sucked from the entryway. The history of the world begins in ice, and it will end in ice. So sing the Celtic bards and Mande djeliw of the north. The Roman historians, on the other hand, claimed that fire will consume us in the end.

Ice, or fire? As the two men faced down, I had a sudden and terrible premonition I was about to find out.

A trill, like speech, slid down from the stairs to interrupt the end of the world. Chartji descended from the first floor with the odd hitching walk typical of her kind. She reached the entry and stuck out a hand in the manner of the radicals. "Magister. Here you are."

Andevai shrugged as if letting anger roll off him. Then he turned, taking her hand in his without the least sign that he, the scion of an influential and wealthy mage House, found this style of greeting plebeian. "My thanks for remembering our earlier meeting and agreeing to my request for an appointment."

She was taller than he was, with the wide-set eyes and feathered ruff typical of trolls. When she opened her snout in imitation of a smile, her sharp teeth certainly presented a threat, but her greeting was pleasant enough and her speech so human that its precision sounded peculiar.

"Well met, Magister. I admit, I was not sure you would venture to this district, where lies so much technology to disturb you. I am pleased you did so. If you will follow me to my office, we can discuss your business."

Drake said, "What business might that be?"

She bared teeth at Drake, bobbed her head at me, and gestured to Andevai. "We guarantee privacy for all who seek our services." Opening the nearest door, she indicated he should precede her into the office.

He hesitated. "Will you be here afterward, Catherine?" he said in a low voice.

This was one answer I could honestly give. "Until Four Moons House gives up all attempt to claim my cousin Beatrice, I can have nothing to do with any mage House or magister."

He stiffened. "Of course. I admire you for standing loyal to your family above all."

He sketched an ambivalent gesture, halfway between greeting and leaving, before he crossed into the office. Chartji shut the door behind them. With my exceptionally good hearing, I heard the rustle of curtains being dragged open inside.

"How do you know this arrogant cold mage?" asked Drake.

"The tale is quite a labyrinth of intrigue," I said, wishing he would leave me alone so I could eavesdrop.

"Phoenician spies must be quite at home with labyrinths of intrigue." Yet he smiled to take the sting out of the words.

When in doubt, we'd been taught to distract through

misdirection. "We call ourselves Kena'ani, not Phoenician. *Phoenician* is a Greek word, and it's the one the Romans called us."

He chuckled. "I'll remember that, Maestressa. I make it a point never to trust a cold mage. I hope you don't think it might be possible to do so." His eyes had the strange quality of seeming vivid in the dim entryway. He watched me, waiting for an answer.

I did not want to speak, but I kept wondering if Camjiata's armed attendants might decide to attack Andevai. "I'm very sure the cold mage doesn't know the general is here. I don't know what his business is, but it's not about Camjiata."

"Your insight interests me, Maestressa," he said with a smile meant to flatter, and indeed I blushed, because I was not accustomed to flattery. "Nevertheless, I'll need to go report the cold mage's arrival."

He went downstairs.

I sidled to the office door and leaned against it. First I tightly furled my senses, blocking out sounds, sights, and smells around me. Then I reached to the threads of magic that permeate all things, the insubstantial threads that can't be seen or touched in any common way. My awareness crept on those threads into the office.

Andevai was talking. "...If the principle of *rei vindicatio* were turned on its head. What if people bound by clientage could say they want to reclaim ownership of themselves? Is it possible?"

"*Rei vindicatio* means to take possession of something you already own. Such a ruling would turn on the legal status of those people bound by clientage." Chartji spoke in her eerily perfect diction and accent. "Is clientage legally equivalent to slavery? If they do not possess their

own persons in any legal way, then there is nothing to reclaim. Unless the law declares slavery to be illegal, as the
law does among my people. So it is difficult for me to say
if it is possible here. I will need to make a thorough exam-
ination of the law codes and the rulings of jurists. I will
need to interview bards and djeliw, because they keep the
oldest laws in their memories. I know of no such case being brought before the princely court in the principality
of Tarrant. In Expedition, the law is handled quite differently. Just a moment..."

I was straining so hard to hear that when the door exhaled away from my face I stumbled forward into the
office. The way the troll pulled back her muzzle was not
unfriendly, but it was distinctly unnerving to stare down
those predator's teeth. The crest of yellow feathers raised.

"When I assure people that I offer private meetings, I
must be able to fulfill that promise."

I am sure my face turned as scarlet as if I had been
painted. "My apologies."

Andevai was seated on a settee by the desk. "You may
as well let her stay, solicitor. There's something she needs
to hear."

"I thought you said this appointment had nothing to do
with me," I retorted.

Chartji shut the door. Because I was not about to join
Andevai on the settee, I remained standing. Chartji
waited beside me. Fox Close lay quiet but for the noise
of a coal man shoveling coke into the coal chute and the
rumble of a wheelbarrow being pushed along the lane.

"Your chin is bruised," Andevai said, touching his own
chin.

I clasped my hands behind my back. "It was slammed
into the floor when you fought that cold magic duel in

the factory." I did not add: *against your own master, the mansa, to stop him from killing me.*

"Ah." He seemed stymied and uncomfortable. "My apologies."

"Since you saved my life, I'm sure you need not apologize."

With a wince as at a sour taste, he firmly said nothing and looked at me as if daring me to talk. Silence swelled like a bubble expanding to fill the chamber. I looked around. One wall was lined with bookshelves stuffed full of leather-bound volumes shelved in a hodgepodge, some upright and some lying flat. An elaborate map of the world, printed on fabric and tacked up askew, covered part of another wall. The troll's desk looked like a bird's nest in the way books, papers, nibs, and a number of odd-looking notched sticks were woven together into a mess that made my hands itch to tidy up. Most strangely, the fire was still burning.

Andevai rose. "Obviously you are wondering why I am here, Catherine. The main reason is business of my own, as I said, none of your concern."

"*Rei vindicatio* is none of my concern? When you arrived at my aunt and uncle's house two months ago, you invoked *rei vindicatio* to reclaim ownership of the eldest Hassi Barahal daughter. Four Moons House had forced the Barahals to sign a contract giving that daughter to the mages, but she had been allowed to remain in the possession of her family all the while she was growing up because the mages were worried that the presence in the mage House of a girl who walked the dreams of dragons might be dangerous. Isn't that correct?"

"Why ask me the question when you already know the answer?"

"Just to hear you say it." I was shocked at how snide my tone was, but I could not control the surging tide of my emotions: He had thought he had to kill me, yet he had saved my life; I had escaped him and then kissed him. I could not make sense of him.

His lips thinned. I knew some cutting retort was coming. He had a habit of trying to cover his emotions with expressions of scorn. "Yes, I invoked *rei vindicatio*. But I married the wrong woman, didn't I? Instead of marrying your cousin, I married *you*."

His gaze was too sharp. I decided I would rather look at the ceiling, which was painted blue and flecked with curiously vibrant representations of clouds.

He went on, his voice clipped. "So I have asked Solicitor Chartji if she knows of any legal way to undo the chain of binding which was sealed on our marriage."

His comment shocked me back to earth. "There is no way to undo a magical chain. No way, short of *death*." The word stung like a mouthful of salt.

"So we are told. But that does not mean it has never been undone before. Or cannot be undone by other means."

"Such a matter lies a very long way out of my field of expertise," said Chartji. "However, it would be interesting to look into as a legal technicality. I can promise nothing. Nor can I figure in what manner of legal court you could adjudicate such a case. However, I can investigate and report back on what I find, if that is what you want."

"Do you want to be released from our marriage, Catherine?" His stare challenged me.

"May I speak bluntly?" I asked.

"When did you ever not?"

"You'd be surprised how many times I bit my tongue!"

"If you'd done so, I would think I would have seen more blood."

"One drop was enough," I said.

With an intake of breath, he stiffened, looking like a man who has no idea how he came to be standing in a place so far beneath his consequence. "There is no answer to that."

How was it he kept putting me on the defensive? "You misunderstand me. All I meant was, are you willing to hear what I have to say in front of another person?"

Chartji's crest rose slightly.

"I do not fear her censure, if that is what you think. Anything said here won't be repeated."

"I was *trying* to be thoughtful," I said. "I meant only to spare your feelings."

"Please do not begin concerning yourself about my feelings *now*."

"Was there a time before this I would have had some reason to be concerned for *your* feelings? Perhaps after I was forced to marry you and you treated me with cruelty instead of kindness? Or perhaps when I was running for my life after you were commanded to kill me?"

The troll's faint whistle shivered the air. I fisted my hands, waiting for Andevai to cut me down to size.

He shut his eyes, then opened them to look right at me, his voice tight and his tone rigidly formal. "I regret the high-handed way I behaved toward you on that journey almost as much as I regret not immediately rejecting the mansa's command to kill you. But my regrets do not change the past. So say what you must, Catherine. I am not afraid to hear it."

My heart was hammering so hard I was dizzy. I brushed the back of a hand across my forehead and took a breath to steady myself. "You belong to Four Moons House. Legally, you belong to them. You had to marry me because you were ordered to do it. Once I was forced to marry you, I belonged to them, too, through the djeli's binding that contracted me to you. You knew that's what would happen. So in a way I think it was an attempt at kindness for you to think that you and I—that you thought I was—" Heat seared my cheeks. I could not go on.

"Acquit me of kindness, Catherine. I meant what I said."

I certainly could not forget what he had said: "*When I saw you coming down the stairs that evening, it was as if I were seeing the other half of my soul descending to greet me.*"

I gulped in air and got words past an obstruction. "Even if you believe that now, to Four Moons House I will never be anything except the mistake you made that lost them the person they wanted. The burden of protecting me from their indifference and spite will eventually wear away whatever affection you may currently believe you hold for me."

"I wish you would speak for yourself, Catherine, and stop telling me what I do and do not believe and how I will and will not act."

"Then I'll speak for myself." Because my hands were shaking, I clasped them together again. "I can't live in Four Moons House as an unwanted creature whom everyone will scorn. And I know you said I could live in your family's village, but I wouldn't know how to live there. I'd be so out of place. Above all else, I know better than to chance what may happen tomorrow on a transitory passion felt today."

I had to stop.

He said nothing. Yes, he was physically handsome, and attractive in some other intangible way. After those first disastrous days, he had made an effort to help me. His kiss had certainly pleased me in a most startling manner. But I did not love him. How could I? I didn't even know him. And whatever he might think, he did not truly know me. He only believed he did.

"I am sure it is to your credit that you tried to soften the blow," I went on.

"*Soften the blow?*" His eyes flared.

Had I been wiser, I would have stopped, because the fire in the hearth flickered.

No one had ever accused me of being wise.

"You were commanded to marry a woman against both your own will and hers. So you concocted a honeyed fable in your heart to make an unpleasant duty palatable. Just as you weave illusions out of light, you wove an illusion about us. One soul cleaved into two halves and then like destiny reunited—"

The fire whuffed out with a puff of ash. A glimmer of ice crackled across the heavy iron circulating stove.

"Are you quite through insulting me?" he demanded.

Chartji's crest was fully raised. I felt she was making ready to act precipitously in case someone lost his temper and brought down the house.

"It's not meant as an insult!"

"Implying I don't know my own mind is not an insult?" His jaw was clenched, his eyes had narrowed, and I heard a whispery groan of iron under strain. Yes. He was very angry.

"That's not how I meant it. You didn't kill me when you had the chance. You aided me when you could. You defied the mansa by telling him you would stop anyone who tried to kill me. So I thank you for that. But Bee and I have our own problems. A husband is one complication too many." My hands were squeezed so tightly my shoulders ached. I untangled my fingers and separated my hands. "I'll make no objection if a way can be found to dissolve the marriage. Let you go your way, and me mine. It's for the best."

"So be it." His gaze flashed up, and if there was a murderous piercing spear in those fine brown eyes I am sure he did not mean it literally. Perhaps he was finally reconsidering the wisdom of believing he had fallen in love at first sight. People could convince themselves of anything.

"Will that be all, then?" Chartji said to me.

"Yes." I was barely able to croak out the word. Over here, it seemed terribly hot, although the rest of the chamber shivered with cold.

"If you will." She indicated the door. "The magister and I aren't finished."

I let her usher me out, and as I turned back to see if Andevai had watched me go, she closed the door in my face.

5

Let him go his way, and me mine. Our lives led down different paths. I was well rid of him and the way he was contemptuous one moment, a proud cold mage from the top of his well-groomed head to the tips of his gloriously polished boots, and then the next might be mistaken for a staidly polite and provincially traditional—if unusually good-looking—village lad who was trying too hard to fit into a world where he was not welcome but could not be turned away.

Impatient with these niggling thoughts which like bad-mannered visitors simply would not leave, I ran downstairs. That idiot Bee had not left, although she had put on her coat. Seeing me, she opened her mouth, perhaps to comment on the way my eyes were red from unshed tears or that I had been parading around in my unkempt bodice and skirts like an overworked scullery maid. Then she closed her mouth and instead handed me my riding jacket. Rory was lounging by the fire as might a cat sunning itself on a rock.

We were not alone.

Kehinde sat in a chair opposite Bee, holding a parsnip. Brennan leaned against the wall beside the door, so perfectly at ease it took a moment to realize how quickly he could block the door. The contrast between them was striking. He was muscular, blond, and white-skinned, with the look of a man used to waiting until he had to explode into action. Small-framed, she was fidgety, touching each unsliced parsnip as if her hands needed something to do while her mind worked; her skin was black, and she wore her long black hair in locks.

"We need to talk." She pushed her spectacles up the bridge of her nose.

"I didn't say anything to him about the general being here!"

"Sit, please." Kehinde spoke without force or anger. I sank onto the bench, all energy drained. "Why did you come? To seek our help to return to the Hassi Barahal motherhouse in Gadir?"

"No," said Bee, with a glance at me. I let her talk. "We're not returning there."

"Why not? They are your community. What are we, if we have no community and no family?"

"'*We*' are left to fend for ourselves," said Bee. "Let me just say that our family betrayed us and we no longer trust them. We hoped to find refuge with radicals. We thought you of all people would understand why we don't want to be bound into clientage, practically legal slavery, to a mage House or a prince's court...or some patrician household from Rome." Her voice fell to a whisper, but she recovered. "We can be useful to the cause. We are not without skills."

"The Hassi Barahal house is known to be employed in the business of selling information," said Kehinde. "You might be spying on us. After all, after you came, the cold mage arrived."

I was getting annoyed. "Turn that around! Why would

Chartji make an appointment for a cold mage to come to your office at the same time the most wanted man in Europe is to be here?"

Brennan laughed. "An unfortunate case of bad timing, and close calls. Rather exciting, don't you think?"

"For you it will always be a game, Du," said Kehinde, measuring him with a frown. "The more you skate onto the thin ice, as you say here in the north, the better you like it."

He shook his head, watching her closely. "Oh, no, Professora, you know it is not a game to me. Risks must be taken if we mean to get what we want." He flashed his enchanting smile at Bee, and then at me. "I think the girls are a risk worth taking."

"Maybe we're the ones who should be asking if we can trust *you*," said Bee. "Like Cat said, you're the ones meeting with the general. And the cold mage!"

"She's got us at knife's point there," said Brennan, still looking amused.

Bee's brow furrowed and her gaze darkened as if storm clouds had swept down. We were in for a blow. "It's easy for you to laugh. You're a man. Maybe you're entirely legally free, or maybe your northern village is entangled in some kind of clientage to a mage House. I don't know. But you, Professora, surely you as a legal scholar will understand our situation. Even though my cousin and I are twenty and legally adults, the Hassi Barahal elders in Gadir can dispose of us however they wish simply because we are female and unmarried." She flashed me a glance to remind me to keep my mouth closed about the unfortunate fact that I was already married. As if I wanted to brag about it! "So you can see that radicals who speak of overturning an oppressive legal code might interest us."

"I understand perfectly." Kehinde glanced at Brennan. To my surprise, he looked away, biting his lower lip. She toyed with the ends of several of her locks. "We dispute the arbitrary distribution of power and wealth, which is claimed as the natural order, but which is in fact not natural at all but rather artificially created and sustained by ancient privileges. Of which marriage is one. Yet we still have a problem. It appears you are being pursued by the same mage Houses and princes who wish to capture the general. Until Camjiata leaves Adurnam, you cannot stay here."

"You're turning us away," said Bee wearily.

"Not at all. I have been formulating an idea that our organization might have a use for two young women trained by the Hassi Barahal clan. Godwik agrees with me. Indeed, Maester Godwik finds you to be of the greatest interest. I consider his judgments to be based on sound reason."

"Unlike mine," murmured Brennan.

She did not by so much as a flicker of the eye indicate she had heard this. "It was odd to hear the general say his wife had had a vision that he would meet a Hassi Barahal daughter who, as he declaimed so poetically, will walk the path of dreams. And then of course there was the oracle about Tara Bell's child. Such oracles being clouded and obscure exactly so that any outcome can be acclaimed as the prophetic one."

"I wouldn't discount such words," said Brennan. "But I am no city-raised sophisticate. I'm just a miner's son who has seen too much death."

"When people die in troubling and violent ways, we seek a story to explain it, however far-fetched." She raised a hand to forestall Brennan's retort. "That forces exist in the world which we cannot account for is manifestly true. Through observation and experience, scholars seek to describe the natural world and plumb its depths. I have for years been in correspondence with a well-regarded scholar who lives in Adurnam. I have now had the chance to speak with him in person, and I find him every bit as impressive as his letters indicated. He will shelter you until such time as it is safe for you to join us. You must ask to share a shot of whiskey with Bran Cof—"

"Everyone knows the poet Bran Cof is long dead," said Bee. "If you can call that death, when your head is stuck on a pedestal and everyone is waiting for you to speak."

"I like that whiskey stuff!" said Rory, sitting up.

Kehinde eyed him as if trying to decide whether his insouciance was an act that disguised a razor-sharp mind and will, or if he was exactly as he seemed. "The name is a code to show you are part of our organization."

"Wait," I said. "Why Bran Cof? Where do you mean to send us?"

"There is an academy in Adurnam. Its headmaster will shelter you."

Bee slanted a glance at me, and I scratched my left ear, and Rory stood to stretch with an exaggerated yawn, because he understood we were speaking with gestures, warning each other and him. Bee and I had attended the academy for over two years. We knew the headmaster well. We had trusted him. When Bee had stayed behind in Adurnam after her parents and family fled on a ship bound for Gadir, she had gone to him for shelter. And he had turned her over to the custody of Amadou Barry, whose home had been a gilded cage that dazzled Bee until the legate made his insulting proposal, offering to make Bee his mistress. But Kehinde and Brennan didn't need to know any of that.

I took a step back to leave the stage to Bee. With her black curls, rosy lips, and big brown eyes, she looked entirely adorable and innocent and trusting. "It is so generous of you to take an interest in us. But you know the risks we face. The factions hunting us. Why help us?"

Kehinde extended a hand, and to my shock Bee handed her the knife. The professor used the tip to investigate the ranks of sliced parsnips. "It is quite remarkable how evenly they are each sliced, as if each cut were measured beforehand by something other than your eye. Unless you find an isolated barbaric village, perhaps in the wilds of Brigantia"—she glanced at Brennan—"you must see you have entered the conflict whether you wish to or not. If it is true your dreams reflect a cryptic vision of the future—and I assure you I will need evidence—then you will never be let alone. *Never.* I am no different than anyone. I can think of ways to employ your gift to benefit the cause I cherish. But I will only ever approach you as a partner, and you will be free to leave our association at any time. It is your decision." She set down the knife.

"What about your alliance with the general?" I asked.

Brennan smiled wryly. "Harsh conditions make for odd bedfellows. Our organization has its own reasons for considering an alliance with the general."

I nodded. "That makes sense. He's a soldier. You're only radicals. He must be better able to fend off princes and mages than you are."

"You will have to decide whether swords and rifles, or words and ideas, are more likely to win the day," said Kehinde.

"I'm all for swords and rifles," I said.

"Do not discount the power of words and ideas," she said with a smile I dearly wished I could trust. "Their touch seems soft at first, but you'll find it can be lasting."

"Well, then," said Bee. "We'll take you up on your offer. We'll leave right away."

Rory collected the two bags as I pulled on my riding jacket, coat, and gloves.

"I'll arrange for someone to escort you across the city who knows the backstreets to keep you out of sight of the militia," said Brennan. "And may I ask, what *is* in the bags?"

My father's journals, our sewing baskets, some clothes and diverse small necessities. What coin we had was sewn into Bee's gown, with a few coins tucked into my sleeve. He had such a charming smile, but I hardened my heart against confiding even such innocuous information.

"Our things," I said.

Kehinde rose. "I'll come to the academy when it is safe for you to return. It would be best to go out the front so it looks as if you came for an appointment and left. If you'll excuse me, I must prepare for my negotiations with the general." She shook hands with Bee and me.

"Rory," I said.

He stared at me with those golden, innocent eyes. "What am I supposed to do?"

"Shake hands. It's the custom, among radicals."

He set down the bags and shook hands with Kehinde. She left.

With a lazy grin, Rory gripped Brennan's hand a bit too hard and a bit too long. I felt a shift in the temper of the air as Brennan took his measure, like coiling up rope in readiness to snap it out.

Bee said, "Rory, stop that."

With a put-upon sigh, he let go, leaving Brennan to shake our hands.

He leaned toward me—too close, for I flushed—and murmured, "Is he really your brother?"

After all, I just could not resist. I daringly drifted close enough for my lips to brush the tips of his hair as I whispered, "What confuses you is he's really a saber-toothed cat who followed me home from the spirit world."

I expected him to laugh, but instead he pulled back and gave first a very searching look at Rory and then, less comfortably, a long and intent look at me.

"Well," he said, ambivalently, and with his forehead creased thoughtfully, he went out.

"That was naughty." Bee shut the door so we could have privacy. "Are you smitten?"

"Men like that don't look at girls like me."

"I think he likes the professora. It's almost tempting, isn't it, to join *the cause* just to fight near him. Or it would be, if we didn't now know they are in league with the headmaster! Who handed me over to Amadou Barry. Who is a Roman legate. And the Romans are allied with the mage Houses against Camjiata. Who has come to this house to negotiate with the radicals. It doesn't even make sense!"

Rory circled back to the stove. "Are we going back out into that awful cold? I'm starving."

"So am I," I said, "but we've got to go."

"Camjiata knows something about walking the dreams of dragons," mused Bee. "Maybe we *should* ally ourselves with him."

"An alliance with him comes with a price."

"I think he says what he means," said Rory, "and means what he says."

"Yes, and so does any lunatic." Bee stirred the parsnip slices with the knife. "Alas, all I see right now in my future is dismemberment."

I crossed to embrace her. "I'll never let the Wild Hunt take you, Bee. Never!"

She sniffled, and put down the knife to hug me. "I love you, too, Cat."

I released her. "There is another choice. I don't know where my mother came from, so there's no use seeking her kin. But Rory and I have a common sire. Someone Tara and Daniel encountered when they were part of the First Baltic Ice Expedition. The expedition was lost, and the survivors were only found months later. It's certain that's when she got pregnant. My sire must be a creature of the spirit world. How else could he impregnate both a human woman from this world and a saber-toothed cat from the spirit world?"

Bee grimaced. "I don't like the way this conversation is going."

I smirked. "Oh, come now, Bee. Nothing we saw in anatomy class ever made you blush."

"That's not what I meant, although now that you mention it, how could that be managed? Gracious Melqart, Cat. What an unseemly shade of red you've turned!"

"I'm going to pour a handful of salt in your porridge for a month, you monster. Don't distract me. The coachman and footman who conveyed Andevai and me from Adurnam to Four Moons House were not...human. The footman was an eru. She addressed me as *Cousin* before I ever had any idea that Daniel Hassi Barahal was not the male who sired me. I have kinfolk in the spirit world. My kin are obliged to aid me. Isn't that right, Rory?"

For an instant, his upper lip began to curl back, and I

thought he was going to snarl. He spoke instead. "As I am bound, so must those bound to me as kin come to my aid. That is the law."

"Cat, you think you can call your sire once you are in the spirit world." Bee's smile had a frightening effect on me: a tingling rush through my body that made me boldly wish to engage in a reckless act. Perhaps being exhausted and feeling cornered made us more reckless than usual. "If he is anything like Rory, he can cross back into this world in the shape of a man. That would bring a new piece into the conflict no one expects. How do we get to the spirit world?"

"When my blood was shed on a crossing stone, I crossed from this world into the spirit world. Once in the spirit world, I crossed back through a different gate. The hunters of Andevai's village crossed likewise, so I was told. How would you get back, Rory, if you wanted to go?"

"My existence was very boring before you came, Cat. I lazed about, hunted a bit, sunned myself, ate, slept, and rested. I never had any fun. I don't want to go back, and neither should you."

"Oh, Rory." I went to the door and put an arm around him. "You've asked for nothing. You're the best brother I could ever have. But our situation here is impossible. We can't keep running. You don't have to come with us. We'll give you money and you can wait with the bags at an inn. We'll come back, I promise."

Because he tended to laze about and look as sleek and indolent as any healthy cat, it was easy to forget he was a dangerous predator. He shook off my arm in a way that made Bee grab the knife as if she thought she might have to defend me.

His voice reverberated like the warning clangor of a bell. "Beware what you call, lest you be devoured by a creature hungrier than you. To drink from the fountain of mortal blood is to drink the essence of power. Every step in the spirit world is a perilous step."

I did not fear him He was my brother. I grabbed his hand. "What choice do we have?"

He seemed to get smaller, as if his fur were flattening. "It's a bad idea."

"To bring the knife, or not to bring the knife," said Bee, "that is my question." She set a denarius on the table before tucking the knife in her coat. "Where do we go?"

I said, "To the plinth that marks the foundation stone of the first Adurni settlement. Where two ancient paths met, according to the history of the founding of Adurnam. If any place in this city opens on a crossing into the spirit world, that must be it."

"I don't know, Cat. That part of town is filled with taverns, dogfights, and fatheaded young guildsmen seeking any excuse for a duel."

"That sounds promising!" said Rory with a cocky grin that made me think he'd already forgotten his frightening words and our bad idea.

I fastened my cane to its loop and buttoned my coat as Rory picked up the bags. A saber-toothed cat, cold steel, and dreams that revealed the future. That would have to be enough. As we headed up the stairs, Bee began to hum under her breath the famous aria "When He Is Laid in Earth" from the recently staged opera *The Dido and Aeneas*, in which the queen of Qart Hadast, after defeating the Roman prince who sought to subdue her rule through marriage, presides over his funeral procession.

The Amazon waited in the entryway, shoulders against

the door and arms crossed. "So here yee is," she remarked in an odd accent. "Already, the general know yee lot shall leave."

But instead of blocking our path, she opened the door. A blast of wintry air swirled in, numbing my face and chilling my heart. The history of the world begins in ice, and it will end in ice. So sing the Celtic bards and Mande djeliw of the north whose words tell us where we came from and what ties and obligations bind us. Here, we dare not forget the vast ice sheets and massive glaciers that cover the northern reaches of Europe. In the old tales, the ice is called the abode of the ancestors. Brennan hadn't mentioned the phrase in his story of gruesome death, but Daniel Hassi Barahal had written it in his journals. I steeled myself, for wasn't I seeking my ancestors?

The winter wind stirred the hem of the Amazon's knee-length jacket. She wore a soldier's boots, kept polished not to a fashionable mirror gleam but with an attention to cleanliness and wear, so they would last longer and support her when she hit rough ground.

"If yee wait with the door open, then the cold air come in. Make up yee mind. Go, or stay."

"You're not going to try to stop us?" Bee asked.

"They who fight with the general, fight of they own will. One thing I shall tell yee before yee walk. If ever any of yeen wish to contact the general, go to the tavern called Buffalo and Lion, in the district called Old Temple. Yee shall say the words 'Helene sent me.' We shall see yee again."

"Our thanks." Bee touched gloved fingers to her chest like a great lady of the theater about to make an exit. "And yet, farewell."

She swept out the door and down the steps. Rory took

in a breath as if scenting for danger, then followed, swinging the bags as if they weighed nothing. I could not stop myself from looking toward the closed door of Chartji's office. Whatever went on there between the lawyer and Andevai was no longer my business. I had to leave that part of my life behind.

Yet I hesitated on the threshold. The clamor of the city assaulted me with the noise of rattling carts, ringing handbells, market-folk calling out their wares, and men crying the morning's news: *The Northgate poet begins fourth day of hunger strike on the prince's steps!* For a moment, I reveled in the sweet familiar sounds, the ones I had grown up with.

Then, out of nowhere and with no warning, a clangor shook me down to my boots. The sister bells, Brigantia and Faro by the river, rang to life with their alarm: *Fire! Fire! Call the watch!*

Doors opened all along Fox Close and people crowded onto their front steps, their breath like white mist in the air as they looked into the sky for the origin of the trouble.

"The war begin," said the Amazon. "But the princes and the mages don' know. Not yet. So, gal. Go, or stay?"

"Cat?" Bee's plaintive voice called from the street. In the house, I heard footsteps, people moving toward doors that were about to be opened.

"I'm going," I said. And I went.

6

"A good morning to you, Maestressas and Maester." A young man with dusty blond hair and a freckled white face stood beside an empty coal cart. "Is all well with you?"

"I have no trouble, thanks to my power as a woman," I replied in the traditional way, and received a scathing look from Bee for my pains. "And you, Maester? Is all well with your family?"

"We have peace, thanks to my mother who raised me," he said with a grin. "Though I wonder at the bells. I hope the fire's not around here."

He looked down Fox Close toward Enterprise Road. With the bells tolling the alarm, the streets of Adurnam had turned, like the snowmelt-fed streams of late spring, into foaming rivers full with a raging flow of people hurrying to get somewhere else. I didn't relish making our way halfway across Adurnam in this tumult.

"Are you from this district?" I asked.

He made a flourish with his cap. "That I am. And my ancestors before me. Eurig is my name. Brennan Du asked me to get you across the city."

I exchanged a glance with Bee. We would have to lose him, but not too soon. A shame, for he seemed nice enough. "Our thanks. We can't give our names. My apologies."

"I understand. This way."

He picked up the handles of the cart and began pushing not toward Enterprise Road but deeper into the narrow lane of Fox Close. We walked alongside as he talked. "We'll take Ticking Lane through the Lower Warrens. They're perfectly safe despite the name. Most of the old buildings here have been knocked down and rebuilt. And there's gaslight everywhere in this district. We used to be nothing more than a fishing village. Now we're quite the most modern district in Adurnam, thanks to the trolls and the radicals."

"How did you become a radical?" Bee asked.

"As the Northgate poet says, it's no crime to think men have natural rights that ought not to be trampled on by ancient privileges."

"Just men? Or women, too?" asked Bee with her most dangerously pretty smile.

He blinked, taken aback by this thrust. "Nature has suited women for a different role than that given to men."

"Like Professora Kuti?" Bee demanded.

"Cat!" Rory nudged me with a bag. "I smell a lot of horses nearby."

Angry shouts of protest rang from Enterprise Road: "The dogs are come to bite us with their teeth of steel." "We need step aside for no man!" "Which will it be, lads? Freedom or fetters?"

A whip cracked. A man screamed. A column of mounted soldiers swept into sight around the corner where Fox Close met Enterprise Road. About half wore tabards marked with the four moons of full, half, crescent, and new: turbaned mage House troops, leading a spare horse. The rest wore the uniforms of the Tarrant militia except for a half dozen in red-and-gold hip-length capes, the mark of Rome's ambassadorial cavalry. Pedestrians stumbled back to the stoops and railings.

"Keep walking," said Eurig. "Don't look back."

"Eurig," I said, "did the ancient village here have a crossroads?"

"What? The Fiddler's Stone down by Old Cross Gate? The fishermen would bring their catch up from the shore and trade it to the folk who came over from the Roman camp. That was a long time ago." He glanced over his shoulder. "Let's move faster. Just don't run."

I looked back. The soldiers pulled up in front of the law offices of Godwik and Clutch. A man wearing a Roman cape dismounted just as the door opened and Andevai appeared on the steps. The rigid set of his shoulders betrayed his annoyance, and made me think he really had come to consult with Chartji on a matter so private he hadn't told the mansa. From the steps, as if drawn by my foolish stare, Andevai looked our way down Fox Close. I saw him see me.

Quite deliberately, he strode down the steps, mounted, and turned toward Enterprise Road.

"He's leading them *away* from us!" I said.

"Just keep walking," said Eurig.

"Cat!" Bee was breathless. "Didn't you recognize him?"

"Andevai? Of course I recognized—"

"It was Amadou Barry, with the Roman guard."

Eurig turned his cart into a lane lined with craftsmen's shops. Behind one window, clockwork toy horses and dogs clattered along a display counter. Behind another, four women sat at a table, filing and polishing tiny gears.

Rory, lagging behind, ran to catch up. "They're coming back. That Lord Marius is with them now. He must have told them to turn around."

Eurig whistled shrilly. Five shops down, a burly man wearing an apron streaked with grease stepped out onto the lane. He nodded, and we hurried past him into a large room where persons bent over an alembic from whose unstoppered rim rose a misty thread. An acrid smell made my eyes water. Rory sneezed. From behind a curtain came the sound of hollow clapping.

"Up on the roof and over to the troll nest," said the aproned man. "They're all out at the steamworks, and I've got their permission. I'll put your cart out back. Lads, get your masks on."

"What's that awful smell?" Bee asked.

"A scent to keep the prince's hounds at bay, Maestressa," he said. "You won't be able to come back down, but they won't be able to come in." He dragged aside the curtain to reveal stairs.

A handbell rang three times. We climbed the stairs to the first floor in pace to the odd clapping noise. Workbenches filled the first-floor chamber, strewn with glass pipes, gleaming gears, and a discarded tartan cap. A dozen workers were grumbling as they reached under their benches for cloth masks. Scars mottled their ashen faces. The second floor was crammed with crates, and the third with neat rows of cots. A stair-step ladder led to a long, low attic with a dormer window and more cots.

I pressed a hand over my nose. My eyes were really beginning to sting.

Rory was staggering. "Poison!" he choked out.

"Move," said Eurig. "The fumes will kill us."

I pulled down the latch and opened the window. The

winter air hit like a blast. A crow sat on the peak of the roof opposite. I was so sure it was watching me that I could not move.

Bee pushed past me and out the window. Shaking myself, I followed. We chivvied to the right around the chimneys and out of sight of the lane. Across a warren of roofs, it was possible to see the river embankments and docks crowded with vessels. A massive flock of crows wheeled in the sky.

"Look!" Bee's fingers tightened painfully on my arm.

A fire blazed on the wide pewter expanse of the Solent River.

Greasy smoke billowed. Ripples of heat rolled upward against a dawn sky made dank and low by clouds. A hulk anchored beyond the docks was burning with fiery abandon.

"Isn't that a prison ship, Cat? All those people chained in the holds must be trapped."

Rory crawled into sight, wheezing. Eurig slouched after, dragging the bags.

Upriver, a sloop flying the prince of Tarrant's ensign flowed into view. The deck was covered with uniformed men, some in clusters around the guns, others with swords, pikes, and crossbows ready to board.

Eurig shaded his eyes. "They mean to sink the hulk. Follow me."

Bee released my hand. "They'll let the prisoners burn? Or drown?"

He cast her a disgusted look. "Of course they will. That's the plague ship."

"A plague ship?" I stared at him. "What plague?"

"The salt plague."

"The salt plague never left West Africa. It can't cross water or survive the desert."

He laughed in a coarse way that made me blush with shame. "Of course it can cross water. In a ship. That's how our noble prince keeps agitators in line. There's a cage of salters on that hulk. A political prisoner gets put in that cage, and he will get bit. The plague will infest his blood, and he will become a salter just like the others. He'll crave salt and blood as his mind and body rot."

Bee's fingers closed over my forearm, grip tightening as Eurig took a step closer.

By the tension in his shoulders and the cant of his head, he meant us to feel intimidated. "My sweet lasses, there is no cure for the salt plague. And every person who is bit gets infested and becomes a salter in their turn. It would be better to be dead. So don't wonder why we send those salters to rest at the bottom of the tide where they can't bite us. Scarred Hades! Get down!"

A corner of Ticking Lane was visible between two chimneys. Horsemen rode past. We ducked, then crawled to where a sloped plank gave access to a higher roof. We climbed up, but once there, Rory vomited a vile spew that, horribly, had the slimy remains of feathers in it.

"Just…need…moment…rest," he murmured, sinking to hands and knees.

"You're turning green," said Bee as I covered my mouth and nose with a hand. "You scout ahead. I'll stay with Rory and the bags."

Wincing with distaste, Eurig was eager to lead the way over the uneven rooftop with its chimney pots, then up steps to a wide ledge boasting a decorative wrought-iron bench, as if people sat up here. We looked over the rebuilt warrens. Trolls in pairs and threes, never singly, hurried through interconnected lanes and alleys, intermixed with men and women carrying goods on their heads or backs.

One of the trolls cocked its feather-crested head, spotting us but moving on. Two bright-plumaged trolls leaned out an attic window several houses down, looking toward the conflagration. A woman hanging out washing had paused to stare at the disaster out on the water.

A voice from an unseen watcher cried out: "Militia in the warrens! Bloody Romans, too. And mage House soldiers! Quick, lads, stow the rifles."

"Get down!" snapped Eurig. "Anyone might see you."

I stepped behind a chimney as he tugged open a trapdoor. We descended steep steps through an attic crammed with crates, baskets, and sealed ceramic jars. The floor below had no walls, only support pillars. Mirrors fragmented me into a hundred pieces: etched mirrors, hand mirrors, bronze mirrors, mercury mirrors, all hanging from the beams or propped on racks or braced on stands. Among them, displayed on a maze of shelving, lay gleaming objects of every shape and size: polished gold bracelets, bowls of metal gears, glass pipettes sealed over liquid mercury, steel blades, a flintlock rifle recently oiled. The shadow threads that bind the world seemed to have caught in the maze, tangling through my head. A discordant melody echoed faintly through the maze, the disharmony making my temples pound.

I rubbed my aching eyes. "What is this place? A thieves' den?"

"Careful where you step! Trolls are the most amiable creatures imaginable. Unless you take or break something that belongs to them. Come on."

We ducked under mirrors, sidestepped a column of pewter candlesticks, and traversed a labyrinth woven of wire. The path doubled back, dead-ended, and once rewound us back the way we had come. The mirrored reflections made my vision throb. I feared that if I brushed anything, the entire collection would crash down. Dizzied, I leaned on the banister as I descended.

The second floor had three doors standing open to bedchambers. We had reached the first-floor landing when a thunder of hooves rattled the entryway on the ground floor below us.

A shout: "That roof, there. Yes, this building. I saw someone up there, my lord."

"The door is locked, my lord captain."

"Break it down."

"Camlodus's Balls! It's the militia." Eurig turned. "Go up and hide. I'll divert them."

I knew better than to argue. I raced upstairs just as the front door was smashed open and soldiers exploded into the house. The maze seemed a bad bet for hiding, so I bolted into one of the second-floor bedchambers. The room looked as though a whirlwind had hit it, clothing scattered in heaps across six high square frames with mattresses, which looked more like nests than beds. The bright patterned fabrics gave the beds a patchwork feel: here a gold-and-green floral extravagance that might have been a barrister's robe suitable for law court, there a ruffed dash jacket sewn out of a cotton printed with orange bars, blue scallops, and elongated rose-colored spectacles winged with peacock feathers whose eyes watched me.

"Stop!" cried a martial voice.

On the landing below, Eurig replied, "Here, now, my lord captain, Your Mightiness. What gives you leave to come barging in here?"

"I might ask what gives you leave to speak so disrespectfully to a man who holds both kinship to the prince, and a sword," said a stentorian tenor. I recognized the voice of Lord Marius, whom I had first met at a ruined fort on a hill northeast of Adurnam, not more than a week before. Then, laughter had lightened his voice. Now, he blared.

"The prince of Tarrant?" retorted Eurig. "The man whose honor drains away drop by drop each day the Northgate poet refuses to eat? Our voices will be heard."

"In the law courts, at least. What brings you to an empty troll's nest?"

"They're partners in a consortium with my employer."

"I do believe you are lying. Are you angling for a ride on the plague ship, man?"

"Do you mean the one that's sinking right now? So will injustice founder."

"Arrest him," said Lord Marius. "Search the premises."

Threads of magic are woven through every part of the world because our world and the spirit world that lies athwart our own are intertwined. As footfalls approached the door, I drew the house's shadows around me like a cloak and hid myself. Two men walked into the chamber. One was Lord Marius, a tall, lean Celt with a thick mustache, a clean-shaven chin, and short hair stiffened into lime-whitened spikes. His gaze swept the chamber with a smile of amusement brushing his lips, as Bee's pencil might coax into life the humor of a man who prefers to laugh. He did not see me.

With him walked his brother by marriage, the young Roman legate Amadou Barry, whose father was both Roman patrician and West African prince and whose mother had been born into a noble Malian lineage. His Roman ambassadorial cape and the cut of his old-fashioned uniform certainly flattered him, although he had a frown on his handsome face.

"I admire his bravado," Lord Marius was saying. "But I'll have to have him fined for disrespect. I can't challenge a laborer to a duel."

"You Celts argue too much over fine points of honor. This seems like a chase after a wild goose, as you say up here in the north." His gaze flowed right past me as he scanned the room. "Jupiter Magnus! Have you ever seen such a mess?"

Lord Marius had a hearty laugh. "Perhaps it merely belongs to a mind whose idea of tidiness isn't the same as ours. It's no worse than your sister's dressing room."

Amadou Barry halted three steps into the room. I eased back to the bed on which lay the peacock jacket. "Sissy was ever so. I'm amazed by the resourcefulness of those two girls."

"Everyone has underestimated them, that is sure. Not least you, Amadou. Were you just that sure she would accept the—ah—position as your mistress?"

"I am a prince and a legate. Her family is impoverished and not respectable. She can't ever hope to receive a better offer."

Unless it was an offer to throttle him. As if a fire had been laid in the hearth and lit, my temperature rose.

"Quite so. I'm surprised to hear a Phoenician refused a lucrative contract—" Lord Marius broke off, gaze tightening. "Did you see something?"

Calm. I had to remain *calm.*

"In Beatrice? Faithful Venus, Marius! Even you must see something in her. She is the most delectable—"

"If I have to hear you praise her shining eyes and cherry lips one more time, I will have one of my men shoot me to put myself out of my misery."

"She will not sigh when I am dead," said Amadou.

"Nor will she lie with you for gold, it seems, which is the next line in the famous poem by the Thrice-Praised poet Bran Cof."

Amadou sighed. "I misplayed my hand. I was too accommodating."

Lord Marius paced the chamber, passing an arm's length from where I stood with my buttocks crushed against the high metal frame of the bed, holding my breath. "Women are hard to please. I could have sworn I saw a flicker of movement. Must have been the light."

"How do we know the girls are anywhere near this district? Much less in this house?"

"The mansa specifically told me to follow the cold mage. We're not to trust him. If *he* says to go left, then we go right."

"Ah, so that's why you turned this way when he wanted to ride back to Enterprise Road."

"That's right. Then one of my soldiers saw the cold mage see someone up on this roof, and my man thought it was a female, so here we are." Lord Marius paced to the door and glanced into the hall. He gestured to someone before turning back. "You know, Amadou, whatever you think about your Beatrice's raven-black ringlets and bonny curves, this business of hunting down girls makes me uneasy. It's beneath us. Meanwhile, that commoner in the hall is right, curse him. The Northgate poet sits on the steps of my cousin's court. Each day the poet does not eat, he heaps more shame on my clan's honor. I fear we are not getting out of this without a bloodbath."

"The plebes will mob and riot. It's in their breeding. We've known that in Rome for centuries. The sooner the militia drives the rabble off the streets, the better for all. If more blood were spilled, there'd be less trouble."

"Do you suppose so?" drawled a far-too-familiar voice. "I would think a timely hailstorm would drive people inside without causing undue harm."

Andevai walked into the bedchamber. I could not call his expression a smile.

"That's an interesting thought, Magister," said Marius. "Can you manage such a storm?"

Andevai's cool vanished like frost under the sun. "Of course I can!"

"I meant no offense, Magister. It would be a cursed sight better way to restore order than cutting people down. In my experience as a soldier..."

Gaze straying from Lord Marius to the bright disorder of clothing and fabric strewn across the beds, Andevai saw me.

He saw me.

Lord Marius had broken off. "Magister? What's wrong?"

Andevai blinked. "I was...just...stunned..." His gaze flickered to the bed. "That jacket. Orange bars. Blue scallops. Peacock-winged spectacles. And a ruff! Quite stunning. You would have to really...wear colors...and lace...to pull that off in a jacket."

"Yes, you would have to," said Lord Marius with a laugh, glancing toward me—at the jacket—and back at Andevai. The look he gave the man I had to call my husband was so frankly appreciative that I blushed. "You're quite the decorative specimen yourself."

"My thanks," said Andevai in the most absent-minded manner imaginable. I blinked so hard I thought he must surely hear me warn him with my eyes to *stop staring at me*.

Amadou Barry sighed in the manner of a man wanting

to change the subject. "Speaking of shooting oneself. Do we search the roof?"

"What say you, Magister?" Marius's amused and avid gaze remained fixed on Andevai.

"I say nothing," said Andevai, glaring right at me in the most shockingly idiotic way.

"We were told you could lead us to the girl you wed."

Andevai looked sharply away and appeared to be searching walls and ceiling for any remnant of good taste. "Is that what you were told? I wonder if this is meant to be a tailor's shop, or if they only raided one and got all the pieces mixed up."

Amadou Barry whistled. "You didn't come to this district to get information on where she fled?"

"I was on my own business."

"You're not going to give her up, are you, wherever she's gone?" said Marius. "Good for you. I liked her. That girl has spine and courage."

"We should check the roof," said Amadou.

Andevai's gaze skipped back to me.

I widened my eyes and mouthed, broadly, "*Yes. Say yes.*"

"Ye-es," he said slowly, brow crinkling with a question.

"Yes?" said Lord Marius with a surprised glance at Amadou.

I lifted my chin and mouthed, "*Say yes. Say go up on the roof.*"

"Yes," said Andevai more decisively. "By all means, go up on the roof." Then, with what was even for him an excess of haughty pride, he turned his glare onto a startled Lord Marius. "Are we going up? The soldiers told me they found a troll's maze. Whatever that is. I'd like to see."

The captain raised a hand as if catching a tossed ball. "A troll's maze! We're leaving."

Amadou glanced at Andevai. "They could have come over the roof."

"There's a goblin workshop locked up for the day on one side. On the other, they're poisoning themselves with arsenic or some such. I don't see how the girls could have gotten in here before us. And I'm not risking a troll's maze. One foot wrong and the whole thing will crash down. Then we'll be years haggling in court for damages. Trolls love haggling in court. Amadou, I suspect you're right: This detour is a chase after a wild goose. Let's go. They're out there somewhere. I promised the mansa I would recover them and return them to him."

Lord Marius went out. Amadou Barry followed.

Andevai crossed to the bed and picked up the jacket, holding it high so it swept along my left side. "Now I understand how you were able to get out of Four Moons House without being seen," he whispered. "What magic conceals you? None I've ever heard of."

"Listen! The mansa told them not to trust you. If you say left, then they'll go right."

Anger flashed in the flare of his eyes. "Is that so?"

"They were following you, to try to find us."

"Were they, now?" His gaze narrowed as he contemplated an object, personage, or situation that annoyed him very much.

"Magister?" Amadou Barry stepped halfway back into the room. "Is something amiss?"

"I just can't keep my eyes off it," said Andevai, gaze skating above the collar of the jacket as his eyes met mine. "There's so much about its tailoring I don't comprehend. But it doesn't truly belong to me, so I fear I must leave it behind. Although you never know. I haven't given up on gaining something so very close to my heart."

My cheeks were so on fire that I was amazed the legate could not see me.

Amadou Barry appeared startled by Andevai's passionate words. "It's a bit...over-complicated for my taste. We're leaving now, Magister."

"My thanks for the warning," Andevai said, his gaze on me.

He tossed the jacket over the other clothes and turned away. At the door, he paused with a hand on the frame. I tensed, waiting for him to glance over his shoulder one last time.

A deep heavy boom shuddered the house.

"By Teutates!" cried one of the men. "They're firing cannon on the river!"

Without looking back, Andevai walked out.

"Bring the prisoner," said Lord Marius from the passage.

I heard Andevai. "By the way, Legate, how did you come to seek me out at the law offices?"

They clattered out, taking Amadou's answer with them, and leaving me with a cold wind rising up through the shattered door and the jangling tinkling off-key chime from the chamber upstairs.

7

The jacket Andevai had held glared at me accusingly through its rose-colored spectacles with their peacock wings. *I haven't given up.* I was standing there, as congealed as cold porridge, when Bee appeared in the doorway, radiant with alarm.

"Cat! We heard raised voices. What happened?"

"I don't know whether to be annoyed or flattered."

Rory slouched into sight beyond the threshold, hauling the two bags. "I feel like a half-dead antelope my mother has just dragged in for dinner."

I hastened to his side. "I'm sorry. Let me take one."

"Never again peahens. I'm off feathers forever." He dipped his head to touch his cheek to mine. "You're all right, though. So I'm better already. What happened to our guide?"

I hugged him. "Eurig sacrificed himself for us. We can't risk going back to the law offices to warn them. We've got to find this Fiddler's Stone at Old Cross Gate."

"It's a bad idea," said Rory.

"Did Andevai betray us?" Bee asked.

"Quite the opposite. He's the one drawing them off. The mansa is having him followed."

"He seems strangely loyal to you, in an exceedingly

peculiar sort of way." She paused, examining my stiffening expression. "I won't tease, Cat. Let's go."

In the wake of the militia's passage, the lanes had emptied. We crept out a maze of back alleys that let onto the crowds of Enterprise Road, east of Fox Close. Women hauled baskets and pots balanced atop their heads. One gray-haired woman staggered along beneath a whole sheep, which was quite dead, all light gone from its eyes. The third person I asked told us to head east. I led with the cane, Rory hauled the bags, and Bee took the rear guard with the knife in her pocket and a small knit bag in which she kept her sketchbook and pencils slung over her back.

A band of young males swaggered past. They bellowed in perfect four-part harmony a song about the misadventures of an "ass" who was not a donkey but the prince of Tarrant. We reached an open area where five roads met. A line of carts and wagons loaded with casks, sacks, and open crates of unfinished hats had locked to a complete halt. The singing youths blocked the intersection. Arms linked defiantly, they began singing a familiar melody. Its usual lyrics, about a lass abandoned by a worthless lover, had been replaced by the challenging political phrases of the Northgate poet: *A rising light marks the dawn of a new world.*

I grabbed the sleeve of a passing costermonger. "Maester! Where's Old Cross Gate?"

"Why, this is it! Trouble brewing. You don't want to be caught in this." He shoved on, using his cart to part the crowd.

I stepped in front of a pair of women with baskets on their heads. "Where can I find the Fiddler's Stone?" I cried.

"An ill-starred day to be looking in the stone for the

image of your future husband, lass," said the elder. "But it's past the arch and then in the little court to the right."

It took us a moment to spot an arch in an unimposing old wall to our left. The opening was barely high and wide enough for a wagon. We fought through the crowd and slipped through it onto a side street lined with dilapidated old houses ripe for the transforming dreams of architects. A tiny lane pitted with ruts and filthy with crusty and yellowed snow took us to a little crossing where three alleys met. The Fiddler's Stone was a squat granite monolith listing over like a drunk. The surrounding buildings were dank. Excrement had frozen in mounds alongside broken steps that led to ramshackle doors. All the windows were boarded up. But a wreath of frozen flowers draped the stone's peak like a flaking crown.

Rory licked his lips. "I smell summer."

"Give me the knife, Bee." I pulled off my right glove, set the blade to my little finger, and sliced. The skin creased and reddened, but no blood appeared.

Bee snickered. "Do you want me to do it?"

"No! You'll hack off the whole finger just to be sure."

"Give me that." She pulled off her own glove, took the knife, and neatly opened a delicate cut on her palm.

"Let your blood fall on the stone," I said.

Warmth stung on my own hand as a bead of blood oozed red down my finger. All at once, I tasted summer on the wind.

"Like this?" Bee held her hand above the stone. Her blood dripped onto the grimy surface.

"Cross now! Hurry, Bee."

Bee slammed into the stone.

"Ouch!" said Rory.

Bee took three steps back and tried again, as if sheer

force of will could force rock to open. She thudded into stone, then cursed with pain.

My drop of blood slipped. A stain appeared on the stone and was absorbed. A roll of distant thunder whispered. A crow fluttered down to land atop the stone. The earth sank beneath my feet as stone and soil melted away.

"Cat's going through," said Rory.

"Not unless I go with her!" Bee dragged me stumbling back as Rory snarled and that cursed crow cawed like a captain alerting its troops.

"This won't work," said Bee. "That *hurt*."

"Bee can't cross," said Rory, "but you will, Cat. Your blood opened the gate."

Heaving, I dropped to my knees into a crackling carpet of snow. Nothing came up. My finger smarted. My tongue burned, and I swallowed blood.

"Someone is peeking at us through the boarded-up door," said Bee. "I don't like this place. And that crow looks like it's hoping to peck out our eyes."

Recovering from the wash of weakness, I groped along the wall with Bee in the lead and Rory behind. Unearthly voices rushed and mumbled in my ears as if I stood with one foot in the spirit world. A magnificent stallion cantered out of the wall, muscles rippling along a coat more brown than bay, and then it was gone. A saber-toothed cat lolled in our path, huge jaws widening in a startled yawn as she saw me, and then she was gone. A winged woman emerged from the coal haze that smeared the sky, her skin as black as pitch and yet glowing as with hidden embers, and then she was gone. A leaf trailed across my cheek with a glistening line of dew.

A shining face, masked and unkindly, filled the alley like a towering cliff of ice ready to calve and bury me.

Chill fingers closed on my heart until I couldn't think or breathe.

"Cat?" Bee's fingers closed over my hand.

Then it was gone, and the voices fell silent. I sagged against Bee, and she held me up.

"There's blood on your lip," she said hoarsely.

I licked it off, its tang as bitter as seawater.

We staggered out to the old arched gate just as a company of soldiers rode up the lane.

"Beatrice! You'll not escape me this time!"

Legate Amadou Barry reined up beside us, accompanied by a dozen Roman guardsmen in swirling red-and-gold capes and carrying burnished round shields more decorative than useful. Amadou bent from the saddle with the ease of a man accustomed to horseback and reached for Bee, meaning to sweep her up. She leaped back, the kitchen knife flashing as she took a swipe at him.

"I'm not yours to take!" she cried.

"You must get out of here! A riot's about to break out. It isn't safe."

"Safer here than in a golden cage."

"Beatrice, you have no idea of the cruelties of the world. I will protect you."

"Legate, you have no idea of how condescending you sound. I'm not interested in your kind of protection."

Had I ever thought him a diffident and humble young man? He was not even arrogant. He was simply a man of such exalted rank that he existed above considerations like arrogance and humility. He grabbed Bee's wrist and twisted until she dropped the knife. "You're coming with me."

Rory leaped. He slammed into Amadou, and Bee jerked free as both men went tumbling to the ground. Guardsmen converged. A sword flashed down at my brother's head. I parried with my cane as Rory rolled away. A cane made of wood would have been riven by steel, but the soldier's blade shivered to a dead stop with a ringing *shringgg*. Rory jumped to his feet, yanked the rider's leg out of the stirrup, and heaved him off the other side.

Bee grabbed the knife and sliced the bridle of Amadou's mount. The harness slipped. We retreated toward the gate as Amadou Barry got to his feet, his expression so blank I wondered if he had actually lost his temper. The bridle was a loss.

On the other side of the gate, the crack of firearms split the air, punctuated by furious howls and the stiffly barked commands of a military captain: "Turn! Make formation!" More reports answered, sharp and short. The Roman guardsmen looked startled. Those were not muskets.

"Rifles!" shouted a male voice from afar. "Fire again, lads! We've got the muscle now! They've only got swords and pistols!"

From the militia, in answer: "*Charge!*"

"Run!" I cried.

We pelted up the lane away from the old gate. The roar of a full-fledged battle crashed over us. People squeezed through the archway, disrupting the Roman guardsmen as they tried to assemble around their legate. With swords drawn and crossbows leveled, the men drew into a tight formation. Bricks flew from the crowd. The curve of the lane took us out of sight.

"Blessed Tanit!" cried Bee, near tears. "Let him not be harmed! Oh, how hateful he was!"

"I wish you would make up your mind!" The noise of a district ablaze with fighting echoed around us, as if every lane, alley, and dank alcove had gone up in flames. "He's not at all what I first thought he was."

"That's why it makes me so angry!" She looked ready to carve her anger into one of the houses we passed. "I thought I could trust him, but I can't!"

A deep vibration knifed through my body. The somber bass of the bell dedicated in the temple of Ma Bellona, he who is valiant at the ford, cried across the city. The authoritative tenor of the bell dedicated in the temple of Komo Vulcanus, who keeps his secrets, answered. The sister bells joined, followed by the droll bass of Esus-at-the-Crossing and Sweet Sissy's laughing alto. Last and most unexpectedly, because it was so rare, the raw contralto of the queen of bells, the matron of plenty and protection who guarded the shrine of Juno Lennaya, filled the air with a din that shook houses. Through the voice of its bells, Adurnam had joined in the conflagration.

We pressed on. The cursed lane tossed us straight back into the churning chaos of a street as wide as Enterprise Road. Its pavement was lined with the newest gaslight fixtures, although half of the glass shades had been shattered. The sheer mass of people surging along the street brought us up short. Everyone was shouting and cursing, the buzzing of voices like a nest of angry bees.

Rory used the bags to batter a way through the crowd. We plowed in his wake.

"Watch it!" A man threatened me with a cane. My blow broke it in half, and he fell back.

As we reached another intersection locked with wagons and carts, thunder rumbled.

Rory cocked his head. "That's not horses."

Bee pointed to a shop whose sign bore a clock-faced owl. "There! We have to go in there."

We reached the awning. Bee opened the door and went in with Rory. An icy taste ground through the gritty flavor of coal smoke. My ears popped as the air changed. My sword's hilt burned. I shut the door hard behind us, shop bell jangling.

The man at the counter had silver hair, spectacles, and a shop full of ticking clocks, no two of which showed the same time. He set down calipers.

"Maester," I said, "begging your pardon for the intrusion, but if you have shutters, I recommend you close your shop now. A storm's coming."

"Maester Napata, they're here," he called, not to us. "Just as you said they'd be."

A howl of wind shook the windows. Hail pummeled the streets like the peppershot of muskets. People scattered, seeking shelter anywhere they could. The shop door burst open and a dozen weathered toughs in patched laborers' coats staggered in. One had a bloody nose, which he was staunching with a crumpled handbill. Another held a hand over his ear. A third brandished a brick, cursing magisters and princes in equal measure. They fell silent as a young man stepped out past a curtain.

The man's uncanny blanched features might have been those of a ghost called from the miserable gloom of Sheol. Then he saw Bee, and he blushed, easy to see because he was an albino. He was no ghost. He served the headmaster of the academy.

What on Earth was the headmaster's loyal dog, as we had always called him, doing here?

"If the head of the poet Bran Cof once spoke to you," said the young man, his words burred by a foreigner's accent, "please to come with me now. The Thrice-Praised poet spoke to the headmaster at dawn."

"Blessed Tanit!" muttered Bee, looking at me. She remembered as well as I did the day we had sneaked through the headmaster's office and heard an uncanny voice say the words "*Rei vindicatio*" as if to warn us. Mere hours later, Andevai had showed up at her parents' house to use those same words to claim legal ownership of the eldest Hassi Barahal daughter.

The men huddled by the door murmured to each other at this mention of the famous head of the poet Bran Cof.

"What said the head of the poet?" demanded the man with the brick.

The headmaster's assistant ignored everyone except Bee. "The head of the poet Bran Cof said he had a message for Tara Bell's child. He said to meet you here."

I was glad he was looking at Bee, so he didn't see me shudder.

"Last time, the headmaster turned me over to the Romans," said Bee. "How can I know he won't do so again?"

"That was a mistake." He gazed at Bee in the way a well-trained but hungry dog stares at a bone out of its reach, for he was yet another young male who had fallen in love with her beauty during our time as students at the academy. "On his honor and dignity, he will not allow it to happen again. If you wish to hear, come with me." He vanished behind the curtain.

"He smells clean of lies," said Rory.

The man with the injured nose straightened out the bloody handbill. "You think these two is the ones mentioned for the reward?"

"What's that?" said the man with a hand on his ear. "The head of the poet Bran Cof speaks at last, did you say? Did he recite a poem to the just cause of our discontent? Or pronounce on the legal principle of men being allowed to vote for a tribune to represent us on the prince's council?"

The other man scanned the print. "This says the prince of Tarrant offers a reward for the recovery of two Phoenician girls. They belong to one of the mage Houses."

"Why should we hand girls over to the cursed mages?" said the man with the brick.

"It's a cursed lot of money, enough to split twelve ways and still make us all rich."

Outside, the street lay empty except for Roman guardsmen trotting up the streets using their round shields to shelter their heads from the pounding hail. In a moment, Legate Amadou might look in the windows and see us. The man with the bloody nose put his red-stained fingers on the latch and opened the door.

"Over here!" he shouted.

"Go," I said.

The clockmaker flipped up the counter. Rory went first, Bee after, and me at the rear.

"Thank you," I said to the clockmaker, and I shouldered past the heavy swags. Ahead, the hem of Bee's skirt snaked along the plank floor under a second curtain and then too many more curtains to count. It was like chasing a serpent's tail through baffles down a hallway. An oily smell made my lips pucker. I collided with Bee as the last curtain's weighted hem slapped down behind me.

We stood in a chamber quite black except where flashes of luminescence flared and died like levers rising and lowering. Taps and creaks and rasps played out as if they were slowly winding down. There fell a last flare of movement. Then the dark poured like pitch over my eyes. The chamber's air lay heavy with the rancid scent of old oil and a tang of char. My ghost-sword, which outside had flared in response to the cold magic of the storm, hung inert in my hand. A ripple of soft barks, snaps, clicks, and pops spread within the room: goblin chatter.

"Gracious Melqart," breathed Bee. "We've stumbled into a goblin's den. This must be one of those illicit daytime workshops the prince's inspectors are always searching for."

"Cat," said Rory in an aggrieved and alarmed tone, "many small fingers are touching me."

"They'll just guide you to the stairs," said the headmaster's assistant from the darkness. "They don't want you in here any more than you want to be here."

Fingers tapped up my arms to my shoulders and around my back, as if measuring me for a new riding jacket. Like most people, I knew little about goblins except that sunlight burned them, they hid themselves beneath masks and robes even under starlight, and they were shaped much like humans. They sold their wares at night markets, and their workshops were legally required to close during the day. Which meant we were standing in a place where we could all be arrested.

A voice as brittle as winter grass spoke on my left side as a hand traced my arm. "One stinks of dragons. One smells of the summer sun. This one is bound between the worlds, like her sword. There is a price."

"You and I have already agreed on the price," said the headmaster's assistant. When you could not see his skin, he sounded like an ordinary man, calm but displeased.

"For these three, it is not enough."

Bee and I had, on a few occasions, bargained with masked and veiled goblin merchants at one of the night markets. "What do you want?" I asked.

"To call on you, spiritwalker, one time, at need."

"Cat," whispered Bee warningly. "Be prudent."

"Done," I said, for, unlike Bee, I could hear very faintly a commotion in the shop, maybe even the sound of a clock falling and shattering. The soldiers had arrived.

"*Ah*," rippled down the Stygian depths of the chamber.

"That was rash," said the headmaster's assistant.

"It's her other name," said Bee.

"There's trouble in the shop," I said.

"We know." The goblin's cool grasp encircled my wrist. "This way."

We were led to stairs. The foul breath of the undercity was exhaled in our faces. Into the noxious sewer we descended step by greasy step. The air was like a wet blanket full of rot pressed against my face. That slurping endless sigh was the sound made by oozing sludge. I could see nothing, but a channel yawned to my left like the mouth of a charnel god, or at least his outhouse.

Rory said, "Euw! Is this where the dogs bide?"

"Quiet!" murmured the headmaster's assistant from ahead of us. "From this point forward, you must not speak. If we're discovered, we will die, and the goblins who guide us will lose ownership of their breath." He did not explain, and we dared not ask lest we break silence.

Descending, we left behind the sewage's reek. Where the stairs ended, we continued in pitch-darkness along a tunnel whose pavement was smoother than any Adurnam street. The touch that guided me never pinched or slackened. The road ran straight and true, punctuated by alcoves and archways sensed as spaces of air rank with a charred scent like the ashes of a dead fire. At intervals I heard gears ticking over steadily. We would walk close and yet closer to the sound and then a gap would open to right or left with a tickle of warmth and a pressure like wind confined by a veil. With a swallow, I would pop my ears, and as we moved on, the ticking would fade.

Goblins were so legendarily ingenious that I had always doubted the impressive tales told of them could be true: Could they really breathe life into stone and metal? But these deep, smooth paths mined beneath the city made me wonder if it might be true. What had I bound myself into? What did goblins who worked in an illegal daylight workshop want? What was "ownership of breath"?

The beat of a tick-tock measure brushed my ears. To our left, a glow limned a vaulted chamber. Its depths lay smothered in darkness, but seen through arches, the front of the chamber gleamed with a milky luminescence. Creatures were lined up in ranks whose columns vanished away into the gloom beyond the aura of light. At first glance, I thought them soldiers at parade rest. But as my steps faltered and I stared, I realized they were not breathing and not human. Their slender limbs and torsos were speckled as if they were stone. Their faces were human in having lips, noses, and ears, but the hollows where they should have had eyes glistened with patches like wet velvet. Most wore sleeveless tunics woven of a fabric that might have been thread spun from fog. In the shadow-drenched depths, unseen sleepers inhaled and exhaled.

My guide hissed faintly. I looked at it. It was almost as tall as Bee, golden in color, lithe as a dancer, and not remotely human in expression, having no eyes to mark its heart and soul. Beyond it stood Bee, Rory, and their guides, but the headmaster's assistant led the way without a guide. How could he see in blackness so complete it blinded *me*?

An emphatic *thud* sounded from the back of the chamber. A ticking ratcheted up with a groan of air as of steam being released. Mist like a cloud of fireflies chased along a murky shadow. Gears whirred. A head slewed around, and claws like edged blades winked in the pale light.

The goblin whispered, "Run."

We ran. For the first twenty steps, I thought the gods were with us, Blessed Tanit offering sanctuary beneath her hand, Gracious Melqart a shield, Ba'al a harbor against the storm. I looked back over my shoulder.

A creature stalked out from the arches. It looked like a troll skeleton knitted out of gears and metal bars. Its head swayed as it turned to look back the way we had come, into the black pit of the far passage. If it just looked that way a moment longer we might escape into darkness.

With a dip of its head and a menace of teeth, it swung around and bounded after us with weighty tick-tock steps. A hiss of steam sprayed from its gaping mouth.

Rory stepped past me and heaved a bag at it. The bag slammed into its shoulder and knocked the creature sideways. It jolted to a stop against the wall, groaned and shook, the head rearing back before it lowered again to seek us. Rory kept spinning all the way around and with the extra force gained released the second bag. It sailed across the gap and smashed into the head. The creature toppled, hitting the wall hard, then staggered the other way, hit the opposite wall, and tumbled down. A spark spiraled up and winked out. Gears whirred busily as the creature strove to right itself.

The cursed creature was not getting my father's precious journals.

"Cat!" cried Bee as I bolted past Rory.

"Go! I'll follow!"

I grabbed the closest bag. Metal claws closed around the ankle of my boot. I dropped the bag on the elbow joint. The weight slammed the arm into the floor. But it was already shifting to dislodge the obstacle. The head reared up, metal jaws gaping. Teeth gleamed. A red heart of fire pulsed deep down in that throat, as if making ready to scorch me.

From far above, linked as by an intangible chain threaded through the earth, cold magic—Andevai's storm—flared down the length of my sword. The hilt flowered; I twisted it free, and thrust the slim blade down that yawning gullet.

Combustion died. The creature sagged on a final stuttering *tock tunk tick*.

My heart lurched as if under a pounding of fierce hail, and my gaze hazed as a pulse not my own roared in my ears: "*Catherine!*"

I was hallucinating Andevai's voice. I sheathed my sword, grabbed both bags, and ran blindly after the others. My head was reeling and I am sure I could not have told anyone my name or indeed anything except that I was not giving up the bags, not even to death.

"Cat! This way!"

I followed Bee's voice past a series of curtains whose fabric slithered like woven metal. As the last one slipped down my back, my leading boot stubbed a step.

"Now we owe you a debt for saving us," said a goblin, hidden behind the last baffle. "Your price is paid." I could not tell if it was grateful or disappointed.

"I'll take them up from here," said the headmaster's assistant. "You'd best scatter before your lords come looking for the trouble we've caused."

I heard the rustle of the baffles as the goblins slipped

back into their underworld so quickly I didn't have a
chance to thank them or ask them a question or even to
think. Startled by the sound of footfalls, I set down the
bags and drew my sword. A young man with a long black
braid dangling over his shoulder like a rope took the bags
from beside me. After a moment, I realized it was Rory,
and there was light enough for me to see. They were already climbing. I followed.

Up! The steps went on forever. My air came in bursts.
Did I hear ticking? What if there were other creatures
stalking after us? *What was that thing?*

The headmaster's assistant glanced back.

"Your sword is glowing," he said in a low voice.

The light came from my blade. Its harsh glow revealed
him clearly. He hadn't the creamy-white complexion of
the northern Celts, although he was very pale. He had
broad Avar cheekbones and the epicanthic fold at the eyes
commonly seen among people who lived in the vast lands
east of the Pale. It was his white hair that was most startling. It had been cut in an awkward approximation of
the short local Celtic style, swept back over his ears. His
fashionable indigo dash jacket was too strong a hue for
him. The backs of his bare hands bore tattoos, like faded
blue ink, of a curling design that might have been vines,
or serpents. It reminded me of the old Roman saying: *Beware the serpent in the east.*

"Bee does stink of dragons," said Rory, pausing on the
steps, "and so does he. It wasn't a good idea to come with
him."

"I do not stink," said Bee, "and you will apologize at
once to Maester Napata. It's very rude to tell people they
stink."

"Even if they do?"

"He's sorry for being rude, and I'm sorry he was rude to you," she said as she halted two steps below the head-master's assistant. He had the expression of a man used to hearing people whispering about his looks, and not in the way Andevai was likely accustomed to admiring sidelong glances directed his way.

"If *you* are sorry, that is enough." Having made this bold statement, he hastened up the stairs as if his own courage were about to bite him.

"Really, this isn't the time for you two to fight so childishly," I said as I climbed past them. Rory looked offended and Bee surprisingly chastened. "Maester Napata, what was that thing? What kind of agreement do you have with these goblins? How do you know about these tunnels?"

"I am not the one who can answer your questions," he said. "The men in the clockmaker's shop will not have much trouble tracing us if they wish to alert the militia. Hurry."

We climbed with my sword as our candle, but the gleam on its blade faded as a pallor of natural light seeped in from an unknown source, turning darkness to gloom. We emerged into a musty vaulted chamber.

"Just give me a moment to catch my breath." I leaned against the stone wall, coughing.

Rory set down a bag and put a comforting hand on my shoulder. "I smell bones and ashes."

"We're in a tomb," said Bee, looking around.

Alcoves sheltered votive statues, dusty jars sealed with painted lids, and hammered metal plaques recording names and clans. Two stelae guarded the space. One was cracked through and listing. The second was carved on one side with the sigil of Tanit—a triangle capped by a small circle and straight arms—and on the other with a bull, a lion, and a crescent moon sheltering a sun.

I ran a hand down the length of my now ordinary black cane. "What *was* that thing?"

Bee glanced nervously toward the darkness that hid the stairs, but we heard no ticking. "It looked like someone built a clockwork automaton in the shape of a troll's skeleton, powered by steam. Do you suppose goblins really are that ingenious?"

"I killed its combustion with my sword just as it was about to breathe scalding steam over me," I whispered. "I shouldn't have been able to do that. It felt like I pulled Andevai's cold magic through the blade."

Bee frowned as she touched my cheek with the back of a hand. "I hope you don't expect me to explain what just happened. I must say, dearest, our lives were a great deal quieter before that awful night when my parents handed you over to Four Moons House."

Maester Napata beckoned. "Maestressas. This way. Please to hurry."

He led us up steps. The air grew wintry as we breached the surface through a marble tombhouse. We staggered blinking into what seemed a fierce brightness of day. Overhead, the sky was rent with blue. The storm had passed on, although cold soaked through our coats. Hailstones littered the ground. The city's growl rose from beyond high walls.

Rory looked around with a bemused expression. "So many little stone houses. What people live here?"

"Only the dead," said Bee.

"Do dead people live? I thought if they were dead, they did not live. It's very confusing."

"It's the *tophet*," I said. The walls had been reinforced

with a spiked chain along the top to keep out vandals, treasure-seekers, and mischief-makers.

"What is a tophet?" asked Rory.

"Every Kena'ani child who died untimely in the first eighteen hundred years of the Kena'ani settlement in Adurnam was interred in this cemetery," I explained.

"The remains of infants were placed here in dedication to the gods." Bee sank onto a moss-covered stone bench as if exhausted. "But it was closed when my papa was a child, forty years ago. There were riots in the city after rumors spread that the Phoenicians were sacrificing children on Hallows' Night and mixing their blood with wine and bread to keep away the Wild Hunt. Here in the tophet." She sighed. "Just give me a moment. My legs are shaking."

"I don't think blood and wine would taste well together," said Rory. "Why drink that?"

"It wasn't *true*, you imbecile," she snapped. "It was a *pernicious lie!*"

A gust of wind stirred my hair, like an unwanted premonition. "Bee, why did you notice the sign on that clockmaker's shop?"

"The clock-faced owl? I saw it in a dream. I sketched it. When I saw it today, I knew we had to go there." Her gaze, on me, looked so weary and worn that I wanted to tell her it would be all right, but I knew such words would be a lie. When I did not reply, she shook her head as if shaking off her fears and offered a teasing smile. "By the way, Cat, I saw a man's face in the Fiddler's Stone."

"Who?" I demanded, remembering the woman who had told us girls went there to see the faces of their future husbands in the stone.

"Knives," she said cryptically, mouth creasing down as if she was herself not sure.

Footsteps crunched on gravel. I should have heard sooner. A figure appeared where the gravel path hooked around a gaudy monument which was crested by a weathered representation of the lashing, intertwined sea monsters known as the Taninim.

"So here they are, the Hassi Barahal cousins." Leaning on a cane and accompanied by his assistant, the revered headmaster of the academy Bee and I had attended regarded us with an expression whose depths I could not fathom. Even though I knew he had sent his assistant to find us, I stared at his regal features, seamed face, and silver hair as surprised as if I had been cast adrift on a wave-tossed sea to confront the toothy maw of a sea wolf.

With a snarl of rage, Rory dropped the bags. In a blur of gold too bright to be fully seen, he melted from man into huge, deadly saber-toothed cat, and sprang at the headmaster.

8

I threw myself into Rory's line of attack.

Even as I was twisting, bracing myself to slam into him, the air distorted. An undulation of intense heat sucked the cold as into a vast shimmering furnace. A scaly beast gleaming of polished copper shuddered across the sky: eyes like burning emeralds, claws the length of my arms, wings that spanned the tophet wall to wall. Its jaw gaped to swallow him and us and all the city and then the world and finally all of existence.

I smashed into the cat's massive fore-flank. I did not stop Rory, but we were both carried far enough sideways that he landed out of reach of the headmaster with me draped over his rippling shoulders. I leaped back and whacked him on the neck with my cane.

"Stop! Rory! Stop!"

The big cat cringed and dropped to a crouch. Its pelt shone with a pulse of light, and smeared into a black-haired young man.

"Let go of me!" cried Bee in a tone I recognized as exasperated rather than alarmed.

Stepping between Rory and the headmaster, I turned. The headmaster's assistant had a hand on her arm, and was in the act of pulling her out of the way. He released her at once.

The headmaster looked as he had always looked: He was a tall, elderly black man of noble Kushite ancestry, a princely scholar of the most cultured and civilized of peoples, a man who was always calm. Why had I never noticed the fulgent green glamour of his eyes?

"Who are you?" Bee demanded.

Remnants of clothes hung like rags on Rory's body. Even half naked, he appeared predatory. "I have to kill him, Cat. Surely you understand!"

"I'm beginning to think I understand much less than I ever thought I did!" I cried.

"And that wasn't much," muttered Bee, as if she could not help herself.

Had the light changed? The headmaster's eyes were a pleasant, ordinary brown, not green at all. "Begging your pardon, Maester," I said politely, "but if I am not mistaken, something rather strange just happened."

"Indeed it did," he agreed with the careworn smile of a man who has seen everything and has yet to be surprised. "Your young companion turned into a rather large cat and then back into a man. Certainly an unexpected occurrence. He must be cold. May I offer my coat?"

"No!" snarled Rory. I pressed the cane across his chest to check him.

"Kemal," said the headmaster to his assistant. "If you will."

The assistant took off his coat and gloves. Bee brought them to Rory.

I said, "Put them on."

He obeyed, although by the curl of his lip I could tell he was affronted.

"Why do you think you have to kill him, Rory?" I asked, digging for patience.

His tone suggested he was completely disgusted with my callous disregard for his needs. "He's one of the enemy!"

I could tell from Bee's busy, bitten expression that she was thinking as wildly and desperately as a runaway coach careens over rugged ground.

"Are you a cold mage, Maester?" she asked. "Perhaps an un-Housed cold mage, making your own way in the world? Hiding your power?"

"I am no cold mage. But I invite you to return to the academy, where I will serve hot tea and we may conduct this conversation in decent warmth."

Bee delivered her reply with queenly obstinacy. "I mean no offense, Maester, but the last time I took refuge with you, you handed me over to Legate Amadou Barry. I became little better than a prisoner in his exalted house, and I must say—" Her cheeks flamed, and she thought twice about what she must say.

He nodded. "You have my deepest apologies, Maestressa. I was mistaken in believing the Barry house was a suitable refuge for you. The offer of a cup of hot tea comes without price. On my honor as a Napata, I will not reveal your presence in the academy to anyone. No one will know except me, and my servants, who are bound to me."

"I have to kill him," said Rory. "Let me go, Cat."

"No." I kept the cane pressed to his torso, its hidden cold steel a leash on his straining form. "Maester, will you explain to us what we just saw? If that was not magic, then I surely have no idea what to call it. My cousin and I have had enough of being lied to, betrayed, and kept in ignorance."

His grave smile made me ashamed of the impetuosity of my speech, and I lowered my gaze so as not to seem to be staring directly at him in a disrespectful way. "These are hard matters, Maestressa, as you correctly comprehend. Did the head of the poet Bran Cof speak to you two months ago?"

Tell no one. I bit my lip. Bee fisted her hands.

"By your expressions, Maestressas, I will take that for a yes. A pity I was not informed at the time. Although I suppose when two young women are waiting in my office, perhaps with a purloined book in their keeping, they may prefer to keep silence rather than be subjected to questions. Might we go? My old bones feel the cold deeply. I note also your companion has bare feet now that his shoes have torn off."

Rory said, as if he had decided he would have more success with being reasonable, "Just let me kill him, Cat. It will only take a moment." He tensed, readying to spring.

A tongue of fire licked the wintry cold. The air pulled at me as if I were being drawn into the maw of a fiery furnace. Green flickered in the headmaster's eyes, but his expression remained impassive as he examined Rory as if seeking beneath the skin to the cat beneath. I had a heart-squeezingly strong premonition—nothing magical about it—that our young, healthy, strong Roderic and the old, frail, fragile-looking headmaster were not remotely evenly matched. With the cane, I pushed Rory behind me. He was trembling, although I could not have said whether with anger, fear, or sheer shaking eagerness to pounce.

Bee's delicate little hand caught hold of my wrist, tightening as I imagined the coils of a snake might crush

the ribs of a larger animal. "Cat, we have to hear what the
head of the poet Bran Cof has to say."

"Ah! Ow! Yes! You go ahead. I'll come after with
Rory."

She released my wrist and swept a courtesy to the
headmaster as I tried to shake the pain out of my wrist
while still holding Rory in check.

"Maester," she said, "we will accompany you out of
respect for your age and lineage. But it is likely the Roman legate and his minions are already on their way to
the academy."

"Then there is no time to waste, Maestressa. I give you
my word I will not be party to your being taken prisoner
by Romans, mage Houses, or princes."

"Very well." She nodded at me before accompanying
them down the path.

A cold breeze chased up from the east, the last breath
of the hailstorm Andevai had called to quell the crowds. It
was better than muskets and swords as a weapon against
people out on the streets, forcing them to flee inside. But
the weakest and most desperate huddling in alleys or un-
heated hovels would expire in the deadly cold. Yet winter
killed the weak anyway, didn't it?

I cautiously drew back my cane. "Rory, explain yourself."

"I have to kill him."

"Those seem to be the only words you know any more.
How can that respected and honored old man be 'the enemy'?"

"He's not a *man*! That body is just the clothes he's
wearing."

I sat down hard on the bench, my heart knocking about
my chest as if it had come loose from its moorings: *wings*,

claws, heat. I covered my face with my gloved hands, and realized how horribly cold my flesh had become. "What do you think he is?" I said through my fingers.

"I don't *think.* I know. He's a serpent. A dragon." He paced around the bench. "These stupid words you use aren't the right ones! He is one of the enemy who encircles the world and traps us. You've seen what happens when the dreams of the mothers of his kind catch us unawares. Where I live it's not like it is here in the Deathlands, where their dreams don't reach. You can walk abroad day and night without fear of being caught and changed. They have always been and always will be the enemy."

"Rory, sit down, your pacing is making me dizzy." But it was his words that made my head reel. "How can he be a dragon?"

"He'll eat me first. He's much bigger and stronger. But I have to try." If he'd had a tail, he would have lashed it. "Because he must want to eat you, too."

"I have attended the academy for over three years. He could have eaten me at any time. Why wait until now, when he couldn't have expected to see me again?"

"Dragons are cunning and patient and never strike until you least expect it."

"I least expected it all these years. He's no threat to us."

"You just can't see it! I can't let you go to his lair."

"This is not your decision!" Watching his bare feet tread the freezing ground made me wince. My lips were so stiff I could scarcely form words. I had to move, or I would die, too. I leaped up and grabbed his arm. "You'll die of cold if you don't get shoes and clothes! I couldn't bear to lose you. But I have to go to the academy to hear the message."

"Maybe he won't eat Bee," he admitted sullenly. "She

does stink of dragons, like they licked her when she was sleeping and she just doesn't know. I didn't say anything about it, because she's right, it is rude to say so, and I could tell neither of you knew or suspected."

I embraced him, petting his arms and back until he relaxed a tiny bit. "Rory, how about this? You will go right now to the Old Temple District, to the inn called the Buffalo and Lion."

" 'Helene sent me.' "

"Yes, that's what you say when you get there. Right now I'm thinking Camjiata's the only person we can trust to be interested in us purely for his own selfish reasons. That makes it easier to negotiate. You'll keep the bags with you. Don't lose them! You know how precious my father's journals are to me."

"Cat, you and I don't know who our sire is."

"I meant, my father who raised me, not the male who sired us. Bee and I will join you after we hear the poet's message. We can't stay at the academy anyway, so we won't be far behind you. Then you can tell me everything you know about dragons."

"I just told you everything I know," he said indignantly. "Do you think I'm keeping secrets from you?"

I searched his face. Was he really my half brother? His eyes and hair were so very like mine, and yet he was not human but a wild creature, nothing tame. Yet I trusted him with my life. "No, I don't think you're keeping secrets. But it has to be this way. Promise!"

As if the words were forced out of him, he muttered, "I promise."

I released him. "Ask on the street for Old Temple, and then the inn. Tell people the militia roughed you up during the riot. They'll help you. Use your charm."

"Oh!" he said, distracted by the thought of using his charm. "I *am* cold and hungry and thirsty. I could use some petting, too."

"I don't need to hear about that kind of petting." I wiggled fingers into the hem of my jacket's sleeve, fished out the last of my coins, and pressed them into his hand. "Buy yourself clothes and shoes, but try them on first, then haggle over the price, and make sure you get correct change."

We ran down the path together. Kemal waited at the tophet gate.

"Tell me, Maester," I said as he chained and locked the gate, "did the headmaster save you from the Wild Hunt?"

His hand paused as he was turning the key. He did not look at me. "Yes."

"How?"

He slung the key, on its chain, over his neck. "It is not my place to speak of it."

"Is he a dragon?"

As if goaded beyond measure, he met my gaze. "The headmaster of the academy is a man."

"One just like you?" I demanded, for I sensed a riddle in his words.

His smile twisted scornfully, which startled me, for I had thought him a passive young person. "In the empire of the Avar, every albino child like me"—he touched fingers to his pale cheek—"belongs to the emperor. It is a crime punishable by death to hide such a child from the imperial governors. So I would answer you, 'No.' He is not a man just like me."

"I take it that is all I am to hear on the matter."

So returned the diffident exterior, like a shell covering vulnerable flesh. "My apologies, Maestressa." He inclined his head with a polite bob of his shoulders and followed his master.

Bee and the headmaster were making their way slowly up the hill, the old man leaning on his cane and she with a hand beneath his elbow quite oblivious to his desire to eat either of us. Rory watched the headmaster's back with a hooded gaze that did nothing to hide his wish to pounce.

"You promised," I said.

"Yes, I promised."

I gave him simple directions based on the bell towers and the high plinth that marked the site of the ancient village founded by Adurni Celts. I kissed him on either cheek, to seal our agreement, and waited at the tophet gate as he walked away down the main thoroughfare, lugging the bags. The wide avenue with its shops remained deserted, everyone in hiding.

I watched until he walked out of sight. Then I hurried up the hill, catching the others as they passed the old Kena'ani temple complex that was the original structure built on Academy Hill centuries ago. All that remained of the old complex was the walled sanctuary dedicated to Blessed Tanit and a grove of votive columns in commemoration of the holy trees felled during the Long Winter of 1572 to 1585. The gate into the sanctuary stood open. Within, a man wearing a heavy coat swept the porch of the priests' house.

"The gate is always open," the headmaster was saying to Bee, "due to an agreement made during the Long Winter, when the priests kept the gates open to provide warmth and sustenance to the destitute. It was that, or have the entire complex be burned down."

"But it was destroyed anyway," said Bee.

"Much of Adurnam burned at that time. Do you know what saved the city?"

"I do," I said. "The arrival of the refugees from the empire of Mali. Certain of the refugees had secret magical knowledge, and they found common cause with the Celtic drua. From that union sprang the cold mages. With the rise of the cold mages, the Long Winter was vanquished. Or at least, that is the story we learned at the academy, Maester."

"So it is. It makes you wonder, does it not? Is there some link between cold magic and the more clement weather of our time? For according to history and the evidence of old Roman ruins found north of Ebora in the uninhabitable Barrens, the climate was less clement, and the ice more advanced, two thousand years ago. What causes these changes?"

"There were no cold mages in the times of the Romans," said Bee. "Were there?"

"Not as we know them, no. Ah, here we are."

His chief steward waited on the front steps of the academy entrance.

"Owain," said the headmaster as he paused at the top of the steps to catch his breath, "the academy remains closed to all callers for the day. Admit no one."

"As you command, Your Excellency."

A cascading *boom* cracked outside. Whoever was shooting off muskets and field cannon was nowhere near the hailstorm. The hum rising off the city reminded me of maddened bees being smoked out of their hive. I hurried after Bee and the headmaster, who had already crossed the wide entry hall.

Surrounded by buildings, the central court lay quiet under its glass roof. No one was around. Midwinter festival wreaths of mistletoe and pine withered atop a trellis arch. The trellis covered the grated shaft of an ancient sacrificial well. A hundred years ago, a now-famous labyrinth had been laid out as a paved walkway spiraling around the well, ringed by stone benches.

I followed the others upstairs to the headmaster's office. The circulating stove set into the hearth gave off glorious warmth.

"Please," said the headmaster. Bee and I took off our coats and draped them over the back of a red leather chair. His assistant closed the door and took the headmaster's coat.

The headmaster's office had the odd quality of seeming larger than it was because mirrors hung on the backs of the doors. I saw everything twice: the wall of windows, the ranks of bookshelves reaching from floor to the crown moldings, the wide table with paper and books covering its entire surface, and the severed head of the poet and legal scholar Bran Cof atop a pedestal. The headmaster was watching me in one of the mirrors. I could see things in mirrors that others could not, threads of magic like the fine lines of spiders' webs. In the mirror, he looked like a perfectly ordinary old man. No threads of cold magic wove around his form as they did around Andevai. No vast winged shape billowed from his slender frame. He looked as solid as the furniture.

"Natural historians speculate that mirrors reflect the binding threads of energy that run between this world and the unseen spirit world," he remarked, as if he had divined my thoughts. "Do you suppose that is true, Maestressa Barahal?"

I glanced down at my scuffed and muddy boots. The ends of the laces had been chewed up as by hungry mice. The longcase clock ticked like the pacing of ethereal feet.

"My apologies, but we don't have time for speculation," said Bee. She walked to the corner where the head of the poet Bran Cof rested like a stone bust. I broke into a prickling sweat. I could not bear the thought of those eyelids snapping open, yet I could not look away no matter how much I wanted to. "When did the head speak? What did he say?"

The headmaster smiled enigmatically. "The very questions I meant to ask you. It was at dawn. I was seated here at my desk reading aloud, as is my habit. This day it happened to be a monograph on the salt plague which I recently received from one of my correspondents at the University of Expedition. Perhaps the same words will waken him again." He glanced at a printed pamphlet lying open on his desk. "'According to report, if a human is bitten by a ghoul, the onset of the disease is so swift and implacable that the victim will become morbid in less than seven days. However, if a human is bitten by a plague-ridden human, there are three distinct and slower stages through which the disease progresses, although the disease remains invariably fatal.'"

The head remained fixed. Bloodless lips kept their disapproving pinch. The lime-whitened spikes of his hair and the luxuriant droop of his mustache made his features look younger than what the heavy crow's-feet radiating out from his deep-set eyes told of years and trials. Three scars like ritual marks formed a column beneath his right ear. Maybe the head was just stone after all.

Maybe it was all a mistake.

"If you have something to say, Bran Cof, speak now." Bee's voice rang above the whispering crackle of the fire burning in the circulating stove. "My cousin and I cannot wait forever."

"Bee!" I cautioned.

"And furthermore," she continued in the tone of an Immortal Fury who has just remembered an ancient slight and means to pursue vengeance to the ends of the Earth, "if you are really bound between this world and the spirit world as it is said poets and sorcerers and djeliw and bards can be—which I admit seems quite unpleasant, for wouldn't it be rather like being forced to stand in a doorway all the time, neither going nor coming? Anyway, if you are so bound, then I wish you would not be so coy about it. I know you are a very famous legal scholar, one of the Three Even-Handed Jurists of the old Brigantes Confederation, so I would hope you would show us consideration now we are come before you, at your request. Yes, I am aware we are required to defer to poets, whose words reveal the world in ways we who are not poets could not otherwise see. And your fame as one of the Three Silver Tongues of the western Celts is naturally enough to awe and impress humble students like ourselves. But I must say, the constant references to women as roses with thorns seems a bit much. Men torment women far more than women torment men."

Did the sun escape a cloudy veil outside? A gleam shuddered within the reflecting angles of the mirrors like the spark of fireflies. A cowl of silvery light writhed around the head of the poet Bran Cof. Color washed the pallor of his face. There crawled beneath his skin a straining like insects swarming or a trapped prisoner trying to claw its way out.

She rolled blithely on. "I can't *endure* these constant protestations about the chains women bind on men. In truth, the chains all bind women at the feet of men."

His eyes opened, corpse-still one moment and full of ire the next.

"Bold Taranis spare me from the complaints of virgins!" His voice was resonant, as lovely as a caress, even in anger. "Especially ones whose black hair is a snare to entwine the helpless and whose dark eyes provoke the tenderhearted to grief. How I despise the beauty of women!"

"Only because you feel entitled to something you have no natural right to possess!"

"Your words dance like sun across ice, but their cruelty is sharper than the winter wind. You must be aware that whatever I might wish for in the Three Matters of Desire has long since been severed from me. You stand there, out of my reach." He looked younger when he was angry. As the cut of his lips softened, he seemed to age. "A kinder woman would kiss me."

"A kinder woman might well! I am not she. Anyhow, Your Honor, the last man I kissed *died* soon after."

His gaze took her in from head to toe. "That I can well believe! An axe may be forged with all the cunning of a master smith. It may be decorated with the skill that draws the unwary eye as a lure coaxes a hapless trout. But an axe's purpose is to sever the living heart of trees. Why are you here if not to persecute me with the promise of the sweet pleasure I can never again taste?"

"We were told you have a message."

"You are not the one I bear a message for."

"Perhaps my dearest cousin Cat is."

His gaze did not waver from her bright face but something very unsettling happened in his eyes. It was as if his gaze turned inward.

"Yes, yes, you've interrupted me," he said irritably, yet with an edge of fear. *He was speaking to someone we could not see.* "Of course you may speak. How am I to stop you?"

His eyes rolled back in their sockets until they showed only white. Shadows—not from this room—settled a curling pattern of insubstantial tattoos across his skin. His craggy features remained the same, but Bran Cof was no longer the personage looking out from those wintry eyes. The gaze studied Bee, then caught on the headmaster with a narrowing like a bow bent but not released. An arrow stabbed my heart. Maybe I gasped. Maybe I moved, shaking with apprehension. Maybe I made no sound and no movement and it did not matter.

Because the head of the poet Bran Cof looked at me. White ice eyes without pupil or iris fixed on me. My chest felt as hollow as if a killing claw had just torn out my beating heart to suckle dry its rich red blood.

The mouth spoke with a sharp, deadly voice.

"So after all, Tara Bell's child survived and grew, as I had hoped. Your blood spilled on the crossing stone woke the bond between us. As I am bound, so must those bound to me as kin come to my aid. That is the law. Come to me, Tara Bell's child. *Now.*"

9

"Who are you?" Sheer rushing terror propelled me three steps back.

Bran Cof's eyes rolled down, the return of blue as startling as a sweep of piercing blue sky seen after days of snow. For all he was a cantankerous old lecher, his gaze had a keen intelligence that made me uneasy, for he knew things he wasn't telling. "What message did my lips speak?"

I took another step back, thinking fast. "I'll tell you, if you'll answer a legal question."

"Ah. A bargain. Done."

Surprised, I took another step back to steady myself. "I want to know if there is any way to unbind a marriage sealed by a magical chain of binding."

"Yes. Your turn."

"I mean, besides *death*!" Why must my voice tremble so?

"Your turn."

Curse him! "You said, 'As I am bound, so must those bound to me as kin come to my aid. That is the law. Come to me, Tara Bell's child. Now.'"

"Bad fortune for you, lass. In pity, I offer this: Only death can unchain a chained marriage. But there is one other way." He attempted a coaxing smile that made him look grotesque. "I can tell you. But a poet has his price. A kiss from you, the girl whose eyes are amber, whose lips are the red of berries, a promise both succulent and sweet."

I cringed away.

His smile broadened lasciviously. "I will have the kiss that already softens your mouth. You are waiting for a man to claim its honey."

I flushed with utter, obliterating embarrassment.

He chuckled, enjoying my consternation. "He must be young and very handsome."

I choked.

Bee said, "I'll kiss him for you, Cat. I have experience kissing lecherous old men as well as young and very handsome ones."

"You will not!" His bushy eyebrows shot up, and the corners of his lips spiked down. "I will have no kiss from you, serpent!"

"How can you stop me, stuck there on your pedestal?" She took a step toward him as I took one back. "I may kiss you however and whenever I please! I'll suck all the life from you—such as you have life—and keep it for myself!"

He squinched his eyes and lips shut, and I thought the head would harden back to its slumbering stone state without ever answering my question. Yet still the veins on his neck throbbed as with anger...and how could that happen, since he had no heart?

"I'll be gentle." Bee took another step toward him.

To my amazement he laughed with an unexpected flowering of charm. "Alas for the men trapped by her love! Alas for the men set free! She is the axe that has laid waste to the proud forest. Where she treads, desolation follows."

"Enough!" I cried. "I'll kiss you, if you'll just answer my question."

His eyebrows rose to a peak. "I was not finished declaiming! It is always so. The young lack manners, and the women like crows cannot stopper up their chatter!"

Imagine all this time I had been in awe of the famous head of the poet Bran Cof!

Bee offered a mocking grimace. "It's me, or no one. Anyway, Cat, I don't think he knows. All those stories about how he mastered the Three Paths to Judgment. How his tongue silenced birds and humbled princes. He isn't really a legal scholar. He's probably just an old drunk."

"Shame, girl! I'll have you know there are three forms of marriage commonly recognized in the courts of the north. How the Romans and Phoenicians do things is a different matter, but I'll come to that afterward. A flower marriage flourishes while the bloom is still on it and dies when it withers. It may bloom for a month, a season, or a year, depending on the verbal agreement between the two parties involved. A contract marriage is a business arrangement signed in the law court between two houses, clans, or lineages. A chained marriage is a binding marriage sealed by arcane keys known only to the wise, to the drua and the bards, and it draws a chain of binding magic around the couple. When there is a question of possible treachery, or a treaty or other obligation at stake, it binds the couple so there need be no concern among those who arranged the marriage that another party will default or there be trouble later. Thus, the only way out of such a binding marriage is the death of one of the parties involved. But do not forget that without consummation, there is no marriage. Has the young man had sex with you yet?"

The headmaster had politely turned his attention to the monograph. The assistant stared at the motion of pendulum and weights behind the glass door of the longcase clock, a blush curdling his white complexion.

Bee said, "Cat, you look like a fish. Close your mouth."

"A year and a day. If the marriage is not consummated, and there is no prenuptial agreement for an extension due to a known and forced separation of the two parties, then after a year and a day, it is no marriage. Does no one teach the law these days?"

All blood and breath drained from me. A year and a day. I could be unbound from the marriage. Released from its chain. I sagged back, to find myself at the door.

Bee glanced toward me, then back at the head of the poet Bran Cof. "Who spoke through your mouth?" she demanded.

The head of the poet Bran Cof flinched.

My pulse thudded in my ears. My hands curled to fists, nails biting into my palms. "You know who it is!" I said.

Blessed Tanit! He wasn't going to answer! But then he did.

"*He is my tormenter.*" An ember of sympathy lit in his face, brief and not bright. "And soon, Tara Bell's child, he will be yours as well."

"Answer her!" cried Bee.

"My lips are bound. Of what passes on the other side, I cannot speak—" Then he was gone. Features as rigid as if carved from stone faced us in petrified silence.

"Oh!" said Bee. "What happened?"

The headmaster murmured, "So. That explains *her.*"

An overwhelming compulsion to get out of the chamber took hold of me.

"My apologies, Maester," I said as I forced down the latch and pushed open the door. "My heart is so disturbed. I'll just go pace out the labyrinth. They say it calms people down."

"Take Beatrice with you," said the headmaster kindly. "You really mustn't go alone."

"That explains her *what*?" said Bee to him, and turned. "Cat, where are you going?"

"I have to go to the labyrinth. I don't want to. But I just can't stop." I was amazed by how calm my voice sounded as I stepped into the hallway even though I did not want to.

Hoofbeats rumbled on the street. Three shrill whistles pierced the peace of the academy halls. Orders were shouted in a ringing tenor: Lord Marius had arrived. "In here!"

Bee grabbed our coats. I dashed to the stairs and ran down to the glass-roofed central courtyard, Bee behind me. "Cat! Stop!"

"I can't! It's like I'm being dragged by the throat." I wasn't frightened, just numb. Something horrible was about to happen, and I wouldn't be able to stop it.

In the courtyard, benches ringed the outermost paving stones of the labyrinth walk. Four fountains anchored the four compass points, each surmounted by one of the beasts who symbolized the four quarters of the year: the bull, the saber-toothed cat, the horse, and the serpent.

"There she is!" Lord Marius's battle-honed tenor filled the space as he and his soldiers appeared in the arch that led to the entry hall. "Catherine Barahal! Beatrice Barahal! Surrender yourselves. You are under arrest at the order of the prince of Tarrant and the senate of Rome."

I sprinted for the nearest bench as soldiers ran after us, some circling wide in order to cut off all roads of escape. Patches of snow like lichen mottled the roof. The sky was dark with fresh storm clouds, flaking a lazy trickle of snow.

Lord Marius shouted, "We won't harm you. I give you my word. It's for your own good."

"So reassuring!" yelled Bee from behind me.

A crow landed on the glass roof, and beside it five and then ten more. The din they made caused men to look up. A crack shattered the roof. Shards sprayed; men ducked and retreated. I leaped a stone bench and found my feet on the beginning stone of the labyrinth walk: This was not a maze but a winding walkway built to hone meditation and to help minds focus. When my cane touched the stone, the path blazed with the breath of the ice. My cane flowered into cold steel.

"Halt!" A soldier overtook me.

I thrust. Surprised, he parried, but it was clear he was hesitant to press for fear of hurting me. I drove him back ruthlessly. He slammed into the bench, tripped, and hit his head. Lay still. I whispered a prayer to Blessed Tanit: *Let me not have killed him.*

More converged on me, too many to fight off. I raced inward on the labyrinth walk, my boots crackling on broken glass from the roof. The soldiers followed like wolves in pursuit, both they and I forced to stay on the path now that a glamour pulsed through it.

A crow flew past so close I ducked. Black wings filled the air. Their caws deafened me. The roof cracked again, more glass showering down. On the blast of frigid air, yet more crows poured through the shattered roof to mob the soldiers. The courtyard became a smear of darkness, men flailing with swords and cursing, crows tearing with beaks and swiping with talons. Many voices clamored as the mobbing crows drove the soldiers back, but only one word had hooked me: *Now*.

"Cat!"

"Bee! Don't follow me!" Slipping on shards, I cursed, trying to turn to go back, but my body lunged forward.

"Never! I'll never abandon you!"

As the path spiraled in toward the grated well, my sword grew so bright and cold I thought its touch would sear my palm. If I let go, I might break free, but I could not uncurl my fingers.

"You can't escape!" Lord Marius's voice sounded as far away as the distant explosion of musket fire. Or were those the cracks of illegal rifles?

"*The war begin.*" So the Amazon had said. Had Camjiata's agents set the prison hulk on fire? Had he coordinated his arrival in Adurnam with the Northgate poet's hunger strike? Who had smuggled rifles into the city? Was it all just a coincidence?

What had the headmaster meant? *That explains her.*

I staggered to a halt beside the ornamental trellis. The grated opening of the well yawned at the toes of my boots, a round, stone-lined pit like a mouth waiting to swallow me. In ancient days, so the story went, the Adurni Celts had cast living sacrifices into this well. The iron grate that covered the maw had hinges and a lock, but the lock was missing. Shaking, I heaved open the heavy iron bars.

O Goddess, protect me, for I am your faithful daughter.

The hand of summer reached up from the well to choke me. It was fetid and rotting, and I could no more re-

sist it than I could resist breathing. On that breeze I heard
the exhalations of the dying and tasted the power of the
blood that had sanctified the ground centuries ago.

"I won't go," I whispered. "You can't make me go."

Instinct—or Barahal training—tugged my head
around. A huge crow plummeted down. That cursed crow
had been following us for days. It beat the air before my
face, and for an instant we stared, eye to eye. It had the
same intelligence I did: thinking, planning, doing.

I shrieked as it stabbed at me with its bill. I connected
my sword's hilt to its body, felt bones give way and
crunch. Another crow was on me, stabbing as I wildly
swung blade and arm, and then a third and a fourth. I
twisted, dropping to one knee, and still they came.

A crow stabbed me above the right eye with its beak.

Just like that, they all flew off.

No pain, only pressure. My eye clouded with warm
liquid. Drops of blood scattered with a hissing like a nest
of disturbed serpents. The stone rim crumbled away beneath my boots.

"Blessed Tanit, spare me!" I pried the hilt of my sword
into the ground but could get no purchase as I slipped.
The spirit world was dragging me in.

"Cat! Grab my hand!" Bee's strong hand gripped
mine.

The stone rim steamed away like mist under the sun,
and we fell.

We plummeted, me beneath and she tumbling after.
How deep was it? At midday, in summer, one could see
the still surface of water glimmering far below.

I tangled with Bee's arms and the billow of her skirt.

Water split beneath my back. My head went under, and
then solid earth slammed me to a halt. Choking, drown-

ing, I came up gulping and spitting beside her. We sat chest deep in the slimy muck at the bottom of the well. My sword gleamed faintly; no brown muck adhered to its length. A withered bundle of herbs floated on the surface half wrapped in a satin ribbon: someone's recent offering. Far above, the opening narrowed to a round eye as if the day stared down on us. The ragged splinters of the glass roof shuddered in a wind we could not feel down here.

A crow peered over, its eyes like twin eddies of black night swallowing all that is light and ease and hope. Satisfied, it took wing, flapping away.

My hand groped for purchase in the sludge. My fingers slid across coins and fixed on a sloped, smooth object. Feeling along its length, I realized it was a bone. With a curse, I let go and tried to slither away, but I could not get my feet under me. Foul matter smeared my clothes and matted in my hair. The odor was like chewing on a hank of moldering cloth.

"Cat," said Bee in an oddly faint voice, "I feel strange, like the well...is swallowing me."

Dread cut like knives. I grasped her wrist and pulled, but she was receding as in the current of a river in flood.

Panic ripped through me. I was going to lose her, as I had lost my parents when they had drowned in the Rhenus River. She would be torn out of my grasp and I would never see her again. I fixed my other hand around hers and dragged for all I was worth.

"Help!" I cried, to no one. To anyone. "Help us!"

"Beatrice! Catherine Barahal!" Faces appeared at the mouth of the well, so far above they might as well have been in Rome. With the daylight behind them, it was difficult to make out their features, but I recognized the voices of Lord Marius and Legate Amadou Barry.

The legate shouted. "Is anyone down there? Call if you're there!"

"We're here! We're here!" But they couldn't hear me.

"You don't suppose they've drowned?" said Lord Marius. "What a stink! I can't see or hear a cursed thing down there. It might as well be tar."

"Get the magister. He'll be able to see if they're down there."

"We can't trust him. His own master told me so. He'll try to help the girls escape. He's got the power to do it. You felt the force of that storm. Bold Taranis! If I had a regiment of such mages, I'd never lose a battle."

"God of Lightning, Marius! Listen to yourself. If the girls die it won't matter either way, will it? Isn't there rope? We'll lower down one of the soldiers to look for them."

"Cat!" Bee's voice came as from the other side of a river, calling across a turbulent channel.

Her hand, trembling in mine, turned to sand.

My fingers closed on grains dribbling away.

She was gone.

Gone.

I had lost her.

My thoughts shattered. I could not see or hear or think.

Then I heard Andevai's voice, shaken and hoarse. "It's worse than I thought. I feel the wind of the spirit world. This is a crossing place, and it is open. Why haven't you gone down already? Get me rope! Hurry! Catherine, speak to me."

"I lost Bee." My voice was scarcely more than a whimper. It was all the breath I had.

"I hear you, Catherine. I'm coming. Hold on." His voice changed timbre as he turned his head away. "Cat's down there, but she's fading."

Lord Marius's voice was sharp. "Is she dying?"

"No. She's fading into the spirit world. It shouldn't be possible for humans to pass from this world into the spirit world except at the cross-quarter days."

"Are these the cold mages' secrets? That they can move at will between this world and the abode of the ancestors? The ancient poets spoke of spiritwalkers. I never thought it was true."

"I'm tied in. Lower me down. Catherine, hold on!"

His body appeared as a shadow, covering half the lit circle. I felt, as on my own body, skin parting beneath a slicing edge of glass as he cut himself. Blood's hot stinging scent drenched me as in a waterfall. Did a cold mage's blood have more power than that of an ordinary person? On the threshold between this world and the other side, the force of his blood swelled and surged like the ocean tide, for it was the essence of life in the undiluted form of salt and iron. I suddenly understood why I had not crossed. My blood had opened the path, but the stinking spew of muck we'd fallen into had coated my skin, sealing away my blood.

A rope's end spun down before my face. It bobbed, bounced, swayed. Clumps of dirt peppered the muck around me like grapeshot, loosened from the slime-dried stone shaft.

"Catherine! I'm almost down. Hang on."

"I have to follow Bee. I can't lose her, too."

I scoured away the mud above my eye. Pain burned where my fingers gouged out the clogged wound. Liquid pushed, trickled, and then streamed down my face.

His voice rang closer now, almost on me. Astonished. "You're all light!"

A rich fat drop of my blood struck the slime in which I floundered.

"I'm here! Grab my hand, Catherine."

His fingers brushed my hair, but his touch was as insubstantial as mist.

His next words came as from the far side of the world. "The gate's closing. I can't grasp you. And I can't cross. Catherine, I will find a way. I promise you, I'll find you—"

I fell through.

10

Into a river whose rushing waters tumbled me over and dragged me under. Skirts tangling in my legs, I pulled upward but my hands could not break the flashing surface. I sank into my past.

I am six years old and the water closes over my nose and mouth as my mother's strong hand slips from mine. The furious current wrenches her away.

My lungs were empty. I was drowning. The current dragged me toward a shadow that resolved into a vast maw rimmed with razor teeth. The spirit world was going to devour me.

Fingers with a grip like death fastened around my wrist. I thrashed.

"Cat! Don't fight me!"

Bee's voice! I went limp as she pulled. Then my mouth was above the water. I retched as air hit my lungs. The current tried to drag me back down. In panic I lunged upward through the shallows, shoving aside the body that was in my way and scrambling until solid ground met me. I collapsed, face pressed against a hot skin of stones.

"There's thanks for you!" Bee sprawled on the rocky shore, water purling around her.

I heaved up a spew of sour-salty water. My whole body

spasmed. "I thought…I was going to…lose you…just like my papa and mama…" I coughed out frantic sobs.

"There, now, Cat. There, now." The warmth of her hand on my back soothed me.

Heat baked down on my hatless head. Wind murmured in leaves. Insects buzzed. A tremulous peace calmed my galloping heart. I hadn't lost her. I hadn't lost her. I hadn't lost her.

I rose. We had floundered to shore on a rocky island trimmed with a sandbar. The sleepy horizon smelled of the sea. A wide, estuarine river flowed past, alive with a flashing presence. A feminine face with skin the blue-green of turquoise breached the surface. Eyes like stones tracked us. A slick shoulder streaked with long hair the color of twilight rolled away beneath the water.

Across the river stood tall trees leafed in summer glory. Far away, a winged creature perched on the blasted tip of a fire-scorched pine. On the far bank sat four wolves looking death in our direction. I was absolutely sure that they looked hungry and we looked delicious.

Bee tugged on my elbow. "Do you think they can swim across?"

"I wouldn't like to stay and find out."

The brushy sandbar on which we stood was separated from the other bank by a stagnant, muddy channel. Downstream, where the back channel met the river, the water was covered with algae. A foul substance stirred beneath that green surface in the same way heating water shrugs just before it boils.

"I guess we have to wade across that slimy-looking mud to get off this island," I said. "Let's get out of these winter clothes first."

We stripped off coats, gloves, and petticoats. I peeled

off my wool challis riding jacket as well, because it was so hot. We rolled up our gear into separate bundles. She still had the knit bag.

"At least you saved your sketchbook and the knife," I said, my courage plunging. "I lost—"

Light winked on steel. Not ten paces away, my sword rocked in the wavelets along the shore. In the spirit world, it appeared as the sword it was rather than disguised as a black cane.

I pounced and swept it up. The blade flashed as if it had caught the rays of the sun, only there was no sun, nothing but a flare of gold on the horizon. The winged creature on the distant tree opened its wings and launched upward. It was not a bird of prey, as I had thought, but a winged woman, her skin as black as pitch and yet glowing as if she were a smoldering torch of power.

"Beware! Beware! A dragon is turning in her sleep!"

Did I imagine a voice, or actually hear one?

The wolves tested the river's shallows as if they had decided they were indeed hungry enough to try to reach us.

Bee turned as she slung her bundled gear over her back. "Did you say something, Cat? Oh! Incredible! Your sword washed up!" She raised a hand to shade her eyes. "Is the sun rising?"

A line of fire limned the sky. A blast of wind shook the trees like an unseen hand wiping clean the slate on which all is written. What came behind it was sharp and painful and obliterating.

"It's the tide of a dragon's dream," I cried. "Grab hold of me and don't let go! If we're swept away, we'll go together."

I threw my arms around her in an embrace so tight she

grunted in protest. Across the river, the wolves plunged into the current and began swimming across.

A low bell tone shivered through the world. Its sonorous vibration splintered air from water, stone from fire, flesh from soul, here from there, now from now. The tone like a taut string passed through us as a knife slices parsnips, as a kiss unexpectedly filters through your entire being, as cold magic flows down a sword's blade, as a choice propels you down a new path whose track you can never retrace once you have set your feet on it.

My heart, my flesh, my bones, my spirit; all thrummed as if caught within the enveloping thunder of a drumbeat that boomed on and on. Within the hollow rolling sound, the space between the beats, there unfolded a long white shore of glittering sand washed by lapis-blue waters and trimmed by thick vegetation with fanned, fringed leaves and flowers so vivid in their reds and oranges and whites they were almost molten. I felt I was looking through a window onto another shore. Then, like a vase shattering into pieces, the world tipped and parted beneath me. An abyss loomed.

I did not fall because Bee did not fall. Bee was an immoveable pillar of stone.

With a howl of rage, a shape writhed out of the channel where the water had run so green. It was far larger than could possibly rest under the surface unless the channel's depths reached all the way to Cathay. It seemed not so much to unfold as to expand as a balloon expands when air is heated inside it. It spread a net of tentacles. Its maw was rimmed with razor teeth so white they hurt my eyes. This was the creature that had meant to eat me in the river. One huge appendage lashed overhead and snapped down to crush us.

·

"Hold on to me!" I shouted as I slashed at it with my sword.

My blade severed the limb. The tentacle fell writhing on the stones, spraying a stinging black ichor that hissed and bubbled across the earth. More appendages lashed over us. The tide of the dream cut through the creature. Its moist hide parted like peeled fruit. Light mottled the body, slithering in and twisting out until my stomach clenched. I shut my eyes, waiting to be smashed.

The air quieted, and the world grew still. The river flowed deep and dark and wide. The trees stood green and lovely. Bee still held me. We hadn't moved. Nothing had changed around us.

Of the monstrous creature, there was no sign. The surface of the back channel was a sheet of glassy calm. Only a single patch of green remained, rimming the steep bank, and as I watched, it scuttled along the shore like a little green crab trailing a black spume behind it and missing one claw.

"The cursed wolves!" I released Bee and spun.

The current streamed undisturbed except for a large leafless branch floating past. Four white birds perched with the most amazing insouciant balance on the uppermost swaying spur of wood. One dove into the water and came up with a gleaming fish in its cruelly hooked beak. The wolves had vanished.

Bee grabbed my arm. "What happened? What was that?"

I lowered my sword. "That was the tide of a dragon's dream. That's what Andevai told me. Any creature caught outside a warded place is washed away and never comes back. But that didn't happen, did it? I guess *he* doesn't know as much as he thinks he does!"

"Do dreams have tides?"

"Dreams can change course suddenly. Once you're dreaming, you are pulled along without knowing how far into the ocean of dreams you'll go. That might be like being caught in a tide."

"I thought walking the dreams of dragons meant sleeping, and waking up to sketch my dreams. I was thinking of it in a...metaphorical way, not an actual one. I don't like it here. And I was never bleeding, so how can I have crossed?"

"Let's get off this island. Then we can talk."

We splashed across the muddy flats and climbed up a sleepy bank carpeted with a bank of intensely gold flowers like chiming bells. No, the flowers were *actually* chiming as the wind's caress made them bob and tinkle.

"Those flowers are making noise," Bee said in a small voice.

She struggled up to a patch of ordinary grass and sank down. I sat beside her. It was a beautiful day. The landscape with its splendid trees and golden bank of flowers looked perfect enough to be painted. A searingly blue butterfly fluttered past. My whole body felt as heavy as a sack of sand. I could not have moved if the great general Hanniba'al and a thundering herd of elephants had borne down on us at that moment, although even had they done, I fully expected some horror would materialize out of the soil to flay them to ribbons, crack their bones to pieces, and suck out their marrow.

"Blessed Tanit," I said in a voice that did not sound like my own, "the spirit world was nothing like this the first time I walked here." I thought of the wolves who had pursued me and the coach as I fled Four Moons House. "Well, I guess it was. We should have listened to Rory.

This is not a safe place. Merciful Ba'al. Now he'll wait at the Buffalo and Lion wondering what became of us! Do you know what he told me after you went off with the headmaster? He said that the headmaster is a serpent. A dragon. That illusion we saw looked exactly the way I imagine a dragon would look. But the headmaster is a man."

"Cat," whispered Bee.

"Did you hear the headmaster say those two strange things right before the militia arrived? He said, 'That explains *her*.' He meant me, like he was watching me all those years in the mirrors trying to figure out what I was. Then he said by all means to take you with me, but that was *after* I said I was going to the labyrinth. If he knew the labyrinth would lead me to the well, and the well was a crossing into the spirit world, that would mean he wanted you to cross into the spirit world. That he *knew* you could cross. But your blood didn't open the Fiddler's Stone, so how could—"

"Cat." Bee's fingers clamped so hard on mine they cut off my words. Her voice was a murmur. "Don't move except to turn your head to your right."

A thousand pins would not have made the skin along my neck and back prickle more violently. I slowly turned my head.

A woman sat cross-legged on the bank under the canopy of a massive yew tree whose wide crown and split trunk I had, strangely, not noticed until just now. She simply sat, saying nothing, looking over the river, her hands folded peacefully in her lap. She had the look of the locals who lived in the countryside northeast of Adurnam: tightly curled black hair with a reddish cast, dark brown skin, and brown eyes, features that spoke of Celtic forebears as well as West African ones. It was her ordinariness that made me uneasy. She was dressed in the commonplace, practical summer clothing of the villages: a skirt sewn from bright cloth printed with red and orange paisleys on a butter-yellow fabric and bulky from petticoats beneath, and a high-necked blouse with a kerchief tucked around the collar. The apron she wore over all looked recently laundered, not a stain or a crease. She held a strip of fabric of the same pattern as the skirt. Folding it, she deftly bound it over her hair to create three decorative peaks in the fabric.

Perhaps I sucked in air too hard.

She turned. Her eyes widened with the same surprise I had felt a moment before.

Hers was a face that arrested the gaze. It had a familiar look to it, especially about the eyes, which were deeply lashed and finely formed. I trusted that face at once, although I knew I ought to trust nothing here.

"Greetings and peace to you, Aunt," I said, for there is never any harm in being polite. "Is all well with you?"

Bee's hand tightened on mine.

The woman spoke in a voice I had heard before. "No trouble, through my power as a woman. And you, bride of my grandson? I did not expect to find you so quickly."

Bee tugged on my hand. "Run."

"Do I know you?" I asked, for I was dumbfounded, although not struck dumb.

"Before this, one time I and you have met. I am Vai's grandmother."

I don't know how many times I blinked, or how wide my mouth gaped. Bee's tugging on my arm grew quite insistent, until I realized she intended to rip off my arm if I did not do something.

"Are you a spirit sent to confuse and tempt me?" I asked, and added hastily, "No offense intended. It's just a question."

The woman held out a necklace. A locket shone as if sunlight burnished it, although the silvery sky revealed no sun.

"That's my locket! With my father's portrait." I pulled my arm out of Bee's grasp.

"Cat!" Bee lunged, pinning my hand to the ground. "Don't you dare take it!"

The locket dangled like deadly fruit from the woman's hand. "To walk with wisdom and caution in the spirit world is wise," she said. "This amulet Vai tucked in my hand. He gave it to me after he made an offering to the ancestors. He asked me to look for you. He thought this locket might draw me and you together."

"Who are you?" demanded Bee.

"Do not speak your true name aloud in the bush. The creatures who live here eat names as well as blood. You can call me Fati."

I twisted out of Bee's grip, snatched the locket, and opened it. The image of Daniel Hassi Barahal, with his black curls and ironic smile, stared at me. When I touched the locket to my lips, I *knew* this was my very own locket. I had been forced to trade it to two girls in Four Moons House in exchange for their getting me out through a locked door.

"How did Vai obtain this?" I asked as I slipped it over my head.

"He did not tell me. He asked me to find you and guide you, for I know a little of the bush. Already I find you on open ground where any spirit animal may eat you." She lifted a scolding finger. "You must stay on the path. Or on warded ground."

"We were in Adurnam an hour ago," said Bee. "How can he have been at your village? How could he even know we fell into the well? Cat, you need to give that locket back."

"He came down the well after us, trying to help us, Bee. I haven't had time to tell you yet." I surveyed the woman for signs of razor teeth or hidden tentacles. This was not the frail old grandmother whose bedside I had attended in the village of Haranwy on Hallows' Night. Here, in the spirit world, she appeared as a younger woman in the prime of life, old enough to be the age of my mother, had my mother lived, but not so old that she had begun to bend beneath the burden of age. Vai had the same beautiful eyes. "He would have come after us into the spirit world, but because it wasn't one of the cross-quarter days, he couldn't cross. It's so obvious!"

"What's obvious?" demanded Bee.

"He went home to ask the hunters of his village to hunt for me in the spirit world."

"His actions you understand perfectly," said his grandmother.

"It's what I would do, in his place," I said.

"Very noble of you, I'm sure, Cat," retorted Bee, "but it must be many days' ride from Adurnam to his village, so he can't have gotten there yet."

"The days pass differently here. An hour here might be a week there. He would have plenty of time to go ask his kinsmen for help. I understand the locket is a talisman. But I don't understand how you are come here, Grandmother."

She said nothing. Heat settled over us in a sweltering mantle.

"You must be dead." My words emerged stiffly.

Bee sat back with an exhalation.

Fati looked at me, still saying nothing.

"He must have found you when you were dying. Because the dead cross over into the spirit world, he asked you to seek me out once you got here. I never thought..." My fingers curled over the locket. "If you're here, then my parents are here somewhere as well. I could find them."

"Maestressa, please forgive our bad manners." Bee shifted forward. "I hope you suffered no pain. I hope we find you at peace. I'm sorry."

"For what are you sorry?" she said with a gentle smile. "The crossing awaits us all."

Belatedly I lowered my gaze, as one did with elders. I absolutely believed she was who she claimed to be, although I could not explain why. "My apologies, Grandmother. You and the villagers helped me at great risk to yourselves. When I said I wasn't sure I could trust you, when I was there in your house, I didn't mean it to be rude."

"Mmm. Yes. You were rude. But you were frightened, and you are young. We all make mistakes."

"You are generous to forgive me."

"Have I forgiven you? I choose to help Vai because he is a very good boy."

"He wasn't that good of a boy," I muttered. "He was arrogant, contemptuous, and unkind."

"Then he forgot the manners his mother and I taught him." She bent a gaze on me that made me duck my head like a scolded child. "Do you appreciate what he has done? To come so far, against the will of the mansa, is no light choice for him."

"I appreciate his efforts to make sure Four Moons

House doesn't recapture us. But I can't believe the mansa would do anything to harm such a powerful young cold mage."

"I do not believe you comprehend what he risks for you. You think you know what it means to be born into clientage, to be bound by law and custom to serve another, but you do not know."

"We in the Kena'ani are raised to serve our households," I retorted, not nearly as belligerently as I might have. "As I did, when my aunt and uncle gave me to Four Moons House against my will. They would have given me to whatever cold mage came to collect me. It happened to be him."

"Do you suppose that was chance? Your destiny was chosen before you were born."

"I don't believe that!"

"I don't either," said Bee stoutly, and loyally. "Although I do have to wonder why I was cursed with this gift of dreaming."

"You're no help," I muttered with a grimace at Bee.

Fati gave me a look that made me feel small and petty. "He placed three strands of his hair behind the portrait in the locket, to help you find him. A thread ties you together, because of the binding the djeli wove over you, which is a chain that reaches between worlds. Seek him in your heart, and you will know where he is. But if you have no heart to seek him, then he is the one who will search in vain."

"Cat didn't ask to be married to him," said Bee. "I am sure you cherish your grandson. I'm sure he is loyal to his family. But it isn't fair to scold her as if she had asked for a pretty bauble and then tossed it carelessly away because it didn't match her gown. She was betrayed by my mother and father, by our entire clan. She shouldn't be taken to task for something she never asked for."

"It's all right, Bee," I said, for I couldn't bear to see his grandmother's expression harden into disapproval. "My apologies for my sharp tongue, Grandmother. I can't truly understand what it means for your village to have endured clientage for so many generations. We studied law at the academy, but... well... it was words in a book. I admit I feel a more personal concern now."

"You can be sure," said Fati, "that Four Moons House has bound you tightly to him. And he belongs to them, just as my village does. When they wish to make use of you, they will do so."

"Unless I free myself."

"Do you think it is so easy to free yourself?"

I glanced at Bee, and held my tongue.

Fati raised her eyebrows as if she knew we had secrets we weren't sharing. "Anyway, girls, enough talking. We must seek a path or a warded place." She rose, brushed off her skirts, and walked away from the river.

Bee and I exchanged a glance.

"I like her!" whispered Bee.

"The hunters will cross at Imbolc," Fati called over her shoulder. "My grandson plans to be with them."

"How romantical!" said Bee as we hurried after her. "I wish some man would rescue me!"

"Isn't that what Legate Amadou Barry was trying to do? During the riot? Rescue you?"

"He was trying to capture and cage me," she snapped.

And wasn't that what Andevai would end up doing, if he brought me back to Four Moons House? Uneasiness rose in my heart, like a chain being reeled in. The world seemed made of cages. Walking gave me something to do instead of think about chained marriages and forbidding mage Houses and a voice commanding me to come *now*. We strode through a grassy landscape, skirting thickets of flowering bushes. Tiny translucent unicorns flitted between the blooms, wings flashing like thinnest glass.

Bee ventured closer. "How pretty!"

They coalesced into a swarm and stung at her. Stumbling away, she batted at the cloud as a haze of scintillant wings engulfed her. I swept my sword back and forth through them until they scattered to settle on the bushes, snorting, with teeth bared.

"Ah!" she said, pressing a hand to her face. "They attacked me!"

Fati said, "Let me see your chin."

After a pause, Bee lowered her hand. Several bumps swelled redly, but otherwise she appeared unharmed. "Nasty creatures!"

A few took to the air, and I brandished my sword, and they retreated.

"Stay beside me," said Fati.

We walked on. In places, the ground bottomed into swales, thick with white-barked aspens, their round leaves flashing like mirrors. Butterflies and dragonflies winked where pools of water had given birth to thickets of reeds and flowering lilies. Overhead, a pair of crows paced us.

"Do all the dead bide in the spirit world?" I asked. "Could I really find my parents?"

Fati had a long stride. "See this grass around us? You might say it comes from a seed, but a seed alone is nothing. It needs water and soil, and it needs the desire to grow. Without these, no grass can become grass. No thing is only one thing unchanging. Right now I walk in the body in which I walked on the other side. This form remains mine only until the tide of the spirit world reaches me. Then I will change, as all things change. So I cannot know what form your parents have taken, or how they have changed."

"Vai said that those who are caught in the tide of a dragon's dream never come back."

"How can you come back if you have not departed?" A smile softened her mouth. "Vai is a very clever and a very obedient and a very hard-working boy, but I am sorry to tell you, Cat, that he does not know everything he thinks he does."

Bee laughed.

I said, "But if all the dead people come here after they die, then where are they all?"

"A fish sees the eagle only as a shadow within the water, but the eagle sees the fish for what it is."

I scratched my bruised chin. "You're saying we can't look at things here in the spirit world and assume that what we think we see means what we think we see is what we think it is."

"Cat, that made no sense at all," said Bee.

"It made perfect sense! Think of the headmaster! We think we see a man, but maybe he's the eagle and we're the fish who only see the eagle's shadow. Grandmother, do you know anything about dragons?"

"I know a story, a long story. I am no djelimuso to tell it with the proper introductory remarks and blessings. It is the story about how my ancestors the Koumbi Mande came north across the desert out of the Mali Empire to escape the salt plague. So it happens, after many trials, the remnant reached the city of Qart Hadast and did not know where to go next."

Bee looked at me, and we didn't mention that Qart Hadast was the city the Barahal family had originally come from, the city the Romans called Carthage.

"The mansa's sister Kolonkan was a powerful sorceress. She stood on the shore of the sea with one foot on the sand and one in the water. She saw beneath the waves smoking mountains which the Romans call Vulcan's Peaks. In the very fire of one of those peaks, a female dragon had coiled in its nest and laid its eggs, and now she slept. Into the creature's dreams, Kolonkan walked. 'Maa, please advise me,' called Kolonkan. 'Where shall my people go?' The serpent answered, 'One of the daughters you will bear will serve me, and your people will go north, to the ice.'"

"How can a dragon nest in a volcano?" Bee said. "Wouldn't the molten fire destroy eggs?"

"My apologies, Grandmother," I said hastily, poking Bee. "We are listening."

"Mmm." Fati was clearly a woman not accustomed to being interrupted. "The tale goes on. That is the only mention I know of a creature the Romans would call a dragon or serpent."

We walked a while in silence. Grass swished along our legs. Insects buzzed sleepily without massing in a swarm to afflict us. The cursed crows floated above. A jumble of shapes like boulders came into view on the horizon.

"Grandmother," I asked at length. "Do you know who my sire is?"

She looked me up and down. "Why would I know that?"

"You can't tell somehow, because you're an ancestor now?"

She chuckled. "I have no such power. I am newly born

into this place. I know nothing more than what I knew before. I would tell you if I knew. A child ought to know its sire. For if you do not know what ropes hold you, then you might as well be a tethered goat. So it seems you and your cousin have undertaken a journey to discover the heart of your own selves."

"I would like to know what it means to walk the dreams of dragons," said Bee with a look a mule might give its handler. "Did this sorceress Kolonkan's daughter walk the dreams of dragons? Is that what the story meant?"

"Mmm. This is knowledge that is not mine."

"Not yours to share? Or you just don't know?"

"Bee!" I said in an undertone, pinching her arm. "It's rude to interrupt an elder."

"I'm the one fated to be dismembered and my head thrown into a well! I assure you, Aunt, I do not mean to be rude."

"Mmm, yes, you are drenched in *nyama*."

"What is that? Energy? Heat? Light? Magic?"

"It is the foundation stone. It is a thread. It is that which can be shaped. A potter molds nyama like clay. A blacksmith forges nyama into steel. A hunter must know how to protect himself from the dangerous nyama released when he kills an animal, by adding it to his own. Cold mages manipulate nyama. How any of them do this I do not know, for I do not know their secrets."

"Cat told me she once met a djeli who called nyama the handle of power. Is that like an axe handle? If you can grip it, then you can wield the axe's blade?"

"I would not say so. But those who can shape nyama can shape and change the world."

Bee nodded. "With the right connections to power and

a strong will, you can shape and change the world! Like Camjiata did, and means to again."

"Bee!" I whispered. "We're supposed to listen to elders, not interrupt them!"

"How are we supposed to learn if we don't ask questions?" cried Bee.

"We are here," said Fati.

Slump-shouldered sandstone towers rose before us, marking the four corners of a walled town. The eroded walls looked much as a seashore castle built of sand looks after a wave runs over it: melting ruins soon to be obliterated. No dogs barked. No wagons rolled or voices called. Not even the wind moaned. If anything lived in the dusty, deserted ruins, I could not hear it.

A road as black and slick as obsidian speared away from the half-collapsed main gate. As straight as a Roman military road, it cut through uninhabited countryside toward distant hills. A shadow raced toward us from those hills.

"The tide comes," said Fati. "Get up on the road, for it is warded ground. Hurry."

I grabbed Bee's hand and ran, even though I was suddenly sure that the instant I touched the pavement something terrible and irrevocable would happen. Yet I had to get there. Perhaps that desire was part of the compulsion that had driven me to the well.

"Aunt, hurry!" called Bee over her shoulder.

"Onto warded ground I cannot cross," said Fati. "You must go forward alone. This is your journey. My path is different."

The knife of darkness cut over us just as we stumbled up onto the road. Bee flung her arms around me. Fati stood in daylight, surrounded by grass. With me in shadow and her in the bright, I could see clearly how my husband resembled her in the planes of his face, the glow of his complexion, and the clarity of his eyes. A vibration rumbled like drums in the earth. A towering wall of fire washed toward us, scorching the grass to ashes. Fati smiled, lifting her hands in greeting.

"Blessed Tanit!" I breathed. "Grandmother!"

Flames obliterated the scene. The town walls rang like a struck bell as the ripple of fire boomed out around the stone.

The tide passed. Pale daylight, like dawn, rose on a world utterly changed.

Fati was gone.

11

On either side of the road lay fields. Three-horned antelopes grazed on grass as green as emeralds. Fields tilled in spirals marked patterns on the ground that would, I felt sure, create beautiful images if seen from the sky. Thick-leaved vines of sweet potatoes flourished on a field of dirt mounds, the only crops I recognized. Elsewhere, huge stalks were crowned by flowers whose petals blazed with streamers like orange flame; that is, unless they were really burning. Others wept green tears. A vine strung along posts burst pods into a cloud of butterflies. Small winged creatures with faces like bats swooped down, snapping them up, until the air drifted with shimmering scraps.

Fati was gone. She might have been anywhere or anything. A stone about half the size of my fist lay on a patch of earth beside the road. I scrambled down.

"Don't touch that!" said Bee.

But I did. The stone was waterworn to a smooth finish, deep brown in color, like sard. The veins in its surface flowed like speech against my skin. I felt I knew its voice. "Do you think the tide . . . turned her into this stone?"

"And you thought *I* was the credulous one?"

"Spirits change, just as the land does." I touched my father's locket, the familiar ache in my heart, the one that could never be filled. "So after all, maybe I can't ever find my parents, not if they were caught in the tide."

"Wouldn't everything be caught in the tide? How could you escape it?"

"You escape it by sheltering on warded ground, like this road." I closed my fingers over the stone and, ignoring her protest, tucked it into a pocket sewn on the inside hem of my jacket. "Although that doesn't explain how we escaped being swept away at the river—"

"*Cat.*"

A sound like the rushing of river water swelled behind us. I turned. Out of the walled town, human-like creatures rose in a tide of dark wings.

Bee said, "Blessed Tanit protect us!"

A mob circled above us. Their vast wingspans half blotted out the sky. They swept down over us, claws gleaming.

"Down!" I snapped.

Bee dropped, and I straddled her back, feet braced on either side of her. My sword blazed with an icy light so bright it burned. I slashed and stabbed as they attacked. Where my blade nicked flesh, they shrieked, scattering in all directions.

"Cat, what are they?"

"Don't move." I shifted so my skirts belled over her. "They don't like my sword."

The mob resumed its circling above us. One landed out of reach of my blade.

Tall, broad-shouldered, and powerfully built, she looked much like a human. Her short black hair stuck up in spikes. Her narrow face was as translucently pale as watered-down milk, and she had the stark blue eyes we in the north called "the mark of the ice." A line of purple-

blue tattoos like falling feathers spun down the right side
of her face and neck. She wore a sleeveless calf-length
tunic covered with amulets sewn onto the fabric much as
hunters fixed such talismans onto their clothing to protect
them in the bush. Her wings certainly amazed me. But it
was the third eye in the center of her forehead that riveted
my attention.

"You are an eru," I said, choosing offense over defense. "My greetings to you and your people. May we be
at peace rather than at odds. I ask for guest rights, if such
can be offered to peaceful strangers who have stumbled
here by accident."

She spoke in a voice like a bell. "You are well come
here, Cousin. Our hearth is open to you. All we have is
yours. All we are is at your service. But we have to kill
the servant of the enemy. That is the law."

"Cat," Bee whispered from under my skirts, "I think
they mean *me*."

The eru cried out the same way the great bells of Adurnam cried out the alarm when the city was threatened. "It
speaks! Beware!"

I shifted my sword's angle; the eru took a step back.
"She is not my enemy, and therefore she is not yours."

More eru landed out of my reach, ranging in a circle
around us. The tall ones had third eyes as bright as gems.
The shorter bore marks on their foreheads like a mass of
cloudy veins, and I had the oddest feeling they could see
with those blinded, blinkered third eyes onto sights invisible to me. It was very disturbing. Worse, it seemed likely
these eru could rip us to pieces in short order with their
claws. And how could I predict what damage they could
do with their magic, for weren't eru fabled as the masters
of storm and wind?

"Never mind," I said. "We'll just go on our way."

"She must be sacrificed," said the eru who had spoken before. "As a courtesy to you, if it is your wish, we will kill her and eat her at the welcoming feast, all except her head. Her head we will cast in the well to give strength to our water. Out of respect for you, our guest, we will show her this honor."

Bee's choked exclamation hit me in a wave of fear. I swept my blade in a slow circle, to mark each eru, ten in all. "I will take as many of you with me as I can, before I let you touch her."

A melody like words flowed around the circle, then ceased when the first eru raised an arm. "Do you serve her, who is a servant of the enemy?"

"Why do you believe her to be your enemy?"

"Did she not come to seek a serpent's nest? Do you not feel the enemy turning and turning again? Doesn't this rising tide aid their servant because it forces us, who would drive her away, to hide within our wards rather than pursue her?"

"I think you are a servant of the night court," I said, re-membering the eru who had pretended to be a footman in the service of Four Moons House and what she had told me when we had stopped at Brigands' Beacon so Andevai could make an offering. "Because servants of the night court have to answer questions with questions."

She nodded in the manner of an opponent acknowledging a hit. "I am she who speaks for this hearth when the night court commands."

Black wings fluttered. Out of the sky dropped a crow. No ordinary crow could cause such a reaction among fearsome eru. They took flight in a cacophony of wings until only the speaker remained. With a self-satisfied air, the crow folded its wings and cocked its head to consider me. A smear of dried blood mottled the tip of its scabrous bill. I was sure the blood was mine.

I could not resist a jabbing feint at the crow, just to make it hop back. I had feelings, too, even if Bee sometimes called me heartless.

"Don't think I've forgotten you," I said as I touched the clotted wound above my right eye.

With its third eye, the speaker looked at the crow, and then at me with all three eyes. For an instant, I thought I saw a reflection in her third eye: turning wheels flashing along a road.

"The master comes," she said. "The enemy's servant will not escape."

Bee had shoved her head out from under my skirts. "Look!"

She scrambled up, pointing toward the hills. At first all I noticed was eru fanning out like herders. They were shepherding antelopes toward the town walls, or corralling them within sturdy copses of shimmering trees. Beyond, a blur of fog avalanched down the distant slopes. Claws sharpened in my chest as though a foul beast had burrowed inside me and latched on to my heart.

"I don't know what else to do, Bee," I said as the fog grew. "You have to run for it. Take my sword. If I offer it to you freely, you can take it." I held it out.

Sparks leaped from the blade, and where they struck her hands and arms, a shower of spitting flames poured like a sheath over her limbs. She yelped and snatched back her hand.

"Cold steel burns the servants of the enemy, so she cannot wield it," remarked the speaker with a cruel smile. But her smile vanished as she looked past me. She knelt.

How the vehicle had bridged the distance so quickly I did not know. An elegant black coach pulled by four white horses rolled to a stop beside us. The horses had a polished sheen, like pearl. The first pair stamped, hooves striking sparks from the obsidian pavement, while the second pair waited patiently in their traces.

The coachman was a burly man wearing a perfectly ordinary wool greatcoat. He wore his short blond hair in the lime-whitened spikes traditional to Celtic warriors in the ancient days when the Romans with their land empire and the Phoenicians with their sea trade fought to a standstill, and the barbaric Celts shifted allegiance depending on what benefited them the most. Seeing me, he did not smile, but the corners of his eyes crinkled as with an inward chuckle. He tapped two fingers to his forehead in greeting.

A figure swung down from the back. I recognized the tall, broad-shouldered eru with skin the color of tar, her third eye ablaze with a sapphire brilliance, her wings a swirl of smoke. Power roiled in her like a storm about to burst free. I stepped between her and Bee as if I could fend off the brunt of the blow. My blade shone like a torch, its hilt turned to ice against my palm.

"Let it be," said the coachman to the eru. "We are here for Tara Bell's child, not for the other one."

She settled back, wingtips fluttering as if a wind spun off them. I swallowed; my ears popped; the wind died.

"Greetings, Cousin," the eru said. "The master has sent us to fetch you."

Such a wave of despair washed through me that my strength failed. I stared at the two creatures I had first met in the guise of a humble coachman and a humble footman. Bee grasped my hand. Hers was cold.

I spoke in a pleading whine I did not like but could not help. "We just want to go home."

The splendor of her third eye sparked rays of light along the surface of the black road. "The master has summoned you."

"Help her return to the other side, and I'll give you no trouble," I said desperately.

The coachman's lips curved in a wry, weary smile.

"You will give us no trouble regardless, Cousin," said the eru, not in anger but in sorrow. "You are bound, as we are bound. Get in the coach. Both you and the serpent. We have a long way to travel. The master is not patient."

"Indeed, he is not," said the coachman with a glance skyward as the crow flew. "We outraced the storm of his anger. Now it is time for you to take shelter."

Over the hills boiled a black wrath of clouds. In the cloud's heart, lightning writhed like so many coiling incandescent snakes. Its power hummed in my bones and my blood like a fever. The crow sped toward the storm as if to welcome it.

A horn wept from the walls as the herding eru chased down the last of their charges, and the kneeling eru broke free and fled.

My knees were turning to jelly. "Blessed Tanit. If we run, that storm will destroy us. If we go with them, you'll be killed."

"One thing at a time," said Bee with astonishing calm as her hand tightened on mine. "Right now, our best chance is the coach."

The eru opened the door and swung down the steps with the ease of practice. I sheathed my sword, climbed in, and sank onto the forward seat, into the same place I had sat when I traveled in this coach with Andevai.

Bee sat down opposite, her knees shoved against mine. "Don't give up hope, Cat."

The door closed. With a crack of the whip and a shout of "Ha-roo! Ha-roo!" the coachman got the horses moving. We turned in a sweep, and the coach lurched as the eru jumped on behind. We picked up speed. No coach in the mortal world ever ran so smoothly and so fast.

A blast of wind shook the coach. The shaking and shuddering pitched us off our seats. The coach bounced up, thudded down, pitched halfway over, righted itself. Like a ship caught in a typhoon, it rolled and yawed. We clung to each other as the gale roared around us with a howl so loud I saw Bee's lips moving but could not hear a single word, nothing except the frightful mocking caws of a murder of crows flocking around us as if their flight were the wind.

Unseen claws squeezed my heart. If I did not obey, the master would crush me.

Terror, like grief, can make you numb. But when the first edge passes, as the storm gusts on and the coach settles, it can also make you angry. For who wishes to be subject to terror?

We struggled up to sit. After the battering we had taken, I was grateful the cushions were so soft. We caught our breaths.

"That puts Papa's temper tantrums into perspective, does it not?" said Bee with a gaunt smile.

I looked at the two doors, the one to my right which we sat up against, and the other door, closed and shuttered, by which Andevai had sat on the first journey we had made together. He had warned me never to open the other door, but when he had said that, he had meant the door to my right, the one we had just used to enter the coach.

I grinned. "This coach is a passageway between the worlds. One door leads into the spirit world. But that one leads back to our world. We'll jump out and run for it."

I scooted over to the other door. Sliding my sword half out of its sheath, I sliced a stinging, shallow cut in my right hand. I grasped the latch, smeared blood on it, and pushed down.

The latch bit me.

I yelped, jerking back my arm. Three tiny puncture wounds in the back of my hand prickled red with my blood. The latch glowered, having acquired a dour, brassy gremlin face as wide as my hand and as thin as a finger. Incisors sparked as if tipped with diamond. A thread of a tongue licked along the brass, and my blood vanished.

Bee slid her knife from the knit bag and, with all her considerable strength, chopped where the latch was attached to the door. The blade thunked, and bounced off. The force of the blow redounded back up her arm. She cried out, dropping the knife as she doubled over.

"We'll see about that!" I cried, fully drawing my sword.

The nasty little gremlin latch-face *winced*.

The coach slammed to a stop so abruptly I was thrown back against the seat and Bee thrown forward, narrowly missing my unsheathed blade and banging her knees. The coach rocked violently. The door to the spirit world was flung open to reveal the coachman.

"Out," he said.

It wasn't that he looked angry. He didn't look angry. It was just that I was suddenly sure he could yank both my arms out of their sockets if I did not obey. Not that he would want to, or would enjoy the act, but that he could.

Bee's face was a grimace of pain as she tried to uncurl her fingers. "My hand! My arm!"

"Out."

We got out. I sheathed my sword as we huddled together at the side of the road. Bee had left the knife behind in the coach but made no attempt to dart back inside to grab it. She could not open or close her left hand. The knit bag sagged at her hip. He got in, and we heard him talking and a soft buzzing voice in reply, but no words I knew, nothing I could understand.

The eru strolled over. Her two ordinary eyes gazed at me; her third eye narrowed, as at a nastily ugly sight, on Bee.

"I'm not sorry we're trying to save my cousin's life," I said.

"He is slow to anger," she said in a reflective tone. "But one thing will do it: assaulting his coach or his horses."

"I thought the coach and horses must belong to the master," I said.

"No more than he does. No less than he does. No more than my wings belong to the master, and no less than they belong to me."

He hopped out and regarded us for such a long time with such a steady stare whose emotions I could not possibly guess at—not anger, not sympathy, not rage, not pity—that Bee began to snivel, as if she had at last reached the end of her rope.

He said, "The door into the mortal world is locked."

"What do you expect from us?" I burst out. "You can't expect us to lie down and give up."

He said, "Go sit on warded ground. I'll make tea."

He indicated a fire pit ringed by a low inner wall of bricks and an outer circle of marble benches. A fire burned. A lofty tree with red bark and white flowers shaded one side of the pit; there was also a granite pillar and a stone bowl from whose center burbled clear water. Bee and I sat side by side on a bench as the coachman brought over a kettle, filled it at the bowl, and set it across an iron grating over the flames. He carried two full buckets to water his horses. The eru flew ahead, scouting. Passed through the storm, we had reached the hills.

"It's a triangle," said Bee.

"What is?" I asked, watching the ease with which the eru flew, her smoky wings skimming the air. I had first seen her in the guise of a male human footman, booted and coated for winter, and it was not so easy to shake that image from my mind to see her as female.

"The tree, the spring, and the pillar form an equilateral triangle," said Bee. "I wonder if the form creates the ward."

"I think there has to be a tree, a stone, and water," I said, remembering the djelimuso Lucia Kante's fire. I had sheltered there, argued with Andevai, and met Rory. I had told her stories from my father's journals, the price I had to pay so she would tell me how to leave the spirit world.

Bee massaged her left hand with her right. "Did you see that sneering face on the latch?"

"The one that bit me? Of course I did!"

Around us lay open forest, trees spaced apart and grass and bushes grown thickly in the gaps. Four big animals trotted into view and settled onto their haunches to leer at us. They looked something like what a dog and a cat and a pig would look like if smashed together, with coarse short hair and hind legs shorter than their forelegs. They had the teeth of carnivores and the gazes worn by the cold-hearted who have nothing better to do than plot the ruin of all they see. When the coachman looked at them, they ambled out of sight, but I had a feeling they were hiding in a tangle of undergrowth, waiting hungrily.

Bee pulled her sketchbook out of her bag and paged through it.

I identified the faces of young men, studies from life, some shaded to fine detail and others a few deft lines that caught an essence. "Maester Lewis. That good-looking Keita lad whose family left for New Jenne. Here's that laughing bootblack Uncle Jonatan scolded you for flirting with."

She turned another page without replying.

I went on, unable to bear her silence. "Now we're at summer solstice, when the Barry family arrived at the academy. My! Isn't Legate Amadou Barry pretty? To think all those months we thought him a student at the academy, when instead he was a Roman spy. Do you suppose he was spying only on us? Or are there other pupils from disreputable families worth investigating?"

"I'm not the only one who has endured an unpleasant romantic interlude, Cat. I won't hesitate to remind you of yours if you don't stop teasing me about mine."

The unyielding rigidity of her tone convinced me to change the subject. "Here's Cold Fort. With Amadou Barry standing at the gates—not that I mean anything by mentioning him! Is this from the dream that made you ask him to look for me there?"

"Yes. Last summer I began to realize that sometimes I would dream an ordinary event, like people meeting at a shop or a fruit seller's wagon overturned at an intersection. Later I would encounter the very thing. Or hear it had happened, like when Banker Pisilco was rude to a troll at the Merchant's Exchange and the troll had to be restrained from killing him by its companions."

"I can see that might be disturbing," I said cautiously. "I wish you had told me."

She wasn't really listening. "I don't think walking the dreams of dragons is divination, seeing into the future."

"That's what the mansa thinks it is," I said.

"I think it's a way to find things. So the question is, what am I trying to find?" Her expression reminded me of the brooding of clouds before a storm. "Did it ever occur to you, Cat, to wonder why we act the way we do?"

"I often wonder why you act the way you do!"

She rolled her eyes, and I was cheered by her brief smile. "You know what I mean. Why should I obey the strictures we've always been told must fence in our lives? We must learn the skills appropriate to Hassi Barahal women. We must marry to oblige the family. We must serve the house by bearing children and by carrying out all orders given by the elders. Travel to a new city and spy on a princely household? Very well. Take a position as a governess or factotum and serve the clan that way? Shiffa and Evved are as deep in the family business as my parents are. My parents threw you away to save me because they were told to do so."

I swallowed a lump in my throat. Bad enough that Uncle Jonatan had betrayed me by handing me over to Four Moons House, but for my beloved Aunt Tilly to have gone along with it was a knife in my heart I could never shake loose.

"I can't expect to be like my mother," she went on. "She married where the family told her to marry, to a man she does not love and never expected to love. She has never complained, although she does not always approve of what Papa does and says. For the sake of the clan she gave birth to three daughters—"

"She loves you!"

"Yes, she loves me, and Hanan, and Astraea. And despite everything, she loves you, Cat. That's why it's so unpardonable that she betrayed you. But she serves as she was brought up to serve. I can't. The dreams that bind my life have changed everything for me."

I took her hand in mine. I had nothing to say. There was nothing to say.

"So I ask again. Why should I feel bound to strictures that won't protect me from being torn to pieces by the Wild Hunt and having my head thrown in a well?"

"Bee, that's such a horrible thought. Why are you blushing like that?"

The rosy glamour creeping into her cheeks brightened. "In ancient days, Kena'ani girls like us could offer their first night to the goddess, at Her temple."

"Which, if you recall, is why the Romans called us whores."

"I don't care what lies the cursed Romans told! The point is, those girls could give their first night to whomever they wanted. So why shouldn't I take Amadou Barry as a lover?"

"*Bee!*"

She skewered me with her gaze. "I might be dead tomorrow!" Her fingers brushed across an infatuated portrait of Amadou Barry: the tight curls of his cropped hair, his pretty eyes, the single gold earring, the gracious smile on his lips. "Don't you wonder, Cat? I saw you kiss him."

"I did not kiss Amadou Barry! He's very pretty, but not what I look for in a man. And after the way he spoke to you, I'm surprised you still think of him—"

"You know who I mean! I saw you kiss the cold mage!"

I hated blushing. "Of course I wonder! But if I were to . . . bed Andevai, then I'd belong to Four Moons House. I'd be trapped."

"He seems very loyal to you. Likely to treat you kindly. You would live well."

"In a gilded cage? Can you even imagine Rory at Four Moons House? Oh, Bee, I had so hoped we would find shelter with the radicals. I was shocked to my heart when Camjiata showed up and said those troubling things. Honestly, Bee, didn't you find it creepy that his wife had seen you and me in her dreams?"

"Once I would have." She closed the sketchbook. "Not now. If we can escape from these two, maybe we can track down your sire and he can help us get out of the spirit world."

"Coming to the spirit world was the worst idea I ever had and I'm grateful to you for not reminding me of how stupid it was! Haven't you asked yourself yet, who spoke through Bran Cof's mouth? Someone who could put me under a compulsion? Someone Bran Cof called '*my tormenter*'?"

"Bran Cof is obviously not the best judge of character. He compared me to an axe."

"So did Camjiata's wife." I drew the sketchbook off her lap and opened it to a picturesque drawing of a summer carpentry yard where half-dressed and well-built men worked. "You were magnificent, Bee."

"I was, wasn't I? I couldn't believe he fell for the old 'I don't think he knows' trick."

I laughed, too. "He *was* an awful old lecher. I wish we knew what the headmaster wants, and who he is! At least

I can imagine Rory will survive a while in Adurnam without us. No doubt he already has women arguing over who gets to feed and pet him."

She chuckled, then snatched the sketchbook off my lap and stuffed it into the bag. "Oh, la! How thirsty I am!"

The coachman approached, carrying four mugs, a tin basket, and a small white ceramic pot in the shape of a boar with a pair of tusks for spouts. He busied himself measuring tea leaves out of the tin basket and into the pot.

"I suppose it's difficult to run away from things that fly," Bee said, looking for the eru.

"I suppose it is," he agreed as he poured water from the kettle into the pot to steep. "Not to mention the four hyenas awaiting you in the bush, if you proved so unwise as to leave warded ground and strike out on your own."

Bee said, with cool politeness, "Is *hyenas* what you call them?"

"There are other names. Like most creatures, they don't always wear the same clothing, but their souls don't change."

"Have they been following us?" I asked. "We saw four wolves. Then four kingfishers."

He set down the kettle on stone and covered the pot. "It is certainly possible they are the same souls in different clothing, hunting you."

"Why do the creatures here attack my cousin?" I asked.

His blue eyes had the remote intensity of the winter sky, but his gaze did not seem unfriendly. "She is the servant of the enemy."

"That's no answer," retorted Bee. "It doesn't really explain anything."

The lines at his eyes crinkled, although his lips did not smile. "It is an answer, but not the one you wish you had. What you do not understand is that I cannot speak as I might wish to speak, because I belong to the one who breathed life into me."

"You belong to the gods?" Bee asked.

"I belong to the one who owns my breath."

I nudged Bee. "The headmaster's assistant said that, about goblins losing their breath."

"You've seen a goblin!" The coachman's lips parted in almost comical astonishment.

Bee looked at him, then at me, a question in the lift of her brows.

"What do you know about goblins?" I asked.

"The goblins are my makers. But it is my master who owns my breath."

"Your *makers*!" Yet when I thought about the clockwork troll, and the lifelike statues waiting in ranks underground, I wondered if he might be not flesh and blood, even though he looked exactly like a man, but something far stranger.

"Cat, close your mouth." Bee twisted the strap of the knit bag through her fingers as she addressed him. "The creatures here don't like dragons because the tides of dragon dreams keep changing this world. They can smell dragons on me because I walk the dreams of dragons in the mortal world. That's why they call me the servant of the enemy. But I'm not."

"You cannot escape what you are," he said.

"What are you?" Bee demanded.

"I am a coachman."

"You work as a coachman. Surely that is not all you are," she insisted.

"You may think this part of my body"—he touched his chest—"is the only part, because you are confined in a single body. But this is only one part of me. The horses and the coach are the rest of me. So when you take a knife or a sword to my person, naturally I will defend myself."

As with one thought, Bee and I looked toward the coach and four horses steaming on the road, and then at each other with raised eyebrows, and then back at him.

"Tea?" He poured out four cups. One he took over to the pillar, where he emptied its steeped contents at the base. Returning to the fire, he handed a mug to Bee and one to me.

Bee found her voice. "Food and drink in the spirit world may pose a risk for us."

He took the fourth. "This tea will offer no harm to either of you, and may do you some good."

I cupped hands around the mug's warmth. "You saved my life once. Can you promise me you will save my cousin's life, if it comes to that?"

"It is not my intention to see her come to harm. But I cannot promise what I cannot be sure I can deliver. I will do what I can. That is what I promise."

"Why would you alone of the creatures of the spirit world not wish me to come to harm?" asked Bee in a low voice.

"I was not created in the spirit world." He sipped from his mug as he glanced toward the road. What hands had built that road? "But you may call it kindness, if you wish."

I crossed to the pillar, spilled a few drops as an offering, and drank the rest. The brew tasted of drowsy summer afternoons adrift in a field of flowers. How tired

I was! I lay down on the bench, and as soon as I pillowed my head on my hands, my eyes closed. Bee sighed, trying to say my name.

The world faded as the drugged tea took hold. We had been betrayed.

12

How had I come to find myself standing beside Andevai, on a ship in the middle of the ocean? He was leaning on a railing, looking queasy, his mouth drawn tight. A female hand as black as his own wiped his sweating forehead with a stained kerchief. It had to be a dream, because he was wearing homespun laborer's trews and an ill-cut wool tunic badly dyed in a squamous nettle green, nothing like the flashy, expensive, fashionable clothes he spent so much effort on wearing decoratively, as Lord Marius had said. How fortunate Bee had not been there to hear Lord Marius's comment, for certainly no mention of Andevai would then have passed without a reference to decoration. Where had she been that she had not heard? Where was she now?

"Bee?" It was my own voice mumbling. I opened my eyes.

For an instant, utterly disoriented, I thought myself back in the bedchamber Bee and I had shared in the house on Falle Square. If the bed were as cold as stone and twice as hard.

No, I no longer had a home. No place was safe.

Bee slumbered on the next bench, the rise and fall of her chest as steady as a clock's pendulum. Above, the sky remained a leaden blue-gray color. It might have been an hour or a day we had slept there, and by the creased state of my skirts and the rumpled mess of Bee's hair, I would have called it closer to a day than an hour.

We hadn't been drugged; we had just been exhausted. I felt rested, and absolutely gut-gnawingly starving. I heard murmuring over by the stone bowl, so I let my hearing take wing.

"I think we should help them," the coachman was saying in a low voice. "The master expects us to bring the little cat. I see no reason we should bring him the other one, too."

The eru hissed, as at hearing an ill-mannered insult. "The other girl belongs to the enemy."

"Maybe she has no more choice than we have, beloved. Even so, are we simply to hand her over when we weren't specifically commanded to? He will plant her in his garden."

"So he should! You can stand there and know you will not be changed when the tide washes through. She's no threat to you."

"That's not fair! I may not be changed, but my master owns my breath. My master can unmake me with a word."

"True enough. I spoke in anger, and I apologize. I cannot be unmade. You cannot be changed. But the master will smell her out sooner or later. He will be angry if he knows she was here and escaped. Even if I agreed, how could it be done so we aren't punished?"

"Isn't servitude a form of punishment? Why should we do one more thing for the masters except what is required and commanded?" Passion trembled in the coachman's voice. "Listen. Water is the gate for her kind. We can say she swam away. The little cat will keep silence. She will not fear the master's anger."

Water is the gate! Was that how Bee had crossed? The crawling play of the flames coalesced into sinuous bodies twisting and slithering until I was sure I saw fiery salamanders alive within the flames, whispering *Fear the master*. Was the fire taunting me, or warning me?

"Of course she will fear him," hissed the eru. "I fear him and even you fear him. It is impossible not to fear him. The little cat is vulnerable. He will exploit that. How can we trust her to play her part in such a scheme?"

"To give trust is to gain trust. To withhold it until there is no doubt, is not trust. She will defy him, even if she fears him. She'll do it for the sake of the other one."

"Maybe it is possible," said the eru, in a tone of great reluctance. "We could travel by the road that leads past the river. We need do nothing, as long as the girls act."

"I knew you would say so, beloved. I knew you would risk it, if only to defy him."

One cannot really hear a kiss, but a texture in the air can change, like the charge of a lightning strike. Could the creatures of the spirit world love? Could a personage who had just told us he was part coach-and-four feel desire and affection? I shivered from the top of my head to the tips of my toes, remembering the kiss I had shared with Andevai. I had disliked and even feared him at first, but as I had slowly come to see a different side of him, I'd become curious and perhaps confused, not sure of my feelings for a man who was so handsome and so obviously interested in me.

A flap and flutter of wings disturbed the silence. A black crow settled on top of the pillar. I made a business of waking, and touched Bee's head.

She stirred, yawned copiously, and sat bolt upright. "Cat! The villains! They drugged us!"

I indicated the crow with a lift of my eyes. "Of course they drugged us. They fear you will escape, so they hope to keep us docile. But we're awake now. We must plot our next plan of action." Keeping my face concealed from the crow, I waggled my eyebrows.

Without moving her head, she slanted a glance toward the crow. Then she exaggeratedly glanced toward the coachman and eru and spoke in a loud staged whisper. "I would never have drunk that poisoned brew had I known! And yet, what can we poor young females do?"

"Here comes the villain!" I declaimed.

The coachman approached carrying a leather bag. By no sign or blush or hint of perturbation in his face could I detect that he suspected I had overheard his conversation. He pulled out a loaf of bread and a wedge of cheese.

"How can we know these morsels are not drugged, like that tea you forced us to drink earlier?" I asked haughtily.

He regarded me for one long breath. "From the mortal world. Thereby safe to eat."

Holding the blade, he offered Bee her knife, hilt first.

A tremor ran through her, and she thanked him prettily before politely taking it.

"There is enough to share," she said, holding his gaze.

He gave her look for look, and for a marvel, she was the first to look away.

"We are already fed," he said.

"Can we not eat the food grown in the spirit world?" I asked.

"I would be wary of such delicacies, were I born from the womb of a human mother."

I wanted to ask how he had been made, but the question seemed rude, and the crow watched. Bee sliced, and we ate as daintily as we could manage being so hungry we might have preferred to bolt our meal as dogs gulp meat.

"We have still a distance to travel, and a stop to make at the river for you to wash so you can be made presentable for the master." When the coachman looked at me, I knew he knew I had overheard their conversation.

"I am sure it would be polite for us to wash before meeting the master," I agreed.

He rinsed out the mugs as we brushed crumbs off our skirts. The coach awaited us. We settled inside, keeping open the shutter that looked onto the spirit world. The eru swung up on the back. As the coach rolled forward, the crow took wing.

In time, we came to a crossroads. We took the left-hand path, striking out along a ridgeline track from whose height we could see across vales and rises. I leaned out to let the wind blow into my face. I smelled a peppery spice so hot its aroma made my eyes water. I heard plucked strings in a waterfall of notes. I tasted the tears of the dead whose salt was the memory of voices I had not heard for years: *My mother and father, conversing in low, loving voices as my child self drifted off to sleep, safe in their arms.*

"Cat!" Bee was shaking me. "Wake up! We've come to the river."

I had fallen asleep. My head was swollen with uneasy dreams, but when I patted my hair, everything seemed in order. I hadn't sprouted cat's ears or an eru's wings. I looked out the window and saw a field of black rocks. Beyond the field flowed a wide river as pale as molten pewter. Light glinted over the water and thrust through my eyes to open a shaft of memory: *I am six, and I am drowning alongside my parents. Water pours into my mouth.*

"Look!" Bee's shriek jolted me free.

She pressed open her sketchbook. At the bottom of the page, I saw myself wearing a very irritated expression no doubt because the clothes I wore in the sketch looked like a printed curtain wrapped around my waist topped by an immodestly low-cut blouse of a fabric so gauzy it was almost translucent. Blessed Tanit! As if I would ever dress so indecently! Above, Bee had drawn a field of black rocks. One rock, split in half as if by a bolt of lightning, was circled and had an arrow pointing at it. A river lay behind it and, on the far shore, five mighty ash trees.

I looked out the window. Five mighty ash trees rose on the other side of the river.

"Stop!" She hammered on the roof of the coach.

She shoved the sketchbook into the bag as the coach slowed. Before we came to a stop, she flung open the door and leaped out. Knit bag flapping behind her, she dashed into the rocks like a dog let loose in a trash pit.

The coach lurched to a stop. I jumped out and with sheathed sword in hand ran after her. The rocks were like the oozing remains of a porridge that has congealed into a crusty, jagged blanket. I slipped, caught myself on the nearest rock, and scraped my palm.

Glancing back, I saw the coachman holding the arm of the eru as if restraining her; her wings were half open. Crows cawed. I heard a buzzing noise, like the whirr of a factory floor. A loud *splash* disturbed the river. Could Bee really escape the spirit world through water?

Bee walked in widening circles, picking her way along the rocks with the knife in her hand. Her body stiffened as she saw something. She dropped to her knees and hacked at the ground.

"Cat, help me!" Dirt spat up.

I hurried over. "What are you doing? Go to the river!"

Ignoring me, she knelt in the cleft of a rock that was split in half. The hollow between the split halves was as wide as my out-stretched arms; rotted debris matted the ground like felted cloth.

"Help me!" She chopped and dug without cease.

The ground heaved. Fissures splintered the earth like veins swelling and bursting. I grabbed her arm to drag her away, but she shoved the knife at me and began digging with her hands.

"Something terrible is going to happen if I don't uncover them," she cried.

Her fingers scraped dirt off a roundish *thing* that had a coppery shine. Fractured streaks of light chased patterns along its sheeny surface. Beneath the dirt she uncovered ten; no, twenty; no, fifty. Packed tight and deep, the fist-sized smooth objects filled the hollow.

They were *eggs*.

With a faint *pop*, one of the coppery eggs cracked. A sliver like a shard of broken glass thrust through the gap. Away in the distance rose the howl of an enraged beast. Gingerly, I poked at the egg with the knife and peeled back an inner shell wreathed with tendrils of translucent goo. A pasty mass pulsed vilely inside, a slimy grub the color of mottled vomit and metallic yolk.

I dropped the knife and raised my hand to smash it.

"We've got to help them get to the river!" Bee grabbed the knife and kept digging.

Horrified by my urge to kill something so small and helpless, I scrambled back to perch on the rock. The grub slithered out of the egg. No bigger than my hand, it had four limbs, a tail, a long beast-like torso, and a deformed back all crinkly like mashed-up paper. It had a snout for a face, with pasty-white strings striping its muzzle and head.

It was foul, and I hated it.

It opened its eyes to reveal molten fire, a blaze of blue-white heat. With a shudder, its outer skin hardened and sloughed off as I might shed a coat on going indoors. Beneath shimmered scaly skin as darkly red as the dregs of smoldering coals.

I could not look away from its eyes. That brilliant, fathomless gaze devoured me.

I had seen a gaze like this before: an old man sitting in a library with no fire and three dogs sprawled close, basking in the heat he radiated. He had kissed Bee on the forehead and on the lips.

I had seen jewel eyes like this in the headmaster's emerald gaze before the spark was subsumed by ordinary brown.

A shadow fell over us in a flutter of black wings. A crow snatched up the tiny creature and gulped it down in one bite.

Bee screamed with pure rage, but she did not stop digging. Around her, more eggs cracked. A crow landed beside me, intent on the nearest egg. On the rock opposite, a bold creature with the look of a plump rodent poised; it had a meek, chubby face, but a frightening mad gleam in its little black eyes as it fixed on a hatchling squirming up out of the hollow. It lunged and caught the thing, which spat and hissed in vain as the rodent ripped off its head.

I jabbed at the crow, which hopped back. Bee dug. The

grubs emerged, shed, and crawled. Their sluggish swarm crept toward the river. Predators descended: more crows; a cruel-billed eagle; stinging flies like a cloud of misery that covered the hatchlings with vibrating wings.

The hatchlings had no voices. They just died.

But the wind had a voice, a rising chatter and roar. Shadows boiled on the horizon. My heart froze in my chest. The creatures of the spirit world were racing or shambling or flying toward us in their tens and hundreds: proud eru, gracile antelopes, sleek wolves, clumsy six-legged oxen.

"Bee." I crunched over broken copper shells. "You've got to get to the river."

"I have to save them." Her hands were smeared with the grease and mucus of their rising, and still they writhed upward, on her, across her, for she was oblivious to their blood and slime. "I can't leave until they're all dug out."

"We have to go. Pick up what you can carry in your skirts. I'll cover your back."

She gathered up her outer skirt and scooped up what hatchlings she could into the cloth. Then she ran, light on her feet despite the rugged terrain. I cut at crows diving at her head. I swiped my blade through a cloud of glittering-winged creatures that had tiny fox faces and grotesque, elongated limbs like grasshoppers. I stabbed a rat, and shook it free just in time to spear a ghastly huge moth trying to fly away with a hatchling.

A chuckling rolling laugh surprised me. To my right, the four hyenas loped closer. I thrust at the closest, my blade catching in the loose skin of its neck. It swung its head back and forth, almost jerking me off my feet, but I wrenched my blade free and raced after Bee. I stepped on a hatchling, crushing it, but there were a dozen crawling beside it. Birds dropped, snagging up the morsels. Some ate them; others flew higher and dropped the grubs to smash on the rocks.

I grabbed up one of the little pathetic creatures, but it bit me with nasty stinging teeth, and I yelped and let go.

"Cat!" Bee splashed into the shallows and opened her skirt.

Hatchlings spilled, flashing and undulating as they began to swim.

Fish with bulbous eyes and teeth like thorns rose out of the water to feed. Pikes and golden-red salmon breached the surface. The water churned with their thrashing. Blood ran in threads. Hatchlings she had not helped reached the shore, nosing into the water.

I stood with one foot on the bank and one in the water, my blade unsheathed. But with so many hatchlings to feast on, even the hyenas had forgotten us, all except the one I had cut. It looked straight at me with black, intelligent eyes, and gave that unsettling laugh.

"Bee, you have to swim."

She did not answer.

"Bee!"

I spun around. She was gone.

A hatchling crawled over my boot and into the water. A fish rose up with mouth gaping. I stabbed the cursed fish and flung it high. Its body spun off my blade and hit the water. Following its arc with my gaze, I saw Bee.

She was *under* the river, walking through a coruscating whirlpool that had created a tunnel of water leading to a bright net flung deep within the current. Hatchlings swam on all sides of her; many had latched on to her clothes. She should have been drowning yet she walked as if through air. So fixated was she on herding the hatchlings forward that she didn't even look back for me.

The last little hatchling launched after her, diving fearlessly into the water.

I slashed my blade through the water to keep biting fish away from the last one. I waded in past my hips, past my chest, my skirts sodden and dragging, calling Bee's name, but she could not hear me. Water slopped into my mouth. The current dragged at me, pulling me down. The river wanted to *drown me*. Panicking, I struggled back toward shore, gasping with fear and swallowing more water.

White light splintered the horizon. The frenzy of feasting ceased abruptly. A distant vibration, as of a village bell heard across miles of empty countryside, sounded like the toll of death. The feeding eru in the field rose in a battering of wings and headed for the road. Earthbound animals scrambled after.

"Little cat! Hurry! The tide comes!" the coachman called from the road.

I leaped from rock to rock past the smashed remains of hatchlings and one little grub still working its way toward the river. The coachman stretched out a hand and hauled me up onto the road just as the knife edge of the dream cut over us. I covered my face with my hands, coughing and choking on the memory of the river's water filling my mouth. *I hadn't been able to follow her.*

As the bell's long reverberation faded, a rush of sound filled its silence. I looked up to see hundreds of eru rising off the road and flying away. Closer, my eru waited beside the coach-and-four. Blood smeared her mouth. I winced away, and my gaze swept the landscape.

Only there was no land. We stood on a causeway, surrounded by a wild gray sea. Waves broke over shallows in foaming white caps. Spray stung my face. I saw not one sign of life, nothing except a single black crow fighting the wind, the eru watching me as she wiped blood from her lips, and the coachman checking the traces on the horses.

My voice trembled. "When the tide came, Bee wasn't on warded ground. She'll be changed."

"Little cat, she who walks the dreams of dragons cannot be altered by their tides," said the eru.

I thought of how I had clung to Bee when the tide had swept over us at the first river. Other creatures had changed, but she and I had remained as we were.

"You see why we who live in this world hate such as she," added the eru.

A wave spilled over the causeway. I pressed against the coach, clinging to the open door. "So she's crossed back to the mortal world?" I said desperately. "I couldn't follow."

"You are not as she," said the eru. "What binds her does not bind you."

"What binds me?" I whispered.

The eru laughed in a way that made me cringe.

The coachman nodded toward the door. "The master is waiting."

Bee had escaped. Surely that was all that mattered, the best outcome I could have hoped for. Weary to my bones, my face moist with sea spume and my body battered by a tearing wind rising off the wide, dark sea, I climbed into the coach and sank onto the cushions.

"What were those grubs she dug up?" I asked, looking out at him.

Without answering, he shut the door, although he left the shutter open. Outside, four gray birds with long beaks swept into view, battling the wind. One dove and snatched a fish out of the water. They flapped to rest on the rocky revetment that shored up the causeway and began pecking life and entrails out of the fish. I looked away, down at the brass latch. Glimmering eyes watched me.

The coach rocked as the coachman climbed up into the box. As we began to move, the latch spoke in a hissing gremlin voice, its elongated mouth drawn tight in a mocking grin.

"Dragons. Silly girl. Those that survive will become dragons. Some will breed, and some will nest, and sleep, and dream, and then the tide of their dreams will wash through this country. It can never end until they are all dead. The master is waiting. He is very angry."

We rolled on as night poured over the sea and blinded me.

13

I did not sleep. I could not sleep. I closed my eyes, but my thoughts tumbled in time to the rhythm of hooves and the rattle of the turning wheels. As the wheel turns, we rise and we fall. So say the Romans, who rose and fell and rose again, even if their second empire was smaller than the first.

Take Beatrice with you, the headmaster had said. Bee had walked unchanged through the tide of dreaming when everything around her was altered. She had known where to find the nest because her dreams had told her, and she had drawn the landmarks and the actual spot. The hatchlings that survived had crossed back to the mortal world, and through water Bee had shepherded them home.

I could not rest, and I had no one else to talk to. I looked down at the latch.

"Is that what it means to walk the dreams of dragons? That you aren't changed by the tide?"

The gremlin face snickered.

"You remind me of my young cousin Astraea." I folded my arms on my chest.

After a long pause, it said, sulkily, "Why?"

"I'd like to tell you, but we haven't been formally introduced. What can I call you?"

"What can you call me? A good question. Names, like blood, can be eaten in this country. Do not spill names lightly. I have no name. What can I call you?"

"You already know my name."

It added a smirk to its repertory of unpleasant smiles. "True. The cold mage called you Catherine."

A sudden inquisitive urge overtook me to learn more about the man I'd been forced to marry. "Did the cold mage talk to you?"

Light glinted where its eyes should have been, like lantern light picking up the sheen of polished brass. "Why should he? If he didn't know I could talk? He doesn't know as much as he thinks he does."

"No, so I've discovered. What else do you know about him?"

"He weaves threads of magic into images. That was nice. It is a bit boring, you know."

"Is it? Can't you see outside?"

It sighed, with a squinched grimace. "No. That's the other latch. We never talk."

"Did the cold mage do anything else?"

"Not until you got into the coach. And I must say, except for looking at you a lot when you were asleep, he sat very still, not like you, shifting about and rubbing the cushions and snoring when you sleep."

"I do not snore!"

"You do! So did the dreamer."

I realized that every word Bee and I had said, in the privacy of this coach, the gremlin had overheard and could repeat.

It spoke as gleefully as that little beast Astraea when

she had been thwarted of something she wanted and felt her only leverage to sway you was just being mean. "The Wild Hunt knows she exists. Her scent is on me, on you, on these cushions, on the wind. When next the gate opens to the Deathlands, they'll ride through, hunt her down, and kill her."

I riposted with an attack. "Are you glad of it?"

"Oh, I don't care," said the gremlin, mouth flat as if hiding another emotion. "Why should I care? She would have hacked me to pieces."

"No, because I would have hacked you to pieces first. No offense intended. We just wanted to run away. Can you blame me?"

The gremlin shut its burning eyes and remained silent for so long that I bent closer, my breath visible as a shimmering glamour on its brass face.

"Remember one thing, little cat." Its voice altered, as if someone else were speaking through its mouth. "You must have his permission to ask questions. Do not ask questions."

A gust of wind sprinkled salt spray over my face, and I blinked. When I looked again, the latch was just a smooth brass latch. Cautiously, I touched it, but it did not bite.

"Hey, there," I whispered.

It did not answer.

On we rolled through the restless sea-swept night. Every time a big swell struck the causeway and splashed, I flinched as droplets spattered my face. Yet I could not bring myself to close the shutters, for then I would truly feel I was in a cage.

Bee had crossed. She would find Rory. They were safe. That belief I clung to.

On we rolled, and I did not sleep.

After forever, night lightened to day. The wind-washed sea spread to a horizon so gray it was impossible to tell where the sea ended and the sky began. At first I took the pale shapes rising and falling along the swells for boats, and then I realized they were rafts of ice. I shivered and drew my coat tighter around me as the coach slowed to a halt.

The horses stamped.

A footfall clapped on stone.

I clambered out because I could not bear to sit inside for one more breath. Better to plunge into the storm than cower to await its blow.

We had come to the end of the road.

The causeway ended in a pile of rocks. Breakers boiled at their base. The gray sea was whipped by a stark wind under an iron sky. Islands of ice peaked and troughed as swells passed beneath them. The wind chapped my face, and when I licked my lips to moisten them, I tasted my own blood, for the wind's icy claws had cut them.

"Go to your sire," said the coachman. He pointed to a rowboat leashed to a post among the rocks, waves breaking beneath its fragile ribs. "We have brought you as far as we can."

Once or twice in your life the iron stone of evil tidings passes from its exile in Sheol into that place just under your ribs that makes it hard to breathe. That makes you think you're going to die, or you're dead already, or that the bad thing you thought might happen is actually far worse than you had ever dreamed and that even if you wake up, it won't go away.

"My *sire*?" I whispered, my mind recoiling.

All that was out there was cold, deadly water.

The coachman said, "Remember, he seeks what you

fear most so that you come to him most vulnerable. Courage, Cousin."

"Look for the tower," the eru called.

My feet moved under the master's compulsion. My heart squeezed as in a vise, I picked my way over the rocks while fixing my sword into the loop at my hip, tied three times so I wouldn't lose it. I closed a hand around my locket as I splashed into the pebbled shore break.

"Blessed Tanit. Father and Mother. Watch over your daughter." What hold did he have over me, the creature who had sired me and yet left me to be raised by others? Why had my mother never spoken of this? Or had she and Daniel been waiting until I was older?

The water hissed, mocking me. I stuffed the locket beneath coat, jacket, and shift, against my skin. Caught on an incoming swell, the boat slammed into my knees and I sprawled forward into it, facedown in the choke water of the bilge. I inhaled a miasma of foul brine. One of the oars whacked me on the head. I grabbed at it as the boat pitched sideways. Water sloshed in, so cold I could not breathe.

The boat came loose. It began to tip and spin as the waves brought the prow around. In a moment, I'd be swamped.

I sucked in air, battled up to the seat, and grabbed the oars. Already, impossibly, the boat had drifted a hundred paces from the pier of stone where the coach-and-four waited. If the tide of a dragon's dream washed the spirit world now, I would be lost. Changed. Obliterated.

"Tanit protect me! Melqart grant me wisdom. Ba'al give me strength!"

I set to the oars, working the prow back around. With my back to the swells, I rowed into the sea. The prow lifted and dropped, lifted and dropped, my backside slapping on and off the seat each time. Water slurped in with each plunge.

I rowed, glancing over my shoulder as I set my sights on a nearby floe of ice that appeared as a sculpted tower. I rowed until my shoulders ached and my back throbbed. I rowed until the causeway was nothing more than a smear on the sea like a smudge of charcoal on one of Bee's sketches that she had forgotten to erase.

The rowing kept my body warm and my boots kept my feet mostly dry, but I had begun to lose the feeling in my fingers. I could not think of the watery deeps. Instead, I thought of Bee, dragged away by a call neither of us understood. I thought of Rory, compelled to kill the enemy. I thought of Uncle Jonatan and Aunt Tilly. Of Bee's sisters, amiable Hanan and annoying little Astraea. Of the charismatic general, Camjiata. I thought of handsome Brennan and thoughtful Kehinde, and of the trolls and their odd charm. Most strangely, I thought of my husband.

I thought: *He would row beside me. He would not have left me here alone.*

I was getting awfully tired of being someone else's puppet. The salt that stung worst in my eyes was the pressure of angry tears. I was not going to give up now, even in the middle of that which I feared most. A wave crashed over the prow, and the boat sank up to its gunnels. The water embraced me with an icily heart-stopping grip.

Breathe.

In and out. That was the first thing. In and out, measured and steady. I fumbled at the buttons of my winter coat and tugged it off just as a wave plowed into my back, flinging me sideways into the merciless sea.

The ice of the water robbed me of breath. I had no air.

I dragged an arm free of the water and heaved myself over the gunnel, using the swamped boat to keep me afloat. The waves wrapped my sodden skirts around my legs. The shocking cold made my throat close and my chest tighten, and I was sure I would pass out. But I bit at the inside of my mouth until the pain brought me reeling back.

Breathe.

Kicking my way around to the stern, I pushed the boat toward the ice floe. As my legs grew inert and my heart grew numb, the shadow of the ice covered me. The boat nudged onto a shelf.

Gasping, spitting, retching, I crawled out. I had no feeling in my hands and little strength in my limbs, yet by fixing fingers onto knobs of pitted ice, I pulled myself out of the deadly water.

For a while, an eternity, I lay on the ice like a suffocating fish.

A whisper of warmth pulsed against my skin where the locket pressed between my breasts. It aroused me from my stupor. I took in a breath, salt water fouling my mouth. Shaking, I rose. I checked my sword, the loop twisted so tight my frozen fingers could not untangle it. The locket's throbbing heat fed strength to me as I stared across the shelf toward a vertical fissure in the ice. The fissure led into blackness.

Really, what choice had I?

"Brave enough for my purpose," said a male voice, smooth and cold. I saw no one, not a single sign of life. "Come, Daughter. I will look on you now."

"I hate you," I whispered to the empty ice.

He laughed, as if my squeak of outrage amused him. As if he could hear everything. And maybe he could, for would it not explain me?

Maybe that would teach me to keep my mouth shut and not speak when I ought to be silent.

My legs were as heavy as logs as I stumped into the fissure. If he hadn't killed me by now, he might actually wish to see what manner of creature he had sired on Tara Bell. A warm breeze stirred the passage. A bell tolled three times, the vibration passing right through my flesh. I felt as if my soul were being rung to check its temper, as a person might flick a finger against a finely wrought glass vessel to see how pure the sound is.

Light bloomed to reveal an arch made out of two massive ivory tusks. The tusks were carved with crows and hounds and saber-toothed cats and an eru, and with the image of a girl no more than six years of age. She had long, straight hair and held a sheathed sword far too big for her.

The girl was me.

My body began to prickle and stab as sensation returned. I stumbled under the arch, which vanished, leaving me in a blast of humid air so fetid I hid my face behind my hands. The smell faded, and the light sharpened.

I lowered my hands.

To find myself and see myself in a maze of mirrors, reflected over and over again. Blessed Tanit! I was a mess! My complexion looked as lifeless as the underbelly of a dead fish; my hair clumped in knots and tangles to my hips; my clothes wrung around my body.

"Find me," his voice said. "One is a gate, not a true mirror. Walk through it, and I will answer three questions."

I turned, seeing myself turn over and over, I and I and I, each one of me alike. My thoughts lurched sluggishly

as I blinked, trying to signal myself as I had blinked at
Andevai in the troll's nest. Why did I think of the troll's
nest? Of course: The upper floor had formed a maze of
mirrors.

What was it Andevai had said that time in the carriage
when he had thought I was asleep? He had been weaving
illusions. He had woven my face in light.

*"The light and shadow must reflect and darken consis-
tent with the conditions of light at the time of the illusion."*

I had it: In every mirror except one I saw my reflection.
My jacket's buttons were sewn on the left so when I drew
my sword it would not hang up in the cloth. I looked for
the one image of me with the buttons on the image left
not the mirror left.

When I found her, I walked into myself. Heat cut
through me to banish the chill that numbed my bones. My
steps sank into a thick pile of lush rug, and I halted.

I was the candle that lit the chamber, for its depths
were shadow as layered as draped cloth dyed black. At
four points equidistant around me, as if at the four points
of the compass, loomed four monstrous toads with bel-
ligerent stances. Their skin had the yellow-green color of
fouled mucus. They did not move, nor did they blink, if
toads even blinked. The only way I could tell they were
alive was by the pulsing beat in their throats.

A personage sat cross-legged on the back of a turtle. He
was clothed in amulets, or perhaps his body was covered
in an illusion woven to appear as a shimmering fabric. He
had long straight beautiful jet-black hair just like mine and
Rory's. The skin of his bare arms had the same coppery
burnished-bronze shade as Rory's. His face was hidden behind a mask like a sheet of ice. His eyes had neither colored
iris nor black pupil, only fathomless light.

He regarded me in silence, masked and unkindly. On a perch next to him sat that evil crow, watching me with its evil black eyes, and I understood that what it saw, he saw, because he had bound it to his will.

I tried to marshal my thoughts, but I could not keep the accusation from popping out.

"Would you have let me drown?"

"You must be both clever and strong. Otherwise you are of no use to me. That is one."

"What manner of creature are you, that you can breed with a saber-toothed cat and a human woman, and no doubt other females besides?"

"I am the Master of the Wild Hunt. That is two."

His words hit as a blow. I sank to my knees as the truth poured over me.

My sire was the Master of the Wild Hunt, before whose spears even cold mages were powerless.

Had Tara Bell known? Blessed Tanit! Of course she had known!

"Did you kill my parents?" I whispered.

"Yes. That is your third. Now, Tara Bell's child, I will ask you three questions."

"Even though it wasn't Hallows' Night, you found a way to kill them," I cried. "It was your voice that said 'Daughter,' not my father's. It was your arms that pulled me out of the Rhenus River while leaving them to drown. You killed them, and saved me."

"Your destiny was chosen before you were born because I made you. Tara Bell promised to bring the child to me, but she disobeyed me. So I punished her."

"I hate you."

As if hate blazed, the chamber grew brighter. The shadows retreated to reveal a seething mass of creatures ringing the edge of what I now realized was a vast cavern whose walls were ice. Everywhere frozen within the transparent ice I saw hunters caught in motion: sleek hounds striped in gray and gold; hulking dire wolves; scowling hyenas; carrion crows; big spotted cats; men with dog faces and four paws instead of hands and feet; creatures half moth and half woman with soft gray wings and wicked sharp teeth; a cloud of wasps; slumbering snakes in coils and layers; furred spiders with faceted eyes; owls; and rank upon rank of bats with folded-up wings. Did they sleep, or were they suspended by the power of the ice?

"You can't hate me because you do not know me nor do you know anything of me." His voice's timbre was limned with an indifference so supreme it was like asking the sun what it thought of you and receiving no answer. "You are a mortal creature bound and ruled by the tides and currents of the Deathlands. The tide that surges through you, you name as hate because you have no other way to describe it. But you need not remain bound and ruled by the tides that govern other creatures. How do you cross between the worlds?"

His question compelled my answer. "With my blood."

"In the Deathlands, in what ways can you weave the threads that bind the worlds?"

"I can see in the dark. I can hear exceptionally well. I can conceal myself."

"What is your name?"

I gritted my teeth in stubborn resistance, sinking to sit on my heels as I pressed my right hand to the locket. Its heartening pulse rose and fell like my father's breathing when as a young child I had sat on his lap as he told me stories. I grasped my sword's hilt and thought of my mother. With my elbow I brushed the hem of my jacket, feeling the stone I had picked up from the road. I remembered what Vai's grandmother had told me: Names are power.

I pressed my lips together. Keep silence. Tell no one.

"Do not defy me. You do not have the strength. *What is your name?*"

Despite my struggle to keep them closed, my lips parted. For all my life I had been told to call myself Catherine Hassi Barahal. Yet the name his command called forth was the name Camjiata had given me, the name that linked me to the mother who bore me and the father who had chosen to raise me. "Catherine Bell Barahal."

A black fleck like ash flickered in those blank bright eyes. "Now your name is mine, and you are mine. You are both my offspring and my servant, obedient to me because you are part of me, bone of my bone and blood of my blood. I will tell you this one thing, Catherine Bell Barahal. I admired your mother. Tara Bell was a female strong of will, with the strength of iron, and with the heart to accept fear but not succumb to it. You are like her. What I did not understand until later was that she harbored a reckless disobedience deep in her heart. But I now understand better how chains bind the vulnerable. In the end, she agreed to all I demanded because she was a slave to the threads that bound her to other creatures."

I thought of my mother, tall and strong, a loyal Amazon in Camjiata's army, sworn to celibacy. On an expedition to explore the Baltic Ice Sheet, under the light of the aurora borealis, she had debated with Daniel Hassi Barahal, using words as a form of flirtation, maybe even courtship.

To honor her, I stood. "No one knows what happened during that expedition, just that most of them died and a very few survived. I can only think of one way to interpret what you've just said. You trapped them somehow, on the ice, maybe even in the spirit world. She agreed to have sexual congress with you to save the lives of the others. She did it to save my father's life, because she loved him."

"That male did not father you."

"He fathered me in every way that counts. You only sired me." My voice rasped with unshed tears, thinking of what my mother had agreed to, and how she must have loved me anyway and risked her life and everything she knew to make a life for me. Had Daniel known? Or had she borne this secret alone, hoping the hunter might forget both her and the child? I would never know.

"That you are as you are is a gift that comes from me only. You must be what I made you to be. Forged like cold steel out of many layers, you are strong, resilient, and able to adapt in a moment's reaction."

"What do you want from me?"

He extended an arm. The crow hopped from its perch to tighten its claws over the bronzed muscles of his forearm. I thought the tips of those claws drew blood, but because of the way the crow's shadow—the only shadow my light could not dispel— fell across his body, I could not be certain.

"I want you to spy for me, Daughter."

I am not a young woman who craves attention or draws notice to herself through dramatic gestures or heedless bravado. But I admit it. I laughed.

"To spy for you! That would be no hardship for a person of my background and training. But I'm sure there's a hook in the bargain that is about to catch in my lip."

"You may address me as 'Your Serenity,' or 'my prince.' Or as 'Father.'"

"Are you mocking me?" I demanded.

"No, I am suggesting it would be both prudent and wise for you to show respect for your master and procreator."

"I have never been told I am prudent or wise. But I suppose I could address you as 'Sire.'"

He betrayed no reaction to my impertinent words and sardonic tone. But the turtle came alive, head easing out from the shell as its eyes opened to look toward me with an unfathomable gaze. My sire tapped it on the head, and it withdrew again. He clapped his hands twice.

Ice smoked over between two of the toads. Within an alcove, a stout man who had no head sat upright on a bench. Two dripping-wet women clothed only in long hair the oil-brown color of seaweed pressed to either side of him. The headless man lurched up, shedding the females leeched to him. With the shuffling gait of a blind man in a strange room, he carried over a tray with two glasses on it. He paused in front of me, and I took a step back, for I had a sudden fear that he might grope me, and I was sure I would scream if he did. He wore a patched tunic with trews beneath, calves bound with cord over soft leather summer boots. Rings adorned his fingers. A buttery-gold torc spanned his neck, whose severed trunk oozed greasily, as if it had never quite healed but could not quite bleed.

"Drink with me to seal our bargain," said my sire.

"I dare not drink or eat what is served to me in the spirit world lest some property within trap me further."

"Take the cup, Catherine Bell Barahal."

My hand took a cup. It was filled with an amber liquid. The headless serving man carried the tray over to my sire, who plucked the other glass from it. The headless man shuffled back over to the bench. The water spirits clutched at him. Their clinging seemed obscene, for while their hair in streaks concealed most of their bodies, what made the display so disturbing was that, beneath his trews, the man was visibly and powerfully aroused. Dear me. Blushing, I looked away to examine the carpets on which I stood, many layers strewn haphazardly across the floor as if to cover a mighty stain seeping upward.

No, this was not helping at all.

Mastering myself, I looked toward my sire. By now my clothes were half dry, my skin coated with a sticky salt grime, and my hair lifting away from my neck in knotted tangles as it dried. I was exhausted—that went without saying although naturally, as Bee would have commented, I would have mentioned it anyway—but I was no longer frozen and disheartened. He hadn't smitten me yet.

"Is that Bran Cof, the poet? The one you torment?"

He sipped at the amber wine as if considering its taste or my faults.

"Are the creatures who sleep in the ice your slaves? Or do they serve you willingly out of their own natures?"

Despite his silence, I was beginning to get the impression that my bold manner amused him.

"Does the Wild Hunt hunt at your pleasure, or for some other purpose?"

"Does no one teach the law these days?" he said mockingly. "Let me educate you, little cat. On Hallows' Night, the Wild Hunt rides into the Deathlands. It culls the spirits of those who will die in the coming year. I am sure you already know the story. The hunt rides on the night of sundering because that is its nature and its purpose."

I bowed my head, for I remembered the story my father had told me long ago about the Wild Hunt and a young hunter who had sought and found the other half of his soul. I remembered the day I had escaped from Four Moons House, when I'd heard a horn's call on Hallows' Eve rising out of the earth like mist and filtering down from the sky like rain. That call had penetrated my bones and my blood and my heart. No one fated to die in the coming year could escape the hunt.

"But that is not the only reason the Wild Hunt rides. Blood, Daughter. We must have blood. One mortal life feeds the courts for a year. The stronger the blood, the richer the feast."

"The day court and the night court," I whispered. "That's what they're called."

"All serve the courts," he agreed.

"The enemy doesn't serve them."

Movement stirred in the ice, and I realized I had gone too far. An owl swooped out of the empty air to settle on the perch. Its golden eyes chained me. I fell into the rip current of its gaze.

I was trapped in the banded, breathing heart of the ice. It was as cold as death and as heavy as the weight of an ice shelf groaning down to crush one fragile human heart. Beneath winter's aching cold lies a deeper cold that leaches blood and heat into a vessel where stolen sparks can be shaped into more obedient forms.

"The ice is alive. Not as you and I are alive. It's not a creature or a person. But it lives, although I couldn't tell you how or why." The recollection of Brennan Du's words roused me.

I had been standing. Now, as if I had been brutally hammered by the power of a cold mage's anger, I found myself on hands and knees although I had no memory of falling. I had dropped the cup, and it had rolled an arm's length away.

I inhaled hard, air hit my lungs, and the dizzy whirling dread subsided.

Until I looked up to his masked face.

"The blood of the enemy is poison," he murmured, as if he had once sipped it. "But the enemy found a way to enter our world through mortal hands, through the females who walk the tide of dreams. So must the courts enter the mortal world likewise, through mortal flesh. You will go to a place in the Deathlands that is surrounded by the Taninim, they who rule the seas. You can reach there because of the flesh you wear that you inherited from your mother's blood and bone."

Did "surrounded by the Taninim" mean an island? Was it possible the Wild Hunt could not reach islands? Or only one particular place? I knew better than to ask such a question directly.

"Sire, you already have servants who walk in the mortal world. Like the eru and coachman who brought me here. They pretend to serve the mage Houses, but they are really there to spy on the cold mages, aren't they? To make sure no magister becomes too powerful a threat?"

Had he not been wearing a mask, I would have guessed he smiled, yet it would have been a smile one could not wish to see on a face. "Cold mages serve the courts without knowing they do. They comprehend in an attenuated way the power of the courts and do their best to avoid the Wild Hunt's notice. They understand that if they spread their net of power too widely or grasp at too much, the courts smell a scent of power, and the Wild Hunt is unleashed to hunt them down."

"That's a clever way to control the power of the cold

mages," I agreed with what I hoped was a smile of rueful admiration, preparing my flattery in order to attempt a leading question.

"Do not play false with me, Daughter. I can smell it."

To give myself a moment to think, I picked up the cup. It had not lost a single drop of the amber wine. "How shall we communicate while I am in the Deathlands? Can you see through my eyes and speak through my mouth?"

"Ah. You've pleased me with a clever question instead of an impertinent one. No. Your mother's flesh blinds me to you except on Hallows' Day. I will send my servants if I need to speak with you."

My heart's pulse thundered in my ears as a sense of relief flooded me. Well, then. Once I left this hall, he could not oversee or control my actions. Yet perhaps he was hiding a hook. "If that's so, why send me? Why not send your other servants?"

"By your service, you shall receive answers. Until then, you will simply obey."

He raised his cup to his lips, gaze on me; my hand raised my cup to my lips. Without drinking, he lowered his hand; without drinking, I lowered mine. I had to; his will forced me.

"You take my point," he said. "We have reached a turning in the path. A power stirs in the mortal world. It pours from one vessel into another, and its motion churns and heats and cools the threads that bind the worlds. The courts whisper, for they are troubled. Has a cold mage reached too far and grasped for too much? Does an unknown power rise out of the lair of the enemy? This is your task: Find that power, identify it, and lead me to it, on the coming Hallows' Night."

My heart constricted. Or at least, that's what the tightening sensation in my chest felt like. I touched my chin, where Andevai had cut me with cold steel. I knew what it was to discover, too late, that you have been chosen to be the sacrifice.

"Why should I betray anyone, when I know it means you'll kill them?" I demanded.

"On Hallows' Night, the Wild Hunt will ride, as it does every year. We will cull the spirits of those who will die in the coming year. And we will take the blood of one mortal creature. Why should you find that power, identify it, and lead me to it? Because otherwise I will choose which mortal's blood we take. My eyes and ears have followed you and your companions, Daughter. I know you walked into the spirit world with a servant of the enemy. She walked in these lands and released a nest. My own servants should not have allowed her to escape, but their actions serve me regardless. You will spy out a fitting sacrifice, one whose blood is rich and strong. Because if you don't, then on Hallows' Night the hunt will track the girl you call your cousin until we corner her."

Dismembered and her head thrown in a well.

I felt my courage flayed off my skin, an obsidian dagger slicing away filaments of hope.

Oh, Blessed Tanit. Gracious Melqart. Noble Ba'al. The threat of mage Houses, princes, and Romans hunting her through Adurnam seemed pathetic now. The mansa had been right, hadn't he? We should have gone with the cold mages, for then none of this would have happened.

None of this would have happened *now*. But the Wild Hunt would track her down eventually, if not this year, then the next. It was only a matter of time for Beatrice Hassi Barahal, who walked the dreams of dragons in the unwitting service of the courts' enemy. No one could stand against the Wild Hunt. No one. Unless the story was true that the headmaster had snatched his assistant from the jaws of the hunt. Yet he had sent Bee into the spirit world, despite its dangers.

"Let me repeat myself, so you fully understand me." The Master of the Wild Hunt did not need to shout. His voice pierced me to the bone and crushed my heart. "There can only be one sacrifice. And there *will* be one. That is the law."

So he settled his chains on me, for there was no one to help us, and no one to trust.

I'll do anything to save her.

Anything.

Would Bee forgive me when I did?

"Now we seal our bond with a drink, Daughter. Pick up the glass."

He drank, and therefore I drank. The liquor tasted of bees and fate, nothing more. I hated it.

But he was satisfied.

"You serve me now. I release you to your hunt."

The crow flapped off his arm and straight for me. As I flung up my arm to fend it off, it raked me above the left ear with its talons. Pain burned along my neck. Blood welled. The crow plunged at me again. I jerked sideways, unable to fix myself on the springy ground made by the carpets. My blood spattered, flecks spraying around me.

The owl's eyes spun like time's hands racing forward. The hall of ice began to blur and distort as if it were melting. The carpets dissolved as the ground gave way beneath my feet.

I cried out as a warm wave washed over me.

Then I was drowning in a wild wind-capped sea under a hot bright blue sky.

14

I had always been too frightened of water to learn how to swim. Salt water streamed into my nose and mouth, its taste foul and warm. My feet were weighed down by my winter boots, and my legs tangled in my skirts. The salty brine caressed my face.

It's all over. Give up. Let go.

A solid object thumped into my legs. The force of its impact lifted my face above the water. I sucked for air, inhaled more water, and sank. From beneath, I was pushed up again. I breached the surface flailing while being dragged sideways by my skirts.

My hand scraped across the gray-white flank of an aquatic creature with a massive fin and dead, flat eyes. Its viciously sharp teeth were caught in my petticoats and skirt. Thrashing and mauling, it dragged me along as it tried to get its jaws out of wool and linen.

The thought of becoming supper for this monster concentrated my mind wonderfully. I fixed my hand around its fin and hauled myself over its wide body. Part of the skirt ripped free, strips of fabric fluttering like ribbons through the water. My cane caught against its teeth but did not break. I punched its eye. It peeled away more quickly than I could move.

I floundered toward a curtain of white and green and blue that bobbed above the waves. A drop of blood stained my sleeve. Had it bitten me? Oh, Gracious Melqart, let me not be bleeding to death here in the unkind sea! But then I remembered the crow tearing at me to draw blood to open the gate.

A shadow circled beneath me in the water.

My boot scraped a prominence. I braced on the excrescence as the monster streaked toward me with astonishing speed and breathtaking decisiveness. My sword was again a cane, so it was no use. As the cursed monstrous fish drove in with its maw widening, I fisted a hand.

Look for the opening. Do not flinch.

I punched its snout. The impact sent me floating back. To stop myself I dug my boots in among the knobs of the underwater shelf. The monster sheared away. I stood with head and chest above the wind-whipped wavelets. Land lay a short swim away through waters more green than blue: a long stretch of white sandy shoreline backed by lushly green trees swaying in a strong wind. Above, the hard bold blue of the heavens spanned existence. Was that the peak of a tower jutting above the trees to the right?

Two shapes moved out of the trees. Human shapes. People!

Blessed Tanit! I might be saved if I could just reach land!

I scanned the waves but spied no gliding predator. Kicking and stroking, I paddled clumsily through the water until my boots touched sand. I did look back then, but saw nothing except a school of fish flashing away. As I walked out of the sea, water streamed from my hair. My skirts and petticoats wrapped in tatters against my legs.

I dropped to my knees on cool white sand as fine as

the sugar we tasted at festival days. The warmth of the wool riding jacket toasted my skin, making heat prickle down my arms and across my back. I fumbled with the buttons and yanked it off. My tightly laced linen bodice and the loose linen shift plastered my body. Sucking in air made me retch. I coughed up seawater and my dreams and hopes and fears until my throat was raw. But I was pretty sure I was going to live.

Two people limped toward me across the beach, a male in front and a female behind. He wore a dirty sleeveless shirt and loose trousers unraveling at the hems. She had on a patterned skirt tied around her hips and a loose, sleeveless shirt that exposed her brown arms from shoulder to hand, a sight rarely seen in Adurnam except in high summer.

As the man lurched up, I rose warily and spoke in a friendly way but without cringing.

"Greetings of the day to you, Maester. Maestressa. Salvete."

He extended a hand in the radicals' manner of greeting.

I reached out in answer, and only then did I think to wonder why his skin had an ashen cast instead of being brown and healthy; only then did I notice the dead, flat shine of his eyes.

He grabbed my wrist and yanked me toward him.

The woman screamed.

And he bit me.

He bit me.

I shrieked. I kicked him in the knee hard enough to topple him as I yanked my arm out of his grasp. I freed my cane and began pounding him over the head and shoulders. Yet he kept trying to get up. He grasped for me with my blood on his lips, smacking them together as if I were water and he parched.

"Let up! Let up, yee!" The woman stumbled to a halt out of range of my cane, holding her side as if winded. She was my age, with black hair twisted into locks and dusted with sand.

I leaped back, cane raised. She crouched beside the man. My blood smeared his hand, and he started licking it.

From the direction of the barely-seen tower, a high sweet bell tolled over the island like a warning call.

"He *bit* me!" He had bitten right through the sleeve of my undershift just below my elbow, leaving a tattered edge.

She jerked her chin sideways, and the spasmed blink of her brown eyes made me recoil. "Reckon yee wait. Dey come quick."

My blood spotted the sand. When I glanced toward the green-blue sea, I was sure I saw a finned shadow churn the depths. I raised my bitten arm toward my lips.

She said, "Yee don' want a touch dat. Let dey behiques suck it. Or yee become he."

"I don't understand you."

"Where yee hail from, maku?"

She had a firm grip on the man's ankle. He was *sniffing* the air and groping toward me, but she was strong enough to hold him down.

A greasy slime of fear slid right down my spine. "What's wrong with him?"

"He a salter."

"A salter? Like *salt plague*?" I reeled backward. His dead flat eyes skimmed over me, looking not at me but at what lay beneath my skin: my hot, pumping, salt-laden blood. "Are you saying he's riddled with the salt plague? The salt plague which makes your mind and body rot? The salt plague for which there is *no cure*?"

"Owo," she said, which meant *yes* in one of the Mande languages.

The urge to retch rose so strongly I ran to the shade where vegetation probed the sterile sands. On hands and knees among the stiff-leafed plants I vomited up bile. My arm throbbed as if hot needles had been jabbed into my flesh and were engaged in a frantic dance aided by a swarm of impatient wasps. His flat, mindless gaze, as dull as an imbecile's and less cunning. His lurching gait. The salt plague ate your body and your brain. There was no cure, no palliative, no hope, only a slow deterioration into living death.

The thud of footsteps made a counter-rhythm to the fear and pain drumming in my head. Maybe I was going to die, but I wasn't dead yet. I shoved myself up. Figures swam into my vision.

"Salve. Salve, Perdita."

Greetings, lost woman. The formal Latin soothed my ears.

A person moved toward me with palms outstretched in the sign of peace. "By Jupiter Magnus! It *is* Catherine Bell Barahal. How in the unholy hells you got here I cannot imagine."

I brandished my cane. I wasn't going to get bitten again. "Don't come closer. I'll kill you."

"Catherine Bell Barahal. Look at me. We've met before."

Five people stood in a cunning circle around me, so I couldn't bolt. Behind, still on the beach with the sun's glare washing their skin to the color of rotting corpses, the young woman was tugging on the thing that had bit me, trying to drag it away as it strained toward me. Three men and two women faced me. Four of the strangers were foreign. They had thick straight black hair very like my own and they looked a little like Rory but a lot more like someone else entirely: broad across the cheeks with high, flat foreheads and deep-set brown eyes, fit and healthy. In fact, they looked like people, nothing like the lurching man-thing that had bitten me. At least the monster in the water had been terrible in its perfectly awful beauty. Wouldn't it have been better if it had killed me and I'd bled my life away in the water?

Blessed Tanit! I was going to die in the most horrible way imaginable.

My knees gave way. First I was standing and then I was on the ground.

One of the men crouched beside me, out of range of my cane.

"Catherine," he said in a quiet voice. "I'm not a salter. Hold out your arm."

His calm tone convinced me to hold out my arm. A woman upended a vessel. Salt water poured over the wound. I must have yelped, but all I could hear was the pain.

"You're faint. Drink this."

I was dead anyway so if he meant to poison me it would be preferable to die quickly instead of slowly. He handed me a hollowed-out gourd and unsealed its cork. I lifted its rim to my mouth. A sweet liquor with the kick of strong alcohol coursed down my throat. I began to chug it, until one of the women spoke curtly, and the speaker took hold of my undamaged wrist and stayed me.

"Wait. Let it settle. Then you can have more."

Its searing after-bite blasted along my throat. Finally

he came into focus. He had hair the reddish-gold color commonly seen in western Celtic tribes who had not mixed with Roman legionnaires and the Mande refugees from the empire of Mali.

"You were with Camjiata," I whispered. "In the law offices."

"That's right. I'm James Drake. You do remember me?"

The liquid churned in my belly. I broke into a sweat. "Was that man a salter who bit me?"

"Stay calm." He spoke to the others. By their voices, it seemed they were haggling.

"My mind must be rotting already," I cried. "I can't understand a word you're saying."

They came to a grudging consensus. The others moved off, taking the creature and the young woman with them. For some reason, the creature did not attack them.

"That's because we're speaking Taino," he said, turning back to me. "It's the common language in these parts. Drink up. It's the local drink. It's called rum."

I drained the vessel. The liquor cleansed my mouth; it numbed and dazzled, spiking straight to my head. "Will rum cure me?"

"No. Rum can't cure the salt plague. The seawater has flooded his saliva away. But I want to wash the bite again. You have to come with me. Please put the sword back in your belt. No need to wave it around."

The sight of the jagged tooth marks bruising my forearm and the blood leaking sluggishly along my skin made me clumsy. I fumblingly fastened the cane to its loop. With a hand pressed to my back, he steered me to a sandy path that led into the trees. Birds clamored in a brazen assault on my ears. Where it was bright the sun was a lance piercing my eyes and where it was shadowed the earth was a monstrous presence trying to devour me. I could not get my balance despite my companion's solicitous hand and respectful silence although I would have liked it better if he had talked to drown out my whirlpooling terror.

We came to a clearing around a circular pool filled to the brim with water as intensely blue as James Drake's eyes. Next to the pool rose an unwalled shelter, just a roof thatched with dried fronds that shaded a table and bench. He sat me on the bench and gave me a second gourd of rum.

"What's this for if it won't cure me?"

"It's to numb the pain and the fear. We don't know each other, Cat Barahal, but you're going to have to trust me."

"Why does it matter if I trust you? I'm going to die. There's no cure, and every bitten person dies." Shaking, I took a long swallow of the rum. It was better than thinking.

A pot and several baskets hung under the eaves. He took down the pot, filled it with water, and hung it from a tripod. Then he put his hand on the wood beneath it. His lips parted, and flames curled up.

"You're a fire mage," I said, intelligently I am sure. I was finding it challenging to put words together because, between the rush of alcohol and fear to my brain, words wriggled away as soon as I had them in sight. "But fire mages all burn up when their fire runs out of control. Unless they learn the secrets of the blacksmiths." I pressed my fingers to my brow, trying to reel in my scattering thoughts lest I start babbling secrets. "That drink went straight to my head."

He came over, caught my chin with a hand, and looked me over carefully. "My apologies. I'm going to have to ask you to kiss me."

"Kiss you!"

He offered a rueful smile. "As you so astutely observed, I'm a fire mage. If I press my lips to yours, the contact will allow me to know if the teeth of the salt plague have gotten into your blood."

"Because you're a fire mage, you can tell if I'm infested with the salt plague if you kiss me?"

"That's right. And if I catch it quickly enough, I might be able to heal you."

"Heal me!" I sucked in a shocked breath, mouth parted, heart pounding, blood pulsing through my veins and horrible, horrible death spreading through my blood. "Don't mock me. There's no cure."

"In Europa they believe there's no cure. Here in the Antilles, we know better. Healing is one of the gifts of fire mages. There are certain diseases we can heal by killing them within you before they kill you."

If he was lying, I was no worse off than before. But what if he was telling the truth!

I leaned into him, and I kissed him on the mouth. He returned the kiss decisively, his lips warm at first, and then his kiss turned hotter until its heat coursed like sun through my body. I forgot I was dying and felt quite astoundingly alive.

He released me abruptly.

Panting, I sank back, hands propped behind me on the bench to hold me up. I was very confounded, warm and tingling all over. The liquor was making my head swim.

He stared at me as intently as if he saw something odd.

My bodice had been pulled askew, exposing half of my left breast. Blushing, I straightened the cloth. I could not catch my breath, and there was a part of me that badly wanted to kiss him again, as if his kiss or his magic had roused a slumbering beast within me.

He carefully eased my torn sleeve back and with a finger traced the bite mark. The jagged wound had gone pink at the edges, with ragged clots of darkening blood and clear oozing plasma. "It broke the skin."

"Can't you help me?" I whispered. I grabbed for the gourd of rum and drained the last of it.

"I can't quite tell... but if I had your permission to try again..."

Why not? The last thing I wanted now was to be alone. When I nodded, he caught me close with another kiss. He was fire, and I burned into the core of me because I was being caressed by tendrils of sweet flame along my skin, and within my skin, and against my lips. Was this fire magic? For as it twined through my body, I wanted nothing more than to run my hands along his back and do more of this kissing; much more; much, much more. He broke off the kiss.

"Cat! Your claws are out." He grinned. "Desire suits you. You're all flushed."

"I was bitten by a dying man with a rotted mind. Of course I'm flushed!" I was sure my bosom was heaving, because I still couldn't catch my breath. "Can you really heal me? You're not just saying that to take advantage of me? Offering me one chance to live before I die?"

His gaze narrowed, as if a spark of anger flared in his eyes. Drawing back, he released my arm. "Is that what you think this is? Let me tell you a few things about the salt plague. If a person is bitten by a salter, that person will become infested with what we call the teeth of the ghouls. They're so tiny they are hidden from sight. At first, the bitten victim is harmless to others. But inside, they're slowly deteriorating as the infestation grows within their blood. On the day the infestation flowers, they forget everything they ever knew except that they have to drink warm, living blood because their own is dried up. Now they bite. It's all they live for. It's all they know. In time, they become like salt, unmoving. Morbid. Worse than dead, for they crave and can never be satisfied, trapped in a pain-wracked, paralyzed body."

"Stop! Please, stop!"

He softened. Pressing a finger under my chin, he held my gaze. "Cat, you have one chance. You've been bitten. But the teeth of the ghouls haven't yet caught in your blood. If I can burn out all the teeth before they catch and hook in your blood, then you won't become a salter. But we have to do it right now. It's like a snake's venom. I have to burn it out before it's too late to stop it."

The water he had set over the fire was boiling. I heard its burbling chatter, and the titter of birds in the trees, and the pulse of the sky like blood in my ears. My head floated as on clouds.

"Of course I want to be healed! Why are you waiting?"

His lips lifted into a faint smile as he brushed a hand lightly along my shoulder, pulling the fabric of my shift down just enough to expose the curve of a shoulder. Where his fingers touched my skin, desire purred into me. "A fire mage's healing is called the kiss of life. I have to be much, much closer to manage it. My lips to your lips. My bare skin to your bare skin, all of it. For me to find and burn out all the teeth of the ghouls swimming in your blood, there must be no barrier—none—between us. It's the only way I can heal you."

I could not think. But oh, Blessed Tanit! I wanted to live.

So I just said, "Yes."

15

I woke with my bitten arm throbbing and my hair in my mouth. Sitting up, I wiped the strands plastered across my cheek off my face so I wasn't chewing on them. The movement of my arm across my breasts made me realize I was stark naked. *My bare skin to your bare skin, all of it.*

Blessed Tanit! I had really done it. And it had been pretty nice.

By the sour feeling in my stomach and the woozy way the world smiled on me, I was sure that not only had I been drunk but I was still a little drunk.

Proud Astarte! No wonder Rory behaved the way he did, wanting to be petted all the time!

I found my cane under the bench. My drawers, shift, bodice, and jacket lay discarded across the table. I sat on the ground on top of the remains of my overskirt and petticoats, spread open like unfurled wings to provide a blanket of a sort. The jagged tears in the fabric made me wonder what manner of teeth could shred tightly woven wool challis and fine linen quite so spectacularly. I brushed a leaf off my bare hip and flicked an ant off my ankle. Despite the drink, I had a clear memory of how the clothes had come off and the rest of the events had proceeded. And although I was a little sore, I otherwise felt good.

Some would have said I ought to be shamed, but I could dredge up no shame in my heart. I had done what I needed to do to save my life. Anyway, to whom was I beholden? Andevai and I had already agreed to seek a dissolution. The Hassi Barahals had sacrificed me, and the mage House did not want me nor did I want a marriage I'd been forced into. According to the ancient rites, a young Kena'ani maiden had the right to offer up her first sexual encounter to Bold Astarte in the temple precincts. So be it. I had made the offering that was mine to give.

"You might want to wash before you dress." James Drake looked up from where he crouched by the cheerful fire and the pot of hot water. I felt a blush creeping out on my skin, and he grinned. It was difficult not to smile back at a good-looking young man who admires you so openly. Especially when you've just had sexual congress with him. "Although no need to put on your clothes for my sake. Even half drowned with your hair all in tangles, you're a remarkably pretty girl."

"*You* put on clothes," I said, for he had: He wore trousers with a white shirt hanging loose over it, the sleeves rolled up to his elbows. His hands were darker than his arms; his torso, for I remembered quite a bit about his torso, had been as pale as cream. "Am I healed?"

"Do you doubt me?" He seemed a little offended. "I washed. You'd best wash, too."

I pulled on my shift and stepped out from under the shelter to consider the pool. Its sides were so round that the fathomless blue waters seemed like an eye staring heavenward.

"How deep is this pool?" I asked.

"It's a sinkhole. Around here, they say it goes down forever, into the subterranean world that is not this world but another world linked to ours."

I jumped back from the edge. *Into the spirit world.*

"You can't wash there," he added as he pulled a length of wet linen from the pot. He wrung it out as he walked over to me. "The Taino call it a sacred place."

Trembling, I accepted the blessedly hot, damp rag and washed my face and, more gingerly, the skin around the bite. "Did you really heal me?"

He took my arm and pressed his lips to the bite. A tickle of heat spread through my body.

Maybe I gasped. Maybe I sighed.

He released me with a chuckle. "You're not one bit shy. Alas, I have duties I must return to, or I assure you we'd linger awhile in the shade. However, you fell asleep and I'm in trouble already. They don't like me because I'm a *maku*. A foreigner. They despise us foreigners. You'll see."

I handed him the cloth. "But did you heal me?"

He took my chin in a hand and met my gaze with a serious one. "No taint of the plague, no teeth of the ghouls, runs in your blood. That's the truth. Avoid the pens, and don't get bitten again."

"What are pens? Where are we?"

"We're on Salt Island. Under Taino law, all salters must be held in quarantine here."

"Who are the Taino?"

"The Taino are the people who rule this entire region, all the islands of the Antilles. I'll answer the rest of your questions later at the *behica*'s table."

"What's a behica?"

"A fire mage. Like me. I warn you, she'll want to know

how you got here. Don't tell her anything. She's an impatient, grasping sort of woman. Like all Taino nobles, she has a great sense of her self-importance. Do me a favor and don't mention we met in Adurnam. I promise to explain why later. Now I really have to go. Here is Abby. She'll find you a pagne and a blouse."

"What's a pagne?" I saw the girl from the beach lurching toward us through the trees along the sandy path. I was being abandoned to the care of a stranger. "Can't I come with you, James?"

With his gear in his arms, he kissed me on the cheek. "We'll be together later. Call me Drake. Everyone does."

He set off down the path. Passing the girl, he spoke phrases that sounded like a forgotten tartan of Celtic, Mande, and Latin, the cadences a different music from the melody I was used to.

The girl limped up. She ventured an awkward smile, as if she wasn't used to smiling and thought perhaps she had forgotten how. "Yee want a bath and cloth."

"Is your name Abby?"

"I have dat name Abby. Yee have dat name Cat'reen?" A dapple of sunlight through leaves caught on her face to give her dark eyes an odd gleam as she looked down the path to make sure Drake was out of earshot. "Dat maku heal yee?"

"Can he really heal people?" I held my breath.

She wheezed in a breath, as if at a stab of pain, and let it out. "All *behiques* have dat power. He one, even if he a maku."

"A maku is a foreigner. A behique or a behica is a fire mage. Is that right?"

She scratched her nose, sorting through my foreign way of speaking. "Dat right. *Na*." Come.

She limped away down the path. I drew on my drawers and laced up my bodice, then gathered everything else and hurried after her. It was not, I reasoned, that she was unfriendly. But even the most generous soul might envy a gift of priceless worth granted to a stranger that has, even if by chance, been denied to a friend, if the man on the beach was indeed her friend.

"Drake told me we're on Salt Island. In the Sea of Antilles, which is the sea that lies between North and South Amerike. Is that right?" She threw a bewildered glance at me, and a knife cut my heart, for I felt I was bullying her without knowing why. "It doesn't matter. How pretty it is here!"

The shadows drew long as we emerged from the trees and walked along a shoreline where vegetation met a sandy white beach. It was really quite beautiful, and it would have been even more beautiful if it had not been so cursedly hot. I was sweating even though dressed only in undergarments that, in Adurnam, would embarrass a prostitute to be seen wearing in a public venue. The path wound up a headland. Birds dove in squalls. A turtle flipped sideways and skimmed away. The water was so clear I could see every stone and fish beneath the surface against shimmering stretches of sand.

In my boots, my feet felt swollen. Abby walked barefoot. An iron-gray lizard with a lacy frill and a pouchy throat sunned itself atop a rock, watching me with the grave disinterest of an elder.

"I'm going to melt," I informed it as I trudged past. "I have never been so hot in my life. How do you stand it?"

It did not blink. Nor did it answer.

The bell rang as we crested the prow of the headland. I walked in Abby's wake down into a pretty half-moon bay with a fine curved beach that faced east. A ring of houses set on low stilts formed a circle around a grassy central plaza distinguished by a circular earth platform. North of the plaza lay a long dirt field fenced by straight stone walls on either side. To the west, in the shadow of a forested ridge, sat roofed cages surrounded by an impressively tall iron fence.

Kitchen gardens stretched between the houses; there a few figures toiled, in no hurry. Beyond, the forest ruled except for several clearings marked by mounds planted with dusty green vines and young fruit trees. A stream sparkled down from the ridge to spill into the bay.

My thoughts scattered every which way as I slapped down the steep path into the settlement. What would Bee say when I told her? *"Really, Cat, did you fall for that tired excuse? 'Fornicate with me and you will be healed'? Or was he so irresistible?"*

But I smiled anyway. I felt cut loose from my old moorings. I might be frightened, miserable, and overheated, but I was also unbound.

My smile vanished. Never unbound. My sire's command was the noose around my neck. His magic had thrown me onto a shore where fire mages dwelled. That was surely no coincidence. Was this why he had wanted me to come to the Sea of Antilles where the Taino ruled? How powerful were these fire mages called behiques? Did the sea hide them from him? Or was it possible that on an island in a hot climate there was no ice from which he could launch his spies?

Abby halted at the verge of a garden plot and kneaded her feet in newly-turned earth. She took my hand in a sisterly way. "Yee safe now, Cat'reen. No need for such a frown."

"Are those the pens?" I asked, indicating the cages. Their thatched roofs and lattice walls made it difficult to see inside. Figures shifted like animals in stalls.

She winced, let go of my hand, and began walking. We skirted the central plaza, kicking up sand. Gracious Melqart, but there was sand everywhere in this place! Its grit rubbed my neck. Grains rubbed between my toes.

Abby led me to one of the round houses. Behind it, tall screens woven of reeds shielded a copper tub, four empty buckets, and soap. We hauled water from the stream to fill the tub, by which time I was sweating so foully I was glad to immerse myself in cold water. I scrubbed my skin, washed my hair, and rinsed myself off with water Abby kept bringing, for she seemed tireless. After I washed my clothes, I hung the clothing over the screens to dry.

"As I thought, you clean up wonderfully." Drake stepped within the screens, looking me up and down so boldly I was not sure whether to be flattered or shocked. I had never been admired so brazenly before, for men in Adurnam would flirt with women but not maul them with their gaze. Andevai, who had after all claimed to have fallen in love with me at first sight, had certainly stared rudely at me and said things to me in the most arrogant way imaginable, but I could not help but think he would never look me over the way a hungry dog eyes a slab of meat.

"I would think a man would ask permission first before stepping into a woman's bathing chamber," I said, lifting my chin. I refused to humiliate myself by trying to cover bits of my body with my hands, especially since he had seen all of me anyway.

"My apologies. You just can't know how unexpected this all is for me. You here, like this." A smile played on his lips. "Anyway, out in the Taino kingdom, outside Expedition Territory, young unmarried women commonly go about their daily business wearing little more than you are right now. Here." He tossed me a rolled-up piece of cloth.

"But I'm naked!" I shook out a piece of bright yellow fabric printed with orange and red shell patterns, and wrapped it around my breasts and hips like a shield of modesty. "What am I to do with this? If you've sewing scissors and a needle and thread I can fashion a—"

"That's your pagne. The women of Expedition wear it as a skirt, with a blouse. You definitely need to cover yourself. You're darker than I am, but the sun can still burn you."

"Expedition is a famous trading and technological city in the Sea of Antilles. This village can't be Expedition."

"As I told you, this is Salt Island. Where salters are quarantined."

"How soon can I leave, now that I'm healed?"

He met my gaze and, oddly, looked away. He had a pleasing profile, with a narrow chin and sharp features. He wore a cap to shade his face, but even so his nose and cheeks were freckled from the sun. "We'll talk later. Abby will bring you supper."

"No supper at the behica's table, with you?" My voice faltered.

"I'm sorry, Cat. I shouldn't have mentioned that before. You're not allowed to eat with her and especially you're not allowed to eat with the *cacique*'s nephew."

"What's a cacique?"

"The cacique is the ruler—we might say king—of the Taino. The Taino have very strict laws. For instance, all fire mages in the Taino kingdom are required to serve periodically on Salt Island. So are any fire mages who live in Expedition Territory."

"Wait. Does that mean Expedition Territory is part of the Taino kingdom?"

"No. Expedition is a free territory, on the island of Kiskeya. The rest of the island is part of the Taino kingdom. Expedition's Council requires all local fire mages to serve here for a season every few years. We're the only people who can live with and guard salters without risk of getting infested with the plague. That's why I'm here. While we're on Salt Island, we serve under the command of whichever Taino behique is eldest. In this case, a woman."

"So behique is male and behica is female."

"Yes. Listen, Cat, if you run into her, there are a few things you must know. Never speak to her unless she addresses you first. Don't speak to the cacique's nephew at all. He is a fire mage newly kindled and thus frightfully dangerous because he can't control his power. And he's terribly highborn. He is one of the possible heirs to the cacique's honorable duho, the seat of power. The throne."

"That means he could be cacique someday."

"That's right. The old bitch has come here to train him. Bear all that in mind. I'm off to supper. I'll come by after. That is, if you're minded to speak to me. The truth is"— his startlingly blue gaze bored into me—"you were irresistible beyond any question of healing you."

I could not resist his smile. "Well, if that's what you call 'speaking.'"

He chuckled. "I never quite expect pretty girls to possess wit as well."

By the time I had decided I could not tell if he was teasing me or insulting me, he had walked away. Abby stepped into view, watching him go with a frown. But when she turned to see me trying to tie the cloth, she laughed in a delightful way and showed me how to tuck and fix the fabric to make an ankle-length skirt. I pulled on my damp shift as a blouse.

We stowed tub and buckets in a lean-to. Inside the single room of the house, baskets hung from the rafters and what looked like a pair of fishing nets were strung lengthwise under beams. A bronze pot half filled with water sat in a wire stand, with a pitcher hanging from a hook and a basin tucked beneath. Otherwise, there was no furniture. She unrolled a mat woven from rushes and, after a hesitation, I sat on it.

"Yee wait. I get food." She went out.

Waiting, hungry, I brooded with my cane across my crossed legs, fingering my locket. Where was Bee? Had she returned safely to Adurnam? Had she found Rory? Touching the locket made me think of Andevai, who had returned it to me. I still had the sard stone. In a strange way, I felt I was saving it for him, and yet the likelihood I would see him again seemed small. I could not be sure if I was relieved or sad at the thought.

From nearby, voices erupted into an argument. It took no great acumen to guess it was Drake at odds with the behica and her noble pupil. Fire mages, all. Including one newly kindled. Was the cacique's nephew the *power* my sire had spoken of? Was he, highborn and superior and a foreigner, a man I might hand over in place of Bee without feeling the shame of treachery? Yet fire mages could not become truly powerful, not like cold mages. Wake too much fire, and the fire consumed you.

I hated my sire all over again. To save Bee, I was going to have to hand someone else over in her place. Just as my aunt and uncle had done, when they had given me to

Four Moons House. For the first time, I felt a tremor of sympathy for their dilemma.

"Cat'reen?"

My eyes flew open. Abby set down a tray.

"Will you eat with me?" I asked, but she lifted her chin to indicate the negative.

I was ravenous. I choked down four flat grilled rounds that were more cracker than bread. Succulent yams had been baked to perfection with tiny red vegetables whose taste turned my mouth to fire. I gulped down the entire cup of smoky brown liquid, which proved to be a mistake, because it was rum. *Slow down*, I told myself.

All this time, Abby watched me. My hazy memory of my arrival on the beach cleared like clouds parting to reveal the sun. "Are you a fire mage, Abby?"

"Ayi." No.

"How can you be safe from the salters if you're not a fire mage?"

Gracious Melqart did not spare me from being a complete ass who could not think before she spoke. There could only be one reason. Quite by instinct, I scooted away from her.

She looked down, shoulders slumping.

"Oh, Blessed Tanit," I muttered. "I'm such an idiot. I'm so sorry."

Lamplight spilled through the door. Drake entered, a lamp in one hand and a gourd bottle in the other. "Is something wrong, Cat?"

"Does Abby have the salt plague?"

Maybe it was the way the lamplight lanced through the room, but for an instant the girl looked like a dead thing, skin the wrong color, lacking the blood that gives life. She sucked in a sob.

"That was rude," Drake said. "I thought better of you, Cat. Abby's no danger to you."

"Cat'reen mean no rudeness," Abby said quickly.

I clamped my lips tight over excuses. "I was rude and thoughtless. My apologies."

He hung the lamp from a hook, caught Abby's arm, and pressed a kiss on her forehead as a father might kiss a child. "Be patient a day longer, Abby."

"I so scared," she said, and my heart cracked.

"I gave you my promise, Abby. Now go."

She shuffled out with the tray. Drake sat down beside me, unsealed the round bottle, and filled my cup with liquor. He drained the cup, then filled it again and offered it to me.

I gulped it all down, the rum smooth in my throat. "It's so horrible."

"More horrible than you know. The salt plague drove out tens of thousands of refugees from the Malian Empire and other parts of West Africa. I'm sure many died as they fled. Most went north to make new lives among Celts and Romans, for the salt plague is rare in Europa. Some say winter kills it. Some in Europa even say the plague was a good thing." He filled the cup with more rum.

"How could they say that?"

"The salt plague brought the West African Mande and the northwestern Celts together. The mages and sorcerers among the Mande and the Celts found they had a great deal in common, and thus the mage Houses were created. As these cold mages amassed power, they bound more and more villages into clientage until with the power of their magic and the power of the law, they rule like princes."

I did not want to discuss cold mages, clientage, and the

law. "Drake, Abby seemed surprised when that salter bit me. Does that mean he was in the harmless phase before and not yet biting?"

Judging by the upward quirk of his lips and eyebrows, I had surprised him. "Yes. Had you spoken to him yesterday, he would have seemed as normal as you or me except halting in speech and lame. Something kicked him into the active phase. Maybe your blood."

"I did not!" I drained the cup as if the taste could drive out the memory of the bite.

"I'm not blaming you! It's unpredictable. The harmless phase, more properly known as the infestation phase, can last days or months or in rare cases years. Yet between one breath and the next, the border is crossed. Poor Abby knows the disease is eating away at her mind and body—"

"Stop!" I grabbed the bottle out of his hand and took a slug. I had drunk too much too quickly, but I was exhausted and disoriented and hot. To think of Abby made me sick at heart.

He took the bottle with a shake of his head. "You have a tender heart."

"Much good my tears do for her! Why haven't you healed her?"

"Abby's family are plantation workers in the cane fields. It took too long to get her to a behique. Her blood was infested before they got there."

"But if a behique could do nothing, what do you think you could do now?"

Passion makes a man attractive, so the poets say, and he blazed with purpose in a way that seemed attractively admirable. "Something they don't want me to do."

"Why would they not want you to save her?"

"Do you know how dangerous fire magic is, Cat? To the fire mage, I mean."

"I'm no fire mage, but I've read that fire mages usually are consumed by their own fire." I met his gaze, realizing how close he sat beside me. "Did you risk your life to heal mine?"

He considered me in silence. Then his mouth turned down in a way that sparked my interest. He leaned back onto an elbow. "I suppose I did. I didn't think about it at the time. Anyway, under Taino law, any person bitten by a salter must be quarantined on Salt Island."

"Unless they're healed. That's what you told me."

He poured more rum. "No. Any person bitten by a salter, whether healed or infested. The law dates from the arrival of people from Europa and Africa. It was part of the original treaty that allowed the Malian fleet to set up the independent territory and city of Expedition on the island of Kiskeya. By ruthlessly enforcing the quarantine, the caciques stopped the disease—and other diseases that came with the fleet—from spreading as much as they would otherwise have done."

"Are you telling me I can't ever leave this island?"

"No, I'm telling you I have plans to get you off this island. You must keep your mouth shut about this conversation and especially about my association with Camjiata. Don't tell anyone. Be patient, like Abby. When I tell you to act, act immediately, no questions. Can you promise me that?"

"What choice do I have? Drake, what day is it?"

"The second of Augustus. As we Celts say, Lughnasad."

Seven full months had passed while I had floundered in the spirit world. Lughnasad was one of the cross-quarter days. Was that why I'd been drawn back at just this time?

"How did you get here, that you don't know what day it is?" he asked.

With a racing heart and a stab of fear, I suddenly realized I could not answer the question even had I wanted to. "How do you think people commonly arrive in the Antilles?"

He took a swig from the bottle and offered it to me. When I hesitated, he lifted it to my lips. He had a delicate touch, and the rum did calm me. "Come now, Cat. There can be no reason I could have expected to see you ever again, much less on the other side of the Atlantic Ocean from Adurnam."

I felt like a cornered rat, but I had to say something. "I was kidnapped. I ended up here."

"Floating in the sea?" He laughed. "Did you get thrown off the ship or did you jump?"

"Since I can't swim and I am terrified of water, why would you think I would jump?"

"Since I don't know, you have to tell me." He glanced heavenward and then back to me. "That's why I asked."

The secret belongs to those who remain silent, as Andevai had once said to me. "It's too painful. I'm not ready."

An expression brushed by a glimmer of impatience creased his face and vanished into a gentler smile. "When do you think you might be ready, Cat?"

Sitting in the dark house with him reclining so close beside me made the memory of our sexual congress by the pool very strong. I was adrift and restless, and I just did not want to be alone.

"Did you think it was nice?" I whispered.

For a few anxious, embarrassed breaths, I wasn't sure he had understood me.

"Ah!" A warmer smile softened his mouth.

He leaned in to kiss my lips, his moist with liquor and mine no different. I needed someone to cling to, and anyway it felt so good, even on a mat on a floor.

16

"I have to go," he said afterward, rising and pulling on his clothes. "Salters are most active at night." He lit a glass-shuttered candle set on a shelf fixed to the wall by the door. "There are centipedes and scorpions. You'd best sleep in the hammock."

Then he was gone. I barred the door as I wondered what a hammock was. The gleam offered enough illumination for me to use basin and pitcher to wash myself with water drawn from the big bronze pot. I pulled on my shift and drawers so as to be decently covered. The air inside the chamber was like hot viscous porridge. How could I possibly sleep?

Fingers scratched at the barred door. Had my heart not been firmly embedded in my chest, it would have slammed back and forth around the room like a rabbit gone wild. After the rabbit calmed down, I picked up my sword and leaned an ear against the door.

"Who is it?" I asked.

"Abby."

As my left hand tightened on the hilt, my right crept to my throat. The only sound I could get out was a soft "*Gaaah.*"

"I not here to bite yee. Mebbe after we chat."

Horribly, we both started giggling. I fumbled with the bar, set it aside, and opened the door.

She slipped in. "I don' have permission to walk out at night. They put we in di pens. Most times dat change come at night."

"Sit down. Although it's horribly hot in here."

She looked surprised. "Think yee so? If yee want, we go up a di roof."

I laced on my bodice, and she tied the pagne for me. We climbed a rope ladder and settled side by side on a ledge rimmed with a railing. I sat cross-legged with my sword across my thighs. The clouds were breaking up, mottling the sky. Waves soughed on the beach. The sound was restful until you began to wonder if the steady lift and drag of the waves was really the breathing sleep of leviathan.

"When were you bit?" I asked. "I mean, if you don't mind speaking of it."

"I don' mind. Dat bite sit on me thoughts all di time. Di teeth of di ghouls eat me."

"Are there ghouls here? I thought they only lived beneath the sands in the Sahara Desert."

"Dey behiques tell dis story. First time, di salt miners in dat place Mali broke open dat ghoul nest. Di ghouls wake and dey bite. Dey left dey teeth in di miners. Dem teeth a go eating all through every person, every man and gal dat wen bitten. One person bite another person and dey ghoul teeth keep eating on and on."

"Blessed Tanit." I took her hand in mine.

A howl like that of a beast with its leg caught in a trap rose from behind us, and fell away.

"What was that?" I am sure the hair stood up on the back of my neck.

"After di teeth eat yee mind, yee don' have no more thoughts. But mebbe for one moment yee wake up and yee remember and dat make yee scream. Don' cry, Cat'reen."

I wiped my cheeks. "It's so terrible."

"I mean, yee tears have salt." I felt her lick her lips, as if she wanted to lick my cheeks to taste the salt of my tears but had enough control to restrain herself.

With an effort, I kept hold of her hand and did not shift away. "If Drake can heal you, why hasn't he done so already?"

She remained silent for a long time. He had kissed her forehead, so it wasn't as if he recoiled from touching her. Far out over the sea, a light winked and vanished. Perhaps it was the lamp of the moon shining on the water, for where the clouds shredded away at the zenith, a quarter moon watched. Under its light, Abby's skin took on a peculiar crystalline gleam, and her eyes showed no irises, only a flat white circle.

"I don' like dat dis man Drake decide so quick to make yee he sweet gal."

"I said yes! He didn't force me, if that's what you mean." A certain giddiness, and the rum, still warmed my flesh. Yet a new uneasiness crept like gossipy whispers along my ears. Now that I was no longer terrified and disoriented, it seemed unlikely that the only way for a fire mage to heal someone was to have sexual congress with them. Had I mistaken his words? Because I certainly hadn't mistaken his intentions. "He told me that to heal me he had to touch my skin with his."

Startlingly, she laughed. "Di kiss of life. We call it by dat name. But I reckon dat maku give yee di kiss of life and den take a little something more."

"Bold Astarte!" I muttered. *A little something more.*

Abby patted my arm. "Dem fire mages reckon dey can take what dey want. So he tell you dat, and den he get you drunk and he take it all. I don' like it."

"Oh," I whispered. "Was I an idiot?"

"Not a bit like dat, Cat'reen!" Her quiet compassion shamed me, for in the midst of her own terror she had opened her heart to feel for me. "If dat man said so to me, right after I got bit, I a done di same as yee for dat chance he heal me. But I don' like it."

I leaned against her as I often leaned against Bee, and her smile was all the gift I could ask for.

Out of the darkness, a male voice spoke.

"Salve, Perdita."

Abby hid her face behind crossed hands in an awkward genuflect. I looked over the railing to see two figures standing below. One was a stocky adolescent wearing as ornament a blocky stone collar. The other was a man perhaps ten years older than me with impressively heavy gold armbands on his bare upper arms and a gold pendant around his neck. He was dressed in white cloth draped over his body something in the manner of a Roman toga. He looked oddly familiar, and not just because I thought he was one of the mages I had faced on the beach.

"I intend to speak with you. I will climb up so we may have privacy." The man spoke in a formal Latin whose antiquated flavor heightened the princely expectation that he was not asking but telling me.

Abby quivered but did not speak.

I had faced down the Master of the Wild Hunt with his evil crows, monstrous toads, frozen minions, and masked face. For that matter, I had dealt with Andevai Diarisso

Haranwy. I knew how to handle a young man who might be arrogant, vain, and besides that a bit of an ass.

"We have not been formally introduced. In my country, a proper introduction is necessary before a man and a woman who are in no other way acquainted may speak to each other. But in deference to what I am informed is your exalted station in life, I will certainly agree to speak to you as long as my companion is allowed to climb down and go on her way unmolested and unpunished."

Just as different fabrics have different textures, silence can display various qualities. In this case, I was sure that if astonishment were like rain, it would have been pouring sheets.

Yet he replied in the tone he had used before. "Your conditions prove acceptable, Perdita."

Abby's dry lips brushed my cheek, and she clambered down the ladder and tottered off.

My interlocutor climbed up and crouched beside me. Straight coal-black hair fell loose down his back. His dark eyes smoldered with the suggestion of buried heat. "You have a name."

"I do have a name. You have a name as well."

He blinked, as at an unexpected drop of rain in his eye. "I have learned to speak the Europan tongue. Perhaps I speak wrongly and you do not comprehend. Your name I wish to know."

"In my country, it is usual for people to introduce their names each to the other. So if I say that my name is Catherine Bell Barahal, then you would say, 'Greetings' and afterward you would tell me by what name I can call you."

"Perdita, it is not possible for you to speak to me as one of my kin. You must address me in the proper way."

"Because you are a king's nephew? He is not my king. We have no kings in Europa."

"But many princes and generals, the histories tell. Perhaps for this reason you fight so much."

"There is no answer to that! I feel obliged to remind you that you are the one who wanted to talk to me. I mean no offense."

It seemed he had taken none, for all this time his manner had not changed. He was beginning to seem less like an arrogant and proud man and more like a reserved and formal one. "You speak with bold words. And you carry a *cemi* with you. Are you of noble birth?"

"What is a cemi?"

"It is that person you hold, who shows her power at night." He indicated the sword.

"Why do you call it a person?"

"Perhaps you have a different name. Here, we say you are accompanied by one of your ancestors. This person travels with you in the form of a three-pointed blade."

Even Andevai hadn't been able to see the sword unless I unsheathed it, but it appeared fire mages could see it at any time. "You see it as a blade?"

"A puzzling question. I see what it is."

"What do you mean by three-pointed? It has only two, the hilt and the tip."

"This person has two points in this world, as you say, but a third point in the other world."

Which was true enough, if you considered the hidden blade the third point. Could a person's spirit live in cold steel? As some memory of the spirit of Vai's grandmother might reside in the stone I had picked up, could some part of my mother's strength reside in the sword? I stroked the hilt, wondering if her spirit walked with me, and it seemed I felt an icy radiance and a trembling sense as of a thin wall that kept me apart from the vast and echoing landscape of the spirit world.

"I wonder why a maku carries a cemi," he went on. "Also, never have I met and spoken to a woman from across the sea. You are disrespectful, but I think that is just your way. My mother the *cacica* tells me I will marry a woman from across the sea. Maybe it will be you." He did not speak the words lasciviously. He said it as he might remark that rain clouds presaged rain.

"I think it unlikely it will be me." Two could play this game. "You call your mother the cacica. Is she queen? I thought your uncle was king."

"My uncle is very ill. Because of his illness, my mother, who is his sister, rules as cacica."

"Ah. I understand now. Then I expect a princely clan from Europa will send a princely daughter to seal a princely pact between your two noble houses. That daughter would not be me."

Yet I eyed him, feeling quite like a vulture as I did so. Was his fire magic enough to attract the Wild Hunt? Could I sacrifice him to save Bee?

From the foot of the ladder, the stocky adolescent spoke in Taino.

A glimmer like the breath of a firefly resolved into James Drake and his lamp. Upon finding the door of the house unlocked and unguarded, he came around to the back.

"Here you are," he said with a frown as he held up the lamp to examine us.

The prince regarded Drake with a splendid display of indifference.

Drake's lamp flared. "What is Prince Caonabo doing here?"

"Why do you think I am obliged to answer for my actions to you?" I asked.

We spoke in the mixed speech common to northwest Europa, not in the formal Latin of the schoolroom, and my face was surely so red that its heat alone might have lit the night. Prince Caonabo glanced at me, then climbed down. He and his companion walked away into the night.

"Well," Drake said grudgingly, "it isn't as if he could be trying to seduce you."

I thought of Abby's words. "You would know, I suppose."

"Dear me, Cat. Have I done anything to provoke such a mean-spirited reply? I only meant that a nephew of the supreme ruler is not in the business of marrying the daughter of an impoverished Phoenician mercenary house. But we have to speak of this later. Where is Abby?"

She would not get into trouble on my account! "Why do you think I know where she is?"

He sighed. "Your insistence on being contrary in every answer is really quite annoying, Cat. A woman who is always contrary is unlikely to please a husband."

I experienced a sudden and painful revelation that it was important to converse with a man before you became intimate with him, or else never to converse with him afterward. "I am sorry to inform you that not every woman wants a husband."

"You're very young. And very naïve."

I felt my ears turn to steam. "All the better to be taken advantage of?"

The wick flared again, flame licking upward in a flash. Yes, he was definitely angry, and not in a way I found amusing. "Is that what you think? That I took advantage of you?"

I pinched my lips together. I had to accept that Abby was right: I had been bitten, and he had healed me. Anyone would have said yes. He had also promised to get me off this cursed island, on which I was, evidently, meant to be trapped for the rest of my life. I could be caged at the vast estate of Four Moons House in more gilded comfort than this! Best to keep silence.

He went on. "I saved your life, Cat. At considerable risk to my own! Do you know why Prince Caonabo walks everywhere with his young cousin?"

"How could I know that?"

"A rhetorical question, I assume. Really, Cat. This affectation of showing opposition to everything becomes ridiculous and does not do you any credit for you seem otherwise a sensible girl. Naturally, fire mages are rare. They are so revered among the Taino that even mages born among the *naborias*—we would call them the plebeians— are married into the noble clans. Each fire mage is given a catch-fire. The great risk of being a fire mage is that you overextend your power—"

"And burn up," I finished. Yet I had felt his magic not as fire but as tendrils snaking through me, drawing my desire out of its innocent sleep.

"And burn up. I wish you would not interrupt me."

"You have no catch-fire?"

"Who would volunteer to be my catch-fire? Would you?"

My fingers tightened on the railing. "Wouldn't it be an awful way to die?"

"To burn to death? I don't intend to find out. Anyway, in Expedition Territory, it is forbidden by law for any fire mage to employ or enslave a person as a catch-fire."

"Is the prince's catch-fire a slave?"

"No, he is a cousin. That is his family duty. Among the Taino, catch-fires are honored. If they die, as they often do, they become a god—as we might say—and their skull—if a skull is left—is woven into a figure of power which the Taino call a cemi."

I lowered my gaze to the gleam of my sword. "Prince Caonabo said my sword was a cemi."

"That's probably why he came to talk to you. If he considers it a cemi, then you carrying it would make you seem a person of consequence, with powerful ancestors."

"How do you know this is a sword?"

He glanced away as if thinking someone else must have spoken. "Because it is one. Now. Where is Abby?"

The question popped out unbidden. "Why do you think I know?"

Raising the lamp, he frowned as if genuinely puzzled. "Are you angry at me?"

I fisted my hands, suddenly furious at myself. Wouldn't it be better to be honest about my anger instead of making all these petty retorts and always answering questions with questions?

The thought stunned me into muteness. *Answering questions with questions?*

He sighed, as if my silence was my answer. "I'll get a hammock for you. It will be cooler to sleep up there, but I warn you, the mosquitoes will feast on you at dawn." He went into the house and emerged with a bundle of netting, which he tossed to me. "There are loops at each end. String it from the hooks in the posts. Draw up the ladder. Salters can't climb, and Taino princes are too proud to ask for a ladder to be lowered. Although I'm not." He blew me a kiss as he left.

I strung up the netting. I had a difficult time finding

a comfortable position because my sword kept getting caught against my body at awkward angles. Once settled, I stared at the sea as the breeze stirred my shift against my sticky body. My eyelids were sweating.

Footsteps paced nearby, wearing a circuit. A man sobbed, "Kill me, kill me before I rot," but no one was listening. No one but me.

I wrapped my arms around myself, wishing I were not alone. Yet how could I wish Bee or Rory here on this terrible island? I thought of Drake and of Prince Caonabo. I did not think the prince was interested in seduction. I was pretty sure he had simply been curious about my cold steel and my foreign origins. Drake's motives seemed simpler: He was a man who might die at any moment. He had risked his life to heal me, and evidently he was the kind of man who thought it fair to get something in exchange. I had my life.

I dozed restlessly, woken once by a resounding splash. I smelled smoke. A smear of light like the flames of a bonfire dusted the ridge. My elbow itched. An annoying buzz whined by my ear. A twisted wail of despair descended into heartbroken sobs. Shuddering, I closed my eyes.

The sway of the hammock lulled me. The night wind kissed my lips as I clutched the locket.

A thread of magic draws taut, a path down which I can feel the presence of a bright, proud, and rather arrogant soul whose light is balm to my lonely shadow. A figure remarkably like Andevai turns with a surprised exclamation, speaking in a tone that suggested I had deliberately encouraged this untenable situation. "Catherine? I'm looking for you! Where are you?"

Wasn't I on Salt Island, wondering how I would save

Bee and recover Rory? Had the locket's touch made me think of Vai because the djeli's magic bound us through the spirit world? Was I always going to have to answer questions with questions? Yet the first time the eru and I had spoken, hadn't I asked her, *"Isn't it said the servants of the night court answer questions with questions?"*

Drowsily I smiled. The eru was a servant of the Wild Hunt, and now so was I. Drake was wrong. I wasn't just being annoying. At last I slept and, thankfully, I did not remember my dreams.

17

I woke as a rising light marked the dawn, my first in a new world. The curve of the sun's light flashed as I untangled myself from the netting and stretched. The air was pleasant, not quite cool but not sweat-making either. The sea was utterly gorgeous, so deeply wrought a green-blue color that it reminded me of a vast pulsing jewel. A flock of large birds with ungainly necks and fanned tails wandered out from the trees, searching for breakfast along the verge. The bite mark on my arm was pink, bruised, and sore when I gingerly pressed on it. But it was healing. I murmured a prayer to Blessed Tanit, protector of women.

After climbing down, I ventured into the brush beyond the stream to relieve myself. Back in the house, I washed, straightened my pagne and bodice, and took an accounting of my worldly possessions: a sword, a locket, a stone, a wool jacket and undervest, boots, and the slaughtered skirts.

It was time to spy. Wrapped in shadow, I crept up to the biggest house and poured myself up the steps onto the porch as if I were the wind. The door was a curtain, roped aside. Inside, baskets hung from the ceiling. A sloped wooden chair was placed in the center back of the room, its back carved with an animal face. Another door, draped with a curtain, led into a second room whose interior I could not see. Since I guessed this to be Prince Caonabo's exalted residence, I had no desire to penetrate its secrets.

The next two houses lay empty except for mouse droppings and chickens squawking as they wandered in and out. In the fourth I found Drake asleep in a hammock, wearing no shirt, his pale torso as smooth as that of a man who labors with pen instead of axe.

I crept into the next house only to find myself face to face with two Taino women, one young and one old enough to have a lined face and strands of silver in her black hair. Hale and strong, the older woman wore a sleeveless tent of a robe woven from white fabric that covered her to the ankles. Worst, she saw me right through my shadows. Her lips curled up.

I let the threads fall. "Salvete. I am Catherine Bell Barahal. My apologies. I got lost."

Her half smile vanished and she surveyed me from top to toe as I bunched my hands into fists. I had forgotten Drake's warning: *Never speak to her unless she addresses you first.*

She grabbed my wrist just as Prince Caonabo entered the house with his doomed young relative tagging cheerfully after him. Without so much as a word, she pushed up my torn sleeve and pressed her lips to the wound. This was the kiss of life. Heat coursed up my veins and spread through my flesh, even to the stirring in my loins. Male or female, what did it matter, really, when the body yearned? As she straightened, still holding my arm, a corner of her lips lifted with unexpected humor and perhaps even sensual interest. Prince Caonabo made a comment in Taino, and the two catch-fires smiled. I snatched my arm out of her grasp, my face burning.

She spoke in a slightly hoarse alto. The prince translated. "Your blood does not harbor the teeth of the ghouls."

"I know," I said as evenly as I could. "James Drake healed me."

She laughed in a curt way that made me want to sink into the dirt floor. Instead, I stared at the printed fabric of my pagne, sure that the secret architecture of the universe could be discerned in its patterns of shells. When the silence dragged out, I looked up.

The prince rubbed his forehead with a frown. "The maku did not heal you."

"I'm not healed?" The room went hot, and my pulse thundered in my ears as I swayed.

"If a bitten person is brought quickly, then we can burn out the teeth before they infest the blood. But always the touch leaves a remnant. Like the ashes from wood that is burned. You have no ashes, Catherine Bell Barahal. There were never ghoul teeth in you."

"But how...?" Words evaporated like mist under the sun.

"This mystery the behica also wonders at. You were bitten by one of the afflicted ones, that is certain. But there are no ashes and there are no teeth. No one healed you. You had nothing to heal because you are clean."

"But Drake told me I would die if I didn't—!" Now and again, I had the unfortunate and unpleasant experience of blurting out words I immediately regretted.

The prince's brow creased in puzzlement, then lifted in enlightenment. "Did James Drake say that in order to heal you, he and you must mate?"

The behica examined me with an expression blended of pity and disgust, just as offended as my once-beloved

Aunt Tilly would have looked had I brazenly informed her I had married and abandoned one man and taken another as a lover. Which some people might say I had.

I hope I am not a rude person. Bee and I learned good manners and proper deportment, and I am sure I value courtesy. But this was too much. I looked at the blameless catch-fires, then met the old woman's gaze with a blazing fire of my own.

"People who throw others to the wolves ought not to judge where they end up running." I turned my back on her, pushed past the prince and the catch-fires, and walked out of the house.

Blindly, furiously, I strode across the open space until, like a brain-rotted salter, I bumped into the tall iron fence and found myself staring through the narrow gaps between bars into the crystalline white eyes of a man.

I yelped, leaping back.

He said nothing. He simply stood with face against the bars shifting ever so slightly as if some hours or days or months ago he had been walking this way and, having fetched up against the bars, did not know how to turn around. For all I knew, he would stand there until a strong rain dissolved him. His gaze had neither soul nor intelligence. He was an empty vessel.

I caught my heel on the ground, and sat down so hard on my backside that I began to cry. What a fool I was!

But tears get boring very quickly. I wiped my face on a sleeve and rose. Better to face the truth than run away.

The high fence ringed an open area of shelters with thatched roofs but no walls. In some, clothed figures dozed in hammocks. Other figures lay on the ground or stood with slack faces and lax limbs staring at nothing. Closer stood actual cages whose prisoners paced and muttered and then, catching sight of me, began to gabble and claw at the bars that confined them. I recognized the man who had bitten me more by the rip in his singlet than by his features, which were smeared with dirt. Red rimmed his mouth; was that my blood? He rocked from one foot to the other, eyes shut, keening and moaning: "Kill me. Kill me before I rot."

How long did it take them to die? For how long did their minds hang on, screaming, as they slid inexorably into the claws of the plague?

I saw Abby. Her hair was bound in a head wrap of brown-and-gold cloth. She was running a hand along the bars of an empty cage as if counting in time to the tune she was singing. "On a fine *batey*, do yee hear, me sissy-o? We want one of they, do yee hear, me sissy-o? Which one do yee want? Do yee hear, me sissy-o?"

"Abby! It's Cat'reen!"

She looked at me without recognition and walked on.

I fled back to the house and barred the door. I washed my face and hands once, then twice, and then a third time, but what I had seen and heard would not rinse away. I sank down on the mat and let the exhaustion of despair drag me down into sleep.

"Cat?" James Drake's voice woke me. "Here's food and juice. I haven't seen you all day."

I opened the door. Drake stood with a half smile on his face and his hair darkened by being sopping wet; his clothes stuck to him; he looked as if he had been swimming. He was not alone.

"Abby!"

She smiled awkwardly at me, as a friend might when caught in a situation where you can't admit you know each other. She held a tray.

"Go inside," said Drake to her. "Set it down. Then come back outside. That's right."

I stepped back as she lurched inside and set down the tray.

"Pardon, gal. I just set dis down." She again offered that awkward smile and limped out, holding her side, not looking back.

"She doesn't know me!" I hissed, my voice breaking.

He gave off an odd scent: almost sweet and with a bite like a spark settling on the tongue. "Cursed bad luck for her. She could slip into the active phase tonight or tomorrow, and then it *will* be too late to help her. Bastards!" He was in the grip of a fever, words rising. "What high and mighty creatures they all are, so proud of their virtue! The truth they will never admit, none of them, is that a fire mage can burn out all the seedlings of the disease, all the teeth, just as long as an infested salter hasn't yet entered the active phase."

"But then why don't they?" I cried, thinking of her blank stare.

"They don't want to pay the price. Be on the beach by dusk with all your things."

He left.

I forced down the griddle bread with its bitter aftertaste, drank the juice, and ate the strips of dried chicken. The gourd bottle still redolent with rum I filled with water and tied to my bundled skirts and boots. I walked to the deserted beach and dabbled my toes in the water. Cool feet make a cool head. Clouds had built up, sliding in from the northeast, and a squall swept through, soaking me to the skin and pounding across the bay in a sudden boil.

Hair plastered to my body and my clothes utterly sodden, I laughed. I pressed a hand to my breast, the curve of the locket beneath my bodice shaped to the curve of my palm, and I thought:

Vai.

Vai? It was as if the cursed man would never stop plaguing me. And yet he had done his best to help me.

Shadows darkened the sea as the sun lowered west behind the island's ridge. A shape like a dark cloud floated against the sky in the east. Did a lamp flare over the water? A faint *clut-clut-clut* like the clatter of factory machinery teased the edge of my hearing, growing louder. The tang of burning wood and oil tingled in my nostrils.

As twilight poured into night, the sword flowered to life. A crash shivered, felt through the soles of my bare feet. A shout rang out, followed by the clang of an alarm bell. I turned.

Flames glowered in the pens. Smoke streamed skyward. Someone had set the cages on fire.

People yelled from the roof of the prince's house. Were they waving at me? Or trying to attract the attention of the figures moving through the houses? Where had they all come from?

In the red gloom, the figures swarmed into view, moving toward the beach. I saw them clearly.

A mob of salters staggered toward me like a pack of rabid dogs.

Running seemed the stupidest thing to do, trapped as I was against the sea. I drew my sword. The flat white eyes of the salters glinted in its light. The forward edge of a wave shushed up the beach to kiss my toes and slide away again.

Legate Amadou Barry and his sisters and aunt had escaped the salt plague by boat. I had once mocked his story because I hadn't understood how salters could reach an island, but I knew now that all you had to do was to be bitten. Invisible teeth would gnaw away at you with no sign of the disease showing until it was too late.

I ripped off my pagne and wrapped it around my neck to keep it out of the way as I backed into the water. Could the monster that had attacked me in the deeps swim so close? Did it matter? The salters halted at the limit of the waves, and there they licked their teeth and grasped with unwashed hands. The man who had bitten me stood among them, saying, "Kill me, kill me," as he strained to the edge of the salty brine and retreated as foam tickled up the sand.

A weight knocked into my legs, bumping me sideways. I shrieked as a huge shape surfaced and a round head blinked solemnly beneath my gleaming blade. The world stilled and the wind hushed. For an instant I stood poised between the mortal world and the spirit world, feet in one and head in another and my heart shoved so hard up into my throat I could not breathe.

It was a cursed turtle. Watching me like a messenger come to remind me that the Master of the Wild Hunt had his spies everywhere: *You belong to me, Daughter*.

Or maybe it was just a sea turtle, as surprised as I was.

From the roof, Prince Caonabo called. "Perdita! Wade to the point! Wait on the rocks!"

An oblong shape blotted out stars and clouds alike. Lamplight flared overhead.

"Cat! Don't come out of the water!" Drake shouted, but I could not see him.

A thread slithered down from the sky to slap the water. It was a rope ladder, lowered as by Ba'al's heavenly messengers. I stared at it as if it were a serpent sliding close to strike, for its swaying bounce hypnotized me. Two figures scrambled down. The first gripped a lamp's hook in strong white teeth. As he turned to take in the scene on the dark shore, he spotted me, let go one hand from the ladder, and drew a very impressive knife from a harness crossed on a dark chest.

I brandished my sword to make sure he knew I had it. I could take a cursed knife, but I wasn't so sure about taking him, for he had the posture of a man who knew how to fight and kill. Although his willingness to raid a plague island filled with brain-rotted dying people who could easily infest him did not inspire confidence in his intelligence.

The person above, the one without a lamp held in his mouth, spoke. "Gal! Speak if yee can hear me."

"I'm just a lost woman, no threat to you," I cried. "Can you get me out of here?"

"No salter, she." By the voice it was a woman. She seemed to be explaining things to the man with the lamp and the knife, thus giving me even less faith in his wit. "She be in the water, see? Therewise not a salter."

I kept my guard up although he sheathed the knife and swung around to peer at the beach.

"Cat! Get on the ship! Go up now!" Definitely that was Drake's impatient voice.

He pushed down through the salters without fear, dragging Abby. She lurched like a broken toy, sobbing in fear. He led her to the edge of the water. A wave brushed up over her bare feet and she whimpered with a horrible hurt dog sound. The salters backed away from Drake as from poison, but yet they so yearned for my blood that they kept coming back and retreating, all in time to the sough of the waves.

Drake tugged Abby against him as in an embrace. He ripped away her blouse, uncovering her torso and breasts. The gleam of my sword and the light of the ladder man's lamp illuminated a suppurating wound gouged into her side. The wound oozed with a slime that glittered like phosphorous. Drake pressed a hand against it, fingers smeared into the oily mess. She cried out, then stilled as abruptly as if he had stabbed her. I yelled a protest and splashed forward to save her.

A salter grabbed at me. My training snapped me into a lunge, weight and force thrusting the blade's tip into his shoulder.

His gaze met mine, unreadable. Blank and dead.

Cold and hot together, blood racing, I rotated my elbow out and yanked free the blade, able to think only that it hadn't been a killing blow. The salter dropped at my feet. A wave spilled over the body, and it turned white and began to dissolve like a ridge of salt crumbling away.

Maybe I screamed in sheer shocked surprise. Someone screamed.

The salters scattered, stumbling away from me. The two closest to Drake began to croon in a moaning whoop whose rise and fall made my skin crawl. A glow like fireflies winked along their skin until their complexions shone as if they were turning alchemically into burnished gold. Flames licked along their ragged clothing. Sparks spun in their eyes.

Furious shouts and curses rose from the rooftops.

A fourth salter limped toward me, his white gaze fixed purposefully on me. He was the one who had bitten me. As he licked his teeth and smacked his lips with the obsession of hunger, he looked me right in the eye with what I knew, like a knife to the gut, was the dregs of the mind that had once dwelt happily in a youthful, healthy body.

"Kill me. Kill me."

I thrust. My blade caught him just below the ribs. Then I pulled free.

He toppled into the sea, and the crystalline remains of what had once been a man hissed away in the swells.

I fell back as a wave of heat blasted off James Drake. The two glowing salters burned in earnest. A third joined them. Their greasy, bitter smell gagged me.

A hand caught my arm. I jerked around to stare straight at a muscled and very bare black chest wrapped with knives. Two old, ropy scars drew a starburst pattern over his left shoulder and across his heart. Once, he had taken the worst of a bad knife fight. Or perhaps he was the one who had won.

"Up! Hurry, Perdita!" With a disturbing shriek of a laugh, the woman leaped off the ladder and landed with a resounding splash next to me.

The burning men weren't even screaming because the flames were consuming them so quickly. The reek of singed flesh dizzied me. I sheathed and fastened my sword, grabbed a stiff rung, and began to climb. I had to work around the knife man, and as I passed he spread a hand across my backside most invasively. But he merely shoved, with astonishing strength, to help me on my way.

Up!

My mind had shut down. Keep climbing. One foot. The next foot. One hand. The next hand. My shoulders strained and my fingers cramped, so I concentrated on pushing up with my legs. One more, and one more again. Keep climbing.

Hands grabbed me from above and hauled me up. I half hung over the rim of a huge basket. Below, fire roared through the pens. A figure stood in the flames, not moving. If you were dead already in every way that counted, wouldn't true death come as a blessing?

Kill me.

I collapsed onto a swaying floor, wet, exhausted, and numb.

18

Clut-clut-clut.

The sound penetrated my dulled mind the way Bee's little sister Astraea's whining complaints in time pierced even the most heartlessly impervious. Not because you cared, but because you just wanted it to stop.

The basket pitched. I grasped at the rope railing, clinging as my rescuers hauled in the rest of their catch. First came Abby, then Drake. Was he glowing slightly?

I shut my eyes. Glittering salt crystals poured onto the sand in the shape of a man's body, hissing away as the sea dissolved them. *I had killed two men.* Yet were they still men if their minds and maybe their souls had been eaten?

As the basket rocked again, I looked up. The knife man and the woman who had laughed swung easily into the basket and rolled up the ladder behind them. Abby was led toward the stern by a young man who had his arm around her. A seventh individual, small and agile, clambered in the rigging to investigate the bloated creature above us. An eighth person fiddling at the stern of the basket worked a crank. As the *clut-clut-clut* increased its clamor, the creature under which we labored began ponderously to part the currents of air. Heat rose from a metal cylinder like the breath of a dragon, pouring upward into the oblong whale with its thrumming skin.

We were sailing in an airship.

A small airship, to be sure, but an airship nonetheless.

I pulled myself up to see the isle falling away behind us, looking like leviathan at rest in the midst of the slumbering sea. The wind rumbled in my ears. Knife man and the woman who had laughed braced themselves against the basket, examining me. They were kissed by the pearly glamour of a waxing moon now sliding free from clouds.

Drake settled beside me. "You were slow. You need to do a better job following orders."

"Yes, certainly I was slow, since it's every day I have an opportunity to be trapped on an island filled with victims of the salt plague and then be rescued by buccaneers in an airship. No reason to be surprised by any of that!"

The eerie glow around his person had faded, but his blue eyes shimmered. "Please don't be so annoying."

I was so angry that I thought maybe the top of my head was going to blow off. And, if we were fortunate, propel the airship faster. "You lied to me!"

"Maku bastard!" The man who had had his arm around Abby grabbed Drake's shoulder, threatening with a hand in a fist. "She mind rotted. Yee promised to heal she!"

Drake's eyes burned hot blue. "Take your hand off me. Or I'll burn it off."

Knife man rocked the basket. Abby's man stumbled to his knees. Drake caught himself clumsily, bellying against the basket's rim. I shifted to balance, and the woman who had laughed grinned at me.

The young man burst into tears. "She me dear good sister. Dey behiques tell we it too late. Den dey take she a Salt Island. But den we hear dat in Expedition der some folk can heal any salter. Dat how I find yee. Now she don' know she own name. She don' know *me*, she own brother."

"She is healed. There's no salt plague in her. You have what I could save. And you thank me for the risks I took by assaulting me?"

"God's blessing for saving she," wept the young man.

Drake rested a hand on the man's plaited hair. "What happened to the salter who bit her?"

"We drive dat salter in a pit and we pour salted water over he."

"That was done well. I would have acted sooner, but if I had, I would have been arrested and imprisoned and she would never have gotten off Salt Island. Go back to her. She needs you."

With both hands on the guide rope the brother staggered back to where Abby sat as in a stupor at the stern, her hands lax on the untidy mess of her rumpled pagne.

I shook out and retied my pagne. I was not ready to talk about Abby. "Drake, when did you leave Adurnam? What happened to the general? Why are you here?"

"I'm here because Expedition is my home. I was born in the Ordovici territories, but I left home at seventeen. I've lived in Expedition Territory for twelve years. Once my business in Adurnam was complete, I sailed back to Expedition."

"What was your business in Adurnam?"

"Why, to rescue the general and bring him over the ocean to Expedition."

"He's in Expedition?"

"At the moment, he is not. He went west to a city called Sharagua to pay his respects to the cacique's court and person."

"You didn't travel with him?"

"In the Taino kingdom, all fire mages serve the cacique. So I'm forbidden from traveling into Taino country. I wouldn't want to anyway. Their laws are unreasonably strict. They won't allow me to heal people."

"Heal people? You burned those salters alive!"

"I used them as catch-fires, that's true. Was that life, what they suffered? I ended their misery through a quick, merciful death that healed Abby. To burn out all the teeth in someone as far advanced in the disease as she was would have killed me. I think it was a fair trade."

"So speaks the man who said he could heal me if I would just have sex with him."

"Cat, you were drunk. You can't expect to have understood exactly what I meant. Anyway, I thought you knew your own mind. You're an independent young woman, traveling on your own. And you're a Phoenician girl."

I put a hand on my sword's hilt. "I would be very cautious about what you say next."

He took a step away from me just as it occurred to me that it might be a mistake to make a fire mage angry. But his voice remained patient. "I meant only that a young woman of your background can do as she wishes. I would never have suggested otherwise had I thought you were under the thumb of a father or brother." He smiled pleasantly. "Or beholden to a husband."

I could not speak out of sheer choked consternation. My cheeks flamed.

Then he surprised me. "My sincerest apologies, Cat. I meant no harm, and certainly no disrespect. A remarkably pretty girl like you is hard to resist." He raised both hands in a conciliatory gesture. "I hope we can make peace."

"Whatever else," I muttered grudgingly, "you did get me off Salt Island."

"So I did." With a nod, he groped his way by guide rope to the stern, where he began to chat with the sternsman at his rudder.

I did not want to drown in my anger, so I went over and knelt beside Abby. "I'm so sorry," I said to her brother.

"I know yee," she said with that horribly puzzled smile.

She began to comb through the tangles of my hair with her fingers. I did not want to interrupt something that comforted her, so I settled cross-legged in front of her. Knife man brought over a comb, and Abby worked through my hair, never yanking although the snarls seemed intractable. The woman who had laughed offered me a gourd bottle, and I swallowed a juice that made my eyes water and my mouth sting. Or maybe I was just tired and shaken. With Abby still combing my hair, my eyes fluttered and shut.

I woke leaning against the side of the basket, my hair a smooth curtain falling over my shoulders to my hips. Abby stood at the prow of the basket with her brother, his arm around her, watching phosphorus dance its glamour on the waves. Staring into their future, which must have seemed very dark. Wasn't it sometimes better to be dead?

I shut my eyes rather than look.

I woke as the air changed, and we bucked like a skittish horse. The *clut-clut-clut* slowed to a lazy *clunk-cluunk-cluuunk*. I rose. We drifted over land, a hulking beast of ridges grown with a breathing exhalation of forest. I remembered Bee's sketches of airships. What had seemed funny then, when she had drawn hapless passengers falling from the basket to deaths far below, seemed indecent now. Easy to joke about a thing you have no experience of and will never suffer.

Off to our right, firelight dappled a hollow.

Knife man paid out the ladder, and the woman who had laughed went over with a grace and strength I admired. I grasped Abby's hand just before she went over, and she smiled at me, and her brother said, "Thank yee, maku," in a way that made me glad she had been saved, even what was left of her. Even in the face of the deaths of others, two of which I had caused. Even so.

Over they went, climbing away into a life hidden from me. Below, on the ground, a rushlight shivered into life. After some time, it wavered away and vanished. The woman who had laughed swung a leg back over and hopped in. We began to move as knife man hauled the ladder back up.

A shape dropped beside me, startling me so badly I cried out. The fourth crewman was a petite, white-haired woman with a lined and leathery black face, her eyes hidden behind goggles. Her sleeveless singlet exposed wiry arms, and she wore loose trousers, a harness with four knives, and a bracelet molded in the shape of a running wolf. She said a word whose meaning I could not guess at, and swung back up into the rigging.

"Uncommon quiet, this night." The woman who had laughed leaned companionably beside me against the basket's rim. The land slumbered silent beneath like behemoth asleep. We watched together. I was content not to speak, and she felt no need to chatter. After a while, knife man moved up on my other side.

"We saw what yee wrought, there on the beach," murmured the woman. "That blade yee carry turned them to salt. They dissolved when salt water washed them. Yon fire mage never saw. Peradventure, yee don' mean to tell him."

Under the circumstances, I settled on a truthful answer. "I don't. Do you plan to tell him?"

"We's paid for the conveyance, that only. Not for secrets."

I smiled, for she sounded exactly like my uncle, scion of the Hassi Barahal clan that made its living stealing and selling secrets. "Who are you, if I may ask?"

"Folk hired to do a job," she answered.

"Yon fire mage is right, yee know," said knife man, the weight of him very noticeable on my other side.

"About what?"

"It were a kindness to let they salters die." He nodded toward my belt. "No ordinary manner of blade, that one."

I fixed a hand possessively on the hilt. "Only my hand can wield it."

He said, "Surely bound to yee. Some manner of cemi."

"It's just a sword."

The woman laughed with a kind of wavering howl. It was not a laugh I would soon forget.

"Have it that way, then, Perdita." Knife man grinned. "Kiskeya is a beauty, is she not?"

"Who is Kiskeya?" I asked, pleased I could frame a useful question to move the topic on.

"Why, Kiskeya is this island. She is the mother of we all."

The hills plunged in jagged shadows down to the foamy white rim of a beach. The airship skipped and rolled as air currents eddied and battered us from two directions. Then we turned and headed parallel along the coastline. Under the moon's light, the sea became a dark mirror in which stars were caught. I smelled a flowery fragrance, a heady perfume blown into my face by the night wind. A bird called in a mournful loop. Far in the distance, I saw a shimmering glow as of a city burning night candles.

"What city is that?" I asked.

"Expedition," said the woman.

"So this island is part of the Taino kingdom. While Expedition is a free city on this island ruled by mage Houses and princes. But how could a free city have been established here?"

"When the first fleet, that one out of Mali, come across the Atlantic, it come to land here, on the south shore of Kiskeya. The island was then ruled by many caciques, each with he own territory. One of these caciques, named Caonabo, dealt with the fleet's officers. He gave them territory in exchange for allowing the Taino to trade and ship through they port."

"And in exchange for the maku not starting a war," said knife man with a sardonic chuckle.

"Is that where the law about the salt plague comes from? The one that all salters or anyone bitten by a salter have to be quarantined on Salt Island?"

"Yee have it right," she said. "'Tis all written down in the first treaty, that one which established Expedition Territory. But yee's mistaken in thinking Expedition ruled by princes and mages. A Council rule in Expedition. Why, mages is not even allowed to form professional associations or corporations or guilds in any wise. The Council don' like mages much. So besides the insult to Taino law for a take yee two gals off Salt Island, Expedition's wardens shall be after yon fire mage for another reason. Because in Expedition 'tis against the law for a fire mage to use a catch-fire."

"Will you tell them?"

"Not good for business to tell tales," said knife man.

"The Taino on Salt Island shall tell them," said the woman. "Yon fire mage shall have some trouble here-after."

I could only hope! But their words puzzled me. "Are there truly no cold mages in Expedition?"

"What is a cold mage?" asked knife man.

I was too surprised to answer, but fortunately the woman did.

"Fire banes," she said.

"Fire banes? I suppose cold mages could be called fire banes."

"They who come from Europa speak such stories of fire banes as mighty as hurricanes, but I don' believe them," remarked knife man. "Yee ever see such power in a fire bane, gal?"

I was really too astonished to answer. In the east, the light had changed yet again, black of night easing to a charcoal pallor. The wind began to soften as dawn crept up the horizon. We were drifting down, sinking closer to the waves and a length of beach.

"Why would there be no powerful cold mages here?" I asked.

I could see them better now: He was a big man, broad-shouldered and powerful, with black skin and a shaved head. The ropy scar that patterned his left torso was not the only old wound marking a violent life. Yet the woman who had laughed scared me more. Not that I thought she was about to strangle me to get my sword, but that she surveyed me with a measuring eye, as if wondering if I were a secret she could steal and sell to the highest bidder. She could have walked down Adurnam's streets without looking the least out of place, with brown skin dusted with freckles from constant sun, reddish-brown kinky hair, brown eyes, full lips, and a thin Celtic nose. But then when she laughed, you would shudder.

Knife man smiled. "Because 'tis just a story di maku tell. I hear they don' even have gaslight in they cities in Europa, so they tell this story about cold mages to fill dem shoes."

"It's true!" I retorted indignantly. "In Europa, cold mages can extinguish fires, call down storms of ice and snow, and twist and shatter iron—"

Knife man began to laugh, and he punched me on the shoulder as at a good joke well told. "With dem honest eyes and fierce look, yee almost had me believing, Perdita," he said, grinning. "Until that yee said about iron. That was too much."

From the rigging shrilled a whistle.

"Time to go," said the woman.

"Where are we?"

"Why, we have crossed into Expedition Territory, Perdita. We don' go into the city. The wardens shall shave off we asses and chop off we hands to decorate the council square. We shall drop yee and yon fire mage at Cow Killer Beach. Yee can find a canoe to take yee along."

"What's a canoe?"

Knife man punched me again on the shoulder, not quite so lightly this time. When I held my place by sinking into the blow, his grin widened. "Yee a real maku, ja? New come to the Antilles?"

"A foreigner? Isn't it obvious?"

He was still grinning, but the amusement faded from his eyes, and it took every thread of courage I had not to step back from the edge that cut through his voice. Not only physical scars can mark you. He was a killer, and not one bit sorry to be so. He just happened to like me, and to have been paid. "Remember, Perdita. Yee a pretty gal, and yee healthy and shapely and with that fine fall of hair. Yee brave, and yee strong, and yee have that cemi yee carry. But Heaven's Breath, gal, yee are but a babe fallen in wild country." He raised a hand, forefinger up to scold me. "Don' yee go getting drunk around men. What yee think will happen?"

He clucked disapprovingly as he shook his head at me, so like a fussing old uncle that I blushed bright red rather than getting angry.

"Yee think about it, Perdita," he finished, and he went over to toss out the ladder.

The woman had a scar along the line of her jaw, so fine it was easy to miss. "Me grandmother was Phoenician-born. No man ever lied to she daughters and lived to speak of it. For the insult, she'd a stick that arseness of a fire mage with a knife in he gut before he knew what hit him. Then twist it and pull his entrails out, to make sure he suffer longer."

She wasn't teasing. "Your grandmother was Phoenician-born! What clan?"

"Don' go asking, for I don' want to have to refuse to tell yee. We's just folk hired to do a job. One piece of advice. Wear long sleeves until that bite heal."

"My thanks." I offered a hand in the radical's manner. With a grin she shook it.

Knife man slapped me hard on the ass as I went over the side. "Don' forget what I told yee!"

I climbed down first, Drake coming after. As soon as his feet hit the sand, they drew up the ladder. A hand waved; I waved back as the little airship took a course out to sea.

"Cat! Come along!"

He was already halfway down the beach, walking toward a ridge beyond which smoke rose. I winkled out my jacket from the bundle.

"Hurry up!" he called.

"I'm covering the bite with long sleeves." I considered the boots, and decided it was better to walk barefoot on the sand. "Who were they?"

"Criminals of the worst sort. You must keep the bite covered until it heals. Tell no one where you were. I hope to reach Expedition before any word of the incident on Salt Island gets there. I've got to sort out what I have to do, and there's you besides to complicate my situation."

Dawn rose as we climbed on a sandy path over the ridge and down to a hamlet ringed by garden plots. Smokehouses steamed with the savory aroma of meat being cured.

Gracious Melqart! I had forgotten how hungry I was!

Women walked out of the forest, carrying pots of water on their heads. Round houses circled a raised plaza paved with stone and a long dirt field where children were playing a game with a ball. Except for the cry of brightly plumed birds, the soft wash of waves, the blat of a goat, and the casual morning chatter of folk and chickens going about their daily business, it was too cursed quiet. If anyone saw us, they gave no sign. We might as well have been ghosts.

"Stay here, Cat," said Drake.

I waited as he walked to the beach where men were loading baskets and barrels into a pair of long, narrow wooden boats. I watched as he negotiated. The men looked my way, and the bidding got steeper. I knew this dance. They'd be arguing: "Ah, but Maester, you understand that if we add the girl, we'll have to take out two baskets, and then where's our profit?"

At length Drake gestured to me, and I walked over, all too aware of the men's scrutiny.

"Get into the canoe," Drake said.

"I hate to mention this, but I'm terribly thirsty."

"I only paid for passage. Have you any funds at all, Cat?"

"Do you think I wouldn't offer to pay my own way if I could?"

"I wish you would stop that. A simple 'No' would suffice."

I thought it wiser to say nothing, so I clambered into the canoe and arranged my bundle to cushion my backside. He sat in front, his back to me. The men paddled with long blades that cut the water. I clutched the gunnels, too paralyzed at being surrounded by water to worry about thirst.

It was not such a long distance, no more than an hour or three, but my life crawled past my eyes at a creeping baby's pace and then limped back as an aged crone before we came around a headland. There, spread before us, lay the infamous city of Expedition.

Buildings stretched along a jetty that ran for at least a mile along the shore. At a river's mouth, the embankment broke into a harbor where masted ships clustered. Proper city walls rose down by the harbor. Where the river opened onto the sea lay a flat island ringed by six skeletal towers like the points of a prince's coronet, stately airships moored to two of them. On the eastern side of the river, a pall of drifting smoke darkened the morning sky, streaming in billows into the west on a stout wind. Smokestacks grew like shafts of blackened grain. The distant clatter of engine works and busy machines hammered a faint counterpoint to the wind's bluster and the slap of swells against the canoe's hull as we parted the waters.

Founded by refugees from the Empire of Mali and their Phoenician shipmasters and allies, the population had swelled with the ranks of criminals, indentured servants, unscrupulous merchants, fortune hunters, and the discontented and maladjusted flotsam and jetsam borne across the ocean from Europa and Africa. More recently, so history told, trolls had emigrated south from their homeland to make common cause with like-minded rats, as Chartji would call them. I wondered if there might be an office of Godwik and Clutch I could approach for aid in securing passage back to Adurnam and Bee once I had accomplished my task.

We passed slim canoes and chubby sailboats, men out fishing who waved to us in a friendly manner that our boatmen returned. We skimmed not toward the river's mouth and the big wharves where the oceangoing ships lay to harbor but toward a crowded comb of piers farther west. Boats crammed the shore.

I pressed a hand to my breast, feeling the locket's warmth like a promise that I would soon find a safe haven. Caught by an inexplicably sharp thrill, I leaned forward. The jetty spread before me in all its magnificently confounding bustle, folk hauling and carrying and bargaining and loitering and tossing out line and drawing in skiffs. The life and light of the place seemed about to break over me like the tide of a dragon's dream.

We bumped up against a pier. The steersman offered a gap-toothed leer as I scrambled out with my bundle and my cane. My bare feet slipped on fish guts and less savory spume. I gritted my teeth and plowed on.

"Come along, Cat," said Drake over his shoulder as he strode down the long wooden pier.

Men working on or lounging in canoes and skiffs looked up as he passed, expressions incurious or passively hostile; then they would see me, and a wolfish kind of grin would flash as they took a good look along me from my head to my toes. My pagne had plastered itself down the length of my thighs. I regretted leaving my jacket unbuttoned, because my shift and bodice were still damp enough to cling. I crossed my arms over my chest.

"Fished a river siren out of the water, did yee?" called one young man to the men in the canoe. "Look at that hair!"

Men within earshot all agreed, quite vocally and with a great deal of amusement, about my cursed hair. I could not imagine why I had not braided it back.

I had no trouble keeping track of Drake in the press of bodies, for his red-gold shock of hair stood out like fire. Men stepped out of his way, not making a scene of it, but it was clear Drake need not ask for passage. They knew what he was. And he was glad they knew.

We stepped onto a vastly wide, stone-paved avenue slimed with a thin layer of mud and oil churned by sun and yesterday's rain and the constant trammeling of the exceptional amount of traffic coming and going. A high-wheeled cart driven by a bored-looking man and drawn by a hairy but quite small mammoth—if that was not a contradiction in terms—trundled past as I stared gape-mouthed. A four-winged bird feathered in bright colors reminiscent of a troll's crest glided overhead, a white tube clutched in its fore-talons. Four soldiers casually carrying rifles over their shoulders strolled along the jetty, now and again pausing to speak to young men as if recruiting.

Two men uniformed in red tabards hurried along the avenue, each carrying a long staff and wearing a stiff black cap. Drake dropped at once into a crouch, head bent to conceal his face. He fiddled with his sandals as if he had caught a pebble until the men walked out of sight past a company of women who were striding along with laden baskets on their heads.

"Come along, Cat." He rose and began walking east, in their wake, toward the distant city walls.

I caught his wrist and pulled him to a stop.

"What's that?" I pointed to a wide dusty open work area set off behind a low fence and rimmed with long thatch-roofed shelters with no walls. Men worked at beams and planks. In truth what had drawn my eye was the rear view of a young man stripped to the waist and plying an adze along a beam. I could not help but admire his muscled back.

"That's a carpentry yard. Strange you should need to ask, as they have the like in Adurnam."

He tugged, but I held my ground.

His gaze narrowed. "Didn't you see the two wardens? They can arrest me. I'm taking you to the Speckled Iguana. You'll stay there in hiding until I sort out if the general is back in the city."

I ripped my gaze away from the carpenter's decorative back and stared at Drake as if he had sprouted two heads. "You're abandoning me here?"

"I'm not abandoning you, Cat. You'll lie low in a safe place. I'll pay your room and board, and the innkeeper will watch over you. He's a partisan, an old soldier and countryman. An Iberian." He sighed, as if exhausted by having to explain things to a persistently dim-witted child. "I need you to keep your mouth shut and your head down until I return. As soon as I know what the situation is here, we'll sort things out."

"How long until that happens? What will I do?"

He shook his arm with an angry grimace, and I let go. "The longer I stand here in public view, the more likely it is I'll be spotted. Then I'll be arrested. Is that what you want?"

"Why should I want that?"

"A question I couldn't possibly answer." As if to punctuate his words, a clock tolled down the hour: ten in the morning. Some distance down the jetty, at an intersection of a major side street, stood a squat building topped by a clock tower. A parade of little clockwork children passed beneath the clock's face.

"Blessed Tanit," I whispered, for the clock's workings had finally shaken loose the obvious. "What if I'm pregnant?"

Most inappropriately, he kissed me on the lips. "Don't you know why we fire mages are so sought after as lovers?"

"Why would I know that?"

His fingers tightened painfully over mine. "Cat, I fear no man has ever told you that repeated impertinence in a woman makes her ugly. Take care you do not lose your pretty face. Or perhaps you have complaints beyond those whose linen you have already aired."

The comment so reminded me of the head of the poet Bran Cof that I would have laughed, except I had seen James Drake engulf three men's bodies in flames.

I twisted my hand out of his grip. "I am sure," I said in my blandest tone, "that fire mages are sought after as lovers for their own special qualities."

"I wouldn't know about that. But you'll be glad to hear

we are indifferently fertile. So the chances my seed will plant in you is small."

I pressed a hand to my belly, seized with a horrible foreboding.

"Or are you disappointed? I know women dream of becoming pregnant—"

"I was dreaming about having a bowl of yam pudding!"

"You're very amusing, Cat, when you make your little jokes." He flagged down a man who was pulling along a cart with a canvas awning draped over a seat wide enough for two people. "We've loitered too long. I must get out of sight immediately. Wardens patrol thickly through these districts where most of the trouble comes from."

"What kind of trouble?"

"Go to the Speckled Iguana." He kissed me again on the lips and clambered onto the seat. "Ask for the innkeeper and tell him the usual phrase: *A rising light marks the dawn of a new world.* You can trust him."

He spoke a meaningless phrase to the cart-man, who was wiping sweat from his forehead with a cloth. The man stowed his cloth, gripped the shafts, and off they jolted, leaving me all alone in the midst of an unfamiliar city.

19

I stood stunned and bewildered, surrounded by tramping feet, axes chopping, wheels turning and a man whistling a cheerful tune. People, carts, wheelbarrows, wagons, laden donkeys, and pack dogs with their human handlers walking behind pushed along the main thoroughfare.

A prickling sensation crawled along my neck as the locket warmed my skin. I looked toward the carpentry yard. The young man with the adze had stopped work in order to turn half around. Was the cursed man staring at *me*? What had I ever done to him to attract his rude notice?

He wore loose trousers belted at his hips with rope and above that, as I had already had cause to remark, nothing but gorgeous muscled skin the color of the raw umber worked in painters' studios, a deep, rich, warm, luxuriously dark brown. He set down the adze and, bracing a hand on the fence, leaped over it. Then he strode toward me as if certain I was about to bolt and he must catch me before I did so.

Several carpenters halted their work. One whistled, provoking laughter.

Another yelled, "Don' let this one run away, Vai. Not like that one yee lost…"

I blinked, for the man approaching me so determinedly looked exactly as Andevai Diarisso Haranwy would look if he were half dressed and his chest and back sheeny with sweat from hard physical labor.

Blessed Tanit, but it was hot in this country!

He stopped at arm's length.

"Catherine," he said, the word fading as if he hadn't the strength to get it all out.

I couldn't tell if he wanted to embrace me or berate me. Heat burning up my cheeks, I knew what he was going to say: *Who was that man and why was he kissing you when you are my wife?*

He said, "Did Duvai find you?"

After several years of effort that passed in perhaps five sluggish breaths, I sewed together the rudiments of speech out of the remnants of my confounded mind.

"Duvai?"

"After I lost you in that well, I meant to follow you into the spirit world myself at Imbolc. But I was unavoidably detained, and then—well—then it wasn't possible. So I asked my brother Duvai to hunt for you. I must imagine you recall him well enough, since he was the person who guided you out of my village in order to keep you away from me."

Only Andevai could have managed that hint of peevishness, as if he, rather than I, had been the one inconvenienced by the mansa's command to kill me!

"I recall him with a great deal of gratitude, if you must know."

"I do not doubt it," he said quellingly.

"He did not find me." I fished out the locket. "But your grandmother did."

He recoiled, taking a step back. A trio of passing trolls

skirted him without breaking stride, as if accustomed to crowded streets where stray men lurched blindly into their path. A man not quite in control of a dozen leashed, unpleasantly large, and clearly short-tempered snapping lizards yelled at us to get out of the way.

Vai grabbed my wrist. "This isn't the place to have this conversation."

He strode back toward the carpentry yard, me trotting alongside, my mind whirling and my stride kicking awkwardly against the damp pagne. We went in by an unlatched gate. Wood shavings warmed by the sun padded my footsteps. Every man in the yard had ceased working in order to enjoy the spectacle. If one man among the twenty or so was not grinning or chuckling, I did not see him.

"Ja, maku! That a fine catch yee hauled in!"

"That the gal yee lost?"

"Yes," said Vai in a clipped tone which likely meant he was strangling an intense emotion.

An ominous silence dropped over the men.

He tugged me to a thatched-roofed shelter with no walls where a woman, seated in its shade, was measuring a shaved plank with calipers. She had silver-streaked straight black hair and the broad features I was beginning to recognize as Taino.

"Boss," he said, halting beside her table, "I need the rest of the day off. I'll make it up."

She finished her measurements and noted down the figures in an accounts book before she glanced up. She looked me up and down. "We's not running a stud service, Vai. Nor a sly tavern."

Some of the men had come up to the shelter's edge.

"Never say yee mean it, maku," said one of the

younger ones. He had scarred cheeks and a keen gaze. "She really that one yee lost?"

"Yes."

Soft whistles and murmurs greeted this curt pronouncement.

The boss measured me rather as she had just been measuring the plank. With no shift of expression, she nodded. "That change matters, then. I shall expect yee tomorrow, the usual."

"My thanks."

"I shall bring yee tools when I come for the areito," said the young man with the scars.

"My thanks, Kofi," said Vai in the absentminded tone of a man whose thoughts have already galloped over the next hill. He led me to another shelter, where he let go of me to grab a singlet out of several draped over a sawhorse. After tugging it on, he unhooked a leather bottle from a crossbeam.

"Drink," he said, unstoppering it. "You look sun-reddened."

"What is it?" I asked suspiciously.

"Guava juice sweetened with pineapple and lime. You need to drink or you'll get sun sick."

It was juice, sweet and pure, and after I had gulped down so much that I burped, he slung the bottle over his shoulder. The carpenters had moved off and the boss had gone back to her measuring. After a hesitation, he clasped my hand in the way of innocent children, palm to palm, and examined me, neither smiling nor frowning.

"Will you come with me, Catherine? Or would you rather not?"

"What choice do I have?" I demanded.

His lips thinned as he pressed them tight as if to hold

back words he didn't want to say. Then he spoke. "Why, the choice I just gave you. Which I meant. Is there something I need to know?"

I flushed, utterly embarrassed. "What do you think you might need to know?"

He looked skyward, released a breath, and addressed me without looking at me. "I must wonder if your... affections are engaged."

"My affections are not engaged. I do not love any man, if that is what you mean."

"Of course it's what I mean! What am I to think, having seen what I saw?"

"Did it not occur to you that he's the one who abandoned me? In a strange city? Oh, la, darling! I have secret business of my own and I'll return to fetch you when I get around to it?"

He looked at the ground, his expression flashing through a series of emotions too complex to unravel. Hard to imagine the man who had worn perfectly polished boots and expensive, tailored dash jackets standing in worn trousers and dusty bare feet in a carpentry yard! "I'm sorry to hear you were abandoned."

"You don't sound sorry. You sound pleased."

"Very well, Catherine." His gaze flashed up to sear me. "I'm not sorry. And I am pleased." He brushed the scabbed-over wound above my right eye, his touch cautious but his tone trembling as on the brink of a cliff. "Unless he's hurt you. In that case, I'll kill him for you, if you like."

"I don't find that amusing."

Thank Tanit, he looked down again, for I could not have borne the intensity of those eyes for one more heart-stopping breath.

I went on. "It would be better just to let it go."

"How like a woman to say so!" he muttered.

"What?"

"Nothing," he said too quickly. When he looked up, he had veiled that boiling glare behind a screen of prickly disdain. "My offer still stands. Come with me, if you wish. I ask nothing of you, except that you allow me to offer you shelter. Or go your own way, if that is what you prefer."

"I'll come with you." I didn't want to let go of a hand that was like a lifeline in a storm-tossed sea.

He closed his eyes briefly, making no reply. Nor did he let go of my hand.

We walked inland. Once away from the carpentry yard we were just another young couple, although I am sure I looked as if I had just been fished out of the sea, so bedraggled was I. The neighborhood was laid out in a grid plan, two-story buildings behind gates and walls, mostly workshops and residential compounds. In the streets, children played a game by hitting a ball with their knees and elbows and calves, and it was quite astonishing how they kept it from touching the ground without ever catching it in their hands. Women dyed cloth in vats and hung the cloth from lines to dry. One pretty woman looked up, began to smile as if to call out a greeting to Vai, then saw me. As her eyes widened, she nudged a companion, and they whispered as they watched us go.

We walked up a quiet boulevard where men were sewing companionably under cloth awnings. The streets were paved with smooth-fitting stone swept clean of debris, and posted with gas lamps for the coming of evening. Past every gate opened a courtyard where more people, of all ages, lounged under shaded shelters or busied themselves at some manner of work. Women carried baskets of vegetables and fruit on their heads. More than one smiled at Vai with a friendly—or over-friendly—greeting, only to notice me with surprise or disbelief. He was polite to everyone, but he plowed forward without stopping.

We turned a corner onto a dusty lane shaded by trees. He led me in through an open gate to a sprawling court-yard with a cistern, a tree, and a two-story wing abutting the back. About a third of the space was taken up by ta-bles and benches set out beneath a vine-swept latticed roof. Behind the tables stretched a counter like a bar in a tavern. To the left lay an open-air kitchen. In its shade, two girls were grating tubers into moist pulp.

A healthily stout woman of middle age stood at a stone hearth, cooking on a griddle. Seeing Vai, she smiled as might an aunt who spots her favorite nephew come to visit. Seeing me, she abandoned the griddle to a girl and, wiping her hands on a cloth tied over her pagne and blouse, walked over to us.

"Never tell me!" she said with a laugh.

"Yes, this is Catherine." He turned to me. "Catherine, this is Aunty Djeneba. She owns this lodging house."

"Peace to you, Aunty," I said, in the village way, be-cause she reminded me of the women of the Tarrant countryside and Adurnam's markets for whom a long ex-change of greetings was the measure of politeness. "Do you have peace?"

"Good morning, Cat'reen," she answered. "'Tis pleas-ing to make yee acquaintance."

"Cat is fine."

"Cat it shall be, then."

I wasn't sure how to go on, so I glanced at Vai for help.

"Catherine, I'm sure you're hungry. Rice and peas, or fish?"

I had never in my life been too stunned to eat. "Might I have both?"

Aunty Djeneba smiled as if I had called her children the best-mannered in the city. "'Tis good when a gal likes to eat," she said with a knowing glance at Vai as if to congratulate him.

I blushed, although I am sure I did not know why.

"Things is still cooking, for 'tis early yet," she added. "Yee like a bath first? Yee look a bit mucked. The gals shall fetch clean cloth, and yee shall wash and hang that yee have on."

"Yes, please," I said with a reflexive courtesy, dipping my knees.

Two girls somewhat younger than me hurried over giggling, and I wasn't sure if it was me and my muck and my foreign manners they were giggling over or the fact that Vai had not yet let go of my hand.

"Lad," Aunty said as she patted flour dust off her hands, "yee run down to the harbor and get pargo from Baba. Cat shall still be here when yee get back."

"Will you?" he asked, looking at me as if he expected me to vanish in a puff of smoke.

"Where else would I go?"

The girls giggled. Aunty swatted them on the arms. His expression got more rigid. With an exhalation that could have been no more pained if he had been pulling a nail from his flesh, he released my hand. For an instant I thought he was going to grab it back, but Aunty nudged him.

"Go on," she said. All the folk in the compound—at this time of day five women, the two girls, an older man and a lad at the counter, plus two old men lounging in sling-backed chairs and an ancient crone likewise, and several toddling children—were watching with evident pleasure.

He walked to the gate. There he halted to look back at me.

"Go on, maku!" There was nothing insulting in her tone, despite what Drake had said about the word. She sounded positively affectionate.

Still, he hesitated.

"I will still be here when you come back," I said, not adding: *Where else do I have to go?*

With a grimace, he left.

The girls led me past the big tree. In its shade two women were washing dishes in a trough fed by a pipe and drained by a ditch lined with ceramic. They greeted me with what appeared to be genuine kindness. Yet the lilt in their speech and the number of unknown words made them difficult to understand. Everything was so strange, and my head was beginning to hurt.

Oh, glorious! A brick-paved platform behind screens made a washhouse. After I set aside my cane, the locket, and the stone, the girls took away all my clothing except for my jacket, which I draped over my arm to hide the bite. By a cunning mechanism with pipes, pumps, a big cistern below and a small one on the roof of the two-storied wing, water flowed through a sieve to create a waterfall of refreshingly cool water. In this shower, I scrubbed away salt and spume and grime with sweet-smelling soap.

I dressed in fresh drawers and a sleeveless bodice tightly laced up like a vest with no blouse over or under it, which the girls assured me was perfectly acceptable attire

for a young woman. I tugged the filthy jacket on over it
anyway. They brought a green cloth whose print depicted
a pattern of fans opening and shutting, which I wrapped
for a skirt. Then they had me sit on one of the benches in
the courtyard while they combed and braided my hair.

The older girl had just finished tying off the end with
a strand of beads when Vai returned with a bundle of
wrapped paper. He took the bundle to the kitchen, washed
his hands, and, at a word from Aunty Djeneba, grabbed
a tray of drink and fruit she had prepared while I was
bathing. He set it on the table and sat on the bench opposite me. Aunty called to the girls, and they giggled and
left us alone.

He poured liquid into a cup, which he pushed across to
me. "You must drink, Catherine."

With his hands, he began to peel an orange object.

I drank. "This juice is the best thing I've ever tasted."

He separated off a wedge of fruit and held it out.
"Here."

It looked moist and cool, so I set down the cup and
tried it. I had to close my eyes because the texture melted
so sweetly inside my mouth.

"Just spit out the seeds," he said, holding out a piece of
the peel.

He fed me half the fruit wedge by wedge before I rec-
ollected myself and said, "You have some."

"You look sunburned and yet you're pale beneath it,
so you've got to eat," he said. "You'd be cooler with that
jacket off."

My healing bite itched like an accusation. "It comforts
me to keep it on."

He shrugged, and fed me the rest.

I licked the sticky juice from my fingers, watching him

self-consciously carve the knife through the peelings as he tried not to stare at me. "Am I still in the spirit world?" I asked.

"No. Why would you think so?"

"Are you really wearing a rope as a belt? Working as a carpenter?"

Had he been a horse, I would have said he bridled. "It's perfectly respectable work. I'm good at it."

"Of course you're good at it. You're good at everything you do."

"Is that meant as a criticism?"

Here was the haughty Andevai I knew! The other one—the polite, caring one so intent on feeding me—was beginning to unsettle me. "Why would you think it a criticism? Mightn't it have just been a description?"

His mouth twitched down. "I'm not sure how I'm meant to answer that. Agree, and I'm proud and vain. Disagree..."

"You'd still be proud and vain, and worse, you'd appear falsely humble. You, a cold mage of rare and unexpected potency. The favored son of Four Moons House."

"Is that what you think? That they favored me?"

"You can't mean they kicked you out?"

"No. I just meant they resent me."

"Yes, I can understand that. A village boy raised to be a laborer whose entire clan serves Four Moons House in clientage. It must have been difficult for the young men raised in all the privilege of the house to see you walk in and best them all."

His mouth twitched up, shading his expression to one of nostalgic triumph. "They hated it."

"And they hated you, too, evidently. But the mansa cannot want to lose you. Nor would your family, for though you were taken away from them to serve as a cold mage, it was clear *they* love you. So why are you here?"

"I might ask you the same question."

"Yes, you might. I'm amazed you haven't yet done so."

He crossed his arms over his chest in a way that unfortunately displayed his muscular forearms to advantage. "Good manners and simple common sense dictate that I should wait until you have a chance to eat."

I laughed.

"Why are you laughing?" he demanded.

"Why do you think I'm laughing?"

"Why would I ask if I already knew?"

"Don't you remember our first meal together, at the inn in Adurnam? Weren't you the one who kept rejecting every dish as not good enough for your consequence?"

"Are you comparing that meal to this one?"

"Comparing the food itself, or just your behavior?"

He shoved the platter aside and rested both arms on the table, gazing at me with a furrowed brow and head cocked to one side. "Why are you answering all my questions with questions?"

"What makes you think I'm answering all your questions with questions?"

"I can't possibly imagine, Catherine." He refilled the cup with juice, as if to give his hands something to do rather than throttle me. "Unless one supposed that hearing you answer all my questions with questions makes me think you are answering all my questions with questions."

"Yes," I said hopefully. My lips parted as I released a breath.

He raised the cup, took a swallow, and lowered it. "Catherine, you are answering all my questions with questions."

My heart began pounding as if I were running. "Yes, I am."

He turned the cup once all the way around. "Past experience suggests you may be doing it purposefully simply to annoy me."

"No, I'm not." I slid the cup out of his hand. "Although it's a tempting thought."

He propped his chin on a hand and considered me until I bit my lower lip. When he spoke, it was as if we were sharing a secret. "You and your cousin crossed into the spirit world in Adurnam. You met my grandmother there. Let me guess. You're under some manner of binding."

"Yes!"

"You have to answer questions with questions."

"Yes. Thank you for realizing!" I reached out impulsively to grasp both his hands.

He looked down, eyes widening.

I snatched my hands back and tucked them out of sight under the table.

He made a business of coughing. "It's easy enough to get around. You're under a binding. If you can tell me what or who has set this binding on you, maybe I can help you break it."

A crow fluttered down to land on the roof of the building in back. Its gaze like a hammer nailed my mouth shut. I just sat there.

Irritation flickered in the tightening of his eyes. Then a thought occurred to him, and his expression cleared. "It makes sense that a binding would *bind* you so you can't speak of it."

"Cold magic can't break this," I whispered, warning him off, for that cursed crow was still watching us.

"Don't think you know what I can manage with regard to cold magic, Catherine."

"Here in the land of the lowly fire bane," I agreed, noting how his gaze narrowed at the phrase. "You haven't answered my question. What could possibly bring you to Expedition?"

He looked past me. Rising, he left the table. Resolutely, I did not turn to watch him. He returned with a huge platter of steaming rice and peas topped by a slab of fish still sizzling from being fried in oil. The smell almost flattened me with its anticipatory aroma. He set down the platter and offered me utensils.

"Don't think to distract me from my question," I muttered as my traitorous hand accepted spoon and knife.

He smiled. I did not like that smile. That smile could peel the clothes right off a woman's body.

"Go on," he said coaxingly.

To my horror, I felt the heat of a blush rising just as if he had voiced that very suggestion and I was actually considering it.

He rocked back, caught himself, and let out a deep breath.

"Aunty makes the best rice and peas in the city," he said in an altered tone.

He dug in. The sight of him eating with such gusto shocked me into temporary immobility. Then the smell of the food seduced me. The rice and round beans had been cooked in a creamy milk, and had a peppery flavor not burning but warm. The fish was white and flaky and perfect. It was so good and I was so hungry.

He paused. A disdainful frown creased his face. "Someone hasn't been feeding you properly."

I dropped my gaze back to the food so I didn't have to

look at Vai in case he would guess that I was thinking of Drake, for it seemed obvious *he* was referring to Drake. "You still didn't answer. What brought you to Expedition?"

"A three-masted ship."

"Don't lie to me!" I set down my spoon.

"I didn't lie to you. It was a three-masted ship. As for why I am here, I came to help my sister make a new life here."

"Kayleigh? And the mansa just let her go?"

He tucked away several spoonfuls of the rice and peas as he considered. "Obviously it is not that simple, but it's all I can say. If you thereby feel you cannot tell me what brings you to Expedition, then I will understand your reluctance to trust me. But you must know, Catherine, even if you can or wish to say nothing, I will give you whatever shelter and help you need. Anything."

The word hit so hard I closed my eyes briefly out of sheer gratitude and relief. I was not alone and friendless. But I had to be pragmatic. "*Anything* encompasses a great deal. I have nothing except the clothes on my back and my sword. And my father's locket, which I have thanks to you."

"I won't abandon you."

Mercifully he did not add *as your lover evidently did*, but when he looked at me with that accusatory gaze, I knew he knew I knew he was thinking it.

"Thank you." I lowered my gaze to the mundanity of the platter. Gracious Melqart! Between us, we had eaten through almost all of it. "Are you sure we're not still in the spirit world?"

"I'm sure. But I wonder why you might think so."

"I just never saw you eat like a normal person before.

You said once that cold magic fed you. Doesn't it here?"

"The secret belongs to those who know how to keep silent."

The words ought to have annoyed me, but instead they reminded me of the other thing I possessed. I fished the stone from the jacket's hem. "I found...this." I handed it to him.

He gasped.

"Your grandmother walked with us for a while. I must say, she scolded me on your behalf. She favors you. It was very irritating."

His smile twitched but did not quite bloom. Wisely, he said nothing.

"Then she was caught in the tide of a dragon's dream. It swept over her, and she was gone."

"Not gone, Catherine. Changed."

I dropped my voice to a whisper. "Is the stone your grandmother?"

"Of course it isn't my grandmother!"

"Her—uh—her soul, then?"

"What odd notions you hold, Catherine. Is this some sort of Phoenician belief?"

"Can't you remember that it is properly Kena'ani, not Phoenician?"

"I beg your pardon. You told me before, and I forgot." He closed his fingers over the stone. "Something of my grandmother touches this stone. By holding it close, we are close to her. If we sit down to a meal and pour the first drops of our wine on the stone, then she will be called to dwell close beside us." He rose, still clutching the stone. "If you'll excuse me..."

"Go and do what is proper. I'll see if Aunty needs help."

He took a step away but turned back to brush my hand with his own as if checking to make sure I was a solid creature and not an illusion woven out of light like the one he had once woven of my face. He walked to the two-story wing, hurried up the stairs, and vanished into a room.

If I had a thought, I am sure it was too faint to register. At length, I stopped staring after him. I finished the food and carried the tray back to the kitchen sideboard.

"A good appetite is a precious thing," Aunty Djeneba remarked. She was back at the griddle.

"The food was splendid. My thanks. Can I help in some way? I'm a good worker. I know how to sew, cook, read, and write. I must tell you, I have nothing, no coin, no possessions, nothing but my labor to offer you."

"Yee's married to Vai, is yee not?"

I blinked. At least four times. I had no idea what my expression looked like, but Aunty Djeneba glanced away, and the girls giggled.

"Is that what he told you?" I demanded.

She considered me thoughtfully. "Everyone around here know the story. He and he sister come here six months ago. He is handsome and charming. He work hard. Know how to make friends. He manners is so very good, I should like to meet he mother. Such a young man is like a flower. The gals will come round to see if they can pluck it. But yee know, Cat, never a hint of that with him. Always he is talking about the gal he lost, that one he married. How can he look at another when he don' know what had become of she he had lost? Yee know all this, don' yee?" She grasped my arm. "Yee need to sit down?"

"Why would I need to sit down?" But I could not get out the other questions foaming up in my thoughts: How had the world come unmoored? Who was this baffling personage pretending to be my husband the arrogant cold mage? Was I actually going to be safe here? How could I save Bee?

"Yee's looking unsteady, gal." She guided me to a sling-backed chair next to a toothless old woman who smiled at me but spoke no word. "Sit."

I sank into the sway-backed canvas and shut my eyes, overcome by a sense of extreme disorientation and by the unrelenting heat.

I dozed off. When I woke, the shadows had drawn long across the courtyard and a dozen children of varying ages were standing in a semicircle watching me with great round stares. As soon as my open eyes registered, one of the little lads raced across the courtyard over to the long counter where men gathered, drinking and talking. Vai was deep in conversation with men his own age who looked vaguely familiar, likely carpenters from the yard, the ones I'd thought had been teasing him. Except they hadn't been teasing him at all.

Someone laughed; a couple of the men made sparring gestures, play fighting. The little lad tugged on Vai's arm, and he turned. His gaze met mine, and he made excuses and threaded through the crowd and over to the shelter. The children crowded around as he crouched beside me.

"Catherine, I hope you are feeling well, not ill."

"I'm just so hot and thirsty."

He tapped one of the little girls. "Juice." With a bright grin, she hurried off and returned in triumph with a full cup. "Best if you rest until you get your feet under you."

I drank. My head hurt and I felt queasy, but I did not want to complain. "Let me just sit."

"Send one of the little lads if you need anything. The

girls can fetch you juice. No giggling or talking." As he rose, I belatedly realized the last was a command meant for the children.

He went back to his friends. I shut my eyes, because the shifting angle of the sun's rays beyond my patch of shade was making me dizzy. The lilt and cadence of voices comforted me. Rain pounded on the shelter's roof, kissing me with a cooling draft. Then it was hot again, and I tried to wake up, but I kept fading.

I heard them talking, but it was too hard to open my eyes.

"Are you sure she's not a shade come to haunt you? Like what they call *opia* here?"

"Of course I'm sure, Kayleigh! She and I are bound by threads of magic chained by a djeli through a mirror. I *knew* the locket would bring her to me."

"She doesn't even like you."

"I wouldn't be so sure about that." His tone had a smile in it.

"Could you be more vain? You can't think she came here to find you! Kofi told me she came in on a canoe up from Cow Killer Beach. It's all criminals, witches, and whores down there."

"Don't you talk like that, Kayleigh!"

"I'm just saying it's got a bad reputation. That's a nasty gash at her eye. How did she get it?"

"It doesn't matter. What matters is she's here, and she's safe."

"I heard she was with another man."

A breath of cool breeze soothed my fevered brow.

"Don't get mad at me, Vai. It's the truth. Kofi saw you see him. He said it looked like you wanted to plant your adze in the other man's...face."

It got a little colder. Then, alas, the breath of ice eased. "I see now. You're jealous."

Her voice did have a touch of discontented whine. "You promised you would come with me to the areito. But now you're going to sit here all night and stare at her."

His anger faded entirely. "I can't leave her to wake up to unfamiliar faces. Here's Kofi. Doesn't he look all cleaned up for you! Because I assure you it's not for my benefit. But before you leave for the areito, he and I need to have a talk about what we tell little sisters."

I opened my eyes into a blur of confusing images: The young carpenter with the scars wavered into view wearing a colorful jacket and with his locks ornamented with beads; he was smiling at Vai's younger sister Kayleigh, who had on a blouse and wrapped pagne in the local way, her blouse ornamented by white necklaces whose polished gleam bore me under into a white-capped sea turgid with ice; a masked face, bright and unkindly, turned to look at me; a latch winked with glittering eyes; a crow swept down in a shroud of black wings. I moaned, trying to get away, but it pecked at my weeping eyes, and I turned to salt and dissolved into the foaming ocean water.

"Catherine?"

I gasped, bolting upright, heart pounding and breath ragged.

Night had fallen. A finely etched and exceedingly delicate bauble of cold fire illuminated Vai's face. Beyond, by lamplight, people were clearing the tables and setting the benches in order.

"I don't feel well," I whispered.

"No," he agreed. He got his arms under me and lifted me bodily out of the chair. "If you can use the privy yourself, I'll take you there. Otherwise I'll ask Aunty to come help you."

"I can do it myself."

I could, and I did, although I got confused by the pipes and the bowl and the water-flushing mechanism that the girls had showed me how to use earlier, very elaborate and hygienic and unlike anything I had ever seen in Adurnam. I was reeling with dizziness when I came out, so he carried me up the stairs and into a room and onto a narrow cot.

He peeled me out of my jacket, and there was a sudden silence even though it was already quiet. Afterward he let go of my arm and wiped down my face and neck and arms with a cool cloth. He made me drink in sips and then he moved away and I heard him talking in a low, urgent voice but I couldn't understand the words.

I tossed and turned. As in a restless dream, an old man with feathers and shells in his hair entered the room. His calloused hand traced my navel; his lips pressed against my forehead with a kiss that snaked through my body to kindle my blood.

His unfamiliar voice spoke. "*She is clean.*"

20

Later, it was quiet, a hint of breeze pooling around my face.

"Aunty, it was the worst moment of my life, when she slipped away from me down the well. I thought I'd lost her forever. And then, when I took off her jacket and saw that bite…"

"Don' borrow trouble, lad. The behique say she is clean. Anyway, better if yee go on to yee work, else yee shall be a nuisance all day. See how she stir, because she hear yee voice? She need to sleep, for she is sorely tired and worn. Go on. I shall watch."

I woke to daylight and a stifling heat like sludge in my lungs. Rain broke overhead, a downpour so torrential I could hear nothing but its drumming on the tile roof. The air cooled. My headache eased. The rain stopped.

I lay on a cot. I wore only drawers and a thin muslin blouse. There had been a cover over me but I had kicked it off. My cane was tucked along one side. I swung my legs over the side of the bed and cautiously rose, but my head seemed fit on properly. I found a pagne hanging over the screen that divided the little room into two, with a cot on either side and baskets hanging from the center beam. A sheathed sword lay tucked into the rafters, safe from stealing because no one could touch Vai's cold steel except him. A basket on the floor contained my folded clothing. I bound on the bodice and wrapped the pagne. The blouse's sleeves were long enough to cover the healing bite.

My mouth tasted of unpleasant memories. Drake had deserted me to make my own way to the Speckled Iguana, where I would have fallen sick all alone. Not like here, where people—Vai—cared what happened to me. Blessed Tanit! The thought of possibly carrying Drake's child and what would become of me if I did made me determined to forge my own path. I was not going to crawl to Drake to beg for help.

"Ja, maku!" One of the girls peeked in at the open door. She looked a bit older than Bee's sister Hanan, perhaps fifteen, and with her springy black hair and brown complexion resembled Aunty. "Yee feeling better? Eh! Never mind the question. Yee look not so like fouled cassava paste. I thought sure yee would faint right away last night."

"I am better, thank you. Never mind what question?"

"Vai say never to ask yee a question. 'Tis almost supper, if yee's hungry."

I had to pee, and I realized I was, indeed, hungry as well as furiously thirsty. "My thanks for the folded clothes. What's your name? If you told me, I forgot."

"Lucretia."

"No. Really?"

She grinned. "Me dad's a Roman sailor. He turn up once a year, all faithful like. 'Tis why I have eight little sisters."

I laughed and followed her downstairs into the courtyard where men and boys were setting out benches and hauling in barrels, and women and girls were cooking. Aunty Djeneba ran not only a lodging house but an eating and drinking establishment as well, the sort of place people, mostly men, came to relax after a day's hot work. The low-hanging sun peeking out from a tumult of clouds gave the light a muted glow.

In the outdoor kitchen, Aunty Djeneba greeted me by looking me over. "Yee stay quiet this evening. Tomorrow we shall talk. Here come Vai."

He had wood shavings caught in his hair, and a residue of sawdust streaked his bare arms. He gave me a long, searching look, which I endured by drawing out my locket and playing with it. "You look like you feel better."

"I slept all day." I wanted to say more, but my tongue had turned to stone.

"You know, Aunty," he said, "I need to go out to the Moonday gathering, if I can."

"I shall see she come to no harm."

"What gathering?" I asked.

"I'll take you another time. If you'll excuse me. I'll just stow this in my room." He had a canvas apron slung over his back with tools tucked into sewn compartments. He hurried upstairs, and when he came down, his friends, including Kofi, had appeared at the gate. They stared curiously at me but did not approach, and they left with Vai.

"I reckon yee shall be most comfortable by Aunty Brigid," said Aunty.

I crept to the sling chair in the shelter behind the kitchen, next to the toothless old woman who smiled and spoke no word. There were always at least two children hovering, anxious to fetch me juice. I was not hungry, but I could have drunk the sea and then some.

Kayleigh came in as night fell, wearing a pretty pagne,

her locks brightened with ribbons. She looked exactly as she had last year: tall, robust, and if not as stunning as her brother, still she was a good-looking young woman, one who had not fully left girlhood behind. As she came closer the lines of weariness on her face became evident.

After a hesitation, she came over. "Cat Barahal. You must be feeling better." She mopped her brow with a scrap of cloth. "Vai went out. He'd not have if he thought you were sick."

Lucretia appeared with a cup of the cloudy ginger beer everyone here drank. "I hear a rumor the general came back today."

Kayleigh accepted the cup with a grateful smile. "He is still in Taino country."

"Me father said the cacica would kick him out when he came a-courting."

"Your father is Roman, Luce. He sees the general as the enemy. Word at Warden Hall is that the cacica and the general are negotiating. That has made the Council very nervous."

"Do you mean Camjiata?" I asked. "This cacica, would that be Prince Caonabo's mother?"

Both girls looked at me as if I had sprouted wings and a third eye.

Kayleigh drained the cup and handed it to Lucretia. "I'll go wash up." She strode off.

"Have I done something to offend her?"

"Never mind she," said Lucretia. "She do work very hard at Warden Hall."

"What is Warden Hall?"

"Ja, maku! Yee know nothing! The wardens keep order in Expedition and enforce the law."

I could not help but think that working as a servant at

Warden Hall would be a cursed good way to eavesdrop on delicate conversations.

"So I's just saying," Lucretia went on, "that she is nice. Truly. Not so charming as she brother, but...I mean, all they women come around all the time. Yet he never look twice at any! Being he sister, she always that one who count with him. And now here yee come."

"Washed up on shore like a three-days-dead fish."

She giggled. "Yee's so funny."

I went back up to the room with a candle. Kayleigh had fallen asleep on the other cot, which meant I had slept on Vai's cot last night. Tomorrow we would obviously have to discuss other sleeping arrangements. I slept soundly. When I woke the next morning, Kayleigh was gone. I didn't know where Vai had slept.

The courtyard had a calm beauty in the soft light.

"Where are all the children?" I asked Aunty Djeneba, who was grating the white root called cassava. "Where is Lucretia?"

"At school. They finish at noon. As for yee, we shall start yee easy today. Yee said yee can sew. I have got some mending by. Usually we take it down to Tailors' Row but it would be a quiet job for yee in the shade."

I pulled a bench over so I could sit under the kitchen roof. We were alone in the courtyard.

She said in a low voice, "One thing first. Yee must keep that arm covered until the wound heal. Yee must never speak of what happened. Never."

I touched my sleeve, feeling the tender wound beneath. "Vai must have seen the bite when he took my jacket off."

"Yes, and came to me at once, exactly as he should. I went out me own self and brought in a local behique, a good man, very discreet. Only we four know."

We four, and everyone on Salt Island, but I didn't volunteer the information. "I know what will happen to me if the wardens track me down. But would something happen to you, Aunty?"

She paused in her grating. "It speak well of yee that yee ask, gal. I would be arrested and lose everything I own."

"That is a terrible risk. Why take me in?"

She indicated the sewing basket and a folded stack of old clothes. "Here is a great lot of torn hems, ripped sleeves, and holes worn in elbows and knees. We people who live outside the old city have come to believe Expedition's Council see us as these old clothes to use and throw out. If yee was the daughter of a Council family, we would hear no talk of sending yee to Salt Island."

"My father wrote that if all are not equal before the law, then the law is worth nothing."

"A wise man, that one who sired yee. Walk he still among the living?"

I looked away because I could say nothing.

"Seem the grief is still fresh," she said kindly.

She returned to cutting, grating, and grinding, while I found peace in mending as she talked about how her people could trace their descent to sailors on the first fleet. She had herself married a man whose grandparents had left Celtic Brigantia to make their fortune in the markets of Expedition. Her husband had passed on a night three years ago when an owl had roosted atop the roof. Her three sons worked a fishing boat with their uncle her brother, and her only surviving daughter Brenna, the one with the Roman sweetheart, helped her run the lodging house. Uncle Joe, widower of Aunty's sister, oversaw the part of the establishment where folk came to eat and drink.

"Do you have gaslight on all the streets in Expedition? Only a few places have gaslight in Adurnam."

"All of the old city and the harbor district and troll town, of course. We here in Passaporte District got the street lighting three years ago. Only because we took to the streets in protest that we pay land tax and excise tax and we shall see something for the coin we pay to the Council's treasury. But Lucairi District and them on out there? Nothing. They must still rely on fire banes to light they way at night."

Here was my chance to find out more about mages in this part of the world.

"Fire banes work like common lamplighters and linkboys here?" I finished off mending a threadbare elbow with a pattern darning and held it up.

She looked surprised. "'Tis as good as tailor's work. Yee have a neat hand for a woman. Fire banes likewise work for the fire wardens and at areitos and other night gatherings."

"What's an areito? A festival of some kind?"

"'Tis the Taino word for a sacred or community gathering, what the Romans would call a festival. As for the other, all fire banes must register with Warden Hall. That is the law. At that time they swear never to enter any association with other mages."

"I've seen the power the mage Houses hold in Europa, so I can understand people in Expedition might be cautious about mage associations. Is there a button for this?"

"In the tin. It need two. If yee's not registered as a fire bane, yee can be arrested. If yee go to register, yee's not yet registered, so yee can be arrested if they want to arrest yee."

"That's exceedingly unfair! Why would the wardens want to arrest fire banes anyway?"

"Because they sell them to the Taino. The proceeds go to Council's treasury."

"Why would the Taino want fire banes?"

"Why, as catch-fires. No Taino fire mage take a first breath come the morning without a catch-fire nearby."

I paused, needle frozen in midair, remembering the three salters Drake had used to catch the accelerating fire of his magic so it wouldn't consume him. "That's awful! Why would anyone let fire banes be taken and sold?"

"Because the wardens only take them who have no one to protect them. Fire banes born into a family with much money or a big house in the old city never go missing, never is sold out, nor never is they forced to work for the fire wardens. There is one rule for the rich and another for the rest. So a maku come to these shores is easy game. Yee shall find, Cat, that folk round here say nothing to the wardens no matter what we go a-seeing. Yee understand?"

Since I understood she was telling me that she knew Vai was a fire bane and that I was never to mention it to anyone, I nodded. I fished out another button and began sewing it on. "Are there many powerful fire mages in the Taino kingdom?"

She lowered her voice. "'Tis best be cautious and not speak of behiques, Cat. Yee would not want to come to they notice."

I moved on, for now. "When did General Camjiata come to Expedition?"

"He and his people landed in Februarius. That man have caused so much trouble over where yee come from. And now he come here and go asking for we help. He want us to pay for he to start up a new war back there in Europa."

"He traveled here to get aid from Expedition's Council?"

"He asked. 'Tis one thing the Council done right. They said no."

"They refused to help him! Is that why he went to the Taino capital? To seek Taino aid?"

"So it look. Any reckoning we look at it, 'tis bad news for Expedition. One time long ago there was many caciques on Kiskeya. Now there is only one, and that one rule over all the islands of the Antilles. I foresee nothing but trouble if the Taino decide to look this way."

"So they're an empire, like the Romans. But if the Taino cacique and his clan are so powerful, why don't they just take over Expedition Territory and its factories and port?"

She smiled. "A smart gal, too, to ask that question. No wonder Vai is so smitten with yee."

I pawed through the tin looking for a button I did not need. Feeling her gaze on me, I poured buttons onto my palm and scrutinized them.

She said, "If the Taino is one thing, they is holders of the law. In the First Treaty, the Taino caciques swore they shall never cross the border between Taino country and Expedition Territory. So by Taino way of thinking, to break the treaty is to dishonor the cemi. Yee know, they ancestors. By the by, Cat. When I speak of agreements, it remind me. Vai ask me last night about renting a hammock in the common hall. I thought he mean for Kayleigh, but he mean for he own self. Yee and she is to share the room, which he pay for, and he to sleep elsewhere."

The buttons were bronze and formed out of the same mold. In a household practicing economy, it was wise to buy plain buttons so they could be interchanged on various garments.

"Not that 'tis any of me business," she added in a tone that implied the opposite, "but peace in the house make peace in the heart."

The buttons stared back at me. Not that it was any of their business!

"It's not my place to speak of such intimate matters," I said in a tone I hoped walked the fine line between being polite and absolutely crushing this subject into oblivion. "I was hoping to ask to borrow thread. I'll pay you back, of course. I can salvage a great deal from my skirts and petticoats by piecing together one skirt from the remnants. I could manage a few work vests—singlets, I mean—from the scraps if your little lads have need of such. It's quite good quality wool challis…" I trailed off, surprised to find my hands in fists, buttons biting into my palms.

She gave me a measuring look. "Happen that young man ever hit yee?"

"Hit me? Like, beat me?"

"He don' seem like that kind. But I reckon I best ask."

"No. That's not what happened. Although he's said some pretty awful things to me."

She smiled wryly. "I admit, that lad have a sharp tongue when he wish, not that he ever use it on he elders! And he think very well of he own self."

"That is a way of describing it," I agreed.

She chuckled. "Yee may use any of the thread in the copper tin. If yee's feeling up to it, I reckon I shall set yee to serving food and drink in the evenings. Yee's a pleasing gal to look on, and yee have a bold way of speaking. 'Tis hard to get help these days with the factories hiring so many."

"I can do that. Aunty, I'm grateful to you for taking me in. I mean to earn my keep."

"Seeing that look on Vai's face when he brought yee back is keep enough, but fear not, gal. I shall see yee earn yee bed." She laughed merrily at whatever expression blanched my face.

I fetched my ruined skirts and borrowed scissors from one of the neighbor men. At a table in front of an interested audience of children and the regular customers who always came early, I began dismantling the ripped and torn remains while I spun a carefully worded tale that left out Salt Island, James Drake, and Prince Caonabo, and jumped straight from the watery attack to my beach rescue by buccaneers. The rains came through, as they did every afternoon, and more people gathered as folk left off work for the day and came to drink and relax.

"Yee say yee was attacked by a shark? Describe what yee saw, gal."

"It was very large, and a nasty shiny gray, and it had dead flat eyes. I must say, I've never been so terrified in my life." *Except standing before the creature who sired me.* "I punched it, and it swam off."

They laughed and whistled. Several began debating whether it was a *carite* or a *cajaya*, two different kinds of sharks known to attack people. I looked up to see Vai standing in the back with arms crossed, glowering as if I had personally offended him. By the evidence of sawdust dusting his skin, he had only recently come in and not yet washed; he'd tied a kerchief over his head today, making him look very buccaneer-ish, a man about to sail off in an airship except of course for the minor issue of his deflating the balloon and thereby causing a spectacular crash.

"That shark is not the predator yee shall have been feared of, gal," said Uncle Joe. "'Tis they buccaneers yee shall have feared more. Seem yee was rescued off the beach by the Barr Cousins. They is called Nick Blade for he knives and the Hyena Queen for the way she laugh."

"The Barr Cousins? Likely so. We were never formally introduced."

"Yee's killing me, gal!" said some wit in the crowd. " 'Never formally introduced!' "

"She said her grandmother was a Kena'ani woman. That makes us cousins of a sort. Maybe more, since I'm a Barahal. We might be truly cousins, if their ancestors shortened the Barahal name to Barr. That must be why we got along so well."

My bravado sent my audience into gales of laughter as I measured cloth against the waistband. As Vai's gaze swept across my audience, they stepped back just as if he had pushed each one. Maybe he had, for the air had a sudden bite. All hastily moved away to other tables.

He sat down opposite me, arms still crossed. "You'll get sick again if you overdo it."

I kept my voice low as I pinned cloth to the waistband, for although the customers had gone to sit elsewhere that did not mean they weren't watching. "I need to earn my keep, Vai, not as your kept woman. It does amaze me how you felt able to tell everyone the gripping tale of how you lost your darling wife and have searched for her ever since. How heartbreaking. How noble."

"It keeps away the women."

Irritation marred the features of most men, making them look small-minded or ill-tempered. Not Vai. Irritation sharpened his features, made a woman want to kiss him until he relented. I imagined hungry young women buzzing like bees to a succulently annoyed flower.

He raised an eyebrow, in supercilious query.

"How nice for you," I said, since he was clearly expecting a response to a statement meant to provoke me. "Or not."

"Don't change the subject, Catherine. I don't see how the tale I told is much different than the one you just embroidered."

"It's all true!"

"I'm sure it is. If anyone could punch a shark in the eye and survive to tell of it, it would be you."

"I would thank you for the fine praise, except you looked so annoyed when I was telling that part of the story."

"Yes, annoyance was certainly my first reaction on hearing you had been attacked by a shark. I couldn't possibly have been shocked or terrified on your behalf. Although you left out the part about exactly how you found yourself floating in the middle of the sea in the first place."

"Would you have turned me over to the wardens if I hadn't been clean?"

His chin raised as sharply as if I had slapped him. A breath of ice kissed my lips.

Because I was suddenly, inexplicably furious, I pressed my attack, leaning closer with an aggressive whisper. "You would have been right to do so. I was on Salt Island."

He stood so quickly that all around the courtyard people jumped, and looked forcibly away. He grabbed my arm and dragged me closer, across the table. The table's edge dug into my thighs.

His voice emerged in a hoarse murmur. "You just dreamed that. *You were never there.*"

"Let go," I said, rigid beneath his hand. All I could see was Abby's face.

He released me. Sat down. Shut his eyes, breathing hard, as the cold eddy of air around us faded. I fought to recover my composure. As I straightened out the disturbed fabric, I wondered what people were making of all this. It would be an easy plate to garnish: The long-parted lovers quarrel over the circumstance that precipitated their separation.

When his breathing had settled, he opened his eyes and considered me with the haughty arrogance I knew best. "Which explains the presence of the fire mage. Although I can't quite figure how a fire mage might have come to be working with the notorious Barr Cousins."

I parried. "I don't think the Barr Cousins liked the fire mage much."

"Good for them. I don't like him much either."

"I didn't ask you to like him. You don't even know him."

He set his elbows on the table, heedless of the fabric I was neatly piecing back together. "There is where you are wrong. I met him in Adurnam. In the entryway of the law offices of Godwik and Clutch. Where I also found you. I remembered that when I saw him again today—"

Jerking up, I stabbed myself with a pin. "Ah!"

"—Wandering around the harbor with a ridiculous cap pulled down to cover his red hair and asking about a girl he had lost track of after he had rescued her from a shipwreck on a deserted islet. I'm surprised you forgot to mention the shipwreck in your otherwise flamboyant tale."

I licked a spot of blood from my finger.

"I must wonder why he was in Adurnam then, and why he came here now," he finished.

Vai didn't know General Camjiata had been in the law offices in Adurnam. And I wasn't about to tell him since it was none of his cursed business and nothing to do with me anyway no matter what the Iberian Monster claimed.

"I never met Drake before that day in Adurnam," I said quite truthfully, "and then not again until that which we won't speak of." But I sat down, resting my head in my hands because otherwise I was going to touch my belly. "Blessed Tanit! Did anyone tell him where I'd gone?"

"No one did in the carpentry yard. I did find out you can leave a message for him at the Speckled Iguana. Shall we go over there now?"

I found the courage to look at him. "Can't I just stay here?"

He exhaled sharply. Then the self-satisfied lift of his mouth betrayed him. "You can, if that's what you want."

I began to tremble. "You couldn't just come straight out and ask me what you really want to know, which I must suppose is whether I want to go back to James Drake. At least the infamous murderer Nick Blade was honest with me!"

That made him sit up straight. "Do enlighten me!"

"He scolded me. He said, 'Don't you go getting drunk around men. What do you think will happen?'"

"Did he, now?" said the arrogant cold mage thoughtfully, drawing forefinger and thumb down the line of his jaw in a way that dragged my gaze toward his lips.

"Do you think I'm lying about that?" I snapped.

"Did I say I thought you were lying?"

"Are you going to ask me questions to annoy me?" I considered stabbing him with a pin.

"Who do you think can keep this up longer?" he said with an aggravating smirk. He rose, snagged a cup from a tray being carried past by Brenna—who smiled on him as if wishing him good fortune!—and handed it to me. "Have a drink?"

"Are you trying to get me drunk?"

"Why would I want to get you drunk, Catherine?"

"Isn't that a way men seduce women—?" I broke off, so flustered and ashamed that all I could do was take a drink. It was juice, sweet and pure.

"I've heard it is the only way some men can manage to seduce women." He took the cup from my hand, drained it, and mercifully changed the subject. "I wish I could know how you are able to stand hidden in plain sight in a chamber where I can see you but others cannot."

I leaned toward him confidingly, and he caught in a breath.

In a low voice, I said, "The secret belongs to those who remain silent."

He laughed quite charmingly, curse him, for it was the laugh of a man willing to be amused at his own expense. "How long have you been waiting to say that to me?"

"How long do you think I've been waiting?"

"I would suppose, since the very first time you heard me say it. Well, Catherine, I am nothing if not persistent. I *also* wish I could know if you sailed from Europa to the Antilles, or if you made the journey here while still in the spirit world."

"And I wish I could know why you and your sister are here. I don't believe the mansa is generous enough to let go of a girl who might be bred for the hope of more potent cold mages."

He smiled in a way that made me wary. "There show the cat's claws. It's a fair assessment. I will not lie to you, Catherine. Like you, I have things I am not free to speak of. Let me know what I can do to help you with settling in."

I bundled up the skirts. "I'll sew in the mornings and serve in the evenings. I start tonight."

I challenged him with a glare to protest that I needed to rest another day. He merely smiled a soft smile that made my heart turn over, an anatomically impossible maneuver that had the unexpected consequence of heating my blood to a boil.

I had been bound into marriage against my will and chained by magic in ways I did not understand. If the head of the poet Bran Cof had told the truth, I could be released from the marriage as long as I did not succumb to an inconvenient attraction to his physical form. I had a dreadful task assigned me. I could not afford sentiment, or distraction. The master of the Wild Hunt was not interested in sentiment, nor would he be distracted. Bee had already called me heartless, and years of living in an impoverished household had taught me how to be sensible.

Taking a deep breath, I began folding up the fabric. Having to be careful with the pins was good practice. Pins drew blood if they pricked you hard enough.

"Just so you understand, Vai. I am grateful for your help. But nothing has changed between us that we have not already discussed."

I glanced up to see how he was taking my implacable declaration, only to surprise a look on his face which I could only describe as calculating.

"What?" I demanded. "You look like you're plotting a crime."

He looked away so quickly it was as good as a confession.

"We're finished here." I pressed cloth to my chest like a shield and stepped back from the table. Around the courtyard, people were pretending not to watch, but they were watching.

He let me go without saying one more word.

21

To wait tables, you had to have a good memory, be quick on your feet, and know how to keep men laughing while you avoided hands touching you in places you weren't keen on being touched. Whatever tips they gave me—small coins but solid—were mine to keep. And I needed money, for Aunty was paying me in room and board. So I worked long hours, every afternoon and evening from the first arrival to the last departure.

At first I stuck close to the boardinghouse, going out only with Aunty, Brenna, or Lucretia as I got to know Tailors' Row, the local market, and the larger neighborhood. I needed to reconnoiter my ground. Above all, I did not want to stumble across James Drake.

The following Jovesday afternoon Vai returned from work carrying a pair of sandals. I delivered a tray of ginger beer to a table of men arguing over the results of a batey game and brought a cup of juice to Lucretia and her next youngest sister. Under the shade of the big tree, they were straining pimento-soaked rum through cheesecloth for liqueur. Luce accepted the cup with a smile, then glanced toward Vai, who was waiting by the stairs. I went over.

He held out the sandals. "Catherine, these are for you."

"I can't afford them. And I won't accept gifts from you."

He glanced up at the tapering, oblong leaves of the ceiba tree as if to find patience hiding in the lofty branches. "Don't take them for your own sake. Do it for Aunty. You're walking around here all day and night, and to the market and up and down Tailors' Row—"

"How do you know what I'm doing during the day when you're at work?"

His glance toward Lucretia betrayed him. "If you cut your feet, you can't wait tables…" He paused.

I turned to see two trolls standing in the gate, looking around with predatory gazes. One was tall, drab, and likely female, and the other was short, brightly crested, and likely male. They wore the long cotton jackets commonly worn by men of business in Expedition, the cloth a plain dark green, smeared with soot and oil stains. The customers looked toward them with the same mild disinterest they showed when a street vendor appeared with a tray of cigarillos or taffy, and then at Vai.

He said in a low voice, "Catherine, don't be an idiot. You've been walking around barefoot for over a week."

"I can't wear my winter boots."

"I didn't say you should. These are cheap sandals. Just take them. I have to go out."

I took the sandals. He joined the trolls at the gate and left. Why would a cold mage be fraternizing with trolls?

"Oooh me stars!" Lucretia sidled up beside me, smelling of pimento, cinnamon, lime, and rum. After prying the sandals out of my hands, she found the maker's mark on the sole. "These cost him a pretty bit of coin!"

"He said they were cheap sandals."

She rolled her eyes as she handed them back to me. "Yee believe that if yee wish, Cat."

I measured them against my dust-smeared feet. "How did he know my size? Luce? Did you sneak him my boots and then put them back? Are you telling him tales on me?"

She grabbed one of the sandals and whacked me on the hip with it. "Yee's so stubborn. Just wear the sandals and be glad yee have such, since there is many who have no shoes."

It was, I realized, a point of pride in Aunty's household that all the children had shoes and could afford the fee for the district school. For however busy the courtyard was every night and however full the boardinghouse stayed, signs of economical living crept out everywhere, things I recognized from my own upbringing. Chastened, I washed my feet, put on the sandals, and went back to work.

"Sweet Cat, a round of beer! I see yee have new sandals."

Sweet Cat was what the elderly regulars had decided to call me. "Nice of him to bring them round before he had to go off again."

"Yes, he go every Jovesday with those two. Yee know them, I suppose."

"The only trolls I ever knew were lawyers." I cast my lure. "Are there many troll lawyers here?"

"Many troll lawyers! Yee's such a maku, Sweet Cat! Now, yee listen."

They liked to explain things to me, because I listened so well. Trolls loved the law the way batey players loved the game. They were known as specialists in scratching over the finer points of the law and pecking through every least step in the contractual procedures on which legal arrangements were created and implemented. Troll-owned law offices tended to congregate in areas by specialty;

law houses that worked maritime law or that anchored branches gone overseas could be found in the harbor district just outside the old city.

By the end of the second week, I had begun to make friends with several of the tailors. Useful and pleasant of themselves, these acquaintances allowed me to have an excuse one morning to depart with apparent innocence on a stroll down Tailors' Row, where I might chat the morning away over the intricacies of patterns, stitches, and the weight and tensile strength of threads.

As I walked away from the boardinghouse, I turned over in my mind the things I had learned. The old city was ringed by an old fortress wall, and these days only families eligible to serve on the Council were allowed to own property there. East and north of the city, along the river, lay the burgeoning factory district. West lay the sprawl of residential districts like Passaporte, where Aunty Djeneba had her boardinghouse. Beyond the city lay farming country, and beyond that the border with the Taino kingdom.

I made my way seaward. The jetty was both a stony barrier between land and sea, and a long avenue running along the shore. It linked the old city with the districts that had sprouted up outside the original walls. I set my path east past the squat clock tower and toward the airship towers and the ships in the main harbor, which lay perhaps a league away. It felt good to stride. Because it was early, the heat hadn't grown too thick.

I bound threads of magic around me, not concealing myself so much that a cart might ram into me but shifting myself into that space of things no one much notices: I was nothing more than the cobbled street, or a dog curled up in the shade of a mango tree, or a burgeoning of weeds down a disused lane where four soldiers were taking a piss against a wall.

Trolls passed in small groups and never, ever alone. Often they glanced my way as if they could sense me, but I felt it safest to ignore their glances. I sidestepped a dog-cart whose driver had not seen me, and hurried out of the way of a wagon pulled by one of those sleekly astonishing dwarf mammoths. Its stubby trunk swayed in my direction, and the trunk's lip delicately brushed me as it lumbered past. An earthy scent washed over me. I hurried on, heart pounding.

I crossed in front of a huge boardinghouse with an open deck and bar overlooking the bay. Beside it lay a raised plaza and a batey court whose length was lined with raised stone seats in the manner of a Roman amphitheater. A team of young women was practicing. They wore sleeveless bodices and short skirts dyed green to mark their affiliation. I drifted to the side of the road so I could watch, a wistful longing rising in my heart. They were astonishingly good, bouncing the ball off legs, arms, shoulders, and even their heads and never letting it touch hands or feet, as they sought to claim a goal through stone rings.

Onlookers sat in clumps on the stone seats, watching the practice. A slender man with flame-red hair and sun-tanned white skin stood toward the rear among a retinue. I lost track of my breath, clenched my hands, and backed up so quickly I almost collided with five trolls. They parted around me with admirable agility. One looked at me and said, as Caith had that long-ago day in Adurnam: "Ooh! Shiny!"

I tugged the edge of the pagne over my cane. When I glanced back toward the ball court seats, seeing the man from a different angle proved him not to be Drake at all. He sauntered down the risers with a coterie milling admiringly around him. The way he carried himself, expecting a degree of deference as cold mages did in Europa, reminded me of Vai.

"Whhh!" whistled a passing woman to her companion. "Isn't that Jonas Bonsu?"

Her friend nodded. "They say the Greens shall pay the transfer fee to get him as striker. Them Anolis shall be called fools if they let him go."

Bold Astarte! Surely I had done enough maudlin dwelling on my own troubles today.

Ahead, the boulevard ended in the old city gate, a lofty stone arch fitted with warden's boxes on either side and lit, even in broad daylight, with eight lamps, four on each side. Traffic flowed through the gate unimpeded, but once a warden stepped forward to question a man pushing a cart heaped with cassava. The harbor's stone piers and wooden wharves pushed beyond the walls along the river's wide mouth.

Before I reached the gate I turned landward into the harbor district. Densely packed with three-story buildings, this commercial district filled the gap of land between the ball court and the city walls. Alongside sailors with their rolling gait and merchants briskly about errands, I walked down a street lined with a raised walkway on each side and gaslights awaiting nightfall. I perused the streets and peered into each side lane, mapping my ground and noting signs and businesses. Down one side lane hung a weathered sign with orange letters against a feathery brown background: GODWIK AND CLUTCH.

My pulse raced. I had not quite dared hope, but Gracious Melqart had smiled on me.

Two steps led to a shaded porch and a slatted door. A bell tinkled as I pushed into a chamber fitted out with so many mirrors set at angles that I gritted my teeth. Clerks labored at sloping desks set as haphazardly as though someone had shoved them in at haste and forgotten to tidy up. All looked up from their ledgers, then bent back to work. A troll appeared from behind a screen. Approaching me, it whistled.

Its height and the muted brown of its scale-like feathers decided me. "Greetings and good morning, Maestra."

It bared fearsome teeth in what I desperately hoped was meant to be a smile. "This way, Maestressa. Yee's a maku."

"I am." I followed her behind the screen to an area with a bench, three square high platforms cushioned with pillows, and a table set with a pitcher, basin, tray with cups, and platter heaped with nuts and fruit. "How did you know?"

She chuffed, which I took as the kind of laugh you make when you suppose the other person has made an obvious joke and you wish to be polite. "How may I help yee?"

This was not going to be easy. "Are you associated with the offices of Godwik and Clutch who have branches in both Havery and Adurnam?"

Her purple crest rose. "We is."

I stuck out my hand in the radical's manner. "I am Catherine Bell Barahal. I have met Maester Godwik. And Chartji. And Caith. That's why I'm here."

"I am Keer." No feathers covered the palm of her taloned hand. The press of her skin against mine reminded me of summer in the north, when the long sun pulls the earth's sweat up out of warm soil.

She released my hand and indicated the table.

"That's right," I murmured. "Wash, drink, and eat before beginning negotiations."

I washed and dried my hands, after which Keer washed and dried her hands and rinsed her mouth, so I went back and copied the mouth rinsing. She settled on one of the high platforms. Her height and sleek predator's muzzle made me feel I would be at a disadvantage if I sat lower, so I hopped up onto one of the other square platforms.

Her gaze flicked to my cane. "Shiny, that."

"Yes," I agreed.

She flashed me a view of sharp incisors, an intimidating gesture meant, I hoped, to express amusement at my laconic answer. I desperately wanted to know how trolls, like fire mages, could see my cold steel in daylight, but I sensed this was not the time to ask. A troll came in and poured us each a cup of a fragrant tea whose bitterness made my eyes water. We drank as the serving-troll peeled and cut fruit into ceramic bowls small enough to cup in the hand, and sprinkled it with nuts.

As we ate, I looked around. The office was fitted out with interior gaslight, which I had never seen in Adurnam. Slatted windows opened into a chamber where two trolls and a man wearing ink-covered aprons were setting type in a press. Discarded sheets of paper with uneven printing advertised a citizens' meeting: in support of the Proposal for an Assembly composed of Representatives elected from the entire Population of Expedition.

When we had finished eating and drinking, Keer cocked her head, looking at me first with one eye, then with the other, then full on, muzzle slightly pulled back to hint at teeth within.

I found my voice. "My business is this. I need to send

an urgent message to two family members in care of the Adurnam office of Godwik and Clutch. Since your office must exchange dispatches with your Europan offices, I thought I might be able to include a letter with your post."

"Yee shall have better fortune after hurricane season."

"Hurricane? What is that?"

"*Hurricane* is the local word for cyclone. The cyclone is a violent storm which forms over water. Hurricanes rise most commonly in July, August, and September. Elsewise the ocean waters is too cool to sustain them. Therefore few ships risk the voyage to Europa until late October."

Beyond the screen, pens scratched across paper. *Late October* would be too late to warn Bee. "Is there no way to send a dispatch now?"

Keer shifted her shoulders in a sliding way that struck me as quite inhuman. She said, "Tell me how yee met with Godwik and Chartji?"

A shiver of alarm crawled up the skin of my back, for with a lunge she could rip off my face with her talons and then eat me neatly down with those teeth, as long as I didn't fix my sword through her heart first, if I could even find her heart and if she only had a single one. Instinct urged me to trade information for information.

"First, we were chance met at an inn. Later, my cousin and I went to the law offices because Chartji had told us to come to her if we needed legal services. We were offered employment. Not by Godwik himself, mind you, but by his associate, a professora named Kehinde Nayo Kuti."

Keer exuded an odor, like sun-dried grass, that made me think of a creature waiting for its prey to creep into view. "Tell me a story of Godwik."

A cautious smile carried me forward. "He told me a tale about his fledging trip with his age cohort. Six to a boat and six boats in all, north to the shores of Lake Long-Water. They planned to battle into the teeth of the katabatic wind that sweeps down off the vast cliff face of the ice. But I never heard about that, for meanwhile, and before they even reached Lake Long-Water, he and his thirty-six companions were reduced to twenty-seven after battles with saber-toothed cats, foaming rapids, a marauding troo, gusting winds, and a party of young bucks from a territory whose boundaries they had violated. You may wonder how it all started!"

Keer chuffed, crest rising. "I hear his voice in yours. Therefore, I will help you. A sloop may be embarking this coming Venerday if the weather holds. Have me your letter before then, and I shall see it posted with we usual pouch."

"How long will it take to get there, and an answer to return?"

"Who can know? A month each way, if the weather holds fair and the winds cooperate and the ship does not sink. So, likely it will be longer."

A month each way! That would be barely enough time for me to hear back from her before Hallows' Night at the end of October, and then only if all went well. What choice did I have? I had to try. "In truth, Maestra, I am destitute. I have neither pen nor paper, nor payment for delivery costs."

Keer bent forward, examining me in the same way, I imagined, that a bored and fed hawk considers a squirming mouse trapped within reach of its talons. "I can offer you work in our clutch's corporation. In recompense for the employment you were not able to take up in Adurnam. The cost of letter and dispatch can come out of your earnings. You can nest in a room above our offices."

The words hit me like a blow. *Employment. A room.* I need never see Vai until a year and a day were up and our marriage dissolved. Never again.

"Here is more tea," said Keer.

I had to drink another cup, because I could not speak.

"My offer has surprised you," Keer said at length.

I dredged for words. "I am unexpectedly over-whelmed, Maestra. But I already have employment and a room." I could not bear to disappoint Aunty Djeneba. Surely it was easier to hear all the gossip at the board-inghouse than confined in an office. *Surely.* What if the wardens caught a glimpse of me so close to the gates? Where was Drake, anyway? "Let me start with a letter," I finished weakly. "I'll bring one before Venerday."

"No one enters into an association without a great deal of negotiation and thought."

"No, of course not." My thoughts tangled and collided as if I stood in a maze of mirrors, staggering from Bee to Vai and back again, she whom I might not be able to save and he with whom I had no future.

Keer let out a hiss of breath like steam escaping from a kettle. "You rats. If you simply agree, without contesting, then I will always stand above you in the—as you call it—the pecking order. Really, where is the fun in that? You rats are too fond of your entrenched hierarchies."

The words charmed me into a grin. "My apologies. I was preoccupied by another matter." I roused the part of me accustomed to being sensible. "I assure you, I will re-turn ready to duel."

The teeth showed again. "That, I will enjoy. Now. You require paper, pen, and ink." Was it my imagination, or had her way of speaking changed as she spoke to me, vowels shifting sound, cadence altering?

We began bargaining over the cost. The troll did not strike me as discourteous or greedy; if anything, I sensed that each transaction was a chance to play a game I could barely perceive whose rules I did not understand. Even after hard bargaining, the few coins I possessed did not suffice to buy a sheet of foolscap and a dram of ink, much less the dispatch service.

With polite words I took my leave, in my confusion turning the wrong way. The crowded shop fronts and offices debouched into a square on the north vault of the old city walls where rose a huge gate carved with a lion on one side and a buffalo on the other. A hulking palace sprawled along one side of the square, marked with the lamp and staff of the warden's service. This edifice was Warden Hall. A tall, powerfully built young man with scarred cheeks was pushing a flat cart laden with baskets of fruit toward a side entrance. After a moment, I recognized Vai's friend Kofi.

Wreathed in shadow, I followed him. Clouds were piling up in the east, heavy with rain and streaked with gray smoke rising from the factory district. I sneezed, grit in my eye. Kofi paused at the corner, wiping his forehead with a kerchief as he studied the clock tower of Warden Hall.

When the hour tolled nine, he pushed his cart to the kitchen entrance. Kayleigh came down steps hauling a bin of rubbish, which she set beside a stinking wagon hitched to a sleepy donkey. Pretending to be nothing more than chance-met servants, they exchanged murmured words.

"Word has come by bird that the cacica and the general

have concluded their negotiations. He and his people will set out on the next auspicious day to return to Expedition."

"What manner of deal have the general struck with the Taino?" he asked.

"No one knows. But everyone is very nervous. The five Council members who voted to support the general are scolding the twelve who voted to reject him. The five say that by refusing to aid him, the Council has driven the general into Taino arms."

"I wonder what other services the cacica demanded of him."

"That's very rude."

"Rude? She have taken more than twenty husbands, and sent eight to they deaths."

"I won't gossip, for it is wrong to do so. There was another thing I overheard. The Commissioner was talking to one of his deputies. Two salters, both women, escaped from Salt Island. The wardens fear riots if the news leaks out."

As my heart stuttered, Kofi whistled, then bent to rearrange the baskets as an older woman came out to examine the fruit. He turned his whistle to a merry tune, while Kayleigh dumped the bucket into the rubbish wagon as if she had just this moment come out.

The woman scolded her. "Get on then, maku. Yee's so slow. Housekeeper say yee have not even finished the grates yet today."

Kayleigh went in just as the wagon's driver came out munching on a roll. Between bites, the wagoner engaged in a peppershot round of casual batey team gossip with Kofi: so many Blues, Greens, Barracudas, Cajayas, Anolis, Rays, and Guinchos that my head reeled. After the

older woman picked through the fruit, Kofi trundled off.
I shadowed him along the jetty to the Passaporte market,
where he delivered the cart to a compound whose family
rented out transport. By the way they treated Kofi, he
seemed to be a son of the house.

Aunty Djeneba looked up when I came in, nose wrin-
kling as if I'd brought a whiff of rubbish. "Yee was gone
so long I sent Luce out to look for yee. Never could she
find yee."

My parents had drowned when I was six. My father
had left behind his journals, which I had read over and
over again, but there were only five words I remembered
my mother saying to me:

Tell no one. Not ever.

My expression must have changed, for Aunty set aside
the bread she was slapping into shape and came over to
me. "Is yee well, gal?"

"Do you suppose I'm tired, or is it just the heat?"

Yet I *was* tired, after my duel with Keer. A nap with
one of the toddlers tucked alongside refreshed me, and
I went down as the early regulars came in to start on
their ginger beer. Vai appeared with a net bag of guava.
After getting Aunty's permission, he distributed them to
the children before sitting at a table and smiling at me until I sat down opposite.

"Papaya is good for the digestion," he said, cutting
in half a large yellow-orange fruit to reveal round black
seeds clustered moistly in orange flesh. "Aunty said you
were tired."

I could not decide whether he was irritating or sweet.
"You'll share it with me?"

"Of course." He scooped out the seeds, took a bite with
evident pleasure, then handed me the spoon.

I could never resist food. "It's delicious! Vai..."

He looked a question, but did not ask it.

"I should have said something sooner. The sandals are comfortable and sturdy. Luce scolded me into accepting them. Thank you. But she says they weren't cheap."

He scraped seeds out of the other half of the papaya, his mouth turned in a faintly mocking grimace. "If you spent the coin I have become accustomed to on clothing, you would have thought them inexpensive."

The confession made me smile. Blessed Tanit knew it was not in my nature to struggle alone, for I had always had Bee. I wanted to give him something in return for the sandals. "The truth is, I went to see about sending a letter to Beatrice in Adurnam. To let her know where I am."

"Because she does not know where you are."

A masked face glimmered where the light sliced down through the trellis roof and across the table. Mumbling, I forced out the words. "'Because she does not know where you are.'"

He sat in surprised silence. Then he handed me a spoon laden with moist papaya and watched as I savored it. "I must suppose your cousin's whereabouts have something to do with the spirit world and your bound tongue. Well. I won't press you. But meanwhile, Cathrine, you must be cautious about traveling around Expedition. I heard a rumor today that the wardens are on the lookout for two salters, both women, who escaped Salt Island."

The sun's angle shifted, and the vise was released from my tongue. "That's a rumor I should think the wardens wouldn't want to get out."

"Exactly. There would be panic. And anger. Because everyone knows the wardens look the other way if a person who was bitten and healed has the right connections or enough money. While poor people, and maku, take their chances. The people of Expedition are very angry, and the Council fears their anger."

"What is this 'Assembly'?"

He cut open a second papaya. "An assembly is like a council, only with more members. An assembly makes laws and governs. These representatives would be chosen from any adult who is a citizen, and would be voted on by the entire adult population."

I blinked. "Really? Anyone?"

"The mechanics remain to be worked out. There is intense debate over who would qualify for election, and who for voting rights, and who would not. Meanwhile, the Council has called for the arrest of all radicals who propose replacing the Council with an Assembly. But since half the territory sympathizes with the radicals and no one knows the names of the leaders of the radical party, the wardens can't act on the Council's order. Still, you must be very cautious."

"Please don't tell me I have to stay like a prisoner in the compound."

He handed me the spoon so I could scoop more papaya. "That would look more suspicious. Establish a routine. Don't stray from it in obvious ways. Luce can dispatch the letter for you."

"That's not the problem, Vai. I can take the letter myself without the wardens seeing me."

"I suppose you can." He waited for elucidation.

"The problem is I don't have money for paper and ink, much less the cost of dispatch."

"I have enough."

His bland assumption annoyed me. "The sandals were plenty. I prefer not to be beholden to you."

He leaned closer. "Then I must suppose you are not desperate to get word to your cousin."

"Yes, I suppose beggars can't be choosers."

He grinned. "I like it when you scratch." I smiled. He slipped the spoon from my fingers in a way that made my ears burn. "You might try the branch office of the law firm of Godwik and Clutch in the harbor district...Ah. That's where you went."

I glanced down at the emptied papaya skins and back at him. "Bee and I were to take employment there. That was how we were going to keep ourselves in Adurnam."

"Were you, now?" He sat back with a narrowed gaze.

I was sure he was thinking of James Drake, whom he had after all seen at the law offices in Adurnam. Despite my best intentions, I brushed a hand over my belly, and he saw me do it. The collapsed papaya skin next to his hands crackled over with a delicate net of frost.

"What makes you think it has anything to do with him?" I muttered.

"I said nothing. You're the one who said something."

"I don't have to be here, Vai. The troll I spoke to today offered me employment. Yet here I am, still working for Aunty Djeneba."

"Aunty Djeneba says you're doing well." His stiff smile grated on my already jangled nerves. "I hear you're learning to play batey."

"Yes, the children are teaching me before they go to school in the mornings."

"Here are Kofi and the lads." He rose as if relieved to be shed of our conversation.

I grabbed my work apron and made my escape.

Yet the next day, Vai called me over when he returned at the end of the day to show me a pale green fruit with little spines. He set it down beside a small package wrapped in a length of burlap. "I brought paper, ink, and a pen. This is soursop. It's not my favorite, but maybe you'll like it." He cut it in half in a bowl. "Go on. Write your letter."

I unrolled the cloth to find two folded sheets of foolscap, and a quill pen and tiny bottle of ink, nothing fancy. "It's what you do, isn't it?"

"You'll have to tell me what you mean by that cryptic statement," he said, not looking up as he pulled off the skin to reveal a white pulpy interior. I liked watching his hands work.

"You're an unregistered fire bane. You can't afford to get arrested. So you've established a routine and don't stray from it. Work. The Jovesday trolls. Moonday and Saturnday gatherings."

Gaze cast down, he smiled as he trimmed out seeds. The man did have lovely eyes, finely formed and thickly lashed. "If I didn't know better, I'd think you were watching me."

I fixed my gaze on the blank paper. "I was raised in a household of spies and intelligencers. It's second nature for me. I watch everything." Gracious Melqart! What ought I to write to Bee? *Dear Cousin, please find a place to hide until Hallows Night is over. You'll know I succeeded in finding a sacrifice to kill in your place if you're still alive on the second of November.* Would the mansa of Four Moons House protect her? No. Cold mages had no power over the Wild Hunt. And the mansa had only wanted her so as to keep her away from Camjiata. If the mansa sacrificed her to the Wild Hunt, then Camjiata could never make use of her dreams for his war.

"Catherine, what an expression you have on your

face!" he said softly. "Please tell me what I can help you with."

I looked up. He had cleared the bowl of skin and seeds and core, leaving a creamy pulp to eat, but it was me he was considering.

I shook my head. "I just miss my cousin. And my half brother, who's probably getting into all sorts of trouble. Don't you have two sisters younger than Kayleigh? Do you miss them?"

He smiled wryly. "The little lasses. They're a bit saucy and impudent, those two. I do miss them. Here. Try it."

"Impudent toward you? Now you simply must tell me about them. Oh, and give me the spoon while you're talking."

But later, I wrote what I had to write: "I am safe but I can't come yet as I must find a way or make one to save you. Meanwhile, throw yourself on the mercy of the headmaster. If he saved his assistant, then we must pray and hope he can protect you."

I accepted Vai's money and made the delivery. I established a routine: batey practice before the children went to school, sewing and visiting in the morning, the afternoon nap, and an evening of serving and listening to the answers to the cautious questions I asked. Each passing day brought me farther from Salt Island, together with the unpleasant thought that I might be pregnant, and closer to Hallows' Night. I had arrived on Salt Island on August second, and now August was drawing to a close.

"I hear the cacica has twenty husbands," I said one evening as I arranged empty mugs on the tray. "Why would the cacica send her husbands to their deaths? Are they soldiers, sent to die in battle? Maybe that's why she's negotiating with General Camjiata, so he can fight for her.

Or maybe men are married to her so they can serve the powerful court behiques as catch-fires—"

"Hush with that talk!" snapped Brenna.

All within earshot glanced toward the gate, as if expecting trouble might burst in like sharks to the taste of blood in the water. Heat boiled in my cheeks.

"My apologies," I said in a choked voice, "if I said something I oughtn't."

"Here, gal," called Uncle Joe from the counter, "cups to serve."

I hurried over and set down my tray, my hands trembling and my belly in knots.

As he replaced empty cups with filled ones on the tray, he spoke without looking at me. "Speak no careless word about fire mages and behiques, Cat. They guide a dreadful power. Best not speak of them at all, any more than we speak of the unseen spirits who trouble the world."

"Are there powerful fire mages at the cacique's court?" I whispered, for the ugly little hope would not die. Was Prince Caonabo strong enough to interest my sire? What about the behica who was training him? What about Drake? It seemed my sire had caught the scent of a powerful mage, and I had to figure out who it was.

Uncle Joe shook his head as a warning. The regulars had gone strenuously back to their cups. At a table too far away to have heard the exchange, four young men with the corded arms of laborers bent together, whispering as they cast glances my way.

"What?" said the youngest of the four. "The Sweet Cat and she man not living as husband and wife? Might there be a chance for me with she?"

The thin one snorted. "Sure, if yee want to risk a chisel through yee eye. None of us reckon 'tis that maku being stubborn. He used to go out every night, he and he radical friends. He don' hang around here for the conversation."

The third, his hair bound back in a dusty kerchief, chimed in. "He bring she a present of fruit every day, like he is courting she, if yee want me opinion on it. I don' fancy she, me own self. Did yee hear she scold that sailor yesterday who put he hand on she ass? Yee want a wife who shall talk to yee like that?"

"She talk to me that way and I shall do she a rudeness," said the fourth and largest, with a crude laugh.

Really, this spying business wasn't so difficult, as long as you could control your betraying blushes and vexed grimaces. Like he is courting she! I sashayed over to the table, enjoying their consternation as I closed in. Even the big, crude fellow looked unsure of how to react.

"Not done with those drinks yet? I've never seen men drink *so slow*." I offered a cutting smile to the big man, who smiled sourly.

"Drink with us, Sweet Cat, and we shall drink faster," said the nice one who admired me.

"What? While I'm working? I'd like to keep my job."

"If yee fancy going to a batey match, I's yee man for it. I play on the Anoli third team. I know moves yee have never been taught."

"There's a bold boast." I could not help but smile, for besides being an amusing flirt, he was very well built, clearly a young man who knew how to use his body.

His friends glanced toward the table where Vai was drinking and talking with friends. By not a flicker of his gaze did Vai show interest in my doings. Yet Kofi, sitting beside Vai with arms crossed, looked at me with a frown that made me feel queasy, as if he thought I was deliberately making a scene. What had I ever done to Kofi? I wasn't obliged to never even smile at another man just because Vai had found me on the jetty. Everything tonight was making my belly ache.

"I'll bring yee back a round," I said quickly to the table, gathering the cups and taking them to the two women who washed up. Then I kept going to the washhouse because something was going on to upset my stomach. Just inside, I leaned against the wall, stricken by cramping and a sudden feeling I ought to at least respect Vai's kindness by not flirting with other men until after Hallows' Night, when I would be free, and Bee would be safe or she would be dead.

Even at this distance I could still hear them talking, more belligerently now, louder, fueled by too much drink and too much male posturing.

I recognized crude man's voice. "If the gal don' want him, why shall she not be free to go with another man? Everyone know that maku never went walking out with other gals. Like he figure Expedition gals not fine enough for the likes of him. Me, I reckon he got nothing in his rifle to shoot."

"No need for this talk," said my nice admirer. "Let's just have another drink."

"Yee reckon I fear him?" Crude man raised his voice another notch. "He got a smart mouth and a pretty face and fancy clothes on festival nights, and what else? For he surely don' got that gal in he bed! Maku! Ja, maku! Yee reckon yee scare me?"

"I reckon either you're very drunk," said Vai, "or you're an ass, or likely both, if this is your best attempt to start a fight. Let's go, lads. I'm of a mind to drink elsewhere tonight."

Was he? I peered out past the washhouse curtain just in time to see Vai, Kofi, and the lads rising from their table. But the moment Vai took a step toward the gate, the crude fellow deliberately placed himself in his path. He topped Vai by half a head, and he was considerably bulkier, with meaty hands and a sneering face.

"Best if yee run, maku," he said. "I shall just give yee a pat on the ass as yee go."

The air changed, charged with a spike of cold that made everyone in the courtyard shiver and look around in surprise.

"Vai, don' do it," said Kofi suddenly. "Yee know why yee shall not."

But he was going to do it. The set of his shoulders, the lift of his chin, and the arrogant curl of his lips betrayed him: He had lost his temper, and now the prideful fury of a roused and exceedingly powerful cold mage was about to hit.

My nice admirer and his friend with the kerchief grabbed their companion and hauled him back. With a confidence that astonished me, Kofi propelled Vai in the opposite direction, murmuring in his ear. Uncle Joe stepped out from behind the counter. Before any of the men could look my way, if they even meant to, which I doubted, I let the curtain drop, my heart pounding.

A moment later, Aunty pulled the curtain aside and looked in. A pale light in the form of a lamp hung from a hook on the wall, but it was not real fire; it was an illusion shaped to resemble it.

Aunty was frowning. "I's telling yee right now, gal, don' come out 'til this blow over. Joe shall take care of this arseness. Bless, gal! Yee reckon this is somewhat to laugh at?"

For I was laughing softly. I was staring at the inside of my ankle, at the smear of blood oozing down the skin. I hadn't been made pregnant with James Drake's seed.

It was like feeling the first chain slip off my body.

22

The next afternoon after work, Vai brought a fruit he called mamey. The smooth pink flesh had a rich flavor, spiked with the lime juice he squeezed over slices scooped out of the rind.

"Perhaps you would like to attend a batey match," he said.

"Perhaps I would. Mmm. The texture is like cream." I licked my lips. "But I have to work."

The intensity of his serious gaze disturbed me more than did the sweetness of his charming smile. "You work hard, Catherine. You've sewn singlets for the little lads, and blouses for the little lasses. If I ask, Aunty will say no harm to miss one afternoon's work."

"If *you* ask?" I examined him. "Does this have anything to do with last night?"

The flare of his eyes told me something, only I did not know what. He obviously did not intend to discuss the incident with me. "Let me know."

"I'll go with Luce and her friends," I said with a defiant lift of my chin.

He agreed so quickly I wondered if this had been his plan all along. "Yes. They're tall gals, too. You won't stand out so much."

"Do I stand out?"

He rose and took a step away, and just as I thought he was going to leave without answering, he paused and looked back as if he knew what I was waiting for. "Always, Catherine. Always."

With that parting shot, more like a taunting volley of stinging crossbow bolts in advance of a battle, he deserted me for the company of his friends who just then surged in through the gate. After an excited conversation they hurried out. For the next three days I barely saw him. Our regular customers talked of nothing except a huge outdoor meeting planned in support of the call for an Assembly. They began a betting pool on how quickly violence would break out and how many would be shot or arrested by the wardens.

"Can I go?" Luce asked plaintively, to which her mother and grandmother united in a staggeringly firm "No," after which they confiscated the money collected by the betting pool and distributed the coins to the beggars and mothers of twins in the local market.

"Yee shall not go either, Cat," Aunty said to me later, "for there shall be wardens out in plenty. Yee must do nothing to come to they attention."

"I won't go," I promised her.

The morning of the day planned for the demonstration dawned red. The winds died, and the air's flavor deadened and then came alive with an odd anticipatory snap. People hurried home early from work, and at the boardinghouse we shuttered all the windows and braced doors and furniture and storage barrels as well as tightly roping down the roof cistern.

I overheard Uncle Joe say to Vai, "They shall have to cancel the demonstration."

At dusk a storm blew through with gusting winds and pelting rain. Flying above it, a shuddering voice sang in a language I did not know, with words like drumrolls and trumpet shrieks whose cadence made me twist and turn all night until dawn came and the winds calmed and the rain ceased. The storm had torn down a few trees and damaged a few roofs.

"Was that a hurricane?" I asked Luce as her little sisters swept away leaves and broken branches while we took down the shutters and unstacked tables and benches.

She grinned cheekily. "Yee's such a maku. That was nothing. I's so angry. I was all set to sneak out to the demonstration. Yee shall not tell, will yee?"

"Will you promise me you'll never go to such a demonstration without permission and someone to keep an eye on you?"

She frowned. "Yee's no help! Anyway, Vai say yee want to go to a batey match. There is a women's game here in Passaporte come Venerday. Yee shall go with me and me friends."

"I'd like that. Luce, how did Vai and Kayleigh get here?"

Two of the little lads had begun bashing each other with broken branches. She chased them down, took the branches away, and returned to me. "Yee can ask him that question."

"I can, but I'm asking you instead of telling Aunty that you meant to sneak out."

She rolled her eyes in that way she had. "Yce just don' want to ask him. I don' know what yee and he fought over—"

"Which is none of your business."

"Ooo! That is a sour face! Can yee make goat's milk curdle with it?"

I laughed, spotted the little lads digging for branches in the sweepings, and gave them *the eye*. They ran off giggling, without branches.

"They came in on the fourth day of Martius."

"You remember exactly?"

"Me father is a sailor. Of course I know all the shipping schedules." She levered up a bench and I caught the end to help her carry it. "They two came here to the boardinghouse on the fifth of Martius. They came in on a vessel out of Porto Dumnos 'twas hauling barrels of salted fish. No chance of missing that, for they clothes stank of herring."

No wonder Vai had been unable to follow me into the spirit world. By Imbolc, at the beginning of Februarius, he had already been at sea, undoubtedly at the mansa's command.

"Do you know the exact date General Camjiata arrived?" When she gave me a curious look, I hurried on. "He is quite the villain in Europa. No wonder the Council isn't happy he came."

"That man shall bring all kind of trouble," she agreed. "He made landfall on the nineteenth day of Februarius on a schooner registered to a local shipping house."

Which meant his breakout had been planned long in advance.

"He came looking for yee, Cat," said Luce with a frown.

"The general?" I asked with real alarm. I did not need that complication on top of all else!

She rolled her eyes again. "Yee's an escaped Amazon from he army?"

"Can't I have made a joke?" I said with a false smile as I realized what she had meant.

"No joke to he who traveled so far to seek yee."

"Is that what Vai told you?" It was a foolish question, answered by the very fact of my asking it. Vai had told everyone he had come to the Antilles to look for the perdita, his lost woman.

Which meant Kayleigh and I were the only ones who knew it for a lie.

Why had he really come to Expedition? More importantly, why had the mansa allowed it? Commanded it?

What did the mansa want that was also in the Antilles?

There was only one thing I could think of: *Camjiata*.

Vai had brought with him a sword forged of cold steel. Cold steel in the hand of a cold mage severs the soul from the body with a cut: They need only draw blood to kill you.

The mansa had sent Vai out to do his dirty work before. Vai had destroyed a magnificent airship and then gloated over his triumph. *"They were sure I was too inexperienced to manage it!"*

Yet he was not a heartless killer. He had refused to kill me. Surely I was the one bred and raised to be a heartless killer, not him.

"Cat, can yee help me with this table?"

My thoughts slammed back to earth. "Where do you want it?"

Because Venerday was Kayleigh's usual half day off each week, she accompanied us to the batey match. Vendors had set up on the open ground outside Passaporte's ball court, selling baked yams, roasted corn, and cassava bread, things that could be eaten with the fingers. A few sold kerchiefs in the colors and patterns by which a person advertised allegiance to one of Expedition's teams. Some kerchiefs bore unusual sigils that marked teams from within the Taino kingdom.

"Do Taino teams play here as well?" I asked.

"Assuredly. And if there is a celebration in the Taino kingdom, like a noble marriage or birth, there shall be games at the border plaza."

Not for us the vendors' expensive food; we'd eaten before we left the boardinghouse. In a jostling delight of girls of whom Luce at almost sixteen was the youngest and I at twenty was one of the eldest, we paid our entry fee for the cheap seats and climbed to the top row. I enjoyed the feeling of being half hidden among them, because the young women of Expedition were, on the whole, tall and big and healthy, quite unlike the frailer, sallower, shorter women of cold Adurnam. I was so accustomed to men and women seated separately in public venues that intermingling forcibly recalled to me how foreign a place Expedition was. Yet my companions felt no compunction about pushing their way through the ranks of young men, seeking a spot where we could all sit together. They were the boldest girls I had ever met, and I loved them for it, and for the way they took me in as if I were Luce's cousin and treated me as if I were no different from one of their own.

We crammed in shoulder to shoulder and thigh to thigh, and I found myself between two tall girls of about my age named Tanny and Diantha.

"Yee husband is uncanny handsome," said Tanny, taking my hand and using it to point toward a group of young men below and to our left, standing in dusty trousers and singlets as if they had just come from the carpentry yard. Vai was fake-boxing with Kofi, laughing, quite at his ease. "Good fortune for yee."

"And you wonder how it is he comes to think so well of himself!" said Kayleigh from the row behind me in a tone accompanied by a long-suffering sigh.

Tanny was a heavyset, handsome young woman who had, I'd been told, cast off two husbands already although she was no older than I was. "Carpenters have the best tools."

I stared at my hands, which had evidently lost hold of my entire store of witty rejoinders.

"Stop! Please!" exclaimed Kayleigh as the girls around her laughed.

"Don' tease Cat," said Luce, popping forward from the row behind us.

"If yee decide to rid yee own self of he, Cat," said Tanny with a shrug, "I shall take a try."

"Good fortune to yee with that," retorted Luce loyally. "He shall not bite. He is devoted to Cat." She cast at me a baleful glare that made the other girls snicker all over again.

"We were married by our families," I said, choking out the words in the hope that some kind Fate would sever the conversation. "I barely know him. Indeed, I scarcely think of him at all."

Tanny buried her face in her hands, shoulders heaving. The other girls tried desperately not to laugh. I determinedly examined the seats opposite where well-to-do folk reclined on comfortable cushions beneath the shade of awnings while servants fetched them food and drink.

"Yee don' want that man's trouble anyway, Tanny." Lanky Diantha had features more Taino than Celtic or Afric and hair as straight and black as mine, cropped short because she had aspirations to play on the Rays' women's team. "He is in deep with they radicals."

"Exactly what radicals is that?" I asked.

"That Kofi-lad was arrested two times for he radical associations. Those is not clan scars on he cheeks, yee know. The wardens tortured him, but he would not talk."

"Cat, close yee mouth," said Luce. "I thought yee knew."

Kayleigh was staring into the crowd to where Kofi was singing and dancing with Vai and the lads to the beat of a hand drum. Those young men could dance! They had the crowd around them getting into a call and response led by Kofi's strong voice: "Give the man yee money, and what do yee get?"

"The wardens must act to keep the peace," said Diantha. "If the radicals get their way, the whole city shall go up in flames."

Luce leaned over my shoulder. "The Council rule unjustly and for they own benefit!"

"The Council was established at the founding to stop a king from taking over!" protested Diantha. "They did it for the best!"

"Just because that was true then, Dee," said Tanny as the other gals nodded in agreement with her as she went on, "don' mean we cannot want to change the way things is now. What chance have we in the districts to be heard by the Council? They line they own pockets with money and we get nothing."

"Think of all the trouble that will come," muttered Diantha.

"Trouble is here already," objected Tanny. "General Camjiata got angry when the Council refused he request for support. Now he is run to the Taino."

"Yee think if them radicals get in power with an Assembly, they will support the general and buy off the Taino?" cried Diantha. "The radicals don' want a king either."

"But the general wants to be emperor in Europa, not here," I said. "You would think the Council, and the radicals, would want to encourage him to go back home, not to hang around because he can't afford to return."

"No one want him to hang around," said Tanny. "There was one time already a man tried to kill the general."

"What happened?" I glanced at Kayleigh but she was whispering to a friend.

"A man shot at the general when he went to Nance's Tavern to meet with the local factory union people. The Council blamed the radicals. The radical leaders had broadsheets printed and blamed the Council. Truth is, the general was always a-meeting with both sides."

The song swept up the risers as the gals joined in: "Give the man yee money, and what do yee get? Yee don' get nothing, not even a kiss!"

A roar rose from the crowd, drowning out the song. Folk leaped to their feet as the two teams trotted out onto the ball court. Three women dressed in white tabards stood as arbitrators for the game, overseen by an umpire seated on a pedestal. Captains accepted the stone belts that marked their status; flags rose. Today, Rays played Cajayas, and the singing of team chants became deafening as the lead arbitrator tossed the ball into the air to launch the game.

At first, I stood with the others, swaying and shouting, yelping when the ball hit dirt, whooping when a well-placed elbow or knee kept play afloat, for teams lost points if a bad play caused the ball to touch the ground. Diantha offered a running commentary on the players.

Yet a disquieting murmur tugged at my ears. A whiff of burning tickled my nostrils. I pushed to the top of the stone edifice to look over the back wall to the ground below. A troop of wardens had gathered, some carrying lamps and the rest carrying staves and pistols.

I dropped down. Vai was easy to find, not because he was particularly tall but because I immediately recognized the shape of his head and the cut of his shoulders. He swung around to look at me, as if I'd spoken. I lifted my chin. He nodded and, with Kofi to cut a path, started up.

I pushed down through the dancing, chanting throngs as the game surged forward, one player making a shot for the hurricane's eye—the stone ring—and just missing to a great shout from the crowd, relief and disappointment woven into a single cry.

On the cry's dying, Vai shoved into view. "Tell me."

"Wardens! With lamps."

The flash of destructive glee that flared in Kofi's face made me wonder how much he hated the wardens and their masters, the Council. "Just what we have been waiting for," he said in a tone that made me shiver.

Vai pulled me close. "Catherine. Go back to your friends. Stay high until the riot starts. Let the gals hide you. Don't break away alone."

"I am not helpless—!"

"Of course you aren't!" His arm tightened around my back. "That's not what I mean. It's going to get ugly. I need you to make sure Kayleigh and Luce get home safely."

I was momentarily taken aback by the realization that he had just entrusted his sister's welfare to me, and that he was half embracing me. "Oh. Of course. What about you?"

"Come on," said Kofi, and Vai released me as if startled to find himself holding me. They took off into the crowd. A hornet's nest of angry buzzing rose in the trail of their passing. Anxious excitement crawled like mice along my skin. I climbed back to the gals.

"There's going to be a riot," I said as I reached them. "Stick close to each other, and we'll get out safely." They were smart gals. They listened. "Dee, you and me in the front. Luce, you right behind me with the others. Kayleigh and Tanny, you two use your size in the rear to make sure no one gets left behind. We have to get off the risers and through the crowd. No splitting up."

A phalanx of wardens had appeared at either end of the long stone risers, on our cheap-seats side only. Not a one inflicted his lit lamp on the wealthy folk avidly watching the game on the other side of the court. The ball arced, struck dirt, bounced, and was sent on its way by a header.

Corncobs, coconut shell bowls, hanks of cassava bread, fruit peelings, and even fragments of broken ceramic cups began to fly. Voices sang out: "Ask for the wardens and what do yee get? Here to bully us, and never a kiss! Who do yee come to arrest? One law for the rich and one for the rest!"

"They shall not trample us today!" Whose voice it was that boomed over the clamor I did not know, but it sounded like Kofi.

Young men shoved forward in a wave. In a tide of linked arms the crowd mowed down the wardens entering at the northern end of the risers. A fight broke out at the southern end, staffs cracking down on unprotected heads but met by fists and knives. People flooded away from the disturbance, many hopping onto the ball court into the middle of the play. In the seats opposite, angry spectators bellowed for order as wardens took up stations to protect them from the crowd.

"The field is clearest!" Diantha quivered beside me like a hound ready to bolt its leash.

"No!" I cried. "We're going straight through the fight."

"But Cat—!" Luce's face washed gray with fear.

"Trust me. In rows, Luce in the center. Link arms. Don't get separated."

I forged forward with Diantha as we shoved down the steps. I steered us to where the melee was like a churning tidal catchwater, current and swell and wind all slapping together to make a deadly confluence. But where the fight was worst, we had least chance of being marked out. The air pressure changed. My ears popped. Lamps shattered; rifles and pistols clicked, combustion was killed. The crowd roared and pushed hard into the collapsing line of wardens.

Luce was gulping down sobs, desperately trying to be brave, but Diantha showed no fear as she and I lanced like a spear through any gap we could see. I used my cane ruthlessly to thwack and thrust and trip. Diantha used her knees, elbows, and hips to make way. Tanny, at the rear, levered her weight against any rioter or warden who crashed against us. Kayleigh had the strength of a big-boned girl accustomed to fieldwork.

I ducked a blow and dragged Diantha sideways as a grasping hand caught at a corner of her kerchief. The other girls shoved us forward into an eddy of open ground where carts lay overturned. Liquid from kettles splashed everywhere, meat pies crushed and leaking their innards.

A pair of wardens spotted me. "Stop, there! We is to detain all maku gals—"

I drew gentle shadows over me, becoming nothing more than the flutter of a skirt and a scuff of dust. The wardens let us pass. Diantha hailed a cluster of huddled batey players in smeared and torn skirts marking them as Rays.

"Hey, gals! Come on!" she cried. "Let us get out of this hurricane."

"Wardens told us to wait until all is cleared," said their shaken captain.

A pistol went off, the report sharp and stunning. What had happened to Vai's magic? If I ran back, I could help him, but Luce was crying and Kayleigh was trying to soothe her in a voice not much calmer than Luce's tears, and Tanny was hauling along another girl who was in hysterics.

"Let them see what we do to them we thought was we brothers," cried a male voice. "Will they fire on us? Or join us?"

A huge surge flooded as men came running and the fight thundered back into chaos.

"Move!" I shouted, startling my gals and the straggle of batey players alike.

We moved.

With the Rays we flowed onto streets hazy with the smoke of late afternoon cook fires. The noise from the ball court rose and fell like a cyclone's winds, and now a drumming hammered into life, hands beating on skin, on thighs, like the beating heart of anger. We made our way first to Diantha's compound, and then to Tanny's, leaving off the girls until there was only me and Kayleigh and Luce to make our way home.

A different sort of drumming rose in counterpoint to the rhythm voiced by the angry demonstrators: the rumbling tread of booted feet, presaging the arrival of armed men from the direction of the old city. We came to an intersection obscured by dusk and smoke. A dozen wardens came running out of the haze. Without thinking, I drew shadows tight around me.

The wardens barely slowed, but as long as Kayleigh didn't speak, there was no reason by looks or dress to think her anything except a local gal. They jogged on.

"Get yee to yee home," called the one at the rear gruffly. "Don' be foolish gals. Move it!"

As they trotted into darkness, Luce began sobbing. "Where is Cat? How did we lose she?"

While their backs were to me, I released the shadows.

Luce turned, saw me, and screamed. "Stay back, spirit!"

"Luce, it's just me."

"Yee's an opia," she croaked out between sobs. "Yee have come to haunt yee husband. Please, don' harm me. I shall never tell!"

"What is an opia?"

"An opia is the spirit of a dead person," said Kayleigh, staring at me with a flat gaze I could not read. "That's what they call them here."

"Why would you think I am dead, or a spirit?"

"How else could yee vanish like that?" said Luce in a choked voice.

I did not want her to look at me as if I had just lumbered down a white sand beach and tried to bite her. But I could not answer her question even with a question.

Kayleigh sighed. "Show her your navel, Cat. Then she'll know you for a living person. Vai's an idiot where you're concerned, but our uncle taught him too well to be fooled by that."

I tugged up my blouse, already pulled askew by our headlong flight. "Luce has seen it often enough when we shower! Touch it! I was born from a human woman just as you were!"

With a trembling hand, Luce touched her forefinger

to my navel. "Yee must be some manner of behica. Or a...witch."

A creature was hiding in the shadows, watching us. Darkness coiled. I heard measured breathing like ghostly bellows as it waited to pounce if I said what I should not.

I grabbed Luce's hand. "I'm not, Luce! I'll never harm you or anyone at Aunty's. But I can't speak of what is secret."

Her lips parted into the admiring infatuation that afflicts only the young and innocent. I had seen it on Bee's face often enough, although never directed at me. "Yee's a secret mage!"

"You're no mage," said Kayleigh. "And if you hurt my brother, I'll dig your eyes out with a spoon. And eat them."

I could not help myself. I laughed, and when I laughed, the listening darkness melted away like a huge shadow dog. Neither Kayleigh nor Luce saw it go, loping away on four long legs into the night. Good riddance. "I'm sorry to tell you this, but my eyes won't taste that good."

Kayleigh's lips curled toward a smile, and I remembered how much I had liked her when we had walked together across a snowy landscape, fleeing the village of Haranwy. Before I'd realized she had been leading her brother to me even knowing he thought he had to kill me. Maybe it wasn't just her who felt resentful.

"Peace, Kayleigh," I said. "Maybe we can start over." Then I looked away, to allow her space to consider the offer. "Luce, I'm lost. Can you lead us home?"

She took my hand with a proud smile. "This way."

When we reached the boardinghouse, Aunty Djeneba and Brenna hugged and scolded us. Luce staggered through an incoherent and disjointed tale, and I inter-

rupted and said, "A riot broke out when the wardens came
through the batey stands with lamps."

"They seek unregistered fire banes with lamps," said
Uncle Joe gravely. "I reckon they hope to bully the radicals into shutting they mouths. It will not work."

The night came alive with drums speaking across the
length and breadth of Expedition Territory, bursts of
mountainous noise rising only to be asphyxiated by ominous valleys of quiet. Wind moaned along the roof, dragging the sounds of street battles in and out of windows
until Djeneba's brother and her sons came up from the
jetty where their fishing boat was moored and told us to
shutter the windows and net the roofs, for the weather was
about to turn bad.

I was glad of the work, for I had grown restless. When
I pressed my hand to my locket, I felt Vai's warmth, but
he could have been anywhere. After the gate was closed,
I paced. I drank the dram of rum Uncle Joe offered, and
then a second larger dram, for I simply could not sit still.

A rap came at the gate, regulars too nervous to sit at
home in darkened compounds. They informed us of what
we already knew: The gaslight in Passaporte District had
been choked off at the Gas Works, as punishment. We lit
candles and lamps. Younger men arrived, bruised and cut,
eager to regale a receptive audience with an exuberant
tale of how they and a pack of sailors had fought off the
wardens down by the jetty. A fire had broken out and been
extinguished by a fire bane of unheard-of power, which
had spurred the wardens into a further frenzy of head-
bashing and arrests.

Their tale was thirsty work, and I felt obliged, asking
them questions about the location and extent of the possible fires, to drink rum with them, for my mouth was dry.

My batey-playing admirer and his kerchiefed friend arrived without their crude companion; they had been down at the Speckled Iguana where lay wounded men.

"I have to go there," I said, my mind churning with visions of Vai all beaten and bloody and of Bee's head floating in a dark well. If Vai was hurt, I had to rescue him. If I knew where Drake was hiding, I could offer him upon Hallows' Night. I would become a killer, like my sire. So be it.

Uncle Joe said, "Yee stay here, Cat. Yee's had too much to drink."

"I really have to go." I drained another slug of rum for courage and went to the gate. They could not stop me as my admirer and his friend followed me out.

23

I gripped my pagne in a fist and hauled the cloth to my knees so I could better stride. "What is your name again?"

My nice admirer had a merry grin and that was something on a cheerless night with anger and fear stalking through the streets. "Bala. This is Gaius."

Kerchiefed Gaius had a frown like a barge.

"I'm perfectly harmless," I said, daring Gaius with my gaze to say otherwise.

Gaius snorted. "If yee say so, Sweet Cat. Yee have that man strung on a leash, or else he have yee strung likewise, I's not sure which."

"I do not! I am a perfectly respectable gal. It is not my fault I was married against my will."

"That is one rumor we have heard," said Bala. "Hearing it for true lend a new smell to the rose, don' it?" he added, to his friend.

"If yee call that a rose," Gaius muttered.

"I shouldn't have said anything." My fingers tightened on Bala's arm. He was a bigger man than I had thought, a full head taller than me and with shoulders that might bear the world on their breadth. His friend with the Roman name and a mass of hair in locks under the kerchief was almost as tall but stockier. For an instant, I wondered if I was safe with them, but then I reflected that should they trouble me, they would have to answer to Aunty Djeneba, Uncle Joe, and the rest of the neighborhood. "Sometimes people say I talk too much."

Gaius made a noise like a choked-off laugh.

Bala said, "Yee have a lovely voice, Sweet Cat. Now, gal, shall we meet wardens in the street, yee shall stand back and let us take care of them."

I removed my hand from his arm. "I can take care of myself in a fight. Do you doubt me?"

"There is the tongue," said Gaius to Bala. "So I told yee."

"We shall walk quickly and keep silent," said Bala with the smile of a man seeking to keep the peace.

I fumed as a thousand wickedly cutting barbs of splendid insults came and went unspoken on my tongue. The Speckled Iguana lay about fifteen blocks away, on the other side of the Passaporte market, whose stalls and grounds lay empty but for the winking eyes of rats bold in the darkness and the leavings of crushed shells that had not been swept up. Clouds veiled the sky, making the intermittent noise of struggle seem both far and close, hard to gauge.

As we skirted the edge of the market, Gaius spoke in a low voice. "Yee meant it, did yee not, Sweet Cat? That yee would fight. Is it true, that story about yee and the shark?"

"Why would I have told it otherwise? Do you think I am a *liar*?"

Perhaps my voice rose sharply. Bala touched my arm. "I see many a shadow at guard."

Belatedly it occurred to me that the wardens might have staked out the Speckled Iguana, if they knew it for a haunt of radicals and troublemakers. Instead, the local men had staked out their ground, flanking the area with clusters of men bearing muskets, pistols, and machetes, the favored blade of the countryside. Lamps burned on the porch and in the windows of the inn, by which I knew Vai was either not there, or was dead.

I ran up onto the porch, colliding with an older man who was no taller than me but twice as wide. A patch covered his right eye, and a horrendous starburst wound had turned his right cheek into a pitted and scoured puckering of ropy white scar tissue. He yanked me to a halt.

"I'll be smited by Bright Reshef if you aren't the daughter of Lieutenant Tara Bell. For you look very like her, but for the hair and the color of your eyes."

"Ja, maku," said Bala, who with Gaius loomed behind me. "What is with the hand on the gal?"

"Is the maku bothering yee, Cat?" asked Gaius.

I stared at my interlocutor. My mind seemed caught in a roof-shattering gale. He saw the stamp of my mother's face in my own. I wanted to demand of him how he knew her, but as I tried to focus the splintering spray of my thoughts, I hung on to one concept: *Tell no one. Keep silence.*

"Drake is here," he said, as if he had gleaned my mind with a rake and pulled forth a nugget. "He's in the back room with the wounded. He has been wondering where you fetched up." He looked over my companions, unimpressed by their stature. "I see you found protectors."

"Let me go."

He raised his eyebrows as if to suggest I was being overly dramatic, but he let go. "Do not say you shall deny whose daughter you are? I fought beside Lieutenant Bell." His Iberian lilt pitched out like the ring of a trumpet. "In the Parisi campaign, when we took Alesia."

Blessed Tanit, how my heart wished to hear the tale! But I was too cunning to reveal myself to him! I drew myself up, matching him eye to eye.

"I came for a drink, for the walk has made me uncommonly thirsty. Bala? Gaius? I quite forgot my coin, so you shall have to buy me a shot of rum." I swept past the man and into a spacious common room crammed with noisy, sweaty, angry men.

"Yee stick close by us, Cat," said Gaius as Bala pushed to the bar. "I don' like this crowd. Yee should be getting home and not drinking any more, for I reckon drink make yee reckless."

The situation would have struck me as amusing—my admirer and his skeptical friend turned into watchful guard dogs—had I not just then seen a flash of bright red hair where a door opened behind the bar.

The old soldier came up beside me and raised a hand to draw James Drake's attention. "He shall want to talk to you, lass. I hear you may be carrying his child."

I slapped him.

He grunted, but although I had slapped him hard, he'd barely been staggered.

I thought: *That wasn't very effective.* So I slugged him, right beneath the curve of his ribs. He doubled over, gasping and—strangely—gurgling as with choked amusement. As a shocked murmur spread out like a ripple, he said, "Your mama taught you to hit, did she? Oof!"

His laugh was a booming chortle whose mirth made me want to strangle him. Gracious Melqart! James Drake! If he had seen me, he would come out. I did not want Vai humiliated by the whole world—or at least every man now staring at me—seeing me with Drake. When in doubt, attack.

I shoved up to the bar, heedless of the men I elbowed aside, and tweaked Bala's sleeve. "I have to go back and check the wounded. Wait for me. I don't want to go home alone."

His interested smile sharpened gratifyingly, and I smiled, for he really was an appealing fellow, but I had to get past that door before James Drake walked out of it, so I hopped over the bar, grabbed a shot glass clear with white rum and drank it down in one swallow, then sidestepped the surprised bartender and thence past him through the still-open door. I shut the door behind me to see a long room filled with shapes lying all a-tumble on the floor or atop long tables on which, on kinder nights, folk might dine and chatter on about politics and batey. Tonight I heard only moans.

By lamplight, Drake bent over a man whose stomach had been opened by a gash, its gaping lips revealing the moist mire of intestines. An old woman with blood splashed across her apron and a serious-looking Taino man whose age I could not guess worked side by side at another table, she sewing shut a gaping shoulder wound with needle and thread while he pressed the ragged flesh together with steady hands. For a moment, I was sure I saw sparks trembling at his lips and a smear of ember light, but when I blinked, I realized I was just reeling. I braced myself with a hand on the door, in case any cursed fool tried to barge in after me.

"This one can't be saved, for I give you my oath his spirit is already one step out of his flesh," Drake said.

The Taino man said, "Take him, then. How many can you save with him?"

"One, for certain." He indicated a man whimpering with the bleats of a person trying to be stoic in the face of unrelenting pain. What appeared at first glance as a kerchief was a leaking mat of blood and, beneath it, the white flag of exposed skull. Drake spread fingers over the wound.

Heat swamped the room, sticky and sumptuous, like sweet pudding that coats the lips until you must lick them clean for the sake of your craving. A kernel of desire swirled in my gut. I opened my mouth, but all that came out was a sighing exhalation.

The woman glanced at me, then at Drake. Blessed Tanit! A skin of glowing fire, not flames but a gleam like coals, washed down the body of the man with the belly wound. His chest arched up, although his mouth made no sound. Drake's hand, on the other man's bloody scalp, turned white-hot, and then I blinked, for it was too strong a light. Had I only imagined it? The first man now lay as if dead, life burned out of him.

Drake removed his hand. "He will live."

I groped behind me for the latch, for I wanted nothing more than to get out of this room with its ashy stench of death and hope. But Drake was as fast and determined as a shark. One moment he stood halfway across the room with his gaze turned to me, as if to decide whether I was worthy prey, and the next he had crossed the space between us and taken hold of my hand. The candles flared. The other two looked up, but none of the wounded men did, and I thought: Maybe they've been drugged so they can't know some men are being killed to save others.

"So here you are. I have been looking for you for weeks now, Cat."

I twisted my hand out of his. "I haven't been looking for you!"

"Why, Cat, I think you are drunk."

"I don't like you, Drake. I just came here to say that."

Was that twitch amusement or anger? "That's not what you said before."

"I was drunk before."

A curling warmth crept up my arm as he smiled. "Where are you staying?"

"Why do you think I mean to tell you?"

"You had better tell me after all the trouble I've gone to for you!"

All the burning wicks snapped out. Just like that.

"*Ah*," whispered Drake, and he smiled.

Out in the common room, the buzzing conversation ceased as if it, too, had been doused.

The Taino man cursed against the darkness, and a single candle feebly wavered to life, just as, beyond the wall, men started talking all at once and in heightened voices.

I pressed my free hand against my blouse, feeling for the locket's curve. I found the thread of him along the chains that bound us. He was nearby on the street, and it belatedly occurred to me that he had gotten home and they had told him where I had gone and this was the inevitable result.

Drake still had hold of my elbow, pouring into me a fierce forceful *need* that was the fire of his magic. Never let it be said I lacked ways to extricate myself from any awkward situation, for I knew exactly what Bee would do in this one.

"I'm going to throw up!" I pretended to gag.

Drake released me and jerked back.

I hauled open the door, slipped through, and slammed it shut. Men were cursing, trying to make light. With a sweep of my cane, I cleared every mug on the long counter, sending them crashing to the floor as I jumped over.

"Wardens!" I shrieked. "*Run!*"

They were not stupid men in the Speckled Iguana. Not many panicked, but enough did to stir the big room and make it hard for them to get order. That made it easy for me to wrap shadows around myself and weave my way unremarked through the clamor and out the doors.

He had paused across the street, hidden by the night. Of course he saw me, although others did not. I raced across the street.

"We have to go!" I whispered hoarsely, trying to grab his arm but missing entirely.

He began walking so quickly I had to trot to keep up, me wrapped in shadow and him hugging the darkness until I wondered if he was using illusion to mask himself, for none of the men loitering nearby took the least notice of us.

I said, "Just think! We could sneak around all over the place and no one would ever see us."

Men looked around, gazes questing like those of scenting dogs.

"Did yee hear that?"

"I see no one."

Vai took hold of my hand and we ran until I was breathless and laughing as we slowed to a walk in the deserted market.

"Catherine, all the shadows in the world will not hide you if everyone can hear your voice."

Catching him by surprise, I shoved him against the wall of one of the empty market stalls. Someone sold spices here during the day. The rich perfumes of cinnamon and nutmeg lingered, and I licked my lips to savor them. "Have I ever told you you're uncanny handsome?"

"Catherine, you are drunk."

He tried to step away from me, but I leaned into him. The rise and fall of his chest caressed me. I was enchanted by his glower.

"I could just eat you up," I murmured in what I hoped was an intimate whisper.

He turned his head away, so my lips brushed the prickly hairs of his decorative beard; he gripped my elbows. "Catherine, if you cannot respect yourself enough not to throw yourself at me while swilled in rum, then could you please respect *me* enough not to treat me as if I were a man willing to take advantage of a woman who is drunk? Because I am not that man."

I nuzzled his throat. "You wish you were that man."

"No, I don't wish I were that man."

I ignored his frosty tone in favor of rubbing against him. "Your body wishes you were that man."

He shoved me away so hard I fell flat on my backside.

He muttered a curse, extending a hand. "I didn't mean for you to fall. My apologies."

I giggled as I reached for him. "You're only angry because you're aroused."

An icy curl of wind kissed my nose as he pulled back his hand without touching mine. "You may think with your body, Catherine, but I. Think. With. My. Mind. I am going home. Are you coming with me, or are you returning to your friends at the Speckled Iguana? Because you can be sure I will not stop you from going where you wish."

He walked away. It took far too long for his words to filter through my muddied brain and then longer still to remember how to get to my feet. I ran after the harried rhythm of his steps. He said nothing as I stumbled up beside him. By the set of his shoulders and the nip of the air pooling around him, I knew he was furious. Aroused and furious, certainly a bad dish to be served.

"I'm sorry about Drake," I said. "I really am. I was drunk."

He did not answer, but I felt his thoughts as if they were knives. Very cold edgy knives.

"I mean, he got me drunk."

"I can now see how well that would have worked out for him."

"Ouch! That was unkind!" I waited, but he fumingly said nothing, so I went on. "Anyway, I had just washed up on that place we're not supposed to talk about. I was so scared and confused."

His anger veered off me and slammed elsewhere. "As I suspected, he took advantage of you. Or worse."

"He saved my life. Or maybe he didn't. I'm still not sure who to believe about that. Do you know what? He uses dying people as catch-fires to heal people who have a chance to live. That seems wrong to me but what if it is right? If they're already dying, I mean?"

"Lord of All, that is a grim tale," Vai murmured. "Fire mages seem rank upon the ground here in the Antilles."

His words caused my thoughts to gallop down a more interesting path, one whose peculiar contours I ought to have surveyed before now. "Vai, what's wrong with you?"

"What makes you think anything is wrong with *me*?"

"When you're angry, shouldn't there be hammering waves of cold? Shattered iron? For one moment there at the ball court, weren't rifles killed and flames extinguished? Yet then didn't a pistol go off? Given you are a rare and potent cold mage, how can you sit in the courtyard and not extinguish Aunty's cook fire? What is going on with your magic? Is it you? Or is it this place?"

He said nothing. We walked a ways in a calm resembling truce.

At length, he spoke. "I'm wondering how you are able to walk unseen. I weave cold fire to form false images. You truly veil yourself from the sight of others."

"From everyone but you."

"I will always know where you are. Maybe you will tell me how you manage this magic."

"You think I will tell you because I am drunk."

"The drink does loosen your . . . control."

I staggered away from him as the abyss that was my future yawned before me to coax me into its chasm. "No, what am I thinking? It's impossible. I have to hold on."

"Why should it be impossible, Catherine? Hold on to what?"

"How can it not be impossible? Haven't we already had this conversation? Aren't I already bound—?" The wind was tearing at the clouds, and in a rent appeared the masked white face of the moon, its light a talon dug into my throat. I halted as if I had slammed into a glacial cliff.

He took two steps, then turned back to take my hand. "Catherine?"

I was a statue, with a statue's grindingly hoarse whisper like a chisel chipping away at my very soul. *"What makes you think he will ever let me speak?"*

The calluses on his fingers made his touch a little rough, and yet thereby their very ordinariness settled his presence over me like balm. "Tell me who 'he' is, Catherine. We will find a way to unchain the binding."

In a rumble of thunder I heard the warning boom of his voice. I broke away from Vai. I hurried, for I was sorely

afraid, and I was not truly sure what scared me most: that
I would never be able to speak or that I would. I came to
the closed gate first and scratched at it.

When Aunty Djeneba answered, I lunged forward to
kiss her. "Aunty! I missed you!"

She stepped back to let us in with a look at Vai that
would have scorched wood.

He was not intimidated. "She's drunk. Did you let her
go out this way?"

She smelled my breath and recoiled. "I did not know
she had imbibed quite so much rum."

He sighed. "I found her precipitating a riot at the
Speckled Iguana."

"I never! I was with Bala and Gaius. They were guarding me."

Aunty set hands on hips and looked at Vai. "I can see
yee would have believed yee had to remove her from that
situation."

"I went there to look for you," I said to Vai, to reassure
him. No need to mention Drake!

Aunty Djeneba made a noise suspiciously like a
choked laugh. By the light of a single candle over the bar,
other forms moved. It took me a moment to realize it was
not a burning candle but a glow of cold fire that had been
illuminated, no doubt, all the while he had been gone.

Uncle Joe called softly, "Is that Vai and Cat, safely
back?"

"Yes, and not going out again this ill-omened night,"
said Aunty Djeneba in a voice none dared argue with.
"Kayleigh and Luce, yee go up to bed. The gate is
barred."

Vai shaped a second floating bauble to light the family
members to their beds, but he and I remained by the

closed gate, him unmoving and me swaying to the surge
of the waves and the voice of the wind. They were living
creatures, calling me. My sire had raked his fingers
through my heart and heard its singing. Now he was sending his minions to cut off my tongue so I could never
betray who I was and how he had made me. Maybe this
was his way to stop me from saving Bee!

Vai said, in the arrogant voice which meant he was
strangling a powerful emotion, "After what you've drunk,
I daresay you need to go pee, Catherine."

"How clever you are, Vai. I do!"

He accompanied me to the washhouse, waiting outside. I did what I needed to do and afterward admired the
fixtures in a glow of cold fire and yanked on the pulley
three times because it worked so cunningly well with water running out and in.

From outside, he said, "If you do not come out
now, Catherine, I will assume you are in trouble and
come in."

I hurried out and wrapped my arms around him. "After
a year and a day has passed," I said, finding in this
thought a glimpse of sun. "Then I can do what I want
without being chained by it."

He squirmed out of my embrace. "What can you possibly mean by that?"

"Who would have thought it, the Thrice-Praised poet
spitting words as crude and unpleasant as an adder's? Can
adders talk? Do they spit venom? Or just bite?"

"I'd like to know which Thrice-Praised poet. It's a
common epithet."

I opened my mouth to tell him, for I ought to have
told him beforehand about what I had learned from the
head of the poet Bran Cof. I had meant to, hadn't I? I

opened my mouth, and there were no words there. Bran Cof's master was my master. I could not speak of him.

"You are tired." He steered me upstairs and into the room. "Kayleigh, put your cot across the door so she can't wander out. She's that kind of drunk."

"What kind of drunk?" Kayleigh obediently dragged her cot to the open door, where he stood poised to escape me.

"Vai," I said urgently. "Why are you leaving?"

"A lecherous drunk," he said.

"Why are you leaving, then, Brother?" asked Kayleigh in a tone whose sneer I could not like.

"Don't you mock me," he said to her, "or shall I have to remind you—"

"I can't be a lecherous drunk," I protested, having finally worked through his comment. "Lechers are male."

She snickered. "This must be very difficult for you, Vai."

He shut the door.

"I recommend a bucket of cold water or a touch of cold magic if you dare," she called, but he was gone.

"You have a mean streak," I remarked, very wisely I am sure.

"No worse than you teasing him the way you do! Come here. Go away. Kofi says you're two-faced like a star-apple tree."

I sat down on my cot. "How can a tree have two faces, when it doesn't even have one?"

"I don't understand, Cat. If you don't want him, then why don't you stay away from him?"

"How can I bear to stay away from him?" I whispered. Lying back, I found that the room, the building, or perhaps the entire island pitched and rolled like a ship at sea.

"I hope you're not going to throw up," muttered Kayleigh from her cot at the door. "Because you have to clean it up if you do."

"I feel fine."

I fell into sleep. Or so I supposed, because a crow flew in through the shuttered window, stirring the air with black wings. Salt poured onto the roof as though ground from a bottomless mill. A rhythmic shaking danced through the room like a procession of invisible drummers at an areito. People were talking, but I couldn't understand their words. They were suckling fruit, the scent of guava in the air. A bat hung from the rafters, its eyes obsidian as it spoke to me in a voice like a rasp. *"Yee should not have defied him. He is angry because yee tried to talk. Now yee shall feel the lash of the master's power."*

24

I woke up.

A shutter was banging rhythmically in a pounding, relentless wind. Rain sheeted on the roof like a downpour of pebbles. Dawn's light suggested the outline of the shuttered windows. Because I had slept in my clothes, everything was rumpled and creased. My braid had begun to unravel, and I had to wipe strands of hair off my sweaty cheek. Kayleigh slept so soundly it was the work of a moment to shift her cot, crack the door, and squeeze through. I paused at the top of the stairs.

The battering gusts of wind forced me to grip the railing. Rain pelted sideways. Uncle Joe, Uncle Baba the fisherman, and Aunty's unmarried son emerged from rooms downstairs, followed by several of the men who rented hammock space. I helped them lash down everything that was not already tied down. The canvas roof over the restaurant was rolled down, leaving a stripped rectangle of ground soon churned to mud. Even the ceiba tree in the courtyard had netting thrown over it and staked to the ground.

"Where is Vai?" I shouted.

"He is gone down to the jetty!" shouted Uncle Joe. "We shall go as soon as we is done here. Got to move people inland. The Angry Queen come. Someone have offended her. Listen." A deep dull boom rolled in the southeast. "Her herald speak. Then the flood-bringer shall come."

I did not ask permission to go to the jetty with them. I simply went. After they had asked me twice to go back, they gave up and let me walk with them if you could call walking what was really leaning into the howl and shuffling forward as against a hand that kept trying to sweep you back. We passed groups of people trudging inland hauling belongings, trundling carts, or carrying cages with bedraggled birds. The city hunkered down like an animal hoping to survive.

When we came to the wide avenue that fronted the jetty, the wind-lashed waters greeted us. Waves clashed and roiled out on the churning brown waters of the bay. Clouds towered along the horizon, as dark as an angry heart.

The wind screamed, blowing my braid parallel to the ground. I could scarcely stand upright as I struggled in the wake of the men toward a damaged building shore-side—one of many boathouses—where folk were trying to hoist a fallen beam. Carpenters had brought tools to cut and split, working beside the wardens they had fought last night. By the evidence of their frantic activity, they were aiming to free people trapped inside as waves pounded at the shattered plank flooring.

A man was laughing.

A lofty shape strode across the bay, flinging shafts. These insubstantial spears ghosted past, curling to become the wind that tore through the streets. The man stood not taller than me, and yet his shadow spanned the sky. His long beautiful black hair writhed, its tendrils growing to engulf every building, every tree, every frail struggling person.

"Run, little sister," he called mockingly. "I's the storm's herald. The Angry Queen follow close behind me. Run if yee can."

Waves rushed up over the revetment and the wharves and onto the avenue, sizzling around my ankles. He stepped out of the air beside me. His face was scored and scarred by zigzag lines so scintillant I had to look away lest I be blinded. A shaft drove into my flesh, and I found myself on my knees in the rising water. The wave that washed around me sucked out, pulling me toward the sea. By the time I struggled gasping to my feet the shadow had walked at least half a Roman mile west along the shore.

A shout rose from the boathouse as three men were carried out of the building, injured but alive. I ran over. Straddling the fallen beam, men were arguing over whether anyone was left inside. The floorboards had cracked to create a splintering hole in the floor beneath which soughed seawater. An arm appeared, tossing a saw and an axe up into the light. A head appeared, and Vai levered himself up to sit on the edge.

An older man shouted to someone still below. "Kofi-lad! Come up! The flood is coming."

I pushed through men stowing their gear.

Vai looked up. "I should have known you'd walk straight into danger," he shouted at me. Then he looked into the hole. "Kofi! You're the last one. Come up!"

In a wreckage of shattered boards and boats below, Kofi slipped and cursed. "I's coming. 'Tis just that he is like my uncle."

"Is someone missing?" I yelled.

Vai said, "The owner is missing. We only found his nephews and the hired boatman."

Before anyone could stop me, I swung my legs over and dropped. Vai swore, and I had no sooner gotten my balance atop a sliding mass of planks than he hit beside me, the heap shifting. I slid. He caught himself on a hand. A bulb of cold fire cast a glow across the carnage. A wave bubbled up from beneath broken boards. Kofi turned.

"Get out of here, gal!" His contemptuous grimace brought me up short. "Yee's not impressing any man except Vai."

With the water coming up, I had no time. "Quiet!"

I balanced across the back of a smashed boat and in a crouch crept up into the nether shadows where the back part of the boathouse had collapsed. I set my hands against one of the ground stilts and leaned there as another wave hissed in, swirling my pagne up to my knees. As the wave subsided, I drew the threads that bind the world into my heart and my ears. And I listened. Nails creaked and groaned as the wind slowly pried at them. Soon the whole edifice would tear loose. Waves slurped beneath the debris. Kofi muttered a complaint, but Vai shushed him.

Human breathing had a distinctive flavor that might flow fast or slowly but that could not be mistaken for a cat's prim proud air or a dog's slovenly panting. Another body dwelled here. Blood tainted the air like a sliver of salt. A heart's erratic pulse cast a fragile line into my hands.

"He is here. Still alive."

I crawled over the wreckage until I found the spot. I began to pull out boards. The bauble of cold fire drifted down to light my way, for Vai had taken no effort to make it appear like a lamp. Kofi and Vai appeared with an axe and a pry bar. We cleared boards to find another overturned boat beneath, with which we grappled until it became clear it was stuck.

"His head is up under the bow," I said.

With four powerful swings, Kofi smashed a hole in the half-buried stern, then used the pry bar to clear out the splintered boards. Vai clambered back over the debris to shout up at the remaining men, asking for rope and a net.

"I'll go," I said to Kofi. "You're too big."

After a hesitation, Kofi stepped back. I squeezed through and crawled up into the marrow of the boat, up beneath the ribs to where a man lay unconscious. I felt along a skinny body to a sunken chest which barely rose and fell. A sticky mat of blood covered his hair, but his skull seemed intact. The ribs of the boat shuddered as Kofi axed a bigger hole in the stern.

"Cat!" he shouted. "Water is rising! Can yee hear me?"

"I've got him!" I tugged him through a slime of mud down to the opening. They got hold of his feet, so I shimmied back to cradle his head as they started to pull him out.

A wave poured in, dragging at Kofi and Vai as they braced to hold on to the old man. I lost hold as water surged into the cavity and slammed me into the ribs of the boat.

Then it sucked out. My foot caught and twisted on the rower's bench above, trapping me under the boat. Spewing and choking, I freed my foot and pushed up to hands and knees. A skin of grime coated my lips. When I breathed in through my nose, a spike of salty water lanced up behind my eyes in a hot knife of pain.

"Cat? Cat!" A shadow blocked the hole. "Throw me some cursed rope, Kofi!"

I heaved, lungs spasming.

Barely heard over the rough tearing rumble of the wind, men cried out in warning.

The whole building rocked as the flood slammed into it and boiled up underneath, filling the entire overturned boat, which was my prison. I had time to suck in one gasp of air before the slippery grasp of the water embraced me. Its moist mouth fastened over my lips to inhale the breath out of my lungs. A liquid voice murmured in my heart: "Let go, little sister. Walk with me and me brother who is the thunder. Walk with us into the storm."

I open my mouth to call for my mother, for it is her hand clutching mine, but the furious water wrenches her away and I am drowning in the churn of the flood.

My head hit a corner and my knee scraped up splinters like a nest of prickling burning bites. I fought, but fear tore out my courage as water streamed through my parted lips.

Then Vai's arms held me, and he dragged me out. Foam popped at my nostrils. My head breached. I gasped in air. Vai hauled me up. I hung on him as a dead weight, for I was a quivering frightened drowning child who had lost her papa and mama to the flood.

He carried me over the wreckage of the under-space, slipping and sliding. Kofi had already gone up with the old man. Distant shouts barked a warning.

Another huge wave slammed into the building, shuddering the structure half off its stilts as the entire building groaned. Water gushed into the under-space, rushing up to engulf everything including us.

My ears popped as the temperature dropped. The wave crackled into a ragged, rippled curtain of ice, stopping just short of washing over us. Above, water poured down through the hole on top of us and slapped into the ice wall, hissing and grinding.

Vai was shaking all over, his skin as cold as winter. He had his free arm outstretched. In the curve of his forefinger and thumb, he was holding a necklace chain with a round metal ring like the eye of a spyglass. Within the ring was a circle of what looked like cloudy glass. He released the ring, and the chain dropped limply against his wet singlet.

"I can't use that a second time," he said in a hoarse voice. "You've got to stand, Cat."

The rippled curve of the ice wave began to pit and sink as a fresh swell surged up below.

"Ja, maku!" Kofi stuck his head down. "Hurry, yee jackass. Another wave coming."

I was not a jackass. I jumped; Kofi caught my hands and hauled me up as another man cast down a net for Vai. I had used the last of my strength. Kofi threw me over his broad back and ran, me retching as water chased us across the avenue.

The tearing baleful wind, most frightfully and dreadfully, ceased.

I wriggled and slipped, and landed on my knees as pain pierced into my brain and every joint in my body screamed with a bone-drilling ache. The sky turned yellow. I looked up into the eye of the Angry Queen. The spirit of the hurricane was a woman, a vast looming face with a brow of thunderclouds and a mouth of lightning. The curve of her arms was the tearing circle of the howling winds. Here, under her face, the world lay still.

Vai splashed up carrying rope, net, and tools.

"She have got the kick of a mule, I swear!" said Kofi. "I shall have a bruise."

"Why did you let her crawl under the boat?" Vai demanded. "She almost drowned!"

"I was too big to fit through. But maku, tell me now, have yee ever tried to stop her doing some thing she mean to do? Had yee much fortune with that? Hurry! The worst is coming, and it shall hit like the hells."

The woman loomed over us. They did not see her, for she was a spirit, not a body.

She bent down and, with a lick of her salty tongue, she ate me whole.

I stood on a beach of fine white sand as cool as silk beneath my bare toes. I wore nothing but a gauzy shift like a caul of light. My lips were cold, and my feet, sipped by wavelets, were warm. The Angry Queen stood on the surface of the water. She was tall, with broad shoulders and powerful arms ropy with muscle, and the girth of one whose appetite makes her strong. Her eyes flashed with lightning, and her presence was the gale.

"Yee sire is waiting. Go to him."

"No."

Thunder growled although the sky lay so clear and blue above me that one might believe it as bottomless as trust.

"Yee cannot fight him. He is stronger and have always been stronger and shall always be stronger. The great ones stir in the abyss. Can yee not hear them?"

On the water's tickling swell I traveled far and deep into the crushing trench of an abyss where the twinned beasts called leviathan shuddered as they struggled to wake from the stupor that bound them.

"Do yee serve the master still? That is the question he ask of yee. He alone must hold yee allegiance or there shall be ill to pay. Yet yee have a defiant heart.

'Tis a spark easily seen, little cat. Better if yee extinguish the spark than if he do, for he shall not suffer rebellion."

"So must we fight," I whispered, "rather than submit."

A turtle rose out of the glassy blue waters, its blocky head a stub above the waves, eye staring until with a flip and a roll it sank back under. For some reason, its presence heartened me.

"Do you serve him, too?" I asked her.

Her laughter boomed, the sound cracking so hard I was driven to my knees. Her fingers like the grasp of death closed over my face.

"Yee talk too much. The secret is not yee own to share."

A mask of water hardened over my face. The foul liquid coursed into my eyes and nose and mouth. But the flood had not ripped me away. Vai had saved me from the drowning waters.

Water splashed in my face. I was being carried through the rain-washed streets.

"Let me down. Let me down!" I struggled free and landed on my knees, first coughing, then heaving uncontrollably until I thought I would retch the entire sea out of my lungs.

Vai knelt beside me. His skin was hot, or mine was cold. "Catherine, we have to keep moving. The sea is flooding inland."

"I have to save Bee!" But when I tried to rise the darkness beneath the overturned boat engulfed me until I saw nothing. Perhaps I flew. Perhaps it was all a nightmare.

For then I was sitting in the chair under the shelter by the kitchen with my muddy wet blouse stuck to me and a dry pagne draped modestly over my soaked drawers.

A poultice soothed my scraped knee. One of the toddlers cuddled in my lap, a comforting presence.

"'Twas bravely done," said Kofi, behind me, "but I still reckon that gal be hiding the truth from yee."

"This is not the time to speak of it," said Vai. "She saved your uncle's life when we all would have left him there not knowing he was trapped."

"'Tis true. She saved him. I shall go over to he daughter's place to see how he fares."

Their voices faded. The wind mocked me in its singsong chant: *We want one of they, do yee hear, me sissy-o?*

The old man was dead. The spirits had taken him. The thread that linked him and me unraveled and its last tendril snapped like a hand slipping out of the hand that seeks to hold it in this world. His spirit sighed, and crossed over. A crow perched on the open sill and watched me as the sun behind it made a cowl of golden light for its form. Weary beyond measure, I went to bed.

I woke the next morning on the cot, wearing fresh drawers and a clean blouse I had no memory of putting on. The sound of hammering and sawing beat at my aching head. My mouth tasted of a vile brew that I could only imagine had been fermented from a stew of rotted worm guts and moldy rat droppings. Gagging, I fastened my spare pagne around my hips and, aching in every battered muscle, creaked down to the washhouse to do my business. After, I hobbled to the kitchen, where Aunty Djeneba greeted me with a cup of fresh juice and a kiss on each cheek.

I drained the cup.

She grated cassava in her calm way. "That was a fierce night and day. Uncommon thing, though. The storm sheared off right after all that happened on the jetty. There was wind, but nothing like what there should have been. Unexpected good fortune for us. How is yee, gal?"

A basket of fruit sat on the kitchen table. "Been shopping already?" I asked.

"That was brought at dawn by the daughter of the man yee found in the boathouse. 'Twas a brave act, Cat."

"But he died anyway."

She paused. "He passed in the arms of he family, not trapped in the flood."

A mask of ice stiffened my face, and my sire's claws sank into my beating heart. Now she was wondering how I'd known, because no one could possibly have told me.

"Is there some mending I could do?" I said hastily.

She studied me. "Yee need mend nothing, gal. Yee rest."

"I just need to do something."

She nodded. "Yee know where the basket lie."

I darned as my heart raged. How I hated them! My sire who had bound me to serve him and sent his servants to mock and torment me. The mansa who had been willing to kill me and didn't even care that he owned me. He only cared that Vai was forced to obey his commands because the mage House owned Vai and his entire village. Princes and Romans who played a game of plots and scheming to which only the powerful were invited. Hidden masters who directed Bee's fate. The Council who sent out its wardens to track down fire banes and arrest people who wanted a voice.

No wonder folk lashed out, rebelling against their chains.

I did not ask where Vai was. I did not have to. I could hear the sounds of repair work all around as the people of Expedition mended the damage done by the storm. He would be working.

For even if he was out hammering and sawing, he was working in the service of the mansa. He was a cold mage first and always. He was bound, as I was bound because I was bound to him.

Today was the eighth of September. What day had we married? It had been late in October, the evening of the twenty-seventh, to be exact. Yet what did that date matter? On the last day of October, the Wild Hunt would ride. I didn't have much time left. I had to stop thinking about anything except Bee.

Aunty Djeneba let me mend in silence as she chatted companionably about the prospects for an areito's being held the next day as usual in honor of the annual Landing Day, the day the first Malian ships had made landfall on Kiskeya. I ate rice and peas although without cassava bread, for the last few days' flour so painstakingly grated and squeezed had been spoiled by the storm.

In the late morning, Luce came running in. Uncle Joe looked up from polishing his best cups. Aunty and Brenna came out of the back, where they had been straining cassava.

It was to me Luce ran. "Cat, wardens is making a sweep. I sneaked out of school. They's looking for a maku gal. They don' say why, except to arrest her."

Uncle Joe set down cloth and cup as Aunty and Brenna looked at me.

"I promise you," I said, seized by reckless fury, "the wardens shall not find me."

I put away the mending and went up to my room to bundle up the clothing I had sewn from my old skirts and jacket, for the wool challis in weave and color was

markedly different from any material sold here. Not that
wardens would necessarily notice cloth, but I could not
take the chance. A trample of wardens announced themselves at the gate before I left the room, but it was no
trouble for me to draw shadows around me and walk into
plain view, nothing more than the railing on the stairs. I
descended to the courtyard as they searched, and I stood
right out in the open against a stretch of wall, one that
providentially captured the afternoon shade.

They searched through every room and shed as Aunty
and Brenna and Uncle Joe demanded by what authority
wardens came trampling into their boardinghouse where
they had never had a hint of trouble and paid their excise
tax just as all folk did.

The wardens left. I waited, leaning against the wall
with my mind a fuming blank, until another brace of wardens showed up. Had I been a warden, I would have used
the same trick, hoping to take my fugitive by surprise after she was sure she had escaped capture. The children
clamored home from school. The afternoon drifted heat-
edly past, and folk whom I had never before seen came
in for a drink. They did not stay long, having not seen a
maku gal.

Yet all the local people knew a maku gal waited tables
at Aunty Djeneba's boardinghouse.

Did folk just not talk? Did the secret truly belong to
those who remained silent?

In the late afternoon Vai returned, shoulders slumped
wearily. After washing and speaking with the others, he
dragged over a bench as if to take advantage of the shade
and placed his tools in a tidy row along its length. He
gently shooed off the little lads who followed him around
and set to work sharpening. The scraping covered his low

voice. "I suppose you've been hiding right here all day. People are furious the wardens made a sweep of the district. I knew they wouldn't find you."

I whispered. "You look tired."

He looked right at me, surprised by my concern, and as quickly away.

Luce had been surreptitiously searching for me all afternoon after returning in the normal manner from school. She strolled over and sat on the bench where Vai had laid out his tools: chisels, planes, three axes, two saws, an auger, an adze, a drawknife, a mallet, and a gauge.

"I shall help yee," she said to Vai, picking up a file.

He smiled. "When a gal offers to sharpen a man's saw, it means she is courting him."

She giggled, a shy smile flashing. I thought: She thinks of him as I think of Brennan Du, a man wholly out of her reach and not meant for her anyway.

He plied a rasp on the edge of his chisel, his hands sure and strong, the muscles of his bare arms tensing and contracting, his lips slightly parted as if he was just about to tell me something. I could not bear to look at him. The sound of the rasp scored a runnel across my heart.

I slunk away and crept up to my room, where I unwound the shadows, stowed my things, hardened my heart, and went back out.

Luce saw me descending the stairs and ran over. "Where'd yee hide?"

"Don't you think I have to keep that a secret?" The others had seen me come down. I walked over to the bar. "Will anyone come tonight, Uncle Joe?"

"Sure." He looked me over with a frown. "Most shall come to drink in thanks we was not harder hit by the hurricane. The rest shall come to talk revolution, for the Council have overreached it own self with this raid."

I ran my fingers along a tray's well-worn rim, smooth from years of use by serving gals before me. "I shall eat something now, and serve if folk do come. If you think it's safe."

Vai had followed me. "Catherine, you took a beating in the storm. Shouldn't you rest?"

Words flooded like the storm's surge in a wild burst of anger that took me utterly by surprise. "Rest? Do you think there is rest for the likes of us? Aren't we the ones at the mercy of the flood and the hammer of the wind? How can it be right that a cold mage who can turn a wave into ice and shatter iron is nothing but the mansa's property? And why would you think you truly own me, Vai, just because your mage House does own me due to a contract I never signed or agreed to? Why would I wrap myself in more chains?"

Leaving everyone gape-mouthed, I ran to the washhouse and blew my nose. A rime of emotion I could not describe or acknowledge coated me, so I stripped out of my clothes and washed myself and my hair and, braiding it wet, fixed it under a kerchief after I dressed. Luce looked in once but left me alone. Everyone else pretended not to see me.

At length I ventured out to a courtyard ringed by soft lamps, an illusion testifying to the power of Vai's cold magic, he who had yesterday said he had nothing more to draw from. Unless that wasn't what he had meant with the words "I can't use that a second time."

Folk came, as Uncle Joe had predicted. The crowd conversed in agitated murmurs. With a laden tray I walked among them as always, and I was grateful to do this ordinary work, just another gal making her way in the world.

Vai had put away his tools and gone over to talk to Kofi, their heads together like conspirators'. Who was this man who looked exactly like my husband? Once or twice or ten times he glanced toward me when he thought I wasn't looking at him—not that I was looking at him all the time—and each time he would look away with an imperious lift of his chin as if to remind me of the way I had raged at him an hour ago in front of everyone. There was the Andevai I had married! I could dislike the arrogant cold mage. I had to.

How old men did ramble! Yet their words had a toothsome bite as they discussed why the Council hadn't supported General Camjiata's original bid for troops, money, and weapons.

"I reckon," said the oldest uncle, "the Council feared the general would-a just turned troops and weapons around against the Council to overthrow them and sit he own self in they place."

"So he is now run to the Taino? The cacica shall be glad to use the excuse to invade."

Several shook their heads. "The Taino shall not invade. They hold their virtue very high. They shall never be the ones to break the First Treaty."

So why would the Taino help the general? Everyone agreed: trade to Europa with no tariffs or wharfage fees and no restrictions as there were now. They could flood the Europan market with sugar, tobacco, and Expedition's cheap cloth, and with the profits fund a war against their perpetual rivals, the Purépecha kingdom.

Oldest uncle considered. "The Council shall get those same benefits if they support the general. Except for the war with the Purépecha. The Council could likewise send over the ocean in the general's service the very lads who trouble the city most with discontent. Yet they refuse to help him. Sweet Cat, yee is from Europa. What yee reckon?"

I paused beside the table, tray balanced on one hand, aware that Vai had looked around to see how I would deal with a question. "Does anyone think the general can defeat the Roman Alliance with a single small fleet from Expedition? Didn't he lose the first war with a significantly larger army? But have you all forgotten there are radicals in Europa, too? Wasn't it twenty years ago that General Camjiata wrote a legal code codifying the natural rights due to men? Wouldn't the existence of such a legal code scare the Council?"

"Gal have a point," said the oldest uncle. "The Council don' like kings, but they like talk of equality less."

"Maybe the Council refuses to help Camjiata because they fear the radicals support him."

Brenna came over to pour more beer. "I hear Camjiata's legal code don' give rights to women. Like the Romans in that, yee know, for on he mother's side he is of patrician descent."

The oldest uncle answered her with a kindly nod at me to show he meant no offense. "Yee know how they is in Europa, very backward. Yee should, with that Roman mariner yee keep."

"Which is why he and me never signed a marriage contract. He is a good man, yee all know it, but he got no rights over me share of this house and me money. Which will all go to me girls."

"With yee permission, Uncle," said Kofi, looming up beside the table. When the old man nodded, he went on.

"I don' know what they radicals in Europa reckon, but if the general wish for the support of we Assemblymen, he shall have to change he code. No troll clan will put a single ship or sailor at he disposal if females got no rights. And neither shall we."

"Not to mention no man in this city who speak against such shall ever again enjoy the favors of he wife or gal," Brenna added before she glided off like a ship under sail.

A judicious silence calmed the courtyard's chatter. Then the men chuckled nervously and got going again. I moved on, and Vai caught the eye of a new customer who had been about to pat my backside but decided to pat his kerchief instead. Vai looked away before I could skewer him with a chiseled glance meant to inform him that I had to take care of myself, not bc beholden to him.

"Say, is it true? After all that big talk about he search for she, the lost woman." The speaker was a young man I did not know, talking in a low voice to his lads. He did not see me passing behind him although his companions had begun gesticulating wildly. "Now the maku found she, he is not getting any—?" He yelped as I upended my tray over his back.

"Oh! My apologies! I tripped." I wasn't sure he could hear me over the guffaws and snorts of laughter that exploded around the courtyard. "Let me get you something to wipe up with."

At the counter, Uncle Joe handed me a cloth. "Yee know, Cat, beer is not cheap. Don' go trying me patience."

"I know. I'm sorry."

Vai slid in beside me. "Did he say something to you, Catherine?"

"The gal just tripped," said Brenna, stacking coconut

shell bowls on a tray for me to take to the women who did the washing up back by the cistern. "Happen sometimes, don' it?"

"Not with Cat it doesn't," he muttered. Then he looked past me, and his eyes widened as he smiled in a disconcertingly anticipatory way.

I turned. Over at the gate, Kofi was greeting a pair of vivacious young women who had the bearing of clever girls who assume men will listen to their words and not just stare at their breasts.

"My pardon, but I have to go." He made his way to the gate.

With a lack of greeting I found peculiarly disturbing, for it made them all seem exceedingly familiar with each other, they went out.

"They radicals mean trouble," muttered Uncle Joe.

"Trouble is what come before change," said Brenna, "for yee know we is overripe for some manner of change."

"How deep in is Vai with these radicals?" I asked, one eye on the gate.

"Why do yee care?" she retorted so tartly that my face flushed. "I reckon yee have made yee feelings known to all."

"Good-looking gals, they two," remarked Uncle Joe right over the top of Brenna's comment. "I would surely have a mind to know them, was I a young fellow."

Brenna snorted and slapped him on the arm. "A sad day for yee should yee be taken blind."

"Surely true," he said, gathering full cups onto my tray. "But I's not blind yet."

"Do you think the Council should be replaced by an Assembly?" I asked them.

Uncle Joe scratched his beard. "Hard to say how an Assembly shall be chosen, is it not? Fools and wise men look a lot alike. But listen here, Cat. Yee shall not go running after the radicals, for the wardens have they eye on them something fierce. Kofi-lad say we shall give the vote to every adult male and female, even the poor and the idle, with no regard to property or responsibility. He reckon it is the natural right of each person, troll or rat, to have a say in they governance."

"*Vai* agrees with that? Do you have any idea how much power he has in Europa as part of Four Moons House?"

Uncle Joe and Brenna exchanged a glance whose contours I could not fathom.

"And Kayleigh is working at Warden Hall, passing on information to Kofi, and thus the radicals, and thence to Vai."

"Keep silence, Cat," said Uncle Joe sternly. "Don' draw notice to yee own self. Or to him."

A memory of the conversation I had overheard in Chartji's office swept over me, the words Vai had said just before Chartji had opened the door to reveal me eavesdropping: "*What if people bound by clientage could say they want to reclaim ownership of themselves?*"

"Cat, yee have such a look on yee face." Brenna put a hand on my arm.

A man came in through the open gate. The man was not Vai. "Fine, I'm fine."

"Take that cloth and these drinks over," said Uncle Joe, "and be certain not to spill this lot."

I walked off, measuring my steps because I felt disoriented, like I was losing track of my path. I had to concentrate on Bee. I needed more information on fire mages, in case Drake wasn't strong enough to feed the

Hunt. I heard them murmur, thinking I was out of earshot.

"That is not like him," Brenna said, "to go running off like that with a pair of handsome gals. Not that I blame him, after what she said to him this afternoon."

"Yee women underestimate him," said Uncle Joe with a chuckle. "He know exactly what he is about. I suspicion he asked Kofi-lad to bring those gals by. Look at she, one eye on the gate. Now she shall wonder all evening what he is up to."

With radicals plotting trouble. What else might he be up to?

They had been good-looking. Far worse than that, they had looked smart and lively. The kind of gals I might be friends with. That is, if I didn't have to put a chisel through someone's eye, most likely my own because I certainly could not succumb to this sort of pathetic jealousy over a man I had to set aside until Bee was safe and I was free. If he would even want me after that.

The hour grew late, and folk went home. We washed up and put the benches on the tables, and I swept. Everyone went to bed, but I was too restless to lie down. I sat in the sling chair under the shelter getting bitten up by mosquitoes and so perhaps that was why sleep did not claim me.

Very late, he came in whistling under his breath, tapping out a rhythm on one thigh. A tincture of cold fire hovered in front of him in the shape of a gas flame burning within a glass lantern latticed by gleaming metalwork in the shape of queen conch shell. He was actually spinning it slowly around, checking to make sure it looked real from all angles. And it did, for I would never have known it for an illusion if it had been stationary. Reflexively, without thinking, I drew threads of shadow around me, to hide myself. He paused halfway across the court-yard, and he chuckled in the manner of a man who, having had a little too much to drink, thinks too well of himself.

"There's a Landing Day areito tomorrow out in Lucairi District. If you want to go, we can. There'll be dancing and singing. And food."

I didn't want to go. I shouldn't go. It was a bad idea to go.

"Yes."

"Then we shall. Good night, Catherine."

25

In the morning I woke muzzy-headed and furious with myself because Vai had already left for his work so I could not tell him I had to change my mind. I'd become selfishly preoccupied and distracted instead of doing nothing but hunting for a way to save Bee. I dressed, grabbed my cane, and tucked into my sleeve a little cloth purse that easily swallowed my paltry earnings.

"Yee slept later than usual," said Aunty Djeneba as I came down. The courtyard lay quiet. Everyone had left already.

"I'm going out," I said as I slipped my cane into a tube of cloth so no troll would spot it.

She frowned but said only, "Be cautious, Cat. The wardens is about."

"Wardens of one kind or another are always about," I muttered, spotting a crow on the roof.

Wreathed in shadows, I walked the avenue down to the harbor district. The storm had done a fair bit of damage. Men labored on roofs; women strung up washing. A dwarf mammoth hauled a wagon heaped with broken bricks and shards of splintered wood. Men had dug up one of the gas lines and were fixing its mechanism. The clock tower had lost a hand. But the city's mood had a cheerful edge, as a person might who has escaped the bite of a tremendous hungry shark.

Yet a taut, anticipatory conversation whispered beneath the work. Something big was up. People stood with heads together. Folk glanced at the sky, as if gauging the weather.

I rang the bell at the offices of Godwik and Clutch. Keer emerged from the back and, with a tilt of her head, indicated that I might enter her office. We drank and ate, and the more we discussed the local batey season the more I thought I was going to have to jump up and start pacing.

When we finished our nuts and raisins and our tea, Keer tapped talons on her desk. "You are impatient to speak of another matter."

I clasped, unclasped, and clasped my hands. "I am here to inquire if the offer of employment is still open."

The troll whistled, crest fanning up. "So we open negotiations. I hope you will tell me what you think we might need."

"You have a printing press out back. Might you need assistance with that enterprise? For instance, I could write a series of reports from Europa. Tales of the people there, and how they do things, and the stories they tell."

"Exotic lands revealed through firsthand accounts."

"My father was a traveler and natural historian. I can reproduce his anecdotes."

"Many foreigners have stories to tell. Yours would need to appeal in a way others do not."

"He knew General Camjiata. He wrote about him, and his legal code."

She cocked her head. "Timely! I am intrigued by this proposition. We can arrange for other duties as well. It only remains to bargain over terms and if you will be needing a nest, a room."

A room. Perhaps my color changed. Certainly I felt all blood had suddenly drained from my body, sucked away by an emotion I had no name for and dared not answer to.

"Yes," I whispered, all the sound I could manage. All that mattered was Bee. The law offices would surely be a better place to scout out information on fire mages and politics. People would be less fearful and more talkative here. Polite words ticked like clockwork gears in my mouth. "I shall return with my things later today."

"Such haste!" Keer rose as I stood.

Her gaze made me stiffen. She reacted with a twitch whose flicker made me instinctively grasp for shadows. Yet when I pulled at those threads, the confusing layout of mirrors and shiny objects scattered throughout the office yanked the threads up short, as if they were caught and tangled.

"Interesting," hissed Keer in a way that made me want to bolt, but I knew better than to run. One had to stand firm, and look bigger than one was.

"Can you see the threads?" I demanded, finding the power of my voice.

She showed me her teeth. "What will you pay me for an answer?"

"What payment do you think you can expect?"

"Do you think I name my price first?"

"Can you suppose I will show my hand by naming mine first?"

She hissed a sound meant, I thought, to be a laugh. "An unusual negotiating technique."

A hammering rush of excitement flushed my body. I

was learning how to use the very binding that trapped me. "Answering questions with questions?"

"Betraying your knowledge of the maze."

"What makes you think I have any knowledge of it?"

Her crest lifted as a strange crease narrowed the bold, watchful eyes. "As you rats would say, you have scored a point. Custom demands I acknowledge your step upward on Triumph Spire."

"Triumph Spire, where the young bucks preen," I muttered, recalling Maester Godwik's words. I had thought it a physical place, like a rocky promontory, but now I wondered if it was more abstract than geological in the way that males competed for intangible but recognized forms of status. "Tell me, Keer, why would a cold mage from Europa work with trolls?"

Keer gave a hiss I took for an indication of amusement or anticipation. "Next round. Yours now the right to draw the circle and step inside."

I hadn't the desire to begin another round. "Mine the right. I will return."

Trolls did not insist on a long ceremony of leave-taking, perhaps because sometimes one did not take one's leave but was merely consumed after a loss. I took my leave, hoping to order my thoughts as I trudged home. No, the boardinghouse was not home. It was for the best, anyway, that I move out, because I was putting them at risk by living and working there.

Aunty's gaze was steady on me as I came in the gate. "I hope yee got done what business yee had a mind for."

I glanced away, for I found I could not tell her I was leaving. "I did."

Her smile put me in mind of a basking lizard awaiting its inattentive dinner. "I don' mind saying we shall miss yee this evening. Yee get a nap. Yee have not yet danced at an areito."

I just could not tell her. "No. I haven't done that."

She exchanged glances with Brenna and Uncle Joe. I was too restless to nap, so I made myself busy with sweeping and mending while Brenna spent hours braiding Luce's hair. Luce chattered the whole while for she was so excited that she would get to go with us. I could not bear to break Luce's heart by not going. And I wanted to go; I wanted to dance and sing at an areito. Bee wouldn't begrudge me one more night. Rory would enjoy such a festival! Tomorrow I could make my farewells.

It rained, but the clouds cleared off under a brisk wind. I washed in the shower, and afterward Luce, her hair done, dragged me upstairs to dress. She wore a lovely pagne and a new blouse. She brought a mirror and, while I dressed, held it to check the way her tiny braids curved in at the ends around the back. When I complimented her, she smiled.

"Oooh me stars!" She angled the mirror to show me the cut and fit from behind. "No wonder yee saved this for an areito! Yee look so fine!"

Normally I wore the wrapped skirt and a loose cotton blouse that was the common fashion, but over the weeks I had labored over piecing together a skirt from my ruined petticoats, one that flattered my waist and hips but gave me plenty of room for my long stride and for climbing if need be. The top had proved harder to devise, since there was no possible reason to wear layers of clothing as we did in the north. I had cut down my wool jacket to three-quarter sleeves and a hem that ended at my hip bones. The wool challis wicked the moisture off my skin; layered over my sleeveless cotton bodice, it was quite comfortable.

She set down the mirror, sat me on the end of the bed, and began brushing out my hair, as she liked to do, humming a popular street melody. I heard footsteps at the base of the stairs. Luce brushed on obliviously, unaware.

The low, sardonic voice was Kayleigh's. "Is that a *bed*?"

"I thought it was time to get off those uncomfortable cots," answered Vai in a tone whose cheerfulness made me suspicious.

"Then why is there only one bed, Vai?"

"I can only make one at a time. After I'm done with my regular work."

A bed!

"Cat?" Lucretia bent to look in my face. "Yee went stiff, like a frog hopped over yee foot."

Vai was still speaking. "Aren't you going to the areito? Kofi hopes so."

Kayleigh's voice dropped to a murmur. "I have to go back. But I had to bring you this news. This is not rumor. General Camjiata returned to the city last night."

I choked.

Luce clucked. "'Tis sweet that yee's nervous."

Kayleigh was going on, voice tight and accusatory. "I'm no good at being a spy. I jump at every noise. I bump into things. I hate being indoors. It's not the cleaning work that's hard. It's that I can't stop thinking they're about to catch me and whip me and then hang me."

"I wouldn't ask it of you if I could do it myself."

Her tone softened. "I know, Vai. I know you'll never stop putting us first. I know you'll never stop trying. It's not fair I get away and no one else does. You know I'll do whatever you ask."

"Then tell me. Do I look all right?"

She snickered. "I cannot believe you just asked that."

"Cat, have a bat stolen yee mind?" Lucretia rapped me on the head with the brush.

"What makes you think I'm nervous?" I rose indignantly as the door opened.

Kayleigh entered. She ventured into monosyllables as she looked me up and down. "That's so fine, Cat. I'm so tired of these cursed lengths of cloth we have to wrap for skirts."

"My thanks," I said cautiously. "I could buy more material and sew you a similar skirt. A jacket will be harder. I'll have to make a pattern for it." Then I remembered I was leaving.

"Me, too, Cat!" cried Lucretia.

Kayleigh looked tired. I suppose a spy's work would be tiring if you didn't enjoy skulking and eavesdropping, and if you couldn't draw shadows around you to hide yourself from everyone except the ones you most needed to hide from.

Her wan smile seemed genuine. "That would be nice, Cat. You look very pretty."

I hoped I wasn't flushed. "I really would love to make you a skirt." Lucretia pinched me. "And *of course* one for pestiferous Luce."

Luce giggled.

Kayleigh sank down on her cot and rested her head on her arms.

"Kayleigh? Are you well?" I took a step toward her.

She gestured with a hand. "I have to go back to Warden Hall. The scullery girl came down sick." She hesitated, then went on into her arms. "I'm sorry I haven't been nicer to you, Cat."

"I hope he hasn't been scolding you. Vai ought to appreciate you better."

She glanced up with a surprised look. I thought she was about to speak, and I braced myself because I was sure it would be words I did not want to hear. But she rubbed her forehead and said, "I'll just rest a bit. Enjoy yourself tonight. I mean that." She lay down.

I grabbed my cane and slid it through the loop I had sewn into the waistband. If I was going to go, then I was cursed well going to enjoy myself. Just this one areito.

Lucretia said, "Cat, we have not braided yee hair."

"I think I won't." Let him see it all unbound!

"A kerchief, then." She followed me out. "Yee shall really look nice with the kerchief."

Vai stood in the courtyard talking with Kofi, who saw me and with a startled expression nudged Vai. He turned, looking up as I swanned down the stairs, Lucretia at my heels. Just for a moment he looked as if he had been kicked by a horse. Or perhaps it was me feeling the hoof slamming into my head, for he wore a jacket I recognized from Adurnam, a chained pattern of red and gold so bold only a confident man could pull off. There was something about the way he wore clothes that choked admiration out of people who wished not to be quite so stifled by a feeling I could only describe as...No. After all, I could not describe it.

"Catherine. There you are. Time to go." He extended a hand, meaning me to take it.

Kofi looked embarrassed. An armature of wood and netted rope rested behind them on the ground: the bed. It was wider than the narrow cot; two might share such a bed if they were willing to lie together in a loving embrace. My arm trembled, for I found I could not decide whether to keep it held firmly at my side as I knew I must, or to reach for him.

Vai smiled in the most annoying manner possible, as if he understood my struggle.

"No!" Aunty appeared, wiping her hands on a cloth. Lucretia whimpered and retreated up several steps. "A kerchief, or a braid, gal. Yee's not leaving me house with yee hair unbound."

"Oh," I said, petrified into immobility. I had never seen her angry before.

She turned on Vai. "Yee should know better, maku." When she said "maku," her tone bit.

The fire in the kitchen hearth flickered out. Over by the bar, Uncle Joe cursed. "Did yee not set that wick properly?" he said to one of the lads.

Vai lowered his gaze and let his hand fall to his side. "I beg your pardon. I wasn't thinking."

"Not with yee mind, that is for sure." She yanked the kerchief out of her granddaughter's hand as Lucretia gave an audible gulp. "I shall tend to Cat me own self. Go sit by the kitchen, Cat. As for yee," she added, nodding to Kofi, "yee take the maku and go on. The gals shall come after."

Kofi stammered an almost inaudible leave taking, grabbed Vai's arm, and dragged him off.

I followed Aunty over to the kitchen, where I sat on a stool. She fetched a comb, gave a look to the children that made them flee to the safety of Uncle Joe, and began a single thick braid.

"Yee do fidget, gal. Never again."

"Never again what?"

"Unbound hair is how sly women advertise they wares, and witches entwine they victims."

"Oh."

"Yee don' know, but Luce ought to have done. I reckon she thought yee was just being daring, for she think the world of yee."

"She tried to give me a kerchief!"

"While Vai was too dazzled to think."

"He was?"

"Gal, don' play that game with me. Nor should yee play it with him, like yee's punishing him for what he done before. Like yee want he to be in love with yee, so yee can throw it in he face."

"That isn't what I want!"

"That is how it look. Either let him be, or let him win yee back. This other is just small and mean, and I don' like to think of yee as a mean-hearted gal."

"But I can't, Aunty," I whispered. "I have to leave. There's a great deal I can't tell anyone." My voice wavered, and almost broke.

"He have secrets also. Yet say 'tis true. If yee cannot, then cut it clean. There is just no cause for this way of going on. Life is too short. There. Yee's fit to go out. Don' be trying that again."

"No, Aunty," I said in my most chastened voice, ducking my head like a cowed dog. And really, what can be worse for a cat than being compared to a dog?

At the gate, Luce took my hand with a compassionate smile, and we went out into the blowsy late-afternoon heat. Rain had slicked the streets, already drying off; the blustering wind had torn the clouds until they looked like crumpled iron sheets. Her arm on mine, we strolled along Tailors' Row, where men greeted us politely from tables beside the gates of their family compounds.

"Yee sew that skirt yee own self, Sweet Cat? Will yee give me the pattern?"

"That's my trade secret, isn't it? How shall yee make it worth my while?"

They laughed. "Going to the areito, gals? Yee two look fine!"

Luce giggled, and it was all worth it, to hear her laugh like that.

The brush of drums spiked the air and made my skin tingle. Shadows kissed and mingled with light as afternoon sank with the sun into the drowsy west. We strode through the quiet streets of the Passaporte District, home to working households of the respectable kind, people who made the things necessary to the daily round of life.

Lucairi District had once been a village where Lucayan immigrants from the Bahamas had settled back in the early days of Expedition Territory. As the city spread, the village had been folded into the outer city and newer immigrants had moved in. The streets had not the neat grid of Passaporte nor its gaslit streets. The plaza was very old, and not large, having once been only a village center, but the batey court had been recently expanded and rebuilt with gaslight, with what the locals called cobo hoods for the glass shell, with its decorative ironwork meant to resemble the queen conch. The drums were already conversing, and rings of dancers moved on the ball court as gaslight flamed into life with the sun's setting. There were a lot of people milling and laughing and eating, but I did not spot Vai or Kofi.

Luce dragged me along toward one of the women's circles where she had seen her friends. I paced along with Tanny and Diantha, the steps easy to follow, the gals chatting like runaway horses. They wanted to know about Luce's hair; my jacket and skirt; they wanted to know about Luce's father's ship; they wanted Diantha to tell them about the latest tryouts for the women's team of the Rays; they wanted to know if kerchiefed Gaius had come courting Tanny with a basket of mamey.

How they talked! I might have said something, but I could not get in one word, and anyway, I kept losing track of the conversation and the steps. I had to scan the restless shifting of the crowd.

But of course he would not come out onto the ball court, not with all those gas lamps.

I tugged at Luce. "I shall be right back. You stay here?"

She rolled her eyes. "Yee's not gone looking for him already?"

Affronted, I meant to make a brilliant counterthrust, but I caught sight of Kofi strolling along the stone risers with one of the gals I had seen at the gate the night before. I hurried after him, only to lose him in the crowd as I pushed out of the ball court and into the plaza where food carts had been set up together with folk peddling such a fine array of amulets, beaded necklaces, and brass or shell earrings that I would have paused to browse had I not been impelled to look for...

Arms crossed on his chest, he was leaning against the closed tailgate of a wagon in whose bed stood four soldiers. One soldier was exhorting the gathered audience, mostly young men, to sign up for the general's army, where fortune and adventure awaited in distant Europa. With his closed expression and detached gaze, Vai looked so like the haughty cold mage I had first met that I could barely stand to look at his handsome face, inviting body, and beautiful clothes. What had I been thinking, to come here? Could a man eavesdrop more clumsily, in his excessively decorative jacket that marked him a mile off?

Could he look more contemptuous, with eyes staring onto nothing and lips pressed together as if he was holding back angry words? I tried to remember all the cutting things he had ever said to me, but there were so many it was hard to recall even one.

My hands clasped and unclasped restlessly over the skirt. Had I dressed up so he would admire me? Or to make him chafe at what he couldn't have? Was Aunty right? Was I just trying to punish him? I felt like a monster, the grotesque spawn of a courageous, bold woman who had protected the man she loved and of a heartless creature who with brutal efficiency and no scruples or compassion hunted down anyone who disturbed his peace of mind.

He saw me, away across the crowd. His entire expression changed. The mask of contempt washed away as in a cleansing downpour. He pushed away from the wagon and arrowed for me.

Blessed Tanit. I could not move. My mouth was parched and my heart was galloping.

Even when a surge of people passing in front cut off my view, freeing me from the chain that linked our gazes, I could not move.

He elbowed his way out of the crowd. And there he was, standing right in front of me. Him. Just him. There was no one else in the world except him.

"Catherine?" He extended his right hand, and somehow my left hand leaped into his grasp. "Are you well?"

I leafed through my extensive mental dictionary and managed to snare a word. "What?"

His eyebrows rose. "You look...stunned. Like a cow that's been bludgeoned by a sledgehammer."

"I look like a *cow*?"

Several people passing paused at my outraged words, and their gazes dropped to my sandaled feet as if they thought to see hooves. Then the crowd's roiling current ripped them away.

He released my hand and pressed his to my forehead. "No fever. Maybe you just need something to drink. Guava juice with lime and pineapple. That's your favorite."

I was riveted by the smile that curved his lips. "Why do you always call me Catherine and never Cat?"

He leaned intimately closer. "A name should be like a caress. Why make it short?"

I am sure I would have spoken a sophisticatedly witty question in reply if my mind had not, just then, lurched to a halt as his lips brushed my cheek with a feathery-light kiss, and then a second and a third, moving toward my ear.

He murmured words like a fourth kiss. "Tell me what you want from me, Catherine. For whatever it is, you know you can have it."

I had made a dreadful mistake. I had left Sensible Cat and Heartless Cat at the law offices of Godwik and Clutch. There was only one way to protect myself.

"I want the truth of why you came to Expedition," I said hoarsely.

He took my hand. "Very well. Let's get something to eat."

He had a small gourd bowl and a spoon slung over his back on a cord. He fished coin out of his cuffs and bought the things I liked best. First, we drank two bowlfuls of lovely juice. Next, we shared a bowl of rice, red beans, and beef with fried plantain, and wiped it clean with a wedge of maize bread. Finally, he filled the bowl with coconut rice pudding topped with slices of papaya.

He sweet-talked a length of burlap from a vendor and spread it on the ground in a quiet corner of the plaza where courting couples had settled down for the serious business of staring at each other like formerly intelligent people who had lost the capacity for meaningful thought. Yet, thinking of Abby, I was horribly ashamed to have made such a comparison. She might have had a sweetheart before she was bitten. Would he love her still, or would he look into her confused gaze and wonder only if the teeth of the ghouls lurked there? Who could ever truly know if one was healed or the infestation only slumbering?

I shuddered.

"Catherine," said Vai, pausing with a laden spoon halfway raised to my mouth, "I hope you are not afraid of me."

I looked at him blankly. "Of you? Of course I'm not afraid of you!"

"There's something. I can see it in your face."

I touched my sleeve where it covered my scar.

His fingers brushed my hand. "It's healed so well no one will guess."

When I did not look up, he sighed. "Obviously I can never let you go adventuring without me. Of course, if I'd been in the water with you, no doubt the shark would have eaten me before you got the chance to punch it."

"I was terrified when the shark hit me," I said, glancing up at him, for I found I could speak of the shark but not of Vai grappling me out of the overturned boat where I was drowning.

"I should think so. For all the words you say, you're oddly silent. It makes it hard to know precisely how to...make sense of your stories. Maybe there is some other thing on your mind you wish to confide in me."

The icy mask that concealed my sire's face shimmered in my thoughts. A bat skimmed past overhead. I was sure my lips had become sewn together. My days of speaking were over.

He leaned closer. "Let me see if I can get that mouth to open."

His tone made me blush in places whose heat made me blush yet more.

His lips parted as he brought the spoon with its scoop of pudding to my lips. As if in mimicry my own lips opened, and he fed me. The pudding was so sweet and rich that I shut my eyes to savor it and lick my lips all the way around in case I had missed one single drop.

"Ah! Mmm. Vai! That's better than yam pudding."

He laughed unsteadily. "You have no idea how much I love the pleasure you take in eating."

A rush like heat and wind poured through me. I swayed toward him.

He pulled back. "Don't distract me. I want you to know why I came to the Antilles."

"You're about to tell me it had nothing to do with me."

"It had nothing to do with you. I told people about you so they wouldn't question me."

"Only you would call that courting talk."

He teased a slice of moist papaya along my lips until I could no longer bear it, so I ate it up and licked its sweet juice off his fingers.

He inhaled sharply. "Is that what you think I'm doing? Courting you?"

"What else would you call it?"

"I could call it a hundred different things, but those are just words. I could use a hundred words to describe cold magic, but none would be this." He pinched a spark of cold fire out of the air and stretched it and wove it to become a golden flower dappled with light as with dew, and then a chain of such flowers like a necklace hammered out of light.

I stared open-mouthed, for it was the most astonishingly lovely vision. "Ought you to be doing that in public?"

"Who will know," he said, bending closer to pretend to loop the chain from my shoulders low along the swell of my breasts, "if you do not tell them?"

Even through the challis of my jacket, the illusion's touch felt like the tickle of bees exploring along my skin. He was still toying with the illusion, darkening the shadows and muting the lights until it no longer glowed like sorcery but only like polished gold catching glints from the lamps that burned around the plaza. None, I realized, were hissing gas lamps or blustering torches.

"Are they all cold fire?" I asked.

"Yes," he said, glancing around at the gleaming lights. "That's the only training they allow their lowly fire banes. Not a one can manage more than the most rudimentary illusion. And they can put out a weak fire. The fire banes who work for Warden Hall are obligated to call light for festivals and hire themselves out to folk who have to run errands at night. Imagine a man of the mansa's stature and pride forced to be a linkboy all his life!"

"I can't imagine it," I murmured, remembering how the mansa had shattered rifles.

"Or the wardens sell them into Taino country. It's against the law for mages of any sort, even fire mages, to form associations to aid and educate each other. They keep them weak by denying them knowledge. I can't wait to go home."

"To Four Moons House?" I asked as my heart hardened.

"More pudding?" He brought the spoon to my lips. As he fed me, he spoke in a voice whose intensity pierced me to the bone. "When you fell into the well and crossed into the spirit world, I thought I would rather die than have to live knowing I had lost you. I left Adurnam and went to Haranwy. There I found my grandmother making ready to cross over. I gave her the locket, hoping it might lead her to you with my message."

I touched the locket. "How did you get it back from those two girls I gave it to?"

He chuckled. "I promised those girls I would never tell. Anyway, I got Duvai and Uncle Mamadi to agree to hunt with me at Imbolc, even though we knew the chance we could track you down was small. Then the mansa summoned me. They'd had news. General Camjiata had taken ship right out from under their noses in Adurnam. No one had even known he was in the city. And he was sailing to Expedition with plans to raise a new army. You can imagine the mansa's consternation."

I said nothing. He fed me another spoonful.

"The mansa commanded me to go to Expedition. My task was to discover Camjiata's intentions. And, if the general intends to launch a new war, to stop him."

A chill knife of foreboding pricked my breath. I did not want him to be that man: the man who would kill in cold blood, with cold steel. "But the general does mean to start a new war."

"I know." He looked away. My glowing necklace of lit flowers faded, as if it were a lamp running out of fuel. "The mansa argued that one death is a small price to pay to avert the deaths of tens of thousands. I said killing is not the only solution. But I also said I would stop the general, *if* the mansa would release the village of Haranwy from its clientage to Four Moons House."

"You didn't ask for yourself?"

He bridled. "Do you think I would walk free if my village could not? Since the mansa has all the advantage over me, naturally he refused. But he said I could bring Kayleigh and establish her here, with a legal writ to release her from clientage. Otherwise they would breed her to see if they could produce more cold mages from my family's bloodline."

"So you were never given a choice, only a sort of a bribe."

"That is how the mansa thinks, because it is the only way he knows how to think. But you must understand, Catherine, that while it is certainly true I am an exceedingly rare and unexpectedly potent cold mage—"

I rested a hand against his cheek, the touch silencing him instantly. The bristle of his beard on my palm made me want to purr. "Such rare potency matched by the inverse of your modesty."

He drew my hand away, his breathing ragged as he went on even more pedantically. "It is also true that in Four Moons House I paid closer attention to our lessons and practiced more diligently and asked more questions and experimented more freely than the others did. Their expectations hurt them, I suppose. They knew what seat of power and wealth was theirs to sit in. It was nothing to them. A few enjoyed the challenge of weaving cold magic. Some felt the weight of duty. But no one worked harder than I did. No one. Maybe my reach is that much greater than the others of my age group. Or maybe I simply am more disciplined and responsible. That being so, how can the children born into the House believe they are somehow in blood better, if my own experience shows they are not? So after the things you said to me, after the mansa commanded me to kill you, I began to question. Why should my village remain under a system of clientage that's little better than slavery just because it has always been that way?"

"You truly listened to me?"

"I did."

"That's why you went to Godwik and Clutch?"

"Yes. I found Chartji's legal knowledge most helpful. She said I could learn a great deal in Expedition, and so I have. All people have a right to liberty. They have a right to the dignity and security of their own persons. Why must we remain chained to an antiquated system that benefits a few on the backs of the many?"

"Are you a radical now?"

He gathered me close, an arm around my back, his lips against my ear. "Oh, yes, Catherine. I am a radical now. I will unbind my village from the chains of clientage. I may not manage it this year or the next, but I will not rest until I find a way to do it, legal or otherwise. I am nothing if not persistent. My village will not be chained forever. Nor should you be. Chartji is still looking into the matter of dissolving a chained marriage. If you wish to wait until I receive word from her, of her findings, then so be it. I will wait for you. And if you do not want me, then you shall not be forced to have me."

He said it not knowing what the head of the poet Bran Cof had told me, words my sire's binding prevented me from repeating to him. Blessed Tanit! I was not drowning. I was being dragged along by the unerring tidal force that was him, or us, or destiny, or—whispered the shade of Heartless Cat—nothing more than proximity and lust.

For it was not that his eyes were beautiful, although they were. It was not that his features were symmetrically pleasing, although they surely were. It was not that his body, which I by now had an arm around, felt so very promising held close against mine, although I could scarcely think of anything except how I yearned to touch him all over.

After all, I had only to wait, hold on for seven more weeks, and then I could get what I wanted from him without being chained by it. If physical love was the only thing I wanted.

Four Moons House owned Vai through his village's clientage, but even so, his magic gave him access to immense status within the House. Yet he had not abandoned and would not abandon his family and his entire village, although he could easily have left them behind for the wealth and privilege his power as a mage granted him. Instead, he made their burdens his own. He intended to risk his own security and no doubt his life to free them. That was the man he wanted to be.

I could take what I wanted as I walked free. Or I could share the burdens and risks with him.

I felt my lips part, as if to speak, but all that came out was a mute exhalation.

He drew back slightly, studying me with the serious look that seemed to see not just me but all the things that made me what I was. That seemed to offer not just him but all the things that made him what he was.

"We can walk our paths each alone. Or we can walk this unknown road together. If anyone can find a way through, it will be you. If you will walk with me, my sweet Catherine, then I will never let go of you. And I promise you that together we will get there."

I thought he was going to kiss me, but that was not what he was about. He brushed a hand along my hair and drew his thumb down the side of my face until I could not remember how to breathe.

Eyes half closed in a way that made me wonder how he might look if I woke up beside him made all drowsy and contented, he whispered, "And I do here ask you if you will come home with me, tonight, to the bed I built for us."

Blessed Tanit, how I wanted him!

Wanting is like the tide of a dragon's dream, sweeping away the safely familiar landscape and all the cautions with which you have so carefully guarded yourself. Those who are caught in the tide can never come back. But maybe they would not regret being changed.

So I said, "Yes."

26

"Vai. Ja, maku! Me wholehearted apologies, but I need a word with yee."

How long Kofi had been standing about ten paces from us, I could not guess. The dance and the drums, the polyrhythm of conversation and laughter and song, the press of bodies and the smell of pepperpot mingling with the kick of dust slammed back up against my awareness.

Vai dragged his gaze away from mine. "I'll be right back." He released me, rose, and walked over to Kofi.

I dredged for a semblance of thought. The intricate voices of the drums throbbed up from the earth. My feet twitched as if drums were a partner who led you into the dance, and of course they were. Rhythm was another thread wound through bone and blood to weave together existence. For one night I could set aside my worries about Bee and Rory. For this night.

I watched as Kofi spoke urgently into his ear. I needed to listen, yet it seemed wrong to eavesdrop on a man who had just confided his secret hopes and dreams. At first he was smiling as if expecting to hear how his conspirator's machinations had brought him triumph. His brow furrowed. Then his eyes widened, and he frowned and shook his head.

I heard him say, annoyed and thus a little loud, "This is not a good time."

With an unreadable glance toward me, Kofi said, "'Tis the message I's told to give yee."

As Kofi hurried off, Vai strode back, pulled me up, and brushed off the burlap. I trotted beside him to the food cart whence he had borrowed it.

"You'd hate it if the last of this pudding dribbled down that gorgeous jacket. What were you thinking to wear it to an areito?"

The coy glance he gave me from under half-lowered lashes was enough to make my breathing stutter and my heart flame. "Only of you. Whatever is necessary, I will do."

Suspicion flowered into a burst of vibrant certainty. "You blinded Aunty Djeneba and Brenna with your good manners and your appealing way of confiding in them. Uncle Joe was right. You haven't been crying in your pillow at all. You've been biding your time. Plotting my downfall."

"You think with your feet, Catherine. That's how you escaped the mansa and fought off a shark. But I"—he offered me the last slice of papaya, his gaze fixed on my mouth as I tried to eat it up delicately and quite failed— "*I* think with my mind."

I should have been angry, but instead I was delirious. I laughed.

He smiled as he wiped out the bowl with a wedge of maize bread and fed it to me. After slinging bowl and spoon on the cord, he twined his fingers intimately through mine and we walked to the jetty. He wore a busy, thoughtful expression, so I let him think and enjoyed the pleasure of walking hand in hand. It was good to have a chance to catch my breath.

After a while, he spoke. "Kofi was just given an unexpected message."

"From the radicals. The Assemblymen."

"Yes."

I recalled I had seen Kofi at the areito earlier with one of the women who had shown up at the gate last night. "Are those two gals really part of the organization?"

"Is there some reason they shouldn't be'?" He pressed a fleeting kiss on my mouth without breaking stride. The touch of his lips made me quite forget who I was for at least ten heady steps. "Were you jealous when I went off with them?"

"Why would you think I was?"

"Why did you wait up, then?"

"Were you drunk when you came back?" I asked, trying not to laugh.

"Only intoxicated by thinking of you."

"I thought so. I could hear the liquor in your voice. Why do the radicals trust a maku who has only been in Expedition six months?"

We turned onto Breakwater Street, the boulevard that ran all the way to the old city. Here in Lucairi lay work yards opposite the stone jetty shore where local canoes and boats came and went. Vendors had set up stalls, selling fried fish, cassava bread hot off portable griddles, green mango on sticks, and roasted crab in the shell whose shattered remains crunched underfoot.

"Kofi trusts me, just as I trust him. I'm an unregistered fire bane. That makes me a good risk because anyone could have me arrested. Also, as a true cold mage, I have something they didn't know they wanted. I've been instructing local fire banes in the most basic teachings any child at a mage House is taught in the schoolroom. Obviously that is also against the law."

"How did you find the radicals in the first place?"

"Chartji's aunt introduced me to Kofi. Trolls have a complex net of affiliations."

"Chartji's aunt? Is she related to those two trolls who come every Jovesday?"

"Why, Catherine, have you been watching me?"

His dash jackets were tailored so exactly to him that they didn't bind, and he knew perfectly well how good he looked. The red and gold of the magnificent fabric set off the deep brown of his complexion most flatteringly. "Why do you ask when you know the answer?"

"Just to hear you say it."

I laughed again. "You are such an irritating man. Where are we going?"

"We're going to Nance's. The boardinghouse down by the gates of the old city."

He drew me over next to the rock wall against which waves slurped so noisily that it would be difficult for passersby to hear. "The radical leadership has finally agreed to talk with me. It's taken months for me to get this invitation. You're right, they're cautious. They can't afford to trust anyone new. They're very close to calling a general strike and bringing the city to a halt until their demands are met."

"What are their demands?"

"The establishment of a committee to compose a charter for the establishment of a new government for Expedition Territory. And a time span to accomplish it in: three months. The Council would arrest them in a heartbeat if the wardens knew who the leaders actually were. In fact, the radicals were ready to call the strike last

Martius. But the arrival of General Camjiata threw the whole city into an uproar. Meanwhile here I am, an unknown agent. That's why I have to meet with them now, at such short notice. If I refuse, they'll think I'm plotting something and won't give me another chance." He looked searchingly at me. "Catherine, I need to know if there is anything you want to tell me about all this. Anything it would be better for me to know now, before the meeting with the radicals. I see you brought your cane—your sword, I mean—as if you are expecting trouble."

The Hassi Barahal house had spied for Camjiata. My mother had fought for him, and then escaped imprisonment at his hands. In the entryway of the law offices of Godwik and Clutch, he had told me he was looking for Tara Bell's child. *Me.* I touched the ghost hilt, for twilight had brought the sword to life even though to the eye it still appeared as a black cane. Was it truly a cemi, of a kind? Was it my mother's spirit that touched me when I felt the shiver of its cold steel? She who had left me with a memory of only five words? *Tell no one, not ever.*

"I always bring my cane because I'm always expecting trouble," I said.

He pressed his cheek to my hair. "There is surely a great deal about you I do not understand."

Water slapped across the rocks. In the distance, thunder rumbled like a warning. I turned my face into the curve of his neck, remembering the voice of the hurricane's herald and his taunting words. The spirit had told me to run, but I was not going to run this time from those chains.

"Vai, I want you to understand—"

Ice weight choke dread throat closing mask blinded. I couldn't breathe. I was slipping below the surface of the water without a sound as my sire dragged me down.

"Catherine! I have you! Don't faint."

I sucked in air, holding on to him as if to my life. "I have to get away from the water."

He eased me away from the rocks and, once we reached the edge of the boulevard, looked me over carefully. "Catherine, I'll never let you drown, if that's what you fear. After I lost you in the well, I swore I would not let go again. Not if you wanted me."

I had my breath back. And I thought: The time to decide about a man is before you sleep with him, not afterward.

"And if I didn't want you?"

He smiled in the most aggravating way. "How could you not want me, Catherine?"

I laughed, because only Vai could have spoken those words in a way that made it seem he completely believed them while at the same time he was making light of his own vanity in needing to believe them. "How much time do I have to answer the question?"

"My sweet Catherine, I suggest we go to this untimely meeting so we can get it over with, the sooner to go home to our bed. And then...then you have as long as you need."

Quite the most reckless surge of feeling swept through me. Before I could kiss him, he slipped out of my grasp.

"We can't start that or I won't get through the evening and neither will you. Let's keep walking."

Walking warmed the cold right out of me and loosened the chains that had been strangling my tongue and my heart. His long stride matched well with mine. I felt comfortable with his silence even if my thoughts wandered all over his body, wondering just exactly how long it would be before we could return to the room and what on Earth we were meant to do with Kayleigh. Being Vai, he had surely already arranged something. Honestly, I could not imagine otherwise.

"Vai, there's one thing, though." I had to say it. "I don't want to get pregnant right now."

"Of course. We'll take precautions. We want no children until we're free of clientage."

"Blessed Tanit! You've already thought about this, haven't you?"

His fingers squeezed mine as he smiled without looking at me. "I've done a lot of thinking about this, if you must know. But besides that, I also suspected...it was something you were worried about before."

Before, meaning Drake. I did not want to discuss Drake with Vai.

"If he hurt you, I wish you would tell me."

I really did not want to discuss Drake with Vai, but I owed him an explanation. "He got me drunk. And he lied to me. He implied he could only heal me if I had sex with him. I suppose that is a form of harm."

"I'd call it harm," Vai muttered.

"Did he *force* me? No, I was willing. I won't lie to you. It was nice."

"*Nice?*" He laughed in a way that made me flush straight through the center of my body. "I would pity the man you said that of, if I didn't know he'd gotten you drunk and lied to take advantage of you. Because I promise you, Catherine, that afterward you won't say it was *nice*."

The air changed not as with anger but with a force so primal I felt I'd been turned inside out and every part of me tuned to him. I had no words, but I did have an overpowering foreboding that the next hour or two was going to advance like molasses down the shallow slope of a platter.

At length and with the grace of a man shifting directions in a dance, he said, "You did a remarkable job piecing that skirt together."

"I am a seamstress of rare and unexpected potency. Vai, when are you going to tell me what you are doing with the trolls?"

"I'll bring you along next Jovesday. And teach you a better thing to call them than *trolls*, which is a human word. Here's a simplified version of what they call themselves." He whistled something short but grand.

"That's not a word."

"It's not a word as we think of words. But it makes you wonder if they dislike being called trolls as much as Kena'ani dislike being called Phoenicians." He tugged me to the left. "Here we are."

Gas lamps burned on the old city walls. We turned aside before we reached the wide plaza, the main batey courts, and the harbor. The boardinghouse was the one I had noticed before, a sprawling edifice raised on squat stilts, its main floor a huge open-air wooden deck flanked by two-story wings. I smelled pepperpot, rum, and urine.

Folk packed the place, many young and plenty male, although more women than I had expected plied their way into the crowd with men on their arms or their arms on men. It was an agitated press lit by cobo hood lamps set along the railing of the outer deck. A burly fellow stood on a box shouting over the noise.

"Yee mean to say yee shall serve in an army overseas for a scrap of pay, the hope of loot, and a dram of rum each night? While meanwhile yee brothers and sisters at home still don' have the right to vote on the Council?

That same Council who claim to govern us as citizens but who act to rule us as subjects? Is yee so easily bribed? Shall yee not stand *here* and fight for the rights we shall hold *here*? Do yee know what they mean for yee to earn there, in they Europan war? Death! Death, for the merchants to get fat off. 'Tis not worth it, lads! 'Tis past time to fight at home."

Vai pulled me close as if to make sure he wouldn't lose me. Rising voices swelled like a gust of wind over us as the one fellow stepped down and another bounded up to take his place.

"I say different! I say, this is opportunity! Yee really believe people shall not be fooled or they vote bought in this thing yee call elections? They who talk of Assembly is either witless or cunning. Let the Council have they triumph now, for I tell you, the Taino shall come soon enough to claim we factories. Them who want to remain free must get out of Expedition—"

Still holding on to me, Vai cut a path through the seething crowd with his stare and, perhaps, a pinch of cold magic.

A wide formal staircase led to a series of upstairs rooms, private parlors whose windows looked over the deck and the sea. He headed for the serving counter in the back, which was mobbed with drinkers. Kofi was leaning over the bar, talking to one of the men pulling drinks.

Appreciative whistles erupted from the area around the crate as the two speakers began talking over each other.

"—These vexatious laws put in place by a Council for which we cannot vote. Why shall we listen to them tell us what to do?"

"Would yee rather have beggars and layabouts rule yee?"

Kofi turned away from the bar with four brimming cups in his big hands as he steered toward a pair of sour-looking men who were scanning the crowd. Were they looking for fire banes? The man behind the bar looked our way, and nodded at Vai.

"Fight! Fight! Punch him in the nose!"

Excitement gripped the crowd as a boxing match broke out at the speaker's crate. Kofi spilled the cups over the two men, who sputtered and shouted. We ducked under the counter and behind a curtain into a corridor that let out into a courtyard in back. The gas lamp burning at the far end of the corridor wavered as Vai paused beside a second curtain.

"This is the servers' stair," he said, pulling the curtain aside to reveal a narrow stairwell illuminated at the top by one of the cobo hood gas lamps. The curtain slithered down behind us just as the lamp's flame was sucked dead by Vai's presence. Shrouded in the darkness of a stifling, windowless space, I halted to let my eyes adjust.

A wan spark of light caught and expanded like blown glass to the size of a fist.

"Oh!" I breathed, for the cold fire he could call never ceased to dazzle me.

Concentration creased his brow. He shaped the light until it appeared as a pewter holder with a candle framed by glass. Even the flame had a pulse and ripple.

"So beautiful," I said in wonderment.

"Yes," he murmured, brushing fingers lightly down my cheek, for he was now looking at me, not at the illusion. I caught in a breath because I thought he was going to kiss me, but instead he stepped back and took my hand. "Upstairs."

We climbed to a curtain made of long strings of beads.

The beads rustled and clacked together as we pushed past into a corridor that ran the length of this floor, with closed doors on either side that led to private parlors. The corridor stood open—unwalled—at either end. The night breeze tickled down its length. At the far end, guarding the main stairs, a burly man with a bandaged head looked our way. He headed for us. He was wearing a singlet over trousers, and his arms were so corded with muscle I expected he could lift me with one and Vai with the other.

"Yee shall be the maku fire bane we have heard so many tales of." He did no more than glance at the "candle" Vai was holding, seeing the illusion as real. By its nacreous light, I saw he had a pair of shockingly green eyes in a face otherwise Roman in its features. "Who is the gal?"

"This woman is my wife."

"The gal was not invited, maku." His appraising gaze lingered too long on my chest.

Vai stepped between us. "I said, she is my wife."

A kind of heat flared that had nothing magic about it as the two men stared each other down. Vai did not have Kofi's height. Although he had a carpenter's back and arms and a dancer's build, that was no match for the guard's powerful girth and loose boxer's stance, ready to land a punch. An eddy chilled around us as my laughing, teasing Vai transformed into the arrogant cold mage who had hammered the mansa to his knees. The guard gave ground with a startled look.

"Which door?" said Vai in an imperious tone that was not really a question.

A woman dressed in the local way appeared from the main stairs, fanning herself with a pamphlet which she lowered the instant she saw us.

"Thank Ma Jupiter yee have come, Jasmeen," said our guard. "Yee's late."

"Who is this, Verus?" Her glance at me was swift and dismissive; she looked Vai up and down in the same way the guard had just measured me. "Surely the fire bane. Who is the gal?"

"His wife, he say," said Verus.

"She was not invited," said Jasmeen, pausing before a door, "although we heard a tale about the maku fire bane's lost woman providentially washing up on the jetty."

"What did you hear?" asked Vai, gaze narrowing.

Jasmeen was a handsome woman of middle years, old enough to have adult children and yet young enough that she might think about bearing more if the appreciative look she gave Vai was any indicator of her state of mind. She smiled, amused by my frown. "We hear everything. Let her come in."

We entered a pleasant chamber with a long table and chairs set just inside the door, and divans and wicker chairs spaced along a row of open doors that let onto a balcony. The remains of a meal had turned the table into a complex pattern of abandoned platters and bowls plundered of their riches. The woman crossed to the divans and chairs, where she greeted the personages already in the chamber: three humans and three trolls; she made a seventh.

They watched Vai and me approach. The only illumination came from Vai's illusory candle. Its pearlescent glow cast strangely distorted shadows along the crests of the three trolls and across the faces of the three rats. One was a vigorous-looking old man, the second a middle-aged man with such a pleasant expression and calm smile that I was instantly suspicious of him, and the third the young woman I had seen at Aunty's gate the night before and walking with Kofi at the areito earlier this evening.

"This is the fire bane, Livvy?" said the old man, looking at the young woman.

"Yes, 'tis he," Livvy answered. "Hard to mistake once yee have seen him. The gal is he lost woman."

"She is the one yee other associate don' trust?"

"Yes, the very one." She considered me with a frown that shaded rueful, as if she was sorry to have to say such a thing. I was certainly sorry to have to hear it!

"Very well. Yee may remain for the meeting, Livvy."

"Mc thanks, Grandfa'." She retreated to a chair in the shadows where she sat with hands clasped, leaning toward the conversation as toward a long-anticipated treat.

Outside, the long moan of a conch sounded. A high-spirited brawl had overtaken the wide deck while drummers out on the plaza started up a driving rhythm.

The old man sighed. "What is done is done. Sit, if yee please."

Vai pretended to set the candle on a shelf by the window, although its light was surely too bright for anyone to be fooled into believing that it was real. We sat on a divan placed perpendicular to the others. The woman with the pamphlet, Jasmeen, sat between the men.

"Ooo. Elegant jacket," said one of the trolls, by the brilliance of his crest likely elderly and male. He was flanked by two younger trolls, one of whom I guessed to be female by her larger stature. About the other I could not tell. "Silk. That pattern look like shiny chains. I love shiny chains."

"Thank you," said Vai so coolly I could tell he was pleased.

The elderly troll's gaze flicked to me and then to my

cane. He showed his teeth but made no comment. The old man and Jasmeen were looking at me the way hungry people look at food that is spoiled. The other man watched with that vaguely pleasant and thereby ominous smile.

The old man spoke. "Ja, maku, this is not a philosophical society where friendly debate is served along with beer and supper in a public venue. I don' like that yee is told yee may meet with us, and then yee bring this gal without permission."

"She is my wife. I have kept nothing from her."

"She know why yee's come to Expedition?"

"She knows everything."

"That yee was sent here to assassinate General Camjiata?"

"That I was sent here to stop him from returning to Europa, by whatever means necessary. Yes, she knows."

Jasmeen waved the pamphlet in Vai's direction. "Our committee have taken a considerable chance in meeting with yee tonight. We have done it at short notice so as to protect we own selves from arrest and, most importantly, to protect the cause of liberty which we champion."

The old man spoke as with the slash of a whip. "Yee services we can trust because yee's an unregistered fire bane. We can turn yee over to the wardens if yee shall prove troublesome. But how can we trust *she* when we know nothing of she? Where did yee lose she? How did she reach the Antilles? Yee own associates don' trust she, so we's told."

Vai stiffened, jaw tight, chin lifted. I knew that expression well. It often preceded his saying or doing something it would have been better for him not to. I had to help him.

I rose. "I have not formally introduced myself. My

name is Catherine Bell Barahal. I was raised in the city of Adurnam, in a Hassi Barahal household."

The middle-aged man started visibly, the first crack in his mask. The old troll's crest rose.

"Some of you recognize the name." I recalled what Chartji had said the first time we had met. "The old histories call my people 'the messengers.' I have been trained in all aspects of the business. My sword craft is rusted, but decent. Also, I can memorize large blocks of text and repeat them later. So you see, I am perfectly suited for the work of radicals. These were my husband's only considerations when the time came to decide whether to bring me along to your society."

In the corner, the young woman made a noise more like a snort than a laugh.

"Have yee aught yee wish to say, Livvy?" asked the old man. "Speak."

"After everything I have heard from me friends, I think it more likely he brought she along to impress her with daring revolutionary deeds."

"That way, is it?" said Jasmeen with a cutting smile, again fanning herself with the pamphlet. "Not so sure of the gal, after all."

The trolls' half-lifted crests I could not interpret, but with the rats I had clearly dug Vai in deeper. I had to try again.

"I am in Expedition because I am a fugitive. If you wish to be rid of me, you need only turn me over to any representative of the prince of Tarrant. I arrived in Expedition because I... escaped from a ship and almost drowned."

"An entertaining tale," said the old troll brightly, although I did not like the look in his eye. Trolls seemed such hospitable companions until you realized they could eat you. "I hope there is more of it."

To avoid the troll's predatory scrutiny, I glanced at the pamphlet now resting on Jasmeen's pagne, its title in bold print: ON NECESSARY CONSIDERATIONS IN DRAFTING A CHARTER OF RIGHTS AND PRIVILEGES ACCORDING TO THE LECTURES OF PROFESSORA KEHINDE NAYO KUTI.

Blessed Tanit had smiled on me!

"As it happens, I was forced to leave the city of Adurnam most precipitously just after I was offered employment with the radical movement by Kehinde Nayo Kuti and Brennan Du."

Had I on the spot burst into fragrant bloom like a nymph seeking refuge from a persistent suitor, they could not have been more startled. Suspicion and reserve melted like ice under Expedition's sun.

"La Professora?" exclaimed the old man. "Yee have met her? What is she like?"

I was not going to let this advantage lie. "Can one truly say one knows a personage of such distinction? Yet might I say she is modest in demeanor and brilliant in aspect?"

"Have yee news of she progress in Europa?" asked Jasmeen, looking flushed.

"What did yee speak of?" asked the old troll.

I racked my mind for memories of that evening at the Griffin Inn. "Was it the color, texture, weight, height, volume, and consistency of ice?" I said ruminatively. Vai was no help because he was staring at me with eyes narrowed. "Isn't she a printer, by trade? Didn't she get a jobber press from Expedition?"

Everyone turned to look at the trolls, then back at me.

"We heard the airship was destroyed," said the old troll.

I did not meet Vai's gaze. "Yes, it was, but she managed to recover enough of the parts from the remains that it was likely the press could be reconstructed." I pressed fingers to my forehead, dredging up words. " 'We dispute the arbitrary distribution of power and wealth, which is claimed as the natural order, but which is in fact not natural at all but rather artificially created and sustained by ancient privileges.' "

"That yee is acquainted with La Professora is quite unexpected," said the middle-aged man, this being the first time he had spoken. His voice was a bass rumble.

"Everything about Catherine tends to be unexpected," muttered Vai.

The young woman called Livvy had shifted to the edge of her chair. Quite beside herself, she spoke without asking permission. "Black-haired Brennan! Have yee really met him? I hear he is the most charming and handsome man imaginable, and that he have never lost a fight."

How I hated my blushes! I smiled at her anyway, gal to gal, and she grinned back. "Well, he's not got black hair. It's likely true about the fighting. Anyone who met him would believe it. And he does have a most enchanting smile and a way of making you feel you are the only person in the room when he speaks to you. My cousin called him the handsomest man she had ever met."

Vai had developed what I could only describe as a thunderous frown.

The young woman clapped her hands together. "Tell me more about him! I mean, begging yee pardon, Grandfa', for the interruption."

"Yee said nothing about a cousin," said the old man, exchanging glances with the old troll.

"I have one," I said hastily. "My cousin and I made

our way to the radicals because we had heard the words of La Professora. My cousin and I have been chained by obligations fixed on us by others. Surely we may wish to contest a vexatious legal code that allows others to bind us without our consent. Surely we may wish to have our dignity respected. To secure the freedom of our families and lineages and clans. And if we wish these rights for our communities, should we not therefore strive to see that other communities and clans also have what we ask for?"

"Bravo!" said the young woman.

But they were a hard, canny lot. I might have amused them, but I was not sure I had convinced them. I sat, quite out of breath. Frown banished by my passionate speech, Vai took my hand in his.

"Very stirring," said the middle-aged man. "So tell me, fire bane, tell me true, is yee sure she is on we side? She who washed up on the jetty in a canoe that came from Cow Killer Beach?"

"She was lost," said Vai.

"Was she, indeed? Yee's sure? Absolutely sure?"

Letting go of my hand, Vai stood. With him rose the candle lantern, drifting off the shelf and twisting like a creature transformed by the tide of a dragon's dream. From candle lantern it bulged into a sphere of glowing lacework, spinning slowly upward to the eaves, and melted into a perfect illusion of a cobo hood gas lamp. If astonished expressions were anything to go by, they had never before seen such a display of cold magic, as modest as it was. As the light floated beneath the eaves, casting oddly distorted shadows across us, I saw that the rafters needed to have a broom taken to them to wipe out the cobwebs. Strange what the eye catches on.

"You have my apologies if it seems my action in bringing Catherine here was reckless or ill considered," he said with a hauteur appropriate to his spectacular jacket and casual exercise of magic. "Or if I seem to have been keeping secrets from you. If you feel you cannot trust my judgment, which I admit must seem to be compromised, then I will understand."

"But yee need us," said the middle-aged man. "Is that not what yee said? That yee would prefer to accomplish yee goals with no killing?"

"That is what I want. No killing."

"But what do yee think will happen, fire bane? People shall die regardless. All that will happen is that blood will not stain yee hands."

"Blood has already stained my hands. I'd rather not repeat the experience. Killing the general does not change your circumstances in Expedition. That's why the best solution is to leave him alive but without support. If he cannot return to Europa, that serves me just as well."

"Alive but without support? No change in circumstances?" The middle-aged man laughed without humor. "Don' yee understand? When he first came and placed he request before them, all the Council could see was trade and profit. The Council would have voted to support him. Expedition is a small place. We's like a basket, all woven together. We radicals is the ones who got that vote to turn against him. And then what did he do? He went running to the Taino. And now he is back, with some manner of agreement with them. That make things worse for us. For the Council can now say 'tis the fault of the radicals that the general made a pact with the Taino. As for the Taino, who know what they mean to do?"

"What are you trying to say?" Vai asked, looking at each one.

The old man gave Vai a bitter look. "Yee have boasted yee have a certain means to kill him."

"It is no boast. It is the truth."

This was not only too much, it was terrifying, for they meant to throw away Vai's life!

I jumped to my feet. "Vai is worth far more to everyone alive. If you demand he try to assassinate the general, you'll only be making him throw away his life on a task he can't accomplish."

"Catherine!"

"One man with adequate fighting skills, pitted against trained soldiers who will have crossbows? The mansa can't have known cold magic is so weak here or I can't believe he'd have sent you. In Europa, there's no one you could not destroy. Here, without truly powerful cold magic to protect yourself, the general's people will *cut you down* before you can get close enough to draw blood."

I desperately needed some way to persuade Vai away from this foredoomed course of action. I recalled Brennan's words when we had been digging through the wreckage of the airship. "Why do you radicals see the general as your enemy? Why do you want him dead?"

The old man waved a hand like wiping away a stain. "We ancestors escaped an empire. Shall we help raise another? A man who is on his father's side a Keita, a descendant of the Malian royal lineage? Even from over the ocean, such an emperor can come back and say he have the right to trample us because we ancestors once served his."

"Brennan Du told me that if you examine Camjiata's legal code, you'll see he understands he can only succeed by offering rights and privileges to the common people that their masters have denied them. Why kill him? Have you considered making an alliance with him against the Council?"

"A question," said the old man, "made more interesting by the fact that yee is the one who have posed it."

"Yee do know, fire bane," remarked the middle-aged man, "that this gal is known to have arrived on the jetty in the company of James Drake, a notorious fire mage?"

Vai's mouth turned down, and his shoulders stiffened. "I know that. Have you a point?"

"Beside the point 'tis rumored he have used unwilling people—dying people—as catch-fires to absorb his magic?"

I choked, but no one was watching me. They were all watching Vai.

"I have heard such a rumor."

"Don' yee know that the reason he is not in prison for these crimes is because he have a powerful protector? One he is careful to hide? He serve General Camjiata. He was one of the people sent to Adurnam to fetch the general out of Europa and over to here."

Vai looked at me.

I swallowed.

"Drake, in the entryway of the law offices," he breathed, as one after another of the connections hit home. "Was the general there that morning, too? Catherine, did you know he was there? Do you know him?"

I shut my eyes rather than answer.

His tone cooled. "I had no idea."

"Seem to me," remarked the middle-aged man, "yee's in bed with yee own enemy."

The temperature in the room dropped so precipitously that everyone, except for the trolls, cried out in alarm.

Several leaped to their feet. The hilt of my sword flowered under the breath of cold magic. I had almost forgotten the way the air bit into the skin, the tingle of power rising from the sword's hilt to sting my tongue. I opened my eyes to see them all chafing their hands.

"What is this?" whispered Livvy, shivering.

I grabbed Vai's wrist. "*This* is an extremely angry cold mage. Come, Vai."

I tugged. He did not budge. Nor did he speak. Had we been in the north, I did not doubt the building would have crashed down around us, but we were not in the north. We were here.

I surveyed the radicals with what I hoped was a look portentous enough to make them let us go without forcing me to fight a way out.

"I'm not part of the general's army. I didn't ask to be brought to the Antilles, or to this meeting for that matter. I won't betray what I've heard here because I know what it means to be betrayed, and I will never do that to another. But let me tell you this. You don't know what you're dealing with, not with Vai and not with the general. And you certainly have no earthly idea of what you're dealing with, with me."

As Bee would say, know when to stop talking and leave.

The cold had intimidated them. I released Vai and headed for the door. He followed me, as I had hoped he would. I got out the door and started down the corridor.

Verus said, "Ja, maku!" but someone called urgently to him from down the main staircase and he stepped out of view.

With his longer stride, Vai caught me just as I pushed past the beads and set foot on the back staircase. He grabbed my shoulders and pressed me back, trapping me between him and the wall, beneath the dead gas lamp.

"It isn't like it might seem," I said. "I can explain."

His cold fire blazed through the gas lamp above us. "I gave you a chance to explain. So why start now when you let me walk blind into that meeting and look like a complete fool?"

I managed words. "What do you wish you knew?"

"What do I wish I knew? Where do I even start? You had no trouble telling them everything you knew about Camjiata, so if you didn't tell me before, it was certainly on purpose. For that matter, why should I believe your story about the binding from the spirit world? You could have made up the whole thing to stop me from prying!"

Such cold surged around him that my breath steamed as mist. "But I didn't make it up!"

He wasn't listening as he stormed on in a voice made icy by fury. "And why stop there? Maybe Drake wasn't the first. I have to wonder about black-haired Brennan, although he doesn't have black hair. The handsomest man alive. A very persuasive man, with his enchanting smile."

My heart was galloping in my breast, crashing between chagrin and exasperation. "I never! Drake lied to me. You know that. Anyway, Brennan Du is the sort of man who isn't interested in a callow young female like myself."

He was absolutely crushing me against the wall, his body pressed against the length of mine. I had never known you could be so agitatedly abashed and yet recklessly excited at the same time. For I wasn't scared of him. I just needed him to slow down and listen to me.

He whispered, his lips a kiss away from my mouth.

"And what sort of man do you think would be interested in a callow young female like yourself?"

Frost crackled up the wall behind me. My lips had parted but I could not speak. All I could do was tip my head back and lick the corner of my mouth in a way that made him suck in a breath.

"An infatuated dupe?" he continued hoarsely.

I slid my hands up his back. I couldn't breathe properly, much less talk.

He raged on. "Can't think of any questions to retort with? Cat got your tongue?"

He was pressed so closely we might almost have been engaged in sexual congress.

"How many nights have I dreamed of doing this?" he murmured in the tone a man uses when contemplating the necessity of cutting into his own flesh to excise a festering wound.

He caught my face in his hands and kissed me.

And he kissed me.

And he kept kissing me.

Nothing existed outside of my body straining into his, his mouth and tongue a glorious pressure on mine. I wrapped my arms around him, explored the breadth and strength of his shoulders. One of his hands splayed along my neck while the other dropped to the curve of my hip, pressing us together. We could have moved closer only if we had taken off our clothes.

"Magnificent Jupiter with he lightning!" said a cheery male voice that sounded a cursed lot like Kofi. "Is there no rooms for that?"

Vai was planting kisses on my lips and my cheek, and my lips and my chin, and my lips and my eyes, incandescently oblivious to his friend's arrival. Hazily, I opened my eyes, trying to recall where I was. Hadn't we been alone in an entirely deserted stairwell? Footfalls thumped along the corridor below. An unknown number of men in wardens' tabards had clustered up behind a big, broad-shouldered man who was blocking the lower stairwell.

Eyes still closed, Vai drew back just enough to whisper. "Wardens. Kiss me so they don't realize we know they're there."

"Yes," I murmured with my lips moving against the caress of his mouth. I could barely grope for and fasten my left hand around the ghost hilt of my sword, but I knew I had to, so I did.

"Move aside, yee lout," said a man below. "I's a warden and we is come to make an arrest."

Another warden chimed in. "Oh, by Venus Lennaya! Have they no rooms for that? Curse it! My wick died."

Kofi laughed with utterly false heartiness. "His have not yet, fortunate man. Good view, too, with that gaslight burning right above him."

"I *said* to stand aside!" said the first warden. "We have arrests to make upstairs."

"So this is where yee got to, Cousin!" Kofi stumped up the stairs making a foul echo of noise. He slammed into us. Vai stepped back so swiftly I realized he'd braced for it.

I sat down on a step, shuddering all over.

"I did not recognize yee at first, yee being so intertwined with the gal." Kofi made a show of grabbing Vai by the back of his jacket. Surely Vai hadn't doused the warden's lamp on purpose; the uncontrolled surge of his emotions would, like a riptide, drag everything with it. But the false cobo hood lamp still shone, to confuse them into thinking he was no fire bane.

"Kofi," I whispered, trying to tell him to warn the radicals. "The meeting... you know..."

"I have no mind to listen to yee, bitch," he hissed in an undertone. Kofi supported Vai down the stairs while talking in a very loud voice to the wardens pushing up impatiently below. "Newly wedded and living with we aunt but no private room for they own selves. No wonder they took advantage of a dark stairwell. Just give them a moment. Would that not be a mercy? Don' yee recall being newly wedded yee own self? Or do yee lot get any pleasure? Or only pleasure from interrupting the pleasure of others?"

"What arseness! I can arrest yee as quick as I can some other lad. Get out of the way. We's here at the order of the Council. Curse it! Cannot even get a spark!"

"Sorry to hear it, Warden," said Kofi with a laugh. "Nothing worse for a man than no spark."

"Let up," muttered Vai. "I can walk... Where is Catherine?"

"There is not enough cold water in this world to cure yee of yee illness, Vai."

Ten wardens crowded at the base of the stairs as if waiting for a signal. I smelled the steel of their unsheathed swords, and felt the exhalation of men waiting to strike.

"*All* we cursed lamps went out," said one at the rear of the group.

Kofi shouldered past them, propelling Vai forward.

"Look down there in the courtyard," the warden went on. "That cursed gas lamp is wavering, too. Here, yee." I could not tell if he was addressing Kofi or Vai. "Is yee a fire bane?"

I shrieked and leaped down the steps, flailing into the

throng of wardens and throwing myself from side to side to knock them off balance. "Spiders! All over me! He shoved me into a web and they're crawling all over me!"

The moaning voice of a conch shell rose from nearby, stark and powerful, as Kofi shoved Vai through the wardens toward the curtain that led to the bar.

"There is the signal," said the first warden. "Yee four, arrest them. The rest, with me."

Six wardens pounded up the stairs. One of the remaining four flung me to one side. I slammed into a wall, pain exploding in my shoulder. Vai jerked away from Kofi and turned. Cold fire sparked, and ballooned. When by its light he saw the wardens with drawn swords threatening me, the air changed, all heat sucked from it. I knew what he was going to do before he did.

I drew my sword. My blade sheared the dark with a flare of light so strong it momentarily blinded me. The hammer of cold hit as icy wind, but the sword protected me. I blinked as the impact slammed into me, but I did not go down. Shouts of consternation rose from the main hall, cries and calls about the lights' going out. My blade's glow lit the corridor. The four wardens lay prone on the floor. Behind Vai, Kofi had fallen to his knees.

Upstairs, the wardens were shouting:

"Yee's all under arrest by order of Warden Hall!"

"Line up, there! Yee, there, don' move!"

"What right have yee to disturb our dinner! What in the ten hells did yee do to the lights?"

"We have orders to arrest an unregistered fire bane and seditionists in league with—"

Arguments erupted from the private parlors above. A fight broke out, chairs crashing over.

"Cat!" Vai flexed a hand.

I ran forward and grabbed his arm. "You've given yourself away. You've got to get out of here. Let's go."

He stared at me, eyes dilated and expression wild. "I don't know you. How many lies have you told me, Catherine?"

"What makes you think I've told you any lies?"

He yanked his arm out of my grip only to grab my hand and pull me past Kofi toward the curtain and the howling clamor of the main hall as people called for light, any light, please light. "We're going to find out, aren't we?"

"How are we going to do that?" I retorted.

At the look he gave me, I ran suddenly so hot that I tripped over my own feet. He wrapped an arm around my back and pulled me against him.

"You know exactly what we're going to do," he murmured, as if he intended to start interrogating me now.

"Ja, maku!" Kofi rubbed his head as he staggered to his feet. "What was that?"

Vai pulled away without releasing me. "My apologies, Kofi. I am overwrought."

"That is not what I would call it," said Kofi. "Yee's going to get taken down for assaulting a warden. Not to mention arrested for being an unregistered fire bane. I did not know anyone could do that. Is they dead?"

Vai barely glanced toward the wardens. "Only stunned."

"I never saw..." Kofi eyed my sword warily but did not mention it, as if it would be bad manners to call attention to an object of such power. The light that gleamed along the blade was beginning to fade as Vai's cold magic eased. "What yee going to do?"

Vai's arm tightened around me as he started walking,

hauling me with him. "I really can't think past the unfinished business I need to take care of."

"Vai, that is not thinking." Kofi hurried after us with hands raised as if to show himself unarmed, although I abruptly realized by smooth lines in his jacket and sleeves that he was concealing at least four knives. "A bucket of cold water first, and then a plan. 'Tis possible the wardens did not get a good look at yee, but we cannot risk it. We shall have to get yee out of Expedition. What a disaster. I told yee she was sent to trap yee."

We reached the heavy curtain that separated the corridor from the main hall of Nance's. Before Vai could grasp it, another hand swept it aside. Beyond lay a churning sea of shadowy movement, the growling murmur of a crowd whose brawl has been dampened by an unexpected change in the weather, and Beatrice's shockingly familiar and beloved face.

"There you are, Cat! The general promised me we would find you tonight. Did I miss it? You two kissing under the lamp, I mean. If you call that kissing! I would have called it more of an act of sexual congress with clothes on, and if you think that's the kind of thing I want to dream about, you are quite *quite* mistaken. I swear an oath I will never again be able to look at you in the same fondly affectionate but innocent way. I woke up blushing!"

My legs gave out. Vai caught me as I sagged against him. My vision hazed into a blurry smear of light, and I thought I was perhaps finally fainting. But it was an actual light, wavering beyond Bee's black curls and dear face. An actual lamp, kindled by James Drake. The fire mage was standing on the speaker's crate looking around as if searching the crowd for someone. For *me*.

Against me, Vai tensed.

The crowd quieted like a hungry beast before it springs. Drake jumped down. Holding the lamp, General Camjiata climbed on the crate with the lamp ablaze as a beacon. By its flame he surveyed the restless murmuring crowd. Or perhaps he was letting them examine him, with his mane of silver-and-black hair hanging to his shoulders, his broad frame, thick arms, and powerful hands, and the sheer penetrating force of his fearless presence.

"Will you let me speak?" the general called into the maw of the surly beast. "For I have something to say, if you will hear it. I have something to say which you do not expect to hear."

Vai's grip on me tightened. "Is he your father? Your true father?"

"Why would you think so?" I whispered, trying to answer in a question, but I could not make words fit together. My sire's masked face swam in and out of my mind's eye.

His words struck my heart like a deadly bolt. "Because it would explain why the Hassi Barahals wished to be rid of you. How you escaped from the custody of Four Moons House. The riots in Adurnam to cover Camjiata's venture into the city. How you got here with his help. You going out this morning to confirm the plans! Kayleigh was right. How could I have thought so well of myself to dream it was any kind of spirit thread pulling us together? That I could feel your soul reaching out to mine? That our reunion was meant to be simply because I woke up every morning thinking this might be the day I would find you? You were seen to be abandoned in the harbor. All part of the plot to infiltrate the radicals. How easily you managed it, thanks to me and my illusions."

"If you would stop to think, you would know that's not how it was. You're wrong."

"There's the truth at last. I was wrong."

Upstairs, footsteps thundered as the wardens called for reinforcements and jailers. They had made arrests.

"We have got to go," said Kofi. He halted dead on Vai's other side to gape like a fish at the sight of Bee in all her sumptuous, poet-defying glory.

She offered him a smile that made him choke and take a step back as she stepped forward. "Cat, I despaired of finding you, but the general assured me he knew exactly where you would be when the time was right." She looked Vai up and down. "Stunning jacket. Are you coming with us? You needn't worry about arrest once you're under Camjiata's protection."

"No." He released me.

As he took a step back to join Kofi, I swayed. Bee put an arm around my waist, tucking me neatly against her.

"You may wonder that I concern myself in the affairs of the common laboring folk of Expedition," began the general in the hall behind us in a wonderfully carrying voice whose musical lilt had a stirring, martial rhythm that caught at the heart and loins. "You may wonder, and even be suspicious, knowing I am born into the Keita lineage. But is it not the concerns of the common laboring folk that propel the ship of revolution out of the night of the old ways? If we say a rising light marks the dawn of a new world, which new world do we mean to measure and describe?"

The gleam of my cold steel dimmed as feet scraped along the darkening corridor.

"Vai," I said.

He was already gone.

27

For a night and a day and a night, I lay immobilized in a bed of unspeakable luxury, unable to think or talk or move. He thought I had betrayed him.

I did drink, because he would have insisted, and eventually I got bored of sleeping and staring. So on the second day I rose in the momentary cool of dawn and washed my face in a ceramic basin while Bee sat on the big bed we had shared, watching me with a gaze I might have described as wary.

"I could not have taken one more day of that," she said. "I didn't know you could stay silent for that long. Even that one time when we were thirteen and you were ill with that terrible fever, you babbled nonsense nonstop sleeping and waking."

I examined her. "You look thinner."

"I was beastly sick on the Atlantic crossing. I only survived because the general sat with me every day and coaxed water and gruel down my throat. He told me about his wife. He told me what he knows about walking the path of dreams."

"You like him!"

She tucked her legs up to sit cross-legged. "I do. I admire him."

"You admire the Iberian Monster?" I looked around the room. "I hope this chamber isn't in the nature of a bribe."

The whitewashed walls had been ornamented with a mural depicting a trellis of flowers swarmed by butterflies in vibrant blues, greens, and golds. The sideboard on which the basin stood had carved legs, the kind of work that took an artisan weeks to finish. The ceramic basin was painted inside and out with an intricate Celtic knotwork with neither beginning nor end. The windows were open, and there was of course no fireplace or brazier, only a gas lamp in each corner.

"It is a fine chamber, is it not?" said Bee. "But I am squelching a horrible temptation to paint nasty pointy-toothed sprites flitting through the trellis. They could be skewering the butterflies with little javelins and darts."

"Javelins and darts? You should give them rifles!"

"Of course! I can't believe I didn't think of that!"

"Neither can I! How did you end up here? What happened to Rory?"

"Questions I might also ask you."

I was so tired of questions! "You tell first!"

"There's the temper! Frustrated, Cat?"

I flung myself onto the bed, which was so spacious and inviting...

"Cat, dearest, you're flushed."

"What can I do, Bee? He asked me straight out if there was anything I needed to tell him."

"And you kept silent, exactly as you should have done."

"Yes. No! Yes, I kept silence, but no I shouldn't have. I should have told him everything."

"Of course you shouldn't have!"

"You don't marry someone with the intent of concealing things from him! To withhold trust until there is no doubt is not trust. He trusted me, but I didn't trust him. Don't you agree he must hate me now?"

"That didn't look like hate to me. And if he really trusted you, he wouldn't have run off like that. So if you ask my opinion—"

"Did I ask for your opinion?"

"Yes, you just did. Blessed Tanit, Cat! *Marry* him? Don't tell me you had actual sexual congress with him!"

"I didn't! But I was going to!"

"I don't understand. The head of the poet Bran Cof said if you don't consummate the marriage, then after a year and a day you'll be free. That's what you want, isn't it? To be released from the marriage?"

Without realizing, I had ruched up parts of the thin blanket in my fists. "Do you think I would walk free if he could not? That I'd take my pleasure, and leave him in chains?"

"Dearest Cat, I always knew you were secretly romantical." She smiled in a way that reminded me of Aunt Tilly at her most tender, and stroked my hair to calm me. "My story is more easily told, which, I note, is commonly true when it comes to your stories and my stories. You witnessed my compulsion to unearth those slimy grubs. I knew I was leaving you behind when I waded into the river but I simply couldn't stop. I floundered to shore in the Temes River of all places, on the wharf in that town Londun. No sign of the grubs. I must suppose they dispersed in the water. As for me, I almost froze to death while choking on rubbish and sewage. But I talked my way into a ride—"

"I'm sorry I missed that!" I found I could open my fists and let go.

She smirked. "I discovered a fatherly carter on his way to Adurnam and weepingly informed him my callous lying sweetheart had abandoned me on the wharf. I went straight to the Buffalo and Lion Inn. You'll be relieved to know I found Rory there."

"Thank Tanit." My heart eased. No matter what else, we had not lost him. "And my father's journals?"

"Rory had everything. He's cannier than he looks and acts, you know. Anyway, six days had passed while we were in the spirit world. Riots still wracked Adurnam. The prince and mages had discovered the general was in the city. There were also broadsheets out with a substantial reward for our capture accompanied by very unflattering sketches, I must say! And of course I couldn't trust the headmaster. Rory kept insisting the headmaster is a dragon, but surely he's a mage."

"I'm no longer ruling out any possibilities. You met the general again?"

"Eventually, yes. He told me his wife had seen in the path of dreams that I would lead him to you. La Professora and Brennan Du had to leave Adurnam also, and they invited Rory and me to go with them to Massilia. But naturally I sailed with the general to Expedition to look for you."

"Where is Rory?"

"He could not bring himself to get on the ship. He's afraid of the ocean. I kept the journals, which are here, and sent him with Brennan."

I closed my eyes. Blessed Tanit! How Vai had kissed me! He couldn't really believe I cared about Brennan Du the way I cared about him!

"Cat, are you blushing *again*? I hope you're not carrying a torch for black-haired Brennan. I suspect he carries a torch for La Professora. But she is married to another, alas."

"That doesn't stop people," I muttered, looking up at the whitewashed ceiling. How must Vai have felt, waiting for me all those months only to discover me with another man?

"It seems La Professora is quite the traditionalist in some ways despite her radical philosophies. Anyway, how would you know about...Cat! You can't hide from me!" Bee grabbed one of my fingers and bent it back. "You said you hadn't done it with him."

"Ouch! I haven't. Although I cursed well wish I had. Ah! Let go!"

"Tell the truth!"

Through teeth gritted against the pain, I said, "James Drake. But I can explain."

She released my finger, and whistled. Wincing, I rubbed my abused hand.

"*James Drake*," she said in an altered tone that made me cringe. She stretched out with elbows planted next to my head. "Gracious Melqart! But then why were you mauling your husband? And why is a cold mage of such rare and exceptional power here in Expedition anyway, where it is against the law to be a cold mage? Most importantly, did you find your sire?"

Like a thwarted child, I rolled over, and pounded my fists and kicked my feet, savoring the smack of my hands and legs on the mattress. I had never hated my sire as much as I hated him at that moment.

"Cat, you're having a temper tantrum." Bee's laughter so sang in my heart that I began to choke and gurgle. I stopped hitting and rolled onto my back to laugh with her.

"Oh, Bee, how I missed you!"

She embraced me, and we laughed until tears ran. Finally, she went to wash her face in the basin. My cane had gotten wrapped up in the blanket, so I stuck it under the mattress.

"What happened to you, Cat?"

I clapped a hand over my mouth and, as she stared at me with an exaggerated expression of surprise on her face, I pointed with my other hand to my mouth. Waggled the fingers covering my mouth. Bit on them, feeling a question rising. Any question. It didn't matter, as long as it threw people off the scent. Curse him!

"You are hungry? No, you are crazed? You've lost the power of speech? You have to pee? You have developed a strange but debilitating desire to inflict pain on yourself? You are trying to tell me something with these bizarre gesticulations that you can't put in words? Ah!"

She dashed to a tall wardrobe. The door was carved with a gourd upended and spilling fish, the sides and top elaborated to resemble a leafy tree. She returned to me with her sketchbook and a lead pencil. The pages fell open to a sketch depicting a man and a woman forcefully intertwined in a kiss. The angle concealed most of the man's face, but the jacket gave him away. I slammed the book shut, embarrassed by the intimacy of the pose.

Bee sighed. "Now you see why I did not want to have had that dream. It was positively *lurid*. The only identifying mark is the cobo hood gas lamp above your head. It's of a type you will find in every establishment in Expedition, so it was hard to identify the place. Try writing."

I grabbed the pencil out of her hand and opened the

book to a blank page. At once, I began shaking, awash in sweat. I bit my lip. The pain allowed me to scrawl: *I cannot speak of what happened after you left. It is worse than we feared.*

"Blessed Tanit, you've drawn blood," said Bee, wiping my lower lip with her thumb. She snatched the pencil and drew in a length of chain like shackles, then handed the pencil back.

I wrote, *Yes.*

She sketched the jetty and harbor of Expedition, as seen from offshore.

Ocean, I wrote, licking a drop of blood off my lip. *Shark. Salt Island. Bitten. Healed. Drunk. Lies. Drake. Rescued. Buccaneers. Cow Killer Beach. Jetty. Vai. Vai. Vai. You.*

She blanched and took in several deep breaths. After, she turned to me with the same look I imagined a surgeon would give a patient who has survived an amputation. "This is quickly going to become tedious."

I wrote, *Don't ask questions.*

"That's an odd sort of binding," she remarked, taking pen and sketchbook from me.

"I do have to pee," I said, rolling off the bed. I trotted to the wardrobe and reassured myself that my father's journals had indeed survived our separation. "And I'm hungry."

With a grandiose sigh, she stowed her sketchbook back in the wardrobe and tossed clothing at me: a featherlight shift and my very own skirt, bodice, and jacket, washed and the wool ironed to a glossy sheen. Over her own shift she buttoned a skirt sewn from strips of gold, gray, and blue cloth. The bodice she wore had sleeves to the elbow

and was embroidered with an entanglement of flowering
vines and axes.

"Where did you get that?" I asked. "I might murder
you in your sleep to steal it."

"I like the axes in particular," she said with a smile that
could have killed a man at twenty paces. "They remind
me of the head of the poet Bran Cof. I had it done here,
at a very nice shop on Avenue Kolonkan. That's where all
the best clothes and finery may be purchased."

"It's very pretty." But I was swamped by a swell of
nostalgic regret for humble Tailors' Row.

"You're not usually this slow to get ready. There will
be food."

Our chamber was one of four on the second story of a
town house whose clean tile floors slipped blessedly cool
beneath my bare feet. Bee handed me the sandals Vai had
given me, now cleaned and oiled. After I slipped my cane
through its loop, we hurried down a stairway at the back
of the house to the ground floor. She showed me into a
tiny room with a water closet and then into a washroom
where one had only to turn a spigot to allow water to flow
into a basin while one washed one's hands.

"How many times do you have to turn that on and
off?" she demanded, clamping her fingers over the faucet
to turn it emphatically off.

"How does it do that?" I bent over, trying to look up
into the pipe.

"Gravity. The water tank is on the roof. We can go look
at it later. Come on."

She led me back up to the first floor and into a chamber
that ran the length of the back of the house. Glass doors
opened onto a narrow balcony overlooking a garden so
green one could almost breathe the color. Guards paced

beneath the walls, swimming in and out of view beneath flowering trees and vines.

The general sat at a table. He set down the broadsheet he was reading, rose with a grave smile, and took my hand between his as he examined me with deep-set, almost black eyes whose gaze penetrated astonishingly. "You are better. Please, join me. I expect you are hungry."

He nodded toward a sideboard laden with covered dishes, a basket of bread, a platter of fruit, a bottle of liquor, and a white ceramic teapot flanked by six white cups on white saucers.

He released my hand and, to my shock, gave Bee a kiss on each cheek in quite an intimate manner. She did not even have the grace to blush. Indeed, she seemed to expect this familiarity.

"I'll pour," she said, going over to the sideboard. "Sit down, Cat."

Steps sounded in the hall. A woman swept into the chamber. She wore a fabulous deep orange boubou of starched, waxed cloth, although instead of a head wrap she wore her black hair uncovered the better to display tiny braids woven with beads and medallions. I gaped at her.

"Darling," she said, kissing Camjiata on the lips.

"Jasmeen!" Never let it be said I could not tally up the numbers. "You're the one who betrayed the radical leadership! Called in the wardens! Why?"

She was not easily discomposed. "The fire bane was sent here to assassinate Leon. Obviously I don' intend to let that happen. Also, as yee own self must admit, he is an unusually powerful fire bane. Such a dangerous sort of man cannot be allowed to run around like a wild stallion with no bridle."

I fixed a glare on Bee, who had paused in the act of pouring tea. "Bee? What do you know about this?"

The general steered me toward one of the chairs. "Sit down, Cat."

I wrenched myself away. "I don't want to sit! I want to know what happened!"

An aroma of wood ash tickled my nose. I sneezed. James Drake walked into the chamber, looking crisp and attractive in a white jacket and gold trousers, his red-gold hair agleam in the morning sun. After all, I sat, for my legs had just gone boneless.

"Cat!" Drake strode over and pressed his lips to mine. I jerked away, ramming up against the back of the chair. He smiled. "No need to be so formal with me, darling. Why did you take so long to come to the Speckled Iguana? And then run away?"

I glared. "Can it be possible you think you have a grievance?"

Drake chuckled. "Must I tender my heartfelt apologies? Were you so hurt by my leaving you on the jetty? Weren't you worried I would be arrested?"

"What makes you think I thought of you at all?"

"No," he said thoughtfully, with a conspiratorial glance shared with Jasmeen, "I suppose there were other men to embrace."

I leaped up and punched him, my fist slamming solidly into his jaw. He reeled back, caught himself. A hot spicy scent sparked in the air as his eyes lit and his mouth thinned.

The general said, "James, calm down. You clearly did not tell me everything. I strongly suspect your conduct in this matter deserves rebuke."

"I want that cursed cold mage," said Drake, his pale

skin gone a blotchy red as he pressed fingers along his jaw. "You told me that if I fetched her and dumped her on the jetty, we would flush him out of hiding and catch him. Instead he escaped."

I made a sound, like choking on the suppurating taste of my own naïveté. Bee dropped the teapot, which shattered on the tile floor, fragments skittering everywhere on a sheen of fragrant liquid. She looked as if someone had stabbed her.

The elegant woman spoke in a plangent tone, as if sorry to be witnessing such unpleasantness. "I shall let yee sort this out, Leon. Send for me."

"Of course, Jasmeen." He took her hand, pressed lips to her knuckles, and released her.

She swept out, gracious enough to close the door behind her to spare the rest of the household my histrionics.

"*How could you?*" I shrieked.

Bee burst into wrenching sobs. "You didn't tell me this was all part of a plot to *trap* him!"

"Sit down," said the general with no change of expression or tone.

I saw as down a narrowing tunnel a brick wall rushing to meet me. "*You used me to get to him!*"

Drake studied me. With a twisted frown that was almost more of a grimace, he looked at the broadsheet. "For information leading to the capture of the rogue fire bane, a significant reward. That's all very well, but how are we meant to arrest him now he knows we know of him? He had to have been living somewhere, and yet no one turned him in. I find it difficult to believe a cold mage of so much power could have hidden his craft. The wardens followed those weather disturbances two nights ago, but they lost his trail, and now ... nothing. No word. No whisper. No ice. No

one will talk. We've lost him." The corner of the broadsheet began to singe and crumple to ash.

"James!" said the general sharply.

Drake exhaled. Shaking flakes of gray from his hand,
he stepped away from the table.

Cheeks wet with tears, Bee got down on hands and
knees to sweep up the fractured pot with her hands. My
flaring exploding rage collapsed as into a dagger of anger,
honed and glittering.

"*You*," I said to the general. "What did you do?"

The door opened and three women came in. Two
cleaned up the shattered pot and spilled tea, while the
third brought a fresh pot and poured four cups for the table. The general thanked them politely. They left without
remarking on Bee, now slumped on the floor in the spread
of her skirt, like a crushed flower.

The general went to the sideboard and uncovered a
rasher of bacon and a plate of poached eggs surrounded
by fried potatoes. He began to load up a plate as he
talked.

"Beatrice assured me you were eager to be rid of the
marriage. Now it seems you aren't."

He looked at me as with a question. I stared sullenly
back, lips pinched shut.

"Jasmeen says he's quite handsome and clearly madly
in love with you. Youth, looks, and admiration are an
intoxicating combination that is difficult to resist." He returned to the table and set down a heavily-laden plate
between a knife and a spoon. Then he steered me to the
chair in front of the plate. "Sit."

I did not sit. "I'll never let you kill him."

The general sat opposite me, touched the rim of a
teacup to his mouth, then lowered it. "Ah! Still too hot."

Drake put a hand on the back of my chair, as if to pull it out for me. I grabbed a knife. He retreated.

"Where you are under a misapprehension, Cat," the general went on, "is in your belief that I want to kill the cold mage. What is his name again?" he asked Drake.

"*Fucking arrogant bastard* is his name. Was there another name that mattered?"

I waved the knife. "What has he ever done to you?"

The general spoke in the voice of command. "Cat, sit." I sat.

"James, you especially must learn to control that Celtic temper."

Drake pulled a hand back over his hair, mussing it, then paced the length of the chamber.

"Cat, hear me out. First, I escape the prison where the mage Houses have held me for almost fourteen years. Quite without legal precedent, I note. I sail to Expedition because my army in exile has taken residence here, out of the reach of my enemies. The Council receives me with great interest, for they recognize that aiding me will open up trade in Europa. Then a man tries to shoot me. Suddenly the Council votes against my request for support, undermined from within. I hear rumor of another plot to assassinate me, one that may involve a cold mage who wields cold steel. Surely you understand I would be unnatural if I did not defend myself."

I thought of how I had given Vai my sword that night in Southbridge Londun. He had killed two men rather than let them kill us. Blood on his hands. He didn't want to kill again.

I thought of the two salters I had killed on the beach of Salt Island. Even as one begged for release. Even so. I would kill them all and more rather than let one bite me again.

I set down the knife. Let out my held breath. "Go on."

He examined me as he sipped at his tea. "Yes, you do understand. Second, Beatrice has a most vivid dream of you and a man." Briefly he looked so sympathetically amused, as if he had been caught kissing once, that I wanted to like him. But I knew better. "By the cobo hood gas lamp in the sketch, we were fairly certain we would find you in Expedition. Soon after this, Beatrice sketched you standing on a beach, little enough to go on. James approached me privately to tell me he recognized the beach, for he had been to Salt Island as part of his healer's apprenticeship."

Bee looked up, mouth a grim line. "You never told me that beach was on Salt Island!"

"I did not want you to worry, Beatrice. You can imagine our concern, Cat! Had you been bitten, you would have been doomed. We had to get you off the island as soon as you arrived. It was easy enough to arrange for James to go there and wait for you." He took hold of my arm. He was a big man, and he had a strong grip. He slid my jacket sleeve up to uncover the scar. "But I was wrong. You were bitten."

"Cat!" Bee scrambled to her feet, to come over to me, but the general raised a hand, and she halted, eyes wide, hands gripping the fabric of her skirt.

"Beatrice's dream saved you, Cat. We saved you. Imagine what would have happened had James not been there to heal you!"

I pulled my arm away and tugged down my sleeve. "He didn't heal me. No matter what he may have told you."

"Then someone did. The salt plague is a terrible thing, as you now understand too well."

"Better than you do." Horribly, the aroma of the salted

bacon had begun to snake its way invitingly down my throat. I licked my lips. He was watching me, perhaps waiting for me to explain how I knew Drake hadn't healed me, but I kept silent.

He went on. "Nevertheless, I knew how to turn the situation to my advantage. Expedition is a city in ferment. Young men and women join radical circles and agitate against laws that vex them. People have new ideas about what rights communities ought to demand. Those outside the old city want assurance the laws will serve all equally. The story of this unusually powerful maku fire bane excited people's interest. It's a nice story, isn't it? Having come to Expedition, the proud Europan lord is bitten by the local radical philosophies. Infested by them, he rebels against the chains that bind the unfortunate and chooses to join those who agitate against the privileges reserved for a few. He comes to see the justice in the complaints of the plebeians and propertyless and laborers. We knew he was here, waiting to strike at me, but we couldn't find him."

He raised the cup to his lip. The tea smelled of flowers.

Hands in fists, Drake muttered, "Dear Lady of Fire, must we hear this entire recital?"

The general lifted his gaze to follow the pacing fire mage. "*James.*"

With a look shot at me, Drake walked out to stand on the balcony.

The general returned his attention to me. "No one knew what this cold mage looked like, except he was a man of noble station, like a prince in bearing and disposition. Because of Bee's dream—it was the jacket more than the kiss—we realized it was the cold mage you were married to."

"Bee knew what he looked like," I said in a low voice.

She wiped her nose with the back of a hand. "I'm so ashamed, Cat. I tried to draw him, but none of the sketches looked right. I thought you truly didn't care for him."

"Because I would kiss someone like that if I didn't care for them!"

She glanced toward the balcony, and Drake's slim back.

"I didn't kiss *him* like that!" I cried. "He got me drunk!"

The general turned his cup once all the way around before he directed his gaze toward the balcony. "James? Are you telling me you took the liberty of your isolation on Salt Island and used it to seduce this innocent young woman by getting her drunk?"

Drake turned, chin lifted as if he had absorbed another blow. "She said yes! She wasn't that innocent, if you ask me."

"There's a tale you told yourself to justify your actions," said the general in a disgusted way that made me understand why Bee liked him. He looked at me. "Cat, eat."

The two poached eggs stared at me as if begging to be devoured in all their exquisite flavor. My stomach growled. Vai would urge me to eat. I set spoon to eggs.

"We realized you could lead us to the cold mage, if we laid our course properly. I thought if we could capture him, then we would persuade him that the mage Houses were mistaken in their goals—obviously he already thought so—and that he should join us."

"What if he said no?"

"You have me there, Cat. I don't intend to die. But I prefer allies to enemies."

"You used me. You might as well have thrown me into the sea not knowing whether I was going to drown." I set to work on the potatoes and bacon.

"We are not so careless. Whether or not James healed you, he did save you from Salt Island. For I assure you, you would not have left the island once you were bitten. The Taino are very strict about that law. We delivered you to Expedition. We didn't realize none of the locals would talk. By then I had gone to Sharagua. We returned to Expedition only three nights ago."

Which Kayleigh had told Vai. In fact, the general appeared to know very little about Vai's situation.

"How did you track us down?" I asked.

"Early on, Jasmeen told me the radical leadership had been informed that a maku fire bane wanted to meet with them to discuss his mission to end the threat I posed to Europa. They didn't want to meet with him because the first assassination attempt was so crudely done that some suspected it was meant to fail in order to raise sympathies for me."

"So after all," I muttered, spearing a piece of bacon as I contemplated Kofi's suspicions, "they might have suspected the meeting with the maku fire bane was a trap. How odd!"

A smile flashed on the general's face. "Spoken like Daniel. But after I left for Taino country, the radicals began to discuss more seriously the need to meet with a man who claimed to have the ability to kill me. Jasmeen heard from one of the young women some trifling gossip about the maku's lost woman. The gal had turned up unexpectedly. Jasmeen sewed the pieces together. With her help, I arranged the meeting and raid the moment I returned to Expedition."

I choked on the last of the bacon, but I forced it down. Then I picked up a roll, still warm from the oven, and I shredded it into tiny pieces.

"The wardens were not going to kill him, Cat. They were simply going to take him into custody and bring him to me."

He returned my gaze with a clear, unguarded look. Either the man was a shameless liar, or he was so deluded that he believed everything he said. Or maybe, just maybe, he was telling the truth. "You make it sound as if the wardens are working for *you*."

He drained his cup and, turning in his chair, addressed Bee instead of answering me. "Beatrice, the world has not ended, dear girl. Your cousin still loves you. Both of you have been sorely used, and it is no wonder you are angry. May I have some more tea? Do come eat."

How any person could say these words and not sound condescending I am sure I did not know, but he did say them, and they were not condescending.

Beatrice brought over the new pot and sat next to the general instead of me. Drake eyed the teapot with longing. Meeting his gaze, I licked egg yolk and bacon grease off my knife. He grimaced before turning back to his view of the garden.

The general set down his cup, and Bee filled it.

"All has been resolved. Once the necessary ships and troops are fitted, the Council will release the arrested radicals into my custody. I'll take them with me to Europa. Otherwise they would be hanged. Everyone benefits."

"If that's what you call benefit. Aren't people afraid the Taino will invade Expedition?"

"That hasn't been announced yet," he said. "We're keeping it secret for now."

"What hasn't been announced yet? An invasion?"

Bee's face flooded with color. She downed a cup of tea in one gulp as if she wished it were rum.

"Our agreement with the Taino," he said, as if such an alliance was foreordained and natural.

"The Taino rule the Antilles! You're nothing but a dispossessed general hoping for troops and money to fight a war in a land an ocean away! What can you have that they want?"

"Besides the spoils of victory to fill a treasury emptied by decades of expansionist wars? An opening of significant trade and export without too much risk to the cacica's authority?" He walked to the sideboard to make another plate of food.

"Is that enough to interest them?" I demanded.

Bee set down the cup and stared at the polished tabletop. Never in my life had I seen her shy from anything. Never. She managed a tremulous smile. "I am to get married."

I sat back, hard, in the chair. "Married!"

She glanced toward the general. He nodded exactly in the manner of a professor encouraging a favored student as she gropes her way toward the correct answer.

She reached across the table to lay a hand atop one of mine. "If the price of hope is marriage, then so be it. To a man of high rank and good manners, so I am assured."

"You agreed to marry him sight unseen?"

"Don't be so naïve, Cat! That's how such things work. You should know! They want me because I am a dream walker. Here in the Antilles, dream walkers are honored because they are so rare."

"I should think they are rare everywhere, given their likelihood of an untimely demise. If that's the only reason you are marrying, you might as well have been handed off to Four Moons House to be their prisoner. What obligations will the Taino place on you?"

She let out a gusty sigh. "Would you please listen for once? They have traditions here about the lore of walking the path of dreams. Once I am married, I will be allowed to learn."

"While you're imprisoned in some hot, dusty palace. Couldn't you have stayed with Brennan and Kehinde?"

"I would have loved to do so, with their fine revolutionary notions and legendary fistfights and buckets of whiskey and beautifully written pamphlets filled with radical sentiments. But that doesn't solve my other problem, does it? Perhaps you have a brilliant plan to stop the Wild Hunt from ripping off my head!"

I jumped up, the chair tipping over to clatter to the floor behind me. "Yes! I do!"

Drake stepped in off the balcony. The door opened and the Amazon captain appeared, sword drawn. The general gestured, and she retreated, closing the door.

"I would be glad to hear your plan," he said, walking over to place the plate in front of Bee.

I dug my nails into my palms, but pain wasn't enough to loosen my tongue. And it was a lie. I couldn't protect her. Only my sire could, and then only for as long as it suited him to do so.

Bee looked at me and blinked twice as a signal. "She's just exaggerating in her usual way."

"Ah, I understand now." He walked back to the sideboard, where he heaped bacon, potatoes, and eggs on a plate. "Helene told me never to ask questions of Tara Bell's child because she dreamed the child was chained by some manner of magical binding."

The chains that bound me to my husband? Or the ones that bound me to my sire? He didn't know everything! I righted the chair and sat with hands clasped in my lap as the general returned to the table with a plate for himself. Drake ventured to the end of the table farthest from me.

"Anyway, Cat," said Bee, barreling on like a fully laden rail car rolling downhill with no brakes, "you're the one who will never be free of Four Moons House because you are married to one of its cold mages."

"I know what I know," I muttered.

"I can't argue with that mulish truism! Anyway, the Taino won't hold me prisoner. The general needs me for the war." She went charmingly pink, like a rose blooming. "The prince is to travel with us. You see, the heir to the cacique's duho, the king's seat of power, is chosen from the cacique's sister's sons. This prince was never considered a favorite because there was a brother better suited for the task. But now he seems likely to inherit so it is felt he must gain worldly experience to prove his fitness and worth."

"What changed to make him worthy?"

She glanced toward the general, and then at Drake. "For one thing, he's a fire mage."

I laughed a little hysterically.

Drake raised a cup of tea to his lips, watching me over the rim. The general ate methodically with only a lift of the eyes to show he had noticed my untimely levity.

Bee scooped up an egg in her spoon and levered the spoon backwards, aiming its trajectory at me. "Tell me why you're laughing, or you'll get egg all over your face."

I needed a drink to settle my nerves. I got up and went over to the sideboard. The bottle had sherry in it. I jiggered out the cork, poured the deep red liquid to the brim of the last teacup, and gulped it down in one go. Turning, I saw Drake frown. I stuffed the cork back into the bottle.

"Cat!" said Bee. "It's still morning!"

The general finished his potatoes.

The liquor's heat rushed through me, and subsided. "I met Prince Caonabo." She gasped. "He seemed...pleasant. He was certainly inquisitive. And he's good-looking, if not nearly as pretty as Legate Amadou Barry. No hardship there." I wiped my brow, for it was already getting warm. "So, General, what exactly is it you want from me?"

He patted his lips with a linen cloth. "That depends on what you want, Cat. Although your choices are constrained."

I wanted to be released from my sire's rule, but I couldn't say that. I wanted a chance to walk beside a man I was finally getting to know, but I refused to speak of that. Maybe the sherry had shortened my temper. Really, I had nothing left to lose except Bee's life.

"What I want to know is why I should trust you when you placed my mother under sentence of death and would have killed her if she hadn't escaped."

"Why, Cat," he said, and I could have sworn he was taken aback, "the matter is entirely different. She was a sworn lieutenant in my Amazon Corps and thus subject to the rules and regulations of that corps."

"Including imprisonment and execution should she become pregnant?"

"The conditions and regulations of service were public knowledge. No woman took the oath of enlistment without fully understanding what was expected of her and where her responsibilities and loyalties lay. Those who serve in my army serve freely, but they are bound once they join to follow the code of conduct. As am I, and any person enlisting. For the Amazon Corps, that code included celibacy. Any woman who had served out her period of enlistment might apply for a discharge if she wished to have children, marry, or make some other change in life. A legal code is worthless if those who enforce it treat persons differently according to consequence, status, kinship, or wealth. All must be equal before the law, or the law is worth nothing."

"That's what Daniel Hassi Barahal wrote."

"In fact, that is what I said when I addressed the committee gathered to write a comprehensive new legal code. Perhaps Daniel recorded my words, and you read them later and thought they were his." An odd sort of smile animated his face, one I could not read. Anger? Amusement? Calculation? He was masked rather as my sire had been: I simply could not fathom what drove him. Except maybe irritation at remembering my mother had escaped the law.

"Tell me what you meant when you said my path will change the course of the war."

"Those are not Helene's precise words, nor did I say them that way." He did not raise his voice, but I realized that something about the turn the conversation had taken was making him angry. "Find a way to win the cold mage to my side, Cat."

"I'm sure she's found a way to prick the man's interest," muttered Drake.

I fixed my gaze on Drake and stalked back to the table. He stared me down, gaze almost fevered.

"Be calm," murmured Bee.

Camjiata said, "Enough!"

Drake leaned back and propped his sandaled feet up on the table. I remained standing.

"Now listen carefully, Cat," the general went on. "A living cold mage serves me much better than a dead one. I would value the services of a powerful cold mage when I return to Europa."

"One like your wife?" I asked.

"She was not a powerful cold mage. She had only a minor gift, enough to call a wisp of cold fire, which was ironic considering how poor her vision was. She was as close to a castoff as a child can be who is born into a mage House. Her House, and she, had no idea she walked the path of dreams. Everyone just thought she recited the most execrable poetry to get attention. But when she was about your age she heard her destiny in her own words."

Despite my irritation, I was drawn into his story. "What was her destiny?"

"Why, I was. Or she was mine. Hard to say. Maybe I should say, we were meant to be together, being each other's destiny."

"That's very romantic," I said caustically. Bee caught my eye, and I knew she was thinking, *Didn't that cold mage call you the other half of his soul?* I narrowed my eyes to let her know that if she spoke one word I would make her life so miserable that dismemberment would seem a mercy.

She ate her egg.

"I meant," I added, "considering what happened."

"Perhaps you mean to note that I am alive while she is dead. Quite true. Believe me, Cat, I intend to do everything I can to keep Beatrice alive. It was what Helene would have wanted. For they are all sisters of a kind, the women who walk the path of dreams."

"Like in one of those quaint cautionary folktales," remarked Bee, "in which everyone dies."

"Yes. Which brings me back to the point I have been trying to make. Cat, my dear, I fear you have not heard me, so I will say it again. If you do not bring the cold mage to me, then I will have to kill him. If that is what you want, then by all means, rid yourself of the magister and your marriage by refusing to cooperate with me. But do not make the mistake of underestimating me."

"Unless he kills you first."

"He will not kill me because I know who will kill me. And it is not him."

"How can you know?"

"On the day Helene and I first met, it was the second thing she said to me. That she had seen the instrument of my death."

"And you married her?" I demanded.

"As soon as I could." He laughed. "Wouldn't you?"

Bee stirred. "You've lived with that knowledge all this time? That's remarkable." She stared at him with none of the sledgehammer intensity that usually characterized her glares and looks. She looked as admiring as an actress in a stage play simpering at the steadfast prince whom she lovingly serves for the duration of the implausible plot.

A chill, as the broadsheet poets wrote in their cheaply inked stories, ran down my spine.

He sipped at his tea as if considering Bee's praise was the weightiest task on his mind, far more than death, war, revolution, love, cold mages, and dream walkers. "Is it? We all live with the knowledge of impending death, do we not?"

"Did she tell you who?" I asked.

He looked at me. But he said nothing.

"Who will be the instrument of your death?" I added, in case he had not understood me.

He poured more tea into his cup, set the ceramic pot back on its trivet, and turned the cup's handle so it lay parallel with the table's edge. His gentle smile had such power that I leaned toward him as if he were about to confer on me a great honor or the princely kiss of approval.

"Why, you will, Cat. You will."

28

I am not a young woman who craves attention. Although people have at times suggested that I talk a great deal, I could maintain silence with the best of them. A stony silence, accompanied by an offended glare, worked wonders on most people when they had insulted me.

Unfortunately, it had no effect at all on Camjiata. He smiled in an accommodating way. "I mean no offense, Cat. Nor do I mean to accuse you or even to suggest that I feel any hostility toward you. I am simply telling you what Helene told me."

I set fisted hands on the table. "You're trying to intimidate me. I won't betray him to you."

"You already have, or so he must believe."

Had he slapped me, it would have hurt less.

"Amazing!" Drake's lips curled into a sneer. "A more pompous, conceited, self-admiring ass I have never before encountered, and yet after all if you add to that a handsome face and expensive tailoring, the gals will crawl at his feet. Really, Cat, I'm disappointed in you."

I slipped the cane from its loop and set it on the table. He looked suitably startled, and shifted his chair away. "I should be careful if I were you, Drake. Because what you don't understand is that I can be the instrument of *your* death. And if you anger me enough, I will. In fact, I'm thinking about it right now."

Heat stung the air. "Don't try to duel with me."

"James!" said the general.

"Why do you always scold me and never her?" he demanded as the spark vanished. "Anyway, what do you expect a man to do when an attractive gal throws herself at him? By the way, that object she carries around so casually is pure cold steel. She's no doubt in league with that cursed cold mage and means to hand him the sword to do you in the moment he gets close enough."

I set my hands on the table and leaned toward him. "He's worth a hundred of you." I took in a few breaths to calm myself, then looked at Camjiata. "No wonder you wanted my mother to die if you believed she would give birth to a child who would kill you."

"It does not work that way." He had the means to hold your gaze even when you wanted to look away. This, too, was a form of sorcery: the ability to command. "Anyway, we do not execute pregnant women. You would have been born regardless."

I pressed a hand over the cane, feeling the quiver of its magic through my sweaty skin. "Babies are easy to dispose of."

"The djeliw teach us that our destiny is already written. As long as you are alive, I can be alive. But if you are dead, then I must already be dead."

"I suppose that's meant to be reassuring. What is your destiny, General?"

"To free Europa from the petty quarrels and greed of princes and cold mages. To unite all its peoples under one just code of law."

"With you conveniently seated as emperor."

His easy smile made my lips quirk despite my mistrust. "I am meant to sit in an emperor's throne. It is the role my mother raised me for."

"How can she have raised you for that?"

"She was the favored daughter of the patrician Aemillius lineage. They cast her off when she betrothed herself against their wishes to an Iberian captain. He was highborn enough. His mother was an Iberian princess and his father was born into the princely Keita lineage. But her people scorned all Iberians and desired her to marry to suit their schemes, so they cast her off in the most public way imaginable. They stripped her naked and whipped her onto the street as a whore. You should have some sympathy for her plight, Cat."

I frowned, thinking of the way Aunt Tilly and Uncle Jonatan had given me to the mage House in Bee's place. At least they had wept.

"She raised me to be the instrument of her revenge. I dare not dishonor her memory. But I have no child to foist off as my heir. The imperiate will dissolve after I am dead, leaving behind a better legal code and the abolishment of clientage. So you must ask yourself if the people of Europa will be better off or worse off than they are now. I must wonder, Cat, if there is something your cold mage wants very badly that I could offer him in exchange for his support."

I sat down as hard as if all the air had been punched from my lungs.

The abolishment of clientage.

Bee placed a hand over mine. "Let's go out to the balcony to get some air."

An uneasy feeling rippled down my spine. I nodded. We rose and went out into a patch of shade. The air was sticky with humidity and thick with the scent of flowers. I closed the doors behind us. A guard clothed in a dark blue tabard and holding a rifle glanced up at us from his station at a gate set into the back wall; his gaze widened; then he looked away.

Bee wasn't looking into the garden. She stared at the railing, her mouth twisted down with shame. "I'm sorry for the part I played in all this. I did truly think you wanted out of the marriage."

"You couldn't have known I changed my mind."

"I truly didn't know most of what was going on. Obviously I was just being tremendously naïve. And he did say he wanted the cold mage alive, in his army."

I leaned against her shoulder in the familiar way. "I've already forgiven you, Bee."

"He doesn't want to harm you, Cat. He told me so many stories about your mother. He speaks of her with the greatest esteem. I think he looks on you as he might look on a niece."

"One with a sword in her hand?" I glanced through the closed glass doors. Inside, Camjiata was working through a second plate of food with the pleasure of a man who enjoys eating, while Drake was picking through fried slices of potato as if looking for an elusive shard of triumph.

"I will tell him I will break off the marriage arrangements if anything happens to you."

"I think he believes what he said, about me needing to be alive. Not that I'm going to turn my back on him. What worries me is that I think you're a little in love with him. I worry he is using your admiration to coerce you into a marriage that benefits him."

She put an arm around me and held hard, whispering. "That's not how it is. Cat, you know me. No matter what it looks like to people outside you and me, you know I've thought this through. Yes, I can learn from the behiques. Yes, I gain an alliance to a powerful kingdom, one which respects and honors the very curse which puts my life in danger. There is one thing else. I was allowed to meet one time privately with the cacica, Queen Anacaona. She is a very powerful woman. I said, what use to me a marriage if I am torn to pieces by the Wild Hunt at year's end? She claimed the behiques have a means to protect dream walkers. This is good for us, Cat. This is hope."

I had met the Master of the Wild Hunt, so I was pretty sure the cacica was wrong. But I wanted Bee to live in hope, not fear. "Then of course I understand why you agreed."

She released me. "As for the other, I think the general will put in place a radical civil code."

"Just for the sake of argument, let us say it is true. What if he changes his mind, marries again, and produces a child to raise up as heir? Or what is to stop his captains from electing one of their own to rule as emperor after he dies? Because he will die. Everyone dies. He said so!"

The general was watching us. Seeing us look his way, he raised the cup to salute our machinations and conspiracies. Drake was crisping bacon into charred strips.

I turned back to Bee. "What is to stop princes and mage Houses from biding their time and restoring the old order with a lot of blood and carnage after he dies?"

Bee's gaze hardened, reminding me of an axe. "Did you listen to nothing that Kehinde and Brennan said? With the right weapons and allies, we can bring them down. A legal code matters."

"You're a radical, too! You and Vai both!"

Her gaze softened. "So it is more than just his looks!"

I fastened my fingers around the wrought-iron railing. The vivid memory of his passionate, angry kisses mocked me. "I wonder how far I'll go to convince him I did not betray him."

"There is something Andevai wants you to think the general can give him. Offer him that."

"Oh, Bee, I thought I was offering Vai so much, to share both the burdens and the risks of trying to break the chains of Four Moons House, when I could have been free of them. But he doesn't even know it. Why should he listen to me now?"

"If he is not willing to listen to you, then he isn't worth suffering over. Really, dearest, this isn't like you. You know you have to try."

Who was I, to feel fear? I, who was the weapon of the Master of the Wild Hunt? In the heart of me, like a shard of obsidian, lay a cruel gleaming kernel that would allow me to do what I must to save those I loved. I need only grasp it, cut my skin on it, and let it drink fully of my blood.

"I'm going to save you, Bee," I said. "I'm the only one who can."

Her lips twisted up. "Really, Cat. The man's vainglorious arrogance has been rubbing off on you. Now, follow my lead."

She opened a door and swept into the chamber, leaving me to follow in her wake like so much wind-chopped flotsam. She threw a smile at Drake that made him wince, and addressed the general. "We are going shopping."

"Of course, my dear." Camjiata began reading a pamphlet whose title was **On the Dynamical Theory of Heat: Some Experiments and Conclusions as Delivered by Professora Habibah ibnah Alhamrai at the Expedition Society of Natural Historians.**

We cut a swath through the shockingly expensive shops of Avenue Kolonkan. After a strenuous morning of examining fabric, smallclothes, footwear, kerchiefs and head wraps and hats, as well as ribbons and beads, necklaces, earrings, and painted gourds suitable for storing such treasures, we rested our feet in the shade of an arbor in a private courtyard. Well-dressed and well-groomed women—no men—drank carafes of sweetened lime juice garnished with mint leaves.

After we had quenched our thirst with an obscenely pleasurable and hotly spiced drink called chocolatl and worked through a platter of pastries, Bee nodded. "We have suitably bored the two men who are following us. Take yourself to the toilet and vanish. The gates into the old city close at sunset. I believe there are secret corridors in the house, so anything we say can be overheard. I should have told you before." She pressed a coin into my hand. "For the washroom attendant."

"The washroom attendant?"

"She has to earn her living, too. That way." She pointed toward an archway set under whitewashed walls, then returned to nibbling on a custard tart layered with slices of star-apple.

The washroom lay tucked in the back beside a lattice that screened off the kitchen. Women worked, chopping, grinding, and conversing about the highest-scoring member of the Anolis women's team, who had begun to hook her elbow shots in a manner that suggested a hidden injury would soon put an end to her glory days. An elderly woman in a faded but scrupulously clean pagne dozed in the shade beside the tiled entrance to a little toilet.

A piercing shriek from the courtyard brought a crashing halt to the kitchen conversation.

"It stung me!" screamed Bee. "The pain! I feel...so
sick...I'm going to throw up!"

I dropped the coin into the gourd, drew the threads of
shadow around me, and slipped out through the kitchen
into a side street. I had left my cane in Bee's room,
shoved beneath the mattress, so even the trolls ignored
me as I strode along the busy streets of Expedition.
Only the occasional dwarf mammoth showed a tendency
to probe in my direction with its exquisitely sensitive
trunk. Folk worked on roofs and walls, repairing the
damage from the hurricane. Mostly people were muttering about the warden's arrest of an elderly man known to
broadsheet readers as the Virtuous Rock, who had spear-
headed the radicals' drive for an Assembly. The Council
had made it known that in the event of a general strike,
the man and his granddaughter would be hanged.

Nerves made me sweat more than the sun. I was chewing on my lower lip as I halted before the gate to Aunty
Djeneba's boardinghouse. It was propped open just
enough for a child to slip through, a sign that the establishment was not yet open for business although I could
hear the comforting flow of voices as the family made
ready. I waited until the street lay momentarily empty,
then dropped my glamour and squeezed past the gate into
the courtyard.

Luce, sweeping, saw me first. The scrape of her broom
ceased as her lips parted. Uncle Joe, at the bar, looked up.
In the kitchen peeling sweet potatoes, Brenna paused.

Silence in surprise has a quality as loud as a scream.
Like a ripple from a thrown stone, it soon laps over the
entire pond. The children, busy braiding streamers as for
an upcoming festival, fixed their hands in their laps as
if they thought crows were about to swoop down and

rip them clean off. In her shaded sling chair, old Aunty
Brigid cackled with a frightful rasp in her sleep, "Nr nr
not the owl. Leave me be. I's not ready to go yet."

Aunty Djeneba turned. For an eternity her gaze measured me as her expression congealed into disgust. Every
voice faded. All movement in the courtyard ceased except
for the drip of water from the rain-soaked leaves of the
ceiba tree.

At last she spoke. "Sly women like to yee is not welcome in this respectable establishment, maku."

My lips had gone numb and my feet turned to dead
weights, impossible to shift. My cheeks flamed. I opened
my mouth but no word came out for there was nothing
left on my tongue except shame and hurt as they all stared
at me until I wished only to sink into the dirt and be obliterated.

All but Aunty Djeneba pointedly looked away, and that
was worse.

"Yee reduced him to tears, if that is what yee came to
hear and gloat over, witch. He is gone and not coming
back so there is no one here for yee to torment. Lucretia
shall fetch yee things, for yee shall not bring the wardens
down on us on a charge of theft."

Beneath the throttling shock quivered words, barely
deliverable in a hoarse mangled voice. "It isn't what it
seemed. I can explain. They used me to get at him. I
didn't know...I had no idea..." How pointless and stupid
the words sounded. How pathetic and cheap. "I need to
find him. I have to warn him he's still in danger."

"Did yee not get yee full payment because yee did not
deliver up the fire bane?" Like storm clouds, she swelled
in indignation as I cowered under the tumult of her anger.
"How did we not see it, yee washed up with yee hair un-

bound on the jetty in the company of another man? With yee magics and yee hair like a net to catch him in? How yee blinded him, poor lad. I must wonder if any of it were true, or if yee even went so far as to bite yee own arm to make him worry for yee. Just get out, maku. We have no more wish to ever see yee again nor hear that lying voice."

I slammed into the edge of the gate and, with eyes blinded by tears, groped onto the street. Yet I had not gone twenty paces when my legs gave out and I collapsed into heaving sobs. The worst of it was that the few folk out on the street passed me by and, recognizing me, walked on as if I weren't there. Whispering. *Look at she, that whore in the pay of the wardens. They say she is really a witch and shall drink yee blood and eat yee heart as she did to the poor deluded maku.*

"Cat?"

I looked into Luce's tear-streaked face. Ashamed, I looked away. I could not bear her scorn.

She pressed a bundle into my hands, my worldly goods as scant as the goodwill left to me. "Tell me why yee said that yee did not know. Please."

Words shook out of half-controlled sobs. "It's true James Drake found me on a beach..."

"Salt Island. So Gran' tell me. But no one can leave there, and yee's no fire mage."

"I never lied about that! The Barr Cousins did bring me to Expedition from Salt Island. It's true I knew Drake was working for General Camjiata back in Adurnam. But I didn't come to the Antilles with the general. I wasn't part of his organization. When Drake dumped me on the jetty, I didn't know it was because they hoped Vai would find me and then they could find him by tracking me. I know it sounds impossible, but I didn't know anything about it. Oh, no one will believe me, Luce. Why should they? I wouldn't believe me. I have to find him, or the general will kill him."

"After everything yee said to him and the way yee acted, I wonder why him dying should matter to yee. If yee's really a witch, yee shall want him dead."

My face was slobbery with self-pity and self-loathing. I could not get over the way Aunty Djeneba had looked at me as if I were a noxious vile cockroach crawling back into sight. But I owed Luce the truth. I wiped my eyes and nose, and I looked up into her solemn gaze.

"I am not a whore or a witch. I know it seems like Kofi was right, that I'm two-faced like a star-apple tree. But I was just confused. I meant to leave here, to take a room elsewhere, but I couldn't bear to leave him. I said yes to him the night of the areito. I meant it, Luce. I love him. Then everything happened so fast." Pain was a knife in my heart. I bit my lip rather than moan.

Her hand brushed my arm. "Venus Lennaya forgive me if I have made the wrong judgment, but I believe yee. He came that night, took he things, and left to go hide. Kayleigh live down by Kofi-lad's people now. She and he is to marry. That is all I can say because it is all I know."

She hurried off, back through the gates where I was no longer welcome.

Blessed Tanit, watch over your heartbroken daughter.

I yanked the threads of shadow around me to hide my shame. Clutching the bundle to my chest, I stumbled back to the old city and through gates guarded against fire banes by lamps. I took a wrong turn, and in retracing my steps found a stone gate overgrown with jasmine and hibiscus and marked by a modest stone column carved with the sigil of Tanit, the protector of women, She who is the face of the moon, sometimes bright and sometimes dark according to Her aspect.

I crept inside to find the place seemingly deserted, dense with flowers and fragrance. I washed my hands in a lustral basin fed by water trickling from a pipe. At the center of the open-air sanctuary, an arcade of pillars ringed a marble altar worn as smooth as if it had been polished for centuries by the hands of petitioners. I pressed my palms against it.

"What must I do, Blessed Mother? How can I be a better sister to Rory? How can I protect Bee without becoming a monster? How can I find him and win him back? How do I not despair? How do I look beyond my own troubles, as he does, to a path that makes a difference not just for our own selves but for others?"

The busy noises of the city had faded. A rain shower mizzled through, stippling the stone walkways. I rested my forehead on the marble.

Perhaps, through sheer emotional exhaustion, I dozed. Perhaps I dreamed that a woman with a brown Kena'ani face, clothed in robes the color of the balmy sea and wearing a crown as pale as the moon, cupped my face in her hands and kissed my lips as a seal to her promise.

Be heartened.

A cold touch on my cheek snapped me awake. I sat back on my heels to find an orange tabby cat nosing at me, tail lashing as it prowled the altar stone. With a disdainful flick of its tail, it leaped away and vanished into a hedge thick with white and purple flowers.

I found myself facing a votive stone I could have sworn had not been there before. A trellis arched over the stone, woven with a flowering vine resplendent in falls of purple flowers. Beneath the flowers, the peaceful stone face of the lady stared into the distance. She asked no questions. She waited with the patience of one who has all the time of passing centuries, as the ice creeps south and retreats north, and seas fall and rise and fall again, and volcanoes slumber or waken.

A five-petaled flower floated in the rainwater gathered in the shallow depression at the center of the altar stone, reminding me that it was proper to make an offering. I had come to the Antilles with nothing but the clothes on my back—and them shredded and since remade—the locket, and my sword. The last of my wool challis, two pagnes, a spare bodice and blouse and drawers, the boots, a comb, and the needles, thread, scissors, thimble, and pins I had purchased with my hard-earned coin were all I possessed besides the little coin purse. I fumbled at the purse's tie to make an offering of coin, but my clumsy fingers could not get it loose.

Coin was not the offering she wanted.

I offered my voice. I gave her the truth.

"My sire is the Master of the Wild Hunt."

In the isolation of the sanctuary, with only the stone to hear, his magic could not stop me.

Be heartened.

There will be a way.

29

The next morning I pretended to sleep late so I could explore the house without being seen. I found Bee sketching on the covered patio that faced the garden. The general lounged on a Turanian sofa next to her, reading aloud from a black book.

"'...The phrase "the span that binds the shores that flank the torrential waters that weep from the ice" likely refers to the bridge at Liyonum. Therefore, move Aualos's division to take that bridge.'" I crept up behind him only to discover that the neat, blocky letters on the page spelled nonsense syllables. "'Jovesday, sixth day of Maius, Aualos advances into Liyonum. Skirmishers report open road to Avarica. If march my divisions north, will split Tene forces and be able to fight each flank separately with full assault. So ordered.'"

"That was the battle of Ariolica?" Bee asked, not looking up from her sketchbook.

He had written a record of his campaign in code. "Yes, although my soldiers called it 'When we shoved that stick up between Tene ass-cheeks.' One might think it easier to recognize places from a drawing than from within the obscure words of a half-blind woman's poetic utterances, but both create a challenge. The words must be interpreted for potential meanings. The images must be recognized and then placed in a season or day. Look how long it took us to find Cat. Your dreams gave hints of where she was, only neither you nor I knew how to interpret them."

"I'm not sure I want them interpreted, now that I see what came of it!"

"Beatrice, if I do not save the cold mage, he will be captured and sold to the Taino."

"If the Taino can hold him!"

"You have met the cacica. Do you doubt her power?"

Her rosy lips pinched so hard they paled. "No, I suppose not."

He chuckled. "Queen Anacaona even proposed marriage to me."

Bee's gaze flew up, her pencil halting in midair. "She did?"

"There is an old custom among the Taino of a stranger king who marries into the royal lineage, but I am not to be that man. It would place me in a subservient position. Also, I promised Helene I would not marry again."

She chewed at her lower lip, her gaze too intent on him. "Why would you promise that?"

He smiled with the expression of a man who means to gently let you know you have gone too far. With a blush darkening her cheek, she set pencil back to page. I sidled over behind her. She had brought life to the leaves, flowers, and branches of the garden so lovingly that a blank spot within the sketch stood out like a wound. I glanced up to identify the spot she'd not drawn in: A man dressed in a sober dash jacket and European trousers stood with his back to us, one foot up on a bench and a hand holding a stub like a little tube whose end glowed with heat. He had black hair in a braid down his broad back.

Bee cleared her throat. I looked down. She had written: *I feel your breath on my neck. You are quite the noisiest breather. I wonder I never noticed before. I said you were feeling poorly.*

The general rose as the Amazon appeared on the patio. "Ah, Captain Tira. Yes, I'm coming. Beatrice, you will join us for supper. Cat, too, if she is feeling better."

"Of course."

He followed the Amazon into the house.

The man at the bench turned.

The shock of seeing Prince Caonabo made me almost lose hold of the threads that veiled me. He set the stub to his lips. Embers flared as he sucked in air. Even at this distance, the smoke made my eyes water and my nose sting. Bee took in a sharp breath, for the man was staring at her with an air of accusation, young men being annoying in that particular way, thinking you owed them something just because they admired you.

Prince Caonabo tossed the stub to the earth, ground it out with his heel, and with a shake of his shoulders walked toward us. He wore knives strapped across his chest, glimpsed where his dash jacket flashed open. Rising, Bee snapped shut her sketchbook. Still in shadow, I stepped back.

He halted. Bee's shoulders squared in a way I knew presaged battle.

"Is it the truth, Bee?" he asked in heavily accented Latin. His voice was nothing like as courtly and measured as Prince Caonabo's. His tone had all the subtlety of a fencer who attacks straight on without feinting. "You are betrothed to my brother? You will marry him?"

"What did you offer me?" she asked coolly.

"What I could! You know how I am situated!"

"I do not have the luxury of joining your exile. You know how I am situated."

He was the one trembling, not her. "Do you cherish any affection for me at all?"

Heartless Cat had never stared down an overwrought man with as much detachment as Bee did now. "Feelings cannot protect me or feed me. Although I daresay I envy my dear cousin for inadvertently falling in love with a suitable man. Not that it helped her, did it?"

"Yes, we have all heard quite enough about the maku fire bane. Will your wedding areito be held in Sharagua?" He made no attempt to touch her, yet I felt I was eavesdropping inappropriately on a most intimate conversation because of the way his gaze caressed her.

"No. It will be held at the festival ground at the border."

His lips quirked up mockingly. "The better for the people of Expedition to be bought off with bread and circuses, as the Romans say. What date have the behiques set for the ceremony?"

"The areito will begin on the thirtieth day of October."

"In the calendar of my father's people, that is the month of the goddess of birds and butterflies. The beautiful woman who brings fertility and desire. It must be thus, must it not?"

She blushed prettily, accepting the compliment without words.

He went on. "I know Romans and Hellenes have odd notions about a woman's knowing no man before she is first wed. But I assure you it will not be what my brother expects."

Bee had gone quite pale although her voice remained steady. "What are you suggesting?"

A grim smile played on his lips. "You know where I sleep."

Without saying more, he walked away on a path that led him out of sight around the kitchen wing. I examined the leafy foliage, the nearby windows with blinds drawn down against the late afternoon sun, and the guards at their stations along the high boundary wall. We were unobserved.

I sank onto the sofa. "I begin to have some sympathy for the head of the poet Bran Cof! 'She is the axe that has laid waste to the proud forest.' You seem to be leaving a trail of felled trees."

She set fists on hips. "Besides Legate Amadou Barry, pray inform me what other man I have admired in *that way*."

"Where do I begin? Your youthful infatuations at the academy were legion." I picked up her glass of pulpy juice and drained it thirstily. Then my face was pulled inside out, for she had not sweetened the lime with pineapple juice or, it seemed, any sugar at all.

"Serves you right! Anyway, that seems a hundred years ago."

"Do you care for this man?" I flipped through the sketchbook but found not a single sketch of the Taino prince. "I see by the blank expression on your face that you are attempting to think. No wonder Prince Caonabo looked familiar. The resemblance is uncanny."

"They are twins. He was exiled for the crime of refusing to live as his brother's catch-fire."

I whistled. "What is his name?"

"Haübey. He fled to Expedition and joined the general's army in exile. That's why he was in Adurnam. Everyone here calls him Juba."

"Juba? Isn't that the name of an ancient Numidian king from North Africa? What happened between you?"

She sighed. "I was quite overcome by the heat of the moment. I am afraid I have come to discover I am susceptible. I begin to worry that more than anything it is the attention I desire."

A year ago I would have teased her. Now, I remained silent.

She sank down next to me and took my hand. "I thought I might as well experience everything life has to offer before my blood soaks the ground and my head is cast into a well." Her voice dropped to a whisper. "And the truth is, his was the face I saw in the Fiddler's Stone. In Adurnam. But now I think it must have been Prince Caonabo's face I saw, not Juba's."

"I recall him now, standing in the entryway of the law offices staring at you. I comprehend he conceived an ill considered and violent infatuation for your beautiful face and blunt speaking."

"Actually, he was quite levelheaded in dealing with my puking on the sea voyage."

"That would certainly endear a man to an impressionable young female." But I thought of how solicitously Vai had taken care of me.

She chuckled. "Why, Cat, you're blushing."

I turned the page: batey players keeping the ball in the air, faces creased with concentration; the masts of ships in the harbor; baskets of fish on the jetty, pargo and cachicata by the look of them. "I wasn't puking, if that's what you're asking. But after Drake dumped me on the jetty and Vai found me, I got sick. He saw the bite mark. The landlady brought in a behique that very night. The man proclaimed me clean, so they let me stay. Vai took care of me, for nothing in return."

"Nothing?" Her eyebrows arched.

"He comes from a village where women can be taken against their will by the mages. He refuses to act that way himself. You have no idea how people fawn over that man. I had no idea he could be so charming and thoughtful."

"Your husband? The cold mage? Thoughtful? *Charming?*"

"What other husband do I have?"

"Kena'ani women are according to ancient custom able to acquire two husbands if it is for the good of the family trade. Maybe you found a charming, thoughtful one to go with the obnoxious, self-important one, like a matched set of opposites."

I trapped her with a smirk. "Like Prince Caonabo and his brother?"

"I shall bury the blade in your skull, just above your right eye."

"That's what I love about you. Your precision." I turned the page, and my heart hammered as if caught in a carpentry yard among busy laborers.

Bee leaned to look. "That's from one of my dreams. Two trolls walking along. I like how their crests are each raised to a different height, as if one is indifferent and the other amused. See here there are two boots. So there is a man walking with them, only their bodies obscure his. I imagine that the man is the one talking, only we can't see his face. Trolls are so interesting. They speak perfectly well, but their own language is all whistles and clicks. There is a course at the university here where people try to learn it, but I heard no person can use it properly."

My mouth parted, as if to receive a kiss. "It's Vai, with the Jovesday trolls. Kofi said Vai would have to leave Expedition."

"Who is Kofi?"

I placed my finger on a small portrait of a young man with a mop of locks and jagged scars on his cheeks, pushing a cart heaped with baskets of fruit. "This is Kofi. Vai's friend."

"The arrogant cold mage has *friends*?"

I pinched her arm.

"Ouch! I meant, friends who are common laborers."

"There's a great deal the general doesn't know about Vai. Kofi is going to marry Vai's sister. Strange to think you're dreaming about Vai." I ran a finger across an arch decorated with four phases of the moon, then paused at a sketch of a wooden bench with a slatted back sitting in front of a brick wall adorned with falls of the flowering vine I had seen in Tanit's bower. "What is this?"

"I don't know. I just sketch what I dream."

"The Jovesday trolls," I murmured. "Could you lie down at night with a specific thing in mind to dream about?"

"I've tried. I can't. I am not dreaming my own dreams. I am walking through the dreams of someone who is already dreaming."

"A dragon."

"Yet I still haven't seen a single plump deer, much less one running exceedingly slowly."

My smile at her jest twisted into a considering frown. "Keer must know where Chartji's aunt lives. Chartji's aunt knows Kofi. There's the link. I have a plan. Well, as long as Keer doesn't eat me for not coming back when I said I would. We have to go to the law offices, in the harbor district."

"There's a statement to send stark fear through my bones."

"My being eaten?"

"No. You're not plump enough to tempt them. I meant, going outside the city walls."

"Where do you think I've been living? Haven't you explored the rest of Expedition?"

"Of course not! Everyone says it's much too dangerous!"

"I've staggered drunk through the streets without being molested and felt ever so much safer than I did in Adurnam! Anyhow, I think it's possible Vai is hiding in troll town. Tomorrow morning I'll go to the law offices. I want anyone watching me to see I'm not living under the general's protection. I could get a room there, too. Could you live with me there?"

Her eyes flared, then tightened as she looked away. "No. I am required to begin learning Taino and also to take lessons in the complicated court etiquette I will be marrying into."

"Then I stay with you here. If he will not believe me, then he is not worth suffering over."

She embraced me, staring into my eyes as if she could pierce the veils that masked me. "Cat, when Hallows' Night comes, are you going to try to sacrifice yourself in order to save me?"

"What makes you think I could?" I whispered.

"Because I won't allow it! I read Uncle Daniel's journals. If you have to answer questions with questions, then when you were in the spirit world without me, you must have been forced to become a servant of the night court. You must promise me you won't sacrifice yourself. Promise me!"

I wanted to say, "*Alas, he will not let me*," but my lips seemed to freeze together, knit by ice.

"Sit down, Cat."

I sat.

"That was an interesting reaction," she said, chafing my hands.

After a bit, I could speak. "When do you go to Taino country?"

"It's complicated, because the wedding is a series of ceremonies that takes place over many days. It all culminates with a five-day areito that begins on October thirtieth."

"I have to be with you when you go to the Taino. Promise me you won't leave me behind."

"I won't, dearest. I was hoping you would offer. I don't want to be alone."

"You won't be because I won't leave you. Now, I feel the need to stab something. Does this city have a fencing academy?"

"I was attending one before we went to Sharagua. It's run by a branch of the Barahal clan."

"Excellent! We have the entire afternoon before supper. We shall go enroll. I'll let you pay my tuition since I have no money."

We came home sore and laughing with just enough time to wash and change for dinner. I had to hope the illustrious of Expedition knew something about powerful fire mages and behiques and were willing to talk. By gaslight, servants bustled behind the windows of the dining room where a table laden for twelve was set out. The chamber's walls were painted with scenes of flowering vines in whose branches nestled half-hidden birds like so many avian eavesdroppers.

The general had assembled a collection of philosophically inclined minds whose ability to lapse into the most abstruse tangents defied my ability to sift through the thickets of natural history, practical science, and political theory to figure out who was a supporter of Camjiata and who was just there to enjoy the conversation and feast on a splendid meal. For the meal was indeed splendid, with platters of whitefish stewed with chilies hot enough to make my nose run, chicken marinated in rum and garlic and ginger, and mounds of sweet potatoes sliced and grilled with yet more rum.

An older maku professora in residence at the university engaged in a lively debate with a toweringly young and prosperous merchant who had been born into one of the city's most prestigious founding families. He betrayed his noble origins with the ostentatiousness of his clothes and the presumptuous way he addressed everyone. Both young merchant and older general claimed Keita lineage, so they could be in some way cousins.

"Yee are a maku, Professora Alhamrai," young Maester Keita was saying in a tone so bombastic that it reminded me of an overstuffed chair in whose pillows you drown. "So it is no mystery that yee shall not fully understand the principles of government here in Expedition."

I liked the bland smile the professora offered in response. "It is true I investigate the nature of the physical world rather than the body politic. Scientific principles teach us that friction creates heat. If a majority of the populace of Expedition has become fractious due to their perception they are being governed poorly, then is it not likely they shall catch fire?"

"Most people have no ability to moderate their emotions. 'Tis why they are unable to govern themselves and need their betters to govern on their behalf. What do you think, Maestressa Barahal?" The young Keita turned his attention on Bee with a smile so condescending it set my blood to boiling.

Bee simpered winningly up at him. "I think you shall be the first one shot when the radicals assault the old city."

Forks and spoons stilled. Glasses thumped, set on the table. Conversations withered. All eyes turned to Bee as she blinked as into the noonday sun with the look that fooled everyone but me.

"For that jacket is certainly very fine. Any young man would be eager to wear it. I suppose most must be too poor and lazy to gain such resplendent garb by any means but foul ones."

The general coughed into a hand as the rest of the table shared a polite and mildly bewildered laugh. The servants brought platters of fruit, but I was too full to do more than stare longingly at a plate of papaya whose slices had been meticulously arranged in the shape of a fish.

Professora Habibah ibnah Alhamrai was seated to my right. She addressed me in the Latin spoken in southern Europa. Judging by her coloring and curly black hair as well as her name, she was a native of the Levant. "You are come but lately to the general's household, Maestressa."

"I do not belong to the general's household. I am here only as companion to my cousin."

"Ah. You are not one of the general's partisans or servants."

"One may have other reasons for sitting at this table or sleeping in this house," I said. "I do not serve the general nor have I ever."

Yet her frank assessment embarrassed me. "You retain some skepticism about the general's motives?"

"Can there be any skepticism where the general is concerned? Is he not exactly what he claims to be?"

"A worthwhile question. If I may change the subject, I am told you are the daughter of Daniel Hassi Barahal. I met him once."

I leaned in too swiftly, drawing notice for my lurch. "Please, tell me about him! For you know, he and my mother died when I was six."

Before she could answer, the general asked her opinion about the efficacy of cold magic in the Antilles. "For I am surprised," he said, "to find there is a general belief here in Expedition that fire banes are weak creatures of little utility."

"So they are," proclaimed the young merchant. "Good for parlor tricks, lighting a path at night in the countryside, and acting as auxiliaries to the municipal firefighting force. These stories of how they call down storms and shatter iron are the credulous fantasies of the gullible natives of Europa, who have been treated for so long to such tales that they have come to believe them."

"In fact, that is wrong," said the professora. "I have studied this question at some length. Many of the properties of cold magic can be explicated using the principles of the sciences. In fact, I suspect testimony from the mages would serve only to confuse precisely because they deliberately conceal what they know. For example, the first question we must ask is, What is the source of the vast energies available to cold mages? Does it lie in that plane of existence often called 'the spirit world'? Or does it lie in the ice itself?"

"Is the spirit world a physical place, Professora," asked the young merchant with a laugh, "or a metaphorical one?"

"Let me complete my thought," she said with the sort

of graciousness that cut him off at the throat. "I believe both may be necessary."

"You know this for certain, Professora Alhamrai?" asked the general.

She inclined her head. "I am an inquirer, General. In the Chibcha kingdom of southern Amerike, in the mountains, rests an ice shelf. I have traveled there to ascertain this for myself. Likewise, my colleagues among the"— here she whistled four notes, denoting trolls—"have a map of the great ice wall whose southern cliff stretches across most of North Amerike. This wall I have seen for myself, although not its entire extent. I think it likely that the cold mages of the Antilles exist too far from these sources to use them with as much efficacy as cold mages can do in Europa, where the ice lies closer to human habitation."

I said, "So a cold mage would have power here, but it would be weaker because the ice is farther away? I mean, is the ice actually farther away?"

Bee looked at me, lifting one eyebrow in an unspoken question.

The professora nodded. "The extent and mass of the nearest ice may also matter. In addition, it is likely that, over the generations, the mage Houses in Europa have developed a particularly skilled and nuanced method of drawing from the source of these energies. Without such specific knowledge, and living in a place where it is illegal for them to form associations to better themselves, the fire banes here in the Antilles would be at an additional disadvantage. In a geography with a number of active volcanoes, it is no wonder fire mages are treasured and ennobled. While, in a tropical climate, the seemingly weaker cold magic is ignored and belittled."

"Are there quite a lot of powerful fire mages here?" I asked. "Where are they all?"

Talk at the table died as quickly as if I had stripped naked.

The general rose. "I believe it is time to move to the salon."

As was typical in Expedition, the company moved with no separation of women from men into a parlor made comfortable with sofas and chairs. Along one wall stood a pianoforte beside two djembes placed atop a wooden chest.

Because I wanted to hear about my father, I tried to slide into the circle that had gathered around the professora by the glass doors that opened onto the patio, but the young merchant had taken her earlier words on friction as an inducement to monopolize her. He began droning on about his theories of the unfitness of most people for governance and the need for the Council to remain a select group chosen by and from those with the virtue, birth, and education to properly shepherd society through difficult times. Bee had been cornered by a pair of young officers in the Expedition militia, specialists, so they were telling her at length, in the new science of artillery. The general sat at the pianoforte to play a complicated fugue, one melodic voice following the next, as two women wearing the rich clothing to be found along Avenue Kolonkan engaged him in simultaneous conversations, one about transatlantic sailing routes and the other about the manufacture of rifles. I faded back to the sideboard. Unlike the general, I could not separate so many voices.

"If yee shall forgive me, Maestressa Barahal. We have met before but was not formally introduced. I's called Gaius Sanogo."

I looked into the face of a man old enough to be my father but not elderly, tall and a little stout but clearly fit and healthy, with more silver in his beard than in his closely shorn black hair. I recognized his face with a shock.

"You were at the meeting at Nance's." My tone sounded too hot to my ears. "One of the radicals. Are you the one who betrayed your own people? I thought it was Jasmeen."

"Did yee?" He had a pleasant face and a pleasant smile and the pleasant gaze of a man confident in his status. "The revelation come too late for they who now sit in prison waiting for the fleet to sail."

My cheeks flamed. *Might the worst have been averted if I'd told Vai everything I could?* "I didn't see you at the supper table," I said.

"I was not at the supper table. Still, I could not help but overhear yee when yee told the professora that yee is not under the employ nor in the service of the general."

"Are there really secret passages in the walls? Do you serve the general?"

He looked amused. "Not at all, Maestressa. The folk at Warden Hall call me 'Commissioner.' The general tolerate me presence here because he must."

"The *commissioner*! Were you infiltrating the radicals?"

"As such," he continued, "I's thinking any gal who can for some weeks evade we search for she, might be a valuable asset for we organization. If she is not engaged elsewhere."

My fingers brushed the spot where my sleeve concealed the scar. "I am not for hire."

"I know about Salt Island," he said in the same tone

he might use to comment about the rain shower pattering through the foliage outside.

"Is that meant as a threat?"

"Only if I choose to disclose that information to the Taino authorities, or to arrest yee. Which for me own reasons I don' choose to do. I's trying to figure yee out. I reckon a Barahal ought to know something of how cold mages fought against the general in the Europan wars."

I bargained. "I might know something, if you tell me where my husband is."

"I must ask me own self, just why it is yee want to know where he is gone. For it surely did look like yee plotted to hand him over to the general. And it surely do look as if the general is protecting yee, even as yee claim not to be under he command."

"He protects me for the sake of my cousin, Beatrice."

He glanced at the floor with a smile caught on his lips that said as clearly as words that he did not believe me. His gaze, rising, met mine. He had eyes as brown as his skin. "I don' think so."

I needed him to believe I wasn't working for the general so he would help me find Vai. "She's far more valuable to him than I am, now that she's to marry Prince Caonabo."

I truly surprised him.

He studied me with the gaze of a man accustomed to assessing criminals. "Yee's either quite naïve or very clever, Maestressa. I suppose time will tell. With yee permission."

As Sanogo withdrew, I glanced toward the general, obliviously playing a sprightly melody as he contributed to the other conversations he was having. When Camjiata rose to allow one of the women to play, Sanogo intercepted him. I escaped through the open doors onto the patio. The wind flecked drops on my head from rain-laden leaves as I stepped into the garden. The debate between the professora and the young merchant seemed likely to go on all night. I sat on a damp bench and folded my hands in my lap, waiting.

The general found me soon enough. "Cat, you and I need to have a talk about the nature of confidential information."

"Had I known you meant to keep your alliance with the Taino secret from your own allies in Expedition, I would have leveraged the information more to my advantage."

"You have no advantage. You eat off my table and sleep in my house. Nevertheless, you intend to sneak off and find your husband. I wonder what you possibly expect to do then."

"Save Europa from your war," I said with an angry smile.

"Thus leaving countless communities laboring in the harness of an unjust social order."

"Which you hope to replace with an empire."

"I am the descendant of emperors both Roman and Malian. I do what I was born for."

"Surely there are other people in the world who are descendants of emperors, but that does not mean they are fit for or eager to rule. Or that they have a right to do so!"

"You are the last person to claim that blood means nothing, Cat. Your mother meant to sacrifice herself in order to make sure you were raised by your own blood instead of by a stranger."

The breeze wove a net that made my lips heavy and my throat thick. I stared at him.

"So you didn't know? Your parents never told you what she risked for you?"

"Don't you know my parents died when I was six? Was that why they were so afraid of Tara being recaptured by your army? Not because she was a deserter, but because of your wife's dream about me? Were they just trying to keep me safe? Because they feared what you might do to me?"

"As the djeli said, destiny is a straight path. We are meant for what we are meant for."

"I can't argue with that mulish truism!"

"Indeed, you can't. Here's something you don't know. Your mother betrayed me."

"How did she do that?"

"She chose Daniel over my cause, her heart over my army, the duty she felt for him and for the baby over the duty she owed to me. She might have waited until her term of service was up, only another five years. But at some point on the lost expedition to the Baltic Ice Shelf, she had sexual congress with Daniel Barahal, and by doing so, broke her oath to me."

The old city's night revelry danced in the excitable rhythm of drums and lutes and laughter, heard from beyond the garden walls. I stared. *He didn't know Daniel wasn't my father.* Yet why should Tara or Daniel have told him? "You can't know what circumstances were like on that expedition," I said. "Many people died."

He set a foot on the bench beside me, braced as if to remind me that he was bigger than I was in every way possible. "Certainly we may do in extreme conditions what we might not do elsewise. But you see, she never claimed so. You can of course understand that when the women in my Amazon Corps swear an oath to remain celibate, it is understood that women may be vulnerable to rape. They less than other women, because of their training and comrades, but it happens."

"Would that have made a difference to her sentence?"

"Of course it would. A soldier made pregnant by rape can serve out her enlistment if she gives up the child to anonymous fosterage. Tara could have claimed rape, given you up, served out her enlistment, married Daniel after, and had other children with him."

"Why couldn't a raped woman give the baby to her family?"

"It would be too easy to circumvent the law. An army must have discipline. No one forced Tara to sign the enlistment papers. She knew the terms. Instead, she hid her pregnancy until she was wounded in battle and her condition revealed. Then we had no choice but to arrest her for insubordination. Yet with my own ears I heard her swear in court that Daniel was the father and she his willing partner, and so he had therefore the right to claim and raise the child after her execution. Yet no pregnant woman can know if a baby will be healthy or even survive birth. So I had to wonder, why she was willing to sacrifice her life for the chance of keeping you with Daniel?"

I knew the answer: because she had hoped Daniel could somehow keep me away from the Master of the Wild Hunt. It hadn't been about Camjiata at all, even though he thought it was.

"Do not defy me as your mother did, Cat. I cannot be merciful. Bring me the cold mage."

I bowed my head to give myself space to calm my thundering heart. Rising, I smoothed down my pagne. "Are we finished, General?"

"No. We are not finished. But this night I am going to have a drink and thence to my bed."

I made him a pretty courtesy in the Adurnam manner, but the heat of my anger had forged my heart into cold steel.

30

In the morning, I went to the law offices and after a protracted duel negotiated new terms: I would write Keer a thrilling monograph detailing the lurid superstitions believed in the primitive villages of Europa, and in payment she would take me to see Chartji's aunt.

For two weeks I followed a strict routine. Early in the morning when it was cool, Bee and I attended the fencing academy. I then accompanied Bee to her morning lessons in Taino, for it seemed useful to learn something of the language most people in the Antilles spoke. She then was carried off by a pair of Taino women, haughty nobles, and their prodigious retinue of companions, servants, allies, hangers-on, and guards. The rest of the day was mine. While I did indulge myself playing batey with off-duty soldiers in the courtyard, mostly I thumbed through my father's journals. I chose tales I could string together to give Vai a glimpse of the truth of what had happened to me in the spirit world. My first two attempts Keer rejected. The third she accepted.

Every evening the general entertained notables, but I was no longer invited. I discovered narrow corridors between the rooms, once used by servants and now convenient for eavesdropping. But at every gathering Gaius

Sanogo or another warden was stationed in such a way that even wreathed in shadow I could not squeeze by undetected. I had to rely on Bee's reports.

The general was visibly displeased when broadsheets trumpeted the unexpected news that a young woman of Phoenician lineage and Europan upbringing had at the general's behest and the cacica's request been betrothed to a Taino prince. Everyone knew the Taino considered the Europans to be uncouth barbarians, nor had any Taino nobles deigned to ally themselves even with the most distinguished of Expedition's noble lineages, so the news was a nine days' wonder.

On the first day of October, I held a printed copy of my monograph in my hands. I showed it to Bee in the privacy of the garden, in the shade of a star-apple tree.

Bee leafed through the pamphlet. "I like this typeface. It's very even."

"All the dialogue is rewritten. I object to having Celtic villagers talk like Expedition locals, with their *yee*s and *shall*s."

She ignored me. "It is tremendously exciting and lurid. 'His kiss was lightning, a storm that engulfed her.' So romantical! I am quite overwhelmed, or I would be if a disturbing image of that terrible dream of you kissing Andevai did not rise into my mind like a dreadful moist and tentacled beast out of the briny deeps. Here. 'He was beautiful and she was young and not immune to the power of beauty.' It would be better as 'He was a beauty and she was a—' "

"Give me that, you beast!" I snatched at the pamphlet.

She skipped out from beneath the tree into the morning sun that was baking into the patio brick, and paused there with her gaze lifted to the east. Her black curls fell—

as the poets said—in a riot down her back, which I had always assumed meant they had some experience in un-tangling a mop of hair that was both thick and excessively curly. I waited. The face Bee showed to the world was only a part of her; despite her dramatic demeanor, she was far more reticent than I would ever be.

She walked back. "Oh, Cat. I'm feeling hopeful. It's very painful." She handed me the pamphlet. "By the way, Professora Alhamrai was a guest again last night. She asked about you. I made sure to let her know the general suspects you of nefarious treachery."

"You used the word *nefarious*? You don't think that was a bit overdone?"

"Now that you mention it, she laughed. As if I were joking!"

I sighed. "Do you think anyone will ever believe I wasn't involved in the raid on Nance's? Besides Jasmeen, that is. As a businesswoman, she'll profit handsomely by the war. I would think people would be suspicious of her since she shares the general's bed."

Bee's gaze narrowed, for the subject of Jasmeen irritated her. "They're very discreet. You need to go meet the troll." She kissed me on either cheek. "May Tanit bless you with good fortune in your hunt, dearest."

At the law offices, Keer offered me a platter of fruits and nuts from which I took one and ate it, and I offered her a pouch of nuts I had purchased on the street, from which she took one and, cracking its shell between her teeth, swallowed it quickly.

"I cannot talk you out of wishing to become acquainted with them?" she asked. "This one whom you would call Chartji's aunt, and her brother, are what you rats would describe as being insane. It comes of being only two in a clutch. I warn you because I like you."

"I have to try. There is one other thing. From here to troll town, you may be startled to not be able to see me. I have to hide myself in case I'm being followed. I can't really explain."

Keer gave a pair of clicks which I was coming to understand in troll speech meant a match of wits in which the players stood at the same level as when they started. "Thus the words of Maester Godwik. 'You will know her because she is touched with the summer breath of the unreachable maze.'"

"When did Maester Godwik say that?"

She cocked her head. "He wrote it. We received dispatches yesterday from Adurnam."

"Any for me?"

"No. There will not yet have been time for you to receive a reply to the letter you sent for your cousin who is after all here in Expedition."

"Then how did Maester Godwik know I was here?"

"We also veil our secrets. If the meeting must be made, let us go."

Let it not be said cats and trolls cannot act decisively and in concert. I wrapped myself in threads of magic. Accompanied by two young trolls who were some manner of kin, Keer and I walked upriver to Iron Bridge. The factories clustered on the eastern bank, smokestacks belching. Like most trolls in Expedition, Keer favored clothing that mixed a wild combination of colors and cuts, the kind of thing I would have pieced out of a ragbag had I no alternative. The few trolls I had seen in Adurnam had had more muted tastes, which had only seemed outrageous because we in Adurnam had never met the trolls in Expedition. But it was not until we reached the glitter-

ing wall marking the environs of troll town that I realized
Keer dressed to fit human taste.

Troll town had a boundary rather than a wall, a fence
of wire from which hung fluttering ribands sewn with
polished shards of glass or metal. The instant I stepped
beneath, my veil shredded as if cut to pieces, leaving me
visible and vulnerable. Ahead lay a confusing maze of
oddly-shaped structures wound about by paths and mirrors.

"This way," said Keer.

As we ventured into the maze, my head began to ache
with a pulse right between my eyes. No pattern or land-
mark distinguished one path from another. Structures like
five- and six-sided gems popped up right in my way,
only to seem to veer aside as the path took a sharp turn.
Copses of nesting houses, some with tiled roofs and others with roofs like plaited hats, clustered around wells.
Trolls busied themselves everywhere, watching me pass
as if they were hungry. Their cacophony assaulted me,
shrills, clicks, whistles, trills, and a constant tapping with
no discernable rhythm that washed over me until I felt
myself sinking. Bile rose in my gorge.

A white-hot pain slicing through my eyes staggered
me. Keer's hand fixed on my elbow, and she steered me
into shadow. Her breath on my cheek smelled of dry summer grass. I was blind.

"Not the place to look weak. You are safe with me, but
some here will be discourteous and eat you, thinking you
need to be culled. Close your eyes."

I hadn't known they were open. I squeezed them shut,
fumbling at the cloth to draw the cane free. "Let them try
to eat me," I whispered.

"Put it away." Keer spoke so close to my ear I could almost feel the bite of her teeth into the inviting flesh of my cheek. "It is too shiny. It will attract vultures and killers."

Blindness gave me no succor. As painfully as the shots and glints had struck me, it was not glass and mirror that made me reel. Not until this moment had I understood how much I oriented myself by winding myself into the threads that bind and interlace the worlds. I did not see these threads with my eyes but felt them through my whole being. Here, I was completely cut loose.

I found a hoarse scrape to serve as a voice. "I am going to throw up."

"Quickly."

I clung to the troll as she guided me what way I did not know, to the slaughterhouse or to rat country, I could not tell, nor dared I look, for all my efforts were fixed on not puking. The most vivid image overtook me, of me on hands and knees on the dusty ground vomiting while lean, deadly predators circled in, watching my struggles until they darted in for the kill...

"Sit," said Keer. I heard the other two trolls whistling to each other, perhaps discussing which part of me would be tastiest.

My legs gave way. Swallowing bile, I sat on a hard surface, face in my hands.

"That was harsh," added Keer. "You must be a spirit-walker. Ditch behind you."

With something I could only call kindness, the troll held me by skirt and jacket while I retched into a rubbish-filled ditch. The stinking remains of my breakfast mottled a sole-less shoe upper and a fraying basket strewn with cracked chicken bones. After a bit, I rose. A man stared curiously as he trundled past pushing a cart filled with bricks. We were back in rat country, on a backstreet lined with ramshackle workshop compounds between weed-ridden empty lots.

"I could use something to drink," I said, my words tasting quite foul.

Keer hissed, her head slewing around. Three unknown trolls wearing only ribbons and strings approached in a crouching posture whose stealth made me extremely apprehensive. Were they about to spring? Had they followed us out of troll town?

"I feel much stronger," I said in a loud voice.

Keer's young relatives dipped their heads, baring teeth as they placed themselves between the strangers and me. The other trolls backed off.

Unmolested, we returned to the law offices, but I felt too queasy to draw the shadows around me. I had to hope the general's spies hadn't been able to follow me to troll town.

A clerk brought a tray in with a steaming pot of tea and a flask of rum.

"Tea, or rum?" asked Keer, talons poised above the tray and teeth flashing wickedly.

"Might I have rum? Why did you call me a spirit-walker?"

She handed me a shot glass and poured tea for herself. The rum burned down my throat. She poured tea again, this time for us both.

"The world is a maze. It is twisted and layered. Like a knot, perhaps you rats would say. No, that is not a good analogy. Anyway. Some of you rats can navigate to places in the knot where none of my kind can go, just as we have our secret pathways."

I sipped at the tea. The flavor breathed with the scent of late summer flowers, dusty and tart. "Your own secret pathways? Does the Wild Hunt hunt your people?"

"Such a question demands we enter the circle."

"I can't play the game, Keer. My head feels like it's being squeezed in a vise. My feet feel like they've been chopped out from under me. If that makes you want to eat me, or if I lose all the height I've gained on Triumph Spire, so be it. Just give me another shot of rum first."

Keer eyed me in the peculiar way trolls had, looking with one eye and then the other. "You have given me the gift of your weaknesses. Now we are like clutch mates. I can either consume you to strengthen myself or . . ."

She had the most interesting eyes, in one way so human with round black pupil and silver iris and in another way so gleaming and deadly, rimmed by the tiny feathers of a metallic golden-brown color. I almost felt I could see in that lens the secret pathways known only to trolls.

"Whatever the second is sounds more appealing than the first," I interposed, for one of the things I liked about trolls was that the ones I knew appreciated a sardonic sense of humor.

She poured me a second shot of the very dark rum. "Your very entertaining pamphlet and its colorful tales is a rat story, not one of ours. We have our own enemies, and maybe you have met them. But no Wild Hunt like the one you describe rides through troll country."

"I don't see how it could track anything in that maze." I raised the glass to my lips, then set it down without drinking. Could Bee hide in troll town on Hallows' Eve? "Keer, do you think the Wild Hunt only hunts humans? Or have you found a way to protect yourselves against them?"

"They are not the ones who hunt us. Once, long past and beyond telling, my ancestors were almost wiped out.

A few pockets survived in valleys amid the great ice shelves. Now we grow again. But the eye of our older brethren lies upon us, and the unwary are taken."

"Who are your older brethren?"

"I think you rats call them dragons. It is not our word for them."

Now I did drain the second shot glass, and followed it with a chaser of tea to purge the sting from my throat. The printing press wheezed in the workshop out back, and pens scritched in the clerks' office. "Fiery Shemesh! Not even my father knew that!"

"Not even the ancients know every secret that exists in the world," mused Keer. "At the heart of all lie the vast energies which are the animating spirit, if you will, of the worlds. The worlds incline toward disorder. Cold battles with heat. When ice grows, order increases. Where fire triumphs, energies disperse."

"Is the ice alive?"

"An interesting question. The worlds are a maze with many paths. That is all I know."

I considered her odd statement that we were now clutch mates. "Keer, troll town seemed to me like a maze with many paths. I want to call on you as my kinswoman. If I send my cousin to you on Hallows' Night, will you hide her in troll town?"

"I will. And not let her be eaten. Today you did not reach Chartji's aunt."

"I'll have to try another path to reach my husband. Why can you see my sword?"

She cocked her head. "How can any not see it? It is so very shiny."

I clasped her hand in the radical manner, and she showed me her teeth and raised her crest, and I did not know what it meant to her, but it heartened me. The headache had passed. Outside, the sun beat down. Clouds glided like airships on an aloof journey, and who was to say they were not? Perhaps creatures of air lived in the clouds whose existence we had no inkling of.

So many mysteries. And yet I had my own burdens.

I left the law offices and, drawing the shadows around me, walked down the long boulevard along the sleepy waters of the bay to the neighborhood I had too briefly called home. I sought out the compound where Kofi's people hired out carts and wagons. I crept in where I had never been invited, feeling like the worst intruder. There I saw Kayleigh boiling and mangling clothes with young women, laughing and easy with them as she had never been easy with me.

I waited. Midway through the afternoon, Kofi came in with an older man who looked enough like him to be a brother. Kofi greeted Kayleigh with an affectionate wink that made me absolutely wild with envy for the simple pleasure they could take in being together among family that cherished them. But I stalked him as he went into a secondary courtyard where three new rooms were going up beside a shed storing broken wheels. We were alone. I let the shadows fall.

He stepped into the shed and picked up a splintered spoke. "A witch, then. Leave Kayleigh alone. She never harmed yee."

"Whatever you think of me, whatever you believe of me, I ask you to remember I risked my life to find that old man in the boathouse."

"That is surely true," he agreed grudgingly. "For he sake, I shall listen." He waited.

We had gone too far too fast to exchange polite pleasantries. "I wasn't the one who betrayed the radicals at Nance's. I knew nothing about it. The general and his people were using me. I was ignorant of the plan. It's a complicated story."

"The stories yee tell always is. Yee shall understand if I's skeptical."

"Jasmeen is the general's mistress. With my own eyes I saw Jasmeen kiss the general and call him darling. She comes at night for assignations. She's the one who betrayed you."

He whistled softly. "Yee's a meaner bitch than even I thought, weaving a tale like that."

A foot scuffed behind us. Kofi whipped his spar forward as if to charge. Just as I shifted to defend myself, Kayleigh stepped in under the shed's roof. Kofi settled back on his heels.

"Maybe Cat is, but if I were you, Kofi, I would look into it."

"Would yee now, love? After she humiliated yee brother as plain as she could?"

My face burned, but I bit down the words I wanted to shout into his doubting face.

Kayleigh sighed. "Even if Cat betrayed Vai, which seems likely, I think she cares for him. People have more than one face, many parts, contradictory feelings. I don't think she wants him dead. I have a very good idea of where she wants him." Her mouth curled into a smirk.

Kofi lowered the spoke. "The same argument Vai made. He said 'twould take a hells good actress to behave toward a man the way she was behaving the night of the areito. But he wanted it to be true. That don' make it true."

"He wanted it to be true?" I asked, so choked with hope I could barely speak.

"Don' think I shall let yee get yee claws in him, gal. Vai is like me own brother. Get out."

"Wait." Kayleigh took a step closer, hand raised. "We hear yee's living with the general, Cat."

"I live with my cousin, not with the general. She needs me. You may have heard she is soon to be married to Prince Caonabo."

"So we have read," said Kofi. "The radicals shall call for a boycott of the wedding areito. We don' like it that the general had a hand in the raid at Nancc's."

I plied my hook, hoping for a catch. "Are we trading information now? I have some for you. The marriage is the deal the general made with the cacica, in return for her support for his Europan war. He promised her that the spoils of victory in Europa would refill her empty treasury."

Kofi took a step back and caught himself with a muttered curse. "Ma Jupiter! I don' reckon that can be true. An empty treasury!"

"I'm just telling you what I heard. I can bring you more information."

"In exchange for Vai?" he asked, his gaze like a machete's cut.

I reached into the pocket sewn inside my skirt and drew out a copy of the pamphlet. "In exchange for this. Can you get this to him?"

"I think not! Likely yee have mixed yee moon's blood into the ink to further witch Vai."

I winced. "Do people really do that?"

Kayleigh giggled. "You should see your face, Cat."

"I don't think it's funny," I said.

"Kayleigh me gal, don' touch that!" said Kofi.

She took the pamphlet from me and glanced through

it. "I saw this for sale today. It's just stories from Europa. If she mixed her moon's blood into the ink then the printers shall have it all in their press, too." She looked at me. "What do you want?"

"I want to meet him, under a flag of truce."

"Sure yee do," muttered Kofi. "The better to witch him. Or claim the reward for he arrest."

"If I was what you think I am, I could have had you arrested already, Kofi, and Aunty Djeneba and all them. And your associates."

"We's small fry compared to the fire bane and the leadership. That gal Livvy was at the meeting. She is in prison in Warden Hall with she grandfather." He shook his head, mouth a sarcastic line. "And yet yee wonder why I cannot trust yee."

There was no answer to that. Voices and footfalls neared from the main compound.

"I'll return on Jovesday. That gives you two days."

"Jovesday next," he countered. "Nine days is soonest I can manage. If he agree."

"Agreed." Nine days was too long, but it was an offer. I drew the shadows around me.

Kofi sucked in a sharp breath. "Is that common where yee come from, Kayleigh? That ordinary women shall vanish that way? She is a witch."

"Not the kind of witch you mean," said Kayleigh. "My grandmother helped Cat twice. She never would have done had she found Cat to have a wicked soul." With her stare she dared Kofi to contradict her, but he wisely kept his mouth shut. "Get the message to Vai."

"I shall, because yee ask it. But yee's wrong about that gal."

"My grandmother was not wrong!"

I crept out past a file of men coming to build on the half-finished rooms.

That night I went early to bed and slept hard. Bee came in late, and she dreamed, because at dawn before I even completed my yawn, she grabbed her sketchbook and drew with such focus and speed that I watched in awe. She filled two facing pages with a landscape of such splendor and detail that we might have been looking through a window: a calm lake surrounded by slender birch and sleepy pine, the flat landscape rimmed with a thin carpet of snow; a rowboat tied to a rickety little pier; mist wreathing a wooded island. An indistinct figure stood on the pier.

She threw pencil and sketchbook onto the bed with a sigh of relief and scrambled up. "All right, now I can pee."

I examined the sketch as she hurried behind the screen to the chamber pot and then back out to pour water from a pitcher into the copper basin. "Too much wine at last night's dinner? What glittering notables did you associate with?"

She washed hands and face. "The professora was back last night. She asked after you again. Something about a story she wants to tell you about Uncle Daniel."

I turned the page, but the next sheet was blank. "I want to hear it. She must be at the university. Bee." She patted her face dry and looked at me, caught by my tone. "Bee, promise me. On Hallows' Night, go to the law offices and ask for Keer. The maze that is troll town will hide you."

She examined me, her gaze guileless and pure. "If you say so, I'll do it. But I wonder how you can be sure."

"Nothing is sure. But there are only twenty-nine days left until Hallows' Night. I don't know what the Taino can actually do. So right now, I think the troll town maze is the best chance you have."

31

The week dragged past, for all I could do was wonder if Vai would meet with me and if the troll town maze could save Bee. If all else failed I would offer up Drake, but I wasn't sure my sire would take him. I found a measure of peace by preparing a distillation of Daniel's extensive notes on the legal congress presided over by Camjiata. Daniel had been a knowledgeable and astute student of the law, careful to note how the new legal code improved the condition of the general populace of Europa, and the ways it imposed restrictions.

On Mercuriday, the day before Jovesday, I stayed at the fencing hall after Bee had to leave for her language and protocol lessons. The fencing master had to scold me twice for too aggressively pushing in on an opponent, but the exercise calmed my foul mood.

I met Professora Alhamrai at the front door as she was coming down and I was going up.

"Peace to you," I said by way of greeting. "Have you been in conference with the general?"

"He is out. In fact, I came to see you." She fanned herself with a copy of my pamphlet. "I thought to invite you and your cousin to dine with me this afternoon. I would

enjoy discussing your monograph. You may be interested
in hearing about my meeting with your father."

"I would be honored and delighted," I said. It might
also help the weary day pass.

"Gaius Sanogo will escort you. He knows how to reach
my house."

Visions of cells buried beneath Warden Hall bloomed
in my mind's eye. "The commissioner?"

She chuckled. "He will not be arresting you. He particularly enjoys showing up at this door to remind General
Camjiata that the general does not rule in Expedition."

I smiled. "Very well, then."

When Bee returned in mid-afternoon, she proved more
skeptical. "The general is out all day at a military exercise
with the new recruits. I wonder if Sanogo knows that?"

"Why do you ask me questions to which you already
know the answer?"

She tapped me on the arm with her painted fan. "To
annoy you, dearest."

We dressed in bright pagnes and matching blouses,
me with my hair braided back and Bee with her curls
partly covered by a yellow scarf that complemented
her sea-struck blue-and-green pagne with its schools
of stylized fish. We might have been any two local
gals walking with a pleasant uncle through the late afternoon heat, except, of course, that we weren't. We
conversed amiably on neutral subjects like batey, batey,
batey, and batey. Sanogo did not ask about the cacica's
imminent arrival at the border or the great areito by
which the Taino queen would celebrate her son's marriage to a humble Kena'ani girl of no particular lineage
or wealth. Maybe he had spies in Taino country tracking
the progress of the cacica and her entourage. Maybe he

had spies in the general's household. Maybe this was just a social visit.

We crossed the harbor in a boat rowed by four silent men. The water was so greasy it was opaque. Bits of rubbish fetched up against the prow as we passed boats and ships tied to moorings. The university lay across the harbor on an artificial island, a vast stone plaza rising from the muddy brown shallows and further reinforced by stone walls. There was only one water gate by which boats could approach, and we waited in line to put in under an archway fitted with a portcullis drawn up and secured by chains. After passing under the archway, we pulled up at a stone pier under the watchful eye of friendly uniformed watchman smiling the way folk do when they know they have the right to bash your head in if you so much as look at them in a way they decide to take offense at.

"Commissioner, no need to ask yee errand. Who is these two pretty gals?"

"Nieces of Professora Habibah ibnah Alhamrai."

They laughed as at a good joke but let us disembark and pass down the pier to a second gate, also manned by watchmen, who waved us through. Beyond the gate lay a public square paved in stone and inhabited by young men napping in the shade of trees.

"This is more like a fortress than an institution of learning," said Bee. "Who is the university protecting themselves against?"

Sanogo smiled his most pleasant smile. "The Council. By a decree passed fifty years ago, the Council cannot interfere with the university. The university guards its independence."

Dusk swirled down over us with a smattering of rain as lamplighters made their rounds. Cobo-hooded gas lamps lit the street at mathematical intervals gauged to provide maximum coverage. As in the old city, the buildings were packed together. We turned out of the built-up portion and onto a tongue of land appointed by fenced gardens and isolated workshop compounds.

A sudden *pop* shuddered the air. Sparks spun skyward. We turned down a dirt path toward the compound the sparks had come from. Overhead, half the sky ran gray with cloud and the other half shaded toward night, stars breaking through. The sea sighed beyond the breakwater. Sanogo indicated an open gate in a whitewashed wall that surrounded four long roofs.

The professora greeted us with a kiss on the cheek. "Peace to you. Come in. Come in."

The courtyard was a verdant garden of fruit trees, flowering shrubs, and a spectacular latticed patio under a trellis that supported a sprawl of hibiscus. The scent of flowers drenched us, but that was not all I smelled.

"What are you cooking?" I asked, licking my lips as if I could lick the flavor of lamb, garlic, sweet potato, mango, and a stew of fine spices as a savor over all. "That smells amazing!"

She led us to a table illuminated by hanging lamps. "Tagines."

"Habibi's specialty," said Sanogo.

Bee waggled her eyebrows suggestively as if to say, "How does *he* know, do you suppose?"

"Do sit." Professora Alhamrai indicated the table, set with an embroidered tablecloth and serviceable ceramic plates of a red clay glazed with brown starbursts.

"Why are there five place settings?" asked Bee.

"Will you help me with the platters, Beatrice?" she asked. "The kitchen is this way."

Bee looked at me, but I shrugged, so she followed the professora. I had of course brought my cane. The sword's ghostly hilt had flowered with the dusk, and it pulsed, tasting magic. I looked up at the pair of glowing lamps and their twisting, flickering flame. Yet there was not a breath of wind. Nor did the lamps hiss.

"Really, 'tis impossible to tell, if yee don' already know," said Sanogo, sitting on one of the benches. He pointed down a brick path laid through a gap in a hedge. "Past the bellyache bush, yee might find somewhat of interest."

My heart had begun to gallop like a reckless horse bearing for home on a storm-wracked night. "Why am I always the last to know or guess?"

"A rhetorical question, I assume. I shall pour the wine. Don' feel yee must hurry back."

Vestiges of daylight clung to the western sky. Far in the distance niggled the *clug* and *clut* of factory machines that, with gaslight, could run all night. Closer, smoke puffed lazily up from one of the buildings within the compound.

Past the hedge the path speared through columns of dwarf fruit trees trimmed into spheres and rectangles; it emerged like the mouth of a stream onto a brick pavement fronting a long whitewashed one-story building. Once, I thought, this wing had served as the living quarters of an extended family, each wife or widow or adult sister with her own room, her own bed, and her own children. Between each pair of doors stood a bench set against the wall. A thick vine had over the years been coaxed along the eaves, and falls of purple flowers adorned the expanse. I stared at a bench and wall and flowers just like the sketch I had seen in Bee's sketchbook. Seeing it, I grew flushed, and then I grew cold, for the workings of a deeper force had spun this moment into being. Not the bench or the building, built by ordinary means, but the energy or will that had directed Bee's hand. This was a meeting place. Or would have been, had the bench not sat empty between two closed doors.

However, there was another bench. On it sat a male figure wearing a dash jacket perfectly tailored to his well-proportioned frame. Eyes shut, he had his head tilted back to rest on the wall, one hand curled lightly on his lap and the other tapping a rhythm on a thigh. A folded paper with a broken wax seal rested on the bench beside him.

I sat at the opposite end of the bench, my heart as fragile as a trembling songbird cupped in sheltering hands.

"Ah," he said, without opening his eyes. "My tormenter."

No, after all, my heart was not a trembling songbird but a hissing, outraged goose in full rampage.

"What puzzles me is how a man willing to spend weeks courting a woman to convince her that she was really in love with him, or could be in love with him if she would just set aside her perfectly reasonable and pragmatical concerns about being in all essentials *owned* by a mage House..." I had to pause to take a breath and sort out my line of argument. "What puzzles me, is how he could spend weeks—*weeks!*—entrenching his plans and carrying out his campaign, and then in one instant be willing to think the worst of her without making any effort to let her explain."

His drumming fingers stilled. "Was I to doubt the evidence of my eyes?"

"Am I meant to conduct my entire explanation in questions?"

"Can you do so?"

"Do you actually think I'm lying about the questions?"

"Can I know what to believe?"

"Did you read my pamphlet? Get my message?"

"Would you be sitting here if I hadn't?"

"You arranged this?"

"Who do you suppose sent Professora Alhamrai to the general's household in the first place over three weeks ago to see how a certain... person was doing?"

"Wouldn't the esteemed professora be capable of sending herself?"

"Do you think she would have thought of you at all? Do you think you are the first person on everyone's mind?"

I opened my mouth, and shut it. The hammering of my heart eased from an erratic cacophony to a mere pounding but no-less-irritated clamor. "Might some vain young man's pride have been hurt?"

"Why would a person trust a person who had lied to him?"

"Why do you think I lied?"

His eyes opened as his head raised. "Was the appearance of the general, his fire mage, and your cousin not reason enough? Not to mention the wardens?"

"What if a lost young woman had had no inkling of any machinations behind her abandonment on the jetty and was as surprised as anyone at the appearance of the general, his fire mage, and her cousin? Not to mention the wardens?"

He cut me a dagger-like glance from his lovely eyes. "Am I meant to believe anyone could be that naïve?"

"Do you suppose I guessed this dinner was arranged by you?"

His brow furrowed in a way that suggested he was calculating my likely ability to be that naïve.

I had had enough. "Is this meant to impress me with your cleverness, Andevai? Wasn't it bad enough when you insinuated in that unpleasant way that I might have had other lovers besides Drake? Do you really think I'm pretending about the questions? Do you think I *like* having to answer questions with questions all the time? *Do you?*"

He exhaled as he pressed a hand to his forehead. "No, you're right. My apologies."

The sudden way he shifted ground took me entirely by surprise. I looked down at the fists I had made of my hands, let out a breath, and opened them.

"Please let me say what I have been thinking about for days, hoping to have a chance to say to you. I want to tell you the things I should have told you when you asked on the night of the areito. I did know Drake was associated with the general. I did know the general was in the law offices of Godwik and Clutch in Adurnam that morning you came to meet with Chartji. But Bee and I were not there to meet him. We would never have gone to the law offices had we known the most notorious man in Europa would arrive there right after we did. We went to the law offices to see if we could get work with the radicals."

"That would be the enchanting Brennan Du," he muttered, hands back to tapping on his thighs.

"It's sweet when you're jealous."

His lips pinched together.

I fought down an urge to jab a little deeper into that soft spot. "We left the law offices *because* the general was there. You know what happened after that. Bee and I slipped through the well and...and then I washed up on Salt Island. A salter bit me. Drake found me."

"You left out the shark."

"The shark attacked before the salter bit me."

"You traveled straight from the spirit world into the Sea of Antilles."

"Yes! But it was the Barr Cousins who rescued us, right off the beach, which I have to admit was very adventurous and ever so exciting...Was that a smile?"

"No." He looked away so I couldn't see his face.

But it had been a tiny bit of a smile.

"I knew nothing about the plot until after the raid. I didn't know the general was in the Antilles until Drake told me. I didn't know Bee was with the general until I saw her at Nance's that night. Camjiata used her dreams to find me on Salt Island. He worked out the whole scheme of rescuing me and dropping me on the jetty as a way to flush you out of hiding. But I didn't know that's why I had been dumped there. I didn't even know you were in Expedition. Yet there you were, at the carpentry yard. And you wore me down. And they sprang their trap."

He whipped around to face me. "I wore you down? Weeks of patient courtship of a woman I can after all already call my wife, and that is how you think of it? That I *wore you down*?"

He pushed to his feet to storm off but I grabbed his wrist and tugged. He was not quite up and not quite stable, so he sat back down hard.

"Am I not flattering you enough?" I was, as the poets said, incandescent with fury, or would have been, if I had not been sitting next to an angry cold mage. "Are you even listening to me?"

An explosion like a fusillade of gunfire shook every building in the compound. Vai leaped to his feet. I ran after him as he cut through an archway in the back of the courtyard and into a cobblestoned side yard that ran alongside a warehouse with shattered windows. At first I thought the explosion had blown them out, but I had heard no breaking glass. Although what glass remained in the windows had jagged edges, none littered the ground; it was cleanly swept. Then my mouth went dry, for I saw flames inside the building and heard whistling in tones of the greatest agitation.

Vai flung open a door and plunged in, undoing the top five buttons of the jacket as if he meant to strip off the fine garment before it could be ruined by smoke and ash. The tang of burning made my eyes water. A line of flames hissed down the center of the open space. Smoke billowed from a tabletop. A troll was bent over the table poking at something and apparently oblivious to the fire burning an arm's length from the hem of its sober gray-and-black dash jacket and the tip of its thick tail. A second troll emerged from a cloud of ashy soot with a glass tube pinned in its talons. Seeing me and Vai, it whistled what sounded like mellifluous birdsong.

Then, with a jolting flash of teeth, it spoke. "No, not toward us. Away."

Vai jerked a chain from beneath his jacket and ran to the table. I spotted a line of buckets at the wall, some filled with dust and others with water. I grabbed one with water and placed myself at the far end of the line of fire, swinging the bucket back to get the best spray.

Vai had turned at the opposite end of the line of flames, holding a ring within the circle of his thumb and forefin-

ger. The two trolls were bent over the table. Gaius Sanogo
and the professora appeared at the door.

Vai shouted, "Cat, no!"

The professora cried, "Not water!"

The water splashed down, and the flames flashed huge.
Heat slapped into me. I stumbled back; the hammer of
Vai's cold magic slammed me to the floor as my sword
pulsed. The fireball vanished as if pulled into an unseen
pocket. A dusting of snow swirled and faded.

Gaius Sanogo reached me first. "Is yee all right?"

My lips were dry and my eyes wept a few stinging
tears, but nothing seemed broken. "I think so."

Vai pushed past him and knelt to rest a hand on my
cheek. "Catherine! Speak to me!"

I fluttered my eyelids, and pressed a hand to my forehead in the hope I appeared wan and fragile. "I...I think
I...don't feel well. Are you worried about me?"

He recoiled. "I would be, if you seemed at all hurt,
which you do not." He rose, running a hand over his head.
"You ruined their experiment," he added, then strode to
the door, where he stopped dead.

Bee blocked it. "Blessed Tanit! Cat, are you hurt?" Her
gaze axed him. She spoke in a caustic tone that would
surely have burned out anyone else's tongue had they attempted it. "Magister, did you do this to her?"

"*Me?* I am the one she refuses to trust! The one she
keeps crucial information from! The one she doesn't respect—!"

"Stop that," said one of the trolls.

Looking startled, he broke off.

"Yee have killed the combustion."

In the silence following this unexpected declaration, I
let the warden help me to my feet.

"Proud young men is prone to nursing wounded feelings," Sanogo observed softly, "as I know from me own experience as one of that very type."

My pagne needed brushing off and straightening, because I dared not meet the warden's gaze. The professora ventured to the table as the first troll rose out of the smoking cloud, crest raised, its feathers smeared with soot and ash. Its old-fashioned knee-length dash jacket was not, I realized, of a gray-and-black splotchy pattern; it was layered with the detritus of countless experiments.

"The ice lens focused the first undulation away," said the troll in a tone I had to perceive as excitement. "That is not what killed this combustion, then. Emotion must also focus and amplify the effect. Or is it only anger? What think yee, Bibi?" It cocked its head, addressing the professora. The tip of its tail lashed twice and stilled.

"He seem unusually high-strung, though," murmured Sanogo. "He would make an ineffective conspirator, but he surely is a cursed impressive fire bane."

"Why haven't you arrested him?" I asked.

He took my hand in an avuncular way. "Maestressa, yee already know everything about me that I can tell yee at this time."

"You can't even tell me who you support?"

With a wink, he released my hand as the professora came up. "The Anolis."

I pounced. "If the Anolis lose Jonas Bonsu, they shall never win the Territory Cup."

The professora appeared beside us to take my arm. "How long have you lived here, gal? They that support the Anolis are radicals. That is why no matter how much the Greens offer Jonas Bonsu, he shall never leave the Anolis. Shall we go to our supper? We need two more

settings, for my associates have had their experiment ter-
minated for the night and will be dining with us after all."

"What happened with the water?"

"Certain chemicals react explosively with water.
Rather like young men who feel they have lost face in
public in front of people whose respect they wish to
have."

"Oh."

At the door, only Bee and her gloating remained. She
said, "He stormed off. Gracious Melqart, Cat, but that
man has a high opinion of his own consequence. Still, it's
clear he's madly in love with you. So if you want him—"

"I really do not wish to discuss this right now, Bee."
Embarrassment had singed me more than flames could.

"You're not hurt, are you?" she asked more solicitously.

"Weren't we talking about batey?" I said to the universe at large.

We had no sooner reached the archway than Vai appeared with the letter in hand. "If I might... your pardon,
Professora... we shall be right there..."

With a look like that, fixed on me, I knew we had to
have it out now. I did not look at the others as the professora released me. Sure that this would end badly, I strode
over to the bench and sat down at one end. He sat at the
other end. The talking of the others faded as they walked
past the hedge and the fruit trees toward the dining patio.

He extended the folded paper, which was clearly a letter. "I read your pamphlet."

I said nothing, for it was obvious Bee, the professora,
and the warden were right. Vai was as in love with me as
ever. And he looked pretty angry about it.

Whistling and clicking, the trolls strode out of the

archway and off along the path, so quaintly oblivious that I realized they were not politely ignoring us.

Still holding the letter, Vai went on in a carefully level voice. "You wrote the pamphlet in the hope I would read it and draw conclusions from the way you strung together the village tales and anecdotes. You have no other way to communicate with me about matters pertaining to the spirit world because of the binding on your tongue."

A weight cold and grim seized my limbs, but I managed one word. "Yes."

"You're not a mage, yet you conceal yourself as if by magic. My uncle said you have the same human flesh and blood as I do but that the spirit world is knit into your blood and bone. The djeli you and I met in the spirit world said you have a spirit mantle close against your flesh."

Ice prickled along my skin, but I did not think Vai was the cause of it. "Yes."

"As impossible as it sounds, it seems likely your sire is a creature of the spirit world who had sexual congress with your mother while he was in the form of a human man. Considering your ability to cross into the spirit world at any time and be blooded by cold steel without dying, it seems the only explanation."

A strange thick clotting swelled to seal my throat. I could not speak, but I held his gaze.

He scooted partway down the bench and tapped my arm with the letter. "The problem, Cat, is that you do not trust me. If you had bothered to write out something when you first arrived in Expedition, I could have worked it out then. If you had told me everything about James Drake, the general, and the Adurnam radicals, this whole situation would have been averted. The radicals could have escaped the raid, and people would not be in prison. You would not have put Aunty Djeneba and her household in danger. Kofi wouldn't have felt obliged to marry Kayleigh—"

"They were courting already!"

"They were flirts. He liked her. She admired him. They married for my sake."

"Everything is not about you! Maybe they were looking for an excuse and this was it. I saw them together. They looked happy to me."

"I looked happy once. For about one hour."

"Spare me your self-pity. That is the one thing I cannot endure from you." I snatched the letter out of his hand and unfolded it, squinting to pull the neatly formed letters out of the darkness. A glow winked to life at my shoulder to aid my reading.

"It's from Chartji," I said, more in breath than in word. In dense legal detail that quoted obscure ancient bardic sources, the letter explained how to dissolve a chained marriage. The head of the poet Bran Cof had declared it more succinctly: *"Has the young man had sex with you yet?"*

Vai had descended to pure incendiary disdain. "'A year and a day.' You said those words to me the night of the batey riot, although of course I couldn't know what you meant at the time. You knew all this time, but you didn't tell me. And yet I am the other person bound into this marriage. You didn't respect me enough to trust me, not even about that."

How I hated my sire.

Crossing his arms, he looked away, toward the hedge. "A marriage chained by magic. Your tongue bound by the night court. It even makes sense that perhaps you couldn't speak of the chained marriage. The two bindings are related if only because they both are chained by magic drawn out of the spirit world. But it wasn't only the marriage and the spirit world you didn't tell me. It was everything. How can we walk a path together if you do not respect me enough to tell me the things we both need to know? The things that mean we are partners?"

A mist mizzled through, not even enough to wet the brick pavement.

He had not buttoned up his jacket, and the flat collar parted to reveal the curve of his throat. I wanted to press my lips just there, where I could inhale his pulse.

"I don't know what your plan was, Catherine, or if you even had a plan. Maybe you meant to wait until the year and a day was up. Maybe you changed your mind that night at the areito. I can't know what the truth is when you never offered me truth or trust."

"Please stop, Vai," I whispered, for Bee was wrong. I wasn't heartless.

Softly, he said, "But I have lasted this long. I can last another nineteen days. Then the year and a day is up, and our chained marriage will dissolve."

My cheeks felt the sting of the flames that had not quite touched me in the workshop.

It was so hard to speak that my voice came out as a husky whisper. "Growing up in the Hassi Barahal household, I was taught to keep silence. About anything and everything, really. It's the only thing I remember my mother telling me."

He uncrossed his arms and shifted back to gaze at me, waiting. Cautious. Reserved. But he had not closed me off yet, for I would know it when he did.

"'Tell no one, not ever.' The words I grew up by."

The widening of his eyes was so brief I would have missed it if I was not staring at him as if his expression held every truth that mattered.

My voice gained strength with surety. "You're right, Vai. I didn't trust you, not the way I should have. So I said nothing except what I thought I had to, to pay my way and tell my story. But I should have told you. And I'm sorry for it. I'm especially sorry for it if it made you think I don't respect you. Because it was wrong."

The sounds of conversation and laughter drifted from the patio. Night eased the heat just a little, and the breeze lifted the intoxicating scent of night-blooming jasmine.

"That's the first time I've understood why you say things the way you say them," he said in so low a voice it might have been the wind muttering over the roofs. He looked toward the clipped hedge of bellyache bush as might a man surprised to see secrets woven into the branches. "Being cruel while being clever was how I learned to endure Four Moons House. Before I could crush them all, that is. But it was wrong to do it to you tonight. I just..." He shook his head impatiently, still not looking at me. "The truth is, I suppose I wanted to know I could hurt you as badly as I felt hurt. And yet I'm the one who thought for one awful day that I had to kill you. I'm sorry, Catherine."

My tongue was lead, but I got it to work. "Thank you for saying it. As for the mansa commanding you to kill me, when I said before I forgave you for that, I meant it."

We sat in awkward silence.

I had to ask. "Vai, what would happen to you if our marriage dissolved? Would the mansa know? Or could you keep it a secret?"

"The mansa would know because the djeli who

chained our marriage would know, and would send him word."

"What would the mansa do? Would he be very angry?"

"Angry?" He glanced at me and quickly away. "No. More likely he'd be relieved. Before I was sent to marry you, he'd had at least ten advantageous offers to marry me. They might look down on me, but no one can ignore what I am. So I'm accounted a valuable catch for mage House women both inside and outside Four Moons House."

"Is such an advantageous marriage...what you would want?"

That other face, the face of the arrogant magister, settled on his features: proud, aloof, and cold. But his voice remained absolutely level. "The mansa won't consult me. He'll seal whatever alliance he wishes in my name and then inform me afterward to whom I am now married. You should know that, Catherine."

"Oh." I did not know what else to say, and maybe neither did he.

He rose. "I was taught never to insult a woman by refusing to eat the meal she had cooked. We should join them at the table."

I folded the letter and handed it to him. He tossed it carelessly on the bench, as if he cared not if a rainstorm pounded it into so much pulp. We walked to the dining patio where the others were already digging into bowls whose contents smelled so delectable my mouth watered. Never let it be said I could not eat. The professora had left a place for me beside Gaius Sanogo and one for Vai opposite, between the two trolls. They were brother and sister, Chartji's aunt and uncle by some arcane measure of kinship I did not understand. Mostly they remembered to speak human language but then they would forget and ascend into flights of trollish that were intriguing to listen to but quite meaningless, lacking words as I knew them. When they remembered to speak human words, they and the professora debated the properties of heat, whether heat was dynamical or undulating, and Bee asked them questions. I ascertained that the caloric theory of heat had been discredited. Vai picked at his food, scarcely touched his wine, and replied with scrupulous courtesy when spoken to.

I, on the other hand, launched into a jocular evisceration of the prospects of the Anolis in the upcoming cup that got the warden laughing even as he vociferously defended his team.

Bee said, "I'd be curious to know where you learned all this about batey, Cat."

Vai glanced at me as if to warn me that to speak of waiting tables might condemn Aunty Djeneba. After all, Sanogo had told me the wardens had never known where I was.

"Batey and politics is all anyone talks about in this city. Might I have another helping, Professora? It's absolutely delicious."

No cook can resist an enthusiastic eater. The way to a cook's heart seemed simple.

She smiled. "I was going to tell you about meeting Daniel Hassi Barahal. It was in Qart Hadast, of all places. I was very young, in my first year at the university."

"You're not Kena'ani."

"I am from the Naqab Desert. But I chose to study in Qart Hadast because of my interest in chemistry. And because they admitted women. And because I had family there, so my parents allowed me to travel so far since I could live with cousins. Your father had beautiful eyes, and hair just like Beatrice, those thick black curls. In fact, Beatrice looks something like him. I suppose you must resemble your mother."

Vai looked at me, then away.

"So people who knew them both say," I said. "I never knew my father went to Qart Hadast. Not all his journals survived. What was he doing there?"

"He had come to see a well-known scholar who at that time was involved in an early attempt to construct a navigable balloon that could cross open water."

"He must already have been planning for the First Baltic Ice Expedition," I said as I leaned forward, trembling. "Go on, please."

Vai's gaze drifted to me, its pressure both bitter and so very sweet.

"I was able to attach myself to a group of students and researchers who went to the caupona for the evening's drinking and meal. At the end of the evening one of the women students made it clear he could share her bed that night. He said he was flattered and honored but he could not. I shall never forget what he said, for I admit in my experience"—here she glanced at the warden with an amused smile, which he answered with an ironic twist to his lips—"it is not a common refrain from the lips of men. He said he had contracted a secret engagement with an Amazon in the army of General Camjiata, and that as long as she must remain celibate so he had pledged likewise. I thought it admirable, which is why I recall him so well."

"Thank you," I muttered, blinking back tears. My gaze strayed to Vai, who was still watching me. "I do believe he loved my mother very much. And she him."

After a moment, we both looked away.

The warden rose. "Alas, my friends, it is late and I have to report to work at dawn. If the maestressas will accompany me, I will escort them home."

I made polite farewells to the trolls and an exceedingly formal goodbye to Vai and walked to the gate with Bee and Sanogo and the professora.

There I stopped. "I'm not coming with you."

Bee examined me as if to make sure I was really her Cat. At length, she kissed me. "Good fortune to you, dearest." She led the warden away, chatting merrily about her sea voyage in a way that made her life-threatening seasickness seem like the running joke in a comedic spectacle.

"You can go around the back way by that path there," said the professora in a matter-of-fact manner that made me grateful, for I was so nervous it seemed impossible to speak one more word.

I cut through the night-shadowed garden and turned each latch until I found the chamber with the bed. There were also shelves, a chest, and a tiny altar with a wreath of fresh flowers and a sard stone on a platter. In the unlit room, I sat on the bed he had built for us. It seemed sturdy.

Mice had made a nest in the eaves, their cozy scrabbling punctuated by the rattling of leaves heard when the wind gusted. His footfalls neared, and halted at the door. I sucked in a nervous breath.

He opened the door. Cold fire ghosted along the backs of his hands like phosphorous. He had the same expression as on the evening I had first seen him, coming up the stairs of my aunt's and uncle's house, but I knew better now how to interpret it. He had been stricken by hope on a night he had expected only an unpleasant and soul-wearying duty. And yet, fearing more of the mockery and condescension he had endured in his seven years at Four Moons House, he had chosen to confront the encounter behind a screen of arrogance.

I spoke before he could. "Vai, the year turns. Hallows' Night comes."

He closed the door. "Beatrice! How could I have not thought of that! She walks the dreams of dragons. The Wild Hunt will come for her."

"Dismembered and her head thrown into a well."

"You want to protect her."

"I can save her."

He sat down next to me, as one might who must utter terrible news to a listener innocent of a heartbreaking truth. "Catherine, even the mansa is not powerful enough to drive off the Wild Hunt. Even with the ice lens to amplify the energy, it's hard to see how it could be done."

"What is an ice lens?"

Drawing out the chain, he showed me a metal ring whose diameter was no greater than the length of my thumb. At first I thought it was empty, but by the light of cold fire it gleamed. When I ventured to touch it, and he nodded to indicate I could, its slick surface chilled my skin.

Startled, I drew back my hand. "It's actually ice! How can they even have ice here?"

"Professora Alhamrai has devised a cunningly engineered cold room. A kind of an icehouse, created with coils that condense vapors."

"What does the lens do?"

"Cold magic is weak here. A lens focuses and amplifies the magic. It has to be made out of ice because other substances like a lens ground of glass don't absorb or transfer the magic. I can keep it cool for a while against my skin."

"That's what you've been doing with the Jovesday trolls."

"The Jovesday...? Ah. Yes." He slipped the chain back under his jacket.

My hands twitched, wishing to trace its path down his chest. "That's how you froze that wave and saved me during the hurricane."

"Yes. Otherwise I couldn't have done it. Not here in the Antilles." He caught my hands in his. "What possessed you to climb into that boat? Trap yourself, knowing the flood was coming?"

"Should I have left that man to die?"

His fingers stroked mine. "No, of course you would never. Give me a moment to work this through. The Wild Hunt will ride on Hallows' Night. You fear they will track down and kill Beatrice. The Hunt must shed blood to be put to rest. I trust you do not mean to sacrifice yourself."

I shook my head. The touch of his hands made me ache.

"It's likely you are not of interest to the Wild Hunt. I can't think of any reasons you would threaten them as dragon dreamers or powerful mages do."

I tried to speak but only an exhalation came out.

"I trust you are not planning to throw me into their path," he added.

"That's not amusing!"

He considered more narrowly. "We'd be well rid of that fire mage. He's very powerful."

"He is? I'm amazed to hear you say it."

"I'm amazed he hasn't burned himself up yet. The only

thing stopping him from torching this whole city is the fact, unfortunate only for him, that he would die."

For the first time, it occurred to me to wonder what it would be like to hold so much power and know you could never use it. To know it could kill you at any moment. "If cold mages are fire banes, then couldn't a cold mage act as a catch-fire for a fire mage? By extinguishing the fire?"

"Catch-fires don't extinguish fires. As far as I can tell, they take the fire into them. Or I should more properly say, the backwash of fire magic floods into them instead of into the mage."

I remembered the way Drake's fire had limned the skin of the dying man at the inn. As the backlash of his fire magic had consumed the dying man, Drake had healed one who could live. "I just thought if a cold mage could act as a catch-fire, that maybe working in concert with a fire mage they might be powerful enough to...to..."

He pressed a finger to my lips.

"To defy the Wild Hunt and save your cousin." By no means did he look astonished. "There you have the real question, Catherine. What purpose does the Wild Hunt serve? Everyone is taught that the Hunt gathers the souls of those who will die in the coming year. A few people know it also hunts down and kills the women who walk the dreams of dragons. But only mages know that any mage who becomes too powerful will be killed by the Hunt. Why would the courts fear us? Do they fear what we might discover? Or what we might become?"

I could not resist gently biting his finger. That was a kind of question, wasn't it? What might he and I become?

He inhaled sharply, but he did not otherwise move.

I had him now.

I released his finger, and he splayed his hand across my

cheek. His touch was firm, promising strength, but also precise in being a question rather than a claim.

"Tell me what you want, Catherine. For the worst of it has been wondering if you really meant the way you looked at me, the words you said, on the night of the areito."

I studied the planes of his face and the precise stubble of his beard. How much time had he taken this afternoon in shaving, trimming, washing, and dressing, knowing I was coming? I considered his eyes, so dark a brown they seemed black, and his lips so full and inviting. Ought a man be allowed to be so handsome? How was a gal to think in the face of such looks?

I put a hand on each shoulder. The damask weave of his dash jacket caressed my palms.

"I want this chain off my tongue, Vai. Just as you want the chains off your village, just as Bee wants to live. I want not to live at the mercy of Four Moons House, or a prince's militia, or the general's schemes. Surely it's the same thing most people want. Health and vigor. A refuge which is not a cage but those who care for us and whom we care for. Like Luce's giggle. Aunt Tilly's smile. Rory's loyalty. Bee's happiness. *You.*"

I pushed him onto the bed and pinned him there with my body stretched atop the length of his. His was a fine body to borrow as a mattress, not one bit soft. He lay beneath me, his dark gaze steady. I drew my fingers down his throat, then spread my hand so fingers and thumb spanned his collarbone, for his jacket was unbuttoned just that far. To measure my skin against his in so simple a way made me almost dizzy. Really, it was provoking how quiet the man could be.

"Vai, I made my choice the night of the areito. I can't

walk free and leave you behind. So I choose the path I walk with you, whatever it brings. Anyhow, I'm not going to let some mage House woman steal you from me."

I brushed my mouth over his. His eyes fluttered as his lips parted and chin lifted to receive a full kiss. But I drew back and slowly counted down the buttons until I got to the sixth. He watched me, not quite smiling. If anything, he looked a bit dazed.

"I've changed my mind," I said as I unbuttoned the sixth and slid my fingers to the seventh. "I am going to take off"—the eighth and the ninth slipped free—"this beautiful jacket... Unless by that quiver of your eyebrows you mean to indicate there is something you want to say first."

"Yes," he said, in quite the hoarsest voice I had ever heard out of him.

"Gracious Melqart, Vai, how many buttons does this garment have?"

He breathed, if you could call that breathing when in fact it sounded more as if he had been running most of the way across Expedition.

"Fourteen?" I demanded as I sat back to undo the last buttons. I spread the jacket to either side to expose not a vest and linen shirt beneath or even a singlet, as I had expected, but only bare chest. "Oh," I said, intelligently. "*Well.* Let me not pretend I haven't been thinking about doing this."

I explored the muscled curve of his shoulders, fondled the necklace chain and, briefly, his nipples, and stroked along the contours of his chest. My hands halted at the line of buttons that fastened the waistband of his trousers. At which point, stricken by the first onslaught of shyness I had ever experienced in my entire life, I lost my voice.

He found his. "If I had stayed in the village, my grandmother would have found a hard-working, placid, quiet young woman for me. I would have married her without expectation of anything except a hard-working, placid, quiet affection that might have arisen after years of going on together. Everyone knows that is the best way. The one least disruptive to the harmonious peace of the community. Not to mention a man's peace of mind."

I bit back a smile and, instead, drew down my brows to indicate vexed consideration. "Is there a point to this pedantic speech? As you know, I'm very hard-working."

He slid his hands caressingly up my hips, and by the tensing of his arms and back, my Barahal training and cat's instincts warned me he was about to attempt an abrupt reversal.

"I don't think you should try that, Vai," I murmured, bracing myself.

"But are you truly hard-working, Catherine? I suppose we're about to find out."

32

I woke at dawn with birds singing and the scent of flowers wafting in through the open shutters, which seemed a little much even considering my euphoric mood. Lying tucked in against him, my head resting on his shoulder, felt the most natural thing in the world. In case he was still asleep, I whispered.

"Vai?"

"Mmm."

"I had *no idea*."

Eyes shut, he smiled in a drowsy, contented way. "Of course you couldn't have had. You weren't with me."

Silence allowed me to contemplate this astonishing statement for a while, during which I stroked my fingers up and down his admirable chest.

"Vai?"

"Mmm?"

"Are you really that conceited? Or are you having a bit of a joke with yourself at times?"

"Catherine, I promise you, no one will ever make you feel as good as I will."

"As the djeli said, 'Men act humble until they get what they want.' Although obviously the djeli who said that hadn't met you. Anyway, wouldn't a person of scientific inclination say that to verify such a statement I would need to make a significant number of comparative tests with other subjects?"

His eyes opened as at a shot. "No!"

"Then I could never actually know."

He pushed up onto one elbow, dislodging my head from its pleasant resting place, and brushed hair from my cheek. "You can't possibly have any complaints."

"But I do."

His hand stilled. "Name one."

"You're talking."

He smiled and bent to kiss me.

Things were proceeding in just the way I had planned when a series of hollow pops rattled the roof. He released me and rolled off the bed.

"Do you need me?" I asked as he quickly dressed in a pair of faded and clumsily mended workman's trousers and a singlet he pulled off a shelf.

"Of course I need you, Catherine, but not in that workshop. You were fortunate yesterday. They're obsessed with my ability to kill combustion. They keep lighting different combinations of things on fire and adjusting me for distance, angle, and substances placed between me and the fire. Eventually they're going to burn the whole place down."

He went out the door so fast he forgot to close it behind him. I used a foot to hook my pagne off the floor and tied it just above my breasts the way we women had at Aunty Djeneba's when we went down to shower, the cloth covering me from armpits to knees. I stuck my head out the door, but the little courtyard was deserted since the professora slept on the other side of the compound and all the other rooms in this wing were empty.

I hurried to the outhouse set out from the compound's outer wall, which Vai had shown me in the middle of the night. Built into the wall was a washroom furnished with a brass tub, and a sideboard on which sat a copper basin, three pitchers, and threadbare pagnes to use as towels. The water we had splashed all over in the middle of the night had dried up. I filled the pitchers from the pump outside. I combed out my hair with my fingers and braided it, then twisted the braid around a stick from the garden and pinned it up on my head so I could wash. Afterward, I refilled the pitchers and hung up the towels to dry.

Back in the room, I tidied up the bed and the precautionary sheaths Vai had been so prudent, and confident, as to obtain the night of the areito. Smiling like a besotted fool, I shook out and folded the clothes we'd strewn all over. In my haste to get off his dash jacket, I had accidentally torn two buttons off a cuff, so I draped the jacket over the back of the chair for mending later. A cedar traveling chest tucked in a corner caught my eye. Kneeling, I opened it. Gracious Melqart! How many fashionable dash jackets and waistcoats could a man own?

How could a woman who loved cloth resist stroking each neatly folded garment? He favored vivid colors: deep browns as dark as his skin, burnished golds, kingly reds, and warm bright oranges, one midnight purple as dark as ecstasy, and indigos so saturated they would drive a peacock to envy. The stronger the patterns the better: plaitwork and interlace, dyed damask beaten and pounded until the fabric was stiff, bold geometric designs, and some strange, crazy block prints. At the bottom, folded between sheets of paper as if to hide it, lay the spectacular red-and-gold-chained dash jacket he had worn the night of the areito.

The door shut. "I have soot all over me, and you look so clean and inviting. But close the chest first."

I kept the lid open. "Don't you dare!"

He didn't shift from the door, but somehow his tone made me feel as if he were nuzzling the nape of my bare neck. "Then wash me like you did last night, my sweet Catherine."

My grip wavered on the lid as my flesh began to melt.

"Oh, curse it." He opened the door just as I realized someone was walking up outside, and he spoke in a changed and entirely polite voice. "Peace of the morning to you, Professora."

"Peace of the morning. My apologies." When he stepped back, she appeared in the door, wearing a loose floor-length robe of cotton dyed in an undulating purple. A four-winged messenger bird balanced on her arm. It had an alert gaze and startling barb-like talons on its forelimbs. What I had taken for the second pair of wings was better described as the feathery ornamentation of its hind limbs. Like her gown, its feathers shaded from a deep purple to a pale gray. "I've a message for you, Maestressa Barahal." She handed me a scroll and, with an understanding smile, stepped back. "There is rice porridge if you are hungry. Just come to the kitchen."

She left.

I unrolled the scrap of paper to see Bee's distinctively grandiose handwriting. *"I hope all is well because I must assume you either found a way or made one and I am sorry to write but I just got word that I am to be handed over to the cacica at dusk so please come."*

I handed it to Vai.

His gaze flicked over the words twice. "Tell me if you think she wrote this herself."

"She wrote it. She quoted the great general Hanniba'al to let me know she wasn't coerced. Had she quoted a Roman, she would have meant otherwise."

"Then we have to go." He went out.

We? I shut the lid and hurried after him to the washroom. "Vai, we can't trust the general."

"I know," he said as he stripped and stepped into the brass tub. "But we can't ignore him. We discussed all this last night, love. As I hope you remember."

"That's not what I remember about last night." I poured a pitcher of cold water over his head; he didn't even flinch. But in fact we had talked for a long time about our situation; it was remarkable how pleasing it was to converse with a man in the dark when he was holding you close and you were both quite naked and well sated. I smiled, watching as he soaped down: He was lean but not thin, not short but not particularly tall either, and the view from the back was simply so alluring I had to clamp my mind to Bee's message and our circumstances.

I said, "It's easy to talk noble philosophy at the table and then change your mind when you're in the mud. Even if the general becomes emperor and abolishes clientage, it will take years of war. By then the mansa could have taken his revenge on you by destroying Haranwy."

"I'm not the only one in Haranwy willing to risk the struggle. Other people in the village have skills as useful in their own way as mine for a radical sort of enterprise."

"Like your brother Duvai? Is he a radical now, too?"

"Perhaps. Rinse me off and hand me a towel, if it pleases you." I emptied the other two pitchers over him and offered to dry him off, but he shook his head and took the faded pagne. "Start that, and we'll never leave. Anyway, I'm not as concerned for myself."

"You should be!" I folded his dirtied work clothes to be washed later.

"I'm simply too valuable to him alive and as an ally. I have to play that drum. But as long as the general believes you're going to have something to do with his death, he's a danger to you."

"No. I truly believe he truly believes in his destiny. So as long as I'm alive, he's alive."

He tied a well-worn pagne around his hips. "Whatever he believes, he's trying to intimidate you. He will use us against each other to get our cooperation. To me he'll say: Ally with me, and I'll spare her life and free your village. To you: Hand him over, or I'll kill him."

Outside, he paused in the sun to brush drops of water from his hair. He looked very fetching, and certainly the glance he aimed at me, to see if I was admiring him, fetched me close. I pressed my face into his neck, his skin moist against my lips. The scent of ash clung to him, odd to smell on a cold mage.

"Keep the ice lenses hidden, but take the cold steel in openly, Vai. He'll respect that. And he won't know your cold magic makes my sword bloom in daylight."

"Yes. They'll be watching my sword, not one that appears to them a cane."

I rested my hands on his chest and looked up into his face. "The general will have crossbows as well as rifles. That's what scares me."

He had a smile that was just for me, intimate and inviting. "You'll have to watch my back. Like you were doing in the washroom just now."

Then after all we had to kiss, a slow sweet morning greeting. Obviously the bliss of love deafened me, because when a twig snapped, I was just as startled as he was.

"Kofi!" He grinned with the laughing smile I had often seen on his face at Aunty's when he was with his friends. He looked so relaxed and appealing I could scarcely breathe for being dazzled.

Stepping away, I gripped the top of my pagne. Fortunately it covered the important bits.

"Yee look like a village man now, Vai. Suits yee." Kofi walked forward to clasp hands with Vai in the radical manner, after which they slapped each other on the shoulder in a manly way. "Or something have suited yee, that is for certain. Peace of the morning to yee, Cat." His grin was just too wicked to endure.

"I'll just go get dressed," I said in a choked voice, and I fled to the room.

"Tamed her, have yee?" Kofi said in a jocular tone that made my ears burn.

"Tamed her? Why would you want to tame a woman who defied the mansa with only her wits and her determination to live?"

"Yee have it bad. I only mean, usually she is quick to scratch. Instead she ran off."

"To get dressed. She's not working for the general."

"I's not yet convinced of it, but—"

"You ought to be convinced by my telling you it is so. If she meant to stab me, she'd have done it to my face while telling me why she was doing it and how I had brought it on myself."

"That is one thing I shall say in she favor: She don' spare words. 'Tis not so lively at Aunty's these evenings, I tell yee truly. But yee know, Vai—"

I shut the door. He let Kofi tease and contradict him because he liked and trusted him. I remembered seeing Vai in the village of Haranwy with his age-mates, the ones he had been forced to leave behind when the mages had come for him. How easy he had seemed with those young men! The mage House had stripped that camaraderie away from Vai, leaving the arrogant magister who used his magic, his status, and his cutting words to intimidate. At first he had probably only used those things to protect himself as a youth bullied and scorned by his new age-mates in the mage House, but after long enough, such things become habit. The worst thing for Vai would be to return to Four Moons House and become the magister the mansa wanted him to be.

When I appeared, Vai broke off in the middle of a sentence about *not letting Aunty believe that about Cat.* "Let me dress," he said.

He left me looking at Kofi. "I trust Kayleigh is well," I said. "And your family. No trouble?"

"We have peace in the house. Me thanks for asking. In yee own as well, I hope."

"My cousin is well, thank you." I essayed the question I most wanted answered, no matter how much it hurt. "Aunty Djeneba and Luce and them. Are they well? No trouble?"

"Certainly no one have spoken to the wardens of they part in Vai's situation." His gaze was not hostile, but it was wary and mistrustful. "Whatever else, I believe yee truly care for them."

I opened my mouth, and shut it, for my face had grown hot. A pause to check on Vai struck me as timely. I took a step back and looked in through the open door. He wore trousers and a thin lawn shirt. Standing in front of a chair, he was holding a dash jacket in each hand, clearly trying to decide which one to wear. "Blessed Tanit! Vai, is that a *mirror* you have set on the chair?"

My gaze caught Kofi's, and suddenly we were both snickering.

Vai's tone had a glacial scour. "Catherine, perhaps you and Kofi shall go over to the kitchen. I am sure you are hungry." He tossed the more soberly patterned silver-gray one on the rumpled bed and began to pull on the purple jacket with stylized orange and black stones.

"That one makes my eyes hurt," I said to the sky. As Kofi and I walked along the brick path toward the dining patio, I decided to dispense with courtesies. "Did you ever trust me, Kofi? Before I was *tamed*, I mean."

He whistled appreciatively. "So yee heard that? Meant as a jest."

"Of course it was! I never doubted!"

He chuckled. "As for the other, yee appeared so suddenly, and up from Cow Killer Beach. Even before, the way he talked about the perdita made me think him witched. It was harder to judge after yee came, for yee would push him away with one hand and draw him close with the other."

"Two-faced like a star-apple tree. It's because the leaves are a different color on each side, isn't it?" I paused at the dining patio, not wanting to take this conversation into the kitchen. "I was very confused. As for the witching, did it ever occur to you he might have set that on himself?"

"Talked he own self into believing he was in love with yee? Could be. Yee know, before the hurricane, I would have thrown yee overboard without a second thought. But when yee crawled under that boat for the sake of a man yee never met nor had reason to care for, I got to wondering. Cat, yee understand I's concerned that yee shall treat Vai well and not betray him."

"I had no idea about the raid at Nance's. As for the other, I shall answer honestly, Kofi, because you have been a good friend to him. I do mean to treat him well. I won't betray him. But I'll tell you truly, the best thing for Vai is not to return to the mage House."

People have all kinds of smiles. Kofi's lips twitched in a way that made his scars flare. "Yee reckon he shall be better served by joining the general."

"I don't trust the general at all. I favor the radicals, but I want to know how people talking around a table think they can win a war."

He crossed his arms in a way that emphasized how big and sturdy he was, the kind of man you wanted at your side when felling trees, or Councils. "Them with the armies and the coin, and these cold mages yee speak of, shall always have the weapons to crush us. Maybe words is a better weapon than yee think they is."

"Kofi, that time when Vai almost used his cold magic when that drunk man insulted him, what did you say to him to calm him down?"

He slanted a gaze at the bellyache bush, as if checking for Vai, and then back at me. "I reckon I have had some practice calming that man down, for that was not the first time he almost got in a fight. This time, I just said, 'If yee want that gal, yee shall not do this.' It worked."

"I thought you didn't like me. Why would you encourage him to keep thinking about me?"

"Gal, yee defied the mansa who rule him and he people. Nothing I could ever say could turn that man's mind from yee. I saved me breath."

Footsteps approached, and Vai came into view tugging on his cuffs. He had chosen a jacket of red, gold, and orange squares limned by black. A slim sword swayed from his belt like a bolt of lightning caught and sheathed. *Cold steel in the hand of a cold mage.* So be it. We would face the general and negotiate our next move together.

His gaze flicked between Kofi and me, and he smiled as if our amity pleased him.

"Best we eat before we go," he said, taking my hand.

He and Kofi chattered about doings in the city, mostly Kofi telling the news of the huge retinue necessary to the cacica's consequence: The Taino had reached the festival ground before they were expected, having been brought by a fleet of airships.

"A fleet of airships?" Vai exclaimed as we came to the kitchen, covered by a roof but open to the air on three sides. "Lord of All! Do they mean to invade?"

"The Taino have always said they would not break the First Treaty. So maybe 'tis just to honor the marriage of a prince who shall likely become cacique."

Kofi greeted the professora as if he knew her well. We sat down to bowls of warm rice porridge steamed in milk and garnished with cinnamon. I was so overtaken by the delicious smell and creamy texture of the porridge that I could only eat and listen.

"No one had any idea the Taino have been building a fleet of airships." The professora paused to study me. "Every cook must love you, Maestressa Barahal."

"'Tis good when a gal like to eat," remarked Kofi.

I looked up to see Vai fail to not look pleased with himself. Flushed, I felt it wiser to set back to the porridge than respond.

"Have they manufactories we have not heard mention of?" Kofi asked.

"So we must hope," she said, "otherwise they have sealed a contract with a troll consortium in the north.

That would not bode well for peace among the trolls. Or maybe the Purépecha kingdom has a hand in it, for Prince Caonabo is son to a Purépecha prince who was at one time married to the cacica. Unlikely, for the kingdoms are rivals."

Kofi shook his head. "I reckon if the Taino have such a fleet, 'tis hard to see how Expedition can survive."

"Sometimes," I said, "a little free territory like Expedition serves like one of those valves where you let steam escape from an engine where the pressure is getting too high. Criminals and agitators can be driven there rather than imprisoning or executing them. Left free, they'll fight among themselves rather than be seen as sacrifices. Competing mercantile interests will stay bogged down. Dangerous technologies can be floated where they won't do harm to the Taino if they fail. If there is trouble, it can be blamed on Expedition rather than the Taino court."

Spoons at rest, they stared at me as if I had sprouted a second head.

"I heard a lot of talk when I was waiting tables. Kofi, why did you happen to come today?"

"I make deliveries every morning to the university."

"I thought you worked at the carpentry yard."

"I work there when they have a big order and I can spare the time. Vai, I can row yee across if yee wish."

The professora fetched a squat ceramic jar packed with straw and ice, from which she drew a pair of ice lenses strung on chains. "These are the last two I have. They are working on more over in the troll town refrigerium."

"Do Chartji's aunt and uncle live in troll town, or here?"

"Their workshop is in troll town. They came here because Vai couldn't move about the city."

Vai slipped the chains over his neck and slid the lenses under his jacket. We gave our thanks to the professora and walked to the pier. Kofi shifted a barrel and crate to the bow so Vai and I could share the stern bench. Vai had brought along one of the faded old pagnes, which he folded over the bench so his jacket would not have to touch the weathered and stained wood. I made a great show of getting into the boat in an effort to not touch anything that might sully my humble but pretty pagne. He leaned enough to rock the boat so I almost lost my balance and he had an excuse to pull me close on the bench with his arm around me.

"This shall be painful, I fear," said Kofi as he unshipped the oars and pushed off. "For I have to sit facing yee two in order to row."

"I was just thinking of leaning here against Vai with my eyes shut and my mouth closed quite tamely for the whole of the voyage."

They seemed happy to ignore me. It struck me how much they genuinely liked each other, how their talk flowed with the ease of people who have spent a lot of time conversing together. That ease, the motion of the boat, Vai's arm around me and his shoulder against my cheek, and the sun's warmth on my head so relaxed me that I dozed off.

The boat's bumping against a pier roused me.

"Good luck to yee," Kofi was saying softly, "for I can see how much she matter to yee."

I felt him kiss my hair. "She's awake. Aren't you, Catherine?"

I opened my eyes to bask in Vai's smile. He gathered up the coiled rope with the arm that wasn't fixed around me. A thin man with sun-lightened hair and the splotched

and freckled sun-weathered skin of a man born in northern climes loped over to help us tie up.

"Ja, Kofi-lad," said the fellow, with a polite nod at me
and Vai. "I's looking for work today. Yee got anything?"

Kofi and Vai exchanged a glance, and Vai lowered his
chin enough to signal agreement.

"Ja, maku," said Kofi. "But here, hold the boat while I
get out."

Kofi leaped up to the pier with the ease of a man accustomed to the harbor and made a show of helping me
out, which I understood as an attempt to make up for his
suspicion of me. Vai shook out the pagne and followed.
Folk on the jetty did notice him, and his clothes, and his
good looks, and I supposed that, like Bee, he desired and
perhaps even enjoyed the attention. But he did not seem
to notice it as he walked a short way with Kofi.

Kofi spoke in a low voice. "As for the other, yee must
promise me yee shall do nothing rash. Don' let yee pride
get in the way of yee thinking."

Vai grabbed my hand to pull me up alongside him. "I
can keep a level head."

"'Twould be the first time," said Kofi, "but listen,
maku. Yee can be the net we throw across the ocean to the
radicals in Europa."

"I think it is our best choice, for I'm sure there's
no other way to force the mage Houses and princes to
change."

"If any man know what power these mage Houses
have, it shall be yee, Vai."

"Yes, it shall be. They will not go down without an
ugly fight."

Shaking hands, they looked each other in the eye with
such grim smiles, like two men about to ride into battle,

that a swell of fear surged up from the pit of my stomach.

I knew then I would do anything to protect him, as my mother had once done to protect the man she loved. When I rested a hand on the top of my cane, the sense that my mother stood beside me, in understanding and support, bloomed so strongly in my spirit that for an instant I was sure I felt her touch on my shoulder. She had been a soldier, and now I must be one.

Kofi offered me a hand in the radical manner. He seemed about to say something but instead he slapped Vai on the shoulder and went back to his boat.

Vai took my hand and we walked along the jetty toward the main gate. Sailors reeled drunkenly toward a ship. A man tacked up a broadsheet with the bold headline BOYCOTT on a public board as people clustered around to read the radicals' call to boycott the wedding areito.

"Why did he look at you and you nod? When that man asked for a day's hire?"

"Kofi's household is poor, Catherine."

"It is?"

"No one in that house goes hungry, so I suppose they are wealthy in that way. The mansa sent a bank draft with me, so I am quite well situated because he assumed I would be living in a manner suited to the consequence of a magister of Four Moons House. I was therefore able to settle a significant sum on Kayleigh as her marriage portion. Because she is not yet legally an adult I am her guardian. If Kofi hires a day laborer, he is using her money, so that's why he was asking my permission. If you want to know, Kofi tried to argue me out of the dowry being quite so large. It does not make it easy for Kayleigh to come into a household as a rich maku bride."

"No, I can see it would not."

"I had a long talk with his mother and aunts. I would trust Kofi with my life, and they raised him to be that man I trust. Kayleigh's a smart girl. She'll find a way to use the mansa's money to help the household prosper."

"Did I miss something when I slept on the boat? What did Kofi mean about you being the net thrown across the ocean?"

"I'll join the general's army but work secretly for the radical cause."

"'Risks must be taken if we mean to get what we want.'"

"I wonder who said those words."

"I just did. But I am quoting Brennan Du." I tightened my grip to make his eyes flare at the pressure. "My next husband."

A pair of wagons sat unattended, loaded with bricks. Vai dragged me to the other side of the harnessed mules where two might pretend to have a little privacy. There, he kissed me until I was breathless.

"You will not be needing a next husband."

"You're so easy to bait. Anyway, you're being jealous of a man you've never even seen."

"Of course I've seen him, twice, which I know you know perfectly well. I saw the way you smiled at him at the Griffin Inn."

I fluttered my lashes. "I was wondering what it would be like to be kissed by a handsome man."

"Wonder no more." He cupped my chin in a hand as he kissed me again.

"Here, now," said the young wagoner, coming up, "none of that. Yee's scaring the mules. Nice jacket, though. Where get yee such tailoring?"

Vai released me and checked his jacket to make sure it wasn't askew or rumpled. "Europa."

"Ah, yee's a maku. No cause to go stealing Expedition gals with yee fine clothes and fat purse."

"In fact, she is my wife."

The wagoner did not look one bit impressed, and as he was a stocky, muscular man, his grin had an air of confidence. "Gal, yee don' want a man who dress he own self better than he dress yee. If yee get tired of that one, come climb me mango tree. I shall buy yee pretty finery and as many ribbons and beads and baubles as yee desire."

"Shall yee?" I asked with interest and in a pretty fair imitation of the local speech. "How many? Shall they come from Avenue Kolonkan?"

"That way, is it?" he said with a roll of his eyes.

"In fact," said Vai, "it is not that way. I am buying her nothing from Avenue Kolonkan."

"Is yee not?" said the wagoner with a look at me to see how I would take this proclamation.

"Shall yee not?" I asked with unfeigned surprise.

"To do so would offend my radical principles. Nor are the mules scared. And by the way, half the tailors on Tailors' Row in Passaporte have taken patterns from this very jacket. So you will not offend your radical principles by purchasing from them."

"See why I love he?" I said, simpering as I batted my eyelids again. "Some men court me with baubles, but he court me with radical principles."

Unfortunately, the wagoner was far more interested in Vai's dash jackets than my wit. "Tailors' Row in Passaporte District. Truly?"

"At a tenth of the price a man would pay on Avenue Kolonkan. And the money goes into the pocket of the tailor who made it and not into the purse of the fancy shopkeeper who pays least wages to workers who are little better than indentured servants."

"I like that talk!" said the other fellow. He and Vai shook hands and had a moment of deep connection with firm, masculine smiles and fiery comments about the corrupt Council, last month's infamous raid at Nance's, and whether the poor of Expedition would boycott the wedding areito despite the bounty of free food sure to be available there. I had to drag Vai away or I would have been left conversing with the mules.

"I hope you have not been spending money on Avenue Kolonkan," he said, taking my hand.

"Looking is not spending! Anyway, the tips I earned at Aunty Djeneba's aren't enough to buy a single ribbon in any of those shops."

"Kofi is going to set Aunty straight about what happened. I hope you don't blame them."

"I admire their loyalty to you. What an awful moment that was, though—"

I broke off as Vai halted. Ahead rose the gate and its watch lamps. A red-haired man stood beside wardens in the shadow of the gate, looking at us. The guard lamps flared as in a gust of oily wind. Vai released my hand and raised his. A slap of heat made the air snap. Vai closed his hand, and the sting vanished as though swallowed. The hilt of my sword trembled, tasting cold magic.

"Stay next to me," he said. With a brisk stride he closed the gap, me beside him. The lamp flames shrank as if losing fuel.

Drake wore the half smile of a man anticipating a long-awaited treat. "Andevai Diarisso Haranwy, you are under arrest—"

"I am a representative of Four Moons House, a magister of the Diarisso lineage. You have no grounds nor means to arrest me."

"We'll see about that." The lamp flames leaped as the air crackled with heat.

Vai curled both hands into fists, and the lamps guttered out. "If you can't do better than that, you shouldn't even try."

Drake took a step toward him. "You're under arrest as an unregistered fire bane. Which you've just let every warden here see. How do you like that, you bastard?"

"I am not a bastard," said Vai so icily I knew Drake's words had truly angered him, "and I will give you one chance to apologize to my mother for even suggesting it. Then you'll know why you should not try to play these games with me."

Drake's grin flashed with a burst of fury. "Fucking arrogant bastard. See how you like fire."

A furnace heat shimmered out of nowhere like a blast of scalding wind. Flames caught on a passing wagon. The poor mules harnessed to it—Blessed Tanit! the very mules who had hidden our kiss!—began to kick and buck in the harness as the wagoner leaped off the driver's bench with a string of panicked curses. How did Drake dare release so much fire?

A fiery glow writhed around Vai's form.

Blessed Tanit! Drake was using Vai as a catch-fire to fuel the flames. He was going to burn him up alive! I leaped forward and punched Drake right up under the jaw with the handle of my cane. He went down hard.

"Vai, douse the wagon!" I cried as I jabbed the blunt end of my cane against Drake's chest.

Onlookers had already run to try to help the frantic

wagoner unhitch the mules, but the wild kicking of the beasts forced them back. My sword's blade pulsed as cold magic bloomed. Flames vanished into thready smoke. I twisted the hilt and drew the blade. As Drake pushed up, I caught the tip in the cloth of his jacket.

I would have stabbed him. I almost ran him through, thinking of the way that glow had lit Vai's body. But Vai had said Drake was an unusually powerful fire mage. So I had to spare him in case I needed him to save Bee.

Yet Drake must have seen the killing lust in my expression, because he flopped back down.

Vai appeared beside me, seemingly untouched by the backlash of Drake's magic. His brown gaze met Drake's blue one.

Men can have a way of looking at each other that is itself a surge of heat and cold warring.

Noble Ba'al! I had been quite mistaken: Drake had never been specifically interested in me, had he? Through me, he had taken a petty but predictable revenge on the cold mage who had treated him so scornfully, man to man, in the entry hall of the law offices of Godwik and Clutch.

Remarkably pretty. Had I really fallen for that line? Twice?

"I am still waiting for that apology," said Vai.

Despite my blade pressed against his shoulder, Drake did not bother to look at me. He sneered at Vai. "You shall be waiting for that apology just as long as you shall be waiting to find out your wife is not a whore."

Vai drew his sword so quickly it took a breath for a satisfying expression of fear to sweep Drake's face. I would have enjoyed his fear longer, but I had to speak fast.

"Vai, don't do it. We need him alive."

Vai exhaled as he closed a fist around his emotions and choked them down.

"You're right, love," he said coolly, sheathing his blade. "His apology would be worthless anyway. Come. I know General Camjiata is eager to meet with a mage who is actually trained and effective. Just as my wife was eager to bed a man who could actually give her pleasure."

Lips pinched and eyes narrowed, Drake raised a hand. "Now I take you down."

Too late I heard the click and release of crossbows from the gate walk above. I slammed into Vai, driving him sideways. A bolt flashed past my cheek. A jolt stung my upper right arm. Then I slammed Vai down onto the ground, my body on top of his and both of us sprawled across the cobblestones.

"Here, now, lads!" shouted the wagoner. "The dogs who serve the Council are attacking we own. Who shall come to the maku's defense?"

Hearts paused and minds considered. Men gathered about the burned wagon. Wardens bristled, raising their staves as they called for the riflemen. From up on the gate walk, crossbows clicked as they were reloaded. I rolled off Vai and grabbed a fistful of Drake's shirt. With a burst of pain in my arm, I hauled him to his feet and yanked him to a halt between the crossbows above and Vai, behind me, who was just now shaking off the shock of the impact.

I shouted. "Have yee had enough of the Council stealing yee own kin? Can we not put a stop to it? If all are not equal before the law, then what is the law worth?"

Pushing up to his knees, Vai pulled at the chains around his neck to drag out an ice lens.

"Stand down! Go about yee business!" cried a warden.

The wagoner called, "They have shot the gal! Look! She arm is bleeding! I say we roust them, lads! Enough!"

Drake spoke. "You bitch. Catch this."

Heat screamed along my skin like the rake of fiery coals. I sucked for a breath as my lungs burned and my tongue withered. My grip on Drake's shirt gave way as the backwash of his fire magic poured into my body as flames. Pain seared me.

Blessed Tanit. Let this agony pass quickly.

"Cat!" Vai shouted.

Cold magic hit like a hammer. First I was standing, about to burst into flame, and then I crumpled to hands and knees, washed cold but alive. My tears fell as ice, shattering on the cobblestones. My belly cramped; I coughed out a drop of blood. But I would be cursed if I would let Drake strike while I was down. I crawled toward my sword, its blade shining as cold magic fed its heart. Drake kicked the sword away. But he was not looking at me but at Vai.

"I guess I'm stronger than you thought, Magister. Because I'm still standing and you're on your knees. You've made a fatal mistake. You've revealed that she's your weakness. This is so easy. You doused me once. But next time you won't be fast enough to save *her*. Beg for her life, bastard."

A brick flew out of the air and struck him on the shoulder. A piece of charred wood clattered at his feet. Another brick shattered an arm's length from my head, and a fragment spat up to gouge my chin.

"Wardens! Arrest these rioters!"

A well-aimed brick hit Drake a glancing blow on the side of the head, and he reeled back as shouts of triumph rose from the wagons. Our friends advanced brandishing bricks, shovels, knives, and axes. Wardens and riflemen pounded up, the captain calling for them to line up. Gouts of shimmering heat surged off Drake as he struggled to control himself. I saw it now through eyes clogged with drifting matter as I blinked, trying to clear them. He was trapped by the power of his fire magic; no wonder he hated Vai, who was fed by his magic, not harmed by it.

"Catherine, speak to me." Vai was groping at the other chain as he got to his feet.

"Don't do it, Vai," I said, my lips stinging and my voice as husky as if I were parched. "He knows if he kills me in public, he'll become a criminal. If you kill him, you'll be arrested."

"I'm taking no chances with you."

I staggered up and found him, pressing my face into his beautiful dash jacket, which was smeared with the slimy churn of the streets. "I'm thinking with my feet. I have more powerful kinfolk than anyone knows. Let him think he's won for now."

"He will not think he has won by the time I'm done with him," he said in that way men have when they have decided their position on Triumph Spire is at stake.

Bricks thudded down, the crowd growing in boldness as Drake did nothing and the militia did not fire. The rippling heat of Drake fumed at my back, like a man wanting more gloat and less stymie. Yet a surly undercurrent dragged on the wind. The city's anger had woken like a beast prodded until it lashed out to bite. I was having a hard time staying on my feet.

"Storm the walls now, brothers! 'Tis time for the Council to dissolve."

A rifle clicked, not firing. A rumble like thunder rose out of the old city.

"Make way! Make way!"

A procession emerged from the gate. Three carriages jolted to a halt as their drivers surveyed the massing crowd and the street blocked by men ready to fight.

Drake took a step toward us. Vai shifted me to one side and again drew his sword.

Drake's fear sparked beneath his anger. "I can kill her faster than you can kill me."

"But you'll still be dead," said Vai.

The door of the front carriage banged open and a man climbed out and strode over to us, expression as thunderous as a looming storm cloud.

"What in the pox-ridden hells is this?" demanded the general in a ringing voice that carried like the boom of artillery.

He marked Drake; he marked me; last of all, he marked Vai and the glittering cold steel that could cut the life out of a man merely by drawing blood. So naturally he planted himself in the path of Vai's blade, between the two mages.

"I'm waiting. What is meant by this disturbance?"

"Besides the insult to my mother, he called my wife a bitch and a whore."

"Yet who could say they were false words?" said Drake with a smirk.

Even I didn't see it coming.

Camjiata backhanded Drake across the face so hard the fire mage staggered back, tripped on his own feet, and dropped on his ass. The wardens and riflemen hissed as in sympathy, and the crowd actually cheered.

"My mother taught me more respect for women than that," remarked the general.

He raised a hand; the crossbowmen on the walls, the

wardens, and the riflemen all lowered their weapons. He surveyed Vai's fixed stare and steady hand. I could practically see the mansa standing as if with shadowy voice urging Vai forward. Not one person could stop Vai from killing the Iberian Monster and ridding Europa of him and the threat he posed forever. Not even me.

"I take it," said the general in the tone he would use to a man he had chanced into conversation with at Nance's over a friendly drink, "that you were coming along either to meet with me or to kill me. I should guess the former, but I am willing to entertain the idea it was the latter." He looked at me, brows knit down. "Jupiter Magnus, Cat. Your shoulder is bleeding."

The point of Vai's sword dropped as he took a step toward me, gaze flashing to my face, then to my shoulder.

The general addressed the restless but notably surprised crowd. "My friends, your generosity is noted. Your courage in standing up for a comrade is evident. But I fear this has been an unexpectedly dramatic altercation between rivals. You know the sort of arseness I mean."

There is a damper that an older man's pointed jocularity can put on a younger man's self-important flash, as unseen as magic but just as effective. That shrank what had just happened down to manageable size, and made Drake look like a man who had lost at love and Vai a hothead who ought to know better than to rub his rival's face in the fact.

"Magister, I suggest we talk after her wounds are tended."

"Where is Bee?" I was startled to hear how hoarse my voice sounded and how much it hurt to swallow. A wave of dizziness rent me top to toe. I was going to have to swallow again and I dreaded it, the raw scrape of pain about to rip through me…

"Catherine." Vai sheathed his sword and swept me into his arms. He looked past me at the general. "She needs to lie down."

The general beckoned. I hadn't noticed Captain Tira and Juba, who stood at the horses' heads. Juba sheathed two knives up his sleeves and walked over to us.

"I have a meeting. Beatrice remains at the house, preparing for her departure. Juba will escort you there. He knows something of medicine. You may rely on him. I shall return at midday." He shot yet one more frowning look of evident concern at me, and headed for the carriage. "James."

The look that sparked between Drake and Vai might have been combustion or it might have been hatred or it might have been the vestiges of unspent magic bursting and melting in the air.

"James! *With me.*"

Drake followed, staring at the general's back with a look I dared not interpret, for men might look so when they are thinking of kissing or of killing or of a sudden change of heart betwixt the two.

"Vai," I said, "put me down. I need my sword."

"I am not putting you down until I see you to a safe place," said Vai in a tone that reminded me that as far as he knew, Drake had gotten to his feet first and unaided.

Why by the starry brow of Noble Ba'al had I so stupidly said, *Let him think he's won*?

Fortunately, Juba arrived and spoke to Vai. "You are the fire bane. I am called Juba."

The two men measured each other and determined on a truce. Juba looked over the crowd, then gestured. A Taino man appeared with a wagon hitched to a donkey. He re-arranged baskets of ginger and chilies, and Vai set me in the wagon bed. He had them wait while he fetched my sword, again appearing as a cane; strangely, he was able to pick it up as if it were his own cold steel.

Juba and Vai walking behind, we jolted through the gate with its iron tripods twisted into freakish shapes by the power of Vai's cold magic, and their lamps completely drained. Swept, quiet streets took us to the general's town house. Juba paid the Taino man and sent him on his way.

I said to Juba, "You became an exile, for refusing to become what almost killed me."

His gaze met mine, and I decided I liked him.

"Cat must lie down," said Vai.

"I return with medicine," said Juba.

He left Vai and me to go up alone. I had to lean on Vai on the stairs. When we reached the bedchamber I realized Vai was shaking. I shut the door as he collapsed over the bed.

"Vai? Blessed Tanit! Drake used you as a catch-fire for longer than he did me. I didn't stop him fast enough."

"I'm not burned," he whispered. "It was so strange...the fire pouring through me like I was the conduit into another place...I can't keep my eyes open."

I pulled off his boots and unbuttoned his dirtied jacket and pried him out of it as he made a faint protest and promptly passed out. I pressed my cheek against his. His breathing remained even and steady, so I stepped back and let him sleep. I scarcely noticed that I handled both my cane and his cold steel until I propped them against the wardrobe and realized his sword had not stung me.

The door opened and Bee appeared. "Blessed Tanit! There's blood on your sleeve!" She ran to me, but stopped before embracing me. "Your skin looks flushed."

"Drake used me as a catch-fire." The words were strangely easy to say, as if I were speaking of someone else. "Vai, too, but it didn't burn him."

She swayed, and it was I who maneuvered her to the bed, where she sat with a look of stunned horror. "What happened to Andevai, then?" she whispered.

"He drained himself to stop Drake. He just fell hard asleep."

She grasped my hands convulsively. When I whimpered, she released me. "How bad is it?"

"I feel like I came up one spit short of being cooked. But it's not too bad, more the shock."

"I should never have sent that note. I mentioned it in front of Drake. I will kill him myself!"

"Leave Drake alone, Bee. I'll take care of him. Believe me, I can."

She had left the door open. Juba appeared at the threshold. He carried a tray with a pitcher and basin, a vial, a ceramic jar stoppered with a bit of cork, strips of linen, and a small glass bottle. With a surgeon's knife he cut away the blood-soaked cloth, careful of my modesty, and washed the wound, which was more of a gouge along the skin. I had been fortunate. Just below my elbow, he paused as a swipe of the cloth cleaned a smear of blood off to reveal the bite scar. He looked up, meeting my gaze although I could not guess what he was thinking. He glanced at Bee and, without a word, finished his nursing. After painting the gash with a white salve, he bound it with linen.

"For the skin," he said, indicating the ceramic jar. He picked up the bottle. "A cup eases the inflammation. Maybe it makes her drowsy or gives her vivid dreams."

He and Bee stood together like lovers who mean to

argue. Bee glanced at me and back at him from under hooded eyes, and he nodded and left.

"Did you?" I asked.

"I did not." She turned the key in the lock.

I stripped. The jar contained a sticky clear ointment that cooled my skin gloriously. Bee rubbed it on my back and then combed a light layer of olive oil through my hair, glancing at Vai all the while. "For if he were to wake up and catch you naked, it would embarrass me beyond belief."

"He's clothed!"

"Yes, but it is one thing for you and me to bathe and change together, and another for there to be a stranger in the room with one or both of us in that condition."

"He is no stranger," I murmured. He looked like a man who ought to be woken with a kiss.

"I take it by that cryptic utterance and unrelentingly fatuous expression that you and he are *reconciled*. Be sure I wish to know no details whatsoever." She filled a cup from the bottle and handed it to me. "Nap for a few hours. I'll wake you. We leave mid-afternoon to take a carriage to the festival gate. The cacica has declared she must undertake my final instruction herself."

"In Sharagua?"

"No. There is a palace at the border, where the areito will be held. It isn't far, but I have to stay there. Cat, you must nap. You look exhausted and stunned. But I must selfishly ask...I can have one attendant with me for the twenty days. I know that you two...it's a long time to be away from him..."

"Of course I will go with you! I have to stay with you until after Hallows' Night no matter what, with or without Vai. But you'll have to tell me what I need to do and not do."

"Don't worry. You know how I love to boss you about. And to show you how much I love you for coming with me, let me take that jacket of his downstairs so the laundresses can clean it."

She departed with the jacket, and I locked the door. After braiding my hair and drinking the liquid with its sweetly chalky taste, I lay down. An attempt to clasp the sleeping Vai met with success: The lotion had soothed my inflamed skin enough that the touch of cloth did not chafe. But when I closed my eyes, I remembered the fire bursting in my heart.

I slept, and I dreamed I was waking Vai with passionate kisses, and he said we can't it will hurt you and I said we have to because what if I'm dead tomorrow and he gave way cautiously and tenderly, and then I woke up. To discover Vai asleep beside me and yet somehow his clothes had come off, which forced me to revisit my memories of what had been dream and what had been real. A sound of clicking and rustling had woken me. The key in the lock was being jiggled from the other side of the door. I slipped out from under the thin cotton blanket and dashed for the wardrobe to grab Vai's sword. Then I picked up my rumpled pagne and tied it hastily over torso and hips as the key worked loose and dropped with a clunk to the floor. Vai stirred. The latch turned, and the general came in.

He closed the door, taking in the scene. "The vigor of youth never fails to amaze."

Vai blinked several times as in confusion, and then recollection settled his expression. Sitting, he caught sight of Camjiata, realized he was uncovered from the hips up, and, after a moment, smiled with the comfortable bravado of the man who knows he looks well in any outfit.

"You have me at a disadvantage," he said, making no effort to cover his bare torso or the two chains and rings, one ice lens clear and one cloudy.

The general smiled. "Which you may suppose is deliberate. I must use what advantage I can make for myself, for I am not a cold mage of rare and unexpected potency." I flushed, not that one could tell, as I was already pinked. "As for you, Cat, I trust you are not too badly injured."

"Do you? Drake tried to kill Vai, too." I placed the sword on the bed next to a startled Vai before I stalked to the wardrobe to get a blouse, pagne, and clean bodice and drawers.

"He will not do that again."

"How can you possibly be sure?" I demanded as I took the clothes, and the ceramic jar of ointment, behind the screen for privacy. Vai kept his gaze fixed on the general.

"I hold the power of life and death over James Drake in ways I am not about to share."

"You'll excuse us," said Vai, "if that seems a slender reed on which to cross this river."

"'*Us*,'" murmured the general as I poured water into a pitcher. "How interesting to phrase it that way. I should like to know how you managed to kill Drake's fire and save Cat. You should not have been able to do that." A chair scraped along the floor and I heard him settle onto it.

"I should like to get dressed," said Vai, "but in all honesty, General, I'm not going to do it in front of you."

"I don't like to have a sword held to my throat, Magister, so I admit to enjoying placing you in a position of discomfort. We'll have the talk here. You may dress, or not."

"Bastard," said Vai, perhaps appreciatively.

"I was very close to my mother," replied the general in a tone so genial it made me pause.

"Then we have a thing in common. My apologies. No offense was meant to your *mother*."

I began dabbing again; the ointment worked quickly; my skin was already better.

"Understood. So, thanks to the mothers who raised us, here we are, Magister. Why did you not kill me when you had the chance?"

"I am not that man."

"Yet you could have been that man. Any reasoned assessment of the situation suggests I will bring war to Europa and many will die in blood and fire. You could have stopped that."

"People already die. There will be a conflagration sooner or later."

"You are the rich and privileged son of one of the most powerful mage Houses. Are you willing to give that up?"

"I am one of their weapons, rather as James Drake seems to be one of yours. I haven't finished discussing the man who tried to murder my wife."

"What do you want, Magister?"

"I want to kill him."

"But not me?"

"You have something I want. The means to abolish clientage."

"A legal code is not the means to abolish clientage. One must have the means to enforce such a code. I can say or write anything I want, and that does not make it happen, or make it true. Why should princes and mage Houses abolish clientage? Whatever your origins, Magister, you have benefited by your association with Four Moons House. You, and your people as well."

"I may have. But they have gained material benefit, nothing else."

"I would not call material benefit 'nothing.' I have seen a man holding his dying child, the one he could not feed because his crops failed and the share for his lord must be met regardless. I have seen a wife hold the broken ruin of her husband crushed in a fall of rock in a mine whose bounty enriches the mine's owner but not those who work in it. Sometimes the gods are cruel, but more often it is the cruelty and greed of men that kills us. You stand in a high place with the waters rising. I would not be so quick to give it up merely for principles."

"Are you a radical, General? Or just an ambitious man who plans to use the blood of others to wash his hands at the altar of victory?"

"As you say, there will be a conflagration sooner or later. Which do you want, Magister? I will bring it sooner, and before the old order is quite ready to combat it."

"They are ready," said Vai. "They will fight you to the last drop of their blood."

"I would expect nothing less. Yet it is long past time for the old order to be strangled in its amply feathered bed of unspeakable luxury."

"You live well," said Vai.

"And I am given to understand that you tailor well. Don't trouble me with the tired old argument that a radical must be poor to be pure. Nothing bores me more than the man who makes a parade of his austerity. You do not trust me, Magister. Yet I have something you want which the mansa will not give you. Since you are talking to me instead of killing me, for I see you keep your cold steel close at hand, I must assume you have already made your choice."

"I have made my choice," said Vai.

I had finished smearing myself with ointment and wielded a cloth fan to dry. From behind my screen, I asked, "General, did you know that Juba and Prince Caonabo are twins?"

"Why, yes, Cat, I do happen to know that."

"Why not marry Bee to Juba? He could come back from exile and take the cacique's seat of power with Bee at his side. Why marry Bee to a fire mage, when she might be caught in the conflagration? Can you imagine I would wish even the chance of this on Bee?"

"Do not think every fire mage is like Drake. Juba's exile is permanent. That is the Taino law. As for Caonabo, recall that he has a catch-fire. More importantly, he is now the cacica's only other living son. But he is said to have the temperament of an unworldly scholar. You see, Juba was the one meant for the throne. Now the cacica fears an attempt by factions within her court to install a different claimant. That is why Caonabo needs the alliance with a dragon dreamer."

Juba's interest in Bee suddenly took on a much more ominous cast. Did he support his brother, or hope to undermine him? I pulled on my blouse and tied my pagne around my hips. "How providential for you, General, that you stumbled upon my cousin so early in your campaign."

"Providential? Never forget that I am an accomplished campaigner." When I stepped out from behind the screen, the general walked to the door and opened it. "Cat, we leave in an hour. I hope you are fit for it."

"I will stand beside Bee for as long as she needs me. But you must promise me, General, that no harm will come to my husband in the twenty days I am with her."

"I promise on my mother's grave that no harm will come to your husband by any intent, plot, knowledge, conspiracy, or neglect of mine. He is too valuable. Magister, will you stay? Ah. I see by your wounded look it was a foolish question. Naturally you will be remaining where you can most quickly be reunited with your wife. Just as well, since I took the liberty of sending for your things."

From the hall came the sound of footsteps. Captain Tira appeared, casting a doubtful glance at Vai and an interested one at me. She ushered in men who were carrying Vai's chest, several baskets, and the bed. Vai and I must have appeared like academy students flummoxed by an unexpected exam they had not prepared for. The four soldiers retreated with disciplined haste and poorly suppressed grins.

"Did someone betray Vai?" I demanded.

"No. I took the liberty of looking through Beatrice's sketchbook. On a page with four phases of the moon, which clearly represent Four Moons House and thus the cold mage, I recognized the bench."

"Bastard!" I said. "That's put us in our place."

"Now, Cat," he said with a smile as sharp as a splinter, digging deep, "were I you, I would not be precipitous in throwing around that particular word. One hour. Captain, shall we go?"

33

The closed carriage rumbled along for what seemed hours. My bold, fearless Bee sat with hands neatly clasped on her lap as she and I poured forth a stream of unenlightening babble about the baubles and fabrics we had admired on Avenue Kolonkan. It passed the time, and alleviated our nerves. We were dressed in the local style, in simple blouses and pagnes. Captain Tira sat at attention in the facing seat, too much like a jailer for us to speak openly about the things we most wished to discuss. Vai had accepted the general's invitation to ride in the other carriage, since he wasn't allowed to travel with Bee.

"And then I said, 'Looking is not spending!'"

"Cat, did he really say it would offend his radical principles to shop on Avenue Kolonkan?"

"Yes, and worst of all, Bee, he meant it in that pedantic way he means things." I glanced at Captain Tira, who met my gaze with the same interested look she had thrown me when she had entered the bedchamber accompanying Vai's belongings. "Not that I can afford to buy anything on Avenue Kolonkan anyway."

"I'll buy you whatever you want, dearest. Never mind what he says!"

I had a sudden and horrific image of being caught between Vai and Bee arguing, a precise cold steel blade pitted against the blunt trauma of an axe. I temporized, because while I agreed with Vai, there had been such lovely trinkets and ribbons. "I thought the Taino treasury was empty."

"I think the situation is more complicated than that phrase makes it sound. We traveled halfway across Kiskeya, to Sharagua and back. I have never seen a more prosperous, orderly, and healthy people. No one stopped me from going anywhere I wished. I saw not a single starving child, and I assure you, I was looking for the wretched and the poor because I wanted to gauge exactly how powerful and rich the Taino kingdom was if I was to ally myself with them."

Despite Captain Tira's presence, I decided to say what really weighed on my mind. "An alliance brought about by the general. He is half *Roman*. We can't trust him."

"Roman on his mother's side. Iberian and Mande on his father's. That makes him of mixed lineage. Just like you. Should I therefore not trust you?" Her curls swayed around her face as she smiled impishly at me. Her hands clutching mine were the only hint of her anxiety at what lay ahead and the huge gamble she had taken. "Of course he is using me to get what he wants, which is the cacica's airships and access to Expedition's wealth and factories because the Council daren't say no to him once the Taino support his cause. I don't care. Because it gets me security. If the cold mage truly loves you, and you love him, then you are both fortunate and cursed, because you two will never be secure. People who want to use one of you can threaten the other one. And they will. But when I am a powerful noblewoman and respected seer among the Taino, I can protect you both. Always, Cat. Always." She embraced me. "And buy you whatever you want on Avenue Kolonkan."

The captain had folded her arms across her chest and closed her eyes, as if the maudlin outpourings of gals like us commonly bored her to sleep.

I muttered, "You would think Captain Tira often delivers innocent young brides to strangers meant to become their husbands." A flicker of movement twitched in her cheek, and her right foot shifted, heel raising and lowering. "Captain, did the general really figure out where Vai was all that time from Bee's sketchbook? Or did someone inform on him? No harm in telling me now."

She opened her eyes. Her silence was her answer.

A growing clamor of sound greeted us: drums, rattles, horns, and singing swelled and ebbed like the sea's surge. We had reached the border, and it sounded like an areito had already started.

The carriage halted.

Bee took in a shuddering breath. We locked gazes.

"Always, Bee," I said. "Always."

The door was opened from outside. The captain went out first.

Bee took advantage of her departure to draw me close and whisper. "Remember, say nothing and do nothing except what I tell you to do. Don't speak unless I tell you to. And especially, don't take orders from others, only from me."

"That shouldn't be difficult, accustomed as I am to you bossing me around."

As Captain Tira looked back in, Bee released me to wave an imperious hand. "You first, dearest, for the last and most dramatic entrance shall be mine."

"You always hog the dramatic entrance, Bee," I said as

I clambered out. "Maybe next time I'll steal it from you."

I had not once ventured out of Expedition's sprawl in the weeks after Drake had dumped me on the jetty. Its streets and courtyard gates, untidy alleys and well-groomed ball courts, cheerful markets and the shimmering presence of the sea and the masts of ships, and even the whistling parties of trolls hurrying about their business, had become my landscape.

We had fallen into another world.

The huge plaza reminded me of paintings I had seen depicting the great public spaces of Rome and Qart Hadast when those empires were in their heyday. The paved open space stretched so far that tendrils of dusk hid its boundaries. Ahead lay entrances to four monumental ball courts, two on either side of a long stone building painted red and blue and pierced with nine narrow archways. The central arch was surmounted by an elaborately painted scene depicting fish spilling from an overturned gourd.

Music, drumming, and singing came from the ball courts. Oddly, the only Expeditioners I saw were a single troop of wardens standing off to my left, and a few local vendors who had set up along the plaza with fried plantains, cassava bread straight off the griddle, seafood being cooked over charcoal, and mounds of fruit. Their customers were Taino streaming out from the ball courts, men from the courts to my left and women from the courts to my right. They wore loosely draped cloth in an antique Roman-like way, although both young women and men wore only a pagne-like cloth wrapped around their hips and no shirts at all, casually bare-chested.

But none of these things robbed me of words. What rendered me speechless were the thirty or more airships tethered at the border between the Taino kingdom and Expedition Territory. Some were scout ships no larger than the one navigated by the Barr Cousins. Many were the size of the ocean-crossing airship Bee and I had seen in Adurnam, the one Vai had destroyed. Among them floated three leviathan monstrous in their glamour. It was a stunning show of wealth and force.

Bee slipped an arm around me. "I have a fancy to be like the didos of old, the queens of Qart Hadast who sailed at the head of a mighty fleet. I shall draw my fleet as a school of bloated silvery fish released from a vast heavenly gourd."

"I can scarcely imagine what it must be like to sail the seas of a noble court, when any courtier is ready to stab you in the back or flatter shamelessly for a step up the ladder. I would far rather wait tables at Aunty Djeneba's."

"Where the customers try to put their hands on your ass? How is that different? Do not worry for me. I shall crush my rivals with smiles and the axe blow of my indomitable will."

"I can't bear it if they take you away from me, Bee."

"Dearest, we shall all return to Europa together like conquering heroes."

The other carriage rolled in, and the general emerged, followed by Vai wearing the dash jacket he had worn the night of the areito. He marked me with the smile that belonged to me alone.

As the sun shimmered against the horizon, the central gate opened. A procession of women appeared. They were dressed in skirts that lapped their ankles and in bodices like wide belts woven with beads. Feathers adorned their long black hair, which they wore unbound. Two at the front walked with hands outstretched and fire—actual flame—rising from their palms as if they contained the oil that lit the lamps. The two fire mages were flanked by four women equally richly garbed, one of whom was not Taino but red-headed, pale, and freckled like a refugee from the Europan north. Were they catch-fires? Hard to tell. By the elaboration and richness of their clothing, they seemed equally honored. Behind walked three more women heavily draped with thick stone pendants and gold bracelets on their bare arms, their skin patterned with lines and dots. When they reached a raised circular platform in the middle of the plaza, they halted.

My sword bloomed against my hand as day crossed twilight's border.

"Come, Cat," Bee said regally, squaring her shoulders.

"Aren't we underdressed?"

"You haven't noticed that many of the Taino women are far more underdressed? I certainly have! I do not intend to emulate them!"

"Beatrice." The general offered his arm. She took it, thus allowing me to drop back next to Vai. I twined my fingers through his as we followed them toward the Taino noblewomen. Captain Tira paced at our backs. I saw no sign of Drake or Juba.

"If you need anything, go to Keer at the law offices of Godwik and Clutch," I murmured. "She'll drive a hard bargain, but I can trust the trolls to like the game better than the prize."

"Tell me how you are feeling, Catherine."

"Well enough. I'm fine, Vai. I don't know how I can bear being apart from you for twenty days."

His fingers tightened over mine. "It's right that you go with your cousin. I'll just hope you come back dressed like those Taino women out there."

"Vai!"

When he smiled, I was so smitten by a rush of affection and desire that all I could do was stare at him in the most besotted manner imaginable. "My sweet Catherine, we won't be apart for long. We are truly married now, love. Nothing can change that."

The gravity and formality of the occasion prevented a kiss, and I would not have tried anyway, not with some of those Taino women staring at me as if I had two faces. Night fell as we reached the platform. The general let go of Bee, and Vai had therefore to let go of me.

The Taino women escorted us under the central arch and through a masonry tunnel across the border and into the country Bee had determined to take on. The smell of tobacco permeated the air. On the other side of the arch lay another huge plaza. From the ball courts rose the joyous sound of people singing and dancing with rattle and drum. Our party walked on a raised walkway to a single-story building. We entered a long room lit by what seemed a hundred lamps hissing as oil burned. Our attendants spoke to Beatrice.

"They are asking if you are my cemi," she said.

"If I am your cemi?"

"They want to see your hair unbound, and if you have a navel. Why would they think you didn't have a navel?"

"They think I'm a spirit of the dead."

"I won't let them bully you. You need show them nothing. Otherwise Juba says they will think I can forever be pushed around." Her reply to them, in Taino, was precise and slow.

They merely shrugged, taking off their sandals and washing their feet before they escorted Bee up onto a carpet of reed mats. Under the heat and light shimmering out of the lamps, they stripped her naked, wiped her down with damp cloths, perfumed her with sweet-smelling oils, and painted her bare arms with lines that crawled up the curve of her flesh like serpents. Then they dressed her in a long wrap skirt of pure white cotton; red and gold feathers for her hair; a bodice woven of cotton and beads; a stone collar carved with turtles and frogs; and wreaths of bells for her ankles and wrists. When they had finished, I could believe she had become someone else, crossing into a new world.

I followed, as ignored as a cane that hides a sword. Her attendants did not speak to me, and she indicated by occasional glances and nods that I was doing exactly as I should. We proceeded down a corridor on soft matting. Bee and the Taino women walked barefoot; I was the only one shod, in the sandals Vai had given me. We came to a porch that overlooked a courtyard crowded with men standing on one side and women seated on the other. Our escort moved aside to reveal Bee. I stayed at the back.

The many elders and proud nobles examined Bee in her finery. The men had stern, striking features; most wore feathers and stone collars. Opposite, women looked us up and down with solemn gazes. They were beautifully adorned in feathers and beads and pure white beaded bodices and skirts. No overt hostility marred their expressions. Neither did they seem overawed by the presence of a woman who walked the dream of dragons. It was hard to judge.

One face caught my eye among the women. I saw the very behica who had grasped my arm on Salt Island and informed me through Caonabo's translation that Drake had not healed me because I had never been infested. In-

stinct jolted me. *Hide.* I caught a few threads of magic to
obscure myself.

Yet the behica saw me at once. She saw me, and she
knew me. But she said nothing.

The assembled people sang in call and response. The
melody seemed familiar, a tune I heard whistled on Expedition's streets, but the pulse and winding rhythm of the
song made it seem like a proclamation. Only I did not
know what for.

When they finished, we proceeded along another walkway to a large wooden building raised on stilts and surrounded by a veranda lit by gas lamps. Bee strode toward
the building as toward her destiny, head high. She was so
beautiful.

We climbed three stairs onto the porch and its carpet
of matting. Past open doors lay a large room draped with
fine netting over the furnishings, a lovingly lathed and
polished table set with gold-plated dishes and shining silver utensils that was flanked by two Europan-style chairs,
and a matched pair of plush Turanian couches suitable
for conversation. On the far side of the chamber, hands
clasped behind his back, Prince Caonabo stood looking
out a window onto the night beyond. He turned, hearing
us. He was so like to Juba in feature that it was only by
the length of his hair that you could tell them apart. Incongruously, he wore trousers, and a dash jacket that had
certainly been tailored in Europa—or on Tailors' Row in
the Passaporte District from a pattern off one of Vai's
jackets—out of sober sea-green cotton. One might think
he was endeavoring to make his foreign bride comfortable with familiar things, although he was also, even
more incongruously, barefoot.

As we paused on the porch for Bee to catch her breath

and steady her nerves, a woman came hurrying around from another side of the building. With a gesture at me, she explained something to the most senior of our escorts.

Bee's serene expression creased into confusion and then darkened to dismay. "They are saying you cannot enter with me. That you cannot stay at all, Cat. There's a misunderstanding...They've changed their minds." She took my hand, but her gaze was on the prince. "But it's too late for me to retreat now. You have to go. I'll be all right."

I shook my hand out of hers. "Wait just a moment."

I charged into the chamber and right up to him as he blinked in astonishment. "Prince Caonabo, I have brought your bride but I have two things to say to you first. If you harm her or let her come to harm, I will gouge out your eyes and then eat them. That is one. As for the other, she must go to troll town in Expedition before the sun sets on Hallows' Night. Promise me you will see that she is taken safely there until a full day has passed."

"Perdita!" he exclaimed, eyes wide with astonishment.

Soldiers swarmed out of the alcoves and herded me back to the porch without touching me.

"That was rash," said Bee, pulling me close as the soldiers melted away under the sting of her glare. "Cat, I shall be fine. I'm sorry to lose you, but Andevai will be glad to have you back."

I crushed her against me, murmuring, "You must be inside troll town before Hallows' Night falls. The maze will hide you. Promise me."

She kissed me on each cheek and gently put me away from her. Her gaze was clear and her expression determined. "I promise you I will live."

She went in as Prince Caonabo stepped forward to

greet her. Women blocked the doors with screens of translucent muslin and lowered beaded curtains to close off the view.

I put up no fuss as the two fire mages and their four attendants ushered me to an adjoining building whose limbs and wings made it resemble a sleeping frog. We entered a small chamber meant, I thought, to be humble, but fitted with wall hangings encrusted with priceless shell and pearl beads. They left me there alone. Baskets and gourds hung from the ceiling, interspersed with unlit lamps. I sat on a mat beside a low table. A woman brought a tray with two cups and a steaming pot of pungent herbs. She did not pour but left me in darkness except for my cat's sight that even in darkness could discern the angles and corners of the room. My skin felt inflamed, and it itched. I was tired and thirsty and hungry, and I had eaten nothing since midday and was coming to the unpleasant conclusion that while Bee enjoyed a feast with the prince, I might be held here all night in disgrace. I hesitated to sneak out since my disappearance could cause trouble for Bee. I wondered where Vai was.

The door opened. Four women entered, one sitting at each corner of the room. Their presence made my sword tremble with a pulse of cold magic. Flames leaped, and the women—north, south, east, and west—shimmered with a glow like the gilding of moonrise on still waters.

The behica entered the room.

"Blessed Tanit," I said, more to myself than to anyone, "they are all fire banes, and you are using them as catchfires."

The behica measured me as Vai's boss at the carpentry yard had once done: marked and tallied. Sitting, she poured two cups, sipped at both, and offered one to me. She lifted to her lips a cigarillo. With an intake of breath, embers gleamed red and smoke curled up. She sucked twice, the smoke quite pungent, then offered the cigarillo to me.

It seemed dangerously rude not to accept. I set the unlit end to my mouth and inhaled. The jolt went straight to my eyes, and I racked out a spasm of coughing as smoke swirled around my face. The room tilted and, as I put out a hand to catch myself on the table, settled upright once. She took the cigarillo back. I gulped down the drink to rinse the harsh taste from my mouth.

"Why have you to Taino country come?" she asked in serviceable Latin.

"Isn't it obvious I came for my cousin's sake? For her only?"

Licking my lips, I tasted too late the chalky flavor of the drink Juba had given me to ease the burn. Was she intending to drug me? I grasped at the shadows and pulled them tight.

But as she drew in the cigarillo's smoke, she merely watched with interest as a cat watches the struggles of a trapped mouse. "That you came surprises me. Your feet rest on Taino earth, Perdita. Thus you are subject to Taino law."

I tried to rise, but my legs had turned to stone. I would have dragged myself out of the room with my arms, but a tall, broad-shouldered, black-haired man blocked the door.

I knew him. He was Camjiata.

My mind produced words, but my lips remained silent.

Watching me, the behica spoke to him. "Was it your intention to send this one across the border when you know

the law would compel me to arrest her? The same law
that forced me to bury my son when he was bitten by a
salter?"

"It was my intention, Your Majesty. I regret it, but it
was necessary."

I could not find the hilt of my sword.

"Do you truly regret it? I must wonder, given your action. I regret losing the son best suited to inherit the duho,
for a day will come soon when my brother will walk to
the other side of the island. My son Haübey was meant to
sit in the seat of power after him."

"You have not lost Juba. I spoke to him this morning."

"You spoke to an opia, not to my son. My son was
killed by the bite of a salter."

"Is he dead? I thought Prince Caonabo had healed
Juba. I thought the brothers put it about that Juba fled because he refused to become his brother's catch-fire. For
Prince Caonabo came late to the fire, did he not? Juba told
me no one thought the twin brothers had any mage craft
in them at all."

"You misunderstood the opia's words. Easy enough to
do. Among my people it is understood that all people
have the seed in them, but the seed does not flower in all
people."

"You think all people could become cold mages or fire
mages if they wished?"

"You simplify. The seed may be buried deep. It may
be too weak to germinate. There are many reasons some
bloom and others never do. My sons showed no such
power. Sometimes people close that gate of their own
will. I was glad of it. Then they went hunting, as young
men will do, deep in the forest in the mountains. Haübey
was bitten. Sparked by the love that binds the brothers,

Caonabo woke the seed in himself and healed his brother.
But Haübey is still dead. That is the law."

Slowly, slowly, I braced a hand on the table, but my
torso had gone numb. I slumped against the wall, but even
that was better than tipping over facedown onto the mat.

"That is the law," Camjiata agreed. "I have delivered
your exiled son as I promised. This girl likewise. Together, they provide the legal excuse you need to occupy
Expedition because Expedition has broken the terms of
the First Treaty by harboring people bitten by salters."

"I acknowledge that you have met your part of our bargain. I will meet mine."

"By the way, I want the cane she carries. It is a sword."

"It is a cemi. It is bound to her. Why do you want it?"

"I think her mother's spirit inhabits it. Her mother was
bound to me also. I want the cane."

"You will have a difficult time leashing a cemi that
does not wish to be bound to you," she said with a hard
smile.

A knife flashed in his hand. He stepped past her and
bent over me. Nothing I could do, no furious diatribe in
my mind, no phantom assault by my paralyzed limbs,
could stop him from slicing the loop and allowing my
sword to roll away from my body out of my reach. He did
not try to pick it up. He merely stepped back to address
the cacica.

"We leash as we must. By the way, I have an exceptionally powerful fire bane you will be very interested in.
If you can control him."

"I should like to see this. There is no fire bane I cannot
control."

She rose, and they departed together. I grunted under
my breath, straining, but I could not move. Women came

in to truss, tie, and gag me. My thoughts plowed a sluggish furrow. To blink took all my effort and concentration.

A shadowy crow settled on my face, talons digging into my cheeks. I could not fight or even scream as it pecked out my eyes and ate them, leaving me blind with nothing but the sting of my fire-burned skin to tell me tales of the world. Hands lifted me into a sling. Rope abraded me as I was jostled along. The close still air within the building melted into the cling of a steamy breeze outside. As through muffling cloth, I heard a clamor of voices as drums rattled a call to battle and men cried out to weigh anchor. Alarm horns sounded far away and too feebly to matter. Then came silence.

Smoke curled up my nose and pooled in the aching hollows where once had been my eyes. In these swirling pools I saw as with the crow's vision from high above. Somehow it was daylight, and Bee and Caonabo sat in a courtyard sharing a large hammock under the shade of a tree, he now dressed in white cotton in the Taino way. He had one leg crossed under him and one on the ground rocking the hammock. Not quite touching him, Bee reclined at her ease, casual in a blouse and pagne. She was talking quite intently and, to my surprise, listened equally intently as he replied. They looked up as the shadows of airships rippled over the ground. Up and up my eyes flew, as airships crossed the border between the Taino kingdom and Expedition Territory. Far below, soldiers marched in neat ranks down the roads and paths that led through the outlying pastures, fields, and orchards toward the city. Wardens shouted down the streets calling for peace and order while brash young men raged in alleys holding machetes and axes and adzes. Luce stood at the gate, staring, as a column of Taino soldiers passed down the street; a few looked her up and down although none broke ranks; Aunty Djeneba yanked her inside and barred the gate.

I woke up, buzzing and swaying with the wind in my face and soldiers behind me speaking Taino so rapidly its lilt was music. I heard the fluttering roar of the airship's propeller. Empty air surrounded me, a chasm whose winds dizzied me. But I could see with my own eyes.

Pale pink light rimmed the east like a rose's unfurling. Below lay briny waters still dark in slumber. I was bound into a large sling and suspended off the prow of an airship, dangling in the air far above the sea. The scream I wanted to make spilled into a torrent of trembling that shook through my whole body. I breathed down my panic as I considered my situation. Rope bound my wrists. I worked my fingers to turn my wrists back and forth, trying to get play in the rope.

But it was already too late. As the sun rose, so a shore rose before us, a band of white beach lapped by blue water. Below, a signal flag was raised from within a familiar half circle of houses.

The airship descended, and the anchor was dropped, the prow swinging clockwise as they lowered me down.

To Salt Island.

34

First they placed me in an enclosure with stout wooden bars, packed earth as a floor, an awning to protect me against rain and sun, and a bucket for waste. But after a day of kicking, prying, digging, chewing, and climbing, I was clouted over the head. While I was stunned, they locked me in a metal cage set on stone with no protection from sun or rain and nowhere to relieve myself except where I crouched. The cage was so small I could not stand straight nor stretch out.

My head ached, and I vomited all down my front.

"Don' fight it, gal," said a woman from behind me. "Yee only harm yee own self."

The ground reeled, only it was me and not the ground reeling. I leaned against the outer wall of the enclosure and shut my eyes as the sun set.

The sun rose. A hand poked me. A cup swam in front of my face. I was so thirsty I drank without thinking, but it was guava juice with lime and pineapple, my favorite that Vai had so often brought me. Such a riptide of longing and fury and fear dragged through me that it was all I could do not to fling the cup at the bars in the hope it would shatter into as many pieces as my broken dreams.

Instead, I choked down my rage and said, "Might I have more, please?"

My voice scraped horribly. But they gave me more. They pulled a length of canvas over the bars so the sun did not cook me. I swallowed as much as I could of the yam pudding my captors offered. My stomach churned, but nothing came back up. In my stinking clothes, I rested to gather my strength. The enclosure sat in a clearing surrounded by trees and backed by a rocky ridge. I saw no sign of habitation. Yet from the distance, sounds remarkably like those of the commonplace work of a village floated on the breeze: grain being pounded with women singing in accompaniment; wood being chopped; a strap being stropped.

The next day they allowed me back into the first enclosure. A crow landed on the palisade, measuring me as if to remind me to measure once again the height of the walls. Then it flew off.

About midday, three shackled women were shoved into the enclosure, one weeping copiously, one stunned, and one with the resigned air of the condemned whose reprieve has run out. They sat as far from me as possible.

"Are you from Expedition?" I asked.

The resigned one called to the man fastening the locks on the gate. "That one stink. Can yee wash her, or put her elsewhere?"

"We got no other cage," said the man. "Women come to this side of the island shall stay in the cage 'til we see if they's pregnant."

"What happens if they're pregnant?" I called, but he was already walking away.

"How did you come here?" I asked the others in a voice I hoped was mild.

After eyeing me suspiciously, one answered. "The Taino arrested us."

"Did the Taino occupy Expedition?"

"That talk of a wedding areito was nothing but an excuse to bring in they army. On the Council steps they read out a proclamation. It say Expedition's Council broke the First Treaty because folk bitten and healed were let stay in the city, not sent to Salt Island. The Taino behiques and soldiers hunted down all them who was bitten and healed. Like us. 'Tis how we come here."

I thought of the way the occupying soldiers had looked at Luce in my dream, and such a spear of killing rage pierced my heart at the thought of the liberties soldiers might take when they had the right of arms, that the three women shrank away from me as if I had snarled.

So I did. "Give me your pagnes. You do not want me to get angry."

I tied the lengths of cloth into a makeshift rope as they cowered in the corner. I dumped out the contents of the bucket and tied the cloth to the handle. It took me six tries to get the bucket over the palisade and properly hooked to take my weight. Though I was shaky, it was not so difficult to climb the rope of pagnes and heave myself over the wall. They began yelling as I lowered myself to the limit of my hands and dropped the rest of the way. I landed on my feet.

Shadows drawn around me, I ran down the path. I had not seen this side of the island before. I was surprised to find a pretty community with fenced compounds strung alongside stands of fruit trees and mounded fields. Flower and vegetable gardens offered a fine view over the sea. Fish and meat dried on racks, but I saw no fishing boats. A plaza, small batey court, and thatched-roof assembly house linked together the sprawling wings of the village. I could, just barely, hear the captive women shouting, but no one here seemed to notice. In the village, folk napped in the heat of the day. Crows fought over a slip of silver ribbon. A woman grated cassava root, chatting with a companion who was plaiting a basket out of reeds. The one thing I did not see was children.

I slipped through the village, stole two pagnes and a blouse from a clothesline, a knife and a machete, a stack of cassava bread, dried fish, and gourds that I filled with fresh water from a cistern. I stashed my bundle in the crook of a tree at the forest's edge. Then I crept to the field farthest from the village, where four men with hoes and machetes sat amid cassava mounds and drank maize beer.

I said, "Know yee of a man named Haübey, or Juba?" They leaped up in consternation, for they could not see me. "Don' bother seeking me, for I's an opia. He made promises to me cousin."

Three of the men looked Taino, and although it was clear they could barely understand me, they set down their machetes. One held out a ripe guava. My mouth watered, but I did not take it.

The fourth man had a shaved head and a bushy beard. "You don' scare us, opia. We who live here is dead to we other life, just as yee is. That Haübey came here on the boat two years back. We knew he was noble-born, but even they nobles is treated the same under Taino law."

"Where is Haübey now?"

"He is gone."

"How could he leave the island?"

"I reckon that question is one we all shall wish an answer for."

"Me thanks." I snatched the guava, startling them. "I crave yam pudding and rice porridge. Just set a big bowl out every night in the ball court, and I shall be no bother at all."

Soon after I reached my stash, a bell began to ring. They had discovered my escape. Yet with no dogs on the island, how could they track me? I walked west toward a rocky out-runner of the ridge that rose like the spine of the island's back. In a tiny cove, I rinsed and wrung out my pagne and blouse. Where a rivulet of fresh water trickled down through a set of rocky pools, I scrubbed my face and hands. The rocks offered a route to the promontory, whose narrow headland broke the waters like the prow of a ship.

I climbed. The wind rippled through my clothes; the sun beat down on my back; the sea shone. White-winged birds sailed above me, riding the currents of air. From that height I could see the contours of the island, with the village on one side and the quarantine pens on the bay on the opposite side: As with life and death, it was a short walk from one shore to the other.

Yet my spirits lifted with the swooping play of the birds. Let them come. They would not catch me.

As the sun set I made my way down. Dusk smeared gold onto the waters. I found a sheltered beach, and there I stripped and waded in. In the sea, I washed fear and doubt from my heart and emerged with the water streaming off me.

So much for Camjiata's promises. Had his wife truly told him I would be the instrument of his death or had he just said that to intimidate and fluster me? Had he been plotting to get rid of me all along, after he had used me to flush out Vai? Was that why he had thrown me into the path of the cacica? She had exiled her own son to Salt Island, and I could not know whether she had engineered Juba's rescue or if another person had. Maybe she had truly acted in the cause of justice, that the law apply in equal measure to all. I did not know her, so I could not be sure.

But I was sure of this: The general had betrayed us. Vai thought I was with Bee, and Bee would think I was back with Vai. They had walked straight into the trap. And while Bee had gone in as a willing pawn with the intent to become a queen, Vai had followed merely to stay near me.

"There is no fire bane I cannot control."

The memory of the cacica's words burrowed into my heart. First they scoured me with despair. Then I got angry.

So be it. My enemies had no idea what anger they had woken. Hard to imagine I would ever be glad to have an opportunity to say it:

My sire is the Master of the Wild Hunt. And Hallows' Night is coming.

35

The last day of October dawned with rain and blood.

On the previous night, 1 had crept to the assembly house to eat my nightly bowl of porridge only to find the village gathered to discuss the weather. A red dawn and the afternoon's steadily rising swells foretold the coming of the Angry Queen. I slept in the rafters of a roofless, abandoned shed, and woke at daybreak soaking wet from a squall of rain and bleeding with my monthly courses. I endured the rain but was glad of the blood.

As the winds began to batter, folk hurried to lash down everything they could before they headed to the ridge for safety. The storm was coming in faster than they had anticipated. Already water flooded up the shoreline far past the high-water mark. The wind had risen to such a pitch that it rumbled. Branches whipped, tearing free. A roof's thatch scattered in a bluster of debris. The sea was streaked with foam as the wind sheared the tops off the pounding waves.

The Herald of wind and thunder strode past high in the sky, his black hair a sheet of darkness. The Flood with his blue-green arms washed around the curve of the promontory, spray spitting so high I thought it would speckle the feet of his heavenly brother. I wanted to be like them. I let go of the shadows and stood with my face into the wind and my braid flying out behind me, sure the gale was about to lift me off my feet. And then I would walk the storm.

Only, of course, I was my mother's daughter, composed of mortal flesh, so the wind shoved me stumbling back. I slammed into a tree trunk. A wind-shorn coconut smacked into the ground beside me, barely missing my head.

A strong hand fastened harshly on my arm. "A remarkably pretty opia be haunting us," said the shaven-headed man. Once I might have been frightened by his lustful sneer and his machete.

I met his gaze. "The storm is coming for *me*. Do you want to be here when it arrives?"

He did not.

So I braved the day alone. I sheltered in the lee of the outer walls of the ball court. Rain tore in sheets driven horizontally by the gale. I could barely see the shoreline. A huge wave crashed across the lowest rank of houses, ripping them off their moorings in a splintering crashing roar. Yet the tremendous and unstoppable power of wind and rain and water transported me into a state of almost unendurable rapture. I was so alive.

Dusk settled as the darkness of Hallows' Night swept over the waters.

My ears popped. The wind ceased between one breath and the next.

A rip like a lance of light sliced through the massed clouds. Her eye opened, vast and terrible, and the spirit who was the hurricane saw me, an insignificant pest far below.

She blinked.

A shining coach pulled by four pearlescently white horses swept out of the embrace of the towering storm wall and coasted over the gleaming foam. The vehicle rolled to a halt on the wrack-ridden shore. Waves parted to flow around it. I ran down to meet them with my bundle of stolen belongings and purloined food slung over my back. The coachman raised his whip to greet me. The eru smiled as she swung down the steps and opened the door. She did not speak, so I merely nodded as I rushed up the steps into an interior lit by cold fire.

I shrieked. "Rory!"

He'd had his legs up on the narrow cushioned bench, lounging, but he swung them down to brace himself as I flung myself at him.

"Oof!" he said, as I hugged him.

"Rory!"

"You already said that." He fixed his big hands on my shoulders and held me away to offer a reproachful look. "I waited and waited for you but you never came. I began to think you just sent me away from that cursed old dragon because you were mad at me for trying to tear out his throat."

"I sent you away to save your life! So much has happened, I can barely remember that now! Why are you here?"

His eyelids closed partway, giving him the hooded look of a man who wants to speak frankly but dares not. "Our sire came to Massilia a moment ago, and leashed me."

Another presence waited in the coach, facing us from the opposite seat.

A young man studied me. A dash jacket, trousers, and kerchief of unrelieved black gave him the severe look of the accountant who comes to tell your aunt and uncle that they have lost all their money in an ill-advised speculative venture. Worn loose, his straight black hair fell to his hips, and there was something about its thick texture that made it seem it might writhe into life and choke me if I was foolish enough to anger him. I could not read his ancestry in his face, because while the hair reminded me of the Taino, his complexion made me think him Afric, and yet the cut of his nose and cheekbones might have been Celtic, and the epicanthic fold at his eyes reminded me of Captain Tira's Cathayan origins. He certainly had the arrogance of the Romans! He was, in fact, remarkably good-looking and no older than Vai.

He sniffed, inhaling with a lift of his chin. "A maiden no longer, it seems," he remarked, "but not gotten with child."

"Cat," said Rory, "your mouth is hanging open."

The coach rocked as we bucked back into the winds. I grabbed at a strap to steady myself as I gaped. How could I ever forget that voice?

The amber gaze, so like mine, pinned me. "Tell me, Daughter. Whose blood shall feed me tonight? That of the girl who walks the path of dreams? Or some other? Son, open the shutters."

Rory slid open the shutter of the door that opened into the mortal world. A tumult of wind and rain shook the coach. Raindrops iced as they spattered inside. A surly little voice hissed displeasure. A glitter of eyes winked on the door handle. With my sleeve, I wiped away a frosting of ice from the latch. Its gremlin face glowered briefly, but it seemed too intimidated to speak.

Rory leaned across and slid back the shutter on the door that opened into the spirit world. The hunt raced on the wind, tangling across the sky. Beasts clamored within the brawl of storm and surge. In their teeth I heard death: owls silent, snakes winding, hyenas cackling with laughter; the shrill of a hawk before it stoops, the pulse of fear that stops a beating heart, the festering that eats at flesh from within. If you are not to be killed then you must kill: That is the law of the hunt. Its drums sang in my heart, and the promise of blood tasted as sweet on my lips as a kiss.

I had that bastard Camjiata now.

"I know who it is, the power you sense rising." I shouted to be heard above the din.

"Lead on, little cat," said my sire, his cruel smile burning.

Expedition.

I leaned out the window to see the jetty lights burning and the masts in the harbor swaying in a blustering wind. Lights riddled the walls that ringed the old city. Sparks spun across twisting braids of smoke from the factories. Like tethered fish, the Taino airships that had spread out to occupy the city bobbed and tugged against the rising wind. We had come in so fast and unexpectedly that the airmen realized the danger too late; Taino sailors began hauling down the smallest airships in a belated attempt to stake them down and save them. The others bucked and rolled. A cable snapped. A stubby prow dipped, slicing across a building's roof and jarring a cistern off its moorings. Water poured down the walls as people ran to escape the crumbling roof.

All across the city, people raced to shutter windows and tie netting over homes and roofs. Yet because of the speed of the storm, their efforts would not come quickly enough.

What must destroy the fleet would devastate the city.

So be it. Ice rimed my lips and chilled my heart. I was the hunter's daughter.

But I was also Luce's friend.

I would have grasped my sire's hand like a supplicant, but I dared not touch him. "Promise me the hurricane will not come here, only the wind of our passing."

He set a hand on the rim of the open window. "The hurricane will come someday, for the hurricane lives in this part of the world. But on this night the Angry Queen walks elsewhere. Then she will sleep until the season turns and the waters warm again."

He leaned out to look. The coach circled the factory district, and one by one every factory engine stuttered and, with a collapsing hiss of steam, died. Gas lamps exploded. All the street lightning went out. A dull *boom* shook through the air.

He licked his lips with the precision of a cat. "Where is the dreamer? I cannot taste her."

The maze of troll town glittered below, cutting through the chains of the magic he used to track his prey. I sought for her in my heart, and for a moment I caught her, but a mirror's reflected light spun her image away and I lost her.

"I have hidden her from you!" I cried as my heart thrilled with triumph.

"So the little cat bites back." His gaze on me could not be shed. He might have drained dry my spirit as easily as cut my throat to feast on my blood. "Where is the blood I'm owed this night?"

"I'm not sure how to find him."

"Hunt down the threads that bind the world to find him, Daughter."

Rory pressed fingers to my knee. "Scent is not only your nose, Cat. Who are you looking for? I can help you."

"Let her sharpen the blade of her senses on her own," said our sire. "How can she hone her steel if you do the work for her?"

My right hand I splayed over my breastbone. In the interstices that knit together the mortal world and the spirit world, I sought the ones I loved. Bee's heart beat so close to mine it was as if my breath mingled with hers, even as mirrors shattered her image into a thousand shards. The locket tingled against my palm, and its warmth tugged me toward Vai's bright spirit to the north. Rory was right here. I could even feel Bee's little sisters, Aunt Tilly and Uncle Jonatan, Luce and them at the boardinghouse, their lives like feathers tickling my skin. They were all safe.

I licked my lips, trying to taste the air as my sire tasted it, trying to sense the land as he sensed it. The mortal world was an impenetrable shadow, here and there pierced by essences I had no other word for except *light*. Scattered across the city and land below shone the spirits of mages strong enough to scent. Some flickered within the mortal shadow like comforting candlelight or gleamed with the steady purpose of gaslight. Others smoldered like half-buried coals. A few flared like pitch torches set alight. One I recognized: Drake simmered in the general's town house, and at first look it was easy to see his magic as nothing more than a sullen red glow of no particular strength. But Vai had been right, of course. That smolder was merely a cap for a vast reservoir of molten power barely tamped down and ready to erupt.

I marked him. But I turned my heart toward the enemy I sought.

"General Camjiata. Lion of war. Leonnorios Aemilius Keita."

I closed my left hand at my waist as if I held the hilt of the sword Camjiata had stolen from me. As at my command, my kinsmen bolted on the paths that net the world: loping wolves, baying hounds, rippling cats, silent sharks, winged raptors. From the smallest to the largest, they raced on the scent I envisioned more as a face and a figure and a presence than as a smell.

My senses slammed up against the border between Expedition and Taino country as against a spirit rope strung with amulets and charms. The Taino had woven a barrier around their kingdom not just with wealth and weapons but with what Vai's grandmother might have called the nyama of their behiques. Yet it took me, half mortal as I was, only a moment's negotiation to tear a rip in the spirit barrier. I slipped through, and the hunt poured through after me.

The island of Kiskeya slumbered, as yet unaware of this invasion, but her beating heart pulsed in the rhythm of the wedding areito. I heard its chant and rattle but I could not see the plaza or the ball courts; I couldn't see the people celebrating. They were hidden from me because they were wreathed in shadow. I knew Camjiata was close, but I could not find him.

Yet the world was lit. Flames like gas lamps marked each behique, some burning fierce and strong while others simmered with a fire humble or frail. Yet in truth the presence of all those fire mages was difficult to distinguish against the brightest blaze. Most were like candles held next to a bonfire. The cacica's magic burned so brightly that she almost blinded all else. How she did not kindle into an inferno I did not at first understand. She ought to be dead. The backlash of her power ought to have consumed her long since, but it had not. Nor was she surrounded by the charred corpses of her catch-fires. She was surrounded by a net of magic that shone as a dew-moistened spider's web might when the rising sun catches in the filaments and breathes light over them.

Threads pulsing as with the flow of energy stretched from the Taino plaza across great distances into the faraway masses of the huge ice sheets, through the spirit world, and back into the mortal world. These threads did not have color, precisely, nor did they glow as flame does. Like spirit, they were animate, or at least shot through with energy and force. Were these threads cold magic? Each led back to a different point, and those points were not flames but intangible wells of power that reminded me of the deep blue pool on Salt Island that Drake had told me was considered sacred by the Taino.

Those wells of power were cold mages. For at last, I understood what I was seeing. Her catch-fires were all fire banes. She was continually casting off heat into an entire troop of catch-fires linked to her as if they were knitted into one garment. She did not pour the backlash into a single catch-fire but divided the stream into many, so no single one was overwhelmed and thus consumed, as I had almost been killed by Drake. Anyway, the fire banes who were her catch-fires were not killing her combustion, or even absorbing it. Their bodies were conduits. The cool depths of their spirits like wells swallowed the constant pillowing outwash of the cacica's fire magic and expelled it through glimmering threads into the spirit world.

The brilliance of her power obscured all scent or taste or sound of the general.

I could not find him.

But there was one spirit she did not obscure. Right next to the cacica, a well of dazzling purity plunged into the bottomless blue waters of the spirit world. Its play of welcoming light and restless energy beckoned like the surface of water seen from below when your lungs are almost out of air.

"Vai," I whispered, but my lips made no sound.

Crows scattered on the vanguard of the storm. Their eyes belonged to the master of the hunt. Clothing myself in their wings, I flew so that I could see into the mortal world with their eyes.

The Taino had chosen this night, Hallows' Night, to receive Expedition's surrender.

Wardens and riflemen knelt in ranks on the main plaza, their faces masked with the anger and shame of the soldier who has had his sword removed by his own captain. I glimpsed Gaius Sanogo standing at the rear of the ranks, hands clasped behind his back as he surveyed the scene with his ominously bland smile. In the darkness beyond the light stood companies of Taino soldiers, but I could not judge their mood.

The crows flew onward to the central ball court, which was ringed by a hundred ordinary lamps. That so many lamps burned despite the presence of so many fire banes made the cacica's power seem even more impressive. In the center of the ball court, the proud Council members, the wealthiest and most powerful of Expedition's ruling families, knelt with heads bowed. Their families and households and kinfolk huddled at the base of the risers like a discouraged losing team. Behind them stood other Expeditioners notable enough to be forced to attend this ceremony. All looked crushed and defeated. I saw no trolls at all.

The Council was surrendering to Prince Caonabo. His fire magic was difficult to see under the glare of his mother's power, and even so it was nothing more than a sober, quiet flame. He stood straight and somber, receiving a copy of a written document that I assumed was the First Treaty. On the stone risers, like spectators to the final game in a prestigious tournament, sat many Taino, both women and men. Some seemed skeptical, even disapproving, while others looked pleased and triumphant.

The cacica sat on a carved duho, her seat of power, placed on a raised wooden platform at one end of the ball court. Some of her catch-fires sat near her, while others were scattered around the ball court and some even outside it. The geometry of their placement was too convoluted for me to follow. Nor did it matter, for out of them all, only one caught my eye.

Vai sat cross-legged on a mat on the ground next to the cacica's duho. With his hands relaxed on his thighs, he looked perfectly at ease as he turned to speak to the queen. I did not like the way she looked at him! Suddenly those rumors that she forced male fire banes to marry her did not seem far-fetched or scurrilous. What did she care about the marriage laws of Europans and the chains that bound him and me? I had a hankering for a chisel.

His demeanor I could not fault, for he displayed toward her the respect he always showed women. She was, I thought, pointing out to him the geometry of her catch-fires, dispersed in a pattern that extended farther than my crow's eyes could see. Like lamps turned low, each visible fire bane was limned by a nimbus of silvery mist. No nimbus touched Vai. She was not diverting any of the backlash into him.

His eyes widened and his head cocked to one side as

if he heard an unexpected sound. After a comment to the cacica, he rose, his gaze lifting to sweep the darkness beyond.

I was sure he had sensed me.

The crows swooped low over the ball court. Behind Caonabo, set between the prince and the platform where the cacica presided, rose six wooden posts. A person was lashed to each post as to a mast. One of the prisoners was Juba, who gazed over the assembly with the look of a man who knows he has been condemned and is not sorry for the crime that has brought him to this place of execution. Juba and Caonabo truly had uncannily identical features, but once you had seen them together, you could never mistake one for the other, for Caonabo was grave and self-contained while Juba was impassioned and impatient.

The crow settled on top of one of the posts. To my utter horror, I recognized the woman tied there. Abby's clothing was so humble and dirt-stained you could tell she had been snatched from the fields. She had her eyes shut. By the way her lips moved, she seemed to be singing.

Yet even she was not the person I needed to find.

The crow looked into the darkness and fixed on the great stone eye through which the players could score a goal. From the shadows, General Camjiata observed the proceedings, flanked by Captain Tira and the one-eyed proprietor of the Speckled Iguana.

On the ball court, Caonabo was speaking to the Expeditioners. He sounded weary but unswerving, a man who does not like the task he has been given but will carry it out to its fullest.

"Always, we the Taino have held in every regard to the First Treaty, which our ancestors made with your ancestors. We respect the words and agreements of those who came before us as if they were our own, for they are our own. You have allowed the threat of salters to live among you. The bitten must be exiled to Salt Island, even if they are healed. They are dead. That is the law. We did not unearth this disease. You brought it on your ships. We allowed you to build your city as long as the agreement we made was honored. But it has not been honored—"

He broke off, raising a hand to test the air. He turned to address the cacica. "Most dignified and wise of mothers," he said, "forgive my impetuous speech for I have not received permission to address you, but this wind is not natural. A spirit comes."

The crow fluttered to the great stone eye and looked down. An expression very like fear pinched the general's face as he looked at the night sky.

"I see him!" I cried, but by speaking I broke the wings that bound me into the crow's eyes. I slammed hard onto the seat, knocking breath from my lungs. Rory steadied me.

"I see him," said the Master of the Wild Hunt, with a smile.

Such simple words to herald death.

The world tipped beneath me as the coach banked sharply, plunging toward the ground. I fell against the latch, and my weight clicked it down with a spark of protest from the gremlin. The door swung out with me holding to it. The wind loosed my hair, and it streamed out behind me like the wings of the storm.

As the coach skated above the paving stones right down the center of the ball court, people scattered out of the way, shouting. They dragged companions with them, or shoved others aside in their scramble to escape. Some flung themselves down, cowering.

The coach rolled smoothly to a halt a hand's height above the ground. The horses stamped and steamed. I released the latch to step down daintily onto the ball court.

Every gaze was turned to me. I would not have had it any other way.

As one, as in greeting or to show respect, the Taino rose.

I paused one breath, to acknowledge them. Then I sought and found my enemy beneath the stone eye.

"I do not like being betrayed, General Camjiata." My voice carried easily, for the wind had ceased so utterly that the very atmosphere, like a rope, stretched taut. Yet my long black hair still rippled and flowed in the unseen tides of magic that washed around us. "Not once did you betray me. Not twice did you betray me. But with every promise or offer you have made to me, you betrayed me. Where are my husband and my sword, both of which you stole from me?"

Camjiata stepped out of the shadows. He was not a man to be beaten down. Whatever fears haunted him, no sign of fear marred his face now. He appealed to the crowd.

"An opia haunts us! In northern lands, we call this day Hallows' Night, and know it for the day when the dead may cross into the land of the living. We cannot trust the shadows that walk out of the night on this night, of all nights."

"I am no opia—" I retorted, but he cut me off.

"Yet she is no opia," he cried, with an orator's gesture that invited his audience to note how he had agreed. "She is a witch and a salter. She has used her witchcraft to escape from Salt Island and means to infest us all *with the salt plague*."

A man who knew how to infest an orderly crowd with terror and strife could make the mob do his bidding. As startled and scared as the Expeditioners had been at the appearance of a coach riding down the wings of night, the salt plague frightened them far more. People pushed and shoved and began trying to climb up into the risers where the Taino, so collected and calm before, were now looking alarmed. Everyone seemed desperate to get away before I lurched over to bite them.

At Prince Caonabo's order, Taino soldiers made a fence around the ball court's exits, while others hurried onto the risers to restore order. But I wasn't worried about them. Captain Tira was pushing through the surging crowd; she had a hand on her sword and her gaze on me, and I didn't have to be my sire's daughter or a Hassi Barahal spy to figure she had just been ordered to kill me.

Rory slipped down out of the coach with the grace of a prowling cat and handed me the machete I'd stolen from Salt Island. I stepped back, weighing the machete in my hand as I looked around for Camjiata. But it was Vai I saw. He shoved through the crowd with a naked blade of cold steel in his hand. He looked stunned and angry and oh so welcome as he placed himself beside me.

Captain Tira halted, too far away to lunge at me with her falcata.

"Catherine, they told me you were sequestered with Beatrice!"

"They lied. I was kidnapped and sent to Salt Island."

As if to reassure himself that I was real and not illusion, he reached for my hand.

A searingly cold wind swept across the ball court. An icy sleet began to drizzle. My sire stepped down out of the coach as into a fine summer's balm.

His gaze met mine just as Vai's fingers brushed my hand.

The Master of the Wild Hunt smiled. It was nothing more than a slight upward quirk of the lips and an infinitesimal narrowing of the eyes, but it was the most horrifying expression I had ever seen. I snatched my betraying touch back from Vai's, but it was too late.

My sire licked his lips, as if tasting the most delicious food.

"Strong and sweet!" His smile mocked me, for he understood perfectly my look of horror. "You are truly my daughter, to have sought and bound such rich blood as this."

"No!" At last I spotted Camjiata making his way toward the end of the ball court, hoping to escape Vai's cold steel and my anger. "That's your prey!"

"The fire weaver?" His gaze lifted to the cacica. "So rare it is to find one such as her. I knew there was tremendous power hiding behind their spirit fence. But I couldn't get through it to find out. Yet after all, the smell of the cold mage's blood delights me far more."

"No! No!" Camjiata was almost out of sight. "Him! Over there!"

My sire stared right where I pointed. "I see only darkness. There is no one there. Do not try to deceive me."

The Master of the Wild Hunt was blind in the mortal world except to the flare of those who channeled the energies that bind the worlds, that weave life to death and death to life, order and disorder. He could not see Camjiata to take him, even if he could be bothered to want to.

"Stand away!" The cacica's voice cracked over the night like thunder. Fire flared in every lamp. Light blazed to reveal the Taino soldiers restoring order. The coach, with the coachman and footman, appeared as a perfectly ordinary coach at rest except for the fact its wheels did not touch the ground. What looked like low-hanging dark clouds churned above, chased by flashes of light like fireflies. The pack of hunters had not yet been released.

"Stand away, fire bane," she called, addressing Vai before she commanded the assembled crowd. "Opia travel at their will. We have no quarrel with them, even if they invite in the spirit lords who are not welcome here. But the salt dead may never walk in Taino land lest we all be poisoned. Those who will not stay on the other shore must be destroyed by fire."

Her gaze touched Juba's. In that exchange I saw her sorrow and his defiance: She had favored him over his brother, and I could not tell whether he had never forgiven her for her weakness in loving him more than Caonabo, or if she would never forgive herself.

"That is the law," she proclaimed.

Sparks shimmered to life on a hot gust of wind as she struck.

"Not my Cat." Vai pulled me hard against him while yanking the last ice lens out from under his jacket.

Fire kindled in my heart. Abby, and the other prisoners, screamed. Prince Caonabo shouted in protest, but there was nothing he could do. The cacica was a fire mage of unimaginable power with a net of fire banes to absorb the conflagration.

Vai's ice lens bloomed as he channeled his magic and his anger and his fear for me into it; the curve of the lens amplified its power. The cacica's fire was vast and complex; its tendrils spanned the ball court and the plaza and farther yet, for the net of her fire magic spanned the island itself. Its threads reached as far as a sick man's bed in distant Sharagua halfway across Kiskeya, where the constant pulse of her magic kept her dying brother alive.

All that fire, the fire bane and his ice lens killed.

Every lamp snapped out.

In far Sharagua, the heart of the cacique stopped beating. Lips parted to release his spirit into the night.

Snow spun down in a beautiful shower of sparkling white, dusting the ground.

"Catherine!" Vai pressed his mouth to mine, just a touch, to mark that I still breathed.

Darkness and silence settled over the land.

Yet out of that darkness, the cacica spoke, unmoved and unperturbed. "I will enforce the law as I must to protect the people. There can be no exception. And I will not be defied."

A flame wavered into life, a single oil lamp catching fire. For after all, there was no limit to the source of fire as long as it had fuel with which to burn. As on an inhalation, she gathered her power back into her and began casting it off into her catch-fires. Filaments of cold magic streamed away in a growing flood, her net brightening as she gathered her power. Cold mages weren't the only ones who could get angry.

She was certainly going to kill me, and possibly Vai in the bargain. I cast one last despairing glance toward poor Abby and the other prisoners, but I simply had run out of time and chance.

"Vai! Run!" I cried.

The cursed fool did not budge. "I'm not leaving you behind."

A shadow quite inverse to the size of its human form loomed over us like a thundercloud.

"This has all been quite illuminating and much more diverting than my usual hunt."

My sire's right hand fell like fate on Vai's shoulder. With his left, he grasped the chain and slipped the now-clouded ice lens into his palm as he might admire a lovely flower, then closed his fingers over it.

"I will take him now. You've done well, Daughter."

I raised the machete. "You will not! He's not the one I mean you to take."

"Whenever did I give you the impression that your wishes, desires, or intentions mean anything to me?" His grasp had paralyzed Vai.

He glanced up at the sky toward the hunters and killers who, when he called, would sweep down to rend and dismember their prey. No human on the ground could see them; perhaps humans could not see the Master of the Wild Hunt either, not really, for he walked half in and half out of the world, perceived as fear and hunger but not truly seen.

The dusting of snow evaporated in a wave of rising heat. I was caught between an immensely powerful fire mage who was about to kill me, and the Master of the Wild Hunt, who was about to kill the man I loved. I could not fight, and I could not run. I had to think with my mind.

For the truth was, why would my sire appear as a good-looking young male? Why would he even care how he looked? I knew something about dealing with vain men.

"Father," I said, "I know you do not hold me in any affection, but I am the weapon you forged, the one you alone can wield. Are you going to let that fire weaver destroy me? It makes you look careless. It makes you look weak. But I guess you can't stop her."

Killing fire pinched at my heart in that instant. I reached for Vai so that touching him would be my last memory before death consumed my flesh and mind.

My sire exhaled. Luminescent snow winked into existence, obliterating the heat. The white flakes were so scintillant they dazzled and blinded. My heart beat on, untouched.

He murmured, "Fire is the serpents' weapon. You know how I hate and loathe serpents."

Ice crackled across the stones.

"Kill her."

The clamor of the hunt dusted down over us as his words released them. They flowed out of the heavens like nightmare, surging forward in a squall of sleeting rain whose icy touch cut skin and caused blood to flow. Deadly hounds loped down the risers, biting and clawing as they passed. I could not tell if they were solid or merely the shadows that haunt dreams, but their touch spread like poison. Hulking dire wolves snarled, and hyenas laughed mockingly as Expeditioners and Taino alike were eaten up by stark fear, even the disciplined soldiers.

Many people tried to run, but the crush was so great they only trampled each other. Others froze, unable to move. A few tried to fight, blocking with arms or clubbing with rifles or slashing wildly with their ceremonial spears. Yet they could do no damage to the sleek cats and men with animals' faces who pushed through the ball court. A cloud of wasps stung, each touch raising a drop of blood. Bats swooped through, accompanied by silent owls. A red-gold-and-black-banded snake slithered over my sandaled foot; tiny frogs with skin as bright as jewels hopped alongside.

All swarmed toward the cacica's platform.

"Son," said my sire. "Did you not hear me? Kill her."

With a glance at me as if to apologize, Rory sighed. He bent, and he flowed. Where a man had stood, a huge saber-toothed cat leaped in silent beauty. The change came so swiftly that people running across the ball court to escape the hunt had no time to break out of his path as he bounded to the platform.

The cacica was no fool. Nor was she a coward. She faced the hunt as she drew deep into the fire, but before she could release it, the great cat drove her down beneath claws and teeth. He snapped her neck with a casual shake.

He, my amusing, insouciant Rory. He was his father's son.

The pack—wolves, snakes, cats, hounds, wasps, raptors, all—converged on the body, rending and tearing.

I had to look away.

The ball court was in chaos, the crowd streaming every which way. The Taino soldiers blocking the ends of the playing field had fled. People stampeded for safety, leaving broken and sobbing wounded behind. A few pockets of order held ground, among them Prince Caonabo who had not panicked but instead had taken advantage of the chaos to cut the bonds of his twin. Juba took the knife from his brother and ran to free the other prisoners. A ceremonial spear in hand, Caonabo approached the raised platform with soldiers at his heels. A shadowy hound loped past, a head hanging from its jaws by long black hair.

Then huge glittering flakes of a heavy snowfall obscured the scene, making it seem I, my sire, and Vai were alone in the world.

My sire opened his fingers. The chain and ring had crumbled into rust. When he blew on his hand, the red dust dispersed like chaff into the blowing snow. Touched by that dust, my machete corroded and deformed as rust bloomed on the blade, creeping up as if to engulf and consume my flesh. I let go. The blade shattered when it hit the ground.

He lifted Vai with one arm and shoved him into the coach.

"But you have this night's blood!" I cried as I scrambled in after Vai.

The door slammed shut behind me like the hammer of fate, leaving my sire outside and us within, his prisoners. A whip snapped. The coach rocked as the horses pulled us upward.

Vai blinked, shaking himself as if motion and will had just returned. "I understand now. Your sire is the Master of the Wild Hunt."

"And I hate him!" I cried as I tried to open latches and shutters, but they were all locked.

"Of course you do, love."

I flung my arms around him, and then we were kissing with the passion of the condemned.

"This is certainly more interesting than the last time you two were in the coach together."

I broke away to glare at the thin gremlin face with its winking gaze and straight line of a mouth. "Shut your eyes!"

Vai drew back, looking startled. "Catherine?"

"I'm talking to the latch! Prying little beast! I'll throw you in a furnace and melt you!"

"Catherine? Did you hit your head?"

"Didn't you hear what it said?"

"What makes you think I let him hear me?" said the latch with a smirk. "But if he weaves me a pretty illusion first, then I'll close my eyes and let you do that other thing in private."

"Catherine, as much as I would love to keep kissing you instead of hearing you rave on about furnaces, we need to do something *now*."

The door to the spirit world was opened from the outside. The gulf of the sky yawned, for we rolled through the void of heaven. The hunt coursed away into a swirl of lightning and black cloud. As calmly as if he were entering the coach from a street corner, my sire stepped in.

I threw myself across Vai to shield him. "You said there would only be one sacrifice."

My sire sat opposite us, raising his eyebrows as Vai set me to one side. Vai left his arm around me but did not speak. We faced the Master of the Wild Hunt together.

"By the terms of the contract, we can take only one," replied my sire. "We have taken this night's blood. But that doesn't mean I can't take a prisoner across to the spirit world with me. I'm going to find out what it was this magister did that he oughtn't to have been able to do." As he spoke, his human face slowly congealed into the mask of ice. "Which means that in addition to assuaging my terrible curiosity, I can release you, little cat, from my service. As long as he resides in my palace, I need only tug on the leash to bring you crawling back."

He leaned forward and pressed a hand on Vai's chest, his touch the embrace of ice.

Then he flung me out the open door.

36

Into the sea.

The warm salty water closed over my face, but I did not have the luxury of panic. I pulled to the surface and breached just as I realized two sharks were circling, drawn by the scent of my blood. My rage and hate leaked like poison into the water, and perhaps that was why they did not dart in for the kill. Or perhaps because they recognized a kinswoman. For they stayed away, merely keeping an eye on me as I floundered toward shore.

It seemed inevitable that I waded to shore at the jetty almost exactly where Drake had dumped me the first time. The few men working the piers turned to watch me emerge from the sea with my blouse and pagne plastered to my body, revealing every curve and mound. My blood streaked one leg. When I glared at them, they backed away.

I halted on the revetment next to baskets filled with fresh catch, slippery pargo with their red tails and little cachicata. Behind, the sun had risen two hands above the horizon, the dawn feed done and the wind no more than a soft breeze. The wide flat expanse of the waters in their constant shimmering reminded me of the trolls' mirrors. At least I had saved Bee.

The sky shone so blue it looked flat; wisps of cloud trailed off the highlands. I scanned the roofs and smoke of the city but saw no sign of the Taino airship fleet. Indeed, there weren't many men on the piers. The streets had a peculiar emptiness, as if most traffic had drained off in the face of a coming storm. The few men gathered into clumps to whisper and stare as I dripped across the boulevard and walked into the deserted carpentry yard. Only three people worked there, despite the early-morning coolness. The two men set down their axes and hurried under the shade of the shelter's roof, where the Taino boss was leaning over her table making tallies in her accounts book. She looked up, saw me, and said something in Taino to them. They bolted out the back as she straightened to greet me.

"The maku's perdita," she said in the local speech.

"Could you ask me a question, please?" I said.

She had the Taino habit of looking at you directly and without fear. "What manner of question shall I ask, Perdita?"

The thrill that coursed through my heart made me smile, not with joy but with resolve. "That was the right one. What day is it? What happened to the Taino fleet?"

"In the Roman calendar, 'tis the third day of November. As for the other, here is the story as I heard it. Three nights back, when the cursed Council surrendered Expedition to the Taino cacica, a witch flew down out of the night, turned she own self into a big black saber-toothed cat and killed the cacica, then tore her to bits and threw she head in a well. That witch was surely angry because the cacica had stolen the maku fire bane the witch loved. Yee suppose that could be true?"

"No, not quite like that. But what happened afterward?"

"The witch flew off with the maku."

"I mean, what has happened in Expedition?"

"Why, the wardens took control of Council House. Yesterday Gaius Sanogo was elected by unanimous vote as president of the committee that shall sit to write a charter for an Assembly. An Assembly we shall now have. 'Tis long past time, if yee want me opinion on it. As for the Taino, they cannot trouble us until they sort out they own rule. If Prince Caonabo wish to inherit he uncle's duho, he and all that army must return to Sharagua."

"You're Taino."

"No, gal. I's an Expeditioner, born and raised. Some say yee killed the maku. Did yee so? Or only fly off with him?"

I raised my eyes to the heavens, so bold and vast and fathomless, like the face of the ice. "I never had wings. I was only the arrow my sire loosed to find his mark. And so the hunt drank the cacica's blood, and then its master stole my beloved to keep me on his leash."

I shut my eyes. In the spirit world, the length of a kiss might stretch to three days. I pressed a hand over my locket and felt the pulse of the chain that bound us. The only thing that could break it now was death, and Vai still lived.

I opened my eyes to surprise the Taino woman with a look of wry pity on her weathered face. "Shall yee like somewhat to eat or drink? Juice, or rum? Guava, perhaps?"

"I am not an opia, although I do like guava. I'm not a witch, either. But I would take a shot of rum and a cup of juice, with thanks."

The rum was potent enough to steady me, and the juice soothed my aching throat. The boss offered me more juice, which I drank.

"Cat?" I looked up to see Luce, chest heaving as she ran up. "Cat!" She hugged me so hard it squeezed the air from my lungs.

Aunty Djeneba proceeded with less haste and more dignity toward us, accompanied by one of the men who had fled the carpentry yard. She spoke briefly with the Taino boss. Her mouth creased down as she turned to me. "Well, Cat, yee have turned up again."

"Like a three-days-dead fish," sniveled Luce, releasing me to wipe her eyes.

I couldn't speak. I knew I was about to start bawling.

"I can see yee need to clean up and get fresh clothes," said Aunty. "Luce, yee run and fetch Kayleigh. Cat, yee shall come home with us until Kofi-lad can come from the meeting down at Council House. He have spoken to us about those things which happened. I hope yee shall forgive me harsh words to yee."

Heart full and throat choked, I whispered, "Yes."

Then I bawled anyway on the way to the boarding-house. A shower revived me. Clean clothes made me feel almost human. A platter of Aunty's rice and peas and a slab of fried pargo with several more cups of guava juice sweetened with lime and pineapple restored my will, as if such humble gestures were magic. Because they were.

I was considering a second platter of rice and peas when Kofi and Gaius Sanogo arrived.

"Were you working for him all along?" I demanded of Kofi as he and the commissioner sat opposite me. "Are you secretly a warden?"

"I's standing for the Assembly, when it come time for

the vote," said Kofi. "As for the other, I's sure me own tale is no stranger than the one I hope yee mean to tell us now."

"There is a lot of it you won't believe."

"That would be a change," teased Kofi with a laugh that coaxed a smile from me.

"I's willing to pass me own judgment," said Sanogo.

The entire household as well as a few of the regulars gathered to listen. It took me two cups of the potent ginger beer to work myself past my instincts and my training to actually tell them things I would normally have kept silent about. But I managed it. With Luce sitting beside me and holding my hand, I told a short version of the tale. Even with the things I felt obliged to leave out, it was the most I had ever told anyone at one time except the night I had spent in Vai's arms. When I was finished, they replied with a measured silence. I could not tell if they believed me, thought I was quite deluded, or reckoned I was merely the most outrageous liar they had ever met.

"Oh, Cat!" sighed Luce. "What shall yee do now?"

I met Kayleigh's stricken gaze. "I will get him back. I promise you."

She nodded, then turned her face into Kofi's shoulder.

I addressed the warden. "What happened to General Camjiata?"

Sanogo's pleasant smile had the bracing effect of a piece of ice sliding down my back. "Jasmeen threw the man out of the town house. She owned it through one of she clan's holding companies. We never knew it belonged to she. That is why we never suspected her."

"She threw him out?"

"He could offer her no profit if there was none to support the Europan war. I believe the man bides at the

Speckled Iguana. We shall send he and any who wish to go with him back to Europa."

"Pay for the whole ship and all?"

"More than one ship," said Kofi. "He have signed up five hundred men for he army."

"We's happy to pay for him to leave," said Sanogo, "and good riddance to hotheaded young fools and they arseness."

"What of Prince Caonabo and his bride?"

"Yee cousin? She I have not seen, although I hear she await the prince at the border. As for the prince, I must go back now, for the committee meet with him this afternoon to seal the First Treaty anew."

"Why should the prince want to renew the treaty? Wouldn't possessing Expedition's factories, university, and port strengthen his position? Especially if he has to fight over the succession?"

"A fight over the succession is no small thing. He have no time to bother he own self with Expedition right now. But it also happen, as yee said yee own self, Cat, that a place like Expedition serve the Taino better as a free city than under Taino rule. Prince Caonabo is young and untried, but to me he seem a pragmatical sort of fellow. We shall see if he succeed, or fail."

"What of the prisoners who were going to be executed?"

"They all vanished in the night."

"Even Prince Haübey? The one they call Juba?"

"That man likewise."

"No doubt with the aid of his brother. It's good to know Prince Caonabo has his flaws. I'm not going back to Salt Island, Commissioner."

"I would not try and make yee. The prince he own self

told me yee cannot be called a salter if there was never any teeth in yee to begin with."

Kofi said, "What shall yee do now, Cat?" Then he laughed at my expression. "Me apologies, gal. I knew better than to ask. Yee's going after Vai. Good fortune to yee with that."

"Come with me to the Speckled Iguana, Kofi. I could use your support."

He rounded up Vai's other radical friends. We walked the fifteen blocks to the Speckled Iguana on empty streets that reminded me of the night I had staggered there in the company of Bala and Gaius and come home with Vai. The streets right around the Speckled Iguana were crowded with young men and their bundled possessions waiting with the look of restless wanderers who think it long past time to hit the road. They watched us walk past as if we were enemies approaching under truce. I climbed the steps with Kofi, and he was a good companion to have, being large, sturdy, and with those wicked scars to show he had survived worse than what you could dish out.

In the common room, a man I did not recognize worked the bar, but he knew me as soon as he saw me. He indicated the door that led to the back. My companions made a path for me through the staring, silent crowd. I ducked behind the bar and pushed open the door into the room in which Drake had killed one man to save another.

In fact, Drake was the first person I saw as I entered, for he was standing to the right of the door. The chamber in which he had healed a dying man was now pristine, decorated with long tables covered with red-and-gold floral-embroidered cloths and runners of magnificent Iberian lacework down the centers. Every seat was taken. People stood all the way around the room as well. At the far end, the general sat at the head of the longest table with a number of broadsheets creased and stacked at his left hand. I recognized Captain Tira and, to my surprise, Juba, standing behind the general like aides. I recognized the young Keita merchant who had railed against the commons at the dinner party. To the general's right, in the seat of honor, sat the proprietor of the Speckled Iguana. He was wearing the gold-braided uniform of a high-ranking officer.

My cane hung from a cord looped over a bracket in the wall.

Everyone turned to look at me as the general raised his cup as in salute.

"I hear the Wild Hunt took him," said Drake with a sneer. "The sad fate of many an arrogant bastard of a cold mage. But I must say, he really deserved whatever he got."

Just out of principle, I punched him, and he went down on his backside, although to my disappointment, not one person snickered. Indeed, a kind of many-throated gasp was inhaled throughout the room as heat spiked and the ornamental candles ranged along the lace centerpieces caught flame. A strange glamour flickered, and the flames snapped out. Drake rose with a peculiarly disturbing smile on his face, as if he had a surprise for me that I would not like. I suddenly remembered that I ought to be frightened of a man who could burn me alive and had been willing to do so before. But I was not afraid, not right now with my fury at what my sire had done still red-hot. He stepped back as Kofi shouldered up beside me and crossed his arms.

The general took a swallow from his cup and set it down atop a bold headline announcing the declaration of a new government for Expedition Territory. "So, Cat, have you come to join my army? I could certainly use a spy of your abilities. I've worked with Hassi Barahals before and hope to again. Or you could join my Amazon corps, as your mother did."

"I'm married."

He sighed. "I know the Wild Hunt took him. My condolences at his death. I have suffered a similar blow."

I had no desire to mock his grief for his dead wife. Nor did he need to know what I knew. So I cut to the chase.

"I am here to reclaim my sword."

"Are you?" he asked with a faint smile.

"I am."

He raised an eyebrow. "An answer to a question."

"You can give it to me, or I can take it. But I'm getting it now, because I hear you're leaving soon to invade Europa with five hundred men."

"One thousand one hundred and thirty-four, to be exact. We may lose or gain a few before the ships sail. I have new recruits, and old guard."

I could not help myself. I laughed. "You're going to conquer Europa with one thousand soldiers?"

He lifted his cup as if in toast to the fifty or so people crowded in the chamber, all of whom watched him raptly. "I started with fewer in my first command."

"You lack a woman who walks the dreams of dragons."

"I have Bee's sketchbook."

"How did you get that?"

"She gave it to me before she went to her wedding."

"I don't believe you. I think you stole it like you stole my sword."

He let this accusation pass. "I also have a fire mage."

"One with no scruples," I said.

"As the Roman poet said, 'The end justifies the means.'"

"A Roman would say that!"

The door into the back courtyard opened. A young man stepped into the chamber wearing a frightfully garish dash jacket of purple fabric printed with stylized orange and black stones. "Cat? I thought I heard your voice."

"Rory!" From across the chamber, he winked at me, and I smiled. "Why are you here?"

"I didn't want to go with our sire. So I stayed behind. This man was the only person I knew."

"You're coming with me now, Rory. The general is a bad man, and you're not to trust him. And while you're back there, I give my cold steel into your hand for long enough to bring it to me. And by the way, my friends, I would not try to stop him, because if you do I will tell him to become the saber-toothed cat he really is, and then he will eat you all up because it looks to me as if you haven't been feeding him properly."

"I wondered why he had your sword." Rory grabbed the braided cord and lifted it off the bracket, careful not to touch any part of the cane or let it swing against him. He strolled down between two tables as the general watched without trying to stop him. I received the cane from Rory and gestured for him to stand behind me.

"My thanks, General, for holding on to that for me until I could retrieve it."

He rose. "Why did the cacica die, Cat? Do you know?"

"'Where the hand of fortune branches, Tara Bell's child must choose.' It isn't always about you, General." I made sure to offer a cutting smile to Drake. "But next time, it might be you, James."

He rubbed his chin. "I only slept with you to get at

him," he muttered, but his resentful tone made me wonder what else simmered beneath the surface.

"Drake. Enough." Camjiata considered me. "You know, Cat, there is another reason Tara Bell might have sworn in court that Daniel sired you. Maybe some other man sired you, someone she was willing to die to save you from by making sure Daniel had custody of you after you were born. Do you suppose that could be true?"

I could keep my lips sealed, but I hadn't Vai's ability to crush my emotions behind a mask of disdain.

The general's bold eyebrows rose, and an expression shuddered across his face like the ripple of a dragon's dream in the spirit world, obliterating the familiar world and replacing it with an unknown landscape yet to be explored. Then the flutter of surprise and disquietude vanished so utterly that I found I feared him for his self-control. "That explains why you look like Tara and not at all like Daniel. And why your hair and eyes resemble neither." He glanced at Rory. "I see this may be more complicated than even I originally thought. We are not done, Cat, you and I."

"No, I suppose we are not. Even so, I don't think you understand destiny as well as you claim to."

He nodded in a way that was both challenge and promise. "We shall see."

With a lift of my chin, I acknowledged the old proprietor, for I did wonder what he could tell me about my mother. He nodded as in reply to my unspoken questions. Unmolested by the general's partisans, we left.

Kofi saw me home and, before departing for the Council House, posted a guard at the gate.

"For I see the general don' care for yee, Cat, and I don' trust him."

We stood in the shadow of the open gate, him outside and me within. "Why, Kofi, whence comes this change of heart about me?"

"Shall I doubt yee love Vai?"

"No, yee shall not. But I am curious."

"Kayleigh reckon yee truly care for him. I trust she to have Vai's interests best in she heart. But also, when I rowed yee and Vai back to the jetty that morning, yee fell asleep. That convinced me yee truly love him."

I flushed, thinking of how strenuously Vai and I had spent that night. "Because I fell asleep?"

He chuckled as if divining my thoughts. "If yee were really after him to betray him, yee could never close yee eyes nor chance to miss one thing he said yee could use against him. But yee just lay yee head against he shoulder and slept. 'Twas sweet. 'Twas the first time I truly saw yee trust him."

He kissed me on the cheek and went off to the business of Expedition's future.

I took Rory in and introduced him to the family. Afterward I took Aunty Djeneba aside. "He is harmless, and very loyal." She indicated the bar, where Rory was already buttering up Brenna, who was giggling like a gal half her age. "All right," I agreed. "That's a problem he has. Just you wait until he turns the charm on you. Is there some mending I can do?"

I mended through the afternoon, too restless to take the usual nap. My thoughts churned and boiled as I thought of Vai in my sire's clutches. When the courtyard began to fill with curious customers, I took a tray. It was easier to move than to sit, and if I had to exchange brilliant quips with the regulars, that kept my mind off Vai, who might only now be realizing I had just been thrown out of the coach, for who knew how time was running for him? Would he think I was dead?

"Gal?" Uncle Joe paused beside me where I leaned against the counter, stricken by a wash of cramping or perhaps only fear. "Yee all right?"

I pressed my hand against the locket, where our hearts pulsed. Vai would know that I lived and that, because I lived, I would come after him. "Just tired, Uncle."

"Yee go up to yee sleep, gal. Yee have the same room as before."

I looked around to find Rory sitting between Tanny and Diantha, lounging at his ease with his long legs stretched out. He was laughing in that flirtatious way he had as Tanny told a story whose words I could not be bothered to overhear. "That will not end well, Uncle, do you think? What if they fight over him?"

He chuckled. "There is that about those two gals I think yee don' know. Anyway, they's of age to make up they own minds, gal. Yee go on up."

I slipped out of the courtyard and went up with a candle to light my weary way. When I closed the door behind me, I stared, for the room was furnished with a bed and chest I knew. I set the candle on the floor and opened the lid to see all his dash jackets waiting for him. As I ran my hands through the folds of the fabric, a tear wound down my cheek.

I did not hear the door open and close. Wind blew out the candle, and he touched my shoulder.

"Catherine."

"Vai? Blessed Tanit! Vai!"

I leaped up and embraced him as the lid banged down. He pressed his lips hotly to mine and in the dark room with the cheerful noise of the evening drinkers serenading us, we kissed until I thought I would dissolve into him.

Then I caught my breath and drew back, peering at him in the darkness, him and his annoyingly handsome face and the strange wisp-light in his beautiful eyes. My hands stroked the buttons and fine chains of embroidery woven down the front of the dash jacket he wore. My fingers itched to undress the man I loved. "Vai, how did you escape...?"

Fear squeezed my heart.

"Let me see your navel," I said.

He laughed, but it was not Vai's laugh. His smile cut like contempt, and although he looked exactly like Vai, his gaze was as hard as stone. "I have come to warn yee, maku. We don' want yee here. Yee cut a path through what was closed. Elsewise that one shall not have taken blood from this country."

"But aren't you a spirit from the spirit world, too? Ruled by the courts?"

"Think yee so? The other land be plenty vast and 'tis not all the same. If yee reckon to force a path from this land back to them, then I promise yee, we shall eat yee before yee can get there. For yee have no right to trample here in places yee know nothing of and don' own."

He vanished in a hissing patter like the scatter of sand melded with the scent of overripe guavas. That, too, dissipated, leaving me with no light, trembling hands, and the burning memory of his mouth on mine. I sank onto the bed Vai had built for us and for the longest time I could not move, until the door opened and Rory squeezed in.

"Cat? What is it? I could smell your tears."

He stretched out beside me, saying nothing more. Soothed by the comfort of his presence, I slept.

I woke at dawn, rumpled and mussed, because I had slept in my clothes. Rory was gone, nor had I any idea how long he had stayed with me. I straightened my pagne and blouse and hurried downstairs to do my business and tidy up. The little lads and lasses were lined up, ready to march off hand in hand to school. I gave them each a kiss and promised to buy them a sweet even though I had no money and no idea how to get hold of the money Vai had been given by the mansa.

The opia's warning haunted me as I ate an orange and considered my options. Yet it was easier to move than to sit, so I went out to walk the old neighborhood. I returned from visiting my friends on Tailors' Row to find Rory sitting on a bench with Luce giggling on his knee.

I marched over to them and dragged her off. "That is enough of that!"

She set fists on hips. "I's sixteen this year. Old enough to know me own mind!"

"Rory, if you do anything with her I would not approve of, I shall castrate you."

He drew himself up, affronted, but before he could speak, I pressed a hand to his chest. "How did you get Vai's jacket?"

"The general gave it to me on Hallows' Night. After we retreated back to the big house. It was generous of him to take me away from the ball court, considering some of those Taino soldiers were beginning to look at me like they thought they would have to try to kill me. My other clothes were all ripped and torn. Then after I had dressed, this woman came, quite shrieking, I must tell you, Cat, for it made my ears hurt. Afterward she had the nerve to put her hand on my—"

"I can guess."

"After the way she complained, I can't imagine why she would think I would want to be petted by her!"

"How did the bed and the chest get here?"

"I don't know everything, Cat! I can't imagine why you expect me to! Someone else came, and there was a great deal of argument but at that moment I was down in one of the guardrooms very involved with—"

"With something I obviously don't need to know. Luce! Go help your grandmother!"

With a mulish grimace, she trudged off, casting glances back over her shoulder.

"I was sure you would not mind if I wore the jacket since I had otherwise nothing but a sack."

"No, that's fine. I suppose Sanogo must have sent the bed and chest over here."

The sound of horse hooves and carriage wheels drawing up outside made me turn. There came a silence, then the bang of a door shut impatiently. A dark head looked in through the partly open gate.

"There you are, dearest! Is this truly where you stayed all that time? How very quaint."

Bee wore the jacket embroidered with axes and a pagne so spotless a snowy white that I winced with each of her steps for fear some tiny smattering of dust would kick up to stain it.

"How very fortunate I was to land here," I retorted, refraining from shrieking and throwing my arms around her. "How did you know I was here? Did Sanogo send word?"

"Really, Cat! Why must you ask questions to which the answer is self-evident? The general stole my sketchbook, but fortunately I dreamed about you last night. Where is Vai?" She looked about with curiosity and just a smidgen of irritating condescension, but she was my Bee, after all. I had to forgive her that.

I had to, because her expression altered as her eyes widened and her voice dropped to a whisper hoarse with genuine alarm. "What happened?" Reaching me, she grasped my hands tightly.

Behind, at the gate, a pair of Taino guards appeared to stand at attention. Rory put an arm around Luce, Uncle Joe set a machete on the counter for them to see he was armed, and Aunty Djeneba politely ventured forward to offer the soldiers juice from a cup, which they politely accepted as a sign of their peaceful intentions.

I met Bee's gaze, as she met mine. "My sire is Master of the Wild Hunt. He killed the cacica for the sacrifice. And then he took Vai."

Her grip crushed my fingers. "Did he kill him?"

"He carried him away alive. Now it is up to me to get him back." I shook off her grip. "Bee, you really must allow me to introduce you to everyone. Do you have some exalted title now with which I must address you? Your Fragrant Pompousness, perhaps?"

"Nothing so splendid. Your Exalted Magnificence will do."

"Noble Ba'al, Bee. Are you really a queen now, like the didos of old?"

"I am something better. I can walk the dreams of dragons, and because of the very clever thinking of my dearest cousin, I know where to hide on Hallows' Night to escape the Wild Hunt. That means there are a great many things I've always wanted to do I'll now have time for."

"Like what?"

"Where do I start? Revolutions to plot. Enemies to crush. Handsome men to rescue."

I actually laughed, because she heartened me so. "But what about you, Bee? What happened to you?"

"Blessed Tanit!" she said portentously. It seemed she had reassured herself that I was for the moment safe, for she turned to look around the courtyard and include every person there in the axe-blow of her smile. "I can scarcely wait to tell you the tale!"

Look out for the final book in
The Spiritwalker Trilogy:

COLD STEEL

by Kate Elliott

You can find *Cold Fire* extras at http://www.kateelliott.com
Extras include *Cold Fire* chapter 31.5, which was not
included in the novel as published because it is not written from Cat's point of view and contains sexual content,
as well as a short story featuring Rory.

extras

orbit

meet the author

KATE ELLIOTT has been writing stories since she was nine years old, which has led her to believe either that she is a little crazy or that writing, like breathing, keeps her alive. Her previous series are the Crossroads Trilogy (starting with *Spirit Gate*), The Crown of Stars septology (starting with *King's Dragon*), the Novels of the Jaran, and a collaboration with Melanie Rawn and Jennifer Roberson called *The Golden Key*. She likes to play sports more than she likes to watch them; right now, her sport of choice is outrigger canoe paddling. She has been married for a really long time. She and her spouse produced three spawn (aka children), and now that the youngest has graduated high school they spend extra special time with their miniature schnauzer (aka the Schnazghul). Her spouse has a much more interesting job than she does, with the added benefit that they had to move to Hawaii for his work. Thus the outrigger canoes. Find out more about the author at www.kateelliott.com.

introducing

If you enjoyed
COLD FIRE,
look out for

THE HUNDRED THOUSAND KINGDOMS
Book One of the Inheritance Trilogy
by N. K. Jemisin

Yeine Darr is an outcast from the barbarian north. But when her mother dies under mysterious circumstances, she is summoned to the majestic city of Sky. There, to her shock, Yeine is named an heiress to the king. But the throne of the Hundred Thousand Kingdoms is not easily won, and Yeine is thrust into a vicious power struggle. Gods and mortals, power and love, death and revenge. She will inherit them all.

I AM NOT AS I ONCE WAS. They have done this to me, broken me open and torn out my heart. I do not know who I am anymore.

I must try to remember.

My people tell stories of the night I was born. They say my mother crossed her legs in the middle of labor and fought with all her strength not to release me into the world. I was born anyhow, of course; nature cannot be denied. Yet it does not surprise me that she tried.

My mother was an heiress of the Arameri. There was a ball for the lesser nobility—the sort of thing that happens once a decade as a backhanded sop to their self-esteem. My father dared ask my mother to dance; she deigned to consent. I have often wondered what he said and did that night to make her fall in love with him so powerfully, for she eventually abdicated her position to be with him. It is the stuff of great tales, yes? Very romantic. In the tales, such a couple lives happily ever after. The tales do not say what happens when the most powerful family in the world is offended in the process.

But I forget myself. Who was I, again? Ah, yes.

My name is Yeine. In my people's way I am Yeine dau she Kinneth tai wer Somem kanna Darre, which means that I am the daughter of Kinneth, and that my tribe within the Darre people is called Somem. Tribes mean little to us these days, though before the Gods' War they were more important.

I am nineteen years old. I also am, or was, the chieftain of my people, called *ennu*. In the Arameri way, which is the way of the Amn race from whom they originated, I am the Baroness Yeine Darr.

One month after my mother died, I received a message from my grandfather Dekarta Arameri, inviting me to visit the family seat. Because one does not refuse an invitation from the Arameri, I set forth. It took the better part of three months to travel from the High North continent to Senm, across the Repentance Sea. Despite Darr's relative poverty, I traveled in style the whole way, first by palanquin and ocean vessel, and finally by chauffeured horse-coach. This was not my choice. The Darre Warriors' Council, which rather desperately hoped that I might restore us to the Arameri's good graces, thought that this extravagance would help. It is well known that Amn respect displays of wealth.

Thus arrayed, I arrived at my destination on the cusp of the winter solstice. And as the driver stopped the coach on a hill outside the city, ostensibly to water the horses but more likely because he was a local and liked to watch foreigners gawk, I got my first glimpse of the Hundred Thousand Kingdoms' heart.

There is a rose that is famous in High North. (This is not a digression.) It is called the altarskirt rose. Not only do its petals unfold in a radiance of pearled white, but frequently it grows an incomplete secondary flower about the base of its stem. In its most prized form, the altarskirt grows a layer of overlarge petals that drape the ground. The two bloom in tandem, seedbearing head and skirt, glory above and below.

This was the city called Sky. On the ground, sprawling over a small mountain or an oversize hill: a circle of high walls, mounting tiers of buildings, all resplendent in white, per Arameri decree. Above the city, smaller but brighter, the pearl of its tiers occasionally obscured by scuds of cloud, was the palace—also called Sky, and perhaps more deserving of the name. I knew the column was there, the impossibly thin column that supported such a massive structure, but from that distance I couldn't see it. Palace floated above city, linked in spirit, both so unearthly in their beauty that I held my breath at the sight.

The altarskirt rose is priceless because of the difficulty of producing it. The most famous lines are heavily inbred; it originated as a deformity that some savvy breeder deemed useful. The primary flower's scent, sweet to us, is apparently repugnant to insects; these roses must be pollinated by hand. The secondary flower saps nutrients crucial for the plant's fertility. Seeds are rare, and for every one that grows into a perfect altarskirt, ten others become plants that must be destroyed for their hideousness.

At the gates of Sky (the palace) I was turned away, though not for the reasons I'd expected. My grandfather was not present, it seemed. He had left instructions in the event of my arrival.

Sky is the Arameri's home; business is never done there. This is because, officially, they do not rule the world. The Nobles' Consortium does, with the benevolent assistance of the Order of Itempas. The Consortium meets in the Salon, a huge, stately building—white-walled, of course—that sits among a cluster of official buildings at the foot of the palace. It is very impressive, and would be more so if it did not sit squarely in Sky's elegant shadow.

I went inside and announced myself to the Consortium staff, whereupon they all looked very surprised, though politely so. One of them—a very junior aide, I gathered—was dispatched to escort me to the central chamber, where the day's session was well under way.

As a lesser noble, I had always been welcome to attend a Consortium gathering, but there had never seemed any point. Besides the expense and months of travel time required to attend, Darr was simply too small, poor, and ill-favored to have any clout, even without my mother's abdication adding to our collective stain. Most of High North is regarded as a backwater, and only the largest nations there have enough prestige or money to make their voices heard among our noble peers. So I was not surprised to find that the seat reserved for me on the Consortium floor—in a shadowed area, behind a pillar—was currently occupied by an excess delegate from one of the Senm-continent nations. It would be terribly rude, the aide stammered anxiously, to dislodge this man, who was elderly and had bad knees. Perhaps I would not mind standing? Since I had just spent many long hours cramped in a carriage, I was happy to agree.

So the aide positioned me at the side of the Consortium floor, where I actually had a good view of the goings-on. The Consortium chamber was magnificently apportioned, with white marble and rich, dark wood that had probably come from Darr's forests in better days. The nobles—three hundred or so in total—sat in comfortable chairs on the chamber's floor or along elevated tiers above. Aides, pages, and scribes occupied the periphery with me, ready to fetch documents or run errands as needed. At the head of the chamber, the Consortium Overseer stood atop an elaborate podium, pointing to members as they indicated a desire to speak. Apparently there was a dispute over water rights in a desert somewhere; five countries were involved. None of the conversation's participants spoke out of turn; no tempers were lost; there were no snide comments or veiled insults. It was all very orderly and polite, despite the size of the gathering and the fact that most of those present were accustomed to speaking however they pleased among their own people.

One reason for this extraordinary good behavior stood on a plinth behind the Overseer's podium: a life-size statue of the Skyfather in one of His most famous poses, the Appeal to Mortal Reason. Hard to speak out of turn under that stern gaze. But more repressive, I suspected, was the stern gaze of the man who sat behind the Overseer in an elevated box. I could not see him well from where I stood, but he was elderly, richly dressed, and flanked by a younger blond man and a dark-haired woman, as well as a handful of retainers.

It did not take much to guess this man's identity, though he wore no crown, had no visible guards, and neither he nor anyone in his entourage spoke throughout the meeting.

"Hello, Grandfather," I murmured to myself, and smiled at him across the chamber, though I knew he could not see me. The pages and scribes gave me the oddest looks for the rest of the afternoon.

I knelt before my grandfather with my head bowed, hearing titters of laughter.

No, wait.

There were three gods once.

Only three, I mean. Now there are dozens, perhaps hundreds. They breed like rabbits. But once there were only three, most powerful and glorious of all: the god of day, the god of night, and the goddess of twilight and dawn. Or light and darkness and the shades between. Or order, chaos, and balance. None of that is important because one of them died, the other might as well have, and the last is the only one who matters anymore.

The Arameri get their power from this remaining god. He is called the Skyfather, Bright Itempas, and the ancestors of the Arameri were His most devoted priests. He rewarded them by giving them a weapon so mighty that no army could stand against it. They used this weapon—weapons, really—to make themselves rulers of the world.

That's better. Now.

I knelt before my grandfather with my head bowed and my knife laid on the floor.

We were in Sky, having transferred there following the Consortium session, via the magic of the Vertical Gate. Immediately upon arrival I had been summoned to my grandfather's audience chamber, which felt much like a throne room. The chamber was roughly circular because circles are sacred to Itempas. The vaulted ceiling made the members of the court look taller—unnecessarily, since Amn are a tall people compared to my own. Tall and pale and endlessly poised, like statues of human beings rather than real flesh and blood.

"Most high Lord Arameri," I said. "I am honored to be in your presence."

I had heard titters of laughter when I entered the room. Now they sounded again, muffled by hands and kerchiefs and fans. I was reminded of bird flocks roosting in a forest canopy.

Before me sat Dekarta Arameri, uncrowned king of the world. He was old; perhaps the oldest man I have ever seen, though Amn usually live longer than my people, so this was not surprising. His thin hair had gone completely white, and he was so gaunt and stooped that the elevated stone chair on which he sat—it was never called a throne—seemed to swallow him whole.

"Granddaughter," he said, and the titters stopped. The silence was heavy enough to hold in my hand. He was head of the Arameri family, and his word was law. No one had expected him to acknowledge me as kin, least of all myself.

"Stand," he said. "Let me have a look at you."

I did, reclaiming my knife since no one had taken it.

There was more silence. I am not very interesting to look at. It might have been different if I had gotten the traits of my two peoples in a better combination—Amn height with Darre curves, perhaps, or thick straight Darre hair colored Amn-pale. I have Amn eyes: faded green in color, more unnerving than pretty. Otherwise, I am short and flat and brown as forestwood, and my hair is a curled mess. Because I find it unmanageable otherwise, I wear it short. I am sometimes mistaken for a boy.

As the silence wore on, I saw Dekarta frown. There was an odd sort of marking on his forehead, I noticed: a perfect circle of black, as if someone had dipped a coin in ink and pressed it to his flesh. On either side of this was a thick chevron, bracketing the circle.

"You look nothing like her," he said at last. "But I suppose that is just as well. Viraine?"

This last was directed at a man who stood among the courtiers closest to the throne. For an instant I thought he was another elder, then I realized my error: though his hair was stark white, he was only somewhere in his fourth decade. He, too, bore a forehead mark, though his was less elaborate than Dekarta's: just the black circle.

"She's not hopeless," he said, folding his arms. "Nothing to be done about her looks; I doubt even makeup will help. But put her in civilized attire and she can convey...nobility, at least." His eyes narrowed, taking me apart by degrees. My best Darren clothing, a long vest of white civvetfur and calf-length leggings, earned me a sigh. (I had gotten the odd look for this outfit at the Salon, but I hadn't realized it was *that* bad.) He examined my face so long that I wondered if I should show my teeth.

Instead he smiled, showing his. "Her mother has

649

even now."

"She will do, then," said Dekarta.

"Do for what, Grandfather?" I asked. The weight in
the room grew heavier, expectant, though he had already
named me granddaughter. There was a certain risk involved in my daring to address him the same familiar
way, of course—powerful men are touchy over odd
things. But my mother had indeed trained me well, and
I knew it was worth the risk to establish myself in the
court's eyes.

Dekarta Arameri's face did not change; I could not
read it. "For my heir, Granddaughter. I intend to name
you to that position today."

The silence turned to stone as hard as my grandfather's
chair.

I thought he might be joking, but no one laughed.
That was what made me believe him at last: the utter
shock and horror on the faces of the courtiers as they
stared at their lord. Except the one called Viraine. He
watched me.

It came to me that some response was expected.

"You already have heirs," I said.

"Not as diplomatic as she could be," Viraine said in a
dry tone.

Dekarta ignored this. "It is true, there are two other
candidates," he said to me. "My niece and nephew, Scimina and Relad. Your cousins, once removed."

I had heard of them, of course; everyone had. Rumor
constantly made one or the other heir, though no one
knew for certain which. *Both* was something that had not
occurred to me.

"If I may suggest, Grandfather," I said carefully,

though it was impossible to be careful in this conversation, "I would make two heirs too many."

It was the eyes that made Dekarta seem so old, I would realize much later. I had no idea what color they had originally been; age had bleached and filmed them to near-white. There were lifetimes in those eyes, none of them happy.

"Indeed," he said. "But just enough for an interesting competition, I think."

"I don't understand, Grandfather."

He lifted his hand in a gesture that would have been graceful, once. Now his hand shook badly. "It is very simple. I have named three heirs. One of you will actually manage to succeed me. The other two will doubtless kill each other or be killed by the victor. As for which lives, and which die—" He shrugged. "That is for you to decide."

My mother had taught me never to show fear, but emotions will not be stilled so easily. I began to sweat. I have been the target of an assassination attempt only once in my life—the benefit of being heir to such a tiny, impoverished nation. No one wanted my job. But now there would be two others who did. Lord Relad and Lady Scimina were wealthy and powerful beyond my wildest dreams. They had spent their whole lives striving against each other toward the goal of ruling the world. And here came I, unknown, with no resources and few friends, into the fray.

"There will be no decision," I said. To my credit, my voice did not shake. "And no contest. They will kill me at once and turn their attention back to each other."

"That is possible," said my grandfather.

I could think of nothing to say that would save me. He was insane; that was obvious. Why else turn rulership of the world into a contest prize? If he died tomorrow, Relad and Scimina would rip the earth asunder between them. The killing might not end for decades. And for all he knew, I was an idiot. If by some impossible chance I managed to gain the throne, I could plunge the Hundred Thousand Kingdoms into a spiral of mismanagement and suffering. He had to know that.

One cannot argue with madness. But sometimes, with luck and the Skyfather's blessing, one can understand it. "Why?"

He nodded as if he had expected my question. "Your mother deprived me of an heir when she left our family. You will pay her debt."

"She is four months in the grave," I snapped. "Do you honestly want revenge against a dead woman?"

"This has nothing to do with revenge, Granddaughter. It is a matter of duty." He made a gesture with his left hand, and another courtier detached himself from the throng. Unlike the first man—indeed, unlike most of the courtiers whose faces I could see—the mark on this man's forehead was a downturned half-moon, like an exaggerated frown. He knelt before the dais that held Dekarta's chair, his waist-length red braid falling over one shoulder to curl on the floor.

"I cannot hope that your mother has taught you duty," Dekarta said to me over this man's back. "She abandoned hers to dally with her sweet-tongued savage. I allowed this—an indulgence I have often regretted. So I will assuage that regret by bringing you back into the fold, Granddaughter. Whether you live or die is irrelevant. You are Arameri, and like all of us, you will serve."

Then he waved to the red-haired man. "Prepare her as best you can."

There was nothing more. The red-haired man rose and came to me, murmuring that I should follow him. I did. Thus ended my first meeting with my grandfather, and thus began my first day as an Arameri. It was not the worst of the days to come.